CHRISTINA

Published by Brolga Publishing Pty Ltd
ABN 46 063 962 443
PO Box 12544
A'Beckett St
Melbourne, VIC, 8006
Australia

email: markzocchi@brolgapublishing.com.au

National Library of Australia
Cataloguing-in-Publication entry
     Munnich, Joyce, author
     Christina : from Denmark to Australia - a young woman's tale
     ISBN: 9781925367218 (paperback)
     Subjects: Australia - Fiction - Frontier and pioneer life -
     Historical fiction
     A823.4

Printed in Australia
Cover design by Wanissa Somsuphangsri
Typesetting by Tara Wyllie

BE PUBLISHED

Publish through a successful publisher. National distribution, Macmillan
& International distribution to the United Kingdom, North America.
Sales Representation to South East Asia
Email: markzocchi@brolgapublishing.com.au

CHRISTINA

**From Denmark to Australia -
A young woman's tale of migration**

JOYCE MUNNICH

*In loving memory of
the real Christina and Carl*

AUTHOR'S NOTE

This book is a novel with an historical background.

All main characters are fictitious, but, because I have relied heavily on the experiences of my grandparents as immigrants from Schleswig (Denmark) and Prussia (Germany), I have used their names.

I have also used the real names of people known from the pages of history and of other early pioneers of the Logan valley and Gold Coast hinterland.

FOREWORD

In December 1859 a new Australian colony came officially into being. This was Queensland, a vast land stretching away to the north of New South Wales, a still-sleeping land, rich in resources, except for the most important of them all – people.

From 1860 onwards, tall-masted ships from distant ports began to appear regularly in Moreton Bay, and they brought a precious cargo: the people who would clear away the jungle, turn the soil and plant the seeds; the people who would lay the foundations of achievement for the Colony, and future State.

Who were they? For the most part, just the poor and the humble, the dispossessed and the persecuted: farmers and factory workers; clerks and teachers; Protestants and Catholics; the young, the not-so-young and the very young. They came from all over Europe and Great Britain, and they asked for nothing more than the chance to build a better life for themselves and their families: to work their own piece of ground, be their own master and bow to none. They were the Immigrants and they would be the lifeblood of the new Colony.

1

The little girl had come through the school gate and walked along the cobbled road with several other children but, when she turned on to the narrow lane, she was on her own and her footsteps slowed. In its own winding, seemingly uncertain fashion the lane led to her home and she knew very well that she should stay on it. But over to her left lay a barley field, and if she cut across that and then the graveyard next to the church, she would be home ever so much sooner. The decision taken, she gathered her bulky woollen skirt and flannel petticoat into a bundle in front of her, and in a series of quick, lithe movements, was off the lane and through the fence into the field. There would be no direct crossing, however – even though that was clearly the shortest way. Christina Cecile Skov, almost eight years old, knew from past experience that the thick sharp spikes left after the grain had been harvested and carried off to the brewery would tear holes in her stockings and scratch cruelly at her legs. So she set off doggedly around the edge of the field, her wooden clogs crunching the rough clods of earth left at the end of each furrow during the spring ploughing.

With the far side gained, she moved quickly across the level ground at the back of the church and into the graveyard. Here, with tombstones looming on every side, she walked more slowly, reminding herself that it wasn't seemly to be rushing where the dead lay sleeping. But there was another reason for Christina's sudden lingering, and it was this which drew her, almost against her will, away from the grassy aisle which would have led her to rejoin the lane only a short distance from her own front gate. In a far corner, beneath the branches of an old oak tree, a number of graves lay clustered within the confines of a low iron fence. The headstones on those at the back were very old, weathered and darkly grey. Others within the plot were not so old, though mottled fingers of

3

mildew and the fading of their lettering marked them as being of a time now well past. But the two headstones at the front were cream-coloured still, the marble unstained, the lettering dark and clear. It was these graves, the one large, the other very small, which had drawn the little girl to this part of the graveyard, and, without hesitation, she opened the small gate and slipped into the enclosure, pausing at the foot of the first one to quietly read the epitaph …

Hans Johannes Christiansen
Died in battle on 7th March 1864
Aged 18 years and 2 months
A much loved Son and Brother
And a brave Danish soldier

Rest in Peace

Christina's softly mouthed words ended on a long sigh. Uncle Hans, the uncle who had died fighting the Prussians and Austrians while she was still a baby. All for nothing. That's what her mother and grandmother so often said and she supposed that it was true. Denmark had lost the war and now Schleswig, their homeland, belonged to Prussia, and, it seemed, would always belong to Prussia, for Denmark was not likely to enter into another war against such a great power. They had fought bravely though, all those young Danish soldiers, at first in trying to defend the Danewerk, then during the siege of Duppel.

"And we are still Danish, Uncle Hans," Christina whispered fiercely. "The Prussians can't change that, even if they did win the war and tear down the Danewerk. We will always be Danish, no matter what they do to our country."

A breeze, springing up suddenly from the direction of the fiord, caught the words from her lips and rustled the branches of the old tree, merging the sounds, so that it seemed to the young girl standing below that they were being tossed back at her: always Danish, always Danish. Shivering, she glanced about her a little anxiously before moving the few steps to the next grave. Just as it always did, its smallness clutched at her heart. Nevertheless, she resolutely read the lettering on the headstone, her lips forming words which had long since been committed to memory …

Madsen Simon Skov
Beloved Son of Simon and Elsie Skov
Born 25th August 1865
Died 2nd September 1865
In God's loving care

Her little brother, who would have been five years old now, but who had lived for only eight days. Christina turned from the grave slowly, struggling to keep her mind free of an old persistent question. Why had he died when he was just a little baby?

"He was ailing," her mother had told her, "and God took him to Heaven so that He could look after him."

"But you could have looked after him, Mother."

"No, Christina, not that little one. All my loving care could not have performed such miracles as would have been needed, and God knew that."

"But He could have helped you look after him. He didn't need to take him away to do that."

"God does what He knows is best, you just remember that, Christina."

Christina gave a deep sigh as she closed the gate behind her. Oh, how stern her mother had become, so stern, all the other questions she had wanted to ask had remained locked away. She had tried to understand though, reminding herself over and over of what her mother had said – God knows best. But, no matter how hard she tried, there were always moments, such as the one now upon her, when doubt loomed. If God had helped her, Mother could have made that little baby well, she mused sorrowfully. She is so good at caring for sick people. Look at how she nursed Father when he was so sick with bronchitis. And me when I had the mumps. And look at how she cares for little Anna ... Anna! Dread, as jagged and piercing as lightning struck at her heart. The baby was ailing. Three times now she'd had the croup and this time the cough had settled deep in her chest. She wasn't eating and there were dark circles beneath her eyes. What if God should decide ... oh no! No! He wasn't going to take her! Not this beautiful baby!

Christina ran, harder than she had ever run in her life before, her resolve not to rush where the dead lay sleeping lost in the turmoil that raged within her. She had to get home. She had to see her little sister, to know that she was all right. Stinging remorse joined forces with her apprehension. Why, she'd hardly thought about the baby all day at school. And what would God think about that if He was about to decide what was best for her? By the time she burst into the warm kitchen with its big fireplace, gleaming pots and scrubbed pine table, Christina was out of breath, her face was bright pink, and her braids, having freed themselves of their ribbons, hung in a tangle of golden curls almost to her waist.

"Christina! For goodness sake, look at you! What has happened?" Elsie Skov dropped the tray of bread she had just taken from the oven on to a bench and turned quickly to peer more closely at her dishevelled daughter. "You look as though you've been chased by some wild creature. What is it? What has brought you to such a state?"

Leaning against the door jamb and with her eyes anxiously searching the worried face bent close to her own, Christina gasped, "I've been hurrying, that's all."

Her mother gave a relieved sigh and shook her head in gentle exasperation as she straightened. "You gave me such a fright, child, bursting in like that."

"I'm sorry, Mother. Is little Anna any better?"

Elsie Skov was a woman in her mid-thirties. Slim and barely five feet three inches tall, she was nevertheless wiry and possessed of a supple strength which made her seem almost tireless. Her hair, a light brown shade in which golden streaks still gleamed when caught by the light, was drawn back tightly from her face and twisted into a bun at the nape of her neck. This severe style and the melancholy expression she often wore combined to make her appear every year of her age, and sometimes more. But, when she smiled, as she did now, the years fell away. "Yes, she is, Christina. She's ever so much better. She has eaten a little porridge and drunk some milk and the cough seems to have broken. The doctor came this afternoon and he agrees that she is improving. She is sleeping now, poor, weary little babe."

Christina released her breath in a long, wavering sigh. Thank you, God. You did see that it was best to let Mother take care of little Anna.

"Are you sure that you are all right? You're not sickening for something?" Elsie's smile had faded and she frowned as she held her hand against her daughter's forehead. "You are quite warm and so flushed."

"No, truly, Mother, I'm not the least bit sick. I'm just hot and puffed from running."

"Well, it's foolish to rush like that."

"I wanted to see how the baby was. She seemed so sick when I left for school this morning."

"Ah, you've been worrying about little Anna." Elsie shook her head sympathetically as she bent to put more peat on the fire. "Poor child, what a day you must have had."

"I wasn't worrying all day, not all day." The words came with a rush, a quick denial spawned by a renewed surge of guilt.

"Well, I should hope not. You have your lessons to worry about. Did you do good work today?"

"I got all of my sums right."

"That's wonderful. Father will be so pleased. He's already fed the geese, by the way."

"Father? He's home so early?"

"Yes, he received some exciting news today, he couldn't wait to tell us."

Only then did Christina become aware of voices floating along the hallway from the sitting room at the front of the house. "We've got company?"

"The Ohlssens have come over to have supper with us and help us celebrate."

"What are we celebrating?"

"Your father's exciting news, of course."

"But what is it? What is the exciting news?" A sudden pleasing notion saw the faint frown that had come to Christina's brow disappear and a quick smile come to her lips. "Oh, I think I know what it is … "

"You do, do you?" Elsie queried with a teasing smile. "And just what do you suppose it is?"

"Mr Johanssen has agreed to sell Father that pony and trap."

"No, no! It's nothing like that!" Elsie gave a soft chuckle. "I hardly think the Ohlssens would come over to celebrate our buying a pony and trap. No, it's something you could never hope to guess."

Watching her mother's smiling face as she sliced carrots into the big saucepan on the range, Christina swallowed back a small groan of disappointment. What could be more exciting that buying that beautiful pony with its especially built trap? Ah, but something could. If her father had managed to save enough money to build a shed and start his own furniture-making business as he'd been hoping to do, that really would be something to celebrate. "Won't father need to work on the new brewery anymore? Is he going to be able to … ?"

Shaking her head, Elsie laughed softly. "No, it's nothing like that, either."

"What is it then? Can't you tell me?"

"No, that's for your father to do. It's his surprise and he'd be most disappointed if I told you with him not here to see your reaction." Turning from the stove, Elsie rested a hand on her daughter's shoulder. "Come, we'll take a peek at little Anna before we join the others. And, while we are in the bedroom, I'll see what I can do about tidying your hair. Guests for supper and you look like something the cat has dragged in." She clucked her tongue reprovingly, but both her eyes and her mouth were smiling and Christina felt a warmth steal through her. It had been days since she'd seen her mother smile in such a way.

A short time later, somewhat more presentable, Christina appeared in the doorway to the sitting room at her mother's side and politely acknowledged the greetings of Maria and Peter Ohlssen, nice, kind-hearted people, whom she had called aunty and uncle all her life, but who were really no more than distant cousins of her mother's. On the rug before the fire their son Lars, a tall, gangling youth of sixteen years, whom Christina alternately liked and disliked, was studying an atlas, and looked up only long enough to give her a brief grin.

But his father declared cheerfully, "Well, little Christina, it's like I always say, you grow prettier every time I see you."

With the smile sliding from her mouth, Christina felt the warm colour rushing to her cheeks. It was true enough, Uncle Peter did always say things like that, and it was something she wished he wouldn't do. It always made her blush, something that Lars seemed to find amusing. Well, she wasn't going to look at him, so this time he could grin all he wanted to. He could grin until his face cracked open even.

Her somewhat satisfying contemplation of such an event was abruptly shattered by her father's excited voice announcing, "Ah, Christina, you must hear our wonderful news! We are to go to Australia!"

Christina, about to cross the room to a chair on the far side, stopped as though suddenly turned to stone, her head jerking in her father's direction. What on earth was he talking about? How could they be going to Australia? Australia was on the far side of the world!

"Oh Simon, what a way to tell her! You've shocked the poor child clear out of her wits." The gently scolding voice belonged to Maria Ohlssen and Christina turned quickly in her direction, her eyes questioning. Was it a joke? Her father liked to make jokes. Was that what he was doing now? Aunty Maria didn't seem to think it was a joke. She gave her a gentle, sympathetic smile, then continued to upbraid her father. "You should have taken a little more time, broken the news more tactfully, for one thing."

"More tactfully! What are you talking about, good woman? Such great news doesn't require tact in the telling. It needs to be shouted from the rooftops. Why, this is the greatest news we have had in a long, long time, perhaps even the greatest we have ever had. Isn't that so, Peter, old friend?" Simon Skov's voice rang with enthusiasm and good humour and he flung an arm about the other man's shoulder, reaching up to do so, for, although he was a strong man with broad shoulders, he was only five and a half feet tall, a good eight inches shorter than his companion.

"Yes, of course it is, Simon." Peter Ohlssen's agreement came readily enough, but there was something in the deep, familiar voice that caused Christina to again turn her head sharply. He doesn't really mean that, she thought. He's only saying it's wonderful news because Father is so excited about it.

Peter Ohlssen's gaze dropped from her suddenly knowing stare and he reached for his beer stein. "Let us drink to Australia, once again."

"For the twentieth time, I should think," Elsie murmured as she settled herself on a chair beside the other woman. "It seems, Maria, that our husbands have found an excuse to drink a goodly quantity of beer this evening."

Still standing in the middle of the room, Christina now stared at her mother incredulously. She was smiling and there was nothing of reprimand in her voice, nothing at all. It's all a dream, she thought, it has to be. Father is getting drunk. We are going to Australia. And Mother doesn't seem to mind in the least.

"To Australia!" the two men shouted, with Peter Ohlssen adding, "And to a happy and prosperous life for the Skov family in that country!"

Christina shifted her gaze back to them, watching wide-eyed as they drank deeply of the strong, frothy beer. To Australia? But their home was here in Haderslev, in Schleswig. Why would they want to go to some distant land? Why would they want to leave this lovely valley where everything was so familiar, so much a part of their lives? It was all so bewildering it felt as though she had walked into a strange dream.

Lowering his stein to the floor, Simon wiped his thick, curling beard with the back of one hand while he held the other out to his daughter. "Come, Christina, sit beside me. I want to hear what you have to say about our good fortune. Free passage to Australia. How about that, eh?"

Christina moved obediently to his side, but, once on the small space he made for her on the end of the settee, she sat stiffly, her mind a confusion of thoughts as she tried to recall what she had learned about that far country. Perhaps she might be able to think of something that would help her understand why her father would want to go there. It was the land of the kangaroo, that amazing, hopping creature that carried its babies in a pouch. And of the koala and other strange creatures that lived nowhere else in all the world. But there were black people there, savages who carried spears and boomerangs and killed with them. And convicts who had been sent there from England and Ireland for doing vile deeds.

"Well," her father persisted, tweaking her ear, "you must have something to say, Christina?"

"I don't understand, Father. Why would we want to go to Australia?"

Simon knew the answer to that question very well. He had been telling it to himself for months now, and in the weeks to come he would tell it to all who asked and to many who didn't. Finally, at the age of thirty-seven years, he had dreamed a dream that was about to become a reality, and he saw no reason why everyone shouldn't know about it, why they shouldn't share in his enormous excitement. A new beginning, far removed from all the disappointments that had thus far clouded his life. That was what had come his way: the opportunity to return to the way of life for which he had been born, that of a farmer.

"Land," he declared now. "That's why we are going, Christina, for the land. You cannot even begin to imagine how much is available in that country. And with all the goodness God gave it still intact. It hasn't been tilled a thousand or more times. It's virgin land, child, thousands of acres of it. Why, it's said that some who have taken up land there can ride for a full day and still not reach the end of their property. And it's nothing for an ordinary man with little in his pockets to own a farm of two hundred acres or more. How different that is from the small plots of spent earth which is all we can ever hope for in Schleswig."

There was a dreamy, far-away look in his eyes and Christina slipped her small hand into his, trying to see what it was that he saw. Two hundred acres? Yes, that would be a lot of land. No wonder her father was so excited. He would be able to be a farmer again, the sort of farmer he had been when he was young, and as her grandfather and uncle in Herning up in Central Jutland still were. But had he remembered how very far away Australia was, or that there were black people and convicts living there? "It would take us a long time to get there, wouldn't it, Father?"

"Yes, several months in fact. But it will be worth it, little one. Not only for the land, but for the security we will be able to feel there. Australia is one complete land isolated from the rest of the world. There'll be no Napoleon, no Prussia, no Austria to make wars or steal its territory."

Christina suppressed a shiver. No wars and no Prussians that would be wonderful, of course. But a land apart from all others, sitting on its own in the vastness of the great oceans. How could that be a good thing?

"If only it weren't so remote," Maria murmured, almost as though she had read Christina's thoughts. "It will be a blessing, of course, to have no Prussians ruling the roost, but there's something rather frightening about such isolation from the rest of the world."

Simon lifted his shoulders in a dismissive shrug. "If it hadn't been so isolated, Maria, Australia would have been settled long ago and we wouldn't have been given this wonderful opportunity."

"I suppose not. But the country is still pretty much a wilderness and I keep thinking about how far it has to go, to catch up, so to speak. There will be so many things missing that we simply take for granted: doctors, hospitals, and have you thought about schools? In this country we are so fortunate in this regard. These days everyone has the opportunity to acquire an education."

"There are schools in Australia, Maria, and, as more and more people settle there, so will there be more schools. If it happens that there are none where we take up land, then I will be responsible for Christina's education."

Peter chuckled and leaned forward to wink at Christina. "I know that you are pretty smart, Simon, but I can't see that arrangement working."

"Why not?" Simon's eyebrows had shot up, creasing his wide brow. "I think I would be a very good teacher."

"Yes, I'm sure you would, but Christina would learn more poetry than would ever be of use to her and probably at the expense of something else, history or arithmetic, for instance."

Simon grinned and, watching him, Christina felt the corners of her own lips curl. Uncle Peter was probably right. Her father loved the works of the Danish poets. He read them at every opportunity and often recited verses from the slim, well-worn volumes out loud. And she loved to listen to him, even though the words he read sometimes had a sadness to them, a gentle sadness that brought tears to her eyes but didn't really make her unhappy.

Peter Ohlssen wasn't the first person to have teased Simon about his 'weakness' as he called it, not by a long way. A passion for poetry had come to Simon, the youngest of four brothers in a farming family, during his adolescent years, and right away the teasing had begun. His older brothers really did consider it a weakness for a farmer to spend his evenings reading verse and they tormented him mercilessly. That this, even when he was still quite young, bothered him not at all may have been due, at least in some degree, to the fact that he had a very strong ally in his mother.

Sidsell Neilsdatter, as she had been before her marriage to Madsen Skov, had never been to school and she could neither read nor write. As a young girl working in a factory and later as the hard-working wife of a farmer with four sons to raise, she had held this to be of little importance. But, when the youngest of those sons took to burying his nose in the books he either borrowed from the schoolmaster or bought with money saved for that very purpose, a strange longing stirred within her and she ached to know what the books contained that could be so engrossing. Simon found her one afternoon frowning over an open volume and began to read to her. Her obvious pleasure added to his and the practice had continued through the years he lived at home. It was largely due to his mother's contriving that he'd been able to acquire the volumes he now treasured – the works of Adam Oehlschlager, Adolf Wiljelm Schack Staffeldt and Bernard Severin Ingemann.

Now he declared cheerfully, "I think Christina might enjoy that. Poetry would be much more pleasant than doing those sums, wouldn't it, little one?"

Christina nodded. "Yes, it would, Father." She wanted to tell him about getting all her sums right, to see the pleased look that would come to his face. But, somehow, this didn't seem to be the time. For one thing, Lars Ohlssen would probably think that she was trying to make out that she was clever and grin all over his face. And, for another, it seemed that all her father wanted to think about right now was going to Australia.

"For a time we'll probably be too busy even to think about reading verse," Simon told Peter. "Whatever land we take up will need to be cleared and fenced, at least in part. And we'll need a house, of course, and furniture."

"Yes, you'll be busy alright. But you're fortunate in that you'll be able to build your own home and make whatever furniture you'll be needing. And I should think there'll be plenty of work available for men able to turn their hands to carpentry."

"That there is, by all accounts, and it will suit me to be able to get some work in the building trade. Naturally, we won't be able to extract a living from the land right away and in the meantime we'll be needing money to live on. What funds we have to take with us will be expended soon enough. But what I really want to do is farm, and the day when I am able to do that full-time will never come quickly enough."

Peter Ohlssen nodded slowly, understanding. Simon had left the family farm in Herning when he turned sixteen, not because he had wanted to, but because it had been necessary. The farm was only large enough to support his parents and the eldest son and his family. Danish laws had seen to that, ensuring, as they did, that there would be no extension of landed property and no union of small farms; always encouraging or insisting upon division, sub-division, and then more sub-division. What fools our law-makers are, Peter mused grimly. No wonder men like Simon are ready to leave for far places at the first opportunity that comes their way.

"I know how you feel, old friend," he said quietly. "But a little patience and the day will come when you'll be the full-time farmer you want to be. In the meantime, you'll have a chance to adjust and take a look at how farming in Australia should be tackled – a quite different proposition from that in Europe, I would think." He frowned suddenly. "Have you thought that it might be a good idea to spend a little time in the more settled areas around Sydney to begin with?"

"No, of course not, Peter! The Colony of Queensland is the place to go. There can be no doubt about that, none at all. It's only been open for free settlement since the forties, and there's good land not far from the coast which has only just been explored; within fifty to one hundred miles of Brisbane Township, by all accounts. I have been told that there are any number of valleys in the region, with deep, rich soil and permanent streams. And the flat lands along the rivers are apparently well-suited to sugarcane. You wouldn't find anything like that still available close to Sydney. In any case, it's the Queensland Government which is providing our free passage, so, naturally, we'll be required to settle in that colony."

"Sugarcane, eh? That would be a crop to be thinking about."

"Yes, there's money to be made from sugar alright. Labour seems to be a real problem, though, not only for the growing and cutting of the cane, but for public works as well."

"I don't know why we don't go too," Lars interceded suddenly and a little sullenly. "Everybody knows that Australia is a land of opportunity where fortunes are just waiting to be made. Look at all the gold they've already found there and they've barely scratched the surface. There's bound to be stacks more."

"There might well be, Lars," Simon told him with a quick grin, "but I don't intend to go looking for it I grant you that it would be a quick way to becoming rich if a man happened to be lucky enough, but it would be too risky a business at my time in life and with a family to support. No, farming in the new Colony of Queensland will suit me just fine."

"Well, you'll probably make your fortune farming if the land is as rich as they say. I still think I'd be going for the gold, though, to begin with, at any rate." He shifted his gaze to his father. "Why don't we go, Father? You know there's no real future for Danes in Schleswig now that it belongs to Prussia."

Peter Ohlssen considered his son for a long moment in silence and, when he did speak, his voice was strangely quiet, as though his words came from thoughts reluctantly acknowledged. "There are those who say there wasn't any great future for either Danes or Germans when Schleswig belonged to Denmark."

Lars flung out a hand in a repudiating gesture. "People who say such things don't know what they are talking about. They keep thinking back to the time before Schleswig and Holstein revolted, but that was twenty-one years ago. Once they were brought back under Danish rule things improved. In any case, the important thing is that we were Danes under Danish rule, which we certainly are not now. We are Danes under Prussian rule."

"Yes, that is so. But it can't be denied that we were more often than not overlooked by Copenhagen. In fact, there were times when it seemed that the king was quite unaware that he had duchies by name of Schleswig and Holstein in his realm."

"Father," Lars protested, his dark eyes flashing, "you talk like a Holsteiner!"

"Well, were we not in the same boat as the Holsteiners?" Peter queried, unruffled by his son's outburst.

"We might have been at one time," Lars admitted grudgingly, "but we certainly weren't when the Prussians arrived. The Holsteiners are all Germans, for God's sake. They welcomed Prussian rule."

"Whereas we in Schleswig are for the most part Danes, who haven't taken at all kindly to Prussian rule," Simon interceded, anxious to clear the moment of tension between father and son. "We all know that, Lars, but let us not forget that Schleswig-Holstein was a united duchy for close on five hundred years. The people of Holstein have never been our enemies, even though the Danish Government tried to force them into assimilation and obliged them to have Danish as the official language in their schools. And they aren't our enemies now even though their nationality did allow them to take more kindly to Prussian rule. Besides, your father is quite right – neither duchy had a fair deal from Copenhagen. If they had, the German Confederation would have had nothing to kick up a fuss about and Prussia and Austria may not have interfered."

"I would have my doubts about that, Uncle Simon. The Prussians have always been warmongers, and the Austrians are almost as bad."

"It has certainly seemed so, I grant you that. But it's Bismarck's Prussia now, remember? As it was at the time of the invasion and when the two powers fell out in '66, and you may be sure there's a deeper reason for anything that man does than seems obvious. We might well ask ourselves, in view of what has happened since, whether he really wanted to annex Schleswig-Holstein or whether he was just looking for an excuse to trigger off a war with Austria? And was the reason, in fact, the German Confederation?"

Lars shook his head. "I could never even try to figure out what might be behind anything Bismarck does."

"Well, what's done is done," Elsie interrupted quietly but firmly. "Please let us not be talking about the war again. It's six years in the past now, and we especially don't want it throwing a cloud over this day."

"No, we do not," Peter agreed quickly, smiling at her. "We have so many other things to discuss, but I think that perhaps you had better save room in one of your trunks for Lars."

Lars was not about to be so easily appeased. "I'll be going one day," he declared resolutely, ignoring the laughter that had followed his father's small jest. "I have heard of lads of eighteen who have gone on their own and, if the truth be known, there have probably been others even younger."

The smile died on Maria's face, the tightness of apprehension taking its place. From the face of her husband, too, all semblance of joviality had fled. Watching them, Christina promptly decided that this was one of the times when she didn't particularly like Lars Ohlssen. Why would he have to go and say a thing like that, for heaven's sake? He must know how his parents would feel, what with him being the youngest of their five children and the only boy.

In the sudden stillness that had come to the room, Elsie got to her feet, smiling down at the woman beside her. "I believe it's time to do something about supper, Maria. These people must be getting hungry and that stew is beginning to smell good."

Maria appeared to give herself a mental shake before exclaiming brightly, "Ah yes, it certainly does. In fact, it smells more than good. It smells wonderful and my stomach is fair doing somersaults in anticipation."

Laughter returned to the room, and Christina was relieved to see that Lars smiled too, his eyes softening as they rested on his mother. Perhaps he did understand how she felt, and, when he really thought about it, he would surely see that he couldn't just go off and leave her, not all the way to Australia. She half rose, intending to go with the women to the kitchen for it was normally her task to lay the table, but her mother gestured to her to remain. "Aunty Maria and I can manage, Christina. You stay and listen. I'm sure your father has a great deal more to tell you."

"That I have, indeed!" Simon declared, giving her a quick hug. "But surely you have some questions, Christina, something you want to know about our great adventure?"

Some questions? She had a thousand questions. So many, in fact, it seemed that her head was getting ready to burst. But they chased each other round and round in her mind, making it difficult to untangle one with which to begin. Finally she asked, "Will we be going to Australia soon, Father?"

"Not right away, love, but fairly soon. And I should think soon enough, for we will have much to do in the meantime. Our ship sails in April." He chuckled softly. "What a year 1871 is going to be for us. And we will be arriving in Australia just one hundred and one years after its discovery by Captain Cook."

April, Christina was thinking, that was more than four months away, but it was the very middle of spring. Just when the countryside was at its most beautiful, they would be going away. The very thought was almost unbearable and she swallowed hard against the lump of tears that formed suddenly in her throat. "Will it be spring in Australia too, Father?"

"In April? No, Christina. It will be autumn in Australia. It's in the southern hemisphere and the seasons are reversed. You learnt that at school only recently, remember?"

Christina nodded. She wasn't really sure why it wasn't spring everywhere at the same time, but she did know about Australia being in the southern hemisphere. In fact, on the globe at school, it seemed that it was under the world almost. And it was so very far away with all those huge oceans around it, at least one of which they would have to cross before they got there. "Will we be going in a big ship?"

"Indeed we will. A big ship with lots of sails, much bigger than any that come into Haderslev Harbour. We will have to go to Hamburg to board the Friedeburg. That's what the ship is named, the Friedeburg. Just think, a train journey and then a great sea voyage. Won't that be exciting?"

"I don't know what it's like to be on a ship, but I do like the train." A train journey to Hamburg, that was a long way, Christina told herself, probably a hundred miles or more. Well, that at least should be fun. When they visited Grandmother and Grandfather Skov up in Herning, they went by train and she always enjoyed that. It was amusing to watch the countryside go rushing by.

"How big is the Friedeburg, Uncle Simon?" Lars asked.

"Over eight hundred tons, around eight hundred and twenty, I believe."

"That's a good size, but there are quite a few ships over a thousand tons now, some even as much as two thousand tons." Lars grinned appreciatively. "Gosh, can you imagine that? A sailing ship of two thousand tons? What a sight that would be."

"They are getting to be big alright," Simon agreed. "And we probably have the Americans to thank for that. They've taken to ship-building in a huge way."

"Perhaps they are getting to be too big," Peter mused. "They'll be needing such large crews to handle them and I doubt that it's really necessary to have ships of such size."

"Well, I suppose, so long as they don't have to sacrifice speed or manoeuvrability … "

Although almost ten centuries had passed, the love of the sea and ships passed down through generations from their Viking forefathers still flowed with the blood in their veins, sleeping only lightly, easily aroused. As it was now. They talked of clippers and schooners; of merchantmen and downeasters; of the Challenge and the Flying Cloud; of the Lightning which, homeward bound on her maiden voyage, had set a new record of sixty-four days from Melbourne to Liverpool; and of the Great Republic, the huge American ship which was the largest ever built and which, a year previously, had been sold to a Liverpool firm and renamed the Denmark. They talked of lengths and beams, of masts and sail areas, of keel plates made of iron. And of the steamships …

"I can't see them taking over from sail, not completely," Peter ventured, frowning thoughtfully at the old pipe he had taken from his pocket but not taken the time to light. "Just think of the amount of coal they would need for a long voyage, to Australia, for instance. The shipping companies would need to have a whole system of coaling stations along the route. And then what of the cost? How would they meet such expenses and still manage to make a profit?"

"That's a problem alright, Peter, but the Suez Canal will be an enormous help to the steamships."

"It will help you, too, Uncle Simon," Lars broke in with a quick grin. "It will make your journey ever so much shorter."

"That it will, Lars. It seems that we have waited for a good time to go. With luck and good sailing conditions we could reach our destination in around a hundred days."

Christina had been paying only idle attention to the conversation, but now she stiffened, disbelief flowing through her. One hundred days on a ship? It wasn't possible! What would they do in all that time? What would they eat? Oh, surely her father had made a mistake. Surely he would correct what he had just said.

But it was Lars who spoke. "It would have been great if you could have gone on the Cutty Sark; you'd have been there in no time at all."

Simon chuckled. "That we would, Lars, my boy. But it's hardly likely the Queensland Government would engage such a new ship for free-passage immigrants. We must be thankful that they have seen fit to put us on one as sturdy as the Friedeburg."

"She'll be sturdy alright. If there's one thing we can't deny the Germans, it's that they build darn good ships." Peter was finally puffing away at his pipe. "There'll be quite a lot of Germans on board, I should imagine. I understand they are going out to Australia in their hundreds."

Christina stifled a dismayed gasp. A German ship! Not only was it going to take them a hundred days to reach Australia, they were going there on a German ship! And German people would be travelling with them, even Prussians, more than likely. And worse. Not only would they be on the ship, they would also be staying in Australia. Oh, what was her father thinking of, for heaven's sake? If they were to share the land with the Prussians, no matter how much of it there was, living in Australia wouldn't be all that different from living in Schleswig. "Will there be Prussians going too, Father?" she asked, unable to hide her anxiety.

"Ah Christina, there's no call for you to be concerned in that respect. Any Prussians who go to Australia will be immigrants just as we will be – people who have left their homeland to begin a new life in a new country. They won't be rulers there, mark my word. For one thing, the country belongs to England and there'll be nothing anyone can do to change that. For another, all who go there, whatever nationality they might be, will do so on an equal basis. And many are going, Christina, from most of the countries of Europe and from all over Great Britain. In time, what we all are – Danish, English, Irish, German, Italian, Greek – won't really matter. We will all be living as one people, that's the only way it can be."

Always Danish? Oh, no wonder the old tree had mocked her. They wouldn't always be Danish. They were going to a country where they would be expected to be something else. One people, but what would that one people be? What clothes would they wear? And, even more importantly, what language would they speak? "What language will we speak in Australia, Father?"

"English, everyone will speak English." Simon chuckled quietly. "Once we know more of the language than we do now, of course."

"Won't we speak Danish at all?"

"We will certainly remember our own language and between ourselves we will probably use it still, but only on occasions. English will be the language in general use and we must practise it at every opportunity until it comes naturally to us." He smiled reassuringly. "You already know some English, Christina. Now you must learn much more. It won't be all that difficult, you will probably even enjoy it."

This time Christina failed to smother the sigh that came to her lips, but a quick glance at her father assured her that he hadn't heard. He was listening intently to something Uncle Peter was telling him about a Danish/English dictionary he'd seen. She wanted to believe him, but something told her that learning to speak English was going to be anything but easy. Besides, she would not only have to learn to speak it, but also to read and write it. And, if all English words were like those she already knew, she was quite sure she wasn't going to like the language. It wasn't at all soft and gentle like Danish. Always Danish ... oh, had it really been only an hour or so ago that she had made that promise? "Will we all be English when we get to Australia, Father?"

"No, Christina. We will all be Australians."

"Even the black people and the convicts?"

"Well, I suppose so. The convicts who decide to settle there after serving their sentences certainly will be. And it could be said that the Aborigines have been Australians for a very long time, the very first Australians."

"But they are savages," Lars exclaimed. "And black. How could they possibly have the same nationality as you and all the other Europeans who are going there?"

"I know it seems a strange idea, Lars, especially when there has been quite a deal of conflict between whites and blacks. But, given time, things will change. The Aborigines will come to accept our presence, and, if we are to share a land with them, we should also be able to share a nationality."

Lars chewed thoughtfully on his lower lip. "I suppose so, but it's an idea that will take some getting used to, and it may not be what other white people going to Australia have in mind." He turned to his father. "What say you, Father? Can whites and blacks share a nationality?"

Peter drew his eyebrows together in a scowling frown. "What would I know of such things? I know almost nothing about the Aborigines and I certainly wouldn't want to be trying to predict how the general run of Europeans settling in Australia will react to such a notion, noble though it seems to be."

"Not noble, just natural," Simon corrected quietly.

The scowl left his friend's face. "Well, I hope it all works out satisfactorily for everyone concerned."

Christina had been listening intently, a new set of visions adding to the confusion in her mind. Did her father mean that they would have black people for neighbours? That she might be going to school with black children? And what about the convicts? Did the fact that they had finished serving their sentences mean that they weren't bad people anymore? She breathed a faint sigh of relief when her mother's voice calling that supper was ready interrupted her search for answers. They were too hard to find, much too hard.

The table in the kitchen had been covered with a brightly checked cloth, on which plates and cutlery and the newly baked bread lay waiting. Christina took her place and waited patiently to be served, her mind turning over all the incredible things she had learned this evening. Suddenly, a question, more vital than all the others, swam free of the many still to be asked. "Father … ?"

"Yes, what is it, Christina?"

"How long will it be before we come back to Schleswig?"

Christina would remember for a long time the stillness that followed her question, the silence that seemed to go on and on. All eyes were on her and she moved uneasily on her chair. Had she said something wrong? Something to annoy her father? The laughter of a moment before had gone from his face and he looked at her so strangely, as though he could find no words with which to answer her.

And then she knew. It wasn't only in the words her father couldn't find. It was written on his face and on all the faces turned towards her. They wouldn't be coming back to Schleswig, not ever.

2

The days that followed brought an onslaught of confused emotions. Anticipation, apprehension, excitement and heartache all came and went in such rapid succession it seemed to Christina that there was scarcely a moment when she felt as she had the moment before. When she was with her father, listening to him planning the things they would do, seeing his happiness, feeling his excitement, she thought only of what they were going to – a fine new life on a farm. But there were other times – times when she could think only of what they would be leaving behind, and that was when the heartache came, on some nights so overwhelming she wept into her pillow.

And the heartache grew, taking on new dimensions, on the Saturday she went into town with her mother and baby sister to inform her maternal grandparents of what they planned to do. She came into her grandfather Christiansen's crowded little tailoring shop feeling none of the pleasure she usually felt on such occasions. Dread had taken its place – dread and a tearful compassion. Not only were such visits now numbered, the news they bore would come as a great shock and bring a lasting sadness to the little shop and the apartment above where her grandparents lived.

They were stricken, as she had known they would be, their faces becoming bleak and incredulous, their eyes filling with tears. Only for a moment though did her mother falter. Then she went on talking, but in a much more animated fashion than was her wont. With her hands moving about nervously, she explained that it was a wonderful opportunity for them, that there was so much land available they would be able to have the big farm they had always wanted. She assured them that Australia was no longer a vast continent inhabited only by blacks and convicts, that ships were sailing almost every week, transporting people from all over Europe and Great Britain. She stressed that there was no real danger since the region they were going to was one of fairly close settlement, and that, although the voyage would be long, there was no cause for concern in that regard either, for the Friedeburg was a sturdy ship and this wouldn't be the first voyage it had made to Australia.

Christina saw that her grandparents had blinked back their tears and were trying very hard to look pleased. It's for our sake, she decided bleakly. They want to act pleased because this opportunity has come our way and Mother has told them it's what we want. She longed to run into her grandmother's arms and have her hug her close. But, if she did that, she would be sure to cry, perhaps even say that she didn't want to go to Australia; that she wouldn't go but would stay here in Haderslev with them. Which, of course, she couldn't do – she would die so far from her mother and father and little Anna.

They all tried, keeping their voices cheerful, making small jokes and smiling often. In spite of their efforts, the silences came and hung heavily as thoughts wandered and fragile holds on light-heartedness threatened to break. The minutes dragged by, pulling the visit to an end they'd all begun to long for, to an hour when the wearying pretence could be cast aside. It came at last, and Elsie and her daughters left the little shop and made their way to where their horse and buggy waited.

On the narrow street leading away from the little shop, Christina heard her mother sigh, a low, grieving sound. When she looked up, she saw that her cheeks were damp and shining. Compassion washed through her and she wanted to weep for her mother. How terrible it must have been for her, having to tell her mother and father that after April she wouldn't ever see them again. That was really what she had done, even though no such words had been spoken. And those gentle, kindly people whom they all loved so dearly weren't the only ones she'd be leaving for all time. There were also her brothers and sisters and their families, and all her friends, people she had been close to all her life for she had been born right here in Haderslev.

Elsie's competent hands soon had the big horse moving briskly away from the centre of town, its hooves setting up a steady clip-clopping on the cobblestones. Christina watched the shops and other buildings slipping by but with none of her usual interest. Even the big new brewery which her father was helping to build received only a brief glance. It's because of Father, she thought bleakly. That's why Mother is going, because he thinks that it's a good idea.

"Mother … ?"

"What is it, Christina?"

"Do you really want to go to Australia?"

Her mother tossed her a swift, reproving glance. "Of course I do. Why would you ask such a silly question? Hasn't your father told you over and over what a wonderful opportunity it will be for all of us?"

Biting her lip, Christina pushed herself further back on the hard leather seat, but not before she had seen the faint pink colour that had come to her mother's cheeks. She longed to cry out, What about you, Mother? Do you think it will be a wonderful opportunity? Do you think we will be happy in that strange new land? Do you really and truly want to go? But her mother had spoken so sharply and been so displeased at her first question, it seemed best to remain silent. Well, she told herself resignedly, she didn't really need to ask. She already knew how it was – her mother didn't want to go. Of course she didn't. Her father, always planning and dreaming, always full of enthusiasm and adventurous notions, had decided they would leave Schleswig and go to Australia, and her mother, believing that it was his place to make such decisions, had agreed with him. It was as simple as that.

The baby had nodded off in her basket and Christina wished that she could go to sleep too. Her eyes were stinging, her face felt stiff where tears had dried, and she longed to forget, even if it was just for a short while, that she had ever heard of a place called Australia. Oh, what a sad, sad day it had been. And to think there was another just like it still to come. It would wait until Christmas when, just as they did every year, they would go up to Herning, and then it would be her father's turn. Just as her mother had told her parents, so would he have to tell his. What an ordeal for him at such a time. And what an unhappy Christmas it was going to be.

"You will be happy in Australia, Christina."

Christina started, her drooping eyelids flying upwards, her gaze rushing to her mother's face, now turned towards her, a gently reassuring smile on the soft lips. "Oh Mother, it's so far away."

"I know, and for a time it won't be easy, having to leave Schleswig and the only life we have ever known for a distant land where everything will be so different. But you are very young and you'll adjust quickly enough. Besides, in so many ways, you are very much like your father, and you'll come to appreciate the wide horizons of your new country. Why, you'll grow up dreaming dreams that would never be possible here in Schleswig."

Christina couldn't see how this would be. Everything she had ever wanted was in Schleswig, right here in Haderslev. Why wouldn't it always be that way? Surely growing up didn't bring great changes in the way a person felt about such things. Though perhaps that wasn't really what her mother meant. "It's all so confusing I don't really know how I feel, Mother. Sometimes, when I think about living in Australia, I'm filled with excitement, but, other times, I'm so afraid I can hardly breathe."

"Well, I'm sure it's quite normal to have such reactions. Most people leaving the land of their birth to settle elsewhere would feel as you do. But you'll be just fine, Christina, you'll see. We all will be. It's just a question of getting used to the idea, and I'm sure we'll do that soon enough. By the time April comes round we'll probably be so excited there'll be no room for other feelings."

Christmas came and went, and, somehow, after an unhappy beginning, they did manage to make it a joyful occasion. Much to Christina's relief. She had spent days worrying that their last Christmas in Denmark was going to be one of gloom. When they'd first arrived at the farm in Herning and her father had blurted out his news, it seemed that all her worst fears were to be realised. Her grandmother had dropped the milk-jug she'd been carrying and begun weeping copious tears into her big apron, while her grandfather, convinced that his youngest son had taken leave of his senses, embarked upon a long and furious lecture. But, later, he'd apparently resigned himself to the fact that nothing he said was going to change things, for he'd done everything possible to ensure that this was their best Christmas ever. Other family members had arrived – uncles, aunts, cousins. So many it seemed that the big old farmhouse would burst at the seams. And there had been such merriment: games and presents; wonderful things to eat; chestnuts to roast; skating on the frozen pond; riding on the sled with its jingling bells.

Simon had also been relieved. Startled by his parents' reaction to his wonderful news, he'd suddenly seen the folly in telling them at such a time. Christmas was a time of joy and in the Skov family it had always been that way. But then, hadn't he been expecting his mother and father to be pleased that such good fortune had come his way? Certainly, he had never dreamed that they would be so against his taking his family to Australia. His father had practically called him a lunatic. Still, after his initial outburst, he hadn't really tried again to dissuade him. Only Madsen, his eldest brother, had done that.

"You're no longer young, Simon," he had declared in his brusque way. "Have you given thought to that? I won't deny that the opportunities seem to be there. But there'll be a lot of hard work before you begin to make any headway. This land you talk about acquiring is probably covered with jungle. Will you be up to clearing it?"

"I'm no weakling, Mads."

"I know that. But you are thirty-seven years old now, and Elsie only a couple of years younger."

"But that's the whole point. It's probably the last chance we'll have to do something like this, our last chance to make a real success of our lives."

"You could do that in Haderslev if you started your own business, as you've talked of doing. You know that Father has always been prepared to help and I could probably do something as well."

"I know, but I couldn't take money away from this farm. There's little enough for improvement as it is. In any case, what I really want is to be a farmer, Mads, a real farmer with a decent bit of land."

"Well, if you would consider returning to this region, we could perhaps acquire a small farm for you."

Simon had laughed, throwing his arm around his brother's shoulder.

"Don't you see, Mads? In Australia there's land such as you've never dreamed of. It probably is still covered with jungle, just as you say, but, once that's been cleared, what will we have? Virgin land. Just think of that, my brother. Hundreds of acres of never before tilled soil just waiting for our plough. How could I possibly forgo something like that for a small dairy farm in Denmark?"

"You're a dreamer, Simon. You always have been, and I'll tell you now that there have been times when I envied you that. I even wished that I could have gotten some of the pleasure you did out of reading those poetry books. But this is not one of those times. The very thought of uprooting my family and taking them halfway around the world to make a new beginning fair makes my blood run cold."

"But you are just the one who should be thinking about it. Three sons growing up, what an opportunity it would be for them. Just compare it to what they will have here in Denmark. How many of them will be able to stay on the farm? One perhaps, no more."

"You are right about that, of course. The two younger boys will have to look to acquire farms of their own or do other work. But you, Peter and Hans, were in the same situation, so that's not something new in our family. And the boys know how it will be. But, whatever you do, Simon, don't go saying anything to them about going to Australia, encouraging them, I mean. I'll never hear the end of it and I can just imagine what their mother will say."

"Of course not. But who knows? Perhaps one day you'll give the matter some serious thought."

"No, all of my days will be spent in Denmark, and those of my sons too, I hope. But you know that I wish you everything of the best, all the happiness and success you deserve. And we'll all be praying for you, Elsie and the girls."

The new year arrived, 1871. The early days of January went flying by and it was the 20th – Christina's eighth birthday. The Ohlssens came over from their farm and her grandparents drove out from town, along with several aunts, uncles and cousins. Flushed with excitement, Christina was sure that it was the best birthday she had ever had. When the thought came that it was also the last one she would be spending with so many people she loved, she resolutely thrust it aside. No such notion was going to spoil this special day.

With February, it seemed that on almost every day a new and important decision had to be taken. A second offer was received for their house and land; better than the earlier one, but not quite as good as they had hoped. Still, time was running out, and they needed to get such matters settled. Perhaps they should accept it. Yes, they would advise the agent first thing in the morning. Other possessions would have to be sold also: their furniture, some household effects, the horse and buggy, the geese, the two cows. Perhaps they should speak to the people interested in the house and land; it would simplify matters no end if they were to buy them. And there was the question of transport. It was finally arranged that the Ohlssens would bring their big wagon and their buggy and deliver them to the Haderslev station, from where they would take the train to Hamburg. Once there, they would hire a horse and wagon to take them from the station to the wharf.

There remained, however, some really bothersome questions. Just what should they take with them? What clothes would they need during the long voyage and when they reached Australia? What other articles? What would they need on their arrival that couldn't be purchased in Brisbane? There came a day when Simon returned from town gleefully waving a brochure and declaring that all such uncertainties were at an end since a person by name of John Capper had seen fit to prepare and publish the Emigrant's Guide to Australia. While his wife prepared their evening meal, he settled himself at the table, the brochure spread before him. "I will read it out aloud," he decided, "so that we will all know what this obliging fellow has to say."

"That's a good idea," Elsie told him. "I just hope that he has some reliable answers to our questions."

"He certainly does! I've already glanced quickly through the whole thing, but I'll start at the beginning. For the steerage or lowest class …" Simon looked up with a rueful grin. "That's us, I'm afraid." He began again, "For the steerage or lowest class, sleeping places are put up on either side of the lower deck, though for married people separate berths are erected."

"Well, thanks be for that." Elsie murmured fervently. "At least we are to have a little privacy. What does he say about the bedding?"

"Patience, wife, I'm coming to that. He says that bedding is sometimes added, and always cooking and mess utensils."

"Sometimes? That's not much help."

"No, it's not. I'll have to check with the shipping company, though I think that, in any case, this fellow would only be referring to mattresses and pillows. I know there's a paragraph further on where he says something about bedding under the heading of 'Other Suggestions', but we'll come to that in good time. It will be less confusing if I go on reading from the beginning." He returned his gaze to the brochure. "Since a long voyage is involved with the possibility of a rough journey at the end of it, too many belongings are a nuisance, besides being expensive to transport. Be sure to cull out your possessions. Books are heavy so ration them. Apart from the Bible, there should be a book or two of instructive tales for the children and, if possible, a few volumes of standard English literature, with a few lighter for the wife."

"Hmmm … English literature," Elsie mused. "Well, English is the language we have to learn so it seems Mr Capper has the right idea." There was a humorous glint in the eyes which sought Christina's and her lips curled in a conspiratorial smile. "If we have only English books with us, then that is what we will read."

Christina giggled and, bending her head over the bowl of peas she was shelling, watched her father out of the corner of her eye. A look of dismay had brought a comical, open-mouthed expression to his face and he seemed to be having trouble finding his voice. "Wha-t?" he stammered. "What do you mean?"

"Just what I said. If we have only English books to read, we are bound to learn the language much more quickly."

Simon noisily cleared his throat. "I don't think we need … well, to be as drastic as all that."

"But haven't you been telling us that the voyage will provide a good opportunity to learn to speak English?"

"Yes, of course, but that doesn't mean … "

"It means we must do as Mr Capper suggests and take a selection of English literature with us." She gave an exaggerated sigh. "I'm sure he would never approve of including Staffeldt, Ingemann and such like in our luggage."

There was such a stricken look on her father's face, Christina was overcome by a fit of giggles and, hearing her, Elsie was unable to contain her own laughter. Simon at once threw back his head on a loud guffaw. "What a joke, by Jove! The two of you really had me on there. The devil take Mr Capper, my books go with me!"

"Before he does," Elsie suggested, "let us hear some more of what he has to say."

"Well, I think that's enough about books for the time being." He gave a deep chuckle before returning his attention to the brochure. "This next part is very important, I should think. He says that one box or bag only may be taken into the sleeping berth, sufficient to contain a month's clothing, at which time the passengers have access to their chests in the hold, replacing the clothes used by clean ones."

"Do we have to wear the same things over and over without washing them?" Christina gasped, dismay quickly disposing of her lingering amusement.

"Oh, I'm sure we'll be able to wash some things," her father told her. "But there won't be much water you know? I think it will be rationed to something like three quarts a day per person. And that's both for drinking and for washing ourselves."

"But there's so much water in the ocean."

"You wouldn't want to be drinking that, child. It's too salty. I don't see why it couldn't be used for bathing or washing clothes, though. However, I suppose that's something we'll find out in due course. Now, listen to what Mr Capper has to say about the sort of clothes we should take. Clothes must be strong and serviceable. Let men, for instance, avoid all sorts of fancy waistcoats, dandy boots, or costly cravats and ties. Let women shun the little vanities of silks and satins, of lace and ribbons, of many flounces and fashionable bonnets. And let both men and women forget that there are such things in the world as kid gloves, lavender water and toilet tables."

Elsie gave a soft chuckle. "Does he really say all that?"

"Indeed he does." Simon tapped the page with his forefinger. "It's all here in black and white."

"Well, we won't have too much of a problem in that respect; we don't own most of those things. I should have thought that lavender water would have been a good thing to take, however."

"I've got some lavender water," Christina said with a faint frown. "The bottle Aunty Maria gave me for my birthday. She said it was for the voyage, and I haven't even opened it yet. Won't I be able to take it with me?"

"Of course you will, Christina. And your mother will take hers too. And her kid gloves. Nowhere in the world do they make such fine leather gloves as they do in Odense. It would be sheer folly not to take a pair. In fact, I think, Elsie, that you should take more than the one pair, since they would weigh little enough and take up almost no space. And I will also defy Mr Capper and take the silk cravat I wore the day we were married." He winked at Christina. "Which I'm sure your mother has forgotten."

Elsie smiled at him. "I don't recall that it was costly, but it is silk and such a nice colour."

She must be happy about going, Christina thought, her eyes on her mother's face. Otherwise, she wouldn't be smiling and joking the way she has been. Perhaps it really was like she'd said, that, as the time for them to leave drew near, they would all be too excited to think about anything else. But a small doubt niggled at her mind. There was something about the way her mother was behaving, something that was strangely out of place. Her father had always joked and laughed a lot, but not her mother. She had always been quieter, more serious, not at all the way she was now, like she was acting, almost.

Her father's voice cut across her wondering. "Now this is something. It's what Mr. Capper considers the minimum outfit for a couple." He glanced up to make sure that he had the attention of both wife and daughter, then continued dramatically, "For the wife: three cotton dresses, one pair stays, four petticoats, sixteen chemises, two flannel petticoats, twelve pairs cotton stockings, four pairs black worsted stockings, six nightdresses and caps, six pocket handkerchiefs, four handkerchiefs for the neck, six caps, two bonnets, cloak and shawl, one pair boots, two pairs shoes, and eight towels." He looked up, grinning widely. "What have you to say to that, good wife?"

"That I will need to do quite a deal of shopping before we leave!" Elsie shook her head disbelievingly. "Sixteen chemises? Twelve pairs of cotton stockings? Whoever would own those quantities of such things?"

"Hmmm ... I think I will be joining you on your shopping venture. This is what the husband is advised to take: Two fustian jackets, waistcoats and trousers, three pairs of canvas trousers, one overcoat, two felt hats, one cap, sixteen striped shirts, two Guernsey shirts, twelve pairs cotton half hose, four pairs worsted hose, six handkerchiefs, eight towels, two pairs boots and one pair shoes, strong but not heavy. Two felt hats, for heaven's sake! Mr. Capper must think I've got two heads. And what need would I have of sixteen striped shirts? I don't like striped shirts."

They all laughed and Christina felt the niggling doubt slip away. It was going to be alright.

"And now for the worthy Mr Capper's next suggestion: a flock mattress and bolster, one pair blankets, one coverlet, six pairs cotton sheets."

"Ah, that really does tell us something. And, regardless of what the shipping company supplies, that's what we will take for each of us. We have so many goose-feather quilts, I can quite easily turn some into small mattresses. They'll be much more comfortable than any the shipping line is likely to supply."

Simon nodded. "So that takes care of the bedding. Now for the rest of it. According to what our friend has to say, we will also need to take two or three tablecloths, six pounds of yellow soap, three pounds of marine soap, metal hand-wash basin, knives and forks, one quart tin hook-pot, one coffee pot, comb and brush, a supply of string, sewing essentials such as tape, buttons and so forth."

Elsie opened her mouth to speak, but Simon held up his hand. "Wait! There's more! And this will really be of interest to you, Elsie. Mr Capper says that, should a little extra means be at command, let it be expended in laying in small supplies of calicoes, brown holland, camlet, fine canvas etc. It will always be desirable that the wife makes as many of her clothes on board ship as possible, as the occupation helps to pass away many an otherwise idle, heavy hour."

"How very thoughtful of Mr Capper," Elsie remarked, tongue-in-cheek. "What does he suggest for the husband? How is he to pass his idle hours?"

"He doesn't say," Simon told her with a wide grin, "but I would expect that it would be playing cards or reading."

"Or maybe sewing on his shirt buttons?"

Christina burst out laughing as her father threw up his hands in mock horror. "I can just picture you doing that, Father."

"And perhaps we should teach him to do some stitching as well," Elsie suggested. "If we are to take material on board, we should take full advantage of all that free time we will be having."

They all laughed, and a feeling of well-being enfolded Christina, everything was going to be just fine.

But neither Christina nor her father knew of the resolve Elsie had made on the drive home after visiting her parents, when her daughter's question had caught her so unawares. Henceforth, she had admonished herself, her doubts and fears would be well concealed. Just as they should be. It wasn't fitting for a woman to be showing weakness or reluctance when her husband was doing something he felt to be right, for all of them. Besides, hadn't she always expected that the time would come when he would want to leave Haderslev? The only real surprise was that it had taken so long.

It was twelve years now since she had married Simon Skov, and almost thirteen since the winter's day when he'd first walked into her father's shop, a not very tall young man with hair and beard the colour of ripening wheat and eyes as blue as the summer sky. He had only just arrived in Haderslev, he'd told her as he selected a jacket, but, if he liked the district, he was thinking to acquire some land and settle there.

Elsie Christiansen had been twenty-two years of age, with two younger sisters married and no beaus on her doorstep. She had been, therefore, both pleased and flattered when the smiling stranger returned to the shop just two days later and asked if she would have lunch with him. Other outings followed and, just eight weeks later, he asked for her hand in marriage. Convinced that this good-looking young man who'd come down from the north was the one their eldest daughter had been waiting for, her parents had been delighted and it was Elsie's father who had heard of the house and land for sale on the outskirts of the town and taken Simon to look it over. He decided then and there to put down a deposit and approach the bank for a loan. But, even as she'd watched him sign the papers, Elsie had wondered whether this quiet little place would satisfy the restless searching she'd sensed within him; whether, if he hadn't asked her to marry him, he would have stayed in Haderslev in the first place. But never had she supposed that, when he did decide to move, it would be to the other side of the world.

They were ready as the first golden rays of the new day streamed into the heavens: the vehicles piled high with their belongings: the horses, anxious to be moving, snorting and tossing their heads as last-minute checks were made. Christina shivered, hugging her shoulders, as she settled herself on a roll of bedding. It was cool still with the fog in no hurry to disperse, but she was glad she had this seat on the wagon. She would be able to watch their house without even turning her head right until they reached the church corner. She waved to her mother and little Anna as the buggy moved off with Lars at the reins. And then it was their turn. She felt her breath catch as the horses pulled the wagon forward and her father closed the gate behind them. For the last time, she thought. Was he thinking about that? Perhaps feeling sorry? It seemed not, for he was smiling widely as he climbed on to the high wooden seat beside Uncle Peter.

Once on the lane, the horses' hooves began a steady clopping and the wagon creaked in protest as it was dragged along, its big wheels rolling with a thump off the edges of the ruts, squelching happily when they settled for a time in a well-worn groove. Christina kept her eyes on the snug little house, the only home she had ever known, but before they were anywhere near the church corner it was gone, lost in the dawn mists. As quickly as that, she thought sadly, her tense excitement giving way to a dull ache. Would it all disappear so quickly, their life before this day? Yes, it probably would. Even before the day ended another family would have moved into that little house the fog had swallowed up – eating at their table, sitting by their fire, sleeping in their beds. Someone else would milk their cows, feed their geese, drive their buggy into town. Why, in no time at all, it might even seem that they had never been there.

3

The train reached the outskirts of Hamburg in the late afternoon, and Christina watched in growing amazement as it began to wend its way over a network of railway lines. How did the driver know which one to follow? A train going in the opposite direction roared past and she jumped back from the window, giggling as the shock ebbed. Another one crept up on their other side and moved with them towards the station. And soon the city surrounded them, massive and sprawling. They had arrived in Hamburg, and what a place it was.

"Goodness!" her mother exclaimed. "Is there no end to it?"

"Well, it's the greatest seaport on the continent of Europe," Simon reminded her, only half-turning from the window. "You remember learning that in your history lessons, don't you, Christina?"

"Yes, Father, I learnt quite a lot about Hamburg."

"Then you will know that, in addition to being a busy port, it's also a free city and actually a state unto itself, though I must say it's rather more than I expected."

A hint of anxiety came to Elsie's face as she held the baby up so that she, too, could see out of the window. "I hope that doesn't mean things are not going to go as smoothly as you expected?"

"Everything will be just fine." Simon assured her. "The station will hold our luggage overnight, and we'll find that boarding house the emigration aid people mentioned in their letter. Something to eat and a good night's sleep, that's all we need now. And then, come the morrow, onto the Freideburg and away we go."

His smile had included Christina and she smiled back at him, but not as confidently as she would have wished. She could understand her mother's concern. Getting all their belongings from the train to the wharf and on to the ship would surely be a trying and complicated business, for all that her father made it sound so straightforward.

But neither she nor her mother need have worried. Hamburg was an emigration port of several years' standing. Thousands of people from all over Europe had already streamed into the city and on to its wharves. Government officials, station-masters and their staff, boarding house proprietors, shipping clerks and vehicle-hirers all knew what was required when whole families in plain, sturdy clothes, clutching an assortment of baskets and bundles appeared anxiously before them. The Skovs were simply another such family, and they would be helped on their way just as those before them had been.

In the bright morning sunshine, the scene on the wharf resembled a crowded, bustling marketplace from which all semblance of order and reason had fled. Horse-drawn vehicles of every possible description jostled for positions with each other and with an assortment of hand-carts and other contrivances being pulled or pushed by their straining, sweating owners. Everywhere, piles of belongings tottered, sagged or sprawled, crowned in many instances by small, bewildered children while older siblings ran noisily around them. There were people in their hundreds. A few were fashionably attired, the women in pastel-coloured gowns with matching bonnets or wide-brimmed hats, the men in morning suits and top hats. But most wore the drab, serviceable garments that marked them as farmers or factory workers: emigrants from half-a-dozen different countries, with their worldly possessions in the carpet bags or baskets they clung to and the trunks and bundles at their feet. Behind all this, with her sails furled but her decks a hive of industry, the Friedeburg waited.

The wagon Simon had hired belonged to a big, red-faced German, with a broad, scowling brow, bulging muscles, and a huge, bellowing voice. The great value of this last attribute became evident to the Skov family the moment the wagon rolled on to the wharf. Their driver yelled at all and sundry, at anything he considered to be even remotely impeding his progress – the other drivers, the people, the horses, his own included, and even the heaps of inanimate objects.

Shifting her gaze from the big man to the people moving out of his way, some quickly, some sullenly, Christina could hardly believe what she was seeing. What was he yelling, she wondered, that he got such results? But then, seeing a young woman quickly put her hands over her ears, she promptly decided that it was perhaps just as well she didn't know.

Her mother, sitting on a roll of bedding with little Anna on her lap appeared every bit as amazed as she was. She seemed a little fearful as well, as though she expected at any moment to be stopped and dragged from the wagon by an irate mob. Her father, though, apparently had no such concerns. Perched on the high seat beside the big German, he was grinning cheerfully, triumphantly almost. Simon was, in fact, congratulating himself. Of all the men with wagons for hire, he had had the good fortune to choose this one. Had he not done so, they could have been obliged to wait for hours before they even got on to the wharf.

Their driver excelled not only at clearing a passage for his wagon, but also, as the Skovs were to learn as they came closer to the ship, at attracting the attention of a member of the ship's crew and securing for them a cleared space on which to assemble their belongings, ready for loading. Once there, he lost no time in removing them and all their things from his vehicle, often moving so quickly, Simon had to almost run to keep up with him. But he stacked their trunks, carpet bags, baskets and bundles carefully, seeming to know just how they should be arranged for transfer to the ship. When this was done to his satisfaction, he pumped Simon's hand vigorously, smiled briefly at Elsie and the children, and was gone, his great voice again bellowing out as he made his way back across the wharf.

The moment he was out of earshot, the Skov family began to laugh, and, overcome as they were by a sense of almost unbelievable accomplishment and sudden release from tension and nervousness, it was difficult to stop.

"Oh, my goodness!" Elsie gasped, dabbing at her streaming eyes with a handkerchief. "What an experience! I thought we would surely be attacked the way that man was abusing everybody."

"I think he was swearing," Christina giggled. "Was he, Father?"

"I don't think there's too much doubt about that, Christina. But they were mostly words outside my German vocabulary, just as well too, I should think. Still, he got us here in good time and that's the important thing. Now, all we have to do is wait for our turn to go on board."

Some three hours later, their belongings had been hoisted on to the ship and their turn had come. Excited, relieved, but with more than a little trepidation, they climbed the wooden ramp on to the upper deck, where the scene, crammed as it was into a more restricted space, was every bit as chaotic as that on the wharf. There was barely room to move, and people boarding were obliged to wend their way through a maze of trunks and other luggage waiting to be stowed in the hold, great coils of rope, bags of potatoes, piled vegetables, crates of live ducks and chickens, a pen containing four goats, and tubs and vats of all sizes. And, everywhere, there was a great bustle of humanity: crewman rushing to and fro, seemingly aware of what they were doing; passengers who were clearly not at all sure of what they were doing or should do next, for it seemed they had a hundred questions to ask, as many assurances to be sought and a great variety of luggage to locate.

Wide-eyed and speechless, the basket she carried weighing her down, Christina followed close behind her parents. Apprehension mingled with her excitement and churned her stomach, while the deck rocking beneath her feet with the incoming tide and the new range of smells assailing her nostrils did nothing to help. But, she assured herself, they were here, dreamlike though it might be. At long last they were on board the Friedeburg, and, within hours now, they would be starting their long voyage. It was hard to believe, though, almost as though it was something that couldn't be happening. Oh, if only people would stop bumping into her, jostling her about. A small frown creased her brow and her eyes narrowed, becoming thoughtful. The ship seemed to have shrunk in size. When they had first come on to the wharf, it had seemed so large, but now that she was actually on board it didn't seem that way at all. It's because there are so many people, she told herself – three hundred and fifty passengers according to her father and all the crew as well. Where would there be room for so many? Their way became blocked yet once again and she lowered the basket thankfully to the deck, staring up at the tall mast with its vast maze of rigging towering over her head.

"That's the main mast," her father told her, following her gaze. "The pieces going across are called the yards. Can you see how the sails are tied to them?"

"Yes, I can."

"The sailors go out on the yards, you know … when they have to attend to the sails."

"Not right up there?"

"Yes, right up there, and in rough and stormy weather too. It will be interesting for you to learn all about the ship during the voyage, Christina. I know there are many things I want to learn. I never dreamed to have such an opportunity."

Christina nodded. "It will be interesting to learn about the sails."

The line of passengers was moving again, shuffling along, carrying or dragging baskets and bundles. Soon there was a ladder to be negotiated, downwards. Christina took a deep breath, put her feet on the rungs and carefully descended. The lower deck was already a great hive of voices and activity, but, within minutes, a harassed ship's officer appeared to show them to their quarters. These comprised two sets of upper and lower bunks, with a space no more than three feet wide in between, but, at least, due to their being a family, they were to have the privacy of an enclosure. Their fixed wall, at the head of the bunks, was the starboard side of the ship and here they had the almost unbelievable luxury of a porthole. Two flexible bulkheads of light wooden panels separated them from similar enclosures on either side, while a stretched canvas screen shut them off from the vast unpartitioned area where bunks lined both sides of the ship, where hammocks were strung between the decks, and where the remaining space was almost fully occupied by long trestle tables flanked by wooden benches.

"Well, this is not at all bad," Simon exclaimed cheerfully as he settled the baby on one of the lower bunks. "I think it best that you stay there for the moment, little one, until we get ourselves sorted out." He turned back to his wife. "What do you think, Elsie? It's not very spacious, I grant you, but we won't be spending all our time in here. It should be perfectly all right for sleeping."

Elsie flicked up one of the thin straw paliasses the shipping company called mattresses, a faint smile coming to her lips. "I think we will have good reason to be thankful that we brought our goose feathers. But yes, it should be comfortable enough." She was critically inspecting the undersides of the paliasses. "And, thank heavens, there doesn't appear to be any vermin, at least nothing that's obvious."

"Well, that's something," Simon murmured absently, his attention held by the luggage piled high at the bottom of the bunks. "It's not hard to see why we are only permitted to bring one trunk in here. Where on earth are we going to put all this stuff?"

"We'll soon get it organised," his wife calmly assured him. "A lot of what we have is bedding and, once we have made up the bunks, we'll have more space in which to see what we are doing. Perhaps you could start untying the mattresses. Christina, for the time being, you can keep your eye on Anna. Then, once the bunks are made up, she can have a nap."

"Can I get on to the bunk with her?"

"That's a good idea. You'll be out of the way while your father and I get things sorted out."

"Will I be able to have one of the top bunks for my bed?"

"If you promise not to fall out. It's a fairly solid sort of rail, so you should be all right, and it does seem that the best arrangement will be for you and your father to have the upper bunks."

All around them similar discussions were taking place as those who would call this deck 'home' during the long months at sea sought to determine the most efficient and comfortable way of utilising the small space they had been allotted. Already, some were taking a few moments off from making up bunks and sorting out luggage to eye their fellow travellers in critical assessment. Before too many days had passed, they would begin, in spite of language barriers, to understand one another: their likes and dislikes; their dreams, hopes and plans. For now, though, there could only be veiled staring, tentative smiles and boundless wondering.

The Friedeburg sailed on the afternoon ebb tide. Hearing a renewed burst of activity above their heads, Christina and her father hurriedly made their way back to the main deck and then up the companion ladder to the poop deck which seemed to offer better vantage points. Here, they joined the many others lining the rails: people who wanted to laugh now that this long-dreamed-of moment had finally arrived, but cried instead; others who yearned for the relief of tears, but found themselves giving way to brittle laughter. People with flushed, excited faces; others with pale, tear-streaked faces. People who called loudly and cheerfully to friends and family on the wharf; others who could do no more than speak in choked voices; still others who could find no voice at all, but stood numbed, their eyes glued to loved faces. All of them, though, caught in this one trembling moment out of time – the omega of one life, the alpha of another.

The fore-topsails were set and at once new sounds joined the confusing chorus: crisp German voices shouting orders, the clanking of chain; the squeaking of the windlass as the great anchor rose from the dark water of the Elbe River. The steam-tug, hovering importantly off the Friedeburg's bow, quickly applied itself to its task, and a gap appeared between the ship and the wharf, widened, and widened. The waving became more frantic, the calling louder, and Christina, averting her eyes from a young woman who had thrown herself, sobbing wildly, into her husband's arms, was suddenly very relieved that their own farewells had taken place at the railway station in Haderslev.

She watched the tugboat manoeuvring to and fro as it turned the ship, marvelling that it was able to do so. "How far will it have to tow us, Father?"

"At least until we are clear of all this shipping, and, more than likely, for quite a way downstream. Then we'll probably just dawdle along with shortened sail until we leave the river. We have some eighty miles to travel before we reach the sea, you know? So we'll have to wait for morning to see the ship under full sail."

The wharf they had left was falling behind, the groups of people still standing there somehow appearing forlorn and forsaken. How strange, Christina mused, it's as though those people are slipping away from us, not us from them. Other wharves and warehouses, fronted by ships and boats of every description, crowded both banks. And, behind these, on the northern shore, the city of Hamburg glided slowly by – the New Town area, rebuilt after the great fire of 1842, clearly distinguishable from the other districts.

"So many large buildings," Christina exclaimed. "I should think there are as many in just a couple of streets as there are in the whole of Haderslev. Can you see that really tall spire, Father?"

"Indeed I can. It must be part of a very important church."

"It's the Church of St.Nicholas and that spire is four hundred and seventy-three feet tall." The soft, musical voice had come from behind them and Christina spun around, as startled at hearing Danish spoken in the midst of so much German as she was at being spoken to. Her father turned too, raising his hat and smiling at the woman who stood there. Not a young woman, Christina saw, not even as young as her mother, but she had a gentle, unlined face with a soft pearl-like skin and dark, merry eyes. She was splendidly dressed in a mauve silk gown, with full lace-edged sleeves, a finely-tucked bodice, and deep, scalloped flounces at the hemline. She wore cream kid gloves and a wide-brimmed hat with mauve and purple flowers covering the crown. She was, Christina quickly decided, the most elegant lady she had ever seen. And then, her lips twitching in sudden amusement, she decided something further – this very elegant lady had obviously never read Mr Capper's brochure.

"The church was built after the great fire," the woman continued after smiling at each of them in turn. "It's still not quite complete, but it's a very fine Gothic structure."

"I'm sure it must be," Simon murmured politely, stepping back from the rail to make room for her beside Christina. "I believe there are some very fine buildings in the new part of Hamburg."

"Ah yes, there are indeed. We Germans have a penchant for erecting magnificent buildings, you know? I sometimes think that the great fire was a blessing in disguise, though not, of course, for the people who lived in the area at the time. For them it was a terrible disaster." She glanced enquiringly down at Christina. "Did you know that Hamburg's great fire burned out of control for four days and destroyed sixty-one streets and thousands of houses?"

Christina shook her head, smothering the quick pang of disappointment that had come to her. She had been so sure the woman was Danish, speaking the way she did, but she wasn't, she was German just like most of the others around them. "No, I didn't know that," she said quietly, returning her gaze to the city. "I can see another very tall spire."

"That's St. Peter's, also built in recent times. You mustn't think that we have only new buildings of importance in Hamburg, though. We have some very fine old churches. St Catherine's is the oldest, it was built in the middle of the 14th century ... " Her voice trailed away and she gave a small apologetic laugh. "How I do go on, but I did warn you as to how we feel about our buildings, and it seems that leaving them has made me feel particularly affectionate towards them."

"We are interested to hear about them," Simon assured her. "We arrived only yesterday afternoon and were sorry not to have had more time in Hamburg."

"Oh, what a pity! You've had no time at all in the city. Did I hear you mention that you have come from Haderslev?"

"Yes, we are from Haderslev."

"That's a very attractive region of Schleswig, I believe? I have been to some of the towns in Holstein and to Copenhagen many times and I always had it in mind that one day I would visit some of those towns further north on the peninsula, but I just never got around to it."

Simon smiled at her. "That's why you speak Danish so fluently, all those visits to Copenhagen?"

"Plus the fact that I have many Danish relatives. My grandparents lived in Copenhagen all their lives and they had several children in addition to my mother, who married a German." She held out her hand. "My name is Eleanor Klaussen. Frau Klaussen, but I am a widow now."

"Simon Skov." Simon responded, taking the hand she held out to him. "And this is my elder daughter, Christina."

"Christina, such a pretty name. And what a pretty little girl she is, such blue, blue eyes and hair like sunshine."

Christina flushed and the gloved hand reached out and rested gently on her head.

"What a wonderful adventure you are embarked upon, Christina. I can imagine how excited you must be."

Christina nodded, a shy smile coming to her lips. "Yes, I am. We are going to live in Queensland."

"So am I. And I am so excited I have hardly slept this past week. I haven't seen my daughter and son-in-law in fifteen years, not since she was eighteen years old. And I have never met my three grandchildren."

Simon gave her an understanding smile. "You have very good reason to be excited then. Have your daughter and her husband been living in Queensland all that time?"

"All except for the first year. Beatrice married an Englishman whose family had some business interests in Sydney and they went there first. But Albert always wanted to go on the land. He seemed to think that he was born to be a farmer. So, when the northern districts of New South Wales were opened up, he decided to seize the opportunity and take up land there." She laughed softly. "It's all worked out quite well for them, so perhaps he was born to be a farmer. He is what they call a squatter, such a name for a sheep farmer."

"Do they live near Brisbane?" Christina asked.

"No, they live out to the west, in a region they call the Darling Downs."

A ship's officer approached, clicking his heels as he came to a halt behind them. "Frau Klaussen … ?"

Eleanor Klaussen nodded, turning from the rail.

He spoke rapidly in German and it seemed that he was apologising for something. Frau Klaussen replied in the same language, speaking with a quiet dignity which seemed to indicate that she was accustomed to being spoken to respectfully. She must be an important lady, Christina decided, perhaps a very important lady. The young officer gave a stiff half-bow, clicking his heels again before striding briskly away.

"It appears that my missing trunk has been found and is now in my cabin, so I must go and attend to the rest of my unpacking." She smiled warmly, first at Christina and then at Simon. "I am sure that we will see each other often in the weeks ahead and I hope that we may talk again, very soon."

Simon returned her smile. "I hope so too. It has been a pleasure meeting you, Frau Klaussen."

"Goodbye for now, Christina."

"Goodbye, Frau Klaussen."

"She probably has a cabin beneath this deck," Simon remarked as he and Christina turned back to the rail. And then with a wry grin, "She has just been invited to dine with Captain Koffer, so I don't think she is a free-passage emigrant."

"She looked very important, and she is wearing such beautiful clothes, but I thought she would be Danish."

"Well, so she is, in part. You heard her say that her mother was Danish, and that her grandparents always lived in Copenhagen."

"But she calls herself German, why would she do that?"

"Her father was German, so she was probably born in the country, and, I suppose, lived there for most of her life. Also, she was married to a German, it seems, so it's really the only thing she could be."

"She might even be a Prussian."

"Yes, she might." Simon's smile faded and he said firmly, "But we are not going to hold such things against the lady, Christina. I have told you several times that there will be people of many nationalities settling in Australia and that we all have to learn to be one people. That's certainly not going to happen if we allow ourselves to become agitated about every Prussian we meet. Do you understand what I am saying?"

"I think so."

She did understand what he was saying, Christina told herself. What she couldn't understand was how it was going to come about. One people from so many, and all so different: different languages, different clothes, different customs. What enormous changes there would have to be, even for people such as Frau Klaussen. "But what about the part of Frau Klaussen that is Danish?"

"Well, I'm sure she doesn't forget that. After all, the lady speaks Danish as well as we do. And that reminds me, young lady – as from tomorrow morning, English lessons begin in earnest. We haven't really made very much progress these past weeks."

"Oh Father, must we? So soon?"

"Yes, we must. I am hoping that we will all be able to speak English by the time this journey ends, and the sooner we begin making a real effort the better. Ah look! We have come to Holstein."

Christina nodded. "I saw that on the map Lars showed me. Holstein will be on our right now all the way until we reach the sea."

"Yes, but we are on a ship, so it's on our starboard, not our right."

But there was no answering smile on his daughter's face. Up there, further to the north was Schleswig, the homeland she had left forever. Two large tears slipped on to her cheeks, but she compressed her lips and a fierce determination took hold of her. No, it won't be forever, she vowed, one day I will come back.

It was going on for midnight when the Friedeburg slipped out of the calm, broad waters of the Elbe estuary and into the stormy North Sea. The ship shuddered as, head-on, she met the first turbulent waters of her long voyage. Then she took heart and, on a brisk north wind, plunged southwards towards the Straits of Dover. When her high, narrow bunk began to heave beneath her, Christina woke with a start, sudden fright forming a knot in her chest. She stared wide-eyed into the darkness while her mind struggled to sort reality from dream, then quickly recalled her whereabouts. Holding her breath, she listened to the creaking of timbers, and the sloshing of water against the ship's side. It was terrifying in the dark and she stirred uneasily, reaching out a hand to grip the rail of her bunk.

At once, her father's quiet whisper reached her ears, "There's nothing to be afraid of, Christina. The ship might pitch and roll a bit now that we've come out of the river into the sea, but you'll soon get used to it."

"Yes, Father," she whispered back. "I was afraid when I first woke up. I couldn't think where I was, but I'll be alright now."

"Good girl. Try to go back to sleep."

His voice had been quietly comforting and Christina wished that she could reach over and put her hand in his. If she could do that, all her fear would go away. It wouldn't matter that her bed was unsteady or that the ship seemed to be groaning. There was movement from the bunk below her father's, and she rolled on to her side to peer over the rail. Her mother was sitting up, checking on the baby. "Is she alright, Mother?" she asked softly.

"She hasn't stirred, bless her dear little heart."

Christina could just see the smile on her mother's face, pale against the darkness, and a smile came to her own lips. "With all this rocking she probably thinks she's back in her cradle."

"Then I wonder who she thinks is rocking it so hard."

"It would have to be a giant, I would think."

"Yes, I agree, but back to sleep now; we don't want to be waking our neighbours."

"Goodnight. Mother."

"Goodnight, Christina."

Christina woke early, impatient to be up and about, to go up on the deck and watch the wind in the sails. But her mother was sick. Between bouts of vomiting, she lay back on her bunk with a damp cloth pressed to her brow, her face a strange greenish-grey colour. Staring helplessly, Christina felt dread sweep through her. She had never known her mother to be sick, not the way she was now. But her father seemed unperturbed. "Seasickness," he declared matter-of-factly. "It will soon pass, I should think."

Elsie forced her pale lips into the semblance of a smile. "I do hope you are right about that, Simon. What a terrible malady it is. And it came upon me so abruptly."

"It's unpleasant alright, and it's just rotten luck that you've been stricken. But you'll be up and about in no time, you'll see."

"Well, in the meantime, I don't think I can leave this bunk, so will you and Christina see to Anna?"

"Of course we will. Don't go worrying about such things. Just concentrate on getting yourself better." He turned to Christina. "How are you feeling after your first night at sea?"

"I feel fine, Father." She glanced to where the baby was sitting on her bunk, chewing contentedly on a dry biscuit. "And she seems to be quite well."

"Yes, she does, indeed, and we may be thankful for that mercy."

The bell signalling the change of watch at eight o'clock also called the Friedeburg's passengers to breakfast. With her father and small sister, Christina went to the long tables, where they took up the places they had occupied for tea on the previous evening. But, unlike that earlier meal, this time there was no excited, chattering crowd to keep them company. There were, in fact, very few people present, and, of those who did put in an appearance, a number departed quickly the minute the food was brought to the table.

"It seems Mother is not the only one feeling nauseous this morning," Simon murmured as he settled Anna on his knee. "I'm afraid the North Sea is not very kind to people so inclined."

"Will they all be well again soon?" Christina asked with an anxious frown.

"Yes, most of them in a day or two. Then, once they get their sea legs, they'll probably be all right for the rest of the voyage, provided there is no really rough weather, of course."

The Third Mate came to eat with the steerage passengers, raising his eyebrows and smiling when he saw the almost empty benches. He spoke to Simon in German and they laughed quietly together before he moved on to speak to others at the next table.

Breakfast consisted of hot porridge, bacon, crusty bread, butter and honey. And there was tea and coffee and glasses of fresh cow's milk for Christina and Anna. While the fresh food lasted, those on board the Friedeburg would all eat well, but, as the weeks passed, the quality would deteriorate. There would be no milk for eight-year-olds, while babies and other little ones would have to be content with goat's milk. Salad greens and other fresh vegetables would gradually disappear from the menu, as would all dishes containing fresh meat. Soup, cabbage stew, corned beef, corned mutton, dried haddock and hake, cheese and hard biscuits would make their appearance on the tables with monotonous regularity. On this first morning at sea, however, breakfast was both tasty and nourishing and those who were able to come to the tables and remain there ate heartily and thanked their lucky stars they were not numbered among those prone to seasickness.

In the hour before dinner, which was served at two o'clock, Christina was finally able to stroll on the upper deck with her father. The baby was asleep and her mother, resting more comfortably, had insisted that she do so. And it was wonderful, just wonderful! Under its great, billowing clouds of canvas, the Friedeburg surged through the rolling ocean, sending spray flying as her bow rose and then fell into the vibrant blue-green water. A crisp breeze blew and there was the tang of salt in the air. Following her father's example, she threw back her head, breathing deeply. How refreshing it was after the stuffiness and unpleasant smells of the lower deck. At first, walking a reasonably straight course along the deck was a real problem and the cause of a good deal of merriment among those who attempted it. But, gradually, most came to realise that it was necessary to adjust their manner of walking. It was, Christina decided, simply a question of planting her feet firmly, a bit further apart than was normal, on the boards of the deck, then letting her body roll a little in tune with the ocean.

Watching her, Simon gave a shout of laughter. "By Jove, Christina! That is how it's done."

Christina's cheeks were flushed with sheer pleasure and her bright blue eyes danced. "Oh, Father, I think I'm going to enjoy being at sea. It's so invigorating!"

"That's exactly what it is, invigorating. And what do you think of the sails now?"

"They are beautiful. And so many. What are the ones above us called?"

"That's one question I can answer. They are the mizzen sails. And this is the mizzen mast, the one nearest the stern."

Christina nodded, smiling as she gazed upwards. Mizzen sails, she should be able to remember that.

"We won't go up on the poop deck this time. It's getting close to the dinner hour and little Anna will probably be waking. We don't want her disturbing your mother."

Christina glanced at the raised deck. There were a number of people up there, but none that she could see even remotely resembled Frau Klaussen. She didn't appear to be on this deck either. "I wonder if Frau

Klaussen is sick like mother. I haven't seen her anywhere."

"She may well be, I suppose. Though perhaps she is sitting in one of the deck chairs or she could even be resting in her cabin. If we don't see her tomorrow, I'll make some enquiries."

"I hope Mother is able to come up on the deck tomorrow."

"Your mother is a very strong woman who hates to be ill. It's not likely she'll let seasickness keep her tied to her bed for very long."

On the following day, though the north wind still blew gustily, the seas were not quite so rough, and, although not completely recovered, Elsie was well enough to spend some time up in the fresh air. The colour came back into her cheeks and she was able to eat a biscuit and drink a cup of tea. It was the same for others. More and more people began to appear on the upper decks, and that evening, there were far fewer empty spaces on the long benches drawn up to the tea table. There were those, however, who were still tied to their bunks when the Friedeburg sailed into the Straits of Dover and, since the waters here were squall-swept and choppy, their recovery was further delayed.

With rain falling almost continuously, there were few who ventured on to the upper decks to see the White Cliffs go by, and Christina, peering through the porthole, heaved a sigh of disappointment. "They don't look very white, they look sort of grey."

"Just as well there are no English people around to hear you say that," her father told her. "They are very attached to their White Cliffs."

"Well, I suppose if the sun was shining they'd look nicer."

The afternoon of the sixth day out of Hamburg saw the Friedeburg off Torbay, with most of the English Channel in its wake. A soft pearly dusk, rose-tinted still, settled over the water and darkened slowly. From Berry Head a flashing light warned of the treacherous rocks jutting out into the Channel from the base of the cliff on which it stood. And, between the ship and the shore, minute dots of light flickered where a group of Brixham fishing boats drifted slowly, their trawls snaking through the dark water. All night long the fishermen would move their small craft back and forth over the banks, racing them home in the first light of day to land and sell their catch at the early markets. On the Friedeburg, moving easily through kindly seas, hurricane lanterns strung from the rigging cast soft circles of light on the upper decks, and, everywhere, people lingered, reluctant to let the last of this mild, pleasant day slip from them. Simon and Elsie Skov and their daughters were among those watching the lights and the shadowy coastline.

"How lovely it all is," Elsie murmured. "So calm and peaceful-looking."

"But they seem so lonely, those tiny lights in all that darkness," Christina said quietly, not at all sure why the flicker of melancholy had come to her.

"Well, have you thought how we must seem to those fishermen?" her father asked with a gentle smile. "Although they are small boats, there are several of them and they are not all that far from shore. We are but one ship, and, even though the Friedeburg is by no means small and we haven't yet left the Channel, we are still little more than a speck upon vast waters."

"And, after tomorrow, we will be an even smaller speck," Elsie murmured as she settled the drowsy baby more comfortably in her arms. "The Atlantic Ocean is rather more vast than the English Channel. Still, let us hope that it's not going to be too rough and that this lovely weather stays with us. It has been such a nice day."

"The nicest we've had since boarding," Simon agreed.

"I hope Frau Klaussen sees the fishing boats. Do you think she will, Mother?"

"I think she might. She did seem much better this afternoon. If only we could have a few more days like this one, she'd be just fine."

On their second day at sea, Simon had learned from the Third Mate that Frau Klaussen was very sick, and, since then, Elsie had gone to her cabin twice daily to sponge the aching body and tend her during her terrible bouts of nausea; her assistance greatly appreciated by Doctor Heinemann, on his first voyage as ship's doctor and feeling anything but well himself.

They passed Land's End in the early afternoon, and Christina and her father joined the other passengers crowding the upper decks to watch the granite cliffs and the lighthouse glide by, then fade into a smudge and become lost against the sky as the Friedeburg surged southwards towards the Bay of Biscay. Almost at once they ran into heavy seas and those who remained on deck were obliged to brace themselves against the ship's heaving. With her feet planted firmly on the replacement mast stowed inside the main-deck bulwarks ... the only way she could manage to see over the side ... Christina watched the spray flying as the white-crested waves of the Atlantic Ocean dashed themselves against the ship's side. Grinning cheerfully, she glanced up at the tiered white sails straining to be free and off on their own soaring flight. "You can't go," she called to them silently. "Not on your own. You are our wings and we'd be lost without you."

Her father's voice interrupted this one-sided conversation. "Rather more boisterous than these past few days, eh Christina?"

Christina's smile faded. "Will it be like this all the time now that we are out in the Atlantic Ocean?"

"It's possible, I suppose. But that doesn't bother you, does it?"

"No, I was just thinking of Mother and Frau Klaussen and all the other people who have been sick."

"Well, they are becoming more accustomed to life at sea all the time, so it may not trouble them too greatly. The ship's carpenter told me that the Bay of Biscay can be very rough, though. He said that he once had to replace a whole section of the main mast when they were caught in a violent storm there."

"Goodness, I hope that doesn't happen to us."

By the following day, the seas had abated, and those who had found the North Sea such a trial were enormously relieved to discover that this stretch of water, contrary to its reputation, was reasonably calm.

Sunsoaked day followed sunsoaked day and a relaxed, almost festive, air began to pervade the ship. Musical instruments made their appearance: accordions, mandolins, banjos, flutes and a lone Jew's harp. Card games were arranged, and activities to entertain the children. Laughter flowed much more readily and voices became cheerful, often ringing out in snatches of song. Friendships were being formed and helping hands extended to those who had need of them.

The learning of English became a much-discussed and high-priority undertaking. Although the task was tackled with great enthusiasm, however, it was with more merriment than dedication, and in the majority of cases progress was little more than an illusion.

When it became known that Herr Schneider, who, with his wife and two sons, occupied the enclosure next to the Skovs, had taught English in a school in Bremen, he was at once greatly in demand, so much so he decided the only way he could have time to himself was to arrange set classes. And this he did with great efficiency and the help of three or four others who had a fairly sound knowledge of the language.

The Friedeburg was more than halfway across the Bay before Eleanor Klaussen was strong enough to leave her cabin. Christina saw her one morning clinging to the poop rail, looking pale and distraught, and she called anxiously, "Are you feeling alright, Frau Klaussen?"

"Ah Christina, just look at you! Striding over the deck as though it were a pavement and not a writhing monster." She clutched at the rail with both hands as the wind veered and the ship gave a sudden lurch. It steadied and she gave a small, rueful laugh. "I don't believe I am ever going to find my sea legs."

"Would you like to take hold of my hand? It might help you to keep your balance."

"That is kind of you, Christina, and I think it might be a very good idea. One of the ship's officers helped me up here and I foolishly assured him that I would be alright."

Christina took the pale, thin fingers in her own and carefully led the woman away from the rail. "It's not so difficult once you get used to the way the ship moves. At first I was real stiff and I was staggering about all over the place. Then I tried letting my body be sort of loose, the way the sailors do, and it was ever so much better," she giggled softly, a little self-consciously, "and you have to put your feet down firmly and walk with your legs a little apart. It doesn't look very ladylike, I suppose, but it's better than falling over."

"Like this?" Eleanor Klaussen lifted the skirt of her soft voile dress and took two or three steps as she had been instructed.

"Yes, that's the way. You kind of roll with the ship."

"Ah yes, I see how it is, Christina. Now all I need is a little practice."

"You're doing just fine."

"Well, as you say, it may not look too elegant, but I'm sure it's much better to be unladylike and on your feet than ladylike and flat on your face, if such a thing is possible."

They both laughed as, hand in hand, they made their way slowly across the poop.

"This is wonderful, Christina. I'm becoming more confident with every step. Now, if only I can regain my strength, I can perhaps begin to enjoy this voyage."

"Oh, I hope you do. It's really very exciting once you get used to the ship, especially on the upper decks." Christina grinned happily. "I'm allowed to come up on my own now, so long as there are other people about and it's not too rough. I love to watch the ocean and the sails, don't you?"

"Well, I must confess that I haven't been feeling very friendly towards the ocean." She glanced up at the sails, filled and taut against the cirrus-patterned sky. "And I haven't had a chance to pay the sails much attention, but I can see what you mean. That is a beautiful sight."

"Father has learned the names of all the sails. He's always asking the crew something or other about them, and about the rigging. He has become very friendly with the ship's carpenter too. Mother said anyone would think he was going to be asked to captain the ship."

Eleanor Klaussen laughed softly. "He just might be able to do that, Christina. After all, his ancestors were great seamen; perhaps he has inherited something of what must have been a natural instinct. Perhaps you have too." Her smile became rueful. "Can you imagine what my Viking forefathers would have thought of my performance these past days? I'm sure I would have been in terrible disgrace."

"You weren't the only one to be sick," Christina reminded her kindly. "And you couldn't help it."

"I suppose not. But, believe me, Christina, there were times when I thought I would never get to walk on Australian soil. In fact, if it hadn't been for your mother … " She smiled, a quick flash of amused recollection coming to her eyes. "She really scolded me, you know? I was lying there feeling so dreadfully sorry for myself, quite convinced that I'd be better off dead, when she came in with Doctor Heinemann and took me in hand. Such a lecture I was given and then so much care and kindness, I will never be able to thank her enough." She shook her head slowly from side to side. "What a wonderful woman she is."

Christina nodded. "Mother is always good with sick people. I think she should have been a nurse."

"I think so too, she has such a gift."

They came to where the helmsman had his hands resting easily on the great spoked wheel and turned to make their way back along the deck. Two young men, laughingly trying to converse in English passed them, and Eleanor Klaussen asked, "How are your English lessons coming along, Christina? Your mother told me that you are all attending classes."

"Yes, Herr Schneider has kindly organised classes." Christina gave a small sigh. "Father is making wonderful progress, but I'm afraid I'm not doing too well."

"Ah, not an easy language to learn, English. The trouble is that it has come from so many different sources it has no really set pattern. I think we may do well to start practising, you and I."

Surprised, Christina glanced up into her face. "But Mother said that you speak English just as well as you speak Danish and German."

Eleanor Klaussen smiled. "That seems to have been my one real talent, a flair for languages. But, believe me, I don't speak English so well that I won't benefit from some practice. When we are together, we will say as many words in English as possible. I think it might be quite fun to converse in a mixture of Danish and English, don't you?"

"If you think I can learn enough English words."

"Of course you can. And you may start by calling me Mrs Klaussen. I will need to become used to that, as it's what I will be in Australia – Mrs Klaussen, not Frau Klaussen."

"Yes, Mrs Klaussen." Christina said with a quick grin.

"Good. And tomorrow morning I'll set down some words and phrases and we'll study them together. If your parents are agreeable, and if it doesn't interfere with your classes, you could come to my cabin."

"I'd like that, Frau Klau ... I mean, Mrs Klaussen."

On a bright, cloudless morning, off the Friedeburg's port bow, the lighthouse of Corunna appeared, an impressive structure over ninety feet tall, well deserving of its title 'Tower of Hercules', and reputed to be of Roman or Phoenician construction. Behind the lighthouse, the port itself, seemingly dozing in the sunshine, gave no indication that violent chapters of history had been written there. At one time part of the ancient Spanish province of Galacia, Corunna had for years withstood Roman oppression, until, in the time of Augustus, it became the 'Magnus Portus' of the Romans.

There were those on board the Friedeburg who knew at least something of the history of Corunna, but for most the port was nothing more than another mile-post on their long voyage, another point to be approached and passed. Now, it was the coast of Spain they saw as a misty blur on the horizon; France had been left behind just as Germany and England had been. The days, too, were slipping by. They were into the month of May and the emigrants had had time in which to review the conditions under which they were being obliged to live; time in which to improvise and do all they could to minimise the discomforts and inconveniences from which they had no hope of escaping. As a result, life on board had settled into a routine that was, for the most part, surprisingly agreeable.

The prevailing winds were now westerlies and, on two successive afternoons, with the breeze blowing from out of the north-west, they had suddenly increased to strong winds which brought thunderstorms flashing from across the Atlantic. Fortunately for the Friedeburg, pushing through the disturbed waters with reduced sail, they failed to live up to the Ocean's reputation for violent storms and were quickly gone, leaving the vast dome of the night skies to the stars, and leaving those on the ship reassuring themselves and each other that, weather-wise, they still had little to complain about.

With each roll of the ship, Christina, lying on her bunk, caught a glimpse of the stars through the porthole. Just a few of the millions and millions, but, she told herself, it was nice to see them, nevertheless. She listened to the sounds of the ship, so familiar now: the creak and strain of its timbers; the fingers of the wind plucking at the rigging as though it was a giant violin; the patter of feet on the deck above as the men on watch carried out their duties; the hungry cry of a baby, quickly hushed; but followed at once by that of a small child unable to sleep or caught in a bad dream.

Christina stretched her legs and wriggled her toes. What lovely days they were having. Why, apart from the storms, there had been only fleecy clouds in the sky for more than a week now. And the storms hadn't really been severe enough to cause much concern. It had been interesting watching them coming, though, the dark clouds sweeping so low over the water while the crew raced to prepare the ship. What dangerous jobs they had: scurrying up the rigging like monkeys; then going out on the yards to reef the sails, while the masts swayed back and forth and tried to tip them off into the ocean. The sailors were used to doing such things, of course, but watching them had been enough to make her hold her breath and ask God to please not let them fall off.

A smile tugged at Christina's lips. The morning would probably be fine and sunny if the night sky was any indication and once again she'd be able to go to Mrs Klaussen's cabin for her lessons. Oh, how much easier it was to learn English with her saying the words and phrases the way she did and making up amusing little sentences to help her understand the meanings. And how pleasant it was in Mrs Klaussen's comfortable cabin, in the midst of all her lovely things. All her most precious belongings, she'd said, and she was taking them to Australia with her because she intended to remain there for the rest of her life and never return to Munich where she had lived for years and years.

Christina's smile faded as she felt again the surprise that had swept through her. Mrs Klaussen had spoken so cheerfully, as though she had no regrets whatsoever at leaving her homeland to live in a strange new country. Of course, her daughter and grandchildren lived in Australia, but not to want to come back? Oh, surely she didn't really mean that. No, she couldn't. Mrs Klaussen was sure to return one day, just as she, herself, was going to do, after she had lived for a time in Australia.

4

Gibraltar was indeed something to be marvelled at, with its massive, fortified rock towering fourteen hundred feet above sea level and dominating the peninsula. Close to one thousand guns were said to be mounted on those seemingly inaccessible heights, but on the Friedeburg gliding quickly through the straits on the strong current from the Atlantic Ocean, such a possibility gave rise to much speculation and quite a few doubts. It was nevertheless generally agreed that Great Britain was justified in considering that, in Gibraltar, she held the key to the Mediterranean. Viewing the great rock from the poop deck with Mrs Klaussen, Christina gasped, "I had no idea it would be so big."

"It is certainly huge, and very formidable-looking into the bargain. In ancient times it was known as one of the 'Pillars of Hercules' and, even then, it was apparently a strong fortress."

"Did it belong to Great Britain then?"

"Heavens no! The Moors were the first people to make a fort of Gibraltar, when they crossed the sea to invade Spain. After that, it changed hands many times before it came into Britain's possession; that didn't happen until the last century. As a matter of fact, even though the Spaniards surrendered the fortress to the British quite early in the century, they spent the next eighty years laying siege to the place because they wanted it back. At one time they even offered to buy it for some quite enormous sum of money. It was really only about ninety years ago that Gibraltar was finally secured for Britain."

Christina listened wide-eyed. How many interesting things Mrs Klaussen knew. If only she could remember them all.

"Ah, there I go, confusing you with snippets of history again." She gave a soft chuckle. "And do you know that, when I was your age, I had no interest whatsoever in history. It wasn't until after I married and discovered that my husband was a dedicated historian that I began to realise that the subject wasn't so boring after all."

"I was wishing I could remember all the interesting things you tell me," Christina told her a little wistfully.

"You have a lifetime in which to learn such things, little Christina. But I have something I really do expect you to remember, a list of ten new verbs."

Christina grimaced, but laughingly. "The hardest part of the language."

"The hardest part of any language, believe me."

"I'll try to know them by tomorrow."

"Well, you'll be excused if you don't. We'll be entering the Mediterranean very soon now and I have a feeling that it's going to be an exciting time, what with everyone so keyed up about finally getting to see this much-talked-about body of water."

For a time, the Mediterranean lived up to expectations. Its waters were a vivid, sparkling blue, as glassily serene as a lake. During the day the sun shone down from an almost cloudless sky and the Algerian coastline was clearly visible through the clean balmy air. At night a full moon climbed into a star-spangled sky and turned the water to silver. Islands appeared, so dazzlingly green they resembled giant emeralds. Aided by soft breezes, countless birds performed a whirling, soaring ballet about the ship. Numerous other ships were sighted, their flags identified, their cargoes laughingly guessed at. And, occasionally, native fishing craft ventured so close it was possible to call to their occupants and to hear their voices floating back in reply. Fish were plentiful in the glistening waters; lines were dropped and a flapping, silvery mound soon appeared on the deck, where it was gleefully inspected, new life for the jaded menu.

A further bonus was that it was time for clean clothes to be brought forth from trunks in the hold, and, to mark the occasion, canvas screens were set up on the main deck to give privacy for bathing with the gallons of seawater being hoisted on board. Passengers and crew alike began to look and feel a good deal brighter. As spirits rose, cheerful chatter, music and dancing sped the hours. But these idyllic days were destined to be all too few. This was the time of the northern spring when winds blew from the south-east or south-west. It was also the season of the dreaded

Sirocco. Spawned by a combination of air and heat in some distant corner of the Sahara, it came hurtling across more than a thousand miles of burning desert wasteland, tearing at the earth, altering the landscape, and continually regenerating itself. And there was no stopping when it reached the northern shores of the African continent. Undiminished, it raged across the Mediterranean's beautiful blue waters, still searing with heat and laden with spiralling ochre dust.

The Sirocco struck the Friedeburg just after midday, and by midafternoon, the dust had coated sails, decks and rigging and found its way into almost every corner of the ship. With the sky and everything else beyond a distance of a hundred yards blotted out, the Friedeburg, writhing in the wind's tortuous grip, crept forward, a strange red-brown spectre in a strange red-brown world. It would be three never-to-be-forgotten days before the ship finally sailed out of the Sirocco's tail, before her bewildered, despondent passengers were able to open up the hatches, discard scarves and face masks and once again breathe sweet, clean air.

Christina stood with Eleanor Klaussen watching the crew tackle the dust with brushes, brooms, mops and buckets. "How will they ever get rid of it all? she asked, shaking her head slowly.

"I'm sure I don't know, Christina. The wretched stuff is everywhere. I have been all morning shaking out my clothes and dusting and it still seems to be on everything I touch."

"We've been doing that too. Even though the hatches and portholes were closed most of the time, there's still a lot of dust on the lower deck. One of the officers has organised working parties."

Eleanor Klaussen gave a soft groan. "It must have been stifling down there."

"Yes, it was terrible, hot and suffocating. Too hot to sleep properly, even. Little Anna cried a lot; the other babies and small children did too."

"Poor little mites, what an ordeal for them. If we'd had time to think about it a bit more, your mother could have brought you and the baby to my cabin, though I don't suppose it would have been all that much better. There was a ton of dust dumped on the poop deck and there was certainly no escaping the heat."

"Anna seems to be alright now." Christina told her. "Father kept her out in the fresh air all morning while mother and I cleaned up. And she's been sleeping most of the afternoon, hardly coughing at all."

"Has she been coughing a lot?"

"Oh yes, a real lot. But Mother thinks it's just from the dust. Nearly everyone has been coughing or sneezing."

"Yes, you are right about that. I know I've certainly done my share of sneezing, the dust was almost as bad as pepper in that respect."

"Once I sneezed eight times in a row," Christina giggled.

"Then you have been outdone, my little friend. My record is ten."

Captain Koffer, his white uniform red-streaked and grimy, his face reflecting his exhaustion, joined them for a few minutes, speaking quietly and seriously with Eleanor.

"He hopes to be able to get the worst of the dust cleared away," she told Christina as he hurried off to speak to one of his officers. "And then, when we reach Port Said, the ship will undergo a thorough cleaning. Thank heavens! It would be terrible to have dust all over the place for the rest of the journey, especially this horrible red stuff."

"Father said we should reach Port Said by Saturday."

"Four more days." She sighed heavily. "And to think how pleasant it was when we first came into the Mediterranean."

A soft gleam of very pleasing recollection came to Christina's eyes. What wonderful days they had been before the dust came. Everywhere, there had been laughter and song. And, each evening, dancing on the moonlit deck while the young man named Fritz played his mandolin and his father and another man took up their accordions. It had all been so romantic and she had seen several of the men steal kisses from their partners as they'd waltzed through the shadows. Her mother and father had joined in the dancing and they had looked so nice, so light-hearted and happy. She had too; she had danced a polka with Henry Schneider, who was just six months older than she was, but almost twelve inches taller. Such a nice boy, not at all like his older brother who was always going on about nationalism, whatever he meant by that, and about what a great country Germany was. He had really deserved that black eye the Swedish boy had given him.

"Do tell me what you find so amusing, Christina?"

Startled at this interruption to her reverie, Christina opened her mouth to explain, but quickly closed it again. Mrs Klaussen might not see anything to laugh about in a Swedish boy giving a German boy a black eye, even if he had deserved it.

"Well … ?" She was waiting, a gentle smile of enquiry o n her face.

"I was just remembering how nice it was dancing on the deck in the moonlight." Only half a lie, she told herself. That's really all it was, half a lie.

"Indeed it was. Everybody had such a wonderful time. And I saw you dancing with that handsome young boy. What a fine polka you were performing."

Flushed with pleasure, Christina told her, "Father taught me how to do the polka and Mother is teaching me how to waltz, but I'm not very good at it yet."

"Well, I'm sure you soon will be. You are so light on your feet and so dainty. And that's the important thing when one dances, to be light on one's feet." A smile came to her soft pink lips and to her eyes. "I have danced the waltz in Vienna, Christina, with Johann Strauss himself conducting the orchestra."

Christina's eyes grew wide and round and she gave a soft gasp. "Mother has told me about Vienna and Mr Strauss. That must have been so exciting."

"Yes, it was. It was madly exciting. I was quite young at the time and I remember wishing that I could go on forever, just floating around with the beautiful music filling my head and lending wings to my feet. Oh, what a magical place Vienna was. What glorious times they were." The smile on her face became wistful and she sighed. "What a pity it is that we cannot hold on to such times, even for a short while. Those precious, glorious moments that seem to fly by more quickly than all the others; if only we could close our fingers around them and hold back the tomorrows."

Christina nodded her head slowly. These were thoughts such as she had never known and it was hard to think of something to say. After a moment or two, she asked, "Did you have a beautiful gown?"

"Oh yes, a most beautiful gown. It was made in Paris from countless yards of rose-coloured silk. It had a tight-fitting bodice worn off the shoulder in a most daring fashion and the skirt was vast and billowing with handmade roses trailing from the waist to the hemline." She laughed softly. "I kept it for years and years, just to look at and remember."

Christina wanted to close her eyes so that she could visualise it all more clearly: the elegant ballroom with its glittering chandeliers, the beautiful gowns of the ladies flying in circles of every colour, and Mrs Klaussen young and lovely in her rose-coloured silk. But she couldn't do that. She was still talking and it would be too rude. The vision would have to wait for another time.

"Those days have gone, Christina, and there will probably never again be anything quite like them. But then, that's the way life is, a great, on-going event. Nothing stands still." She laughed suddenly. "And, instead of standing here watching the dust fly before the brooms and brushes and daydreaming about waltzing in Vienna, we should be practising our English, you and I. We have lost three full days and now that we have a chance to resume we are dawdling."

Thanks to favourable breezes, the Friedeburg reached Port Said on the Saturday morning some hours earlier than had been expected. At once, people began to gather on the upper decks, laughing and talking excitedly. Another milepost – an important one, for here they would be able to go ashore and feel the earth beneath their feet once more. While her crew hurried to furl first one section of her canvas and then another, the ship made her way slowly between the two long piers jutting out into the sea and into the outer harbour, where a grimy little tugboat with a puffing smoke-stack bustled up to take her in tow, guiding her past the lofty concrete and iron lighthouse into the inner harbour, from where she would later enter the Suez Canal. A second tug joined its companion for the task of manoeuvring the ship into position against a wharf teeming with people of a dozen or more races. There were Fellahs and Copts whose land this was, but, mingling with them, were Turks, Arabs,

Armenians, Berbers, Negroes, and a number of Chinese and Europeans.

Watching from the main deck, Christina felt a tingle of apprehension run down her spine, for a moment or two taking the edge off her excitement. What an incredible mixture of people they were. Why, there were shiny black faces, dark brown faces, light brown faces, yellow faces, white faces. And the difference didn't end with skin colour. Some of the faces were broad, whereas others were quite narrow, and there were big noses and small noses, thick lips on wide smiling mouths and thin lips pressed tightly together. And the clothes they were wearing: flowing robes, turbans, strange looking pantaloons. Oh, never had she dreamed that people could be so different from one another.

"Come, Christina, let us see what it feels like to have earth beneath our feet once again."

At the sound of her father's voice, Christina turned quickly from the rail, her smile fading when she saw that he was alone. "Where's Mother?"

"She has decided against coming with us. Perhaps she'll go ashore for a while later this afternoon."

"But why not now?" A small frown creased Christina's brow. "Is she worried about Anna?"

"Not unduly so. She just considers that the heat and crowds would be too wearying for her when she's still a bit out of sorts. They are going to rest in Mrs Klaussen's cabin while the lower deck is being cleaned. It's probably a good idea, it will be nice and restful for them there."

Christina nodded. "And Mother will at least have a good view of all that is happening on the wharves. Is Mrs Klaussen going ashore?"

"Yes, but a bit later on. Captain Koffer is going to escort her."

How strange it was. As though the ground was moving just as the ship did. And it was difficult to walk properly. "Does it feel strange for you too, Father?"

"Indeed it does. What a strange place Egypt is. Ground that moves, for heaven's sake."

Christina giggled delightedly as she skipped along to keep up with him. "Will we look in the shops?"

"Of course. We may not buy very much, but we will certainly look. In a place like this, such things we should see. From all over the world, I would think. I believe that it's even possible to buy some fruit, and what a treat that will be." He stopped abruptly. "Look at that, Christina."

Christina froze in her tracks, then drew back against her father's side. Squatting in the dust at the edge of the road, an old, dark-skinned man with a turban on his head was quietly blowing a whistle beside a tall, cane basket, and, even as they came to a stop, a snake poked its large flat head up over the top, balancing itself in an erect position while it moved to and fro.

"Oh, my goodness, what is it?" Christina gasped.

"It's a cobra," her father whispered, bending down so that his lips were close to her ear. "It's under the influence of the music."

Christina shivered. "It's horrible. Will it bite him?"

"No, it has more than likely had its fangs removed. The cobra is a very poisonous snake and I'm sure the old fellow wouldn't be sitting there as calmly as that if there was any chance of his being bitten."

"But don't go any closer, Father, please don't."

"It won't harm us, Christina. You wait and see, the moment the music stops, the snake will disappear back into its basket. Indian fakirs have been performing such tricks for centuries and I'm sure that very few, if any, of them have died of snake bite."

"It's such a fearsome looking creature, do we have to watch it?"

"Not if you don't want to. Let us find something more pleasing to look at."

The road leading from the wharves to the centre of the town was narrow, dusty, and crowded with people and animals. Donkeys appeared to be the chief mode of transport for those who chose not to walk, but, every so often, tall, bleary-eyed camels ambled along, the bells on their reins jingling as their owners urged them to greater effort.

"Ships of the desert," Simon mused as his daughter stood still, staring in amazement. "Oh, what strange creatures they are. And ever so much bigger than I expected."

"But you're not afraid of these poor, harmless fellows, are you?"

"I am a bit." She giggled nervously. "More than a bit when they come too close. I thought that last one was going to eat my bonnet."

"He certainly seemed interested in it. But come, we should be moving a bit more quickly. If we stop to watch every camel that comes along we are never going to reach the shops."

Just a few yards further on, the shops reached out to them. On blankets or pieces of canvas spread over the dust on both sides of the road, the wares of a hundred or more sharp-eyed traders were spread in a glittering, colourful confusion that contrasted strangely with the drab buildings behind. There was jewellery of every possible description: necklaces, pendants, rings and bracelets of gold or silver, jade or ivory, the precious stones that adorned them flashing in the sunlight. There were leather goods, and scarves and handkerchiefs of silk, wool or cotton. Jars and vases, carpets and rugs, baskets and woodwork, all the result of countless hours of patient toil. And bolts of material piled high, their ends unwound and hanging free so that potential buyers could be invited to feel the quality. There were perfumes and other toiletries, and a myriad other odds and ends, including a bird in a cage and a puppy on a leash.

Further along, the traders bent on tempting jaded shipboard appetites displayed their wares: baskets of dates and olives, of figs and oranges; long, flat trays of hard biscuits and strange-looking breads; crates of fish and vegetables.

Everywhere, there was noise: a great deafening din of voices that shrieked, cajoled, bartered, persuaded, whined, urged and argued. It beat against the eardrums in such a throbbing cacophony it was well-nigh impossible to determine from which persistent trader the best bargains were forthcoming. Deciding finally to take pot-luck, Simon and Christina bought their oranges from a swarthy young man who assured them over and over that they had come all the way from Spain. And then some dates and olives from the neighbour he highly recommended and who just happened to be his brother. Next, they bought a soft blue shawl for Elsie and a leather belt for Simon. Then it was left to Christina to choose something for herself and little Anna. This was no easily-decided matter, and she changed her mind at least half a dozen times before selecting a soft fur donkey for the baby and an embroidered blouse for herself.

They returned to a ship smelling of scrubbed, still-damp timbers, wet canvas and carbolic soap, clean smells that pleased the senses. For months to come, particles of ochre dust would, at odd moments, make their appearance on the Friedeburg, creeping out from corners and cracks, but for now there was none to be seen. The ship had emerged from the shroud dropped over her by the Sirocco.

In the late afternoon, as a pink, purple and gold sunset blazed in the western sky, the tug boats hustled the Friedeburg across the inner harbour and into the dark waters of the Suez Canal. The desert, hauntingly beautiful with reflected colour and the dark silhouettes of camels and Bedouin encampments, stretched away on both sides of the man-made waterway and held those who watched from the ship enthralled. But Christina, pressed against the rail on the poop deck, felt none of the enchantment, only the aching loneliness. She was weeping quietly, the tears slipping unchecked on to her cheeks, her lips trembling over whispered words, "Please, God, don't let her die. Please, please don't take this baby from us."

5

For a time, while the Friedeburg sailed the long, dreary reaches of the Red Sea, sometimes covering less than twenty miles in a full day, the Skov baby rallied, and it seemed that she had recovered from the severe bout of croup which had seized her small body so suddenly in Port Said. But then she became feverish again, crying as though in pain, and it was clear that, although she now had only a short, dry cough, she was having difficulty breathing. Doctor Heinemann, prodding gently at the swelling on her left side, grimly diagnosed pleurisy; the aftermath, he explained, of the croup attack. He tended her night and day, applying hot mustard poultices to subdue the inflammation of the affected membrane, then strapping her chest with strips of cloth in an attempt to restrain the accumulation of effusion in the lung cavities. In spite of his constant attention and the loving care of her mother, little Anna Skov loosed her fragile hold on life just after dusk on the tenth day of June. An hour previously, the Friedeburg had sailed out of the Strait of Bab-el-Mandeb into the Indian Ocean.

Huddled against the deck-house, Christina seemed unaware of the sudden squall sweeping the deck and drenching her clothes. She stared past the fore-sails to where the jibs reached out beyond the prow, their boom rising and falling with the roll of the ocean. Flying white horses against the darkness, that's what they were. Flying white horses pulling the ship on its way, never wearying for all that it was thousands of miles. Almost halfway now. Too late to turn back. Too late to go back to Schleswig. Too late to …

"Christina!"

Someone was calling her name, but the sound was coming from far away, much too far away to answer. Don't listen. Think about the white horses. How graceful they are. How they prance up and down.

"Christina, where are you?"

Her father was calling her from somewhere back there in the darkness. Don't answer. Don't answer.

"Christina!"

So close now, just around the corner of the deck-house. Stay where it's darkest …

"There you are! Thank God, I've found you!"

He was here, right beside her, and he had seen her. Oh, why did Father have to come?

"I must talk to you, Christina."

"Have you seen the jibs this evening, Father? See how they fly, like prancing white horses pulling the ship on its way."

"Listen to me, please! Little Anna … "

"No, no! I don't want to listen! I don't want to!" Someone was screaming. Surely not her. She would never scream at her father in such a way. But why didn't he understand? "Don't tell me, Father. Please don't tell me."

His hands were on her arms, drawing her to her feet, trying to hold her close. "Christina, dearest child … "

Abruptly, Christina ceased her struggling. Her father was crying, she could hear him choking over the sobs in his throat. Don't cry, Father, please don't cry. She took hold of his hand and pressed her face against his side, feeling his fingers tighten over hers. For long, long moments, they stood there, holding each other fiercely, oblivious of the rain beating down on them, the wind tearing at their clothes.

Finally, Simon spoke in a bleak, muffled voice. "I have to tell you, Christina, before we go back to your mother … "

Christina slowly shook her head. "I know what it is, Father. God has taken little Anna."

Under dark, threatening skies passengers and crew huddled together on the main deck. Overhead, the trimmed sails thrashed angrily back and forth, while the ocean pounded just as angrily against the ship's sides. With so much noise there were few able to hear the prayers the Captain was saying over the small canvas-wrapped body. Standing at the front, with her hand crushed in her father's, Christina heard his voice, but the words eluded her. English words? The German Captain was saying the prayers in English. How strange that was. But there must be some words that she knew. Wasn't she learning English? Oh, if only her mind would let her think. If only she could stop crying. She kept her head bowed and closed her eyes tightly, but the tears pushed their way beneath the lids and through the lashes, sliding down her cheeks on to the scarf that covered her head and tied under her chin. Would she never be able to stop? She wanted to. It wasn't helping her mother and father to have her crying all the time. But, no matter how hard she tried, she couldn't stop. The tears wouldn't go away … they were there, burning her eyes, no matter how many fell. And in her throat too, in a lump that she couldn't swallow. And her heart ached and ached, as though all the happiness had been squeezed from it.

Her father was crying too; she could feel his body shaking where it touched her shoulders. And so was Mrs Klaussen, weeping quietly into her handkerchief. She couldn't tell about her mother, though. She was standing on the other side of her father. Still, even if she could see her, she wouldn't know. Mostly, her mother cried inside herself. She must do so, for, even last light when she'd gone back with her father, she hadn't been crying, but just standing there with her face white and stricken and a terrible emptiness in her eyes. There were no tears, none at all. And, even later, up here on the deck, there'd been no tears …

Christina gulped and pressed her free hand over her mouth, fearful that what her mind had recalled would find its way into words that others would come to know what only she did. Oh, if only it had been a dream, the way she thought it had been when she'd first woken this morning. But it wasn't a dream, it was real. It had all happened. First, the empty bunk where her mother should have been sleeping. Then groping up the companion ladder in the darkness with the rungs hurting her bare feet. The deck, wet from the earlier rain, but bathed in silvery light as the moon sailed free of the ragged clouds. And, over by the rail, her mother, with a shawl over her nightdress and the wind whipping her long, loose hair about her face. How strange it had been to find her there all alone and with no nightcap on her head. She'd wanted to run to her and snuggle close, to let her know that she wasn't all alone. But something had held her crouched in the shadows at the top of the ladder. Such a look on her mother's face, a terrible wild grief that twisted it almost beyond knowing. And something else as well. Anger...? But at whom? And then, with a wildly thumping heart, she had known: her mother was angry at God. She was glaring up at the sky and a torrent of harsh, bitter words had begun to fly from her lips. Her mother who had always said that God knew best was now crying out that He knew nothing of love or kindness, that he was a cruel, uncaring God. She was saying that she didn't want to know him any more, that …

"Christina..."

Christina started, her thoughts flying back from the tormented midnight hour. Someone was singing a hymn and Mrs Klaussen was taking her hand. "We'll leave now, dear, and go to my cabin for a while."

Numbly, Christina let herself be led away, along the path people moved to clear for them. But, even though they hurried, with Mrs Klaussen pulling on her hand, the sound of the splash, sharp and different from all the other noises, caught up with them. Christina shuddered and the lump in her throat rose to her mouth as her stomach began to heave. "I think I have to vomit."

"Oh, quickly then."

Mrs Klaussen stood behind her, gripping her shoulders while she leant over the basin and let the retching have its way. Then she helped her to remove her coat and scarf before washing her face with a soft cloth that smelt faintly of lemon.

"I'm sorry," Christina murmured miserably as a warm shawl was settled about her shaking shoulders.

"You don't have to be sorry, love. That was just a normal reaction and you may feel a little better for having got it over with. Just lie down for a while and I'll make us a nice cup of tea. There's no milk, but I'll make it weak and we can have lots of sugar." She smiled gently, trying to coax some response from the small figure sitting so crumpled on the edge of the bed.

"I don't need to lie down."

"Oh … well, that's alright. The tea won't take very long. This little burner is quite a treasure. I'm sure I don't know how I would have managed without it." With the kettle in place on the small blue flame, she came to sit beside Christina, picking up one of her small cold hands and rubbing it between her own. "I think you should try to say her name," she suggested softly.

Christina winced and fresh tears welled in her eyes. "I can't."

"Yes, you can. And you must. You can't lock little Anna out of your heart but you can't lock her in either. She's left you some very precious memories. Don't hide them away. Don't be afraid to speak of her."

"She's dead."

"She's in heaven, one of God's angels."

Spl-ASH!

Christina shivered as the sound, recalled, brought icy fingers to her spine, and her eyes darted to the porthole. How cold and grey the water looked. And where would she be with the whole ocean for a grave? No stone beneath an old oak tree for this little baby, nothing to show where she lay, no lettering to spell out her name. No coffin in the soft earth, just a piece of canvas in the vast rolling ocean.

"Christina, do you hear what I am saying?"

Bringing her gaze back from the porthole she fixed it listlessly on the blue flame. "I think so."

"You have to understand that it's not important where the graves for our bodies are. In the earth or in the ocean, it doesn't matter in the least. Because, you see, from the very moment we die, we are free of these earthly bodies. We have discarded them for something far more wonderful. You do know that, don't you?"

Christina nodded.

"Well then, you must know that it's that way for little Anna. She's in heaven now and has no need of her body."

"She was just one year old, she hadn't even learnt to walk properly."

"I know, but she was a very sick little girl."

"She might have got better … " Her eyes narrowed and she muttered,

"She would have got better if only … " she hesitated, frowning.

"If only you'd stayed in Haderslev," Eleanor Klaussen suggested with a sad, gentle smile. "Is that what you were going to say? Your father has wondered about that too. Poor man, feeling that he is somehow to blame."

Christina's chin jerked up. If only they'd stayed in Haderslev? She hadn't thought of that. She should have, though. If they'd still been at home, it would have been easier for her mother to care for the baby. And she would have had fresh cow's milk to drink and her own little cradle to sleep in. The terrible dust wouldn't have been there, and perhaps she wouldn't have become sick in the first place. "Would she have been sick like she was if we hadn't left home?"

"Oh Christina, no one can really answer such a question. But you, yourself, have told me that little Anna had been sick with the croup on more than one occasion, and Doctor Heinemann feels that her heart may have been damaged in some way. So perhaps it really wouldn't have been any different even if you had stayed in Haderslev." She sighed quietly. "It's not always easy for us to understand God's way, Christina. In fact, it's sometimes very hard."

"He took our other baby, too."

"Oh, I'm so sorry, I didn't know that."

"It was when I was just little." Large tears slipped on to her cheeks, and Eleanor Klaussen took her into her arms, drawing her head on to her shoulder. "It's going to be alright, Christina," she murmured against the soft golden hair. "It's going to be alright."

"I can't stop crying."

"You will, love. Soon now the tears will begin to dry. Even the ache in your heart will ease. That's the way life is, the yesterdays slip further and further from us and even our most terrible wounds heal. The day will come when you'll be able to think of little Anna without tears and then you'll remember all the happy things: what a beautiful baby she was, the great joy she brought into your life, how very much you loved her."

"I'll try, Mrs Klaussen."

"You won't have to try, darling, it will just happen."

With the Equator came the doldrums: calm seas, cloudless skies and feckless breezes. The crew worked hard and continuously at swinging the ponderous yards to trim the sails to every chance puff of wind, but, in spite of their efforts, progress was slow. The sails would billow out; then, with only a few miles gained, slat again, with a sharp cracking sound, against the masts. Each morning the sun rose out of the sea in a blaze of gold, signalling the beginning of yet another long succession of heat-seared daylight hours, which somehow had to be filled. The boredom and frustration, which had begun to stalk the decks of the Friedeburg as it crept through the Red Sea, now spread, taking on new proportions as it did so. Some six thousand miles of ocean still to be crossed, and the month of June into its final week. At the rate they were moving, they'd still be on the high seas when Christmas came round.

In the shade cast by the deck-house, Christina sat at her mother's side, watching her hands flying with needle and thread. Oh, how quickly they moved. And what neat, tiny stitches she was making. "What are you sewing, Mother?"

"A skirt." Elsie bit off the cotton and rethreaded the needle before continuing in a quiet voice, "This cambric is such a pretty blue I thought it would look nice with that blouse you bought in Port Said."

Christina swallowed, feeling again the sharp, stabbing sensation that had marked the end of that shopping expedition, the sensation that comes when happiness is drowned in sudden blind fear.

"Don't you agree?" her mother persisted gently.

"I suppose so."

"It will match the embroidery very nicely."

Christina nodded. It probably would, but she had almost forgotten what the blouse was like. She hadn't even looked at it since she'd brought it back to the ship. Even now, she wasn't sure that she wanted to. To change the subject, she asked, "Are you going to make something for yourself as well?"

"Not out of the cambric. I thought it might please Mrs Klaussen if I made up that lovely piece of silk she gave me." A faint smile passed over her lips. "I'm not sure when I'll ever get to wear such a dress, but it will be nice to have."

Christina's eyes, widening with surprise, searched her mother's face. She was smiling and talking so calmly about making a new dress for herself, it was hard to believe that there had been a night when she'd raged at the heavens with wild eyes and flying hair. It was just as well she had stayed in the shadows and slipped back to her bunk before her mother noticed her. Now that she was herself again, she would want to forget that she had yelled at God and she'd hardly be able to do that if she knew that someone shared her terrible secret.

"Shouldn't you be doing your lessons?"

Christina glanced down at the pages lying neglected on her lap. "It's much too hot just now; it's too hot to think even. I wish the wind would start to blow."

Again Elsie smiled. "You certainly don't have that wish all to yourself."

"No, it's what everyone is wishing for. But some people are saying that we could still be on the ship at Christmas time."

"That's silly. It's simply exaggeration when people say such things."

"When do you think the wind will blow, Mother?"

"I have no idea, Christina. But your father is quite convinced that we will encounter the trade winds any day now and he tells me that we should then have good breezes all the way to Australia."

"I hope so. It's terrible when the ship is moving so slowly and everyone is so bored. There's so much grumbling and complaining. Some of the men are even saying that we should have gone around the Cape of Good Hope like most of the clippers still do."

"The captains of the clippers look to the gales of the southern seas to speed them on their way. All sails set no matter how violent the storm, that's apparently their attitude. I'm afraid that would be much too hazardous for my liking. In any case, had we done that, we wouldn't have escaped the doldrums, we would have had those of the Atlantic to contend with."

"If only the sailors could catch a shark … "

"Oh Christina, that's just superstition. How could a shark's tail tied to the end of the jib boom possibly guarantee fair winds?"

"But they've been trying to catch one for days now."

"I know, but sailors are very superstitious. They no doubt believe a number of such things."

Her mother was right, Christina supposed, and yet, each time she'd gone with Henry Schneider to watch the sailors drop the stout line with its great hook and smelly piece of corned mutton over the poop rail at the stern, she'd felt the same hopeful excitement as all the others gathered there. "A lot of the passengers believe what the sailors do."

"People believe what they want to believe, and quite often it's what suits their present situation. But there's no harm done in believing that a shark's tail will get the wind to blow, and trying to catch one at least helps pass the time." She gave the fabric a quick shake before gathering it back on to her knees. "That's the seams done, now for the waistband."

Christina watched her for a time before asking, "Do you enjoy sewing, Mother?"

"Yes, I find it very relaxing."

"Would you like me to read that little story in English Mrs Klaussen wrote for me?"

"Yes, I would enjoy that."

Christina read slowly, but there was no stumbling over the words and when she finished she looked up at her mother with a small glow of triumph.

"That's very good, Christina. You really have made excellent progress with Mrs Klaussen."

"She said that by the time we reach Australia I might even be able to speak English without having to search for the words. Oh look, here comes Father."

Simon smiled at both of them. "Well, at least you've found a little shade."

"But it's still hot," Christina told him, "even in the shade."

"It certainly is, but it's to be expected, of course." He lowered himself to the deck at Elsie's feet before relating his most recently acquired piece of information. "I've been talking to that fellow Hertzig and a most interesting conversation it has been. He knows such a lot about Queensland, especially the Moreton Bay district. It seems that his aunt and uncle were there for a number of years as missionaries. They returned to Germany only last year, so they've been able to give him a fairly up-to-date account of the place."

"Missionaries, in Queensland?"

"That's right. Mr. Hertzig tells me there was a German missionary community at Moreton Bay as early as 1838. They went there to teach the Aborigines."

Elsie raised her eyebrows. "Wouldn't the Aborigines have been hostile to whites at that time?"

"I would have thought so." Simon shrugged, anxious to return the conversation to its intended course. "In any case, they would have known what they were letting themselves in for, missionaries usually do."

"I suppose so."

"Well, the interesting thing is that it's been largely due to those missionaries that so many Germans are settling in the Colony. It appears that, to begin with, the agents hired by the Queensland authorities to seek out immigrants for the colony gathered together a pretty motley crowd, people who were entirely unsuited for work on the land. They took clerks, shopmen, professional people and such like, as well as a string of neér-do-wells. Also, according to Hertzig, there were hundreds of cotton weavers from Lancashire. Because the manufacturing industry in England was at such a low ebb due to the American war and the shortage of raw cotton, these poor, misguided souls went out to Queensland convinced they were going to help grow enough cotton to keep their fellow workers back home in employment."

"Well, surely, if it was possible to grow cotton in Queensland, that wasn't such a bad idea?"

"It was possible to grow it alright, but these people had no idea what it was like to work on a cotton plantation. For one thing, the work was harder than anything they'd ever tackled in their lives before. For another, there was the fact that they'd always been used to regular hours, and to doing the same job day after day. Hertzig says they were hopeless, even those who went on to small farms. Anyway, as a result of all this, the Colony of Queensland found itself sinking into a deep morass where labour was concerned."

"Then the Germans came and saved the situation," Elsie suggested, tongue in cheek.

Simon gave a deep chuckle. "Well, Hertzig didn't go so far as to say that, but there seems to be no doubt that German immigrants have settled into the country very well indeed. The missionaries apparently undertook to bring out only industrious families of known integrity and the whole arrangement has worked very well for all concerned."

"But surely there are other successful settlers?"

"Of course there are. For one thing, people from Australia's southern colonies have gone north to Queensland. And, since those early days, the Government has improved its immigration policies. It chooses much more carefully now."

Elsie smiled. "Well, that's nice to know, especially as we are among the chosen ones, so to speak. Did Mr Hertzig happen to mention which part of Queensland he's going to. Or hasn't he decided yet?"

"He had decided even before he left Germany. He's going to the Logan Valley. It's not very far to the south of Brisbane and from what he tells me it could be well worth considering."

"Isn't that where they are growing sugarcane?"

"Yes, but there's other farming as well..."

Christina, leaning forward to watch her father's face as he spoke, gave a small sigh of relief. His eyes were not nearly so red and swollen as they had been, and the blank, bewildered look had gone. They weren't really shining the way they used to when he talked about going to Australia, but a soft gleam had returned. And, as he told her mother what he had learned about the Logan Valley, there was something of his former excitement in his voice and the way he moved his hands. Her mother could see it too, Christina decided, for she was nodding her head and smiling gently as she listened to him tell of two rivers not very far apart, of river flats where sugar cane thrived, of the Lutheran community which had been established there for seven years now, and of the land still waiting to be claimed. Perhaps, she thought, in spite of the void in their lives and the ache in their hearts, it would still be possible to have a good life in their new country.

A brisk rain-scented breeze scurried suddenly along the deck and Simon broke off in mid-sentence to glance at a patch of cloud sweeping up into the south-eastern sky. "We could be in for a bit of a squall." He grinned suddenly. "And if Captain Koffer knows his job as well as I think he does, that could mean we are about to pick up the trades."

Simon's faith in the Captain was justified. The squall came and went within the hour, but the breeze continued to blow steadily. With the yards braced forward, it struck obliquely against their after-sides, the sails bellied, dipped and pulled, and the Friedeburg surged forward into the face of a trade wind. Before the week ended, the Great Bear would fade from the night skies and the brilliant stars of the Southern Cross make their appearance.

6

The great storm overtook the Friedeburg as she sailed eastwards across the Indian Ocean in the twelfth week of her voyage. Since picking up the south-east trades two weeks previously, she had met with nothing but fair weather: kindly seas, reliable winds and clear skies. A feeling of well-being pervaded the ship. In spite of discomfort, boredom and the dreary, monotonous food, passengers and crew alike had begun to feel that they had reason enough to be thankful. Soon, they would be off the north coast of Australia and on the last leg of their voyage. When all was said and done, things hadn't gone too badly. There had been no major calamities, no outbreaks of fever or dysentery, no discord of any importance. Sadly, a baby had died and been buried at sea and a sailor had fallen from the rigging and broken his leg, but such occurrences were normal on long voyages and no more than might have been expected. The Sirocco in the Mediterranean had been an ordeal, of course, and the Red Sea and the doldrums had slowed them down dramatically. But, it was generally agreed, such setbacks were always on-the-cards, and, in any case, no one had ever expected the Friedeburg to break any records.

But now, on this eighth day of July, complacency began to crumble. The sky was no longer blue. It wasn't the colour of rain-clouds either, but a strange, yellowish shade, and from it the sun glared down like an angry red eye. The ocean, glassy and undulating, took up the colour and became mud-coloured, as strange and alien-looking as the sky above it. The wind shifted, blowing in short bursts from the north-east. Within the hour the gusts had become stronger and, as the water stirred to a sullen, restless heaving, the crew of the Friedeburg hurried to the task of reefing her great spread of canvas. Tension quickly degenerated into a sense of foreboding and, when passengers were asked to go to their quarters, most did so without question or protest, but with rapidly beating hearts.

Orcan ... orcan ... everywhere, the word was heard.

Orcan, a German word. What did it mean? Christian wondered. Something to be feared, it seemed, for the faces of those who spoke the word and those who heard it and knew what it meant were grim with apprehension. Her father, appearing suddenly from around the rolled back canvas screen, supplied the answer before she had a chance to ask the question. "Hurricane," he announced worriedly. "It seems we are in for a hurricane."

Christina felt a stab of misgiving. That really was something to be feared, a terrible storm which could quite easily wreck a ship such as theirs. She saw her mother's head jerk up, her eyes anxiously searching her father's face. "Will it be a bad one, do you think?"

"All hurricanes are bad enough, Elsie. It's strange that we should run into one now, though. We are in the region for hurricanes, there's no doubt about that. But this is not the season for them. In fact, according to Captain Koffer, we are almost square in the middle of the off-season." He smiled reassuringly. "It may turn out that it's not a hurricane at all, but just some freakish weather conditions building up for a bit of a blow."

Elsie sighed heavily. "The Captain must think that we are in for something more than a bit of a blow. Just look at this place – the portholes battened over, lamps lit when it's still only early afternoon."

"He has to take precautions," Simon told her. "Even if he's not sure what we are in for, he has to do that. He's responsible not only for his ship but for the life of every person on board, and he can't risk just waiting around for something to begin to happen. But there's no call for you to be worrying. The Friedeburg is a sturdy vessel, capable of riding out a severe storm."

"Will the ocean be really rough, Father?" Christina asked in a small voice.

"It will probably roll the ship around a bit, but you're not afraid of that, are you?"

Christina wanted to return the smile he gave her, to let him see that he didn't need to worry on her account, but her lips felt so stiff they did little more than twitch at the corners. "I don't know what the ocean would be like in a really bad storm."

"We don't know that it is going to be a really bad storm, little one. But, even if it is, you'll be quite safe, never fear." He turned back to his wife. "There are some precautions which we must take."

Elsie nodded. "Of course. What should we do?"

Simon was already critically appraising the cramped space. "These are not at all sturdy," he declared, pressing his hands against the timber partitions. "They could quite easily give way if something was to roll heavily against them. I think our best plan would be to get down on the floor between the bunks. They seem to be fixed securely enough, and, if we take the mattresses and pillows and arrange them like a sort of burrow … "

"Will the hurricane last for a long time?" Christina asked anxiously.

"It shouldn't, and we'll certainly be hoping that it doesn't. Now, why don't you help your mother stow away everything we won't be needing?"

In the midafternoon, the yellow sky gave way to heavy black clouds which quickly swallowed up the strange red sun. Lightning streaked across the darkness and thunder began an incessant rumbling. With the wind whipping itself into a howling fury, heavy rain began to fall. On the Friedeburg the hatches were quickly battened down, and the lower deck became an oppressive place where the only light was the ghostly circles thrown by a couple of swinging lanterns. With the ship turned into the wind and all but a storm-jib and a section of the main-sail reefed, the Captain roped himself to the mizzen close to the two men in safety harness fighting the huge spoked helm to keep the hull from swinging about in the surging seas.

Hardly had he done so, when the storm increased its ferocity into an explosion of skies and ocean. Driving wind and rain lashed the rigging and upper decks, while the waves took on the appearance of liquid hills and marched relentlessly down on the Friedeburg, towering their sheer black cliffs for a moment before crashing with a deafening roar over the forecastle head and filling the main deck with foaming water, feet deep. The ship shuddered as she plunged headlong into the boiling cauldron, then, with water pouring from her scuppers, sluggishly recovered, only to have to go through the same grinding torture again and again, while the angry waves, born and reborn at the whim of the screaming, treacherous wind fought ceaselessly to turn her. And finally did. With her fore-topmast and all the section above crashing to the deck in a tangle of canvas and rigging, the Friedeburg slid sideways into a deep trough, where she rolled helplessly from side to side with great walls of water crashing over her bulwarks.

Down below, in complete darkness now, straining, clinging bodies were being flung to and fro, while those unable to retain their grip on some securely fixed object were being thrown about like driftwood caught in a whirlpool. The atmosphere was stifling, rancid with the smell of vomit, sweat and fear. And the noise deafening: thunder which seemed to be trying to shatter the heavens wide open; the crashing of waves against the ship's sides and on the deck above; the banging of the great assortment of articles, large and small, being continuously flung about; the screaming which went on and on.

Crushed between her parents, Christina was screaming, but there was only a strangled whimpering coming from her throat, terror had long since choked off her voice. "It's going to be alright, the storm must pass soon." She had heard the words so many times now they hardly registered, even though it was her father who kept saying them, with his lips close to her ear, while he held her pressed tightly to his side. He doesn't believe that, she thought. He knows that it's going to go on and on and not let us get away. The ship will roll over and the ocean will swallow us. Then our bodies will float around for ever and ever, just the way little Anna's is doing. She shivered violently and her father at once pulled a blanket up over her shoulders. But she wasn't cold, she was hot. Oh God, please let it be over! Please, please let it end!

Suddenly, just when it seemed that the Friedeburg could take no more, the great roaring and pounding eased and there came a strange lull. The wind died and the ship steadied.

"Is it going to be over now, Father?" Christina asked in a small, hoarse voice.

"I don't think so, love, not just yet. If it is a true hurricane, we are now in its centre and before we are free we will have to go through wind coming from the other direction."

"Will it be as bad as before?"

"Perhaps not. At least we'll know it will be over the next time it stops."

"When will that be?"

"I don't know, Christina, but we are going to be alright in our little burrow." He leaned forward in order to see his wife's face through the gloom. "How are you bearing up, Elsie?"

"Still in one piece," his wife told him, attempting a small laugh. Then, shaking her head disbelievingly, "I never imagined it would be anything like this."

"Well, now we have a respite in which to prepare ourselves for the next onslaught."

The respite was short-lived. The wind returned with renewed violence and the terrifying pounding and rolling about resumed. "It's going to be worse than before," Christina cried, clinging frantically to her father.

"No, it will just seem that way until we get used to it again."

The wave hit with a thunderous roar, shaking the ship violently before rolling her into yet another trough. And this time she rolled and stayed, wallowing on her side. Christina felt her father stiffen, jamming his back against the mattress behind them, bracing his legs, freeing his arms to grip the uprights supporting the bunks. And she couldn't stop her own body from toppling hard against his, while her mother struggled to keep from falling on top of her.

"Now," she heard her father plead. "Roll her back now. Oh, Dear God in heaven, roll her back."

The seconds passed, measured in heartbeats. A strange hush took the place of the screaming, as though every breath was being held. Roll her back ... roll her back ... silent begging while hearts hammered. Then, miraculously, the gallant ship was being lifted, thrust upwards by a long, curling wall of water. For a breathless moment she hung on the crest, then with a sound like a long, deep sigh, slid down the watery slope, coming to rest, battered and torn, but on an even keel.

By morning all trace of the hurricane had been swept from the heavens. A kindly sun shone down from a sky so brilliantly blue it was hard to believe that less than twenty-four hours previously both had been grotesquely distorted. The ocean, though, encouraged by a brisk breeze, still displayed remnants of the maniacal fury in which it had indulged, its long, heavy swells driving the crippled ship down-wind and even further away from her course. With his arm in a sling, the Captain held a short thanksgiving on the littered main deck. A helmsman had been quite seriously injured and there were a number of people with broken bones, cuts and abrasions, but no lives had been lost, and this was indeed something to be thankful for. Also, the ship, although badly battered with both fore-mast and main-mast severely damaged, could be repaired, thus allowing them to complete their voyage. Everyone, conscious of the great dangers passed and the richness of their survival, listened solemnly and fervently offered up their prayers. Then they set to, crew and passengers alike, to try to extract some order from the shambles. They slaved at the pumps, at repairing the broken masts, at mending sails and rigging, at restoring fittings and belongings to their rightful places and at reorganising the hold where much of the stowed luggage floated in inches of water.

For Christina, though, the terrifying experience of the hurricane was not yet complete. She had just come up the companion-ladder after helping her mother remake their beds when a deep swell curled and broke against the side of the ship, its foaming waters spilling over the deck. Caught unawares, she was swept off her feet and bowled over and over. Screaming and thrashing her arms about wildly, she clutched at coils of rope, pieces of wood, bundles of canvas, at the deck itself. But there was no stopping; the water rushing to the scuppers had her at its mercy. Through streaming eyes she saw the hole in the bulwark come rushing towards her, knew what it was, knew that even a grown man could be swept through it. She was going to be washed overboard! She was going to die!

The sailor, wizened and ageing, burnt by the tropical suns of half the world, but as lithe as a cat, left the forecastle in one long bound. He caught her within inches of the scupper, grabbing her clothes in his strong brown hand, hauling her back across the deck, then holding her tightly while the last of the water swirled away.

Christina sagged against him like a rag doll, her heart racing, her mind still echoing her screams. But quickly the realisation came: she hadn't died, she was alive! Why was she crying then? Why was she crying when she should be laughing? But the sobs kept coming, choking her, and she was shaking so badly she could hardly stand. She clung to the sailor with both arms, pressing her face into his bony side. She would fall if he let her go, and then if another wave came …

"Oh, thank God! Thank God you are safe!" Her father was sweeping her up into his arms, holding her tightly. "I thought you were down below with your mother. I had no idea you were on deck when the wave hit." His voice broke and there was an expression of such horror on his face, Christina stifled her sobs and slipped an arm around his neck. "I'm alright now, Father."

"You're not hurt?"

"No, not really, just a few bumps. I would have gone into the ocean though if the sailor hadn't saved me."

Simon spun around, reaching for the man's hand, speaking slowly and emotionally in German.

I should thank him too, Christina thought, hiccoughing over the last of her sobs. She lifted her head from her father's shoulder and the thin brown face was there, very close to her own. "You have saved my life," she murmured huskily. "Thank you very much."

He nodded, smiling widely, and, in spite of the terror still trembling through her, Christina felt a quick rush of elation. She had spoken in English, and the sailor had understood. Wait until she told Mrs Klaussen.

After speaking again with her father, he touched her hair gently with the tips of his fingers, then slipped quietly through the ring of people gathered about them. Within minutes, he was back mending the jib stays.

"I wonder what his name is," Christina mused as her father carried her back along the deck.

"We'll find out, little one, and that is one sailor we will never forget."

Elsie met them at the foot of the ladder, her face white and distraught. "Henry Schneider told me that Christina would have been washed overboard if a sailor hadn't caught hold of her?"

"Yes, but she's fine now," Simon told her, setting Christina down on her feet.

"I should never have let her go up there … "

"You weren't to know something like this would happen. No one expected such a wave, it was a real surprise breaking against the ship the way it did. And, with Christina being so small, it swept her right off her feet."

Elsie shuddered. "If the sailor hadn't been there … ?"

"He was there," Simon told her firmly. "And now I think we should try to put the whole incident out of our minds. It's over and done with and the only harm Christina has suffered is a thorough drenching and perhaps a few bruises." He smiled down at the small, bedraggled figure standing beside him. "Some dry clothes and you'll be just fine, won't you, little one?"

"Yes, Father." Christina reached out and took her mother's hand. "I haven't been hurt, Mother, truly I haven't. I was just crying because I got such a fright."

"And why wouldn't you have got a fright? It must have been a terrifying experience." Elsie's fingers tightened over her daughter's, but she brought a smile to her lips, "Couldn't you have managed to keep some part of you dry?"

Christina grinned in response to her mother's gentle teasing. "I'm wet all the way through, right to my skin."

"I can well believe that. And it seems your father could also do with a change of clothing as well."

Simon shook his head. "Mine will dry out quickly enough once I get back up on deck."

"Is any progress being made?"

"I would think so, but everything's in such a mess it's a bit hard to tell. There's any amount of work to be done, so, if you don't need me here, I'll go back up. I'll probably see you for dinner." About to climb the ladder, he glanced back over his shoulder with a faint, rueful grin. "Don't expect anything hot. The cook's fire has been well and truly doused and the galley is a shambles."

Christina smiled as she stepped out of her wet clothes. "I can't wait to tell Mrs Klaussen that I thanked the sailor in English and he knew what I said."

"She will be pleased to hear that, but you'll have to wait to tell her, I'm afraid. She had a nasty fall during the storm and Doctor Heinemann thinks she should stay in bed for a few days."

Christina's smile faded. "Is she badly hurt?"

"Severe bruising and a sprained wrist, according to the doctor. Bad enough, but I suppose it could have been a whole lot worse."

"Shouldn't we visit her? She might be needing some help and Doctor Heinemann will be too busy to spend much time with her."

"He's certainly busy, poor man, but he has assured me that what Mrs Klaussen needs is rest, so we won't disturb her today. We'll see what he says tomorrow."

Within two days, the Friedeburg was sufficiently repaired to move freely, and, within two weeks, she was back on course and sailing across the top of the Australian continent. With a brilliant sun burning down on her billowing canvas, tarred cordage and scrubbed decks and her scars barely visible, she was sped on her way by favourable winds. It was almost, ran the thoughts of those on board, as though the weather was trying to atone for the damage and delay it had inflicted on the ship. And, with their destination now drawing ever closer, they were almost able to forgive. Even those hobbling about on crutches wore smiles and were inclined to regard the whole terrifying experience as a nightmare now firmly entrenched in the past.

On the last day of the month, they sailed into Torres Strait, the eighty-mile-wide, island-dotted stretch of water separating Australia from New Guinea. Now the ship buzzed with excitement. To the south of a cluster of palm-covered islands a smudge of land could be seen. It was, Captain Koffer informed his passengers, the northernmost tip of Queensland. Although there were still close to two thousand miles to travel before they reached Moreton Bay, this glimpse of their new homeland brought the immigrants on the Friedeburg a somewhat satisfying feeling that they had arrived. That land stretching off to the south was the new colony they had come to help settle. It was where they would build their homes and plough their land. It was where their dreams would be realised.

"I can't believe that's really Queensland," Christina exclaimed, hopping excitedly from one foot to the other as she stood at the poop rail with her parents. "After all this time we are really here."

"We still have a long way to go," her mother reminded her, "so don't go getting too excited just yet."

"But we'll be close to land all the way now, won't we? Didn't the Captain tell you that we'd be taking the inside passage, Father, between the coral reef and the shore?"

"Yes, that he did. It's very well charted now and apparently the safest way to go."

"I believe there are people on that island." Elsie exclaimed, pulling the brim of her bonnet down in order to shade her eyes from the slanting rays of the afternoon sun. "There are small huts in between the trees. Ah yes, there they are, coming on to the beach."

Christina had seen them too and her breath caught on a flicker of unease. Black, the people on the island were black. She turned to where her father was standing behind her, "Are they Aborigines?"

"I think they are more likely to be Islanders," Simon told her. "Though I suppose they could be related to the mainland natives. Whoever they are, they appear friendly enough; they are waving to us."

There were now ten or twelve dark outlines on the white strip of sand and more arriving. "There must be a whole community living there," Elsie mused. "I could almost envy them, it must be an idyllic lifestyle."

"So could I," Simon told her. "What about you, Christina? Would you like to live on an island like that?"

"I suppose so, but what would we eat?"

"Mainly fish, I would think. And, of course, there would never be a shortage of coconuts."

"What lovely trees those coconut palms are, especially the ones that stand apart and become silhouetted against the sky." Elsie turned from the rail, a pleased smile on her lips. "Ah, here's Mrs Klaussen."

Eleanor Klaussen still wore a bandage on her wrist, but, apart from that, she appeared to have recovered well from her fall during the hurricane. She smilingly greeted each of the Skov family in turn before moving to the rail at Elsie's side. "Aren't those islands beautiful, so peaceful-looking?"

"We have just been saying how pleasant it would be to live there," Elsie told her. "Unfortunately, though, we have far more complicated needs than those people over yonder."

"Yes, how right you are. But perhaps it has all been in the scheme of things, so to speak. For those people a simple life, filling their stomachs from nature's bounty, then sitting back to watch time go by. For us, something very different." She chuckled softly. "Goodness, how philosophical we are becoming, Mrs Skov. If we continue in this vein, we'll be diving overboard and trying to swim to one of those islands."

They all laughed and conversation between them flowed easily as they watched the people on the beach become mere specks, then disappear as the island faded into a soft green blur. With the sun low in the west other islands appeared, some of them green and palm-covered, others nothing more than blobs of sand carpeted with bird-life. Watching the ceaseless coming and going of the feathered colonies and listening to their constant squawking and bickering, Christina laughed out loud. "What quarrelsome creatures they are. And there must be thousands and thousands of them."

"Gulls and terns, for the most part," her father observed, "but there are others in their midst. All seabirds though."

"If we do decide to live on an island, we must be sure there's no roosting place for birds on our doorstep," Eleanor Klaussen laughed. "Even from this distance the noise is quite deafening."

"It most certainly is," Simon agreed. "I don't think it would … Oh, for heaven's sake, watch out there!"

His sudden shout was drowned in the clanging of the ship's bell and the yells of a hundred other people along the rails. A boat had appeared, gliding out from behind one of the larger islands and heading directly toward the Friedeburg. For one or two breathless moments it seemed that a collision was inevitable, but then, at a shouted command, twenty long, hollowed paddles lifted as one and began to beat back against the water. The craft veered away, then began moving with the ship. And what a craft it was. A great canoe made from a single log some fifty feet in length, elaborately carved along both sides, with a figurehead devised from a plank and adorned with brightly coloured feathers and bleached skulls; with a woven mat attached to the mast to catch the breeze and an outrigger to maintain balance. A craft that brought the glaze of wonderment to the eyes of all who gazed down upon it from the decks of the Friedeburg.

And just as spectacular were the men who rowed it. Twenty of them, standing straight and tall as they plied their paddles back and forth; their sooty-black skins deliberately scarred in strange designs and painted with red and white clay; their thick, fuzzy hair, a giant pom-pom atop their long, sombre faces, ornamented with feathers even more brilliant than those on the canoe. They wore short skirts of plaited rushes and an assortment of necklaces, armlets and anklets made of shells, beads and large teeth, and, horror of horrors, they had bones piercing their earlobes and nostrils.

"Oh, how can they do that?" Christina gasped, responding to a need to press closer to her father's side.

"I suppose it's a custom for them, though I'm sure that doesn't make it any the less uncomfortable."

"Or gruesome," Mrs Klaussen added, shuddering. "And aren't they human skulls on the front of the boat?"

"It would seem so."

Christina gulped. People's heads? And they had used them to decorate their boat! Oh, what savages they must be! "Where have they come from, Father?" she asked in a voice that was little more than a whisper.

"I have no idea, Christina."

"They may be from New Guinea," Mrs Klaussen suggested. "I have a nephew in the navy and, a year or so back, his ship was required to check on the German mission outposts in New Guinea. I recall that when he returned he often spoke of the magnificent feathers the natives wore. I believe he said that they come from the birds of paradise."

"Ah... then that is almost certainly where these men have come from."

"Do you suppose they attire themselves in such a way all the time?" Elsie asked.

"I wouldn't think so," Simon told her. "They are more than likely dressed up for something special, perhaps some ceremony of importance to their tribe."

"They are not going to attack the ship, are they, Father?" Christina asked quickly.

"No, of course not. They've probably happened upon us quite by accident. They may even have got as big a shock at seeing us as we did at seeing them."

"They don't look very friendly. They're not smiling or waving like those on the island were."

"Well, perhaps we've interrupted whatever it was they were doing. Or maybe they object to our being in these waters. It's only been in recent years that ships have begun to use the Torres Strait as a regular route, so they could quite easily still be harbouring some resentment, seeing it as an invasion of their territory, so to speak."

Abruptly, as though taking exception to all the speculation taking place on the ship towering above them, the warlike natives scooped their paddles out of the water in one rippling, flowing movement. At once, the great canoe fell behind, rocking on the creaming wake left by the Friedeburg. Then, again as one, the long paddles were raised against the sunset. A farewell salute? There were few on the ship who thought so. To most it was more like a gesture of angry defiance.

7

In the soft, melting darkness of predawn, one ghostly figure after another appeared on the upper decks – the immigrants responding to a pressing desire to see what the first light of the new day would reveal of this land they would soon call 'home'. Waking to find her father's bunk deserted, Christina dressed quickly and hurried to find him. He was on the poop deck, leaning against the rail and he straightened as she approached. "So you are up, Christina. You were sleeping so soundly I didn't like to waken you."

"All the moving about woke me. So many people are getting up, even though it's still so early."

"Well, this is going to be a very exciting day. We should be able to see quite a bit of the Queensland coastline."

"Are we in the passage now?"

"Oh yes, well and truly. The reef is off to seaward, not too distant at this point, I believe. And the land is just over yonder. It's little more than a dark outline at present, but it should soon be light enough for us to see something."

Christina allowed herself the luxury of one last yawn. Then she looked about her, a quick appreciative smile coming to her lips. What a special time of day this was, the last minutes before sunrise. It was as though the whole world stood still while it waited for the day to begin. "Do you see how still everything is, Father? Even the water seems hardly to be stirring. And look, you can see the reflections of the stars."

"So you can. I've been so intent on watching the coastline I hadn't noticed. The drowning stars. eh? But they seem not to care, they are winking at us quite cheekily." Simon laughed softly and took hold of his daughter's hand. "Oh Christina, what exciting times are before us."

Christina nodded, her heart skipping a beat. It was exciting, even though there had been long weeks when she'd been quite sure that it would never be so, that only sadness would be with them when they arrived in Australia. "How long before it will be daylight?"

"Fifteen or twenty minutes only, I should think. But come, let us enjoy the waiting. We have the heavens over our heads and also at our feet. What more could we ask for?"

As the first golden light struck the Friedeburg's sails and spilled on to her decks, colour and form came back to the world through which she sailed. Puffy white clouds drifted across an azure sky. The water, serene and glistening, took on a deep blue-green colour. A strip of sand, the embryo of an island, pushed through its surface and provided a base for a dozen large pelicans searching for their breakfast. Further to seaward, coral cays in turquoise circles told where the inner reef lay. And beyond, where the great ramparts of coral rose up from the ocean depths, a thin white line beneath a soft haze could be seen – the long swells of the Pacific Ocean being dashed to foam.

For the immigrants who had waited for the dawn, however, these first moments were not for the appreciation of such things. A small coral insect, building ceaselessly and beautifully through millennia, might be responsible for the calm seas through which they sailed. The pelicans might glide gracefully back and forth and dip their huge bills into the water with incredible rhythmical unison. The water might shimmer like sapphires and the sand of the island gleam like silver. But it was the land that held their attention and at this they stared in wide-eyed amazement. At first, with the sun's rays tinting, gilding and shading, it seemed that they gazed upon an ancient city – an Atlantis scooped up from the ocean floor and washed up on these remote shores, where its temples and cloisters, arches and stairways, streets and dwelling places would await the return of its people. But then, as they drew closer and the sun's rays became stronger, they saw that this 'city', stretching for miles along the water's edge, was nothing more than a vast tumble of boulders, sandstone-coloured and densely packed.

And there was something else to bring gasps of incredulity. Behind the natural fortress along the shore, a sandy ridge with sparse yellow grasses marked the beginning of grass-covered plains which stretched away to a distant tree-belt. On these plains, sprawling endlessly, was what appeared to be an African village of domed huts, each structure clearly defined on its own grassy plot of ground. It was left to Captain Koffer, who had himself gazed in wonder at this strange illusion the first time he'd sailed his ship through these waters, to explain that the domed huts were actually solid mounds of sun-baked clay, some as tall as twelve feet, and that they were, of all things, ant hills.

Henry Schneider came to stand beside Christina who was staring in wide-eyed disbelief. "Don't you wish we could go ashore and take a closer look at those things?" he asked.

Christina's mind raced as she searched for words with which to reply. The German boy had spoken in English, fluently, for he had been learning the language for some years now. Christina understood what he said well enough, for they had been conversing in English for some time now. She had soon come to realise, however, that understanding what he said was usually easier than making reply. But the boy had learned something also – it was better to wait while she found the English words she needed than to try to understand when she spoke in Danish.

"Yes, I think that would be very ... ah interesting." She spoke carefully, but with the last word a quick smile of satisfaction came to her face. That was a good word to use, interesting. She hadn't really had to think about it very much either, it had just been there in her mind. She watched for her young friend's reaction.

"It would be interesting alright," he agreed, grinning. "So long as the ants who live in those things aren't ferocious giants. Twelve feet tall, can you imagine ants building something like that?"

"It must have took ... ah, taken a long time."

"Years and years, I would think." A thoughtful frown wrinkled his brow. "It would be good to know more about them. I'm writing a letter to my grandfather, to mail when we reach Brisbane. I'm sure he'd like to know about those things."

"Captain Koffer might know." Might ... ? Was that the correct verb to use? Yes, it must have been. There was no funny puzzled expression on

Henry's face, the way there sometimes was when she talked to him.

"I've already asked him, and all he seems to know is that they are definitely anthills and that there are thousands of them."

"There are thousands of them alright," Simon confirmed, also speaking in English and rejoining them at the rail after a short discussion with the ship's carpenter. "They are spread over that flat land as far as the eye can see." He grinned down at the two children. "Hardly the place for a farm, eh?"

"No, sir," Henry agreed fervently. "I shouldn't think it would be any good for sugarcane either, even if it was possible to get rid of those things. But Father says that they are growing cane in the north of the colony now."

"Not as far north as this, obviously. But I think we shall soon see a marked change in the land. In fact, I know we will, since I have just asked a question or two of my sailor friend."

Christina smiled, not surprised. Her father often helped the ship's carpenter who seemed to have numerous chores to perform. In return, the old sailor provided him with all sorts of enlightening information. Still, her father wasn't the only one with a special friend in the crew. She had one, too. His name was Otto, and, ever since he'd saved her from being washed overboard, she'd made a point of watching out for him. He always had a smile for her, and sometimes, if he wasn't too busy, he would stop and talk to her. Oh, how pleased he would be with the pullover her mother was knitting for him. It would keep him warm when he had to be on the deck in freezing weather, and with the scarf she was knitting he would. Christina's smile faded and she sighed quietly. She really would have to get a move on. Here they were off the coast of Queensland and she still had only twenty-eight inches completed, and that was when she stretched it.

"I'm glad to hear that, Mr Skov," Henry was saying earnestly. "Even though they are quite amazing it would be rather dreary to be looking at giant anthills day after day." He turned to Christina. "Why don't we go over to the other rail, there might be some more pelicans."

Christina hesitated, glancing up at her father. "Will you come too, Father?"

"In a while. But you go with Henry. I'm sure you'll find the birds more amusing than the anthills."

The embryo island with its feathered fleet had faded into a gold-tinted smudge off the stern, but, within minutes, another, in a slightly more advanced stage of development, slid into view and obliged by having its own contingent of pelicans systematically searching the shallow waters off its shores. "What ridiculous birds they are," Henry laughed. "Just look at that crazy fellow, will you?"

One of the group had staggered on to the sand with a fish almost as large as its own body and proceeded to juggle it, still flapping, into the large pouch of its lower bill. This accomplished, it tried, with much gulping and head-shaking, to swallow it.

"Oh, I think it's stuck in its neck," Christina gasped, her alarm causing her to speak in Danish. "I hope it doesn't choke."

The boy glanced at her, enquiry flashing to his dark eyes, but then, deciding that he knew more or less what she had said, he shrugged his shoulders and declared bluntly in English, "It would serve him right if he did choke."

"Oh, that's … that's … "

"Awful," Henry supplied, grinning at her.

"Yes, awful. That's an awful thing to say."

Henry's grin widened, but he said gently. "It won't choke, Christina. Look at the others … they are not at all worried about their greedy companion. In any case, I think he has now managed to get it down."

"Thank goodness for that," Christina murmured, refusing to let her mind dwell on the thought that perhaps the bird's discomfort had been simply transferred from one part of its body to another. "I hope he thinks that's enough breakfast."

"He'll have to be satisfied for a while at least. I'm sure he can't do much more than squat there just now. But look, one of his friends has caught a fish."

"Oh, I hope he's not so silly."

"Well, it's not as big as that other one."

The fish disappeared in a flash and was apparently gone from the pouch in one gulp for the bird promptly strutted back into the water. "He doesn't think he's had enough breakfast," Christina chuckled.

"No, he doesn't. I wish we could have seen the others catch their breakfast."

The islet was quickly falling behind, and soon the pelicans were rocking in the spreading wake left by the ship. For the two children, though, there would be no wondering as to what they would do to fill in the hour still remaining before the breakfast bell. There were hundreds of jellyfish, pale green and transparent, floating aimlessly past the side of the ship, and they laughingly set about the task of counting them.

As had been the case on other occasions, the information given to Simon by the ship's carpenter proved to be correct. By the time the day ended, the land had begun to change, its stark flatness giving way to small green hills, while the line of boulders along the shore became less dense, interspersed more and more frequently with clumps of dark green mangroves. And, by the time the following dawn arrived, a complete transformation had taken place.

The Friedeburg was now sailing through waters of such a deep flashing blue, the eyes were dazzled. Serene, sheltered waters still, where the wings of a gull, sweeping low, were reflected and the shadows of clouds flying north before a south-east trade-wind danced fleetingly; where porpoises came to play beside the ship and the vast aquarium nature maintained on the reef spilled over in shimmering splashes of multi-coloured marine life; where the strange, translucent bell-shapes, counted by Christina and Henry as jellyfish on the previous morning, termed Medusae by scientists of the eighteenth century, and Acalephae by Aristotle three hundred years before Christ, trailed their crystalline tentacles as complacently as ever.

On the land, not far from the shore, tree-clad mountain ranges loomed against the sky, their east-tending spurs dropping abruptly to the water to form picturesque bays and headlands. Between the spurs and behind the long curves of glistening white sand, a wealth of tropical vegetation covered low-lying tracts of deep, rich soil: ferns and orchids, flowering plants and trees, graceful palms and tree ferns, and, towering over them all, the tall pines and mighty cedars. The summits of the loftiest peaks pushed their way up through clouds resembling puffs of cotton wool, while, lower down, wraith-like mists clung to the sides of the ravines and joined with the purple shadows in defying the piercing rays of the sun. In places, the boles of great trees stood out, brown or russet-coloured. Elsewhere, jagged rocks thrust through the dense foliage, while boulders, tumbled down the ravines in ages past, gleamed whitely. On the scarped cliffs, where landslides had broken the surface, rust-coloured streaks and patches were here and there visible and sometimes, against the sheerest escarpment, there was the flash of silver as a waterfall spilled hundreds of feet into a rock pool concealed in the jungle below. But all else was green, a living, vibrant green, revelling in the perfect harmony which existed between it, the brilliant blue of the sea and the soft azure of the sky.

On the Friedeburg eyes gleamed and hearts beat faster. What a land this was. What richness there must be in the soil. What reliable rainfalls must play their part. There was no one to point out that the tropical shore the immigrants gazed upon with such delight was a unique part of Australia; that, here, the south-east trade winds, charged with moisture from the sunny surface of the Pacific Ocean, are intercepted by the lofty peaks of the great coast range, the result being annual rainfalls of up to one hundred and eighty inches. No one to tell them that, although this great line of mountains flanked the eastern seaboard of the entire continent, its influence in the more southerly regions, where it was further from the coast and not so high, may be neither bountiful nor reliable.

The days unfolded one upon the other, or so it seemed, for so full were they of new and wondrous sights to behold, every minute of daylight must needs be spent on the upper decks. There was, as well, information to be gathered, and Captain Koffer obliged by pointing out landmarks bearing names bestowed by Captain James Cook and relating something of what he knew about that intrepid explorer's voyaging along this beautiful, but rugged, coastline just one hundred and one years previously. The mangrove-edged indentation which was just discernible from the ship was the mouth of the Endeavour River where Cook spent seven weeks waiting for his ship to be repaired. The massive cape rising almost three and a half thousand feet above the sea and with its upper regions hidden in clouds was Cape Tribulation, named at a time when Cook was experiencing difficulties after the Endeavour struck a reef. And the broad bay, where a small settlement could be seen on the sandy, timbered flatlands, was visited by Captain Cook on Trinity Sunday in 1770. Captain Koffer smilingly suggested that the children might like to guess its name, and. of course they did, gleefully shouting their response.

Some distance south of Trinity Bay, the Friedeburg moved away from the mainland to skirt a large and beautiful island which rose boldly out of the water, its rugged heights clothed in tangled jungle, the summits, in some places, rising in sheer cliffs for several hundred feet. "It's called Hinchinbrook," Christina's father told her. "And what a majestic island it is."

"There are so many beautiful islands and they seem to be all shapes and sizes. This is the largest one we've seen so far, though."

"Yes, it's about thirty miles long, I understand. Ah, here's another light-ship."

Christina turned her head quickly, following his gaze. The ship, one-masted and painted red and white like the one they'd seen two days previously, was anchored off the northernmost point of the island, and, as they drew closer, a woman appeared on the deck with a baby in her arms. "Oh Father, there's a lady with a baby on this one!"

"So there is." A thoughtful frown appeared on Simon's forehead. "I suppose it could be quite normal for the men in charge of such ships to have their families on board with them. After all, it would be much like being in a regular lighthouse, they'd be completely isolated and, if their wives weren't with them, they wouldn't see them for months on end."

"What a lonely life that would be, living all that time on a small boat and seeing only the ships passing by."

"The ships would stop sometimes, when they have mail or supplies to deliver. You are quite right, though, it would be a lonely existence."

The woman held the baby up, waving its small arm and pointing to the

Friedeburg as she tried to direct its attention. Christina felt a lump come to her throat and sudden tears pricked the backs of her eyelids. If only she could reach out and take that tiny hand in hers, instead of just waving.

"They do a very worthwhile job, those people. There would be a deal of satisfaction to be gained from that and I suppose they become used to the loneliness, they might even like it."

No, Christina told herself, she wouldn't like it, not a woman with a young baby. How would she get the fresh milk she needed? And what if the little one became sick? There'd be no doctor to tend her. Her … ? Was the baby a girl? It was impossible to tell from this distance, and yet she felt sure that it was, a baby girl about the same age as little Anna had been. Christina's brimming eyes spilled over and she turned her head so that her father wouldn't see the tears on her cheeks. Oh, why did the loneliness of others reach out to her in such a way, bringing melancholy to her heart, and, this time, touching that corner which belonged to her little sister?

The light-ship, with the woman and baby still waving, disappeared abruptly as the Friedeburg swung around the headland and again set a tacking course into the wind. "It's a pity we couldn't have taken the channel," Simon mused. "It's supposed to be very pleasant."

"Is it too shallow?" Christina asked huskily.

"At the southern end it is. There are apparently so many bars there a ship of this size would have virtually no exit. It's disappointing for another reason also. There are supposed to be some settlements along that part of the mainland coast and it would have been interesting to have seen them."

Christina nodded, surreptitiously brushing at the moisture on her cheeks with the back of her hand. She was sorry her father was disappointed. He wanted to see all he could of what was happening in the Colony of Queensland, she understood that well enough. But they had already seen a number of settlements along the shore; small huddles of cottages right at the water's edge, with the wilderness pressing in all around them. Those they were missing by not going through the channel would probably be no different.

But Christina was wrong. Here, hidden from their view by the island, was a settlement different in one very important respect from those they had seen further north. It was on the banks of one of a number of small, deep streams which crossed the fertile lowlands and emptied into the Hinchinbrook Channel. And it was surrounded by a carpet of bright, fresh green of such a conformation as no natural tropical growth could have accomplished. This was, in 1871, Queensland's most northerly cultivation of sugarcane.

There were more freckles on her face. Yes, she was sure of it. At least eight on her nose now and a faint line of them on both cheeks. Oh, why were they still coming, for heaven's sake? Hadn't she been very careful ever since her mother had noticed the first small dots? Why, never once had she been out in the sun without her bonnet. And she had remembered every time to check that the brim was shading her face. With a small shrug of helplessness, Christina held the silver-framed mirror further from her face, moving it to and fro so that her reflection came from different angles. There, they were not nearly so noticeable now, and, when she moved the mirror out of the direct light, they really couldn't be seen at all. She gave a deep sigh. They were still there, though, and there wasn't any sense in pretending that they weren't. Though just what she was supposed to do about them she had no idea. Probably, she told herself, she should be worried, for one thing. Her mother had certainly been quite distressed and even her father had seemed concerned. Did they think that she was going to grow up ugly with spots all over her face?

"I'm sorry to have been so long, Christina."

Christina started, guiltily slipping the mirror back on to the small vanity table. "It's alright, Mrs Klaussen., I didn't mind waiting."

"I thought Captain Koffer was just going to show me one or two of the islands on his charts. Instead, he pointed out at least a dozen and left my head in a complete whirl. This present cluster is called the Whitsundays, that much I did absorb."

Christina smiled at her. "There are so many islands in these waters I don't think anyone would be able to remember all their names."

"I agree. But, oh Christina, how beautiful they are, every last one of them! That magnificent Hinchinbook, then the Palm Islands, and now the Whitsundays. It's almost as though every day dawns with the intention of putting on its own breathtaking display for our benefit." She stood for a moment gazing out of the porthole, then spun around, the soft silk of her skirt swishing about her legs. "How naughty we are! Here we are speaking Danish again. And only yesterday we resolved to speak nothing but English for the rest of the voyage."

Christina laughed softly at her assumed dismay, then said carefully in English, "Father says that we are almost halfway down the Queensland coast now."

Eleanor smilingly nodded her approval. "Such an improvement in these past couple of weeks."

"Sometimes I still have to think very hard about what word I should use, and then I think about the Danish word first."

"Well, that's to be expected, but you'll soon stop doing that. You'll find that you are not only speaking in English but also thinking in English. I'm sure that being friends with young Henry has helped you a great deal in that respect."

A quick grin came to Christina's face. "He refuses to listen when I speak Danish, and sometimes he makes me say whole sentences over again just because I'd got one word wrong."

"Well, I shouldn't wonder that he won't listen to you speaking Danish. Why should he bother when he has no idea what you were saying?" She reached for the pages Christina had placed on top of the chest of drawers they sometimes used as a desk. "Now let me see what you have written about our incredible voyage along the Great Barrier Reef."

Christina was preparing to leave the cabin on the conclusion of her lesson when Eleanor said quietly, "You're not worrying about your freckles, are you, love?"

Her eyes flying involuntarily to the mirror, Christina hesitated. So, Mrs Klaussen had seen her with it. "I think I have some new ones."

"When I was your age I had many more than you have, believe me."

Doubt at once shadowed Christina's eyes. Mrs Klaussen's skin was pale and flawless.

"It's true. I think they first appeared when I was around six years of age, and their number just kept growing. I remember my mother being terribly dismayed. I'm sure she thought I would never find a husband."

"What happened to them?"

"They just went, faded away, I suppose. I didn't really notice it happening. And I was quite surprised when I looked in the mirror one morning and realised that I didn't have freckles any more ... well, none that I could see."

"And you didn't do anything to make them go away?"

"No, not a thing." She chuckled softly. "My Danish grandmother used to say that the fairies had sprinkled them on my face when I wasn't watching and that, only when they were good and ready, would they come, just as secretly, to take them away again. To sprinkle them on the face of some other unsuspecting little girl, I suppose."

Christina smiled, her eyes dancing. "Then I might have those very same freckles."

Eleanor gravely lifted the small chin with the tips of her fingers. "Let me see, now. Ah, I do believe I recognise that one on the tip of your nose, the one next to it, also. And yes, those on your cheeks are quite familiar."

Christina laughed and she was still smiling as the made her way back along the deck to the companion-ladder. What a lovely, kind lady Mrs Klaussen was. And how pleasurable she had made the long voyage. Her smile faded. The voyage was almost over. In just days now they would reach Brisbane, and then Mrs Klaussen would go one way while she and her parents went another. The Darling Downs, how far away would that be?

Much too far for visiting, more than likely. So, after they left the ship, she probably wouldn't see that lovely lady ever again. Oh, how sad that would be. It made her heart ache just to think about it. And it would be the same for Henry. His father was talking of going north to start a sugarcane farm, whereas her father talked of going south to the Logan Valley. What distances there would be between them.

And what of all the others who had become her friends. Pretty little Katrina, who was Danish just as she was, where would she go? Her mother and father had no idea; they said they would just wait and see. And Frederick who talked all the time of the goldfields; would he go with his parents, brothers and sister to the small farm his uncle had already started or would he wander off looking for a fortune under the ground? Then there was the young couple who were expecting a baby; the woman who had wept so bitterly in her husband's arms when the ship left Hamburg. Where would they live? And Fritz who could make such merry music with his mandolin? Christina sighed deeply. Why, it was going to be just like breaking up a big family and sending them all off in different directions.

On a morning sparkling after early rain-showers, the Friedeburg crossed the Tropic of Capricorn. Now, although bold hills continued to thrust their rugged shapes up out of the coastal lowlands, forcing the rivers flowing to the sea to meander this way and that, the main range had moved further from the coast and donned the soft blue-mauve of distance. From time to time, over land that seemed silent and empty, the immigrants saw thin columns of smoke rising and drifting lazily. And the sailors shook their heads and mumbled, ever ready to tell of the horrific deeds committed by the black people whose fires those were. Ask in Brisbane, they said, and you will soon learn the truth of what we say. There are many who know well the blacks' hostility and treacherous ways, some of them from first-hand experience.

Christina, having watched the horrified expressions that came to the faces of those listening to the sailors' stories, related for the most part in German, lost no time in asking Henry about them. He told her only briefly, omitting the more gruesome details, but, even so, Christina shivered. "I didn't know they were such savages."

"Neither did I, but Father says they are not all like that. Some of them have become quite friendly towards the white settlers. There are a lot of different tribes, you know?"

"Those we saw on the Palm Islands seemed friendly."

"Yes, they did, but we only saw them from a distance and you can't really be sure. The sailors say they often act that way, as though they want to be friends, and then the first time you turn your back, wham! You get hit over the head with a nulla nulla."

Christina shuddered and he grinned apologetically. "Sorry, Christina, I didn't mean to scare you?"

"Aren't you scared?"

"I suppose I would be if I was out in the bush on my own. If I had a gun though it wouldn't be too bad. Everybody should have a gun, Father says. He's going to teach me how to shoot, my mother and brother too. Just in case the blacks are hostile where we go to live."

"I wouldn't want to shoot them, they are people, not animals."

"Nobody wants to shoot them, Christina. It's just that there may be times when we have to, if we want to stay alive ourselves."

"Well, I hope there are no blacks where we are going to live."

"It seems they move around a lot, so I would think you'd have to be careful, no matter where you live. Is your father still thinking about the Logan?"

"Yes, but he wants to talk to the immigration people before he makes a decision. What about your father, is he still planning to go north after we arrive in Brisbane?"

"Yes, he has definitely made up his mind on that. He's quite convinced that there is a prosperous future for the sugar industry in Queensland."

"But they are also growing sugarcane in the southern regions. Mr Hertzig told Father that there are a number of farms in the Logan Valley and some even further south."

"Father knows that, but he thinks the northern districts will be better suited to cane growing on a large scale. He has done quite a lot of reading on the subject, you know?"

Christina nodded. Everyone knew that Mr Schneider was a very knowledgeable, well-read man. The wonder was that he had given up an important teaching post to journey so far and become a cane farmer.

"There will be a lot of miles between the places where we live, Christina. The Colony of Queensland is a vast land and the distance we must travel quite great." He tossed her a faint smile. "I wonder if there will ever be another time when we can watch the birds together."

"I have been thinking of things like that too," Christina told him wistfully. "It seems sad, the way all the people on the ship will be going off in different directions."

"Yes, it does. Do you suppose we will be able to write to one another? There must be mail services of some sort."

"I suppose so, but what addresses could we use?"

"Well, if I wrote to you at Logan Valley, perhaps that would be enough – Miss Christina Skov, Logan Valley, Colony of Queensland, Australia. Then I could give you my address and you could write back."

The smile returned to Christina's face. Henry wasn't just going to disappear when they reached Brisbane, he was going to write to her. "Yes, I'd like to do that," she told him happily.

Soon, there came a night when the Friedeburg's passengers were woken from their sleep by a sensation they hadn't experienced in almost two weeks, the rolling of the ship in heavy seas. There was little room for regret, however; excitement, growing with every passing hour, saw to that. Those placid waters sheltering behind the great coral reef might be behind them, but Moreton Bay was drawing ever closer. If they had to sail these turbulent seas to get there, then so be it! The sooner it was begun, the sooner it would be over! And so they braced themselves once more against the heaving of the ship and watched with calm resignation as the spray flew and the ocean swelled and surged before lashing itself furiously against the rocky feet of the towering headlands that sometimes seemed perilously close.

Late one afternoon, a massive, densely wooded island swam out of a sharp rain-squall, and the Friedeburg moved further out to sea, the captain having elected not to use the strait between the island and the mainland due to its being fraught with difficulties and unsuited to night-time sailing. "This is Great Sandy Island," he announced from his usual position on the poop. "It is about seventy miles in length and the largest sand island in the world." He supplied no further information, though it had seemed for a moment or two that he was about to do so. Neither did he make small jokes as was his wont. Instead, after staring at the island through dark and sombre eyes, he spun on his heels and walked briskly away.

It was left to his crew to relate the island's terrible story. And they did so angrily and dramatically, for this time it was no isolated farmer and his family the blacks had killed, but a sea captain and his entire crew. It happened in 1836, they said; the Stirling Castle, a vessel of some five hundred tons, was wrecked while on her way from Sydney to Liverpool by way of Singapore. Captain Fraser, the ship's master, along with his wife and the crew managed to reach the island in a lifeboat. Only to find that, there, a death far more horrible than drowning awaited them, they were viciously slain by the blacks. All except for Mrs Fraser, and for her, poor soul, it would have been better so, since her fate was far worse than that of her husband and the other men. Until she was rescued several years later, she was kept as a slave by the savages and subjected to such degradations as were beyond description.

The story horrified, far more than those told earlier had done. They had concerned people who had remained unnamed in the telling: a group on a remote station, a farmer, his wife and two small daughters, a lonely shepherd, a missionary who believed he had succeeded in befriending the blacks, two wandering prospectors, and so on; the locations where the shocking deeds had taken place had been only vaguely recalled; and the events themselves, along with the circumstances surrounding them, had been variously described by different sailors. This time, they all told the same story, stressing the same gruesome details. And not only were there names for the victims, the murders had taken place and Mrs Fraser held prisoner here, on this very island.

"It happened a long time ago, thirty-five years," Christina heard her father tell her mother. "Relations with the blacks are bound to have improved enormously since then."

But her mother appeared not to be listening. "Oh, that poor, poor woman," she murmured over and over.

"It was a shocking tragedy, there's no doubt about that. But, for goodness sake, Elsie, try to remember that it happened back in 1837. Queensland was no more than a remote part of New South Wales at that time." He sighed resignedly. "Unfortunately, such occurrences seem to be unavoidable when civilisation spreads out into lands already occupied by primitive races."

"Perhaps we do wrong to come to such places. After all, if people are already here, even if they are primitive races as you say, they must have some right to the land."

"But usually they do nothing with it. They don't build anything; they don't till the land, plant seeds and grow things."

"They hunt and gather whatever foods are growing naturally and perhaps that's all they were ever intended to do. We should remember that the blacks in Australia have survived for a very long time, close to forty thousand years according to Mr Schneider."

""Well, no one is planning to put an end to the race and there's no reason why the Aborigines shouldn't continue with their way of life."

"How will they be able to do that if their hunting grounds have been cleared and planted with maize, sugarcane and so forth?"

Simon threw out his hands in a gesture of mingled appeal and exasperation. "My God, Elsie, haven't you realised the size of Australia? Denmark would probably fit into it a dozen times over. Besides, it seems there are no huge populations of Aborigines, even if they have been here for thousands of years. So it's ridiculous to suppose that they'd require all the land for their hunting grounds. Surely you can see that?"

"I suppose so."

The words came quietly, almost reluctantly, and Christina nodded over the book she was supposed to be reading. Mother is not sure, she told herself, she's not the least bit sure. It was strange what she had said about the black people having some right to the land because they already lived there. If it was true, then that was probably why they killed the white people, because they thought they were going to take the land away from them. In a way it was like when the Prussians and Austrians came to take Schleswig away from Denmark. All the Danish people had wanted to drive them off, to kill them even. Hadn't they taken up arms and fought a war?

How many times had she heard Grandfather Christiansen relate how Uncle Hans and three other Danish soldiers had set up an ambush in which a number of Prussians died before they themselves were shot? Why, in 1864, the Danish people would probably have killed every Prussian or Austrian who set foot on the soil of Schleswig if they could have.

They weren't strong enough, Christina recalled with a quiet sigh, and it was whoever was strongest who won in the end. Not always the one who was right. Someone should tell the black people about that. They might have spears, boomerangs and nulla nullas, but the white people coming to their land had guns, and even their children were being taught how to use them. Perhaps, if they understood such things, they would stop their terrible murders, and then it might be possible for them all to live together in Australia, sharing the country, so to speak. After all, as her father had said, it was big enough. And the white people who were coming weren't arrogant warmongers like the Prussians had been, even if some of them did happen to have that nationality. They didn't want to be bosses of the land, they just wanted to farm it. Christina sighed again, so heavily both of her parents glanced in her direction. Who, for heaven's sake, would be able to explain such things to the black people?

With the island passed, the mainland came into view once again. At first, a thirty mile strip of beach with a backdrop of incredible cliffs formed of coloured sands, resembling giant canvases on which an impulsive artist had flung his paints, leaving the colours to take up their own patterns. Then, further miles of glistening sands, but with sombre, scrub-covered lowlands in the back ground. From these lowlands, as though by way of relief, the strange basaltic shapes Captain Cook had seen fit to name the Glasshouse Mountains thrust their towering heights skywards, and stayed within view as the Friedeburg surged southwards into the final one hundred miles of her fifteen-thousand mile voyage.

At 6.30 a.m. on Friday, the 11th of August, one hundred and fourteen days after leaving Hamburg, the ship was off Cape Moreton. The morning was fine and golden, but with only the faintest whisper of a breeze, and not until 3.00 p.m. would the anchor be dropped off the pilot station in the bay.

The Friedeburg was destined to have prestigious company at the anchorage in Moreton Bay. On the morning following her arrival she was joined there by the H.M.S.Clio and on board were Queensland's new, and third, Governor, the Marquis of Normanby, his wife, and their son, Lord Harvey Phipps. Brisbane was all set to give these important personages an enthusiastic welcome, and, to the delight of the immigrants, it began in the bay. Excited and happy, they crowded every vantage point on the Friedeburg's decks and were afforded a front-row view of the proceedings: the decorated craft overflowing with laughing, chattering sightseers, which sometimes came so close they were able to talk to those on board; the arrival of the steamer Kate with the officials who would be the first to greet the Marquis; his disembarking from the Clio to board the Kate. And when they heard the three cheers ring out, they joined in with great gusto; then followed with three of their own, for this man was their new Governor also.

They heard the seventeen-gun salute as the procession of boats entered the river for the fifteen-mile journey upstream, and, later, the distant booming of another such salute as the new Governor stepped ashore at the especially constructed landing place in Queen's Park. Any further participation in the celebrations would, however, have to wait until Monday. With business-houses closed and work generally at a standstill for the Governor's arrival, they would be obliged to spend the weekend on the ship.

This was not the case for the few paying passengers. The Customs boat, Francis Cadell, one of several paddle-steamers on excursion with sightseers, suffered a slight mishap with one of her paddle floats and, while she was undergoing repairs alongside the Friedeburg, the few passengers who had cabins were taken on board to spare them the tedium of having to wait another two days before going ashore. Eleanor Klaussen had time for only brief farewells with the Skov family, and this, Christina told herself as she watched the steamer follow the other boats into the river, was probably just as well. With everything happening in such a rush there had been no time for tears. She turned to her mother who was standing at the rail beside her. "What about all her things? She has been able to take only a small valise with her."

"They'll be taken off on Monday, I should think, when the boats come for us and our belongings."

"Then we might see her again?"

"I wouldn't be counting on it. Mrs Klaussen will almost certainly have people waiting to meet her and they'll probably arrange for her luggage to be collected." A faint smile touched Elsie's lips. "I don't think she would be expected to attend to such matters herself."

"I don't suppose so," Christina murmured, not knowing whether to be glad or sorry.

"She is a very nice lady, Christina," her mother said gently, "and it was wonderful having her for a friend during the long voyage. She helped us all in so many ways. But the voyage is over now. We will always remember her as a friend and I hope she will do the same about us, but it's unlikely that our paths will cross here in Queensland. Not only will distance separate us, her family owns a large property of thousands and thousands of acres, whereas we will be farmers with perhaps one or two hundred acres."

Why should that matter? Christina wondered, her eyes growing thoughtful. Her mother spoke as though the sort of farms they had would separate them just as distance did. Mrs Klaussen's family must be rich, of course, but they had been in Australia for some years now. Why wouldn't it be the same for them? After a time, their small farm … and a couple of hundred acres wasn't really small, for heaven's sake! After a time, it would prosper. Wasn't that why they had come all this way, to have a fine farm and be prosperous? "One day we might have a really big farm too," she suggested quietly. "Just like the one Mrs Klaussen's family has. If there is so much land, we should be able to."

Elsie smiled and rested a hand on her daughter's shoulder. "Perhaps we will, given time, but, to begin with, I think we will do well to keep our ideas from becoming too grand. Not everyone with a lot of land is a successful farmer, you know? Far better a small farm that we can work well than thousands of acres we would have no hope of managing."

Christina nodded. Her mother was right. Being rich didn't happen just because you owned a lot of land. The land had to be worked: cleared, ploughed and planted. Just owning it wasn't enough. The Aborigines had done that and they hadn't prospered.

"Well, I don't think we are going to see much more happening now that the Governor has left the bay, and I have some things to do down below. Are you coming?"

"Do you need me to help?"

"No. You might like to decide what you'd like to wear for going ashore though."

"The weather's very warm. Do you think I should wear the new skirt you made for me and the blouse that father and I bought?"

"I think that's a very good idea. It will be nice and spring-like, and this is certainly spring weather even though we have a couple of weeks to go before the season officially begins. In fact, it could quite easily be summer."

"The girls on the pleasure boats were all wearing bright summer dresses."

"Yes, they were, and how pretty they looked. They made us all appear quite dowdy." Elsie moved away from the rail, but paused to say over her shoulder, "If you are looking for your father or Henry, you'll find both of them at the stern rail. There's a lot of chopped seagrass floating on the water, and they are hoping to see some more of those strange creatures we were watching yesterday." She laughed softly, shaking her head. "Seacows, whoever heard of such a thing?"

Christina smiled to herself as her mother walked away. They were strange all right, the dugong, or seacows, as most people called them. Great heavy things swimming about so easily and living on weeds and grasses growing under the water, just as ordinary cows did on land. There were other large creatures in the bay as well, huge turtles which made a strange whooshing noise as they came to the surface and were such fun to watch. Now, though, she had something other than turtles and seacows to think about. She was going to wear the embroidered blouse even though she still wasn't sure how she felt about it. It would please her mother who had gone to the trouble of making a skirt to match. Probably her father also, since he had bought the blouse for her. Christina sighed. It was strange that they didn't seem to understand why she hadn't wanted to put it on. But then, when all was said and done, how could they? She wasn't really sure herself why that was. Was it because she felt guilty that she'd been having such a happy time when little Anna had become so sick? Or did the blouse seem to be associated in some way with those terrible hours after they had returned to the ship? It had been in her hands all the time she'd been standing in the doorway to Mrs Klaussen's cabin watching the baby struggling so desperately to stay alive, and she had wanted to fling it from her, to hide its bright, uncaring colours in some dark corner. She sighed again, more deeply this time. What difference would it have made? None at all. How could it, if God had already decided that little Anna wouldn't be with them in Australia?

The hours dragged by. The doctor who came on board from the pilot boat completed his examinations and gave the ship a clean bill-of-health. The government officials who arrived at the same time completed their documents and made a head count that tallied satisfactorily. Then they all departed in a tugboat, anxious to return to the celebrations which, they assured all who enquired, were on a scale never before seen in the Colony, leaving the immigrants to stare at their already packed luggage and bemoan the fact that they were still on the Friedeburg. Apart from the comings and goings of other ships and boats, there was little to see. Beyond the tangled mangroves at the water's edge the shore was low-lying, silent and still, with nothing to indicate that a busy town in festive mood lay only a few miles up the river. There was more activity on the seaward side of the mangrove fringe. Here, miles and miles of mudflats, stretching well out into the bay, emerged at low tide and came alive with vast colonies of scurrying crabs, a banquet table for the birds which arrived in their hundreds.

8

Finally, Monday arrived, and, even as the sun began its climb into the sky, the first of the tugboats and lighters emerged from the river and made their way to the Friedeburg, where unloading and disembarking at once began. The Skov family's turn came just after eight o'clock, and, as did all of those with them, they left the bay and began their journey up the river with rapidly beating hearts and eyes wide with interest.

The river impressed. Beyond the sandbars at its mouth, it was wide, deep and a clear dark green. It was also very busy. They passed a number of boats making their way to the bay and then, lying at anchor, the large British ships, the Indus and Ramsey, which had negotiated the narrow channel at high tide to enter the river. The swampy mangrove banks soon gave way to high ridges which rose, here and there, into wooded crests. And, now, the breeze drifting lazily over the water came laden with a strange but pleasing fragrance that would be with those come to help settle this land for all the days of their lives – a fragrance gathered as the breeze filtered through the leaves of countless eucalypts.

The river narrowed and, presently, swung around a sharp bend, the first of a number to be negotiated in the final four or five miles. On both banks imposing residences began to appear, surprising the immigrants for such dwelling places had not been expected in the young Colony. The main part of the city, swinging into view as they rounded the sharp bend known as Kangaroo Point, was also a surprise with its busy wharves and numerous substantial buildings. And still the river twisted, around a cape-like prominence given over to luxuriant botanical gardens into yet another of its reaches. Here, the impressive buildings the immigrants had glimpsed across the gardens were seen at close hand and they learned that one was the Governor's residence, while the other, a three-storied block capped with small turrets of galvanized iron, was the Houses of

Parliament. Here, too, about two hundred yards below a bridge in the course of construction, was the government wharf from which they would step for the first time on to the soil of their new country. And, close by, the Immigration Depot where they would all be housed until they had somewhere else to go.

Their quarters, in a solid structure built by convicts, were comfortable and somewhat more spacious than those they had occupied on the Friedeburg, and immigration officials were continually on hand to answer questions and assist with requirements. But, after so long confined to a ship sailing the great oceans of the world, the immigrants had no intention of spending more time than was absolutely necessary in any restricted space, no matter how comfortable it might be; nor were they ready to settle down to lengthy discussions with officialdom. Beyond the heavy doors, the city waited, bathed in sunshine, and they were impatient to walk its streets and see for themselves what it had to offer. The minute their belongings were accounted for, they set off, laughing, excited groups, so conspicuous in their drab, serviceable clothes the city's residents were able to recognise them, even from a distance as 'new chums'.

With the river winding around and through the town, four distinct sections had evolved – Brisbane proper, South Brisbane, Fortitude Valley and Kangaroo Point, but, apart from a temporary footbridge near where a new bridge was being constructed, the only means of crossing the river was by ferry.

The streets had not yet been paved or cobbled, and, as a result, were extremely dusty; it wasn't difficult to visualise what they would be like in rainy weather. The drainage, too, left much to be desired.

The city nevertheless pleased the newcomers. It was bright and colourful and there was no denying the natural beauty of its setting – scattered, irregular hills nearby, blue ranges in the distance, and the meandering river visible in all directions.

Furthermore, it had character. Not yet thirty years out of convict garb, Brisbane appeared to be tenaciously guarding its hard-won respectability, proudly displaying a number of impressive buildings erected by men whose day's labour had often ended with fifty strokes of the lash for some minor misdemeanour. Lining the streets were churches of various denominations, banks, shops, auction marts and residences which ranged from noble mansions to humble cottages. There were distilleries, hotels, meatworks, bakeries, a town hall of three stories, a small general post office dwarfed by the town hall next door, but soon to move into a much more substantial building, and a school of Arts where a display titled The Great Diorama of the American War was presently attracting a lot of attention.

After wandering up and down the main streets, the Skovs spent some time in the botanical gardens before looking for a suitable place in which to have their evening meal. Slipping her hand into her mother's, Christina sighed softly, contentedly. "It's been such a lovely day, hasn't it, Mother?"

"Yes, it has, Christina. And how pretty you look in your blouse and skirt. I think you are the only one out of all of us who doesn't look out of place in this bright, sunny town."

Christina felt a flush of pleasure steal into her cheeks. She was glad she had worn the blouse, it felt so light and cool, and it really was very pretty. "Will I be able to wear these same clothes again tomorrow? I've kept them quite clean."

"We'll see what they look like at the end of the day. We don't have to wear the same clothes over and over now, you know?" She gave a deep sigh of relief. "Oh, what a wash-day I'm going to have on the morrow. Reticulated water, what a blessing!"

"It comes from the Enoggera Dam, a sort of artificial lake fed by some creeks," Simon told her. "A very popular picnic spot, apparently."

Elsie smiled at him. "And who gave you that piece of information, may I ask?"

"The man who sold me the newspaper, which I had hoped to read while I sat in the shade."

"Christina and I weren't the only ones who kept finding new trees and plants to look at," Elsie reminded him.

"No, I grant you that. What a dedicated curator those gardens must have; to have accomplished so much in what would have been a relatively short time."

"I read his name somewhere, on the gate perhaps. It's Walter Hill."

"Well, Mr Walter Hill has good reason to be extremely proud of his efforts. Now, where shall we eat?"

They found the Royal Oak Hotel which advertised family meals at moderate prices. And they were so impressed, both with the quality of the food and the attention they received, they returned the following morning for breakfast.

Breakfast at the Royal Oak was a cheerful, rather noisy affair. Brilliant sunshine poured in through the wide-open windows and spilled on to the bright green tablecloths and squat bowls of geraniums. Greetings and conversation flowed back and forth. Bright-eyed after a good night's sleep, Christina listened intently, once again having good reason to be thankful that Mrs Klaussen had so kindly taken her English lessons in hand, for that was the language most people were using. Even at their own table, where Mr And Mrs Barton, who were staying at the hotel while their new home was being built, once again joined them, the conversation was in English. A smiling girl, wearing a white frilled cap on her dark hair, brought steaming bowls of porridge to the table and Christina moistened her lips with the tip of her tongue. It looked good and, even though she had already eaten two bananas this morning, she was feeling hungry.

She was about to raise the first spoonful to her mouth when there was a sudden lull in the conversation humming about the tables, and she looked up to see a newcomer standing in one of the doorways. Surprised at the impact the man's appearance had had, she glanced quickly about the big room. Several pairs of eyes were turned towards the door, some of them openly like those of Mr Barton who had half-turned his bulky frame on his chair; others not so openly, like Mrs Barton who was watching the man out of the corner of her eye, something that gave the lady's face such a comical, twisted appearance Christina almost giggled. To stop herself from doing so, she returned her attention first to her porridge and then to the man in the doorway. Well, she decided, savouring her first taste of the sweet, creamy oats, he was certainly a strange-looking man: sort of important-looking, even though he was rather shabby. Who could he be, for heaven's sake, that half the people in the room were looking at him?

The newcomer was middle-aged. Perhaps close to fifty, but, then again, perhaps not all that much over forty, it was no easy matter to tell. He had a long, thin face with a stiff, dark moustache and a small clipped beard, and there was something of arrogance in the way he held his head. He wore an elegantly cut morning jacket of maroon velvet and a matching silk cravat, but what could be seen of his white shirt was crumpled and soiled, while the cuffs peeping from his coat sleeves were frayed. His trousers, of some light-coloured fabric, were also stained, and the worn leather of his boots had not seen a polish in a long time. For all that, his gaze slid over the room and its occupants with a certain disdain and he tapped the floor imperiously with the silver-headed cane he carried, both his manner and his actions clearly implying that he expected to be received in the dining room as a person of consequence.

"Boobegan Price," James Barton informed the Skov family, straightening on his chair as one of the serving girls led the man in question to a table in a far corner.

"Boobegan?" Simon question. "What sort of a name is that?"

"It's a nickname." He scratched the bald patch on the top of his head thoughtfully. "And I'm blessed if I can recall what his first name actually is! Do you know, Margaret?"

"Edmund … ?" his wife suggested after a moment or two. "Yes, I'm sure that's what it is."

"By Jove, you're right. It is Edmund. He's been called Boobegan for so long now I'd completely forgotten."

Margaret Barton turned to Elsie. "We weren't living in Brisbane when he first arrived. We were still in Ipswich, and, by the time we did settle here, he had already gone down to the south coast to grow his cotton. After that everyone called him Boobegan. It's the name of the creek where he had his plantation."

"He's quite a character, old Boobegan," her husband explained. "A remittance man, one of England's moneyed gentry who came out here thinking to make a fortune for themselves. He made a big splash when he first arrived, by all accounts, and got the red-carpet treatment almost as thoroughly as the Governor did on Saturday."

"That's nonsense, James," his wife exclaimed. "You know very well it was nothing like that."

"It was most definitely something like that. I'll admit there was probably a lot more pomp and ceremony on Saturday, but old Boobegan got the right royal treatment alright, mark my word."

"Why?" Simon wanted to know. "Because he had money?"

"That was part of it, I suppose, but it wouldn't have been the main reason; any number of people come out from the old country with money. No, it was because he was supposed to have very important connections back there." James Barton gave a short laugh. "The big welcome didn't last all that long, though. The bloke was too fond of booze, high-living and the ladies; wasn't the least bit fussy about whose wife he romanced either. Strangely enough, the final straw didn't come until he took in a certain young woman as his housekeeper." He laughed again, this time a throaty chuckle. "I must say that I've always found that rather amusing."

"You have a warped sense of humour, James," Margaret Barton retorted with a quick frown. "Belle Chadwick has told me on more than one occasion that they had realised what sort of person he was some time before that happened."

"Well, that may be so, but Belle and Brisbane's other society ladies liked having him around nevertheless. From what I've been told, it was more jealousy than anything else that made them take exception to Boobegan's housekeeper. She was apparently a very attractive lady."

"Lady?" his wife queried tartly, her eyebrows raised dramatically.

Hiding a smile, Simon turned the conversation in the direction of Boobegan Price's other activities. "Was his cotton plantation successful?"

"Of course not. How can a man be successful in this country when he's not prepared to work?"

"Not in any country, I would think."

James Barton shrugged his heavy shoulders. "In England you can probably do it, if you've got money enough to get others to do all the work for you. But things are different here. No matter how many people you are able to employ, you still need to give of yourself. Boobegan wasn't prepared to do that. He got this piece of land at the junction of the Nerang River and Boobegan Creek and had a decent sort of house built there. Then he laid in enough liquor … good quality stuff, mind … to stock a pub, and just sat back taking things easy while the men he'd hired cleared his land, planted his cotton, picked it when the time came and even built him a gin."

Simon slowly shook his head. "With all that going for him, he still didn't prosper?"

"No, he didn't. I suppose he just might have made money though, if he'd shown some lasting interest. As it was, once he had produced his first crop, he didn't bother to do anything more. The seeds for his next crop were left lying out in the weather and Boobegan caught a cutter back to Brisbane." James Barton gave a deep, highly amused chuckle. "But I understand that the party he gave to celebrate his first crop was really something. It went on for more than a week and, as the word went out, every bloke from miles around showed up to sample his hospitality: other growers and their hands, timber-getters, sailors from the cutters, drifters and so forth. Then, when all Boobegan's liquor had been disposed of, there was a brawl such as no one had ever before seen the likes of. Down that way they still talk about it and I reckon they'll go on doing so for years to come."

"He's not a very nice person," Margaret Barton whispered in an aside to Elsie. "Not the sort of person you'd want to be knowing. For one thing, even though he had money he was always slow in paying his accounts. All of the people he owed money to had to chase after him to get it and some never did get all that he owed them."

"That's right," her husband agreed, having had no trouble in over-hearing her whisper. "He's a slow payer alright, a damned slow payer."

"What does he do now?" Simon asked.

"Nothing, as far as I know. Doesn't drink as much as he used to, or live the high life in other respects either. Can't afford to, I suppose. His cotton-growing venture would have cost him a pretty penny and I should think the family purse strings back in England would have been tightened as a result."

"Did anyone make money out of cotton?"

"A few probably made a bit in the first half of the sixties, but, for most, it was a somewhat costly venture. Robert Towns, a Sydney merchant whom I have met on a couple of occasions, had over a thousand acres under cotton at the Logan, but gave away the idea in 1868 when the enterprise showed a deficit of close on six thousand pounds."

Simon whistled softly between his teeth. "That would take some getting over."

"You're telling me! But, luckily for Towns, he had a number of other interests, including a profitable shipping business. He was actually the first to bring in Kanakas to work his fields."

"These Kanakas, what are they exactly?"

"Islanders. They bring them in from all over the Pacific. One of the boats is in port now, the Lytonna. You would have passed it as you came up the river."

"I do recall seeing a vessel with that name. A schooner, not very big?"

"Yes, that would be it, around seventy tons. Well, there'd be a dozen or more boats like that engaged in the trade now, and more joining in all the time. They go mainly to the New Hebrides and the Solomons, but their masters are not really particular and they quite often visit other islands as well. The people they pick up are supposed to come willingly … under contract, so to speak … for a period of three years. Then be returned to their homes. While they are here they are paid six pounds a year plus their basic keep."

Simon nodded thoughtfully. "I have only recently heard about them, from a sailor on the ship, actually. I had no idea the practice was so well established."

"It's that alright. There are hundreds of Kanakas working in the canefields and the consensus of opinion is that the sugar industry can't survive without them. There's certainly no denying that they are a cheap source of labour, and, ever since the transport of convicts was stopped, labour has been a commodity in short supply throughout the Colony. Of course, even if there were enough Europeans available, you'd find the canefields still needed the Kanakas. A lot of white men regard such work, especially up north, as nigger work and they won't have a bar of it."

"These Islanders are reliable workers then?"

"A damned sight more reliable than our own blacks. The only thing they've shown themselves to be any good at is stock work, they can ride like they were born on a horse's back. But, even there, you can't count on them. You've got a bloke happily rounding up cattle one day and the next he's gone, trudging off to some God-forsaken place on walkabout." He gave a short laugh. "Damned hard to understand, if you ask me. You'd think that once a bloke took to riding that would be the only way he'd be keen to travel any distance. But no, not the Abo. When it's walkabout time, that's exactly what he does – walk."

"I suppose it's a genuine case of old customs dying hard, and the Aborigines have been here in Australia for thousands of years, I believe."

"Yes, around forty thousand according to those who are supposed to know about such things, and I'll bet they haven't changed one iota in all that time. But, to get back to the Kanakas, they do seem to be reliable enough. Most planters will tell you that they are docile, loyal and carefree." He gave a short laugh that came very close to being a snort. "A nice way of describing them, when, in actual fact, many of them treat their Kanakas as though they were ignorant, uncivilised children. I can tell you, Mr Skov, there have been a number of occasions on which I have heard them described as 'ebony golliwogs.'"

"That's horrible!" Elsie, who had been listening intently, gasped.

A wry smile flickered across James Barton's face. "I agree, Mrs Skov, but, unfortunately, the behaviour of the Kanakas does nothing to discourage such descriptions and, believe me, there are others even less flattering. The fact of the matter is that they really do behave like harmless, ignorant children, always looking to frolic about even at the end of a hard day's work under a burning sun. Actually, it's this attitude which is now being pointed to by those who are against the trade. They say that, even if the Islanders do appear to come willingly, they are really too ignorant and child-like to understand what they are letting themselves in for. On top of that, there's no getting away from the fact that, in some instances at least, they have been kidnapped from their homes and brought here against their will."

"That's out and out slavery," Elsie exclaimed. "The churches must be objecting, surely?"

"With half a breath only, I'm afraid. The very mention of the word 'blackbirding' is enough to make the good stalwarts of our churches turn pale. On the other hand, however, they haven't been slow to recognise the fact that the Kanaka trade has brought them something of a windfall – there are a lot of potential converts to Christianity working in those canefields."

"James, you know I don't like to hear you to speak like that." Margaret Barton protested, scowling deeply.

"It's the truth, wife, and you know it."

"No, I don't know it. All of the missionaries and other church people have it in mind to help these poor unfortunate souls. You know very well that many of them live under appalling conditions: grass huts on the river bank, poor quality sustenance and so forth. Why, Reverend Marlowe spoke only last Sunday about the diseases they get and how many of them die here." Margaret Barton's eyes gleamed suddenly, the problem of the Kanakas gone from her mind. "We have a lovely church on Kangaroo Point, Mrs Skov, not very far from where our home is being built. It was constructed by the convicts and they did such a wonderful job. If you are still in town next Sunday, perhaps you would like to come to the morning service with us?"

Christina, who had been giving more attention to her breakfast than to the conversation passing back and forth across the table, at once ceased crunching on the piece of toast she had just popped into her mouth. It seemed to be making such a noise in the quiet which had come so abruptly. Besides, she wanted to hear her mother's reply. What would she say? Ever since little Anna had died, she had stayed away from the services Captain Koffer had conducted every Sunday on the ship. But this would be different, Mrs Barton had asked her to go to a real church with a real minister.

"Thank you, Mrs Barton, but I don't think that will be possible. Even if we haven't already left Brisbane, we will be fully occupied preparing to do so."

"Of course you will," James Barton exclaimed briskly. "There'll be time enough for going to church once you've settled in."

The smile her mother gave him was a grateful one, Christina decided, swallowing the piece of toast which was no longer crunchable and reaching for its successor. Mr Barton had saved her from having to find more excuses. So, she must still be angry with God, even after all this time.

"We got away from the cotton industry," Simon said, breaking the silence which seemed to be on the point of lengthening. "I was wanting to ask if it was finished."

In spite of his talkative mood, James Barton had managed to dispose of a large bowl of porridge and a plate of bacon and eggs. Now he reached for the honey and a slice of toast. "It's been more or less finished for a few years now. The Manchester Cotton Company got into financial difficulties and ceased operating back in '66. It's been the same for most of the other growers. Once the war in America ended and they started sending their cotton to England again, there wasn't much point in keeping on with the plantations here. The shortage of cheap labour wasn't the only problem; they had no end of trouble with the boll-weevil and they simply didn't have the technical know-how to compete with the Americans. Most of those who started out with cotton have now turned to sugarcane or general farming."

"I believe they are growing quite a lot of cane in the Logan Valley?"

"They certainly are. Further south as well – the Coomera River, Pimpama and down at the Tweed River. Have you been thinking about going in for cane?"

Simon shook his head. "It certainly sounds very interesting, but I should think it would require a large area under cultivation for it to be successful, and more capital than I have at my disposal."

"Well, it would be a couple of years before you could expect any return, of course, but you wouldn't need such a great area to begin with. Captain Louis Hope, who was almost certainly the first successful grower in Queensland, began with twenty acres at Ormiston. That would have been around 1862 and, two years later, he had a mill built and produced three tons of sugar and fifteen cwt of molasses. Since then, he has acquired a much larger area, around eighteen hundred acres, at the mouth of the Coomera River on what is now known as Hope Island."

"That is certainly encouraging, and perhaps the time will come when I can also be a cane grower."

"Why not? But, in the meantime, are you sure you won't change your mind and stay in Brisbane? As I told you yesterday, I'd be able to employ you for years, at good wages too. I'd even help you acquire some land and build a home."

"I wish you would stay, Mr Skov," his wife interrupted. "Then we just might get our home finished. More than three months for a builder's own house, can you believe that?"

Simon's smile included both the woman and her husband. "I do appreciate the offer, but I could have remained in Schleswig and been a carpenter. The very reason we came to Australia was to acquire some land and have a farm."

"It's not going to be easy, you know?" James Barton warned.

"I've never expected that it would be, and we are not really thinking to prosper overnight, as it were."

"Well, I hope you do prosper. The Colony needs men prepared to do such things and every man should have the opportunity to make reality of his dreams." He got to his feet, brushing the crumbs from his clothes. "I have to rush now, I've dallied far too long. But remember, if things don't turn out as you hope they will and you come back to town, be sure to look me up."

"I will, and I thank you, Mr Barton."

9

The Immigration Officer who came to advise the Skov family was a tall, thin man who introduced himself as Charles Walters. He had grey hair, a sparse, rather nondescript moustache, and a worried expression that seemed to leave his face only very rarely. In the small room which served as an interviewing office, he smiled briefly, then at once ruffled his papers, indicating that he was anxious to get down to business.

"It is my responsibility, in the first instance, Mr Skov, to ensure that you are correctly informed as to the conditions under which you may take up land. You have already been given some literature on the Land Code of Queensland, but I hope to be able to explain the relevant sections more precisely."

Simon nodded. "We would appreciate that, Mr Walters."

Charles Walters took time to clear his throat before proceeding, but, once he had begun, it was obvious that he knew exactly what he had to say. "Of most interest to you, Mr Skov, will be the Alienation of Crown Lands Act. Originally, this Act provided for the setting aside, as agricultural reserves, of land on the shores of Moreton Bay, Wide Bay, Port Curtis and Keppel Bay, and also of land within five miles of towns with more than five hundred inhabitants. Such land was not to be for sale by auction, but was to be opened up for selection as farms, with certain conditions applying. The Land Code has, however, been amended a number of times, and I see no point in enlightening you as to what those earlier arrangements were, unless, of course, you wish to know."

Simon shook his head. "Not at the present time, at any rate. It's the conditions now applying in which I am interested."

"Good! We'll be able to get to those without too much beating about the bush then. However, I feel that you should have at least a little understanding of the new Act that was passed three years back, in 1868.

This particular Act provides, in the main, for the resumption for closer settlement of half of each leased run; in other words, the runs held by the squatters." The hint of a smile passed fleetingly across his face. "I won't go into details now; you'll learn soon enough of the haphazard manner in which vast tracts of land have been taken up in this country. Suffice it to say that, had the Queensland Government not taken some action, the squatters would have gone on holding virtually all the land and progress in the Colony would have been throttled."

Simon nodded. "I have already heard quite a deal about the squatters and their vast holdings."

"Not all of it good, I'm sure. Still, no matter how much we might object to the apparent greed of these people, we can't overlook the fact that they have undertaken much of the pioneering work in Australia. The lands they took up were almost always well away from settled areas, and they were obliged to endure, initially at any rate, all manner of hazards and hardships. And, of course, they have been responsible for establishing valuable industries – wool, for instance. Furthermore, they haven't all become successful and rich. In fact, Queensland is not long out of a long drought and many squatters have been so badly hit, with crippling stock losses and so forth, they are finding it difficult to continue. In a number of cases the banks have already taken over their properties."

"The drought was that bad?"

"Yes, '67 through to '69 was a very grim period indeed. Fortunately, though, we have had good seasons since. Even the winter we are just coming out of has been kind to the man on the land. Well, as I have said, half of each leased run is being resumed for closer settlement. This land is being thrown open in three categories. Firstly, there is the agricultural land, to be taken up at fifteen shilling per acre, the area not to exceed six hundred and forty acres. Secondly, there's what had been termed first-class pastoral land, at ten shillings an acre, the area not to exceed two thousand, five hundred and sixty acres. And, thirdly, the second-class pastoral land, at five shillings per acre, the area not to exceed seven thousand, six hundred and eighty acres."

"They are very generous acreages in any man's language."

Charles Walters gave his narrow shoulders a faint shrug. "Not too many people will be taking up thousands of acres, though. They still have to be paid for, and, perhaps even more importantly, they have to be improved."

"Yes, that would certainly be restriction enough."

"Well, to get back to what is actually being done with this resumed land. The conditions of purchase in each case are actual occupancy and improvements, plus payment for the land, which is effected in ten equal instalments termed rents. These would be, as I'm sure you've already worked out, one shilling and six pence per acre, one shilling per acre, or sixpence per acre, according to the category of the land taken up. The payments are to be made annually and, of course, when the final one has been made, provided the other conditions have been met, the selector will be entitled to his Deed of Ownership." Charles Walters flipped his hands apart in an expansive gesture and, for the first time, something resembling a real smile came to his lips. "Well, there you have it. An outline of the free selection system. Is there any point you need to have clarified?"

Simon shook his head. "I don't think so. It all seems fairly clear thus far. As you can see, I've made a few notes and I'll be going over them later with my wife."

"Good." He turned to Elsie who had been listening intently. "It's very important that the wife should have some idea of just what is involved, Mrs Skov, especially since it will be some time before you can expect any return from the land you take up."

"I realise that, Mr Walters, and you may be sure that my husband will have my full support." Elsie told him with a faint smile.

His glance moved on to Christina who had been sitting quietly on a chair against the wall before returning to Simon. "You have no grown sons, I take it."

"No, Christina is our only child."

"That means more work for you then, and it's important that you understand that the land is cheap because the struggle to make it useful is very severe. The advice I give to all new settlers is not to attempt, in the first instance, to make money by selling the produce of the land. Build yourself a home ... I see that you have had carpentry experience among other things, so you'll have an advantage there. Make it something simple to begin with, there'll be time enough for improvements later on. Clear part of your land, build some fences, get a few cows and some poultry, plant a vegetable garden and so forth. But, during a period in each year go out and work for wages."

"I had planned on doing that," Simon told him, letting his eyes skim over the notes he had written. "So, a man may take possession of unoccupied Crown land subject to the terms and conditions you have mentioned. Are there any exceptions that I should know about?"

"Not really. The Selector is at liberty to select freely from the whole area of land opened up for that purpose whatever block seems to be most suitable for his requirements." Charles Walters's lips twitched into the ghost of a grin. "That's why it's called free selection, because you have a free choice, not because the land comes free of charge."

Simon returned the grin before asking, "How have the squatters reacted to this new Act?"

"They certainly aren't delighted about it, as you can imagine. They claim that the selectors are getting the best sections of their runs, along the creeks and so forth. Nevertheless, I think the majority of them are beginning to realise that Queensland needs the small farmer. Besides, they can see benefits in it for themselves. Since the selector usually finds it necessary to go out and work for wages during part of the year, he helps ease the labour shortage on their properties."

"How should I proceed once I have established what land is available for selection?"

"Once you have selected a block, you peg it out. I must point out, Mr Skov, that this is by no means a simple task. The land is usually heavily timbered and care must be taken to include the whole of the area you have chosen. There have been cases where confusion at the time of pegging has cost the selector the very piece of land he most desired."

"Wouldn't I have a surveyor do that?"

"You are required to have the land you select surveyed by an authorised surveyor, but that comes a little later. First, you do the pegging yourself, then you lodge your application to select the land with the local Lands Officer. In doing so, you must, of course, identify the land by referring to the official maps. You will also be required to pay a small deposit. The Lands Officer then submits your application to the local Lands Board. If it meets with their approval, they endorse it and forward it to the Minister for Lands, who, almost invariably, ratifies it and issues a Licence. The Lands Officer will advise you as to just when you should have the land surveyed. This will cost you around eight pounds, by the way."

"Does the whole process take long? I was hoping to be out of Brisbane within the week."

"It won't all happen as quickly as that, I'm afraid. But you can leave Brisbane whenever you wish. Once you have decided on a particular region, you will, in any case, need to go there to peg out the parcel of land you want. My suggestion is that you get all the things you need together: horses, wagon, tools, supplies and so forth, then take off. Once you have selected your block of land, no one will try to stop you camping there while your application is being processed."

Simon grinned delightedly. "That's a great idea. I don't suppose you know offhand what land is available in the Logan Valley?"

"I don't have a lot of details, but new areas are being surveyed and thrown open all the time. You'll find the notices in the newspapers or in the Government Gazette. I'll give you a copy of that. I do know, however, that an area has quite recently been opened up to the west of the township of Beenleigh, back into the hills, I understand. If you care to go to the Lands Office, they'll be only too happy to show you the maps and answer any questions you may have in that regard."

"I'll do that. Do I need to make an appointment?"

"No … " The Immigration Officer had replied absently; he was quickly scanning a page which he'd removed from a folder on his desk. "This just may be of interest to you, Mr. Skov. It was actually handed to me only this morning and this is the first opportunity I have had to read it. It seems that a block of land has just been redeemed in the same general area as the newly surveyed land – two hundred and fifty acres, five of them cleared."

"You said redeemed?"

"That's right. There has apparently been a family on the place for some three years. But, apart from the clearing, some fencing and a well which they put down, very little improvement has been carried out. No house, for one thing. It seems they've lived all that time in a couple of tents."

"Goodness!" Elsie exclaimed. "And there were children?"

"Six, according to this report."

"Were they turned off the land for not meeting the conditions?"

"Good heavens, no! Though there certainly would have been problems when the time came for them to apply for a Deed of Grant. No, they left of their own accord."

"Do you know why?" Simon asked.

Charles Walters sighed, deeply and expressively. "Why do any of them give up the land? Gold-fever, of course. According to this report, the family had already been at the diggings in New South Wales. So I'd say that it's always been there, in the back of their minds – the thought that, if they'd stayed, they might have struck it rich; that, if they were to go back or to some other field, they might find that nugget they see in their dreams."

"That's what has happened with this family, they've gone off looking for gold again?"

"I can't be saying that for sure, Mr Skov, but all the indications are there. They've sold up everything they could and taken off for Bowen, and I'm sure it's not just coincidence that there has recently been a new discovery in that area. God alone knows why the fellow would want to take such chances though, especially with a wife and children. It's not only the conditions under which they'll be obliged to live when they finally arrive, it's the tracks they'll have to travel over to get there – bush tracks that barely exist and with unfriendly blacks on all sides."

"The blacks wouldn't attack without provocation, would they?" Elsie asked with a worried frown. "I mean, people just passing through an area aren't likely to do them any harm."

"The blacks don't know that, Mrs Skov, and they are still very hostile up there in the north. They are continually attacking mining camps and they seem to consider small parties of travellers fair game. Only last week a report came through that two prospectors have been found murdered on a lonely track not far from Bowen, and, in the previous week, a storekeeper met a similar end." The Immigration Officer gave a short, mirthless laugh. "The blacks were responsible in both cases, but do you know how it was that everyone was so sure about that?"

"I suppose the men were speared," Simon suggested.

"The storekeeper was, but not the other two. They had been bashed about the head, probably with a nulla nulla, but there was nothing to prove that such was actually the case. What left no doubt in people's minds that blacks were responsible was the fact that all three men were carrying gold and none of it had been taken. Can you see a white man capable of such murders leaving a fortune on the bodies of his victims?" Charles Walters shook his head slowly from side to side before answering his own question. "No, in this country, only the blacks see no worth in gold."

A thoughtful frown had come to Elsie's brow. "That's interesting, Mr Walters, especially since we were talking to a gentleman over breakfast who remarked that the Aborigines hadn't changed their ways in thousands of years. I find myself wondering what will happen to their way of life in the next one hundred years, or even fifty, now that Europeans have arrived in their country. Will they, for instance, continue to be so disinterested in gold?"

"I don't believe so, Mrs Skov. Already, some of them, those members of vanquished tribes who have remained to hang about white settlements, have come to realise that the white man has some things they don't find too objectionable – rum, for one thing. It's only a question of time before they begin to see gold through different eyes, through white man's eyes, one might say."

"I suppose it is inevitable," Elsie sighed. "But there's a sadness to it nevertheless. Such a relatively abrupt ending to a lifestyle which has gone on for so long."

"I agree with you, Mrs Skov, even though there are those who say that the Aborigines were a dying race even before Europeans set foot on these shores."

"What is the situation with the blacks in the Logan Valley?" Simon asked, a little impatient to have the discussion back on course. "Are they likely to be troublesome?"

"No, there's little chance of that happening, unless you build your house on an ancient Bora ground or something like that. The Aborigines are a very ritualistic people and certain places appear to be of great importance to them. There was one particular instance in which they repeatedly attacked a shepherd's hut and yet never bothered others nearby. It turned out that the poor fellow had his dwelling on sacred ground. Seriously, though, you'll have no cause to worry about them at the Logan. In fact, most of the Moreton Bay region is quite peaceful now. In some places, blacks even trade with the settlers – fish, wild fowl and so forth in return for tobacco, flour or sugar. There are still, of course, those who will have nothing to do with the white population, but they rarely come near the settlements. They might pass through wooded districts on the outskirts as they move from place to place, but they don't usually look for trouble. In fact, you probably won't ever get to see them."

"I won't be complaining about that," Simon assured him with a quick grin.

"You will hear stories of earlier troubles, of course. But the war with the blacks is actually a sort of moving frontier. It was in this region to begin with, and there certainly were some gruesome incidents. But it has now moved inland and to the north, what with settlement spreading out in those directions. There will be clashes in those regions for quite a while to come, I'm afraid. But, as I've said, you'll find the Logan Valley quite safe … so to get back to this redeemed property?"

"I could certainly be interested," Simon told him. "What category does it fall into?"

"It's … ah, let me see. Yes, here it is, first-class pastoral land. That's ten shillings an acre, which would mean … " He did a swift calculation on a slip of paper. "An annual rental of twelve pounds ten shillings, and a total cost over the ten years of one hundred and twenty-five pounds."

Simon nodded. "I do have some capital and we should be able to manage that. Will there be any charge for the work that has already been done on the place?"

"A nominal amount could be charged for the well. That will be up to the Lands Office."

"The well is not the only water supply?"

"No, there's a creek running through one corner of the property. It's quite reliable, according to what I have here."

"If we do decide to apply for this place, what would our chances of getting it be?"

"Fairly good, I should think, but it would probably be a good idea to see the Lands Office people as soon as possible. Tell them that you'll be lodging an application as soon as you get to the Logan and inspect the land."

"I'll make a point of calling on them this afternoon. And I do thank you, Mr Walters. You have been a great help to us."

The Immigration Officer began gathering up his papers. "It's been my pleasure, and I'll be happy to talk with you again if you run into any difficulties. By the way, you'll find that either the City Auction Mart or Tattersall's Horse Bazaar will have the horses and most of the equipment you'll be needing."

"I'll keep that in mind."

"And, as for drapery, Mrs Skov, I don't think you'll do better than Finney Isles and Co. in Queen Street, while Bright Brothers in Eagle Street will have all the pots, pans, and foodstuffs you'll be needing."

10

The Skov family left Brisbane on the following Saturday, taking the first ferry of the day across the river, then moving slowly out through South Brisbane, which, being part of the city, surprised with its gentle, rural appearance, to the flat plains district beyond. Here, they passed a number of small scattered farms, their simple slab cottages surrounded by squares and rectangles of cultivation and grazing lands, while newly cleared tracts with their stark ring-barked trees bit back raggedly into the dense scrub. Just before midday they stopped at a farm with the name, COLLINS, printed boldly across the top rail of a sagging wooden gate; this farmer, they had been told, would be happy to sell them both cows and poultry.

Herb Collins, his wife Marian, and their three teenage sons were English migrants. "Out from the old country for more than ten years now," Herb explained cheerfully. "Since just after Separation, that is." The Collins family at once understood the needs of these newcomers, so much so they actually vied with one another in offering advice and suggestions. By the time the Skovs took to the road once again, not only had their little cavalcade been added to as they had intended, they had been fortified with cups of tea and thick slices of newly-baked bread topped with corned beef and pickles, and pressed into accepting a large bottle of honey which came with the instruction to "lose no time in getting yourselves a couple of hives", two dozen eggs "in case all the bumping about puts the pullets you've bought off laying for a day or two", a bunch of bananas just beginning to turn yellow and a pile of suckers which had been mercilessly rooted up from beside the parent trees and which would "be no trouble since bananas grow like weeds in Queensland".

In the still heat of the early afternoon, they moved slowly over the bumpy dirt road. Simon led the way, driving a big German wagon drawn by a large draught horse and piled high with their trunks, implements and tools, a tent, canvas stretchers and stools, a small table, a hanging safe, an assortment of pots and pans, bags of seed, flour, sugar and potatoes, plus a collection of other provisions. On top of all this, balanced somewhat precariously, was the crate with its dozen protesting pullets and lone bewildered-looking rooster. Tethered on ropes behind, the two newly-acquired cows plodded reluctantly, tossing their heads and mooing indignantly. Elsie and Christina followed in a spring-cart laden with bedding, clothes, food and such other articles as they would be needing on the way, and drawn by a high-stepping brown mare who had lost no time in showing her impatience at the dawdling pace.

"I'm not sure this mare is as placid as we were told," Elsie declared, having cause yet once again to grip the reins more tightly. "Whoa! Whoa there! Settle down, Sally, old girl."

"She seems nice, though," Christina mused. "She has kind eyes."

"Well, I'm pleased to hear that. Let us hope that she has a kind heart as well and doesn't decide to tip us and our belongings out on the road."

"Father said that I might be able to ride her when we get to our farm."

"That will depend on how she turns out, Christina. It might be better if you waited until we are able to get you a pony." Elsie gave a small sigh. "Though I suppose we shouldn't be judging poor Sally by this performance. She has every right to object to this snail's pace we are travelling."

"Can't Father go any faster?"

"Goodness, can you imagine what would happen to those poor cows and all that stuff in the wagon if that big horse should break into even so much as a trot?"

Christina giggled. "I think those hens would be flying all over the place, for one thing."

"I fear they may get to do that even as things are, the way that crate is wobbling about."

But Christina was no longer listening. Her gaze had wandered to a grassy glade and she gasped excitedly, "Oh, look! It's a kangaroo! A real live one! And see how he's sitting up ... just like in the pictures we've seen."

The big grey animal watched them curiously, resting on its strange long ankles while its powerful tail provided central support. "He looks as though he is trying to decide who we are," Christina chuckled. "Oh, I do hope Father sees him."

"He has seen him," her mother told her. "See, he is pointing with his whip." The top of the whip handle had appeared over the hen crate, pointing in the direction of the kangaroo.

"Yes, he has. Oh, I wish he would stop, just for a while."

"It would probably hop away if we stopped. Besides, we are bound to see others. And we must remember to look in the trees for koalas. We haven't seen any of those yet."

"We've seen plenty of birds, though," Christina laughed, involuntarily ducking her head as yet another flock of brilliantly-coloured parrots rose from the trees near the road and swooped low over their cart.

"That we have, Christina. And what birds they are, with such colours as to seem almost unreal." She gave an amused grimace as the birds circled, then settled with a new burst of screeching in a tree only a short distance from the one they had vacated. "But what a terrible noise from something so pretty."

Christina grinned, but then said thoughtfully, "It's strange, though, how the parrots and the cockatoos have such screeching calls while the plainer birds make such music."

"Ah yes, indeed, like those magpies we heard in Brisbane. And the butcher birds, I don't believe any sound could be more tuneful than their piping, certainly none that we humans could make."

"Father said there will probably be a lot of them around our farm, and kookaburras too."

"Well, I'm sure we'll enjoy the magpies and butcher birds, but I don't know that I'm going to appreciate being continually laughed at."

"When Henry and I saw those two in the Botanical Gardens, we stood under the tree and laughed back at them."

"And what did the kookaburras do then?"

"They just peered down at us, as though they thought we were crazy or something."

Christina's smile faded into a soft sigh. What a wonderful day that had been. First, watching the procession in honour of the new Governor, then wandering for hours in those wonderful gardens, just her and Henry, while their parents attended to preparations for their departure from Brisbane. How delicious the soft grass had felt beneath her bare feet. And how cool the water in the small pond when they'd sat on the mossy rocks and dipped their toes in, to the consternation of the small ducks whose home it was. Stealing a sideways glance at her mother, Christina felt again the faint prickling of guilt that had been with her in spite of Henry's assurances that no one would notice. Her mother wouldn't have been at all pleased to have seen her in a public place without her shoes and stockings.

"I wonder what progress the Schneiders have made. It was quite a coincidence that we should set off at virtually the same time. Though I suppose, in a way, it was bound to happen, what with your father and Mr Schneider both so impatient to get to their land. It wasn't likely that either of them would be wanting to hang around Brisbane the way some of the others seem content to do."

"Henry said that his mother would have liked a few more days in Brisbane," Christina remarked in a small voice, recalling the sinking feeling that had come when she'd learned they would be parting so soon.

"I know just how she felt. We really did have to rush our shopping, and. even though we bought so much stuff, I'm still not sure that we have everything we'll be needing. Nevertheless, I can appreciate your father's impatience; the sooner we are settled on our land, the sooner we'll be able to make something of it." Elsie wiped the perspiration from her brow with a limp handkerchief. "In any case, I won't be sorry to have this journey over and done with, it's so warm to be travelling."

"It doesn't seem possible that it's still winter."

"It is, though, the end of winter. Spring comes with September, but it seems that it's very impatient in this country. It just refuses to wait for its allotted time. But, goodness me, whatever is summer going to be like?"

"Very, very hot, I would think." Christina suppressed a sigh as she stole another glance at her mother's damp, flushed face. How hot and uncomfortable she looked. And she must be too, what with her whalebone stays crushing the very breath out of her, her thick stockings, petticoats, and heavy dark dress with its high collar. She was hot herself, and her dress wasn't nearly so heavy; furthermore, she had persuaded her mother to let her wear only the one petticoat, a light one at that. There was no doubt about it, the English lady at the farm where they had stopped had been quite right when she'd remarked that they would have to change their mode of dressing if they wanted to survive a Queensland summer.

The sun was already low in the west when Simon guided the wagon off the road and into a small glade surrounded by towering gum trees … the first area they'd come to in more than an hour that wasn't covered in dense bush. And, although it was deserted now, they saw at once that they were by no means the first to have come thankfully to this small oasis in the wilderness, for the earth was marked by blackened rings where fires had burned through other long dark nights, and, off to one side, someone had heaped some stones together to form a rough fireplace.

"I was beginning to think we weren't going to find a suitable place to camp for the night," he remarked as he helped his wife and daughter from the cart. "But this will do just fine. There's even a gully of sorts with a bit of water in it and I'm sure the animals won't mind that it's not as clear as it could be."

"Are we going to put the tent up, Father?" Christina asked as she glanced a little apprehensively into the thick bush with its darkening shadows.

"Not just for one night, Christina. It would take too long and then delay us again in the morning. It's not likely to rain or be too cold, so we'll just stretch that piece of canvas from the side of the wagon, that will be shelter enough." He grinned cheerfully. "We'll have a nice fire, and it will be quite fun, you'll see."

Unconvinced, Christina had more than a little trouble returning his grin. How, she asked herself, could sleeping under a piece of canvas with the bush all around them possibly be fun? What strange creatures were out there waiting for the darkness so that they could begin their prowling? And what about the blacks? Even if this was supposed to be a peaceful region, you couldn't always be sure about them; how many different people had told them that? Then there was ... Christina's fears as to what dangers might lurk in the night disappeared, and she began flailing her arms and hopping about as a great buzzing surrounded them and swarm after swarm of bloodsucking insects surged out of the bushes.

"Mosquitoes!" Elsie gasped, waving a hand in front of her face. "Oh Simon, there are millions of them! And they are so vicious!"

"I will get a fire started." Simon was already dragging dead branches into position against a partly burnt log. "The smoke should drive them away."

"Goodness, I hope so! We'll never be able to stay here if it doesn't!"

"Dusk is apparently the worst time for them, so I think it would be the same wherever we stopped." He turned to Christina who was slapping at first one arm and then the other. "Christina, do you think you could gather up some twigs and dry leaves? Don't go away from this open area, though."

Father must be joking, Christina told herself as she hurried to obey. Why would she want to leave the open area, for heaven's sake? With the bush all around so dense and growing darker by the minute? Ouch, how they stung! She dropped the first few twigs she had picked up, needing both hands to swipe at the mosquitoes now intent on attacking her through her bodice. And they were getting under her skirt as well and biting her through her stockings. Oh, what cruel monsters they were. Far more savage than the odd few they'd met with in Brisbane and along the road. Those had been quite easily swatted or shooed away, but not these. She danced about, flipping her skirt to and fro. How was she ever going to pick up kindling when they would give her no peace?

"Try swishing this about."

She took the small leafy branch her father handed her, waving it back and forth in front of her face and about her body. It did help, a little. Now, if she could just manage to keep it moving with one hand, perhaps she could gather up the kindling with the other one. What a slow business it was going to be though, especially since she would be obliged to run back and forth to the fire with every handful. Still, it was the best she could manage if she wasn't to be eaten alive. Or be carried off, for that matter.

There were such swarms of them it seemed they could quite possibly do that, just like Mr Barton had said when he'd warned them about the mosquitoes. Such a funny joke, they'd thought, laughing. Well, it wasn't a joke anymore, it wasn't the least bit funny!

Elsie, also armed with a leafy switch came to help her daughter. "I never would have believed this," she exclaimed. "Even though people warned us about the wretched creatures, I didn't really expect them to be so vicious or to be in such large swarms."

"I was just remembering what Mr Barton said about them being able to carry us off and I think that perhaps he wasn't joking after all."

"To think we laughed at him." Elsie tugged at a piece of bark hanging from the pale trunk of a gum tree, grunting her satisfaction when it came away in her hands. "This should be dry enough to burn, and there is plenty of it."

"I will just take these twigs over to father and then I'll ... ow!" Dropping the bundle of twigs, Christina slapped at the hand holding the switch, shuddering at the sight of the small splash of blood which burst from the squashed insect. That was her own blood. How much would she have left, for heaven's sake, if every mosquito that stung her was stealing some? Not very much, that was for sure. She scratched furiously as the full effect of the sting made itself felt, feeling the lump that was already rising.

"Don't scratch, Christina, you'll turn the bites into sores. Just rub them."

"I can't help it, they are so itchy!" Christina's voice was suddenly tearful. "And I have bites all over me, even under my clothes."

"I know," Elsie said gently as she straightened with an armful of bark. "Come, I'll get you a blanket and you can sit under it until the fire takes hold."

"But Father needs me to help."

"I think he might have enough kindling. He's gathered quite a pile himself and with what we have here we should soon have a fire, a nice, smoky one, hopefully."

The fire took hold, sizzling through the dry leaves, curling the strips of bark, lapping at the twigs. And the blessed smoke rose, smelling of eucalyptus and swirling out across the clearing. Right away, the buzzing began to lose its intensity as the swarming mass thinned, then, except for a few stragglers, disappeared.

"Well," Elsie declared on a deep sigh of relief. "I'm sure this is the first time in my life I've been grateful for a smoking fire!"

Christina, crouched on her haunches beside her father, gave a small, soft laugh. "I think even the horses and cows like the smoke. Look how they've crept closer to the fire."

"So they have, poor things. I suppose the wretched mosquitoes bother them just as they do us. I hope that, since they appreciate the smoke, they understand that it's the reason they haven't been attended to."

"Oh. I'm sure they do, Father."

Simon smiled at his daughter's reassurance, straightening as he did so. "Well, I should be able to see to them now; the fire seems to be going along nicely enough."

As they had come to expect, darkness came swiftly, with no lingering twilight such as they had known in Schleswig to soften the transition from day to night. One minute the white trunks of the gum trees wore a soft rosy glow, while the birds in their branches twittered noisily as they argued over roosting places; the next, the gums were pale ghostly pillars holding dark canopies over their heads, and, except for an occasional drowsy protest, the birds had hushed. With the darkness, there came a profound, almost breathless silence. A waiting silence, Christina decided, glancing furtively over her shoulder as they finished their meal by lantern light and the flickering glow from the fire.

It was no stealthy sound that broke the silence. It was a long, mournful howling that sent icy fingers down her spine. With racing heart, she saw that both her parents had been startled and were staring off into the darkness as though they would see what was out there, and that her father had reached for his rifle. Within the space of seconds the call came again, but from a different direction Two of them! Christina gasped to herself. And on opposite sides of their camp. Oh, what were they, for heaven's sake? Crying as though they were in pain or something and yet still sounding so terrifying. Another one! With a small, smothered scream, she scrambled to her feet, heedless of the plate balanced on her knees and scurried the few paces to her father's side. This one was so close, in the bushes just beyond the wagon. She could hear it moving about, the rustling of the bushes and dry leaves, the snapping of a twig. "Oh Father, there's one just over there!" she cried in a hoarse whisper, huddling against his side.

"I know, love, but there's nothing to fear, they are not likely to come near the fire." He gave her shoulders a reassuring squeeze before guiding her around his knees to where he could push her gently towards her mother. "Sit with your mother while I see if I can give them a bit of a fright." He got to his feet, the rifle in his hand. "A shot or two will soon let them know that they should keep their distance."

As Simon walked quietly in the direction of the wagon, the dolorous wailing began again … a chorus now, with new and distant voices joining in and those they had first heard sounding much closer. They are probably coming to be with the one behind the wagon, Christina decided fearfully, shuddering against her mother's side. "Are they wolves, do you think?"

"No, of course not," her mother told her, not quite as confidently as she would have wished. "I think they must be what they call 'dingoes'."

"There seems to be a whole pack of them. Are they savage?"

"If they were dangerous, I'm sure someone would have warned us to beware of them. The Collins family did mention that dingoes sometimes took their poultry, but they didn't really say anything else about them. I suppose they thought that we knew all about the creatures."

The sharp crack of the rifle echoed through the bush, seeming to bounce from tree trunk to tree trunk. The howling, even that coming from a distance, ceased abruptly, and there was a scampering through the undergrowth. In the same instant, a great cacophony of alarmed screeches from the disturbed birds burst forth, spreading in an ever-widening circle.

"Oh, my goodness!" Christina gasped on a small, nervous giggle. "Now, see what Father has done."

Her mother laughed quietly too. "What a noisy protest it is. I suppose they are justified though, the poor things must have got an awful fright. But let's hope they soon settle down again. With such a racket going on we'll never be able to get to sleep."

Christina cast an involuntary glance at the piece of canvas stretched from the wagon and pegged to the ground, the blanket-draped wheel of the cart providing an incomplete wall at the far end, while this end remained open to the fire. How were they to sleep, in any case, in such a meagre shelter? She wouldn't be able to. She was quite sure of that. She would be much too frightened to close her eyes even for a minute.

For a short time she was. She lay, wide-eyed and tense, on the feather mattress, the blanket pulled up to her chin. The dingoes had resumed their mournful wailing, some off in the distance but others not all that far away. The parrots and other birds of the daylight hours had once again settled, but those of the night were now astir. A great flapping of heavy wings as a large owl swooped low across the clearing made her jump, and there was a strange whirring sound as other nocturnal winged creatures set out on their food-foraging expeditions. A mopoke roused and added its monotonous call to that of the dingoes. And there were other sounds, other movements – rustling, stealthy, some so elusive they seemed little more than a breath, sensed rather than heard. Christina watched her mother and father moving quietly about in the firelight. Why, she thought, they are acting almost as though they are clearing up after a meal in the big kitchen back home, washing and drying the cups and plates they had used, talking quietly together, occasionally laughing softly. If she closed her eyes, she could listen to their voices and pretend that they were still back there.

Her mind groped for the pictures she sought: their home and the church, the school, the barley fields, her grandfather's little tailoring shop. They came, but only fleetingly, as though they could not bear to stay, or was it that they couldn't compete with others that seemed bent on leaving them no room? Tears, hot and stinging, found their way into Christina's eyes and pushed under her lowered lashes on to her cheeks. It was no use, no use at all. This was the Australian bush, thousands and thousands of miles from Haderslev, and it was horrible and terrifying. No one would ever be able to pretend that it was something else, especially something gentle and lovely. Oh, why had they come to this strange, wild land? Why weren't her mother and father washing the dishes in their own kitchen instead of out in the open with the dark bush all around them? Why wasn't she sleeping in her own bed under a real roof instead of on the ground under a piece of canvas, with itchy bumps all over her and some of the wretched insects still buzzing about? Why? Why? Oh, there were a thousand whys, far too many to think about, especially when she was so sleepy.

Christina woke as the first rosy glow stole into the glade, setting the shadows to flight. Her father was already up and about, raking over the last glowing embers of the fire, arranging a new lattice work of small branches, dragging up another log. Her mother also; even before Christina saw her crouched down beside one of the cows, she could hear the sharp squirts of milk going into the bucket, a nice familiar sound that brought a soft smile to her lips. The birds were awake too, twittering quietly as they waited for the sun to rise and the real business of the day to begin. Dressing quickly, she hurried from the meagre shelter. With the dark night at an end, the emotions which had crowded her young heart as she'd fallen asleep wavered, then retreated before a new rush of excitement.

"Well," her father observed with a quick smile, "you look bright and cheerful this morning. Did you sleep well?"

"Yes, I did. I didn't think I would, though. I thought I'd be too scared even to close my eyes."

"But they closed themselves, eh?"

Christina returned his smile. "I think they must have, I don't remember closing them." She glanced quickly about her as a sudden burst of golden light replaced the rosy glow. Oh, how different it all was in the light of day. Tangled and wild-looking still, but not horrible. In fact, in its own way, it was very pleasant: the stately gums marching off in columns through the bush as though they always had the right of way; the lovely tree-ferns that lined the sides of the gully; the flowering trees and bushes that were everywhere; and the vines which clambered mindlessly wherever their tendrils reached, but dangled their lovely flower clusters like fragrant tassels for all who passed their way to see. Christina gave a soft self-ridiculing laugh. Had she really thought this bush horrible? Oh, surely not! Even with its mosquitoes and howling dingoes, surely not! Why, every glance brought a new and pleasing surprise, and it smelt good too.

Watching her, Simon chuckled. "Much nicer in the daylight, eh Christina?"

"Oh yes, Father. We didn't really get a chance to see it properly yesterday afternoon."

"No, we arrived too late and had too much to do, and, of course, the mosquitoes didn't help. They are still about, by the way. Fortunately, though, they seem to be keeping mainly to the bushes, so we must take care not to disturb them."

"Do you need any more kindling?"

"No, the fire is under way and we'll only need it for a short time, just for a cup of tea and a bite to eat. We want to be back on the road as early as possible."

Helping her mother roll up mattresses and fold blankets, Christina listened, a smile on her lips to the morning sounds of the bush, so different from those of the night. The birds were now fully active, fluttering about in flashes of brilliant colour, their chorus swelling to a crescendo that was a joy-filled welcome to the day, for all that it was exquisite in some ranges, raucous in others. At intervals, there came the turn of the kookaburra: a low croodle of soft content to begin with, rising to a louder chuckle as his mirth increased, then bursting forth in a loud, riotous guffaw – an invitation to another to join in, and then another, and yet another, until the whole bush rang with their merriment. Christina laughed too as a pair of them settled on a branch nearby and immediately set about contributing to the chorus. "Oh, what crazy birds they are, and it really does seem as though they are laughing at us."

"Indeed it does," Elsie agreed. "What's more, I believe they could be having a contest to see which of them does it best. No wonder they are called laughing jackasses. But come, we must hurry with this bedding, your father is waiting to load it."

"Will we get to the land Father wants to look at by tonight?"

"I don't know, Christina. We are apparently not yet halfway, so we'd have to make better time than we did yesterday. Your father seems to be hopeful of reaching Beenleigh at least, but I don't really see how it will be possible to go much faster than we have been doing."

"Perhaps we could go a bit faster," Christina suggested hopefully. "That's if the road is not too bad."

"I don't expect that the road will improve. Still, we'll just have to wait and see what the day brings."

The day brought slow-turning wheels and a number of delays on a road that seemed to deteriorate with every mile. When it drew to a close, the Logan River was still more than a mile away and they were obliged, once again, to make camp by the side of the road. As on the previous evening, the dusk was mosquito-haunted, and, when darkness came, the dingoes began to prowl and wail. Through the trees, though, a faint light flickered, reaching out to take the edges from their feelings of isolation.

What a difference it makes, Christina mused to herself as she crawled into her makeshift bed, knowing that someone is living not so very far away. There were probably other houses as well, with lights they couldn't see because of the dense bush. Perhaps, in the morning, they would actually see the houses. Certainly, when they reached Beenleigh, they would see some, and shops as well, more than likely. Then, before the day ended, they would have reached their own land, the land her father was hoping to buy. Oh, how good it would be to get there and have their travels over the bumpy road at an end. Why, sometimes she had bounced up and down on her seat so hard all her bones had jarred, even those in her head. And how many times had they had to stop when a wheel became wedged in a deep rut or slipped off the narrow strip of dirt which was all the road really was?

There had been other problems too; like the creek where the water ran so swiftly and the banks were so steep, she'd been afraid that, even if they did manage to get down and across the stony ford without toppling over, they would never be able to get up the other side. They had, though, with the poor horses straining and pulling with all their might while her father yelled and flipped his whip across their rumps. Christina sighed softly ... so many difficulties this day had brought, and just when they had hoped to make good time. Her father was disappointed, she knew. He had hoped to reach the township of Beenleigh by nightfall and here they were, not yet across the river. No wonder he had seemed so annoyed; why, he'd hardly smiled all evening. Her mother hadn't been annoyed though. Even when she'd had to take off her shoes and stockings to help her father lead the horses across the creek, she hadn't minded. Even all the times she'd had to go down on her knees in the dust to push branches under the wheels, she'd never lost patience or complained.

A sudden smile came to Christina's lips and she wriggled her toes into the soft mattress in recalled delight. This morning her mother had laughed, really laughed – for the first time since little Anna died. Oh, she had smiled and chuckled often enough before, but always it had seemed that there was something missing, that she did so with only part of herself. Not this morning, though. This morning, when a magpie had stolen the piece of toast her father had been about to spread with marmalade, she had laughed with all of herself, with her whole heart. How good it had sounded. So good it had made the whole day special in spite of the delays and their slow pace.

Other nice things had also happened along the way: kangaroos and wallabies bounding about, sometimes whole families of them, and once, by the very edge of the road, there'd been a gentle mother with a baby peeping from her pouch. They'd finally seen a koala. They wouldn't have, though, if the man hadn't ridden up as they were having a bite to eat at midday. A tall man wearing a wide-brimmed felt hat and mounted on a big black horse, and who had come from the valley they were going to. What was his name again? Kleinschmidt ... ? Yes, that was it, Mr Kleinschmidt. What a nice man he was, answering all her father's questions while he drank a cup of tea with them. He'd even said that, if her father wanted work cutting cane, he should go and see him. It had been as he was about to ride off, heading north, that he had pointed with his whip handle into the branches of a young gum tree. And there it was, almost over their very heads, and in a tree not yet grown tall. How could they have not noticed the grey furry bundle? How many others had they passed and not seen, for heaven's sake?

"You're still awake, Christina," her mother exclaimed as she came to prepare for bed. "I thought you would have been asleep as soon as your head hit the pillow."

"I have been thinking about all the things we've seen today, especially the animals. Now that we know what to look for, we should see some more koalas, shouldn't we?"

"I hope so." Elsie placed her shoes and stockings tidily under the wagon. "We are certainly learning all the time."

They boarded the ferry to cross the Logan River just before eight o'clock after waiting for almost an hour for it to return from the far side. It was no simple feat, since neither the horses nor the cows were particularly co-operative. Unperturbed, the ferryman, a large, brawny fellow of middle age, prodded and shoved until he was at last able to fasten the chain behind them. "It's a good deal easier when the tide's in," he declared cheerfully as he took up his position at the winch and set about winding the cumbersome pontoon across the stream. "For some reason the animals don't take too kindly to coming all the way down the bank on to the ferry. Some of them, that is, others don't seem to care, one way or the other."

"Well, I certainly appreciate your help," Simon told him.

"Think nothing of it." He grinned, showing large and uneven teeth. "If I didn't hop in and help, I'd spend half me blooming life just waiting to get started."

Simon returned the man's grin before glancing about him appreciatively. "This is quite a fine waterway."

"Yep, she's not a bad river, the Logan. You planning on staying in the valley or going further south?"

"We are hoping to be able to stay, to take up some land and farm."

"That's good. This region can do with more settlers. There's still any amount of land waiting to be opened up. Where are you from, if you don't mind me asking?"

"Schleswig," Simon replied automatically. Then, seeing the puzzled frown replace the smile on the other man's face, he added, "We are Danish."

The smile returned. "Ah, from Denmark, eh? I didn't think that was a German accent somehow. We've got quite a number of German families in the valley. Along the Albert River as well. Some of them have been here for going on ten years now. They do pretty well too, especially those like the Kleinschmidts and Hecks who've gone in for cane in a big way. They've even built their own crushing mills, you know?"

Simon nodded. "We met up with Mr. Kleinschmidt along the road, and it was actually a German immigrant on the ship who first got us interested in the Logan Valley. I have spoken to other people about it since, of course."

"You got favourable accounts, I'm sure. The place is really progressing now. More and more land is being cleared and the town is growing all the time. I can tell you, there's been a big change since I came here eight years back."

"I can imagine. Do you have land as well as the ferry?"

"Too blooming right. The ferry's really only a sideline." He nodded vaguely at the bank they were approaching. "I've got some two hundred acres over yonder, more than half of it cleared and planted. Took it up within a year of coming out from the old country. Best thing I ever did. With three sons it would have to be, wouldn't you say?"

Simon nodded. "Yes, it would have been."

The ferryman shook his head slowly from side to side. "With just the wife and one little girl, opening up new land is going to be pretty hard for you."

"We'll manage," Simon told him, just a little abruptly.

"Of course you will. A bloke can do anything if he's got his heart in it and he's not afraid of hard work. It's just that having some help makes it so much easier. Gives a man a chance to take a breather, so to speak." He grinned again. "Like now, for instance."

The scowl left Simon's brow and he grinned back at the man perspiring over the winch. "I would hardly call what you are doing, taking a breather."

"Well, I do get a break between trips. Besides, you should see what me lads are doing right now – ain't one of them wouldn't be wanting to change places with me."

"Oh … ?"

"Yep, they're digging spuds and they'll be at it all day, unless I get to feeling guilty and let them have a go here. On the other hand, I might just go and help them and let the missus take over here when she's through with her washing." He chuckled deeply. "Monday morning, you know? Rain, hail, or shine, the missus does the washing on Monday morning."

"This would be very strenuous work for a woman."

"For some women, it would, but Mildred's built like a young ox, it don't bother her one bit. In fact, she likes being down here, since it gives her a chance to talk to other folks. The Cobb and Co. coaches cross here, and Mildred's always interested to see who's travelling on them." He gave another of his deep chuckles. "You'd be fair amazed at the bits of information she picks up from people who only got out of the coach to stretch their legs. I bet she knows as much about the functions being held to celebrate the new Governor's arrival as most city folk do."

"We were fortunate enough to see the new Governor arrive in Moreton Bay. Our ship was at the anchorage over that weekend."

"You were out there when 'his Nibs' arrived! Holy mackerel, wait until I tell that to the missus! She's going to be so jealous that she wasn't down here to talk to you. What ship were you on then?"

"The Friedeburg."

"That's right. I read in the Courier about the Friedeburg being out there when the Governor arrived. Didn't some of the passengers come ashore in the Francis Cadell?"

"Yes, a few of the paying passengers. The rest of us were obliged to wait until Monday morning."

"Last Monday? You've really been moving then."

"There didn't seem to be any reason for us to be waiting around in Brisbane."

"Of course not. The less time I spend in that place, the better I like it. The lads like to go there, though, and the missus." The ferry shuddered to a standstill against the strip of stones laid over the muddy shore. "There we are now, .safely across."

"I must pay you before we get these animals moving again. How much is it?"

The ferryman removed his hat and scratched his head, his gaze gliding thoughtfully over the animals and vehicles. "I reckon two bob ought to cover this lot."

"Two bob? That's two shillings, isn't it?"

"Ah, I forgot you were a new chum. Yes, two shillings it is. But I reckon the next time I see you, you'll be calling it two bob, same as the rest of us."

"It doesn't seem enough," Simon protested, a faint frown on his brow. "It cost me a deal more than that to cross the Brisbane River and we didn't have the cows with us then."

"Two bob it is. For people aiming to live in the valley, I wouldn't be thinking to charge one penny more."

"Well, if you're sure …"

"Of course I'm sure. Hell, I bought me land for two bob an acre, and a ferry ride hardly compares with an acre of ground."

"It's not two bob an acre now," Simon told him with a wry grin. "But I do thank you."

"It's been my pleasure and I can't wait to tell the missus about you seeing the Governor arrive. Now, let's see if we can get these creatures of yours off without too much trouble."

Although the bank was no less steep than that on the other side, leaving the ferry presented fewer problems than boarding it had done – due, in no small respect, to the fact that the animals showed no desire to remain afloat.

Within the hour the small township of Beenleigh had crept out from its shroud of trees and bush – an assortment of buildings which, for the most part, religiously followed the more or less straight line of one wide, but dusty, street. If the village appeared to be resting none too confidently on its site astride a small hillslope, it was with good reason

– this was its third location and it had been on it for only three years. The original site, marked out by the Government surveyor on the north bank of the Albert River, had remained only a wharf site; the second, to the south of the present choice, had seen the building of an hotel and a couple of general stores before being abandoned, in 1868, in favour of an area at the junction of four roads, midway between the Logan and Albert Rivers.

The land chosen had been covered with bushy scrub, but, before the year ended, the Beenleigh Exchange Store had been opened; the hotel, post office, general store and butchery had been relocated from the previous site; and a blacksmith's shop set up. Other buildings had since been constructed, and, just six months before the arrival of the Skov family on 21 August 1871, the district's first State school had been opened with an enrolment of fifty-two pupils, the majority of whom were the children of German immigrants.

The Lands Officer who ushered the Skovs into a small, sparsely-furnished room was no taller than Simon but he was heavily built with more hair on his face than on his head. His name was George Hunter and, unlike the Immigration Officer, he smiled often. He listened attentively as Simon explained what had brought them to the Logan Valley, then leaned back in his chair with a wide grin. "So, you could be interested in the O'Reilly place?"

"That's right. It would be a big help to be able to take up land which has been partly cleared."

"Yes, of course." He glanced first at Elsie and then at Christina who was sitting primly on a low stool at her mother's side, and was only a little more tactful than the ferryman had been. "This … ah, this is the whole family?"

Simon's smile faded and he said stiffly, "Yes, this is our whole family."

George Hunter spread his hands in a placating gesture and kept the smile on his face. "I have daughters myself, Mr Skov – four of them, the eldest just turned sixteen." Only in his mind did he add that this was the very reason he worked for the Government and farmed only a couple of acres in his spare time. The son of a ticket-of-leave convict and born in

Australia, the Lands Officer had long since come to the conclusion that the small selector had little chance of making a success of his venture in his own lifetime; therefore, only if he had sons to take over the land and carry on after he was gone, was the never-ending toil, uncertainty and sacrifice likely to pay dividends.

"We would need to see the place first, of course."

"Indeed you would. I think you'll be pleased with the land though. Most of the block is reasonably level and, even in the hilly sections, there'll be slopes that you'll be able to use once you get around to clearing them. The O'Reillys didn't do all that much with it, as you've no doubt been informed. Old Timothy's heart was never really in farming. Still, a few acres cleared is, as you have recognised, a jolly good beginning. Whoever takes up the land now will be able to get right down to the business of ploughing and planting."

"That's what I've been thinking. If the bush in these parts is anything like that we've seen on the way down, clearing it away is going to take quite a deal of effort."

"It's pretty dense alright. Just hope that, when you do start clearing, you don't come up against too many ironbark trees. It usually takes a good half-dozen blows with a sharp axe before you even get a glimpse of the timber under the rough bark."

"Is the timber good for anything?"

"If you were planning to build your own house, that's what you'd be looking at for the walls – ironbark."

"But I am planning to do that," Simon told him with a quick smile. "I'm a carpenter by trade as you will see in my papers, and I've been looking forward to building my own house using my own timber, as I've been told most of the German settlers around here have done."

The Lands Officer's brows had shot up and he eyed Simon disbelievingly. What was he talking about for God's sake? Build his own house with his own timber? Didn't he realise what would be involved before he even began the actual construction of his house: the felling of the trees, splitting of the logs, the sawing of planks and slabs. Sure, the German settlers had done it, living in rough huts while they extended and improved. But, not only were there usually strong sons to help, they were all part of a community only too willing to pitch in and support one another. And here was this man virtually on his own …

Simon interrupted the other man's troubling thoughts. "Are there any others interested in this land?"

"Ah … I've had a couple of enquiries, but no formal application has been lodged as yet. Having to pay something for the improvements is a bit of a deterrent, people don't always have the ready cash. What did they tell you in Brisbane about the value of the improvements, Mr. Skov?"

"Nothing definite. No one seemed to be too sure just what they'd be worth."

"Well, you see, we've been trying to come up with an amount that would be fair to all parties. The Department is planning to make some reimbursement to the O'Reilly family. Even though we have no such obligation, we feel they should get something for the work they have carried out, such as it is. But, actually, Mr Skov, this could be to your advantage if you happen to have a little spare cash. It will certainly lessen the likelihood of there being a whole lot of people interested. In fact, it could well be that yours will be the only application."

"I do have a little capital, but I would like to know in advance what payment would be required. I don't want to be left short of funds."

"Of course not. You appear to have already dug quite deeply into your resources, that's quite a deal of equipment you've got outside."

"We've purchased only what we felt to be essential, but, as you say, we have been obliged to spend a fair amount of money."

George Hunter nodded, suppressing a wry smile. Essentials? What would this very pleasant man sitting on the other side of his desk have thought of the 'essentials' brought to the valley by its earlier settlers … those who had arrived pushing their worldly goods in wheelbarrows, for instance? Still, it was good luck to him if he could afford a decent start. Heaven knew, he was going to need it, a man with only a wife and young daughter. Thinking to build his own house into the bargain …

"If you could just let me have some idea of what you have in mind?" Simon suggested quietly.

The Lands Officer gave himself a mental shake and brought his gaze back from the laden wagon visible through the open window to the papers on his desk. "Yes, of course. Well, even though we still don't have a definite figure approved at all levels, I can certainly tell you what we have been considering. Normally, when we calculate the value of improvements at the time when a Deed of Grant is applied for by a selector, the clearing of the land is held to be worth fifty shillings an acre. On the O'Reilly place, five acres have been cleared. Some ring-barking has been done over a further two acres, but we are not taking that into account. And since this is not an application for a Deed, we propose to regard the clearing as being worth ten pounds, and not the twelve pounds ten shillings which would have been the case." He looked up from his papers, his eyes questioning both Simon and Elsie. "Have I made myself clear thus far?"

They both nodded.

"Good! Well, the next thing is the fencing. A two-rail split fence in good condition is held to be worth fourteen shillings a chain. There are some twenty chains of fencing on the O'Reilly place. It can hardly be said to be of a good standard, but, at least with it being there, the new settler will be able to get on with his other work, he can always improve the fence later on. We have put a value of five pounds on the fencing and that includes a stockyard of sorts."

Again Simon nodded. "That seems fair enough."

"There are no buildings on the place, you realise that, don't you?" This time his glance of enquiry was directed at Elsie.

She nodded. "Yes, we've been told that. We understand that the O'Reilly family lived in tents."

"That's correct. Timothy O'Reilly wasn't a person to be too concerned about providing comforts for his wife and kids. I suppose it could have been that he always intended to return to the diggings and simply didn't consider it worthwhile to build a house. He did put down a well though, and I must say that was something of a surprise to everyone. There is a reliable little creek on the place, and it's not a cheap business putting down a well." A grin appeared on George Hunter's face. "It was probably a surprise to old Timothy too. It's said the blokes who sunk it got on to him at the pub when he didn't have his full wits about him … apparently convinced him that a great drought was coming or some such thing."

"He must have come to appreciate the well though. I understand there was a severe drought a couple of years back."

"That was over before the well went down. No, I think all he ever thought about afterwards was how much his afternoon in the pub had cost him."

"You mentioned that a well doesn't come cheaply. What does it cost to put one down?"

"For a permanent well, you'd be looking at, on an average, one pound per foot for the first thirty feet and anything up to two pounds for every foot after that."

Simon raised his eyebrows. "You are right, that isn't cheap. How deep is this particular well?"

"Around fifty feet. O'Reilly reckoned it cost him eighty pounds. The last of his gold, he always said, and I reckon that figure would be more or less correct. It's in quite good condition, by the way. As it should be, I suppose, since it's not yet two years old. It's good water too, not brackish like it is in some of the wells further downstream. I tried it only the other day when I was out there with the surveyor."

"And is there good water in the creek also, Mr. Hunter?" Elsie asked.

"Yes, there is, Mrs Skov – clear, flowing water, quite fit for drinking. It's still a good idea to have a well though, these smaller creeks can stop running in dry weather."

"Well, I can't say that I'm not pleased the well is there," Simon murmured thoughtfully. "We've been more than a little concerned about the water supply. It's just that, what with it being such a costly undertaking, I would have deferred putting one down until such time as I had an income."

George Hunter nodded his understanding. "And rightly too. It's always a good idea to keep as much capital as you can in reserve when you are just starting out. A new farm won't be bringing in any returns for the first couple of years, as I'm sure you realise. Fortunately, here in the Logan Valley, there's nearly always outside work available, and you'll find that most settlers resort to that during certain periods of the year. As a matter of fact, the cane farmers are looking for cutters right now. That's jolly hard work, but the money's pretty good."

"I'd be quite prepared to do that if the need arises, but I'm hoping that, with the carpentry experience I have had, I'll be able to get some work in the building industry."

"That should certainly be possible, the way this area is progressing. But to get back to the cost of the well, we've been thinking along the lines of forty pounds. With the fifteen pounds for the clearing and fencing, you would then be up for an outlay of fifty-five pounds for the improvements. How does that sound?"

Simon breathed a sigh of relief. "Very fair, provided everything else is satisfactory, that is."

"You understand, though, that you'd be required to pay the improvements money as a cash deposit and then still be liable for the rent of twelve pounds ten shillings a year for a period of ten years – that's two hundred and fifty acres at an annual rent of one shilling an acre."

"Yes, I understand how the rent works. And now what must I do?"

"Go and see the place," the Lands Officer chuckled. "I know you're anxious to do that, and, naturally, the sooner your application comes in, the better. The property is actually some five miles to the south-west of here. I'll give you a map and mark directions on it."

"Will we be able to set up our camp on the land?"

"Yes, you can do that. It's a good idea, actually, since it will give you an opportunity to have a decent look at the place."

"If we are happy with it, we simply lodge a formal application?"

"That's right. Don't take too long about deciding, though. All things being equal, the first person to apply for a particular block of land usually gets it. I'll give you an application to take with you. It's fairly straightforward, but, if you have doubts about any part of it, just leave that section blank and we'll fill it in when you return the form."

"Thank you. I probably will need your help. My English seems to let me down when it comes to completing documents."

"You're not alone in that respect, you may be sure of that. You speak English very well, though. Have you always known the language?"

"I had some knowledge of it, and then we had lessons on the ship." Simon grinned. "I must admit that I have made a lot of progress this past week, however, it was a case of having to."

George Hunter smiled, then turned to Elsie. "You also speak English well, Mrs Skov. What about your daughter?"

"Christina speaks English almost as well as her father and certainly quite a deal better than her mother," Elsie told him, returning his smile.

"That's the way it seems to be, easier for the children than for adults. We've seen that with the German immigrants here in the valley – the youngsters pick up the language much more quickly than their parents do."

He smiled at Christina, who had been staring dreamily at a painting on the wall behind his desk. "Do you know that we now have a school here in Beenleigh, Christina?"

"Yes, a lady in the store told me. She said that it's very new."

"It opened only this year. There are some fifty children attending, though, including two of my daughters. Marie, my youngest, would be about your age, she'll be eight next month."

"I had my eighth birthday last January, on the twentieth."

"Well then, I'm sure you and Marie will be good friends."

"I'd like that."

"But how will Christina be able to go to school if we are living so far out?" Elsie wanted to know, a frown coming to her brow.

"She would have to ride, it's much too far to walk. But you'll find that many of the children ride, and several of them come from out that way."

Christina's eyes widened and a delighted smile came to her lips. Ride to school? Oh, what a treat that would be.

"She hasn't learned how to ride."

"She will, and soon enough. That seems to be another thing children take to without any effort. Around here they get about as though they'd cut their teeth on a bridle, half the time not even bothering to throw on a saddle."

Christina watched her mother's face. She's not the least bit convinced, she decided, seeing the fleeting smile she gave the Lands Officer and the frown which quickly returned. She doesn't think I'll be able to ride to school, even though the other children do.

"I don't think we need concern ourselves with how Christina is to get to school just at the moment," Simon interrupted, smiling as he got to his feet. "We haven't even seen the land yet, let only made application for it. What's more, if we don't soon make a move we won't be there before dark."

"Yes, you should be moving," George Hunter agreed. "You've got quite a load on that wagon and there are a couple of uphill stretches on the way which might slow you down a bit." He handed over the map and application form. "I've marked the land which has recently been surveyed for selection as well as the O'Reilly place. Since it's out in the same general direction, you might care to have a look at it, have a second string to your bow, so to speak."

"Thank you. I had meant to ask you to do that." Simon shook the other man's hand. "I'll see you again in a day or two, perhaps even tomorrow."

"Good luck. I hope you are pleased with what you find out there."

Simon was pleased with what he found; even though it was at the end of a winding dirt track so shocking it made the rough roads they had already travelled seem as highways in comparison. The fences were, as he had been warned, of a poor standard, but they enclosed well-grassed paddocks in which only clusters of shade trees had been left standing. Where the earth had felt the bite of the plough, it wore a faded, sunbaked crust, but, when this was toed aside, it showed dark and rich. After only a brief priming, the well-pump worked and brought forth water that was cool and only slightly discoloured, and the little creek danced its way over rocks and pebbles that were clearly visible on its bed.

On all sides of the cleared acres the bush towered like a great green fortress, and, in places, was backed by wooded hills. But the smile on Simon's face didn't waver. His back was strong and he had purchased good-quality tools. Such a farm this will be, he told himself, even with just the five acres of land presently cleared, and once we move further back into the bush …

Early next morning, with the completed application form in his pocket, he was on his way back into Beenleigh, the mare, glad to be free of the cart, only too willing to respond to his urging.

11

She was lost. The realisation brought a wild thumping to Christina's heart and she glanced in first one direction and then another, her eyes wide with alarm. The bush surrounded her and confused with its sameness: trees that were replicas of others; flowering bushes that flaunted a familiarity born of profusion; tangled undergrowth; ferns and rotting logs as monotonous and unhelpful as the carpet of dry leaves beneath her feet. There was nothing to show her which way she should go. The track she had followed and which had seemed so distinct was now just one of a maze of similar tracks – the highways and byways of the countless creatures, both large and small, whose domain this was. Like the young wallaby she had been following and which had long since taken fright and darted off into the undergrowth.

For a time there had been other distractions: the clouds of small, coloured finches that swept in a startled fashion from tree to tree, twittering wildly and too excited, it seemed, to rest for more than a moment or two; the strange piercing bird call that was like the cracking of a whip; the beautiful long-tailed parrot that had eyed her so fearlessly from a nearby branch; the cluster of sweet-scented violets in a secluded place by the root of a fallen tree. But now, as she stood peering anxiously into the shadows, all these earlier pleasures were forgotten; the bush had become an unfriendly place and she wanted desperately to be out of it.

A terrifying thought leapt into her mind and Christina shivered. What if she was never able to find her way out? If all she could do was just go on wandering around and around, following one track after another until she fell down from exhaustion, then just lay there until she died? No! She wouldn't think such things. Of course she would be able to get out of the bush. If she couldn't find the way herself, her father would come for her. In fact, as soon as he saw that she was missing, he would set out to look for her. Why, he was probably coming through the bush right now. But the confidence at which Christina clutched was undermined by doubts that refused to be thrust aside. How long would it take for her father, who had been busy splitting logs for fence posts, to realise that she was missing? Then, when he did, wouldn't he just think that she had followed her mother when she'd gone back to the tent to prepare their midday meal? After all, that was what she had been about to do, and would have done, had she not seen the wallaby. And, when he did come for her, how would he know where to look? She'd walked so far trying to find the right track back out of the bush, she was probably now nowhere near where he would expect her to be. Miles and miles, it must have been, for her legs were very tired and she was ever so hot, and so terribly thirsty.

Sighing deeply and wiping the perspiration from her face with the hem of her skirt, Christina sat down on an old log. Perhaps, if she rested for a while, she might be able to remember which way it was that she had come. She shouldn't have come into the bush at all, she knew that well enough. Hadn't she been told over and over not to do so? Hadn't she been warned that it was ever so easy to become lost? Why, only yesterday, when that nice Mr Hunter had come out from Beenleigh to see how they were getting on, he'd patted her on the head and said that he was pleased that she hadn't wandered off and got herself lost. And now here she was, as lost as could be.

If only the wallaby hadn't appeared and just sat there as though it wanted to be friendly, and if she hadn't wanted so badly to be closer to it, to touch its fur. In spite of her fears, a faint smile parted Christina's lips. She had almost touched it, moving ever so quietly and holding her breath. If it had just stayed a moment or two longer, or stopped again and waited when she'd followed it into the bush. If it had done that, the short way she had meant to go wouldn't have become a long way and she …

Sighing again, Christina tossed her head in quick rejection of her thoughts. What was she doing blaming the poor little wallaby, for heaven's sake? It wasn't its fault that she was lost, it was hers. It was because she had been so heedless of the warnings that had come her way that she was now sitting here all alone with the bush crowding in on her and hiding the path that she should follow. How could she ever have thought it a pleasant place to be? It wasn't pleasant at all, not now. It tormented her with noises she hadn't noticed before and with shadowy movements that she sensed but never quite saw, no matter how quickly she turned her head this way and that. Why, even the tall trees creaked and groaned in a mournful fashion, adding their voices to the furtive whispering of the bushes and the rustling of the leaves that covered the ground – all secretive sounds that she now heard instead of the chirping of the birds.

Behind her, a twig snapped and Christina swung around with choked-off breath, stifling a scream when she saw the yellow dog-like animal staring at her through ferocious, shining eyes, its sharp teeth bared in a low snarl. A dingo, one of those frightening creatures they heard howling every night and had seen slinking about the clearing where their tent was. Setting her small chin resolutely, she bent forward, her gaze fixed on the animal, her hand reaching for a piece of wood lying beside the log. She wanted to scream, to scramble to her feet, to run for her life, but instinct stayed her flight, warning that the dingo was waiting for her to show fear. With her trembling fingers closed around the piece of wood, she sprang to her feet, waving it above her head and yelling for all she was worth. At once the dingo turned and sped off through the trees.

The flash of triumph she felt was all too brief, lasting only moments before being pushed aside by growing apprehension. Who was to say that the dingo wouldn't come back? Perhaps even bring others with it? Wasn't that the way they usually hunted, in packs? There would be other dangers lurking about as well. Snakes! Why hadn't she thought of them before? Hadn't they been told that the district was alive with them? Hadn't her father already killed a dozen or more, and they'd only been here for seven weeks? Oh, why hadn't she remembered the snakes? If she had, she would never have come into the bush in the first place, the very thought of them terrified her. She moved cautiously away from the log she'd been sitting on. How very foolish that had been. It was where they lived, under logs and things? What was she to do with the bush so full of creatures waiting to harm her? Tears came to her eyes, but she blinked them back, telling herself that she couldn't be crying now, not when she needed to be able to see which way she was going. But which way? Which way should she go?

The sound came indistinctly at first, barely distinguishable from the other sounds around her, but Christina stood still, holding her breath, willing it to come again. It did, and she released her breath on a quick gasp, a faint smile beginning to tug at her lips. Someone was laughing. She wasn't alone in the bush after all. The sound floated faintly to her ears, but there was no mistaking it. It was, Christina told herself, quite definitely laughter, and not a kookaburra, either. There were people over yonder and not so very far away, it seemed. She had probably wandered close to another clearing like their own. Now, all she had to do was go there and someone would show her the way home. Wasting not a moment, she set off in the direction from which the laughter had come. In spite of her tiredness, now that relief surged through her, she moved swiftly over the dry leaves and decaying vegetation, skirting around the clumps of undergrowth that were too tangled to allow her passage through them, clambering over logs, and stooping to pass under low, interlaced branches, no longer thinking about dingoes or snakes, but only of how wonderful it would be to be on her way back to their tent.

So abruptly it made her gasp, she was out of the bush and on the edge of a canefield. New young cane, no taller than she was, it stretched like a gently undulating green sea as far as she could see, both to her right and to her left. But ahead, across the field, there was the unmistakable meandering line of river gums. Christina's gaze darted about. Where were the people who owned the cane? They had to be here somewhere. She'd heard them laughing, hadn't she? But there was no house, no tent, nothing to show that people lived here. There was only the cane, rustling in the breeze.

Christina's heart sank. Someone had planted the cane, and in time someone would come to cut it. In the meantime it just grew; it had no need of people to care for it all the while. Whoever owned it could be living miles and miles away, and the laughter she had heard could have come from another direction. It hadn't always been easy to tell with the bush all around her, and now she wasn't hearing it at all. Or perhaps there had been someone here, someone come to check on the cane but now gone away again. This time Christina made no attempt to check the tears that filled her eyes and slid on to her cheeks. Whatever the explanation, there was no one here to help her, and now she was probably even further away from the clearing where their tent was, miles from where her father would look for her.

The sudden shout of laughter burst through her misery so sharply Christina jumped, then stood still, hardly daring to believe what she had heard. But it was quickly followed by another outburst, a happy, carefree sound that floated clearly to her ears. There were people here. They were over at the river. She darted forward and into the canefield, racing down a long, straight aisle, the crown of her hat bouncing along like a ball on a green carpet. And, all the while she drew closer to the laughter and the happy chatter she could now hear mingling with it. Flushed and puffed, she burst out of the cane where it gave way to the gums and other trees along the bank of the river, and, in the same instant, saw the people whose laughing voices she had heard. They were in the water, swimming and splashing happily about. But ... they were black!

Edging back into the cane, Christina pressed a hand over her mouth to still the scream that trembled there. Blacks? And she had come to them for help. All the things she'd heard about them, all the contradictory things, began darting about in her mind. They were peaceful in this region, harmless people who wandered the countryside, living off the land, afraid of the white man and his guns, wanting only to be left alone. They were savages, burning with resentment, hating all white people, always looking for a chance to kill one of them. Oh, what was true, for heaven's sake? They certainly didn't look like savages, those people swimming so happily in the river. They looked just like any other group of people having a good time. But how was she to know? Perhaps, even as they laughed and played, their spears were lying close by, ready to be picked up in an instant, perhaps in the very instant they caught sight of her.

It was enough. Christina spun on her heel, preparing to flee. But the boy was there, blocking her escape. A boy who was lithe and dark-skinned, a boy who held a spear much taller than himself in one hand, a small furry animal, dripping blood, in the other, and he was naked. This last shocking awareness brought a horrified gasp to Christina's lips, and, for a moment or two, fear was something of only secondary importance. She tried to tell herself that he was only a boy, no more than ten or eleven years old, and that he wasn't going to harm her. But her gaze had settled on the spear and an icy shiver ran down her spine. He had killed a poor harmless animal with that spear, and he could quite easily kill her in just the same way.

The boy stood very still, making no sound, just as he had made no sound when he'd followed her from the bush and into the canefield. And the dark eyes watching Christina so intently told her nothing. They were as expressionless as the rest of the dark face with its high cheekbones and short, flat nose, a face framed by thick shoulder-length black curls and so impassive it might well have been carved from ebony.

"I'm lost," Christina finally managed to stammer, her voice little more than a hoarse whisper.

The boy scowled deeply, then quickly looked all around him in a curiously furtive manner, his lean body taut and ready to spring should the need arise. He doesn't understand, Christina thought bleakly. He thinks there might be others with me and he's afraid. Oh, if only there were. If only her father could come through the bush carrying his gun. Of what use would the black boy's spear be then? None, none whatsoever. He would just run away, taking it with him. Christina's wishful thinking was short-lived and it ended on a soft sob. The boy wouldn't need to run away. There was no one coming to help her. What was more, he now knew that only too well; he wasn't even bothering to look any more.

The young Aborigine had brought his gaze back to Christina's face, and he continued to stare at her for long, silent moments. Then, in an abrupt movement, he dropped the spear and the dead animal to the ground close to his dust-covered feet, and, with a strange whining sound, reached out and struck her in the chest.

Christina jumped back, tears rushing to her eyes, not because the blow had been hard enough to hurt her, but because it seemed to be a clear indication that, even though he no longer held the spear, the boy had no intention of being friendly. Her shaking legs gave way beneath her and she dropped to her knees on the turned earth, burying her face in her hands and sobbing quietly. So she didn't see the black boy strike his own chest in the same way, or the puzzled expression that came to his face when she recoiled from him and sank to the ground. Of course, Christina had no way of knowing that the young Aborigine had simply been greeting her in the ages-old way of his kind. She knew only that the fear within her was a monstrous thing and she wanted the ground to open up and swallow her, to protect her from the black boy and his spear.

The thin dark fingers touched her shoulder so uncertainly and so lightly, Christina, caught up in a renewed burst of weeping, was at first unaware that they had done so. When they moved to her arm, she started, then cringed closer to the ground, her eyes squeezed tightly shut. Now he was going to strike her down. He would take up the spear he had dropped and … But there was nothing rough or cruel in his touch. It was gentle, softly caressing, and the words she couldn't understand were soft and gentle as well. Bewildered, Christina listened, no longer choking over her sobs. Could it be that the black boy wasn't going to harm her after all? She could make nothing out of what he was saying, but his voice was strangely reassuring, hardly the voice of someone who was about to kill her. It was as though he was trying to tell her not to be afraid. Removing her hands from her grimy, tear-streaked face, she looked up in growing wonder. It was true, he wasn't going to hurt her. He had both hands on her arms now and was gently, but firmly, lifting her back on to her feet.

Christina stood unsteadily, her sobs dissolving into quiet gulps. Again the boy studied her thoughtfully, as though unsure as to what he should do next. Then a smile flashed whitely across his dark face and he began to speak rapidly, pointing back in the direction of the bush. He's telling me how he found me, Christina thought, how he saw me come through the bush. The flow of strange words ceased as abruptly as they had begun and the dark eyes searched her face for some sign that she had understood. Christina nodded slowly, and at once the smile returned and he began to talk again, this time gesturing in the direction of the river. He was, she supposed, telling her that they were his people in the water, his family, more than likely. Again she nodded, but the faint hope that had stirred within her began to fade. He would probably want to take her over there, let the others see her. Just because the boy seemed friendly, it didn't mean that the rest of his family would be. His father, for one, might want to kill her. Or perhaps they would decide to hold her captive for years and years, the way the blacks on the island had done with the lady from the shipwreck. And that would be much worse than dying, hadn't she heard her mother say so?

The black boy's voice cut into her misery-drenched thoughts and she blinked rapidly, rubbing at the tears on her cheeks with the backs of her hands. Then stared in amazement as he deftly scooped up the spear with his toes, and, in the next instant, did the same with the dead animal, flicking it effortlessly into his free hand.

"Kappolla," he announced, grinning broadly and proudly holding out the limp bundle for her inspection.

Swallowing hard against the revulsion that rose like bile in her throat, Christina forced herself to look at his prize, at the beautiful fur stained with blood, at the big eyes staring vacantly. A possum, she thought sadly, just like those that came to the trees by their tent night after night and peered down with their bright eyes.

"Kappolla," the boy repeated, his smile beginning to fade as he sensed something of her disapproval.

Christina pushed her lips into a smile she was far from feeling. "Yes, kappolla ... possum."

For a moment or two, he stared at her, a puzzled expression on his face, then, suddenly understanding, he threw back his head on a shout of laughter. "Possum, possum!" he cried, shaking the poor dead creature. "Kappolla ... possum!"

His amusement was infectious and, in spite of her apprehension, Christina felt the smile on her lips lose some of its stiffness. Still chuckling, the boy abruptly turned his back on her and set out for the river, waving the hapless possum over his head in a beckoning gesture. Since there seemed to be little else she could do, Christina followed.

His arrival on the river bank was the signal for a great deal of calling and laughter from those in the water. He called back, laughing too, and holding up the possum for all to see. But, when Christina came to stand forlornly at his side, the chatter and laughter died away. The boy began to talk rapidly, dropping the dead animal so that he could gesture with his hands and the spear. He was explaining her presence, Christina decided, and perhaps he was assuring them that she meant them no harm. But, even as he spoke, she saw two men detach themselves from the group and begin swimming towards the bank. What did that mean? Oh, surely the boy had convinced them that she was alone and harmless, that she was lost and had come to the river quite by accident? But what if he hadn't? They might even be angry at him; they hadn't seemed all that pleased with what he'd been telling them and now he seemed anxious. Oh, but she was so thirsty. There was no moisture left in her mouth whatsoever. If she didn't soon have a drink she would die in any case.

"Water?" she asked the boy. "Could I please have a drink of water?"

He chewed on his lip, frowning deeply, and Christina tried again, pointing to her mouth and then to the river. "Water … a drink of water."

A smile spread slowly across his face. "Tabbil," he exclaimed, nodding his head vigorously before darting off into a cluster of trees. A moment or two later he was back, a container made of bark in his hand. "Minti," he announced, thrusting it at Christina and obviously pleased with himself, "Minti."

The drink was cool and sweet-tasting, and Christina gulped it down thankfully. "That was very nice," she told the boy when she finally handed back the container. "Thank you very much."

"Minti," he said again, wanting her to understand that he had given her something better than mere water, something that was of his own doing, for he had gathered the honeysuckle while the dew was still on it and dipped it ever so carefully in and out of the water so that only its sweetness was captured.

Christina nodded, smiling briefly. "Yes, it was very nice, thank you."

He appeared satisfied for he nodded before raising the container to his own lips and drinking deeply, droplets of water spilling from his chin to form shining rivulets down his dust-covered chest. With his thirst quenched, he held out the container, saying carefully, "Pikki … pikki."

"Pikki," Christina repeated, touching the container to show that she understood.

A gleam of approval came to the young Aborigine's eyes and he glanced quickly about, searching for another word to tell her. A flock of noisy parrots obligingly swooped low over their heads. "Pillin," he said, with a deep chuckle, "Pillin."

"Parrots …"

"Ah, pillin … parrots." He danced happily from one foot to the other, but Christina was no longer looking at him. The two black men had come up over the bank, spears clutched in their hands.

And, this time, her horrified gasp became a wail of dismay, for, like the boy, the men wore no clothes. Their dark skins gleamed with moisture, the tribal markings showing clearly on the upper part of their bodies, their manhood showing just as clearly on the lower part. Christina quickly dropped her gaze to her shoes, sure, even in the throes of her agitation, that this was something her mother wouldn't want her to see. Somehow, with the boy, it hadn't seem quite so bad and, after the initial shock, she had managed most of the time to look only at his face and upper body. But now … now there were three of them without clothes!

The two men came closer, so close Christina could see their black legs from beneath her lowered lashes. She pressed her small chin deeper into her chest, hearing more clearly the thumping of her heart. Oh God, please … please let them be friendly. They were talking now, their voices flowing back and forth above her head and it seemed that they were questioning the boy. Didn't they believe that she was on her own? A trick of some sort, is that what they were thinking? But who did they think would do such a thing, put her life in such danger? If only she knew what they were saying, and, if she could just look somewhere, instead of at her shoes all the time. Already her neck was hurting and it wasn't at all easy keeping her eyes from looking up.

She jumped as one of the men reached out suddenly and lifted her chin with a long black finger, his steely dark eyes searching her face. And he seemed to be asking her something, for, after a short flow of words, he waited, as though for an answer. She shook her head slowly from side to side, hoping that he would realise that she couldn't understand what he was asking her. The man gave a short laugh and, removing his finger from under her chin, turned to the boy who was talking quickly and earnestly, apparently trying to answer for her. After a time that seemed like an age to Christina, he and his companion appeared to be satisfied. They gave the boy what appeared to be instructions, gesticulating a great deal and talking very seriously, then they turned and walked away, disappearing over the bank without so much as a single backwards glance.

Alone with the boy, Christina released her breath on a long, soft sigh of relief. Then she waited patiently while he wrapped the possum in strips of bark before jamming it into the fork of a tree. This task completed to his satisfaction, he gestured with his spear in the direction from which they had come and at once set off with a long, easy gait.

Christina followed, her spirits lifting. The black boy, she felt quite sure, was going to show her the way home. But her relief was short-lived. In a matter of moments he was well ahead of her and she was running to try to keep up, stumbling along between the rows of cane with despair returning. At this rate he would be lost from her view the very minute they left the canefield, and in the bush she'd never be able to find him. She would be lost all over again.

But, about to leave the canefield and enter the bush, the young Aborigine came to a halt and waited for her. At the sight of her flushed and tear-stained face a flicker of something akin to compassion came to the dark eyes. It was quickly gone, though, replaced by confusion. Waiting for a woman to walk beside him was contrary to the ways of his people and something he was loathe to do. He told himself that this was a child still, a weak, white child at that, and that she had already walked far on this hot day. But, soon now, he would be a kippa and it wouldn't be fitting to be too soft with a woman, even a white child-woman. He spent some moments in silent deliberation, chewing on his lower lip and scowling deeply, before coming to a decision. Once it was taken the scowl disappeared and a gleam of satisfaction came to his eyes. It was, he told himself, a good decision, one worthy of a kippa. He would give his brothers no reason to ridicule him, but neither would he walk on, paying no attention to the small figure stumbling along behind him. He would walk more slowly, not so slowly that she would walk at his side, but slowly enough for her never to be too far behind, and, from time to time, he would pause to show her things, so that she might rest a little.

So, in just such a fashion, they made their way through the bush, the young black boy with his pride still intact, Christina tagging contentedly along a few paces behind him, never for a moment doubting that he knew where he was going. During one of their numerous pauses, the boy pointed to a ball of fur wedged in the fork of a tall gum tree. "Oh, it's a koala!" Christina exclaimed. "But it's so high up, I can barely see it."

"Dumbripi," the boy declared firmly, but with his eyes glinting teasingly.

"Koala," Christina responded just as firmly.

"Dumbripi … kwala … dumbripi … kwala," he chanted in a sing-song fashion, and they laughed merrily together before continuing on their way.

Dumbripi ….dumbripi … Christina said the word over and over to herself, liking the sound, even though she was well aware that it came more musically from her companion's lips than from her own. Giggling softly, she let her gaze dwell for a moment on the bare black buttocks no more than ten paces ahead of her. He did look funny, she mused, marching along so proudly with his tall spear, but completely naked. He was nice though, gentle and kind, even if he didn't ever take her hand or let her walk beside him.

He stopped suddenly and, with a finger pressed to his lips, used his head to urge her forward. Christina joined him as quickly and quietly as she could and was just in time to see a fearsome-looking creature waddle out of the undergrowth a short distance in front of them. In the same instant, the spear flew through the air and the creature became a wildly thrashing thing, firmly impaled. With a shout of triumphant laughter, the young Aborigine darted forward, retrieving his spear and holding it up so that Christina might get a closer look at the still-writhing animal. "Barra," he told her and then waited expectantly, his eyes on her lips. But Christina could only stare, for she had no idea what the creature was. A lizard of some sort, she supposed, and yet it didn't really look like any other lizard she had seen; it looked like a reptile from ages past. In time, she would learn that it was a small goanna and that there were many of them in the Australian bush. She would learn, too, that there was a larger species, even more fearsome looking, but that, in spite of their appearance, they weren't really harmful. For now, though, she knew only that it was extremely ugly and that she wasn't really sorry it had finished up on the end of a spear. She shook her head slowly, indicating to the boy that this time she had no word to go with his.

He nodded, seeming to understand, then promptly set about beating the creature mercilessly with a piece of wood. Once its struggling had ceased, he freed it from the spear with his foot, then quickly wrapped it in bark as he had done with the possum. What, for heaven's sake, is he going to do with it? Christina wondered as she watched him push the parcel into a hollow in a nearby tree. And with the possum? Something, of course, or he wouldn't have attended to them so carefully. But what? What could he possibly do with a dead possum and a dead whatever the other creature was? Not even remotely or half-guessed did the answer occur to Christina, for as yet she knew nothing of the ways of an ancient people unchanged by time. Her visions were those of a European and they did not include such things as wild creatures roasting on open fires while hungry bellies waited, or dark, unclad bodies seeking warmth from possum skin rugs on cold winter nights.

Their next stop was at a large mound close to three feet high which the Aborigine's keen eyes had sighted some little distance from their path. "Wargun," he shouted over his shoulder before dashing off through the undergrowth. Christina followed, the bushes scratching her arms and catching at her clothes. Reaching the patch of bare earth where the mound stood, she watched, wide-eyed with puzzlement, as the boy pranced around it in what appeared to be a state of great excitement. What was it, that he should be carrying on in such a way? A great pile of rubbish, that's all it seemed to be – leaves, twigs and loose earth. It was as though someone had taken a broom and swept the area, leaving the rubbish in a great heap.

The bird appeared suddenly, rushing out from the bushes with a great fluffing of feathers and its big feet beating up small puffs of dust. Large and dark-coloured, but with a bright orange wattle hanging from its neck, it rushed towards the mound in a ferocious charge, retreated, and then rushed up again, repeating the performance over and over. It's some sort of turkey, Christina decided, moving warily behind her companion. It must be, though why it should be making such a fuss when they were not attempting to harm it?

"Wargun," the boy said again, brandishing his spear at the angry bird.

"Turkey," Christina replied, but none too confidently.

He tossed her a swift glance over his shoulder, obviously pleased that once again she had a word to go with his. But, right away, he was obliged to return his attention to the bird, which had come rushing forward almost to the place where they stood. Christina was sure that it was about to receive a spear in its breast, but the young Aborigine simply set about chasing it off with a funny, rushing charge, so like that of the bird itself she burst out laughing. Hearing her, the boy laughed too and at once exaggerated his comical actions for her amusement. Back and forth went the ridiculous dance, while the laughter of the two children echoed and re-echoed through the bush. Finally, the bird, as though in disgust at the mimicry of its antics, shook its feathers and stalked haughtily off into the undergrowth. Still laughing, the boy came back to the mound and began scratching away at the mulch and leaves on the top, then, suddenly, gave a loud shout and held up an egg.

Wide-eyed with astonishment Christina stared at it. For heaven's sake, this pile of rubbish was the bird's nest. No wonder it had been so angry.

When four of the eggs lay side by side on top of the mound the boy marched over and took Christina's hat from her head. Turning it upside down, he carefully arranged the eggs and some dry leaves in the crown. Realising that this was to be her share of the spoils, Christina smiled her thanks, pulled the side brims together and took a firm grip, pushing aside the thought that her mother wouldn't be at all pleased to see the hat she had bought in Beenleigh only last week treated in such a manner.

Before leaving the mound, the young Aborigine carefully rearranged the disturbed leaves. The eggs he would take for himself would wait there until he returned after delivering his charge. If he was again obliged to do battle with the old man wargun, that might just be too bad for the stupid bird. Perhaps he would kill it in any case; .there would be much fine meat beneath those feathers. But, even as the idea came, he was shaking his head, rejecting it. There was no need to kill it, not this time. Didn't he already have the barra and kappolla? Hadn't the river been kind to them earlier this morning, letting them fill a basket from its bounty? Hadn't they caught many pillin at yesterday's sunset? He laughed softly, flicking his arm as he recalled how they had flung their boomerangs into the air so that they resembled large birds in the fading light, his eyes shining as they saw again the flashing colours as the parrots flying up the valley to their roosts in the hills dived in terror, right into the nets they had stretched between the trees? Ah yes, this time their bellies would be well filled while they stayed here. Another time it may not be so, and then he would come for the old man wargun, perhaps one of his women as well.

The boy heard the calling some moments before Christina did. Adopting a peculiar stance on one leg with the foot of the other planted against his knee and his head to one side, he was very still, listening intently. When he straightened, a wide smile spread across his face and he murmured softly, "Chrussina … Chrussina."

Christina stopped in her tracks, staring wide-eyed at the dark smiling face. He was trying to say her name, but how could he know it?

He laughed out loud at her puzzled expression, his head thrown back, his eyes dancing, and in a teasing chant repeated, "Chrussina … Chrussina … Chrussina." Then, while Christina still stared, open-mouthed, he darted forward, beckoning to her to follow quickly. Taking a firmer grip on her hat, she hurried as best she could, a small worried frown creasing her forehead. Surely he wasn't expecting her to run. For one thing, she would never be able to keep up with him, and, for another, if the eggs should bounce about and break, there would be an awful mess in her hat. She came to an abrupt halt, lifting her head to listen. Someone was calling her name...

The boy came back, catching her arm and pulling her forward. Then he pushed her ahead of him and pointed to a track.

"Christina! Christina!" There it was again. And it was her father's voice calling her. Oh yes, it was. It was. She began to run, no longer caring about what might happen to her hat. "I'm here, Father. I'm here!" she called as loudly as she could. Right away a joyful shout came back, he had heard her.

"It's my father," she called excitedly over her shoulder, sure that the boy would understand. But the boy was no longer there. Christina stopped and turned completely around, her face reflecting her disbelief. He couldn't be gone just like that. He had to be here somewhere. Why, she hadn't even had a chance to thank him. "Where are you?" she called out. "Come back. Please come back." But there was only her father's voice, very close now, and the twittering of the birds. The black boy had vanished even more thoroughly than the wallaby she had followed into the bush, with not even a stirring of bushes or rustling of leaves to tell which way he had gone.

Her father scooped her into his arms, rocking her to and fro. "Oh, thank God. Thank God."

Christina saw that there were tears on his face and remorse stung her. How worried he must have been, and it was all her fault. She slipped her free arm around his neck. "I'm sorry I came into the bush. I know you told me that I was never to do so, but I followed a little wallaby. I didn't mean to go far, and I would have come back long ago, only I couldn't find the way." The words had come in a rush and ended more than a little tearfully.

"It's alright … it's alright." Simon hugged her to him, speaking huskily. "I've found you now and you haven't been harmed, that's the important thing."

"Will Mother be very angry with me?"

"She'll be too relieved to see you alive and well to have any room left for anger." Simon grinned as he set his daughter down on her feet and noticed for the first time the state she was in. "Though I'm sure I don't know what she is going to say about your appearance. I don't believe I have ever seen a little girl so dirty and dishevelled. And what on earth have you got in your hat?"

"Turkey eggs … well, that's what I think they are." Christina spread the hat brim so that he could look into the crown, breathing a quick sigh of relief when she saw that all four eggs were still intact.

"Where on earth did you get those?"

"They were in a funny sort of nest, a big mound made out of all kinds of rubbish, and the black boy got them out for me."

Simon started, the smile leaving his face. "What black boy?"

"The one who brought me back."

Bending down in front of her, Simon gripped her shoulders. "Christina, what are you saying? A black boy brought you back? What black boy? Where is he? And where were you?"

"I was at the river, Father. When I got lost I didn't know which way to go. I was just walking and walking, and then I heard some people laughing … "

"Who was laughing?"

"The black people who were swimming in the river." Christina wriggled her shoulders against the increasing pressure of her father's hands, grimacing as she did so. At once he eased his grip, letting his hands slide more gently on to her arms, but asking urgently, "What happened at the river, Christina?"

"When I saw them I was going to run back through the cane the way I had come, but the black boy was behind me. I think he must have followed me through the bush." She saw the horrified look that twisted her father's face and went on quickly, "He didn't hurt me, Father. I thought he was going to when I first saw him; he had a spear and he had killed a possum. But he was very kind, he gave me a drink of water, and then he showed me the way back here."

"And those in the river didn't see you?"

"Oh yes. The boy took me over to the bank and spoke to them. I think they were his family. Two of the men came up on the bank to look at me and one of them could have been his father."

"What do you mean they came up on the bank to look at you?"

"I think they just wanted to make sure that I was on my own and that the boy wasn't in any danger."

"What did they do?"

"They talked to the boy mainly. One of them asked me some things but I didn't know what he said, so I couldn't answer."

Simon groaned. "Oh Christina, do you realise what grave danger you might have been in? You know that you can't ever be sure with the blacks."

"But they didn't hurt me, Father, and if the boy hadn't shown me the way back I would have still been lost in the bush."

"He brought you all the way from the river?"

"Yes, he did. And he was still with me when we heard you calling, but then he pointed out the track I should follow and disappeared." Sudden tears blurred her vision. "I didn't even have a chance to thank him, and I did want to."

Her father stroked her hair gently as he gazed thoughtfully back the way she had come. "I know, I would like to thank him also. He may very well have saved your life bringing you back like that." He shook his head, slowly, incredulously. "I can hardly believe that you wandered so far."

Feeling her tears overflow, Christina wiped a grimy hand over her equally grimy face, wincing when her fingers touched a long scratch on one cheek. "Do you suppose that he knows?"

"That we would like to thank him? I'm sure he does. He may even be still watching us."

Christina spun around, her eyes searching the shadows. "Where would he be?"

"Even if he is there, we won't be able to see him."

"Why? Why won't we?"

"Because he doesn't want us to, that's why. And now, little grub, it's high time we were on our way out of this bush."

Although her whole body ached with weariness, sleep eluded Christina. Bathed and with her numerous scratches smeared with ointment, she lay on her narrow bed and stared out through the open tent flap to the glimmering line of embers that was all that remained of the log her father had dragged on to the fire at sunset. From close by, a long, mournful howl rose and hung on the still night air, and, soon afterwards, in the glow from the embers, she saw a shadowy form slink past. Perhaps, the thought, it was the very same dingo that had snarled at her in the bush. No wonder she couldn't get to sleep with such terrifying things to remember.

A restless stirring on one of the other stretchers brought a sigh to her lips. Her mother wasn't asleep either. Several times now she'd heard the squeaking of the canvas as she tossed and turned. She was still worrying more than likely. Yes, of course she would be. Even though she was now safe and sound in her own bed, her mother would still be fretting about what might have happened to her or that something like that could happen again. How terrible it must have been for her having to wait all that time to know that she hadn't been harmed. How white her face had been when she'd come running to meet them. Then whiter still when she'd learned about the black people.

Rolling on to her side, Christina thumped at her pillow with a small fist. Why had the boy run away like that? If only her mother could have seen him, she would have known that her life had never been in danger, not from the black people. Not from anything once the boy was with her. Hadn't he killed that fearsome looking creature? Hadn't the dingo known to stay hidden when he'd brought her back through the bush? Hadn't he just laughed at the ferocious attacks of the angry turkey? Stifling a sudden giggle, Christina snuggled deeper into her mattress. How funny that had been. The funniest dance she was ever likely to see. What was the name he had given the big bird again? Wargun ... yes that was it. And the koala was dumbripi, she remembered that one too.

The sun had long since begun its journey across the heavens when Christina woke. She stretched lazily, but then, seeing that hers was the only bed still occupied, sat up and swung her legs to the ground. Peeling off her nightgown, she began a hurried dressing, inspecting the scratches on her arms and legs as she pulled on her undergarments. Some of them hurt still and she winced as her clothes rubbed against them. But the blood had dried and, although it had left lines that were rough beneath her exploring fingertips, she decided they were a vast improvement on the angry-looking welts she had gone to bed with. It won't take long for them to disappear, she told herself, probably not more than a few days. Why, even the one on her face that had so dismayed her mother was no longer stinging.

"So, you are awake at last? We were beginning to think that you were planning on sleeping all day."

Christina turned around quickly. Her mother was coming into the tent, the ribbons of her wide-brimmed hat tied securely under her chin, her eyebrows raised enquiringly. "How are you feeling?"

"I feel fine, Mother. My legs aren't aching any more, they just feel a bit stiff. And my scratches have already started to get better."

"Let me see." Elsie lifted her daughter's chin with her fingertips, turning her right cheek towards the light flooding into the tent. "Mmmm... that one hasn't become infected, thank goodness. It should heal without leaving a scar, if you take care not to do anything to irritate it, that is." She reached for a large jar resting on an upturned packing case. "We'll give them all another good smearing with ointment. And then how about some breakfast? You must be hungry?"

"I'm starving. What time is it?"

"It's past nine o'clock,"

"My goodness, what a time to be getting up."

"You had a very exhausting day, you needed a good sleep."

Christina watched her mother's face as she concentrated on smearing the ointment on to her scratches. It looked drawn and tired. Perhaps, she thought unhappily, she didn't go to sleep at all. Perhaps she was awake all through the night and worrying the whole time. "I'm sorry I caused you so much worry."

Elsie nodded her head slowly. "I know you are, Christina, and I'm not going to be telling you that you have no need to be. You caused both your father and me a great deal of anguish." She glanced up suddenly, her eyes seeking and holding her daughter's. "Don't you go thinking, even for a moment, that there was no cause for us to be worrying, that your life wasn't in any danger. It was. If not from the blacks you met, then from snakes and other creatures, and simply from being lost. You have heard more than one story about people, adults as well as children, being lost in the Australian bush and never found."

Christina squirmed uneasily, rebuked by the stern ring to her mother's voice. "I won't go into the bush on my own again, not ever."

Elsie's expression softened, and, returning the jar of ointment to the makeshift bench, she caught her daughter's hands in hers, squeezing gently. "This isn't Haderslev, you know, love? This is a land not even fully explored yet, and we are living on a few cleared acres surrounded by dense bush, by an unknown wilderness, you might say."

But not to the black people, Christina thought. It's not an unknown wilderness to them, not when even their children can find their way through it with no trouble at all. And they certainly aren't afraid of whatever dangers might be lurking there, the boy had shown her that. A sudden troubling thought brought a quick frown to her brow. "Will all the bush be cleared away one day?"

"I shouldn't think so and certainly not in our lifetime." Elsie smiled as she took a brush to her daughter's tangled curls. "But I am sure that we will see vast changes. For one thing, there will undoubtedly be a great increase in the number and size of settled areas, especially in valleys like this which are good for farming."

As it so often did, her mother's vigorous brushing brought tears to Christina's eyes. This time, though, there was no 'ouch' of protest. Something more bothersome than the tugging at her scalp held her thoughts. "But, if white people claim all the land and clear all the bush from the valley, where will the black people live?"

"They will go somewhere else, I suppose, those who still want to remain in the bush and be apart from us white people. After all, as you have heard your father say many times, this is a very big country."

"But what if they don't want to go somewhere else?"

"You have to remember that they are a wandering race of people."

"But they have special places and they come back to them after they have been somewhere else. I heard Mr Hunter telling Father that. He said that sometimes they even leave their tools and fishing nets for when they return, that, even though they wander about, they still have their own special districts."

Elsie gave a faint sigh. "Mr Hunter is obviously a knowledgeable man where the Aborigines are concerned, but the fact remains that they don't remain long enough in one place to plant and grow things. They simply don't use the land the way white people do."

"They might learn to do so."

"Yes, they might, now that examples are being set for them. That would probably be a good thing ... after all, there is plenty of land to go around. They could even take up jobs and live as we do." Elsie sighed again as she began twisting her daughter's hair into a thick plait. "If only they would do that, it might well solve the whole problem."

The boy would never do that, Christina told herself. He was happy in the bush, and he was proud of who he was. He wouldn't be wanting to forsake the ways of black people for those of white people. "I don't think the ones I saw would like to live the way we do."

Elsie moved her shoulders in a faint shrug. "That's up to them, of course, but they must surely realise that it's going to become more and more difficult for them to go on living in the old way." She tied a blue ribbon around the end of the completed plait. "There, now you are presentable once again." But when Christina turned her scratched face to look up at her, she smiled ruefully. "Well, as presentable as you can hope to be for a while."

"I won't look in the mirror and then I won't know how awful I look."

"That might be a good idea, but now I have something important to tell you."

"Oh, what is it?"

"You are to go to school."

Christina's eyes widened, dancing with sudden excitement. "Really and truly?"

"Yes, really and truly. Your father and I talked about it this morning, and we agreed that, even though there are a number of problems to be overcome, it would be a good idea. We certainly don't have the time to teach you and, besides, you should have the opportunity to make friends with other children."

"When can I go?"

"Don't be getting too excited just yet. It's not going to happen until the new year. First, we must get you a suitable pony, which you will have to learn to ride properly. Also, we will have to speak with the schoolmaster and some of the other settlers who live out this way. We should be able to arrange for you to ride into Beenleigh with their children."

"My very own pony. Oh, I can hardly wait. I think I must be dreaming."

An amused smile touched her mother's mouth. "I'm afraid you'll soon learn that it's no dream, Christina. You'll need to do a lot of work on your written English in these coming weeks. It's been sadly neglected since we left the ship and we can't have you starting school unable to write the language in which you are to be taught. I'm sure I don't know what Mrs. Klaussen would say about such a state of affairs after all the trouble she took with you."

Christina's smile wavered. Mrs Klaussen would be disappointed in her, there was little enough doubt about that. Even though she spoke English almost all the time now, she hardly ever wrote any. On the two or three occasions when she had tried to do so, she'd had so much trouble trying to decide how to spell the words, she'd quickly reverted to Danish. Her smile recovered and sudden resolve shone from her bright blue eyes. "I've still got all the notes and papers Mrs. Klaussen gave me. I'll get them out right away and I'll practise writing English every day."

"After you've had some breakfast will be time enough to begin," her mother told her, but Christina was already on her knees tugging the wicker port that held her most precious bits and pieces out from under her stretcher. "They are in here, I know."

They were, pages and pages covered with Mrs Klaussen's fine, sloping handwriting, all tied in neat bundles. And with them, bringing a soft gasp to her lips, a painting Lars Ohlssen had done of their house in Haderslev and given to her on the day they'd left. Christina sat back on her heels, holding it with both hands, feeling her throat constrict as a wave of nostalgia washed over her.

"Ah, Lars's painting," Elsie exclaimed. "I was wondering only the other day what had become of it."

She studied the painting over her daughter's shoulder. "What a gift he has. It's such a pity he hasn't been able to go to an art school."

"I should have it out somewhere so that we can see it all the time."

"When our house is built, you'll be able to do that. For now, I think it's best left where you had it. There's just no place in the tent for paintings or such like to be displayed."

Christina didn't need to look around her to know the truth of that. They could barely move in the tent without tripping over something or other, and everything serving as a bench or tabletop was crowded with their everyday requirements. "I'll keep it out for just a little while … oh, how far away it seems."

"It is far away, Christina … very, very far away."

12

As Christina's scars faded, so did the anxieties her experience had brought to her parents. The lesson had been learned, they told themselves and each other; their daughter wasn't likely to go wandering off into the bush again. Also, according to Mr Hunter, the blacks she had encountered were not likely to be a problem, since they had probably been just passing through the district, using as their route the thickly-treed, but relatively undergrowth-free, ridge between the Logan and Albert Rivers. So, although they toiled with blistered hands and aching backs from the first light of day until the very last, and although their hearts sometimes ached unbearably for another land and the sight of other loved faces, Simon and Elsie were content with their lot. All the assurance they needed that they'd been right to come to this country, to this valley, was here for the glancing: on every side the acres they had claimed for their own either smiled in their newly-encouraged productivity, or waited, jungle-covered but beaming promise, to be cleared and ploughed.

The brief flying storms of spring and early summer had regularly drenched the valley before vanishing out to sea and leaving the warm sunshine to resume the responsibility of coaxing and nourishing. As a result, the crops and vegetables planted by the Skovs had flourished. By the time December came round, the first of their potato plants were a healthy eighteen inches high; the pumpkin vines had run riot along the entire eastern boundary of the cleared acreage, flaunting their large yellow flowers as they climbed heedlessly over stumps and piles of felled trees in their eagerness to spread; the first planting of corn stood tall and straight, the young cobs thickening with every passing day; the second planting was growing even more rapidly. In the garden area at the rear of the tent, tomatoes, beans, turnips and carrots thrived, already contributing to the larder, while the banana suckers acquired on their way to the valley had grown into frond-waving trees. The hens continued to lay well, and, in the paddock bordering the creek, the animals grazed contentedly – four cows now and three horses. As an early Christmas present, Christina had acquired a small chestnut mare with a white star-like blob on her forehead, and consequently named Star.

The four-roomed house with detached kitchen for which Simon had carefully drawn up plans had, however, failed to earn for itself a high priority and was still waiting to be started. This was a quite major disappointment, since they had wearied of living in a tent, especially when the storms came and threatened to tear it from its moorings. Still, with everything else going so well and only four months gone by since their arrival, there was much to be thankful for. But, as so many of those who had come before the Skovs knew only too well, this was a land as demanding as it was bountiful, as cruel as it was beautiful. Here, very few dreams came to fruition without setbacks of one kind or another; disappointments and heartache were as much a part of the price to be paid as the never-ending toil. Although there was nothing to warn them when they retired to bed on the night of 12 December, the Skov family were about to learn for themselves how very true this was.

The sulphur-crested cockatoos, induced by some instinct to leave the western plains for the coastal regions, flew out of the trees on the mountain ridges in the early morning. At first, they came in twos and threes, the brilliant white of their feathers taking on a golden sheen as they entered the piercing rays of the rising sun, losing it again as they swooped down along the still-shadowed hillsides. Then, as the sun appeared above the horizon, the small groups became large groups, and these followed each other more and more closely until there soared across the sky a seemingly endless stream – a fast moving cloud of beautiful white birds, whose bright yellow crests matched exactly the under-feathers of their wings and tails.

Shocked into wakefulness by her father's urgent shouting, Christina tumbled from her bed and rushed out of the tent. Once outside, she stood wide-eyed with a mingling of disbelief and astonishment. Her mother and father were both running for all they were worth, her father with a gun in his hand, her mother waving, of all things, a broom! Oh, what were they doing, for heaven's sake? In the next instant, the sun spilled its brilliance over the treetops and into the clearing and her question was answered. It was there before her – the most beautiful and, at the same time, the most terrible scene she had ever gazed upon. The cornfield had been transformed into a fluttering daisy field, but from one end to the other sharp hooked beaks were ripping the husks from the tender young corn, while the tall stalks bent to the ground under the great weight that had descended upon them.

With her nightgown flapping about her legs and her bare feet flying over the ground, Christina yelled as her parents were doing. "Shoo! Shoo! Off with you! Shoo! Shoo!" The harsh sound of the gun being fired brought her to an abrupt halt. Surely her father wasn't going to shoot the birds? No, of course he wasn't. He would be just firing into the air to frighten them away from the cornfield.

The cockatoos had risen, a vast screeching umbrella, but, within the space of seconds, they were back on the corn, their feasting resumed. There was a second blast from the gun, and Christina, closer to her parents now, choked on a horrified gasp, for she had seen what gun her father held in his hands, his shotgun, double-barrelled. Once again the birds rose only briefly. Not until the gun had been fired several times did they finally rise and drift reluctantly away. Christina then saw what her wildly-beating heart had told her she would see – dozens of the birds hadn't been able to fly away. Many, mercifully, were dead, but others fluttered about piteously as they tried to rise on shattered wings, their feathers stained with blood. Oh, father, how could you? But the voice that cried in anguished protest within her was hushed the moment she turned, wide-eyed with incredulity and accusation, to look at her parents.

They were both staring blankly at the torn and ravaged mess that, only an hour previously, had been a neat, thriving cornfield. And they were so still it seemed that they had been drained of both thought and emotion. As though they waited to awaken from a nightmare, Christina thought, feeling the tightness in her throat swell into a lump she couldn't swallow. But this was no bad dream. It had happened, it was all real. Stinging tears blurred her vision and she closed her eyes tightly, not only to blink them back, but also to shut out all the things she didn't want to see – the dead and wounded birds, the ruined corn, the distraught faces of her mother and father.

Her mother turned as she approached, shaking her head sorrowfully, but her father continued to stare at the cornfield of which he had been so proud. "Have they destroyed it all, Father?" she asked quietly.

For a moment or two he didn't answer and Christina began to think that he hadn't heard her. Then, with his bleak gaze still on the devastation, he muttered grimly, "I fear there will be little that we can salvage."

Christina smothered a deep sigh and had to struggle to keep the tears from again flooding her eyes. She thought of how hard her father had worked, her mother often at his side: ploughing the hard earth, dragging away the heavy rocks and tree stumps, prising up stubborn roots with shovel and pick, planting the seeds, clearing away the weeds that grew so profusely. She remembered how happy they had been when the first small green shoots made their appearance and the rain clouds gathered about the ranges before sweeping down over the valley, and a new dismay washed over her. Was this the end of her father's dream, of all the plans he'd had for a farm of his own? "What will we do now, Father?" she asked anxiously.

"What will we do?" Simon repeated the question absently, as though he, too, were asking it. But, when he looked down into the small worried face of his daughter, a faint smile of reassurance came to his lips. "Why, we'll plant more corn, of course. That's what we'll do, love."

Christina was not about to be so easily reassured. "Won't the cockatoos come back again?"

Simon shrugged, indicating an unconcern he was far from feeling. "I suppose they might, but we'll be ready for them next time. There must be something we can do to outsmart them. A few scarecrows might be a good idea. Do you think you'd be able to make one?"

"Oh yes, I'm sure I ..." Christina's voice trailed away and, as her parents were doing, she lifted her head, listening.

From the direction of the track leading to their farm, there came the steady beat of hooves, quickly growing louder. And they were soon able to hear, also, the jangle of bits and the straining squeak of saddle leather as two riders burst out of the trees. They came at a gallop, drawing rein only when they came to the gate, where they dismounted and walked their horses through to where they joined the Skov family in staring wordlessly at the heart-breaking waste spread before them.

The men were Herman Schmidt and his eldest son Wilfred, members of a German family which had migrated to Queensland in 1865. They were also the Skovs' closest neighbours. Like others of their nationality fleeing Bismarck's Germany, the Schmidt family had arrived in their new country with little money and very few possessions. In their hearts, though, there had been courage, determination and a fierce conviction that deprivation and back-breaking toil was a small enough price to pay for freedom and the chance to build a better life for themselves than the one they'd left behind. The price had been extracted in full measure. Hardship and hard work had begun on the day of their arrival and continued through the years.

Not only had there been the need to clear the jungle from the land they would farm, build a modest home, turn the soil and hastily plant their sustenance crops, but also, since there was, at the time, no store or township in the Logan valley and only irregular visits by paddle steamers bringing supplies, the ordeal to be endured in obtaining provisions. Owning neither bullock nor horse and being too poor to pay others for transport, Herman Schmidt, like a number of other German newcomers, had no alternative but to tramp the long, lonely scrub track to Brisbane and back, pushing his wheelbarrow.

Improvements in their lot had come slowly to the German settlers in the Logan and Albert River valleys, but they had come, and for that, being staunch Lutherans with no illusions and asking no miracles, they were thankful. Respect had come their way as well. Though often considered grim-faced and joyless, they were admired throughout the district for their relentless industry, their cleanliness, their hard acceptance of life and the blows it dealt them, and for the fact that they never begged for credit; what German families didn't have the cash to pay for, they went without. Fine colonists they had certainly proved to be, justifying the claims the pastors of the German Missionary Station at Brisbane had made to the Government of the newly separated Colony: "Give us the land and we will bring to it industrious families of integrity."

The recent arrival of the Skov family, so relatively well-equipped, had brought a wry smile to the face of Herman Schmidt, but there had been no envy in him. Even had he not held such feelings to be sinful, this would still have been the case. For one thing, how could he, a man with four sons, be envious of a man with none? For another, Simon Skov was just beginning his farm and, whereas a respectable amount of equipment might soften the blows to some extent, it wouldn't stop them from coming. Until such time as the lessons were learned and the inevitability of the setbacks accepted, this new settler would reel and despair just as he himself had done.

So Herman Schmidt, a big man with a thick beard and bushy eyebrows, turned eyes warm with sympathy on his new neighbour. "We heard the shooting and thought that perhaps you were having trouble with the blacks. Instead, cockatoos! Wretched, destructive creatures!" He threw out his arms in an angry, disgusted gesture. "If it weren't for the cost of the lead, I'd be shooting every one I saw."

"There must have been hundreds," Simon told him dully. "I had no idea they were here in such numbers."

"They aren't as a rule, not in these parts. They are always a pest, of course, but, for some reason, every few years they come across from the west in vast flocks, hungry as can be and as bad as a plague of locusts where the corn is concerned. They got to my first crop." He smiled grimly. "In actual fact, it was my second planting, the bandicoots claimed my first before it was anywhere near the cob-producing stage."

"What did you do, after the cockatoos?" Simon asked, shaking his shoulders as though to physically rid himself of the numbness that gripped him.

"Cleared the whole mess away and planted again," the big German replied in his deep, guttural voice. "Of course I raged and carried on for a time; useless, wasteful emotions we can well do without. Believe me,

Mr Skov, there's never time in this country to sit be-moaning the setbacks. The only thing to do is to strike right back."

"I was thinking that I might be able to save some small sections," Simon suggested uncertainly.

"Don't try it, man. In the first place, it would be too time-consuming. In the second, what you did manage to save would not only fail to justify your efforts, it would also make for awkward handling of the field in the weeks to come. No, get it cleared and replanted as soon as you can. You'll find that, in the long run, it was the best thing you could have done." Herman Schmidt half-raised a hand to indicate his tall, wiry-looking son. "Wilfred here can give you a couple of days, beginning tomorrow if that suits you."

Simon stared at him, finding it hard to believe what he had just heard. Thrusting his hands into his trouser pockets to hide the clenching of his fists against the rush of emotion that threatened to overwhelm him, he said huskily, "I couldn't let him do that."

"Of course you could," he was told in a voice that brooked no argument. "You need help right now, and Wilfred will be only too pleased to give it to you."

"That's right, Mr Skov," Wilfred said at once, a grin coming to his youthful, clean-shaven face. "Between you and me, we'll have that field cleared and replanted in no time at all."

"You can start being helpful right now," his father told him. "There are a number of birds over there needing to have their necks wrung."

Christina shivered, her eyes drawn against her will to the cockatoos still struggling, despite shattered wings and legs, to rise from the ground. Something had to be done for them, she knew that only too well. But wring their necks? That would be just horrible.

Seeing her distress, Herman Schmidt said gruffly, "There's no point in letting them suffer needlessly, little one, and you may be sure that Wilfred will put them out of their misery quickly and cleanly, there's no cruelty in the lad."

In spite of the sick feeling in her stomach, Christina's eyes met his steadily, and she nodded.

"There's a sensible girl." The big man patted her head before turning to her mother. "Be of good heart, Mrs Skov. It's a terrible disappointment, I know. But these things happen and, when they do, we have no option but to accept them along with all the good things this country has to offer."

Elsie sighed heavily. "It's just that it's all been so unexpected, such a shock, coming the way it did when everything seemed to be going along so well for us. My husband and I do appreciate your kindness."

"It's little enough that we do."

Elsie half-turned, preparing to usher Christina back to the tent, but Herman Schmidt had something more to say, "I have been meaning to speak to you about coming to church, Mrs Skov. You are of the Lutheran faith, are you not?"

"Yes, we are, Mr Schmidt." The words came slowly, spoken carefully.

"I know, of course, how busy you have been, but I hope that you, along with your husband and daughter, will soon see your way clear to attending Sunday services. They are conducted for the most part in English and you would all be made most welcome."

"I'm sure we would be, and perhaps we will be able to come, soon."

"I certainly hope so. Our new church is nearing completion, as you have no doubt seen."

Elsie nodded. "Yes, we have seen how well it is progressing."

"A few more weeks should do it. We are all sorry, naturally, that we won't be able to take the time to finish it for Christmas. Still, the old church has served us well, especially when you consider that it was hurriedly built and meant to serve only temporarily. So perhaps it's fitting that we should hold our Christmas services there this one last time." He smiled, but his dark eyes on Elsie's face were serious and quietly searching. "If not before, may we look forward to seeing you and your family on that special day, Mrs Skov?"

For a moment or two, Elsie made no reply, and there was a vague, remote look in her eyes, an inwards look that seemed to be seeing again something that had happened in another time. Then she smothered a sigh and said quietly, "Yes, you may, Mr Schmidt."

Christina barely managed to check the gasp that rushed to her lips. Did her mother really mean that they were to start going to church again? Christmas Day, that was all she had actually promised. But might that not be a beginning, with other times to follow? Oh, she hoped so. Not because she especially wanted to go to church, but because it would mean that her mother was no longer angry at God, that she had forgiven Him for taking little Anna from them. If that could be, of course, forgiving God? Well, perhaps it wasn't really forgiving, it didn't seem like the right word somehow. After all, it was God who forgave people, not people who forgave God. Still, what did it matter who did the forgiving or whatever else it was; the important thing was that her mother and God would be friends again.

"Will we really be going to church on Christmas Day?" she asked as she made her way back to the tent at her mother's side."

"Didn't you hear me tell Mr. Schmidt that we would be?"

Christina nodded, releasing the breath she'd been holding in a small sigh of relief. Even though there had been no real enthusiasm in her mother's voice, she hadn't changed her mind. "That will be nice, won't it? I'm glad Mr Schmidt asked us."

"Mr Schmidt is a good man. He does what is expected of him."

"Is he a Prussian?"

"No, Mr. Schmidt is not a Prussian."

Christina swallowed, the abruptness of the reply and the sharpness of her mother's glance reminding her all too clearly that she was not supposed to concern herself, let alone others, with such matters. The Prussians who came to Queensland were settlers just the same as everyone else, with just as much right to be here. What they had been or done before was of no account; it was what they were doing now that mattered. Recalling the familiar words brought a sigh to Christina's lips. She ought to know them, she told herself, she had heard them enough times, and, in a way, she understood. It was just that there was something that always puzzled her. Accepting the Prussians as fellow settlers was one thing, but both her mother and father talked as though they had never been their enemies, as though they had never marched into their country and claimed it as their own. How could they do that? Especially her mother, who had lived in Schleswig all her life and whose own brother had been killed by Prussian soldiers? Did she really put such things out of her mind completely? Was it possible to do that? Again Christina sighed. She herself couldn't do it, no matter how hard she tried to see things the way she was supposed to. Prussians were Prussians, whether they were in Europe or here in Australia.

"This day hasn't had a very happy beginning, Christina," Elsie said gently as they neared the tent. "But we will recover from this setback. After all, it's the first serious one we've had and it appears that we've been fortunate in that respect."

"We haven't had the bandicoots like Mr. Schmidt did."

"No, we haven't, only the cockatoos." She heaved a deep sigh. "Such magnificent birds to have done so much damage."

Christina nodded, not trusting herself to speak about them. Would she ever be able to forget the sight of all those birds lying dead or struggling so desperately to rise and fly away? And, even though she had kept her head averted, in her mind she had seen with a burning clarity what was happening when Mr. Schmidt's son went into the cornfield.

Her mother interrupted her thoughts almost as though she had read them. "I know how sad you must be feeling about the cockatoos, Christina, but you must understand that your father had no wish to shoot them, he simply had no other choice."

"I do understand that, Mother."

Elsie nodded, sighing again. "It was a most disagreeable thing that he was obliged to do, something quite contrary to his nature. I fear, however, that it won't be the last time we find ourselves in such a situation. This is by no means a gentle country; it seems to demand that we must sometimes harden our hearts, and learn to live with things the way they are. It would be sheer folly to try to do otherwise."

George Hunter appeared two days later, having heard about the cockatoos and their destruction of the Skovs' cornfield. Dismayed at what he saw, he was quick to reassure Simon that the Government would take into account such setbacks when calculating the value of improvements. There was something else he also wanted to talk to him about and this, he told himself, might be a good time … then Simon gave him just the opportunity he'd been waiting for.

"It's all the time that's been wasted," he groaned. "If I'd started on the house instead of spending all my time on the land, I would at least have something to show for it."

"Perhaps, now that you've had this setback, it might be a good idea to have someone build the house for you?' George Hunter suggested carefully. "The men who built the school are still working in the district, they could be interested."

Simon chewed thoughtfully on his lower lip. "I don't know, I'd always planned on building my own house."

"Well, you could help with the finishing off of the place, windows, doors and such like. Then there's the furniture, you could get on with making that."

"They'd be using milled timber, I suppose?"

"Yes, and tin for the roof, much more reliable than bark, believe me."

Simon returned the Land Officer's smile, but only briefly. "I don't have much capital left … "

"Talk to the Bank, Simon. They'll probably come up with an arrangement that puts you in a better position than you'd be in if you took time off from the farm to build the house yourself."

"I'll think about it."

George Hunter had brought their mail from the Beenleigh post office, and there was a letter for Christina addressed to Miss Christina Skov, Care of Post Office, Logan Valley, Queensland.

"It's from Henry," she cried delightedly, dancing about with the letter in her hand. "Oh, I know it is. I know it is."

"Then how about you open it," Simon suggested. "We'd all like to hear how that family is faring."

"Oh, I will! I will! It's just that I'm so excited I'm having trouble getting the envelope open."

There were three pages covered with firm, neat writing and Christina read them out loud, slowly and carefully …

Dear Christina,

I suppose you have been thinking that I had forgotten my promise to write to you. The truth is that we have all been so busy since leaving Brisbane the time has just disappeared, but I'm sure you know all about that as your family would have been busy also. I hope that you are all fit and well and that you like your new home. We are all well and are pleased that we came to Mackay. It's a nice area and very good for sugarcane. In fact, everyone says that this will be the biggest sugar-producing area in the whole of Queensland. At present, we have six hundred acres on the Pioneer River, but Father is hoping to acquire more land before too long. We have some Kanakas to help us but there is still a lot of work that we must do ourselves … jolly hard work it is, too.

We have had some concerns. The blacks around here are still troublesome and there have been a number of raids on outlying farms. Not on ours, as yet, but we have all learned how to handle a gun, even Mother. Do you remember how we talked about that on the 'Friedeburg' and you said that you would never be able to shoot a black? Well, I think you would change your mind if you knew of some of the terrible things they have done up in these regions. I know that I won't be hesitating to shoot if they come near our place.

Our house is not large, but it is sturdy and fairly comfortable. It was here when we arrived, having been built by the man from whom Father bought most of our land. He gave up cane farming to go looking for gold somewhere in the north. Father says the fellow can't see beyond his own nose, because the real gold in the Colony is sugar. I hope he is right about that.

Do you go to school, Christina? I don't, because there is no school anywhere near where we live. Father is teaching Rolf and me at home. He is quite strict and gives us lots of lessons to do every night, no matter how hard we have worked in the fields during the day.

Rolf is always complaining. He says he doesn't see why cane farmers need to know all the things Father insists we learn. I must admit that I agree about that and sometimes also complain.

Mother and Father wish to be remembered to your parents and I send you my best regards. Also, we wish you all a very happy Christmas and a wonderful New Year in your new home.

From your friend, Henry Schneider

P.S. I will be waiting to hear from you.

P.P.S. Did you ever believe there could be such hot weather?

"No, we never did believe there could be such hot weather," Simon declared as he wiped perspiration from his brow. "That's a fine letter, Christina. You'll have to look to your laurels when you write back, no sloppy writing or careless spelling."

Christina smiled too, but ruefully, as she refolded the pages. "I don't think I could write a letter like this, no matter how hard I tried."

"Well, you can think about what you want to say and I'll help you put it to paper."

"Oh, thank you, Father. I was hoping you would say that."

"Christina should write the letter herself," Elsie interrupted brusquely. "It will be good practice for her, having to think about how the words should be spelt instead of just writing down the first thing that comes into her head, especially if she is to go to school next year."

"She is going to write the letter," Simon told her quietly. "I'll just give her a bit of a hand."

His smile had disappeared and Christina saw his eyes go a little unhappily to her mother's face. Shifting her own gaze, she caught her breath on a pang of remorse. How could she have been so thoughtless? So happy with her own letter she had forgotten that her mother had been hoping to receive some mail from Schleswig? A week or so back, someone had told her that the clipper ships often carried the mail from Europe to Australia, covering the distance in a good deal less time than the Friedeburg had taken, and, ever since, she had been watching for letters. How disappointed she must have been. Must still be, for now, with only a little over a week to go, there would be no letter from Schleswig before Christmas. She should, she thought, say something, let her mother know she understood how she felt. But her head was once again bent over the dough she had been kneading, her face so set and expressionless it seemed to warn that tender words would be an intrusion, an unwelcome intrusion.

Christina saw that her father, too, felt the need to say something but hesitated to do so, for his brow was wrinkled and there was a pitying, frustrated look in his eyes. "Well," he finally said, clearing his throat, and glancing at his own mail, "It seems the Government has some more forms for us to fill in, or maybe they are sending us a Christmas card."

On Christmas Eve Simon loitered outside the tent, the sound of hushed voices bringing a smile to his lips. His wife and daughter were decorating a small pine tree, and, any minute now, he would be summoned inside to see the splendour they had created. And he would, of course, be both delighted and surprised, even though he was well aware that treasured ornaments from other Christmas trees had been smuggled into their luggage when they left Haderslev and kept hidden ever since. Well, he mused, tapping the ash from his pipe, at least something about this Christmas will be familiar.

There was little else that was, the very fact of it being Christmas Day serving to magnify everything that was strange. They went to church wearing smiles and their best clothes just as they had done in other years, but they drove their horse and cart over a bumpy track and rutted dirt road lined with trees that had nothing of the rich luxuriant mystery of the oaks, beech and cypresses of their homeland – shimmering box trees with leaves that caught the sunlight like tiny mirrors, iron-barks with their dark hard trunks and clearly defined foliage, grey gums with their trembling leaves of sober green turning first one side and then the other to the sun, their boles so satin-smooth and tall they stood out clearly, dwarfing the acacias and blackwoods beside them. Instead of sleet and snow, there was a golden haze as the sun beat down from a cloudless sky. Soon, they knew, the temperature would climb into the nineties. Rivulets of perspiration would run from their pores and plaster their clothes to their bodies, and, even when the sun went down, there would be little relief – the heat would linger on. There would certainly be no log fires, no chestnuts roasting.

As Herman Schmidt had promised, they were made very welcome by Pastor August Sultmann and the German families gathered at the small church, but they sat in pews with people they hardly knew, and listened to a service read in English by a man with a strong German accent. Christmas Day? It didn't seem that it could possibly be.

A day after Christina's ninth birthday, two carpenters arrived with a wagon loaded with building materials. Due to the bank's stipulations, the house wouldn't be as big as the one Simon had planned, just two bedrooms, a small sitting room, a kitchen large enough to serve also as an eating area and a small verandah. It would be constructed of milled timber, have a tin roof and be two feet off the ground. Simon wasn't too disappointed at the reduced size of his house. He hadn't wanted a large loan, in any case, he told himself, and he could always add a detached kitchen and perhaps another room later on. In the meantime, he would still be contributing to the building of his house; he would be responsible for the doors, windows, and other finishing-off jobs.

Three weeks later, the house was up and the carpenters gone, leaving Simon to continue with the jobs he had claimed for himself.

For Christina, helping him was a treat, not a chore. She handed him the nails and tools he needed, and held pieces of timber in place while he sawed, hammered or rasped away rough edges. And all the while he entertained her. Sometimes he sang songs, insisting that she join in whenever she knew the words. Other times, he told her about his childhood on the farm in Herning, and about his wanderings when he'd been obliged to leave the farm, wanderings that had only come to a halt when he'd met her mother in Haderslev. He related great adventure stories that he had either read or been told. And, to his daughter's delight, he recited poetry in Danish.

"Sorry to be late, father."

Simon grinned as his daughter bounded up the short flight of steps. "Well, did you finish it?"

Christina heaved a deep sigh. "Mother insisted that I do so. She wants me to post it when we go into Beenleigh this afternoon. I don't think Henry will be too impressed, though."

"Of course he will. What a surprise getting a letter from him, eh?'

"Yes, it was. He did say that he would write, but I didn't see how it could be possible for a letter to get to me when we didn't really know where we would be or have a proper address."

"Well, apparently he had faith in the Queensland postal system. It was good to know that his father is apparently happy enough with his decision to go north. He was right, of course. There's good money to be made from growing sugarcane if you can get yourself a big enough piece of ground, and there seems little doubt that the north is the place for it."

"But there's a lot of sugarcane growing around here."

"Yes, and it does very well, I'll not be denying that. In fact, I'm going to be planting some myself, over yonder where I've begun clearing."

Christina glanced over to where newly-felled scrub and small trees had not yet been dragged into piles for burning. It was beyond the replanted cornfield, in the very place where she had gone into the bush on the day she'd become lost. What had become of that young boy? Was he now far away, as everyone seemed to think? Or was he still somewhere in the valley, hiding away where the bush still covered the land? If he was still here, did he sometimes come to the edge of the clearing to watch her? Those times when a fleeting movement caught her eye, was it really only shadows that she saw? And the strange soft sound that sometimes reached her ears, was it only the breeze in the trees that whispered "Chrussina, Chrussina"?

"I'll be needing you to hold the door steady while I mark where the hinges have to go, and then again when I am fitting it. Do you think you'll be able to do that?"

"Yes, I can do that. Oh Father, won't it be wonderful to live in a house again?"

"That it will, love. A tent might be a bit of an adventure for a week or two, but after that it's certainly no fun." He looked up, grinning, from the package of screws he was opening. "Especially when snakes decide to share it, eh?"

Though she returned his grin, Christina was unable to suppress a faint shiver. Twice, during these past weeks, snakes had come into the tent. On the first occasion, her mother had disturbed one behind a packing case. It had slithered away quickly, its black scales gleaming in the sunshine before it disappeared into long grass. That had been bad enough, but not nearly as bad as her own experience: waking to find a monstrous, mottled creature curled up on the foot of her bed. She might be able to smile about it now, but at the time it had certainly been no laughing matter. Rather had it been a screaming matter and she'd still been doing that even after her father had managed to prod the thing into a reluctant departure, assuring her that there was no need for him to kill it because it was only a harmless carpet snake, welcome in the canefields and barns because it ate the rats and mice.

The Skov family moved into their new home in the week before Easter. They would still sleep on stretchers, sit on canvas chairs and use their trunks and an assortment of boxes in lieu of cupboards, for, as yet, apart from a table and a few shelves, Simon had had no time to spare for the making of furniture. But now, instead of the meagre protection of canvas over their heads, they had a stout roof and sturdy walls; instead of a fire out in the open, they had an indoor fireplace; instead of the uncertain shade provided by the tent flap, they had a covered verandah; instead of earth beneath their feet, they had a floor; and, best of all, instead of having to depend on the well and creek for their water, they had a tank. It was enough.

13

The year 1872 dawned to exciting news for the Colony of Queensland. A group of prospectors stumbled across the outcrop of the North Australian Reef and strolled about picking up gold at random. The exploitation of the immense wealth of Charters Towers was about to begin. By the end of February, five hundred miners were at the site, with more arriving every day. And, when the wet season ended in April, eighty bullock and horse teams, accompanied by a string of men on horseback, set out from Townsville. By the time the year drew to a close, the new field, in conjunction with the fading Ravenswood, would have yielded over ninety thousand ounces of gold. As the diggings at Gympie had been a tremendous boost for the Colony in its first decade, so would those at Charters Towers be in its second.

In other areas, also, things were going well. The new Governor was proving to be an active man with progressive ideas, and, to the great relief of most people, the dead-locked situation in Parliament which had, for months on end, obstructed the passage of any new Acts and given rise to no end of arguments, was finally resolved, at least for the time being: the creation of more Seats to lessen the powerful influence of the squatters, it was agreed by all except those worthy gentlemen, being the only way to achieve a permanent solution.

The major problem for Queensland was still, however, the drastic shortage of workers. In both Europe and America the overall economic situation was improving rapidly. Almost overnight, it seemed, a massive demand for labour had brought about increased wages and improved working conditions. The general feeling had become one of prosperity, hardly a feeling conducive to the uprooting of families and possessions to emigrate to the other side of the world. The Queensland Government responded by passing a new Immigration Act, more easily workable than that of 1869, but it was also obliged to cast about for other solutions to the labour shortage problem.

There were now some two and a half thousand South Sea Islanders in the Colony, the majority of them in the Townsville and Mackay areas, but considerable pressure was being applied to have what had come to be regarded as a deplorable traffic in human lives brought to an end. It was clear that the system worked well enough when properly conducted, but there was any amount of evidence to indicate that it was being grossly abused: many of the Islanders did not come willingly as they were supposed to do; the conditions under which they were transported were usually appalling; they were often obliged to live in hovels and be content with rations that barely sustained them; in many instances, they were expected to work without a break from daylight to dark, their masters never doubting that it was the divine right of the white man to use the black man in such a way. It was, therefore, obvious that a new scheme for the obtaining of cheap labour was necessary.

Ever since Britain had abolished slavery, her colonies in other parts of the world had taken to using Coolie labourers from India and China, these being introduced into the country as indentured immigrants and contracted to serve for a period of five years. There seemed no reason why such an arrangement wouldn't also work for Queensland and arrangements were made for a trial shipment to be brought from Malabar in British India.

Christina went to school, gleefully riding Star. Once off the lonely bush-shrouded track and on the road, she met up with other children on their ponies and rode into Beenleigh with them. They were all German and, though the boys sometimes teased her about being Danish, the girls were always nice to her. At the school, however, she lost no time in seeking out Marie Hunter who, instructed by her father to "keep an eye on the little Danish girl", had quickly become a close friend. A sweet-natured child, with wide brown eyes and long dark plaits, Marie, although younger, was a grade ahead of Christina, but this didn't prevent the two girls from strolling about the playground arm-in-arm, sitting together to eat their lunch, giggling over shared jokes, or talking endlessly as they exchanged confidences and experiences from young lives far removed from one another before the day at the end of January when they had met at the school gate.

The sounding of the school bell for the commencement of lessons, however, brought no great pleasure to Christina. Mr and Mrs Nussey, who had charge of the school, were patient and understanding, but they had many children to teach, in a language that was for most of them adopted. They couldn't spend the time with her that Mrs Klaussen had done, and so she struggled along, trying to remember that some words had an e on the end when there was no need for it whatsoever, that others were spelt quite differently from the way they sounded, that there were words with the same sound, but different spelling, and still others with letters that seemed to have been included for the sole purpose of making the word difficult to spell. "I'll never be able to spell properly in English!" she wailed to Marie as they ate their lunch after a particularly disastrous morning.

"Of course you will," the other girl assured her kindly. "It will just take a little time, what with it being a new language and all. Mrs Nussey knows that it's hard for you."

"She didn't seem too pleased with the spelling test I did this morning."

"Oh … how many did you get right?"

"Four, that's all."

"Out of ten?" Marie asked, her eyes wide with disbelief. "No wonder Mrs Nussey wasn't pleased. That's worse than you did on Monday."

"It's the worst I've done all week." Christina sighed heavily as she nibbled on her sandwich. "It was ever so much easier with Mrs Klaussen."

"The lady who taught you on the ship?"

"Yes, she taught me how to speak English, and she had really interesting ways for me to learn how to spell the words and things like that."

"Can't your mother or father help you?"

"Sometimes they try to, but at night everyone is so tired, and there never seems to be any time during the day."

"Well, there's no sense in worrying too much about it. If you practise writing down the words, you'll get used to them and then it will be quite simple. It will be just as if English was always your language." The expression of commiseration Marie was wearing disappeared suddenly and she exclaimed cheerfully, "At least you do well with arithmetic."

"I suppose that's something to be thankful for. It's not much help to me when I write a letter, though. You should have seen how much trouble I had writing to Henry – you know, the boy from the ship I told you about. Even with Father helping me, it took ages. I tore up six pages before I got one to look at least a bit presentable."

"Well, I should think he'd be so pleased to get a letter from you he wouldn't mind in the least what it looked like. Do you think you will ever see him again?"

"No, he lives too far away."

"But one day he might come back this way and ask you to marry him."

"That's silly."

"No, it's not. And you could marry him, you know? You've said that he's not a Prussian, so there's no reason why you wouldn't be able to do so. Though why you like the Germans but not the Prussians is still something I don't understand. They are really all Germans and much of a muchness, if you ask me."

"It's because of what the Prussians did to our country." Christina sighed softly. "But I'm not supposed to not like those who have come to Australia; Mother and Father have told me that so many times."

"It's what my father says too, that we are to forget about nationalities and treat everyone who comes here equally."

"I try to remember that." Christina smiled suddenly. "And I haven't met any Prussians here yet."

"You will, and what will you do if one of them should ask you to marry him?"

"I would never do that. I would try to be nice to him, but I could never marry him."

Marie nodded. "I don't suppose it would be a good idea, not for you." She brushed the crumbs from her lap industriously. "Hurry up and finish your lunch, Christina, or it will be time to go into school again before we've had a chance to play."

Christina considered throwing the rest of her sandwich to the pair of magpies waiting hopefully just a few feet away, but the idea was quickly rejected. No, she couldn't do that, it would be too wasteful. She pushed it hastily into her mouth, scrambling to her feet as she did so.

"I didn't tell you to try to choke yourself," Marie laughed as they linked arms. "I just said to hurry."

From the door of the schoolhouse, Mrs Nussey watched them leave the shade of the big camphor-laurel tree and join a group playing a noisy chasing game. She shook her head slowly from side to side, smiling ruefully to herself. Was she ever going to be able to teach the little Danish girl to spell correctly? On days such as this, it certainly didn't seem so.

"How did she fare in the test this morning?"

Mrs Nussey turned as her husband came up behind her. "Four out of ten," she told him with a faint shrug of her shoulders.

The Headmaster whistled softly. "Four? I thought you said she was improving."

"That was last week." His wife sighed. "It isn't that she's not bright enough, and she speaks English very well, considering she's only known the language for a comparatively short time."

"Well, you have to admit that you always know what it is that she means to write, and her sentences, if you disregard the spelling, are excellent for a child of that age."

"She has a refreshing imagination, yes. But how is she going to be able to get through life not being able to spell, especially now that the need for girls to be educated as well as boys is being recognised?"

"Very well, I should think."

Hilda laughed softly. "You're influenced by the charm of the child."

"That's exactly what I mean. I don't believe that anyone, except perhaps her parents, will be unduly concerned that Miss Christina Skov doesn't spell the Queen's English too well."

"I suppose you could be right at that, but I have to keep trying with her. That's what I'm here for, when all's said and done."

"I wouldn't be too hard on her, though. I'm sure she's doing her best, and besides … "

"I know, she recites beautifully in Danish."

Elsie's hopes that letters from Schleswig and Denmark would arrive earlier than they had originally expected were not realised. It was April before their first mail from overseas showed up. When it did, there were so many letters the postmaster in Beenleigh saw fit to tie them into bundles with pink tape. "Goodness, where on earth will we start?" she cried, as she untied a tape with shaking fingers.

"Anywhere at all," Simon told her, reaching for an envelope with a Herning postmark. "There'll be time enough later to read them in some sort of order."

They read avidly, chuckling over amusing incidents, smiling over good news, sighing over that which was not so good. Two new babies were expected, one by Elsie's youngest sister, the other by Simon's brother Peter. Mads's youngest son was going to marry the eldest daughter of Farmer Svenson ... "a man with a nice property and no sons of his own, as you may recall," Mads wrote. "So I don't think the young fellow will be getting any ideas about going off to Australia. I wish I could say the same about the other two. Perhaps I should be trying to interest them in Svenson's other daughters."

"Ah, ha," Simon exclaimed with a wide grin. "My nephews have been getting a few ideas of their own, it would seem."

Elsie nodded, but absently, as she frowningly reread part of a letter from her mother. "The winter is proving very harsh" the uneven scrawl ran, "and your father has been suffering from a severe chest complaint. He has been feeling a little better these past few days, though, and hopes to be back in the shop by next week" Next week? And the letter was dated 11 December. He would be well again now, then ... Anxiously, she shuffled through the letters scattered over the table. A later one, there must be a later one. Ah ... her father's handwriting. But when had he written? She tore the envelope open, her eyes flying to the date at the top of the page. Christmas Day! Her father had written to them on Christmas Day! Elsie's heart lurched with an aching compassion and she pressed her teeth into her lower lip to stop its trembling, Oh, how like him. "Father wrote on Christmas Day," she murmured huskily.

Simon watched his wife's eyes flying over the fine handwriting. "Is he well?"

"He was when he was writing, apparently. But in one of her letters mother said that he'd been ill with a chest complaint earlier on. Oh, why has he gone back to working in the shop? He should have sold it long ago."

"Because that's what he wants. He loves that shop and he wouldn't know what to do with himself if he sold it."

"But to be working at the tailoring, that's too much for a man of his age. He's never had serious chest trouble before, but now that it has started … why, he could even have had another attack already. Mother said that they were having a harsh winter and it was still only December. What about these past two months?"

"I'm sure he made a good recovery, and now that spring has arrived he's probably as sprightly as ever."

He smiled encouragingly. "While you are over here worrying about him."

Elsie returned his smile, but wryly. "How silly I am being. Waiting all this time for letters and then becoming melancholy when they do arrive."

"Well, it's frustrating to have waited so long and then be reading something written ages ago. I'm afraid that's something we are going to have to put up with, though – old news."

The Ohlssens had written, a long rambling letter to which Lars had also contributed, but had occupied a whole page asking questions.

"For heaven's sake," Simon laughed. "How could he have thought up so many things to ask?"

Elsie shook her head. "I'm afraid that boy still has it in mind to come to Australia. We must remember not to mention the new goldfield when we write back."

"I think he'll hear about it in any case, if he hasn't done so already. It's such a bonanza it's bound to be widely discussed in Europe." He flicked through the still unopened letters. "Christina is certainly going to be excited when she gets home from school. Seven letters, no less. Who are they all from, do you think?"

"Her cousins and some of the girls who were her friends at school, more than likely." She smiled briefly. "Christina's going to be excited about getting them, but answering them will be another kettle of fish."

A grin caught the corners of Simon's mouth but wasn't allowed to spread. His wife, he knew well enough, saw nothing in their daughter's letter-writing ordeals to be amused about. "At least she'll be answering these in Danish."

"Hmmm, that's some consolation, I suppose."

They were still lingering over the mail when Simon glanced up and remarked carefully, "I have news, by the way. Another doctor has taken up residence in Beenleigh – Doctor Travis. So, after years with no doctor closer than Brisbane, the valley now has two."

"Doctor Gunn may not be too pleased to know that he's to have competition, so to speak."

"I shouldn't think he'd mind too much. After all, there are a lot of people living in these parts now and it's quite a large area he has to cover with his house calls." Simon hesitated, chewing on his lip before saying even more carefully, "They say that Doctor Travis is very highly qualified and has had wide experience in Europe."

Faint colour stole into his wife's cheeks and she at once busied herself refolding pages and slipping them back into their envelopes. "Well, I'm sure that's comforting to know."

During the whole of the month of May only sixty points of rain fell in the Logan and Albert valleys. In June, no more than sixty-five points. An exceptionally dry season was under way and an unusually cold winter added its destructive forces to turn the green grasses of the valleys to a withered brown, lay waste to vegetable gardens and the crops in the fields, and rob even the hardy cane of its brightness.

The sugarcane farmers wisely decided to begin cutting and crushing early and they kept the mills working around the clock. The cane from some areas proved to be of poor quality, the density of the juice much too low for a profitable return. But, as the crushing continued, with large quantities of good quality sugar being produced, it was realised that the frosts had not done as much damage as at first feared. On one trip, the barge, Barbara Jane, made its way down the Logan River with a load of forty tons from three mills, causing a general feeling of satisfaction to spread among the district's cane growers. Certainly there was room for improvement in the yield per acre, but, all things considered, the industry was coming along very nicely indeed.

"I should have held out for cane," Simon reproached himself as he and George Hunter considered the brown and dusty desolation of his farm. "There would have been enough land if I had set myself to clearing more right away instead of messing about planting corn on that which was already cleared. I kept thinking that, only with a large acreage, would cane be a paying proposition, but it seems that isn't the case. Look at the return Mr Witty has had from just twenty-three acres of eighteen-month-old cane. And in a poor season."

George Hunter nodded, knocking the ash from his pipe against a fence post. "Thirty-eight tons from twenty-three acres is certainly nothing to be sneezed at."

"I figure that he would have cut around three hundred tons of cane for that amount of sugar, so, even if Davy and Gooding only paid him ten shillings a ton, he would have earned a hundred and fifty pounds or more. That's a darn sight better return than for corn. One shilling and nine pence for a bushell of sixty pounds, sometimes as little as one shilling and sixpence."

"It's a lousy return alright. All of the farmers have been complaining; general feeling is that anything under two bob a bushell is not really a paying proposition."

"It isn't … well, certainly not when you've had a setback along the way as I did with the cockatoos. I barely broke even with my first two crops, even with the good weather earlier on. And, as you can see, this lot is a complete write-off." Simon gestured helplessly at the rows and rows of brown, wilting plants. "I've been feeding some of it to the cattle. Pretty unappetizing stuff, but no more so than the grass the poor wretches are having to eat."

"Cornstalks and leaves make good fodder, even in that state. It may not be too tasty, but there's any amount of nutrition in it. You'll find that the cattle will also eat some of the scrub trees if they get hungry enough."

Simon nodded. "I've already cut a few and dragged them up, but I'm still hoping that the grass I have, sparse though it is, together with the corn, will see me through. Surely this weather is not going to continue for too much longer. After all, in two weeks' time, we'll be into spring."

George Hunter gave a short mirthless laugh. "A drought and a long, cold winter. Wouldn't it just have to happen in the year the Agricultural Society is to hold its first Agricultural Show?"

"Yes, that's the very devil of a pity. I'm sure I don't know who's going to have anything worth showing."

"I don't either. Even if we do get good rain in these next couple of weeks, the damage will have been done. On every farm I visit the cattle are pretty scrawny-looking and they're not going to recover that quickly." He glanced towards the trees marking the course of the creek. "You haven't had any of yours bogged yet?"

"No, thank God. The only water hole I have left has little enough in it, but, thankfully, it's in a stony section of the creek."

"That's one advantage of being a bit further up the creek, I suppose. The farmers further down have had any number bogged. Elsewhere they have too. It's been some time now since most of the creeks ran and what waterholes remain are rapidly shrinking into bogs."

"Herman Schmidt was telling me that he's had to put up a fence to keep his cattle from getting to the creek."

"Well, all he's got left are a couple of holes filled mainly with mud and slush. That's the trouble with these smaller creeks it doesn't take much of a dry period to turn them into death traps for the cattle."

"One thing about this drought, George; it has made me appreciate the well more than ever. I've been thanking Timothy O'Reilly every blessed day, wherever he might be. As you know, we only have the one tank and it's getting close to being empty."

"He just might be pleased to know that someone is benefitting from what I'm sure he still regards as his greatest folly. Unless, of course, he's found gold, in which case, he's probably forgotten all about the well. I suppose that's quite a possibility if he's managed to get himself to Charters Towers."

"It seems to be quite a field they've got there. Can it last?"

"The alluvial stuff? I shouldn't think so, it never seems to. Give it a few more months and it will be left to the companies with the money and know-how to come along and get into the reef itself, When that happens, the prospectors will drift away looking for new diggings, another chance. They could always stay and work for the companies, of course, but that's not part of the dream ... whoever got rich working for wages?"

They both laughed quietly, and, soon afterwards, the Lands Officer mounted his horse and rode off. Well, Simon thought as he watched him turn on to the track and disappear into the bush, at least I've managed to pay next year's rent. Twelve pounds ten shillings. God, it was almost as much as he'd earned in two months, doing four days a week carpentry work. Still, it wasn't rent in a true sense, not when it was going towards paying off his land. And, this time next year, the money shouldn't be so hard to find. Now that he knew what to do, what to expect, it wouldn't be nearly so difficult, and things would be bound to have improved.

As soon as the rain came, he would plant cane, on every cleared acre he could spare. Some areas would have to be kept for other crops, of course, potatoes, for one thing, and some corn, just enough to carry them over until such time as the cane was ready to cut. And perhaps, if there were some good rainfalls, he'd be able to graze a couple of beef cattle, fatten them up, then sell them. They at least were fetching a fair enough price, six or seven pounds for a good bullock. Having a couple to sell would at least take care of the next lot of rent. But the cane, that was the thing. Simon let his gaze roam over his land, his eyes dreamy, his imagination rolling back the dense bush that still covered more than ninety-five percent of it, putting cane in its place. It would, he told himself, be a good farm, in spite of the cockatoos and the drought. In two or three years, perhaps four ...

Christina dug her heels gently into Star's flanks, clucking her tongue and shaking the reins to urge her forward. Not that she wanted to. With the horse paddocks at the school being very close to bare and very little grass in those at home, she would have let her go on nibbling by the side of the road. But they had already stopped a number of times and, if she was late, her mother would begin to worry, perhaps even come looking for her. A few paces further on another tuft of withered grass caught the mare's eye and she again veered sideways. Sighing softly, Christina loosened her grip on the reins. "This is the very last time, Star," she admonished. "If I let you have your way, it will be dark by the time we get home."

But she waited patiently, shivering in the cold of the deep shadows, feeling the weariness of the thirsty bush as a weight on her young shoulders. Everywhere, there was a brittle dryness. Brown and withered leaves lay thick upon the ground, all of the smaller ferns were dead and even the hardy bracken had lost its greenness. Much of the undergrowth had also died, leaving the bush with a strange skeletal bareness, and there were other things contributing to the gloom. Just off the track, in a gully that early in the year had held water deep enough to be home to frogs and small lobster-like creatures, the bones of some animal now lay scattered on hard, baked earth, not the only ones in the bush. She had seen any number on her way to and from school and only this morning she had disturbed a group of crows bunched together on the track. While they'd perched, cawing impatiently in a nearby tree, she'd stared in horror at what it was that had attracted them; the handsome bushy tail on the mangled body telling her all too clearly that this time even the wily fox hadn't escaped the drought.

The dull thudding of hooves approaching rapidly brought a quick frown to Christina's brow. Surely she wasn't so late that her father had had to come looking for her? But who else would come riding along the track like that at this time of day?

"Now look what we've done, Star," she muttered, digging in her heels not quite so gently this time. "Father has had to leave whatever he was doing and come looking for us." But it wasn't her father, she saw with a surge of relief as the horse and rider burst into view, it was Mr Hunter. The Lands Officer reined his horse to a halt, a smile coming to his face.

"Hello there, Christina. I've just left your place. Your father told me that I'd probably meet up with you along the way."

Christina returned his smile. "I think I'm a little bit late. Star likes to eat the grass at the side of the road. She thinks it's better than what she's going to get at home."

"Don't let her keep you too long. Even though the days are becoming longer, darkness still comes with something of a rush."

"No, I won't. I've already told her that we won't be stopping any more times."

"I hope she takes better notice of you than my horse does of me," George Hunter chuckled.

"She doesn't always pay attention, but I'm going to make her move a bit faster so that she doesn't see the tufts of grass."

"That's a very good idea. Off with you then."

"Goodbye, Mr Hunter. I'll tell Father that I saw you."

Watching the slight form bouncing away on the trotting pony, George Hunter shook his head slowly from side to side. She had no easy life, the little Skov girl. It didn't seem that there was some wonderful change in store for her either, not unless some miracle happened to help her father with his farm. He smiled wryly to himself. She was probably already learning that ever so important lesson though, how to live in the Australian bush and survive. She would be a survivor, of that he was very sure.

Spring soon came. Not early or with the confidence of the previous year, but cautiously, as though doubting its ability to heal this ailing land. Not until late September, when the Logan valley farmers woke one morning to the blessed smell of rain biting into dust, did it finally take heart.

14

Christina's schooling came to an end in mid-July 1873. She was ten and a half years old and she had been attending the school in Beenleigh for just eighteen months. There was simply no other solution to the dilemma in which her parents found themselves. Elsie was expecting a baby in September and, although Doctor Travis stressed there was no cause for undue concern, he was insisting that she take things easier, that she put her feet up for at least a couple of hours each day.

Simon, himself, could do little to make this possible. He had to go out to work. Nothing would have suited him better then to be able to stay at home, easing the burden on his wife and devoting more time to his land and the shed he was building, but it was out of the question. It would be another year before his cane was ready for cutting and, even if it did prove to be of good quality, there would be little enough return from three acres. He was counting on both his corn and his potatoes to bring in some cash, but it wouldn't be nearly enough to pay the rent and doctor's bills and keep starvation from their door. So, when the crushing season started in June, he had gone cane cutting. For one thing, it paid better than carpentry which was, in any case, no longer so readily available. For another, the season would be over by the end of the year and he expected to be then in a position to forget about outside work for a couple of months at least. For now, though, on every day except Sunday, he left the farm at daybreak and returned at dusk, exhausted and covered with the black grime left on the cane by the fires lit to rid it of the trash and unfriendly inhabitants – snakes and spiders, rats, wasps and bees. But, mingling with the exhaustion, there was a faint feeling of satisfaction; by the end of the first week, he was cutting six tons a day, which wasn't at all bad for a beginner.

Staying away from school would be only temporary, both he and Elsie assured Christina, when school started next year she would be able to go back again. Christina didn't mind. The thought of not being able to spend mornings and lunch breaks with Marie brought a quick pang, as did the obvious dismay of Mr and Mrs Nussey. But, for some time now, she had been worrying about her mother. She had so much work to do and she seemed so weary, her swollen body making it impossible for her to move briskly from one task to the other as she had been wont to do. Now, I will really be able to help her, Christina told herself. I can do all the milking for one thing.

There was something that did trouble her though, something far more important than whether or not she went to school. It had begun to tangle both her thoughts and her emotions on the morning she'd first realised that her mother was going to have a baby. They had been walking across the dew-covered grass to the cow paddock when a playful breeze had flipped up her mother's apron, revealing the bulge beneath. Christina had caught her breath as a surge of happiness reached for her heart, but it had never arrived. Unbidden, the little grave in the Haderslev cemetery had swum up out of the depths of memory, to be joined, in the space of a moment, by a small canvas-wrapped bundle. Fear had pushed aside the happiness and, although it faded when she looked upon the obvious delight of her parents, it refused to leave.

She saw that there was a tranquility about her mother, for all that she was awkward and often weary, and a gentle smiling in her eyes, while her father made light of the heavy work he was doing, laughing a lot and planning for the future with a new eagerness. Next year, things would really begin to improve for them, he declared cheerfully, looking at her mother with such an expression on his face Christina felt a reassuring warmth steal through her. Next year, when the new baby was with them.

Although the fear sometimes faded, and even on occasions disappeared completely, an uneasiness remained with Christina, nourished by the dark silence of the nights, the loneliness of the bush track, the aching beauty of a sunset. She prayed as she hadn't done in a long time, treasuring the Sundays when they found the time to go to church, for she was sure that was where God was most likely to hear her. "Please God, let us keep this baby. Don't take it away from us. We'll take special care that it doesn't get sick. Please, please, let us keep it." The same words, over and over, until it seemed that she had said them at least a million times. Sometimes, she was tempted to remind God that He already had two of their babies, but she told herself that it might make Him angry for her to be thinking that He could have forgotten. And He wouldn't have, of course, God never forgot anything.

It was going to be a most beautiful spring, Christina decided, as she shooed the cows in the direction of the bails on the afternoon of the last Saturday in August. Already the days were warm, and there were buttercups in the grass; bluebells also, if you took the time to look more closely. Unlike this time last year, the grass was thick and green – new-green, having pushed itself up out of the sodden earth only in these past two weeks. Smiling to herself, Christina threw her head back, watching the fleecy clouds sail across the ever-so-blue sky while she took deep breaths of air. It really did smell of spring – of grass, earth and new leaves. Something else as well, something gently and deliciously fragrant – honeysuckle! Christina's smile became just a little smug. The air wouldn't be smelling like this further down the valley. Instead of new grass and honeysuckle, it would be molasses and smoke, and haze would be hanging over everything. Even from here, she could see it smudging the sky.

"Christina! Christina!"

Christina's gaze flew from the sky to the house, to her mother standing in the back doorway, beckoning frantically. At once she began to run, racing ahead of the slow-moving cows. The baby must be coming, she thought, her heart beginning to race. But it wasn't time, not for another three weeks. Oh God, please don't let there be anything wrong. There didn't have to be, she tried to tell herself; even if the baby was coming early, that wasn't something to be alarmed about. Babies quite often came early; besides, hadn't her mother told her that it wasn't always possible to know for sure when the arrival time would be? But what was she to do with her father off cutting cane? Get Doctor Travis, of course. Yes, that's what her mother would be wanting her to do. And quickly too, more than likely.

Once inside the back door, Christina's hurrying came to an abrupt halt and abject horror washed over her. Her mother was sitting on a chair, crouched over the table, beads of perspiration clinging to her chalk-white face. And, on the floor, something bright red and shining was moving slowly, spreading. Blood! And it was coming from under her mother's skirt. Christina's mouth opened, but she gulped and bit back the scream that had been on the point of bursting from her lips. She couldn't be screaming, not now... she had to do something. "What should I do?"

"You must ride for Doctor Travis, Christina, as quickly as you can."

"Shouldn't I help you first?"

"No, there's nothing you can do here. Just fetch Doctor Travis."

"But you... you're bleeding."

"Just go, Christina!"

Christina turned and ran, grabbing her bridle from its peg by the back door. No need for a saddle; it would waste too much time. Star lifted her head enquiringly as she climbed over the fence, calling coaxingly, "Come Star, good girl, come now." But she was rushing and the horse danced off nervously. Reluctantly, she slowed her approach, moving more quietly, one hand held out, the other holding the bridle against her side. "Good girl. Good girl, come now." The horse eyed her curiously for a moment or two; then, as though sensing her distress, trotted up to her, trying to nuzzle her face and neck. Catching her breath on a small sob of relief, Christina slipped the bridle into place, her trembling hands fumbling with the straps. But at last it was done and, fretting over the time lost, she caught up the reins and ran to the sliprails. Once through them, she climbed on to the fence and swung herself on to the horse's bare back, pulling up her skirt so that her knees could grip more tightly. Shaking the reins she dug in her heels and set out at a gallop for the main gate. Here, she was obliged to rein to a halt and dismount, but she was used to the cumbersome structure, and was soon on her way again, galloping furiously along the track. There was a roaring in her ears and her heart was beating so hard it seemed that it was about to burst through her ribs. But the tears had dried on her cheeks. If she was to get to the doctor she couldn't be crying, she told herself sternly. It was enough that she was riding without saddle or stirrups, she couldn't have the hindrance of not being able to see where she was going as well.

The trees and bushes flew by, her progress pinpointed by the parrots that, startled by the thudding of the horse's hooves, took to the wing and burst through the tree tops in an explosion of colour. A large grey kangaroo, grazing at the side of the track prepared to flee, but then, confused by the swiftness of her approach, headed off down the track, its huge tail thumping the earth only a short distance in front of her. "Get off the track, you silly thing!" Christina yelled, struggling to keep the disturbed pony from veering off the road and crashing into the bushes. But they had covered a good half-mile before the now terrified roo sighted a break in the undergrowth, and, skidding on its haunches, abruptly changed course.

With the rough track behind her, Christina swung on to the road with a sigh of relief. If she kept to the middle, the road, deeply rutted though it was, would be easier for Star than the track had been. "Oh, keep going, Star," she pleaded, knowing full well that the horse had never before galloped anywhere near the distance already covered, and there was still a long way to go. But she had to keep going, she had to...

The big chestnut overtook Christina a mile or so along the road, its rider leaning from the saddle to take hold of Star's bridle and ease the now floundering pony to a halt "What are you trying to do, girl, kill yourself?" The young man's handsome, deeply tanned face was set grimly and he spoke angrily, his dark eyes going from Christina's flushed face to the horse's sweat-darkened neck and flanks, "Or is it your pony you're wanting to kill?"

Dazed, Christina stared up at him. She wanted to be angry too, to brush his hands away from her bridle so that she could continue on her way, but almost numb with dread and her desperate need to reach the doctor, she instead burst into tears, gulping, "I have to get to the doctor. My mother is having a baby."

The young man whipped his lean hard body around in the saddle, incredulity replacing the anger in his eyes. "Now? She's having a baby right now?"

"Yes, she's having it now, and there's … there's …"

"Where is she?"

"Back at our farm, and she's on her own." She choked on a sob that refused to be swallowed. "I think there's something wrong."

The dark eyes searched her flushed, tear-streaked face. "Would you be Simon Skov's girl?"

"Yes, I'm Christina."

"Which doctor do you want?"

"Doctor Travis."

"I'll get him for you. You go back to your mother." He considered the slight figure and distraught young face, then added somewhat dubiously, "There might be something you can do to help her."

Although she longed to let him take over the wild rush to get the doctor, Christina wasn't so sure that she should agree to his suggestion. After all, she was the one her mother was counting on. What if Doctor Travis wasn't at home? This man might just go on about his business and not try to find him. Besides, her mother would be expecting her to tell him about the blood. "I have to tell the doctor something," she murmured miserably.

"Well, what is it?" The big horse was snorting with impatience, pulling against the restraining bit, and the young man, too, was anxious to be on his way. Didn't the child realise how quickly babies could sometimes come into the world?

Christina shivered, seeing again the bright stain spreading over the kitchen floor. How could she tell this man such a thing, that there was a lot of blood coming out of her mother? But he had a fine horse and he'd be able to get to the doctor far more quickly than she would. "There's blood," she burst out. "It's on the floor."

A horrified expression appeared momentarily in the dark eyes, but he said at once. "I'll tell the doctor that." The set line of his mouth softened and, almost as though he'd read her thoughts, he said, "And don't be thinking I won't find him. If he's not at home, I'll hunt him down. I'll go and tell your father, too, after I've found the doctor."

"Thank you, Mr … "

"Eichstead,... Carl Eichstead. I've been cutting cane with your father." He released Star's bridle. "Don't be riding too hard now. It won't help your mother for you to have an accident."

"I won't. I'll just … "

Christina didn't get to complete her promise. Carl Eichstead had pivoted his restless horse and booted it into a gallop. Even before she turned Star, horse and rider had disappeared from her view around a tree-shrouded bend.

The baby, a seven-pound boy, lived for less than an hour. "Placenta praevia," Doctor Travis groaned wearily as he joined Simon on the small verandah. "The placenta didn't attach itself to the wall of the uterus in the usual manner." He sighed heavily. "I can't tell you how sorry I am. He was a fine little boy."

Simon's eyes sought those of the doctor. "But why did he die when he seems so perfect?"

"He would have been greatly deprived in these past hours. The haemorrhage, for one thing, your wife lost a great deal of blood." Doctor Travis reached out and gripped Simon's shoulder. "Be thankful that her life was spared, Mr Skov. In many such cases, both mother and baby die. And, in others, the baby lives, but the mother dies."

"I am thankful," Simon murmured huskily. "My God, I don't think anyone can possibly know how thankful." He took a handkerchief from his pocket and noisily blew his nose. "I talked my wife into having the baby. After losing the boy back in Haderslev and then the little girl on the ship, she seemed to think that one child was all we were meant to have. But I thought … well, a new life had begun for us in this country and it seemed reasonable, somehow, to expect that things might be different from those other times."

Doctor Travis nodded. "Yes, I can understand your feeling that way," he said gently. And then, after a brief pause. "Mrs Skov told me that, in addition to losing the little boy in Haderslev, she also suffered a miscarriage, and it was with that in mind that I kept such a close watch on her." He threw out his hands in a helpless gesture. "God knows, though, there never are any signs with placenta praevia, not until the wretched haemorrhage starts. In any case, knowing is of no real help, we can't change the way things are in the womb." He sighed again and turned his head to stare out into the night. "Rightly or wrongly, my own reaction when confronted with such a problem has always been to do everything in my power to save the life of the mother, and to pray that the baby survives as well."

"Has it ever happened that both have lived?"

"It could have, I suppose, but not to my knowledge."

"Then all these months we have been waiting with joy in our hearts for something that was never going to be. I put my wife's life in danger for an impossible dream."

"No, it wasn't an impossible dream, Mr Skov, it wasn't that at all. Things could have gone differently for you and your wife."

"Could have?" Simon made a sound that was part groan and part bitter laugh. "But they didn't, Doctor, they didn't."

Almost two weeks passed before the Skovs were able to talk about the young man who had summoned the doctor. He had been part of a heart-breaking time and neither Simon nor Elsie was anxious to bring that to the forefront of their minds by recalling what he had done for them. Christina, taking her cue from her parents, also refrained from mentioning him, which wasn't to say that she hadn't thought about him on a number of occasions: about how horrible and arrogant he had at first seemed, but then how kind he'd been when he'd learned why she'd been galloping Star so hard. She'd thought about who he was too. A German, that was clear enough, but there was something about his confident manner that told her he was more than likely a Prussian.

Finally, there came an evening when Elsie, her head bent over the sock she was darning, said quietly, "I hope that young man who went for Doctor Travis knows how grateful we are."

"He knows," Simon assured her. "He's probably sick to death of hearing me thank him."

"Well, it was a very obliging thing he did. What did you say his name was?"

"Carl Eichstead. He came out last year on the Reichstag, arrived at the beginning of August. He was still only eighteen at the time."

"And he came on his own?"

"No, it's all very sad really. He had a sister with him but she died earlier this year."

Elsie looked up from her darning to slowly shake her head. "She came all that way and then lived for only a few months, what a tragedy. What did she die from, do you know?"

"The boy has never said, only that she was working as a nurse in Brisbane at the time. I do know that her name was Ulrike and that she was twenty-one years old."

"So young. How terrible it must have been for that young man, not only to lose his sister, but to be all on his own so soon after his arrival."

"It left a great ache in his heart, there's no doubt about that. But he's obviously made up his mind to make a life for himself here in Queensland and he seems to be managing that well enough." A faint smile touched Simon's mouth. "He has even changed the spelling of his name. Instead of Karl he spells it Carl, and instead of E-i-c-h-s-t-a-a-d-t, he has adopted E-i-c-h-s-t-e-a-d."

"Is it possible to do that, change the way you spell your name?"

"I don't know that he ever bothered to find out whether it was legal or not, I think he just did it. Well, I say good luck to him. He obviously intends to make this country his home."

"He's been cutting cane with you?"

"Yes, but only because the crushing season got off to a late start down at the Tweed; that's the river on the border with New South Wales where they are growing quite a lot of cane. He's been working in that area ever since he arrived. As a matter of fact, he left yesterday to go back there."

"He didn't like our valley well enough to want to stay?"

"He liked the Logan well enough, but he's hoping to be able to take up some land a bit further south than this, and, in the meantime, it seems he can get any amount of work around the Tweed – fencing, cane cutting, stockwork. That young man is quite a toiler, believe me, and mad about the land. Knows a fair bit about it too. In fact, if it hadn't been for that, he wouldn't have been out this way that day. Mr Witty had sent him to have a look at some land he's interested in; he wanted young Eichstead's opinion."

Elsie raised her eyebrows. "And him only nineteen. That really is a feather in his cap, to have his opinion sought in such a way. He must have grown up on the land, surely? What part of Germany did he come from?"

"A district in Pomerania."

Christina, who had been labouring over a letter to Henry, bit back a small gasp. So she had been right about him being a Prussian. That's where Pomerania was, in Prussia.

"That's mainly wheat country, isn't it?" Elsie asked.

"That's right. Highly prized wheat it is too, especially in England. According to what Carl tells me, there's a lot of dairying carried on also, along the rivers and around the lakes."

Christina was no longer listening to her parents' conversation, nor was she concentrating on her letter. She was seeing again the young man galloping off on his fine horse. He had looked like a golden-haired prince, not at all like a Prussian. When he'd first stopped her, he'd been rude and abrupt, the way she expected Prussians to be, but then he'd been kind and gentle, and not the least bit like that. And they certainly had good reason to be grateful to him; her mother would probably have died if he hadn't gone for the doctor. She sighed quietly. Learning that he was a Prussian was not really a surprise, not when she had thought that he might be. It was just that knowing it for sure was disappointing, somehow.

The decision wasn't an easy one for Simon and Elsie. In the end it took them almost three weeks to make up their minds, mainly because Simon, disheartened by the death of the baby and plagued by a growing suspicion that he was losing out to his land, found it hard to discuss the matter without becoming frustrated and angry. "I don't want her to be leaving school any more than you do," he exploded one afternoon after Elsie had suggested that, since Doctor Travis was waiting for an answer, he should decide whether or not Christina was to return to school.

"I didn't say you did," Elsie replied calmly, knowing that his anger was directed more at himself and their situation than at her. "I just think we owe it to Doctor Travis to let him know one way or the other."

They had been digging potatoes all day, and they were both hot, tired and dirty as they loaded the cart preparatory to returning to the house. It probably wasn't a good time to have brought the matter up, Elsie thought, stifling a sigh. But when was there a good time? They certainly couldn't talk about it in the house in front of Christina.

"I'm sorry," Simon muttered, clumsily patting her arm. "You're right, we do have to decide. What makes me so angry is that I don't believe we have any choice."

Elsie nodded. "It does seem that way."

"If only I could count on a good return from the corn. Or find the time to clear more land for cane … " He laughed shortly, mirthlessly. "Time, why is there never enough of it?"

Elsie didn't reply. There was little she could say and, in any case, he wouldn't be expecting an answer to such a question.

"Well, I suppose it's a pretty good offer really: Doctor Travis being prepared to pay Christina a couple of shillings a week and clothe and feed her in return for nursemaid duties. It wouldn't be as though we were sending her out into drudgery."

Only depriving her of her schooling, Elsie thought wearily, but she said, "Of course we wouldn't. She will be well cared for and it will be quite light work that she's doing. Had she been a little older, we probably wouldn't have hesitated about having her accept such a position."

"I suppose not. When you come to think about it, working for the Doctor and his wife will be an education in itself. Christina will learn the refineries that go with living in a fine house in town, and, what's more, there will be any amount of books for her to read. Mrs Travis might even take it upon herself to help her with her writing and spelling." Simon grinned suddenly. "Christina would like that, wouldn't she? Look how she enjoyed having Mrs Klaussen teach her."

"Mrs Klaussen had a lot of time on her hands," Elsie reminded him gently. "Mrs Travis is a busy doctor's wife with two young children and another one on the way."

"Yes, but when she has Christina to help her … "

So, Elsie thought, turning her head to hide a wry smile, it has finally been decided. All that remained now was for them to tell Doctor Travis, and Christina. The doctor and his wife would be very pleased, there was no doubt about that. But Christina? How was she going to feel? Expecting to be returning to school when it reopened after the summer holidays, and then to be told that she was to go out to work instead? She would accept the news calmly enough, of course. There would be no tearful tantrums. Any tears that were shed would be very quiet and very private. Elsie sighed as she helped her husband heave a bag of potatoes on to the cart. Sometimes, she almost wished … No, she didn't wish anything of the kind. The very idea of Christina in a tantrum was unthinkable. In any case, she told herself as a faint hope stirred, the arrangement with Doctor Travis might just appeal to her. When all was said and done, she wasn't very enthusiastic about her school work and she would certainly have an easier life than she would here on the farm.

Elsie gave no thought to the fact that she, as a result, would have quite a deal more to do. Had this been pointed out to her, she would have quickly retorted that she had no complaints with her lot. Her only complaint was with the seemingly insurmountable difficulties coming their way, pushing the realisation of her husband's dreams further from him. Two years gone by, she moaned silently, and, if anything, they were worse off than when they'd first arrived. At least, then, they'd had money enough to keep them going. Now, of course, they had a house and land that was their own, or would be if they could manage to pay the rents for the next eight years and bring about sufficient improvements to satisfy the Government. But there were still less than ten acres cleared and it was all they could do to keep those under control. Always, the bush seemed to be demanding their return, scattering the seeds from its trees and bushes on every breeze, reaching out persistent roots.

The man who farms these lands needs sons. Elsie lived with the thought and the anguish it brought. And she lashed herself with accusation. The failure was hers. Her husband implanted sons in her womb, but she failed in her allotted task of bringing them alive and well into the world. If they had lived, or if even one of them had lived, her husband's hopes would have still burned brightly. He wouldn't be talking about their land in a strangely abstracted manner, leaving sentences unfinished as though, in doing so, he saved himself the necessity of having to find a way of accomplishing whatever it was that had to be done.

Christina was not as surprised as her parents expected her to be. A couple of weeks back Doctor Travis had invited her to his home to meet his wife and children, and this had set her to wondering. There had to be a reason, she had told herself. It would hardly be only the Doctor's kindness that made him go out of his way to arrange such a visit, driving out to the farm in his fine sulky to collect her, then driving her all the way home again. But, when the days following the very pleasant afternoon had slipped by with no explanation coming to light, she'd ceased searching for that reason, telling herself that perhaps, after all, Doctor Travis was just being kind. Now, though, it was all perfectly clear. With her steady gaze on her father's anxious face, she said quietly, "That was why Doctor Travis asked me to his home that day, so that his wife could see whether I was suitable."

"And to see whether you liked them, of course. You do, don't you?"

"Oh yes, they are very nice."

"Well then, wouldn't you like to go and live with them?"

Live away from home? And with people she hardly knew? How could her father be asking her to do such a thing? Like it? She would hate it. Surely he must know that. Surely he must know that the very thought brought an ache to her heart. But … there was an ache in his heart too, and worry on his mind. She could see both reflected in his eyes. There was a need for it then, a reason why she had to go and live with people who were not her family? Yes, of course there was. Her father would never have asked her to do such a thing unless he had to. Christina pushed her lips into a smile. "It would be very pleasant living with Doctor Travis and his family."

Relief spread over Simon's face. "There now," he exclaimed, throwing out his hands as though tossing away the load that had been on his mind. "Didn't I say that Christina would be happy about the idea?"

Christina turned to look at her mother. She was sitting at the end of the table, her face pale in the lamplight, an untouched basket of mending in front of her. "Yes, you did," she said clearly, wondering how her husband could possibly have failed to see the stiffness of the smile on his daughter's face. To Christina she said gently, "It will be nice for you in the Travis home, Christina. Your duties will be quite light and there will be much that you can learn from Mrs Travis. I will be calling on her every Friday to deliver eggs and butter, and, every second Friday, I will bring you home for the weekend so we'll still see you quite a lot."

The smile on Christina's face lost some of its stiffness. She would be home every second weekend, that was more than she had dared hope for. "That will be something to look forward to," she said, then added quickly lest the wrong impression be given, "Not that I won't like being there, they are very nice people."

"You'll come home for Christmas, of course," her father said, smiling at her.

Christina swallowed, her eyes widening. Christmas was just over two weeks away. "I'm to go before Christmas then?"

"Doctor Travis would like you to start as soon as possible," her mother told her, finding a sudden need to delve into her box of yarns. "As I'm sure you would have noticed, his wife is expecting a baby and she's finding chasing after the two little ones very trying in this hot weather."

"When will I be going?"

"Your father will take you on Monday."

So it was that, when the first school term of 1874 commenced at the Beenleigh school, there was no Christina Skov in the roll call. By then she had been working for Doctor Travis and his wife for six weeks and counting the days until every second Friday. It wasn't that there was anything about staying with the Travis family that made her unhappy. Both the doctor and his wife were very kind to her, and so was Mrs Gilligan, the jolly Irishwoman who did the cooking and cleaning. She adored the smiling three-year-old Robert and his rosy-cheeked sister, Elizabeth, and the two children adored her openly in return. She had her own small room with a comfortable bed and frilly curtains at the window, and a real wash-stand with a prettily-flowered pitcher and basin. She wore cool dimity or gingham dresses that Mrs Travis had had made for her, petticoats with lace and ribbons, soft shoes and stockings without a single darn in them. On her eleventh birthday, Mrs Gilligan made her a wonderful cake with pink icing, and, while they were having a special tea, the children, giggling softly, presented her with an elegant brush, comb and mirror set. It was all, Christina conceded, very, very nice. It was just that it wasn't home …

Henry Schneider was still writing to her. Every two or three months she received a long, enthusiastic letter, which she took with her on her weekends at home to read to her parents. In one, received in the middle of March, he wrote that their cane had been of a high standard, one particular section yielding close on three tons of sugar to the acre.

"Hmmm, that's a good yield alright," Simon agreed. "The Schneiders certainly did well to go to Mackay."

Christina glanced up quickly, but there was no scowling regret on her father's face. Relieved, she returned her attention to the letter. "Henry asks whether we know that there are now seventy-one mills at work in Queensland and that the total production for this year is expected to go beyond twelve thousand tons?"

"Well, we do now," Simon chuckled. "I think that boy must have molasses in his veins, he's a born cane farmer if ever there was one."

Christina giggled. "I think you might be right, Father. Just listen to what else he has to say … Father is still teaching Rolf and me about all sorts of useless things, or perhaps I should say that he is trying to do so. I would much rather be learning about the cane … about new varieties and the conditions they need. So I'm afraid that I have to tell you that I now complain more loudly than my brother does."

They all laughed, light-hearted at being together in this stolen hour of relaxation before the evening meal. The late afternoon was clear and calm, with the rosy glow of the sunset spread across half the sky and the purple clouds along the western ranges golden-edged. A heat haze still clung to the land, but every so often a wisp of a breeze found its way to the small verandah where the Skov family lingered.

"It's certainly something to think about, the sugar industry advancing the way it has done," Simon mused. "The Government will be overjoyed, along with the growers. I don't think even the most optimistic of its members would have expected such results at this stage. I wonder what Captain Hope thinks about it all?"

"He was an early planter, wasn't he?" Elsie asked. "I have heard his name mentioned on a number of occasions."

"Yes, he was. He had his own manufacturing plant as early as 1864, and was almost certainly the one who began the industry on a commercial basis."

"He must have had remarkable foresight, or else he took quite a chance."

"Something of both, I would have thought." Simon's gaze wandered to his own cane, standing straight and tall in the gathering dusk, and a quick grin came to his mouth. "I wonder if they've taken our sugar into account in the twelve-thousand ton estimate?"

He really is happier, Elsie thought, returning his grin, and it's not only because Christina is home for the weekend. It's because he has been able to spend so much time on his land these past weeks, and is also close to completing his shed; because he feels that he is making some progress. Her gaze shifted to her daughter. Oh, how pretty she was in her dainty clothes, her hair neatly braided and shining. Why, even the faint freckles on her nose and cheeks seemed to add to her charm. Her smile became just a little wry. Such a difficult decision and, in the end, it had brought nothing but good for Christina. She was sparkling with health and happiness, and perhaps she had even stopped counting the days between her weekends at home.

Mrs Travis had told her about that after she'd found a piece of paper with the days written down and crossed off under Christina's pillow. At the time, Elsie could have wept for her daughter, but now the thought that she had probably stopped her counting brought no great satisfaction; she didn't want the clever and pretty Mrs Travis taking her place in Christina's life.

Mail from Schleswig and Denmark was now arriving fairly regularly, but Simon and Elsie still held their breaths as they tore open envelopes and spread the first pages. There had, however, been no bad news. All the grandparents were in good health. The new babies were doing well. The newly-married couple were already expecting their first child; Mads, to his great delight, would be a grandfather. The seasons had been fair enough. The shop in Haderslev was doing well. In fact, it appeared that the life the Skov family had left behind was going along quite serenely without them. But then a letter arrived that brought gasps to the lips of both Simon and Elsie. It was from the Ohlssens and it told them that Lars had left home at the beginning of the year heading for Australia.

"At the beginning of the year? But that's the beginning of last year," Simon exclaimed. "See, they wrote in October. My God, he must already be in the country."

Elsie wrung her hands together. "How do they seem, Maria and Peter? I do hope they don't hold us responsible."

"Of course they don't. They would never do such a thing."

"Then why did they take so long to write and tell us?"

"I don't know, Elsie. Perhaps they were hoping that he would change his mind before he left Europe and return to the farm. Or perhaps they just didn't want to think about it. They seem to be alright now, though. Peter writes that it was always on the cards, so to speak, and that he's sure that once he's found enough gold he'll be home again." Simon looked up from the letter, grinning widely. "Does that boy really think that he's going to come to Australia, pick up a fortune in gold, then sail off home again?"

"It certainly seems that way, and he's apparently got his parents thinking that too. What else does Peter have to say?"

"He says that Lars has our address and will be looking us up. Well, I should jolly well think so."

Elsie was smiling too, in spite of lingering doubts as to how their dear friends would be feeling towards them. "How wonderful it will be to see him, someone from home." She quickly corrected herself, "Someone from Haderslev." Not long after their arrival Simon had decided that it wouldn't do for them to be always referring to Haderslev or Schleswig as 'home'. Their home was now here, in the Logan valley of Queensland. It hadn't been easy for his wife and daughter and he had had to correct them many times. Now, though, it was only on rare occasions that they erred.

"It will be wonderful alright. So many questions we will have to ask him," Simon chuckled. "We'll give that boy back some of his own medicine, eh Elsie?"

"Perhaps we should start making a list."

"That mightn't be a bad idea. " He flicked the letter in his hand. "Letters never do tell you all you want to know, however much they say. Where is he, for heaven's sake?"

"He may have gone to New South Wales or Victoria."

"No, he would come to Queensland. You can bet your life that he's heard about Charters Towers and the Palmer River and there's no way he'd be passing up an opportunity to get to goldfields like those."

Elsie's smile faded. "But they are so far away. Why didn't he come to see us if he has already been in Brisbane?"

"I suppose he couldn't wait to get to the diggings. But don't be fretting, he'll be back, and before too long, I'd reckon. He would have already had a few months in which to try his luck." Simon got to his feet, grinning. "Won't Christina be excited where she hears this news?"

"Yes, she will."

Christina was, very excited. The things she had disliked about Lars Ohlssen had long since slipped into some remote corner of her mind. Now, she thought only of the nice things about him, and there was the painting, that very special gift he had given her. It was in her hands as she danced about, savouring the news her mother had kept until they reached home. Right away, she decided on a new place for it – a small shelf where he would see it the moment he stepped through the door. Neither she nor her parents imagined that they would wait more than two years for Lars Ohlssen to do that.

In the meantime, conditions on the farm improved slightly, due largely to extremely favourable weather. Simon's first planting of cane returned him twenty pounds. In the following year, the ratoon crop, together with that from an additional two acres, brought him twenty-eight pounds. Corn was fetching a slightly better price, and, even though he lost part of another crop to cockatoos, he still managed to make a small profit. He had grazed four bullocks and had no trouble selling them for seven pounds apiece. They had also made some money from the sale of potatoes and pumpkins, and from eggs, butter and the jams Elsie made from wild berries and bush tomatoes. The day when the farm would support them without the need for outside work no longer seemed quite so distant. Also, to Simon's great pride, they now had a large and sturdy shed, built with timber from his own land, even the bark slab roof.

But they buried another baby, a little girl who came into the world on the 12 September 1875, pale and still, and remained that way, despite the efforts of a distressed Doctor Travis who tried desperately to fan a spark of life, plunging the tiny body first into warm water and then into cold, repeating the process over and over.

She was buried beside her brother in the cemetery beside the Lutheran Church.

15

Lars Ohlssen rode in off the track on a steamy afternoon in mid-December 1876. Elsie and Simon saw him at the gate in almost the same moment; Elsie from the verandah where she was churning butter, Simon from his second canefield, where, with the ratoons recently harvested, he was ploughing the trash and old cane roots back into the earth. They both left their tasks and ran to meet him, waving excitedly

"Lars! Lars! We thought you were never coming!" Simon cried, pulling the lanky figure in faded shirt, corduroy trousers and blucher boots into his arms the minute he leapt from his horse. "And now here you are!"

Beneath the wide brim of his battered felt hat, Lars was grinning broadly. "How are you, Uncle Simon?"

"Fine, fine! And you, Lars, how are you?"

"I'm great." Lars eased himself free of the hands still gripping his upper arms as Elsie, flushed and smiling, rushed up to join them. "Aunty Elsie, how good it is to see you!" He gave her a bear hug, kissing first one cheek and then the other before holding her from him so that his merry eyes could search her face. "And you are just as pretty as ever."

Elsie laughed. "And you, Lars Ohlssen, have grown up to be just like your father. That's the sort of thing he would have said." But when she was able to take a good look at him, her smile faded. "Lars, you are so thin. Are you well, really well?"

"Of course I am. I'm as fit as a fiddle. You forget, I always was skinny. Ah, but it's good to see you both." He glanced about him, nodding his head appreciatively. "And what a place you've got here."

Simon beamed. "It's taken a lot of hard work, and there's still plenty more of that to be done, I can tell you. But we are getting there." He swung his arms out proudly. "We've got two hundred and fifty acres, you know? Some of them hilly and stony, but more than two-thirds with good deep soil."

Lars whistled softly. "That's some farm all right."

"We still have to do battle with the bush for the biggest part of it, as you can see. Believe me, that is a battle. The bush doesn't give up easily. It's a never-ending struggle trying to stop it taking back what we have taken from it, a real tug-of-war, you might say. Nevertheless, we are managing to clear a bit more all the time."

"I can imagine. You seem to be doing alright though, and I see you've got some sugarcane."

"Not as much as I would like to have, Lars. Still, I've made a nice little profit out of what I've grown. That patch you are looking at is twelve months old, it will be cut next season. What I was doing just now was ploughing in the old roots and rubbish after a ratoon harvesting. Not as profitable as the original crop, of course, but not a bad return all the same."

"From what I've seen, cane growing is pretty much the way to go around these parts."

"It's that alright. I've come to be sorry that we arrived too late to get ourselves a piece of land on the river flats at a reasonable price, that's where the cane does really well. A few years back, good quality land along the river could be had for as little as two shillings an acre." Simon grinned wryly, moving his shoulders as though to shake himself free of familiar regrets. "Well, it wasn't to be, so there's no point in complaining, especially since we are thankful for what we have here."

"But tell us about yourself, Lars," Elsie implored as they made their way towards the house. "Where have you been? What have you been doing?"

"At the Palmer, looking for gold."

"We thought that's where you would be," Simon chuckled. "But did you find any?"

"Some, not enough to get really excited about." Lars gave a short, self-ridiculing laugh. "I was at what they call the 'river of gold' … an early comer to boot … and all I got for myself was a paltry sixty ounces. What do you say to that for miserable luck?"

"I don't know," Elsie mused, smilingly raising her eyebrows. "That sounds like quite a deal of gold to me. How much did you get paid for it?"

"Three pounds ten shillings an ounce, that's the going rate up there."

Simon looked at him quickly, both surprised and impressed. "You didn't do too badly then. What ... something over two hundred pounds?"

Lars nodded. "But that was peanuts. Crikey, there were prospectors at the Palmer who were washing a pound of gold a day. One lucky devil got six hundred and forty ounces in just three weeks of panning."

"Good heavens! I had no idea that field was as good as that."

"It was a bonanza! Some blokes simply found the gold in the river or by pulling up tufts of grass growing on the river flats. One character picked up nuggets weighing close on a hundred and eighty ounces from under a stone dislodged by his horse's hoof." Lars grinned ruefully. "Nothing like that ever happened to me, though. I had to work hard for what I got. Not that I didn't try looking under tufts of grass, mind. I must have pulled up a million of the wretched things and turned over just as many stones."

"Well, at least you did find some gold," Elsie consoled. "I should think there were any number of prospectors who didn't find any at all."

"That's right. Even at the 'river of gold' there were those who missed out. I've seen blokes up there who were absolutely destitute, some of them with wives and children."

"Goodness, how terribly sad."

"How did you get there, Lars?" Simon wanted to know. "Did you come to Brisbane first?"

"No, I didn't come into Brisbane at all. I came out on the Herschel, and it went directly to Port Denison. I was planning on going to Charters Towers, but everyone I spoke to after I arrived reckoned the alluvial gold there was running out and it wasn't worth going. I was pretty disappointed, I can tell you. Anyhow, I was still hanging around in Townsville trying to decide what to do when I met up with this old Irishman who had heard some rumours about there being gold further north. He was getting ready to go to Georgetown, so I figured I had nothing to lose by going along with him."

"That's how you came to get to the Palmer?"

"That's right. We were at Georgetown when James Mulligan rode in with the first gold from the Palmer, over a hundred ounces. Needless to say, when he went back, old Patrick and I were with his party. My God, what a trip!" Lars closed his eyes and shook his head as though even the recollection brought pain. But, almost at once, he opened them again, laughing softly. "There'll be time enough to be telling you of such things. Right now, my tongue is hanging out for a cup of tea."

"Of course it is." Elsie exclaimed, throwing up her hands in dismay. "And here we are keeping you out in the middle of the paddock."

"Elsie will take you back to the house and show you where to put your things," Simon told him. "I'll just unharness old Toby. I don't think I'll be doing any more ploughing on this day."

"I'll help you do it tomorrow, Uncle Simon. It will be quite fun to get back to something like that after all this time." Leading his horse, he caught up with Elsie who had begun to walk more quickly back to the house. "Christina's at school, I suppose?"

"No, Christina has been working for some time now. She's nursemaid to the young children of our doctor."

"Christina, working? I can't believe it!"

"She'll be fourteen years old in January," Elsie reminded him.

"So she will. I keep picturing her as a little girl and she's grown up almost." He shook his head slowly from side to side, "Is she pretty?"

"Asking a mother whether her daughter is pretty? You should know better than that, Lars."

"I can see by your eyes that she is," Lars told her with quick grin. They lit up like stars when I asked you that."

"Well, you'll be seeing for yourself soon enough. Christina will be home tomorrow afternoon for the weekend." Elsie glanced up at the tall young man at her side, her smile fading. "You are not going to be in a hurry to leave us, I hope?"

"I should think not! After all the time it's taken me to get here! I plan to be here for a couple of weeks at least. I wondered if perhaps I might stay for Christmas."

"Oh Lars, having you here for Christmas would be just wonderful. But only a couple of weeks? Surely you can stay longer than that?"

"I hadn't really planned on being here for more than three or four weeks."

"Had you thought to return home when you leave here?"

"Heavens no! I don't intend to do that until I've done really well for myself, one way or the other. Perhaps not even then. I've come to like this country. It might be rather wild and demanding, but it's got a lot going for it and it's exciting in a way Schleswig could never be."

So, Elsie thought as she waited by the sliprail while he unsaddled his horse, Peter and Maria won't be seeing their son for a while yet, a long while, more than likely. She sighed softly, feeling for them.

"Does Christina come home only at the weekend?" Lars asked as he rejoined her, dragging his saddle and with a carpet bag slung over his shoulder.

"Not even that. She comes home every second weekend. It's just fortunate that we've got a second weekend coming up. Christina would be most upset if she got to know that you were here and then had to wait for more than a week to see you."

As Christina had planned so long ago, Lars saw the painting the minute he walked through the door. "It's my painting of your house," he exclaimed delightedly. "She's still got it."

"Why would she not still have it?" Elsie asked teasingly. "It's one of her most valued possessions."

"Is it really? I remember giving it to her at the station in Haderslev while we were waiting for your train to come in. Poor little Christina, she was so choked with tears and so bewildered she hardly knew what to do with herself." Lars gave a faint sigh. "It's hard to believe that it was such a long time ago."

"Five and a half years," Elsie said quietly as she bent to stir the slowly burning fire to greater effort beneath the suspended kettle.

"And in January it will be four years since I left home." Lars was gazing at the painting as though seeing it for the very first time. "It's strange really. Sometimes it seems that it was only yesterday that I was there, but, other times, it seems like a hundred years almost." He turned suddenly, the mists of yearning in his eyes. "Do you have any recent news from home, Aunty Elsie?"

Elsie felt a wry smile touch her mouth. All those questions they had planned on asking Lars when they'd first known that he was in Australia, and now here he was asking her for news. "We had mail a week or so back," she told him, "including a letter from your parents. They were both well at the time of writing and everything was fine on the farm and with your sisters. But you'll be able to read what they had to say for yourself. We keep all of our letters from Schleswig and Denmark. I think some of them get read a dozen times or more."

"I would appreciate that, being able to read their letter."

Elsie raised her eyes and let them rest, gently accusing, on his face. "Letters are very important when loved ones are far away, Lars, but it appears that your mother and father haven't heard from you in quite a long time."

Lars moved uneasily, shifting his weight from one leg to the other. "It was well-nigh impossible to be writing at the Palmer. For one thing, there was no writing paper to be had, unless you'd thought to take some with you." He attempted a grin that wasn't very successful. "I wish I had done that. I could have made a few bob selling some of it."

"Well, we have writing paper, so you must get a letter off to your parents as soon as possible. They'll be overjoyed to know that you are alive and well."

"I told them both before I left not to worry about me," Lars muttered a little defensively. "They know I was never a one for letter-writing."

Elsie smothered a sigh. She had no wish to be reprimanding the boy, and certainly not within an hour of his arrival. In any case, she told herself, it was probably better to encourage him to write more regularly. "We parents are worrying people, Lars, as you will learn for yourself one day. Telling us not to worry doesn't mean that we won't. Even though we try to persuade ourselves that we have no need to do so, we worry constantly about our children and, of course, when they are far away from us, it's ever so much worse."

"I suppose so." Lars scratched at the wispy beard on his chin. "I did mean to write home more often. Like I said, it was pretty much out of the question at the Palmer, but I was over in Cooktown a couple of times and I guess I could have written from there, or at least remembered to buy some paper."

Elsie smiled at him. "Well, you can make amends while you are here, at least five pages in your first letter."

"Five pages? It would take me a week to write that much. Not that I don't have a million things to tell them; it's getting it written down that's the problem."

"Christina has the same problem, especially when she writes in English. Which she does to a young boy from the ship. Sometimes it takes her an hour or more to produce just one respectable looking page."

Lars chuckled softly. "Poor Christina."

"That's just what her father says, and, if I don't stop him, he'd be writing the whole letter for her to copy." Elsie flung a tablecloth over the scrubbed pine table. "I'm sure you must be hungry as well as thirsty, Lars. How long since you've eaten?"

"I had a bit of breakfast around five."

"Goodness, you are hungry then. Starved, more than likely."

"Now that you come to mention it, I am feeling a bit that way." He looked around him. "Say, this is a really nice house you've got here. Did Uncle Simon build it?"

"No, he didn't. He wanted to do so, of course, but there was so much else needing to be done. He has made pretty much all the furniture, though, and he has built the shed."

Simon bounded noisily on to the verandah, calling to them as he paused to drag off his mud-caked boots. "How's that for a fast piece of unharnessing?"

"Pretty good, Uncle Simon," Lars laughed. "I didn't expect you for half an hour at least."

"I didn't want to miss any of your news."

"Don't be expecting Lars to have news of Haderslev," Elsie saw fit to remind her husband. "He has been in Australia for almost four years now."

"That's right, he has." Simon came through the small living room to the kitchen, grinning cheerfully. "I'm sure he has plenty to tell us nevertheless. What a pleasure it is to be able to converse in Danish after all this time."

"For me, too." Lars told him. "But I should think your English is pretty good by now."

"Well, passable, at any rate. What about yours?"

"I tell myself that I speak pure Australian, but I sometimes say things that make the blokes I'm with laugh, so I guess I've still got a way to go."

Christina stole yet another glance at the young man sitting across the table from her. It was hard to believe that at long last Lars was actually here, eating his evening meal with them. And, even though it had been such a long time since she had last seen him, he didn't appear to have changed all that much. He seemed to be a boy still, for all that he was twenty-three years of age. The beard that he had tried to grow was no more than a sparse collection of fine pale hairs, more like the fluff from a dandelion than a beard His fair skin was sunburned and against its redness his eyes were the azure blue of a summer sky, a boy's eyes still, ready for laughter and impatient for adventure. From what her mother had told her on the way home he had certainly had quite a deal of that. Christina's brow wrinkled in a faint frown. It was obvious that both her parents viewed some of the things Lars had done with quite a degree of alarm. They laughed at his amusing stories, listened intently to others, and showered him with affection, but there was an anxiety about them, as though, in some way, there was a responsibility they felt they should assume.

Lars was laughingly relating a story now, about someone in Cooktown who had sold his horse to three different men wanting to get to the Palmer and then disappeared, leaving the buyers to sort out the confusion as best they could.

"How did they sort it out?" Simon wanted to know.

"They had a three-man brawl which soon developed into a thirty-man brawl and entertained everyone who managed to stay out of it for a good hour or more. When it finally ended, there was only one of the original three still standing – the littlest bloke, would you believe? Anyhow, he just wandered over to the horse, kind of in a daze, and rode off without so much as a backward glance."

"Good for him," Simon laughingly exclaimed. "I wonder whether he was as lucky with the gold."

Lars shrugged. "Who knows? Perhaps he found a stack of it. But I tell you, Uncle Simon, finding gold wasn't the only way to becoming rich up there. In Cooktown there were dozens of ways you could have done it. All you had to do was find a way of supplying the goods that were in demand."

"A major problem, I take it?"

"It was difficult alright, but it didn't have to be top-quality stuff to find a buyer. Take the horses now ... men were so desperate to get to the Palmer they were willing to pay fifty quid for any old nag, sometimes as much as sixty. And you should have seen what the poor wretches were expected to carry."

"What about the men who couldn't get horses? Did they still insist on going?"

"Yes, there were many who walked to the diggings. Some pulled carts loaded with their possessions, others pushed wheelbarrows, and some even went so far as to drag boats rigged up on wheels so as they'd be able to cross the rivers and creeks when they were in flood. The idea was that, when they got to the Palmer, they'd break the boats up and use the timber to make the cradles and sluice boxes they needed for washing the gold. "

"I reckon that really would be a case of burning your bridges behind you. Did they never think about a return trip?"

"I guess not, or perhaps they thought the place would develop into a town and everything they required would eventually be available there. Not everyone who set out for the Palmer made it though, there are graves all along the way."

"Were any of them killed by blacks? I believe they are still pretty hostile up that way."

"Some were. There are large tribes up that way and it's true that they have no love for the white man. But most died from sickness or the hardships they had to endure along the way, sometimes from starvation when they became trapped between flooded streams and their provisions ran out. The whole journey was something of a nightmare really, especially early in the piece when there was no wagon road, and it was necessary to go north around the top of the Conglomerate Range before being able to head off to the south-west in the direction of the Palmer. That was all through unknown country covered with long dry speargrass and unbelievable anthills that looked like huge tombstones."

"The ones we saw from the ship," Christina exclaimed. "Would they be, Father?"

"I would say so, Christina. We would have been off the coast in that region when we saw them."

"Yes, you would have seen them from the ship," Lars agreed, "but only a comparatively small section. They stretch for miles and miles and cover an enormous area." He gave a short mirthless laugh. "And I can tell you it's the weirdest sensation to be riding through them day after day. You get the feeling that you're not getting anywhere, just covering the same ground over and over."

Christina gave a faint shiver. "That would be strange. I know I wouldn't like to be doing it. When we saw them from the Friedeburg we thought that it might be fun to go ashore where they were, but now I'm glad that we couldn't."

Lars smiled at her across the table. "No, you wouldn't have enjoyed the experience, Christina. In fact, I have never yet met anyone who did. Some of those who came with the first party out of Cooktown swore that the whole place was haunted. They reckoned they often saw the spear grass move where there wasn't even the faintest breeze."

"But you, yourself, didn't go to the Palmer from Cooktown, did you?" Simon queried. "Didn't you mention that you'd gone up from Georgetown with Mulligan?"

"Yes, that's right. I only went over to Cooktown later on to sell the gold Patrick and I had found and bring back more provisions. Actually, I was at the Palmer before Cooktown came into existence, as a town, at any rate." He chuckled quietly. "It more or less sprang up in a day, you know, towards the end of October in '73. Word of the gold had spread like wildfire in New South Wales and Victoria and ships in their dozens were making their way up the coast. Even though it was a hundred and fifty miles from the Palmer, with several rivers and a thousand-foot-high mountain range in between, Cooktown … or rather what was to become Cooktown … was the closest coastal point and that was where everyone wanted to be off-loaded. It didn't seem to matter that there was no road, no track either except for the trodden-down speargrass along the route taken by the first party to go that way." Again he gave a short laugh. "But who am I to be talking about having no track? For most of the way up from Georgetown we didn't have one either."

"Did you have a horse?" Christina asked.

"Yes, I had a horse, and so did my old friend Patrick. We bought them in Townsville and got a much better deal than we would have later on in Cooktown."

"How far was it from Georgetown to the Palmer?"

"Two hundred and fifty miles. And some of those who went that way also walked. They were called swagmen. They walked behind the wagons and drays and carried their belongings in a swag, unless they could afford to pay to have them put on one of the vehicles."

Elsie slowly shook her head. "The endurance of men when gold is the lure."

Lars grinned. "I would have walked if it had been necessary. Old Patrick would have too."

"Oh Lars, please don't tell me such things."

Christina watched him, almost as horrified as her mother was, but he was grinning cheerfully as he gave further attention to his meal. It might have all been hard and dangerous, she thought, but he still seems to have enjoyed his time in Australia. He looked, in fact, fit and healthy, and brimful of energy, in spite of the fact that he had spent the day helping her father in the cane field.

"Was it a big party that Mulligan took up?" Simon asked.

"Yes, it was. A hundred or more miners, quite a few of them with families, some three hundred horses and bullocks, and, I suppose, around forty wagons and drays, all piled high with tents, stores, tools, dynamite and so forth; all in all, a great straggling procession following one man. He was a damned good leader though; got us to the Palmer in fourteen days, in spite of the fact that there was no track whatsoever once we'd passed the last homestead. I have to admit that I had a few qualms along the way though. I just couldn't believe that we could head off into the bush the way we were doing, with Mulligan blazing the trees and the teamsters cutting rough passages for their wagons, and get to where we wanted to go." He laughed quietly, the glow of affection in his eyes. "Not old Patrick, though. He had complete faith and never once doubted that, in due course, we would arrive at our destination. Of course, James Venture Mulligan was an Irishman like himself, and, in Patrick's view, that was just about the best recommendation anyone could have asked for."

"He must be quite a character, this friend of yours," Elsie remarked, smiling.

"He's that alright. Many's the tale I'll be telling you about that old bloke, mark my word. I was really sorry to have to part from him, but I couldn't talk him into leaving the north. But, to get back to Mulligan and the trail he blazed for us. The bush itself turned out to be no real problem, not when compared with the creek and river crossings. They caused no end of trouble. The wet season was over so there wasn't a lot of water to contend with, just this rotten loose sand. Time and time again, it brought the bullocks to their knees and overturned the wagons. In fact, it quite often took a whole day to get everything across to the far bank."

"Elsie held up her hand as Simon opened his mouth to ask another question. "That's enough for now. We must let Lars finish his meal. Just look at him, only halfway through, whereas all our plates are empty."

"I think I must have had more on my plate."

"You've had too many questions to answer, that's what."

"Not too many from Christina, though. Is she always so quiet?"

"No, she is not," Simon told him with a chuckle. "Usually, when she comes home for the weekend, she has so much to relate her mother and I can't get a word in edgeways."

Christina felt the warm colour flooding into her cheeks and was at once angry at herself. Now Lars would know that, even though she was no longer a small child, she still blushed, and he would more than likely laugh at her just as he used to do back in Haderslev. It could even be that he was doing that already. Not openly, but within himself. There was certainly a gleam in his eyes, of amusement, more than likely.

"I have a good idea," he announced. "Since I've hardly had a chance to talk to Christina, I will wash the dishes and she can dry them. That will let us get to know one another again."

"I have a better idea," Elsie told him. "You can talk to Christina on the verandah where there just might be a little breeze, while Simon and I do the dishes."

When Christina and Lars moved on to the verandah, the first stars had appeared in the darkening sky. The breeze stirred only intermittently but the air was fragrant with the scent of the honeysuckle climbing over both ends of the verandah, and of the roses, budding and full-blown, on the lone, petted bush by the steps. The sounds of the night were beginning, those of the day fading From the trees on the hillsides came the call of a mopoke, early astir, the harsh drumming song of the cicadas, and the bickering of countless parrots not yet settled for the night; from a tall gum tree by the creek, the goodnight chortles of a family of kookaburras, unlike their excitable neighbours well content with their resting place; from the creek itself, the cheerful croaking of frogs and the gurgling of storm-fed waters over rocks and pebbles; from the nearby paddocks the soft lowing of a cow and the gentle whinny of a horse, as gently answered; and, from every direction, the buzzing of mosquitoes, kept at bay, except for a venturesome few, by the smoke rising lazily from drums in which dry cow dung had been put to the match at sunset.

"It's the one thing about this country I'm not partial to, the wretched mosquitoes." Lars slapped at his cheek as he lowered his long, lean body to the top step and settled his back against a post. "Flies and mosquitoes, did you ever believe there could be so many?"

"No, I didn't," Christina told him, sitting on a canvas chair and pressing the folds of her skirt down over her knees. "We had our first real encounter with the mosquitoes on our way down from Brisbane. When we stopped for the night they came out of the bush in such swarms I was sure they were going to carry us off." She laughed softly, a little self-consciously.

"That was what a man in Brisbane had jokingly told us they could do."

Lars grinned. "And you thought it was actually going to happen?"

"Not really, but there were times when it almost seemed possible. And they were so vicious, we had lumps all over us."

"I know what that's like, scratch, scratch, scratch."

Christina smiled, relaxing a little. "Mother is forever telling me not to do that … just to rub the bites, otherwise they could turn into sores. It's awfully hard not to scratch, though."

"Hard? For me it's impossible. Sometimes I've even wished that I had an extra pair of hands for that very purpose."

"Or longer arms," Christina chuckled. "So they could reach all over my back."

"Yes, that too. Are they always bad here?"

"No, only in the summer months when there's been some rain. Dusk is always the worst time for them, of course."

"Well, at least you don't seem to have as many flies as I've seen in some places. I've known them to be so thick, it's well-nigh impossible to keep them away from your eyes and nose, and out of your mouth when you're speaking or trying to eat."

Christina grimaced. "Ugh, how sickening that would be. It's bad enough when one gets in the milk or lands in the butter."

"Especially when the heat has turned the butter to oil, eh?"

They both laughed softly, recalling such an incident at the table they had just left.

"You should have seen Father when we first came here. Every time something like that happened he wanted to throw the whole lot out; he was just so disgusted at the thought of a fly swimming in the butter. But now he's quite content to have it removed with a spoon. He says that in this country such things are done in even the very best circles."

"Well, I would hope so. Think of the waste there would otherwise be. But what about this job of yours, Christina? Your mother said that you are a nursemaid?"

"Yes, I look after the Travis children."

"And you like doing that?"

"Oh yes, the children are very sweet, and Doctor and Mrs Travis are ever so kind to me. Mother says they treat me like a daughter."

"That's nice, Christina. I'm glad for you."

"I'm glad for me too. I think I'm lucky to have a position with such nice people."

"So, now I know what you've been doing with some of your time since you arrived in this country. You've been looking after the Travis children, slapping mosquitoes and rubbing their bites, and fishing flies out of the butter. But what else, Christina? You must have a score of things to tell me."

"I haven't done any of the exciting things that you have."

"I should hope not. The goldfield is no place for a young lady, believe me. And neither are some of the other places I've been."

"I didn't really mean that. I should have said that I hadn't done anything as exciting … " Christina floundered to a halt, but a pleased smile tugged at the corners of her lips. He had called her a young lady, even though she had been so tongue-tied all evening and even though she still blushed. A young lady. And he hadn't said it in the same way her father did, or Doctor Travis either. It was as though he really did think of her as a young lady. But what was she to talk about if he was to continue to think that way, for heaven's sake?

"I got lost once," she said at last, with a small, apologetic smile. "Not that it was very exciting at the time. It was more frightening than anything else, but, afterwards, when it was clear that the only harm that had befallen me was a collection of scratches, it seemed to be."

"Where did you get lost, in the bush?"

"Yes, over there." Christina waved a hand in the direction of the dark outline beyond the canefields. "It wasn't very long after we arrived and I followed a young wallaby into the bush. I wandered for miles trying to find my way out again and finished up over by the river. A young black boy brought me home, but not all the way; as soon as he heard Father calling me he pointed out the track I should follow and then just disappeared."

Lars had jerked his head around, his eyes flying to her face. "A black boy … ?"

Christina nodded, smiling, happy in the recollection. "Yes, and he was very kind to me. He walked very fast, but every so often he would stop and wait for me to catch up. And he told me the Aboriginal names for a whole lot of things. I still remember some of them. He was funny, too. Oh Lars, you should have seen how he carried on with a big old turkey that was guarding a nest. It was as though the two of them were doing a funny sort of reel, rushing back and forth at one another and circling around."

Lars was smiling, his alarm vanished in the face of her relived amusement. "This boy must have belonged to a tribe that had become civilised, as they say."

"Oh no, he didn't. I've seen some of those in Beenleigh, and he wasn't at all like them."

"What do you mean, he wasn't like them?"

"Well, he didn't seem to know any of our words, for one thing – English words, I mean. For another..." Christina hesitated, her glance going to the open door, then continued in a whisper, "I have never told anyone before, but he didn't wear any clothes, and neither did the others who were with him, not even the grown men."

The smile had been wiped from Lars's face and he stared at her, aghast. "Grown men? My God, Christina, you could have been killed."

Christina stared back at him, blankly, feeling disappointment wash through her. Why did he have to go and say that? After she had told him about the black boy being so kind and amusing and bringing her back to her father? After she had confided in him about them all being naked?

"No," she said flatly, "they didn't want to harm me. I don't believe it ever occurred to them to do so. They were afraid I might have had someone with me who would have been wanting to harm them, though."

Her words had been pointed, and, after a moment or two, Lars nodded thoughtfully before turning to gaze out into the gathering darkness. "I see what you mean, Christina," he said quietly. "You could be right. We have probably given the blacks a great deal to fear one way and another. It makes you wonder whether perhaps we couldn't have gotten off to a better start with them, looked on them as people instead of savages for one thing."

Christina breathed a faint sigh of relief. At least Lars didn't have a great hatred of the blacks inside him the way some people did. "No one could have considered the boy I met a savage," she told him, "not once they got to know him. I must confess that I was filled with fear when I first saw him though. He had a spear taller than himself and he had killed a possum." She gave a short, soft laugh. "I thought that was a terrible thing for him to have done, but since then I've come to understand that it wasn't a needless killing. He and his family would have eaten the flesh and used the skin to make a rug."

"Yes, they would have. How old was this boy that he was contributing to the family larder?"

"I thought perhaps around eleven or twelve, but it wasn't easy to know." Again Christina laughed softly, this time a little self-consciously. "I've often thought about him since that time, and, when I was younger, there were occasions when I had a feeling that he was in the edge of the bush watching me."

"He might well have been, Christina."

They were silent for several moments, each lost in thoughts that took them back to other times. Then Lars said quietly, "At the Palmer I met up with an old 'Forty-niner' from California, who had been at every major Australian gold rush since Ballarat. He'd come to know quite a lot about this country and he had very definite ideas on the subject of the Aborigines. He reckoned that Europeans coming to Australia should have learned from the Americans and their problems with the Indians, but that we hadn't, that we were making the same mistakes. He had some first-hand knowledge to support his views, too. He told me that when he'd come across from Cooktown with one of the very first parties to go that way, they had seen hundreds of blacks but that they had just stood and stared at them, amazed rather than hostile, and made no attempt whatsoever to try to stop or harm them. That was until a couple of idiots on horseback decided to take a pot shot at them and finished up killing or wounding quite a few. The blacks fled, but that night they were back, and this time it wasn't just to stand and watch. They were out for revenge, and the bloodbath up there has continued ever since."

Christina was horrified. "It could have all been avoided?"

Lars shrugged his shoulders. "I wouldn't be the one to be saying that. Christina, it's something no one can really know. It could well have been that once the blacks had recovered from their amazement they would have become hostile in any case. There are a number of war-like tribes in the north and it's hard to see them taking kindly to white people moving into their territory. Still, the fact remains that a peaceful approach was never really tried."

"What a tragedy it has all been. And is there now no hope of something being done to end the conflict up there in the north?"

"It will end alright, Christina, but only when the blacks have been subdued; either that or wiped out. But, whatever happens, in the north it's going to take longer than it has done in other places for the white man to have things the way he wants them. It's not brief skirmishes with individual clans that he has to contend with up there. It's a different story altogether. As I have said, the tribes are large and strong, but, more importantly, they seem to be able to organise themselves. That has been obvious from some of the attacks they have launched; there's nothing weak or despairing about them, believe me. In fact, a number of small townships to the south of the Palmer, around the Gilbert River area, have had to be evacuated because of continued, well-planned raids. The Kyowarra and Daldewarra tribes have even been bold enough to attack the heavily-armed gold escorts." Lars gave a short, mirthless laugh. "Not that they have any interest in the gold; it's useless stuff as far as they are concerned. What they see as being far more valuable are the horses' shoes … from those they can fashion axes."

"So they leave the gold and take the horses?"

"They always leave the gold. Bodies have been found with hundreds of pounds worth still on them. But they don't usually take the horses either, they kill them and take only the shoes."

"What strange people they are."

"They're strange alright, but then they no doubt think the same thing about us. Can you imagine the ridicule they must feel when they see hundreds of us scratching around in a river bed in the hope of finding small yellow pebbles?"

"I guess they would think that was pretty stupid. Those tribes you mentioned, are they the really big ones?"

"There are others just as big, perhaps even stronger, but the Merkin are the most feared, mainly because they are cannibals."

Christina shuddered. "Are they really cannibals, or is that just what people suppose?"

"They are cannibals all right. It's even said that they are choosey in their search for a meal, that they would rather have a Chinaman roasting on their fires than a white man."

"Why, for heaven's sake?"

"The Chinaman is supposed to taste like pork, whereas the white man is said to be tough and salty."

"Oh Lars, that's horrible," Christina protested with a small half-laugh. "It can't be true, surely?"

"It's supposed to be."

"But do you really believe it?"

Lars laughed. "I think I must, Christina. I know that, whenever I was obliged to go anywhere near where the Merkin might be, I always hoped that a few unwary Chinamen had been there before me."

Christina's laugh was still uncertain. Was she really expected to believe such a horrific tale? It seemed so, since Lars, himself, apparently believed it. Besides, it wasn't the first time she had heard that some of the Aboriginal tribes were cannibals. Why, she had overheard Mr Hunter telling her father that some of them even ate their own people. But, in a way, that was different. In the first place, they didn't kill the person, they only ate him if he was already dead. In the second place, there was a reason apart from that of providing a meal; it was done so that those eating the flesh would inherit whatever good traits and exceptional qualities the dead person had possessed. It was, according to Mr Hunter, a primitive way of ensuring that such things were not lost to the tribe.

Lars interrupted her uneasy thoughts. "Now, look what has happened.

I've done most of the talking again and you were the one who was supposed to be telling me things."

"Well, I did tell you about getting lost … "

"Which led us into a discussion about the blacks. But that happened when you were a little girl. What has been happening to you since you've been growing up? Do you have friends of your own age?"

"Yes, I have a very nice friend, her name is Marie Hunter. I see her quite often in Beenleigh and sometimes she comes out here to the farm on the weekends that I am home. We often go riding together."

"Not into the bush, I hope?" Lars teased.

"No, just around the paddocks mainly. Sometimes we dismount at the first shady tree we come to and sit and talk for the whole afternoon." Again Christina gave him a faintly apologetic smile. "It may not seem like much, but it's very pleasant being with Marie. We laugh a lot, about all sorts of things."

"Well, it's good that you have a nice friend to talk and laugh with. What about at the Doctor's house, do you have anything to laugh about there?"

"Heavens yes! The children are always saying funny things, and Doctor Travis likes to make small jokes at the dinner table; that's when he's home, of course, and if he doesn't fall asleep because he's so tired."

"He's a busy man then?"

"Yes, very busy. He travels miles and miles calling on sick people, and he has to go out at all hours of the day and night, and in all sorts of weather, too. Mrs Travis plays the piano very well, and she likes to have musical evenings every so often, but they are always difficult to arrange with the doctor on call all the time." Christina grinned. "She keeps her own calendar of when she thinks all the expected babies will be arriving. She says it's more reliable than the doctor's because he goes by the book, whereas she goes by instinct."

"What does the good doctor say to that?"

"He just tells her to go ahead and arrange her evenings according to her instinct, but not to blame him if she finds herself without her best baritone."

They both laughed quietly.

"What do you do at these musical evenings?" asked Lars.

"I sing in the choir Mrs Travis has organised. Marie does, too, and her mother. Mrs Hunter has a beautiful voice, better than a lot of opera singers in Europe, according to Mrs Travis."

Having begun, it was easy. Christina discovered that, after all, she had a great deal to relate. She told Lars about going to school for such a short time and the trouble she still had with her spelling; about the Agricultural Show held every year, how everyone looked forward to it, and how, this year, her mother had entered a bottle of wild raspberry jam which had won first prize, and a jar of pickles which had won second prize; about the people she had come to know since going to live in the doctor's house; and about Henry Schneider and how he still wrote to her. "He lives at Mackay," she explained. "His father was always interested in growing sugarcane and they went in for it in a big way."

"And are doing very well, I should think."

Christina sighed, recalling the dismaying news in Henry's most recent letter. "They aren't now. Last year was really good for them. The Mackay district produced six thousand tons of sugar; that was almost half the production for the whole of Queensland. Henry was very excited about their own return; he wrote that it was beyond their wildest expectations. But this year the sugar industry in the Mackay district has been wiped out."

"Goodness! What on earth happened?"

"Some disease they are calling 'rust' attacked the cane. It seems that in a single night every field was blighted."

"Has it only happened at Mackay?"

"So far. Some of the bigger cane farmers here at the Logan were very worried, but, luckily, the disease hasn't spread out of the Mackay district. Henry says that it happened because they were all using just the one type of cane, which was rich in sugar but too delicate for those latitudes. It's called 'Bourbon' and it was really good for a time, but, when the original stock became weak, it only needed a poor season for the disease to take hold. Henry says that he always felt they were taking too much for granted with the cane they were planting."

"This young friend of yours appears to be quite an authority where the cane is concerned."

"He does know a lot, but he would like to know more. He's always said that he would rather be learning about the different types of cane than doing all the lessons his father, who was a teacher in Germany, insists that he and his brother do."

"Well, perhaps his father will let him do that now. Still, it's rotten luck for them, for Queensland, too, what with so much of its sugar coming from that region. What are they planning to do about the setback?"

"Start again, using hardier varieties of cane. Henry says that things will be tough for a time, but that they are sure the industry will soon be thriving again."

With the stars in their millions claiming the heavens, darkness came to the small verandah, and Christina glanced a little uncertainly to where the light from the lamp in the kitchen made an oblong splash on the floorboards. Should she and Lars be going inside since it seemed that her mother and father weren't coming to join them? The clatter of dishes being washed and dried had ceased some time ago. Now, the only sound drifting through the open door was that of muted voices.

"I'm glad that you still have that painting, Christina."

"It has meant a lot to me." Christina at once bit her lip, dismayed at the inadequacy of the words. But what was she to tell him? That there had been many times when the colours had been blurred and misty because of the tears that filled her eyes? Others when her throat had ached with such a tenderness of loss it was almost more than she could bear? Or of how it sometimes seemed that only by looking at the painting was she able to recall what living in Haderslev had been like, so distant and unreal had it become?

"Will you go back, Christina, when you are older?"

Christina started, her gaze flying to where Lars's face was a pale oval against the darkness, her heart beginning a strangely uneasy beating. He was the first person to have asked her that question. Thus, not once during the five years she had been in Australia had she been obliged to bring to the forefront of her mind the promise she'd made to herself as the Friedeburg sailed past Holstein on its way to the open sea. It had always been there, of course, nestling in some remote recess, something she knew, but didn't really think about.

"Well?" Lars prompted. "Will you?"

"It would be much too difficult."

"But you have thought that you would?"

"Yes, I suppose so, but only vaguely. It's not that I'm not happy here, it's just that a part of me seems to belong back in Schleswig." She had spoken very softly and in order to hear her Lars swung his body around. His face came into the top edge of the splash of light and Christina saw that he was watching her intently. "A part of your heart?' he questioned gently.

A part of her heart? Was that really the way it was? Christina wondered. Then, with a soft laugh, she said, "I will have to go back then, won't I? Or is it possible to go through life with part of your heart in some other place?"

Lars smiled at her. "I think it must be, Christina. There would be many people in Australia doing that. I've even seen tough old Patrick with tears in his eyes when he talked about the green fields of Ireland or played some sentimental Irish tune on his fiddle, and he's been in the country ever since he deserted his ship in Melbourne in the fifties."

"Will he ever go back?"

"He has always said that he will, but I don't believe that he'll ever get around to it. Even if he found a fortune on some goldfield I have my doubts as to whether he would go. He has become too much a part of this country, or perhaps it's the other way around and it has become too much a part of him."

Would it be that way for her too? Christina wondered, leaving her chair to cross the verandah and gaze up at the brilliant stars of the Southern Cross. Would this sometimes-green, sometimes-brown land hold her for all the days of her life and then enfold her body when she died? In spite of the promise she had made to herself, was that the way it was going to be? No, of course it wasn't.

Her silent denial was accompanied by an involuntary shaking of her head, and Lars laughed softly. "What are you saying 'no' to?"

"I was just thinking about Patrick and wondering whether … " She gave her shoulders a faint shrug. "It was nothing really. Does he play the violin well?"

"Now, that's a change of subject if ever I heard one."

"It's not, really. We were talking about him only moments ago."

"Hmmm … I still have the feeling I haven't been told something important. There you were, gazing dreamily at the stars one minute, shaking your head the next, quite vigorously, as a matter of fact."

"You are exaggerating, Lars Ohlssen, and you haven't answered my question. Does Patrick play the violin well?"

"I don't know, Christina, I'm no musician. He does seem to be able to turn out quite a range of tunes, some of them quite lively, but others as mournful as the very devil. None of them appreciated at two or three o'clock in the morning, I can tell you that."

Christina's laugh was a delighted ripple. "Did he really play at those hours?"

"Yes, quite often. Whenever he couldn't sleep, he'd get up and dig out his wretched instrument."

"What did you do when that happened?"

"Begged him to stop and might as well have saved my breath. But other blokes in the camp were rather more forceful with their objections. Not only did they bellow out for him to stop but all sorts of things came pelting against our tent. One night a practically new blucher boot sailed in under the flap. That stopped Patrick, but only for as long as it took him to pull the boot on. Then he grabbed the fiddle again, grinning like mad, and began playing with renewed gusto, quite convinced that the second boot would follow."

Christina had burst out laughing as the tale unfolded, but she managed to gasp, "And did it?"

"No, it didn't. The owner followed instead, a great, brawny fellow who tipped Patrick almost upside down to recover his property. Then he marched off, not only with the boot, but with the fiddle as well."

"Goodness, did he return the fiddle?"

"Yes, after a few days. I think he got tired of seeing Patrick's gloomy face around the camp. But he made him promise that he'd restrict his playing to the daylight or early evening hours and that he wouldn't play Come Back to Erin more than twice on any one day."

"That seems fair enough to me. Did he keep his promise?"

"For almost three weeks he did. Then one night he drank more than his quota of whisky and became very melancholy around midnight. The violin came out and he must have played Come Back to Erin a dozen or more times."

"That would have brought a few protests?"

"Protests? It had the whole camp in an uproar. But, do you know, Christina, when we left the Palmer, Patrick still had his fiddle and, what's more, it was still in one piece. To me that was one of the real miracles of that place."

They were still laughing when Simon came to the door and announced that it was past his bedtime.

"We'll have a lot more talks before I leave, Christina," Lars said as he got to his feet.

Christina nodded. "Mother says that I might ask Mrs Travis about having a holiday while you are here."

"That's a great idea. Mrs Travis had better say 'yes'."

Mrs Travis did say 'yes'. In fact, seeing Christina's delight at having someone from Schleswig staying with them, she insisted that, beginning on the following Friday, she take three full weeks, leading up to and including Christmas and the New Year.

16

Lars Ohlssen quickly and easily slipped back into the lives of the Skovs, though in a very different way from that they had known in Haderslev. Every day he toiled tirelessly on their farm, ploughing, hoeing, and planting, or ring-barking, felling trees and digging out roots as more land was tediously claimed from the bush. Every night, when they all sat on the verandah and watched the moon climb up into the star-studded sky, he carried them off to the almost unbelievable world of the gold-seekers in the Colony's far north ...

He told them of how it was at the Palmer at the end of 1873 when, with the wet season about to set in, there were a thousand people at the site, far more than could be fed, since, with nothing more than a pack-trail from Cooktown, the only supplies that could be brought in by the wagon-load were those from Georgetown, which had, in the first place, to be procured from Townsville. Of how starvation was staved off for a time by the arrival from Georgetown of two loaded bullock wagons only hours before the streams flooded and cut the Palmer diggings off from both towns. He told them of the prices paid for the supplies brought in: twenty pounds for a bag of flour, seven shillings for a pound of tea, thirty shillings for a pound of tobacco, and forty shillings for a pair of blucher boots. And of a horseshoe being worth an ounce of gold, while horseshoe nails were bought for their weight in gold.

He told them of how it was in the middle of the wet season in early '74, when men had bags of gold but empty bellies; of how some shot and ate their horses, while others made a stew by boiling their blucher boots with pigweed. Of how hundreds set out, some in large groups, some in small parties, to try to reach Cooktown, many of them carrying a fortune in gold; of how some drowned in the flooded rivers and creeks, while others starved to death when trapped between streams, and still others died at the hands of the blacks. Of how those struggling to reach Cooktown met up with a thousand others struggling to get to the Palmer. And of how, when the wet season ended, decomposed bodies were found with the gold, so jubilantly won and in the end so useless, still on them.

He told of how only the experience of his friend, Patrick Donovan, toughened and knowing after years at other Queensland diggings, had sent him off, as the rains were beginning, on a life-saving ride to Cooktown; of how, knowing he couldn't spare the time to follow the track around the northern end of the Conglomerate Range, he had come and gone through the notorious Hell's Gate Pass, a gloomy defile between massive rocks that was only just wide enough to allow the passage of a loaded pack-horse, its eastern descent so steep and dangerous that a horse losing its footing would fall at once to its death; of how blacks lay in wait at the pass – the dreaded Merkin tribe who could launch a spear from a woomera for a distance of a hundred and fifty yards; and of how, on his return trip, he had had to cross some of the streams clinging to his horse's tail.

He told them about the town that sprang up at the diggings when a road from Cooktown across the range was opened, a town, named Mayfair, that became the capital of the Palmer: a shanty town with three banks, ten stores, twenty or more tiny Chinese shops, two dozen gambling dens and three dozen hotels. Of how, every Saturday night, crowds of miners passed bags of gold across the counters; of how J.S.Denny, the Gold Assayer, had bars of bullion, dishfuls of nuggets, barrels of gold dust and heaps of rich specimens piled on the ant-bed floor and gin-case counter of his bark hut; and of how a miner who had done well during the week would 'shout' for all and sundry, buying a tubful of champagne and carrying it out into the street where everyone was invited to dip in his pannikin.

He told them about the coming of the Chinese in the later months of '74; about how the Europeans, tired of the hardships and the never-ending shortage of food, were at first happy to let them on to the field, but then later became hostile towards them when such numbers arrived they outnumbered the Europeans by seven to one; about how thoroughly the Chinamen worked on the river bed, refusing to move on while there was still a chance that even a single grain of gold remained; about how they lived in squalor, the stench of their camps like that of a pigsty, yet still referred to themselves as 'celestial gentlemen'; of how they worked for a bossman under terms set down in Canton or some other distant place, smuggling the greater part of the gold they found back to China.

"They really did smuggle it out, eh?" Simon asked as he tapped his pipe against the edge of the verandah.

"Yes, whenever they could manage to do so. The gold was worth more back in China than it was here in Queensland." Lars gave a short, ridiculing laugh. "The official records of the gold won at the Palmer are really quite a joke, Uncle Simon. Take 1874, for instance … the total gold won was supposed to be a quarter of a million ounces, but anyone who was up there will tell you that it was a whole lot more than that, something over seven hundred thousand ounces. And it wasn't only the Chinese who were sneaking it out, believe me."

"That's a lot of gold." Simon exclaimed, almost dropping his pipe in his astonishment. "And there's still more up there?"

"Heavens yes! What was taken out up until the end of '75 was mainly the alluvial stuff. It's really only been this year that crushing mills have been set up and a start made on the reefs themselves. They are going to yield a fortune, you can bet your life. But that's not for the small prospector hoping for instant riches, it's for those with capital enough to undertake a long-term project."

"Surely some of those who did find gold in respectable quantities were prepared to risk some of it for what might have been an even greater return?"

Lars shrugged. "It wouldn't have been a risk even, just a case of having a little patience. Who knows? Perhaps a few of them did that. Not the majority, though. They moved on as soon as the alluvial gold began to peter out. Hundreds left the Palmer even before I did, most of them joining in the rush to the Hodgkinson."

"Is it going to be as good as the Palmer?"

"I doubt it. If I'd thought that it was going to be even half as good, I would have gone there myself." He grinned. "And then it would have been another year or more before I got around to visiting you."

"I'm glad you didn't then," Elsie told him. "We waited long enough as it was for you to show up."

The stories both enthralled and horrified, and they sometimes kept Simon and Elsie awake long after gentle snores coming from the makeshift bed in the sitting room told them that their narrator was fast asleep. "Perhaps it's just as well he didn't write to Peter and Maria while he was up there," Elsie whispered one night as they both lay wide-eyed in the darkness. "He probably would have told them a lot of the things he has done and can you imagine how they would have reacted?"

"With a heart seizure, more than likely," Simon muttered. "It's only the fact that he's here, alive and well, that has prevented me from having one myself. I'm sure I don't know how that boy has managed to survive, especially when you consider the somewhat protected upbringing he had back in Haderslev."

"I think that Irishman he always talks about may have had a good deal to do with that."

"Probably, but don't forget that it was Lars who rode into Cooktown for their provisions."

Although the night was stiflingly hot, Elsie shivered. "With a tribe of cannibals lying in wait. The very thought gives me goose bumps."

"Don't be thinking about it, try to go to sleep."

Elsie gave a small exasperated sigh. "I've been trying to do that for the past hour or so." After a moment or two, she asked, "Has he told you what he means to do, when he leaves here?"

"I don't think he knows himself. He's proposed at least half a dozen different things. One day he's talking about going out west, getting a job, and saving enough money to buy a sheep station; the next he's on about returning to the goldfields to get the money he would need. But then he seems to change his mind about the sheep station and talks about going south, reckons he'd like to see something of the other colonies before returning home."

"He does mean to go home then?"

Simon moved his shoulders against his bunched-up pillow. "It sometimes seems that way, but I have a feeling it won't be for a while yet."

Elsie groaned softly. "I keep thinking that we should be doing something, guiding him in some way."

"I feel the same way, but what can we do when all is said and done? He's not a boy any more, he's a grown man. I've assured him that he's welcome to stay on here for as long as he wishes, hoping, of course, that, if he's not going to return home, he might think of taking up some land hereabouts for himself, but he seems determined to be moving on."

"Right after Christmas?"

"That's what he says."

For Christina the time was passing much too quickly. Apart from the times when her mother and father appeared to be worrying about what was to become of Lars, a wonderful feeling of light-heartedness had come into their lives. And such times they had. Why, even her mother had laughingly done things that would never have been expected of her. Like the really hot day when they'd had a picnic lunch on the creek bank and Lars had coaxed her into taking off her shoes and stockings to go wading in the cool water with the rest of them. Or the night she had danced a polka with him on the moon-silvered grass, while her father had played his mouth-organ. How happy and young she had seemed. Lars had danced with her too, Christina recalled, smiling at the dough she was kneading. First a polka and then a waltz in which he'd taken such giant steps he had swung her right off her feet.

"Now what could possibly be amusing about a heap of dough?" Christina spun around, her mouth dropping open, soft colour rushing to her cheeks. He was standing in the back doorway, grinning widely. How long had he been there, for heaven's sake? "Or do you always giggle when you are making bread?"

"I wasn't giggling."

"Yes, you were. Giggling away to yourself as though you'd just thought of something very amusing."

"Perhaps I was remembering how Mother wouldn't let you go to bed last night until you'd finished that letter to your parents?"

Lars groaned. "What a hard task-master she is. But she's right, of course, I do need to write to them more often."

"And more than just one page."

"That too, I suppose."

"Did Father come with you?"

"No, that big pile of rubbish is still burning and he stayed to keep an eye on it. We don't want it setting the whole bush alight. But there seems to be another storm brewing and he thought it might be a good idea to get the milking done early."

"Gosh, I hope Mother gets home before it breaks."

"She's not likely to be dawdling in Beenleigh once she sees those clouds." He glanced down at her hands methodically working the dough. "How long are you going to be with that? I've already brought the cows up. Will I wait or go and start?"

Christina held up her hands, inspecting them for any signs of clinging dough. "It looks as though it's been kneaded enough. I'll just cover it and tidy up a bit and then I'll be with you."

"I'll fetch the buckets."

He was waiting for her by the clothes line. "I'm glad you left that flour on your nose, it looks real cute."

"Oh, for heaven's sake!" Christina exclaimed, at once rubbing at her nose with a corner of her apron.

Lars grinned, his merry eyes on her flushed face. "Father was right, you know? In fact, you are growing into such a beauty, I might come back and marry you, when I become rich, that is."

"You are being silly," Christina admonished, but a faint, involuntary smile touched her lips and Lars was quick to notice. Laughing softly he reached over and looped her long plaits into a loose knot. "Silly, am I? Well, I'm not so sure. Now that the idea has occurred to me it seems to be quite a good one."

Christina shook her head, freeing her plaits, before pulling on her hat. Keeping her thick lashes lowered lest her eyes betray the confusion she was feeling, she forced herself to speak lightly, "I should think you'd already have a sweetheart somewhere. If the truth be known, more than one."

Lars gave her a glance of assumed rebuke as he gathered up the buckets. "Now how could that be when I've been all that time at the Palmer? No, I've been waiting for you to grow up. How old are you now, Christina?"

"I'll be fourteen in January, as you know very well, Lars Ohlssen."

"Hmmm … that means I have another two years in which to make my fortune." He nodded, grinning widely. "That should be time enough."

He turned and strode off in the direction of the cow bails, and Christina had to run to catch up with him. "I'm not going to get married at sixteen," she informed him, the minute she did so.

"My mother did, and I don't think she was ever sorry. After all, look what she got out of it – me."

"And what a reward that was. I had no idea you were so conceited." She grinned up at him. "Though I used to think that you were a know-all, and I suppose that's much the same thing."

Lars threw back his head on a shout of laughter. "Ah Christina, did you really think that?"

"Not all of the time. Sometimes, I thought you were quite nice. And, after you gave me the painting, I didn't once think of you as a know-all, at least I don't think I did."

"Well, thank heavens for that. But you still haven't told me why you don't want to be married at sixteen. It's what most girls want, to be married young."

"It might be, but it's not what I want. I may not get married at all, as a matter of fact."

"Why ever not?" Lars stopped so abruptly, Christina, a pace or two behind, bumped into the bucket swinging from his hand. He stared at her, disbelief wiping the teasing laughter from his face. "You don't really mean that?"

Christina squirmed beneath his suddenly piercing gaze. "There's nothing wrong with not wanting to get married."

"But why would you not want to?"

"Oh, I don't know. It's just something I've … " Her mind groped for words with which to complete the sentence, but found none. And what was there to say when all was said and done? she asked herself. She couldn't be telling Lars that she had no wish to be having babies just to see them die. She shouldn't have told him about not wanting to be married in the first place. If she hadn't done that, she wouldn't be in this uncomfortable situation, being expected to explain why. But then how could she have known that Lars would take her so seriously? Once, she had said the very same thing to her father, but he had just laughed and said that she would soon change her mind when the right young man came along.

"You must have a reason?"

Oh, how persistent he was, staring at her like that with his eyebrows making question marks on his forehead. Why couldn't he have just laughed as her father had done? Well, there was nothing for it, she was simply going to have to make a joke of the whole thing, "Don't you think I would make a nice old maid?"

"No, I don't," Lars replied, with not even the semblance of a return smile on his face. "Old maids are tragic figures. Remember those two sisters in Haderslev who used to come to church every Sunday just to ogle the pastor or any other man who happened to be unattached?"

"All old maids aren't like that. What about Miss Janssen at school? She was lovely."

"She was only an old maid because the man she wanted to marry was killed in the war."

"That doesn't alter the fact that she was both a spinster and a very beautiful lady." Christina gave a sudden deep chuckle. "What a ridiculous conversation we are having."

"It's that all right, especially when there's no way that you are going to be Miss Christina Skov all your life. In a year or two there'll be so many hopeful suitors riding out this way it will be like a parade. Don't be surprised if Johann Schmidt is one of them. I've seen the way he looks at you even now … when he thinks no one is watching him, of course."

"Johann?" Christina gasped. "He must be going on for thirty?"

Lars laughed. "He's twenty-four, just a couple of years older than I am. And he's not only a very likeable bloke, he's what most young ladies would consider very handsome. Now, don't tell me you hadn't noticed that?"

"I suppose I had," Christina admitted, but then added. "He's a German, though."

"So … ?" Lars queried, his eyebrows lifting.

Christina glanced up at him. Surely he wasn't implying that marrying a German wasn't all that different from being friends with one. "You used to hate the Germans," she accused in a small voice. "And now you're more or less suggesting that it would be all right for me to have one as a husband."

"I used to hate the Prussians," Lars corrected. "I suppose I still do, in a way. It's hard to know, though. Since I've been out here, all that seems to belong in another life, almost." He was striding on again and Christina had to skip to keep up with him. He grinned down at her, his eyes dancing. "I wasn't suggesting that you consider Johann as a possible husband, you know? I was just using him as an example of the attention you are likely to be getting. Besides, you are not to be forgetting that I'll be coming back when I've made my fortune."

Christina laughed. "Well, you'd best not be dallying if I'm to have all those suitors on my doorstep."

"We'd best not be dallying now," Lars exclaimed as the banking clouds blotted out the sun and the first low rumbles of thunder echoed about the hills. "Come on, I'll race you to the bails."

The Skov family were agreed, it was going to be by far the best Christmas they had had in Australia. For one thing, there had been no major setbacks during the year. It could even be said that the farm had made more than a little progress. Enough, in Simon's opinion, to justify the purchase of a sulky, not a new one, of course, but one that was in a good state of repair for all that it was second-hand, perhaps even third-hand or more. He drove it home on Christmas Eve to such delighted exclamations from his wife and daughter the last lingering doubts as to the wisdom of having spent so much money fled from his mind, leaving in its place a feeling of satisfaction and the faintest tingling of triumph. Wasn't the sulky a sign that they had begun to prosper? he asked himself. Of course it was. Something purchased that wasn't in actual fact a necessity couldn't be anything else.

It was the same with the presents they bought. This year they weren't as utilitarian as those that had waited under the tree in other years. They were gifts that had been chosen with an eye to the pleasure they would bring, rather than priority of need or likely length of service. Another good sign, as anyone would agree. And, of course, there was something else making this a very special Christmas: Lars Ohlssen would be with them, someone come out of another life to breach the isolation that always seemed, at such times, to rise up like a wall around them.

As they had come to expect, the day dawned hot and humid. It received, nevertheless, a boisterous greeting from the big black rooster who had been boss of the fowl-run for the past twelve months and obviously had no suspicion whatsoever that this was to be his last such function; that, within the hour, he would be reposing on the kitchen table minus his head, feathers and innards, waiting to be plumped up with sage stuffing. The crowing was the signal for the Skov household to fly from their beds and scurry to their allotted tasks. The deliciously-smelling, calico-wrapped pudding was set to reboiling, the custard made, the vegetables peeled; the cows were milked, the fowls fed, the numerous other chores necessary even on such a day disposed of. Then, washed and dressed for church, they gathered about the gaily decorated tree, eager to be caught up in the sheer pleasure of giving and receiving.

Christina had bought presents for her parents and Lars with her own money. It wasn't the first time that she had spent money saved especially from what Doctor Travis paid her on Christmas presents. It was, however, the first time she had chosen entirely on her own what she would give. She'd had a wonderful time, returning again and again to the small shops in Beenleigh before finally making up her mind, but now she waited more than a little nervously as her parents handed out their gifts. Had she chosen well? Would the things she had bought really please? The butterfly brooch she had bought for her mother, for instance? It was the sort of jewellery Mrs Travis took a delight in wearing, but would her mother perhaps see it as something too frivolous?

She held her breath as the small cardboard box came free of its wrapping in her mother's hands.

"Oh Christina, this is beautiful, quite the loveliest brooch I have ever had. Thank you, dear, ever so much."

Holding her cheek up to be kissed, Christina released her breath in a long soft sigh. Her mother wasn't just saying that, she really did like the brooch. She could tell by the way her eyes were shining and the softness of her smile. "I'm glad you like it, Mother."

"How could I not like anything so pretty?" Elsie held the brooch up so that the light streaming in through the front door could catch its vibrant colours. "It looks so real I keep expecting it to flutter its wings and fly away."

"It does look as though it could do that," Simon agreed, smilingly nodding his head. "You'd best take care where you wear it, you don't want someone trailing you with a butterfly-net."

"I'm going to wear it right here on my lapel where everyone can't help but see it. Would you pin it on for me, Christina?"

Christina pinned the brooch on carefully, then stood back so that they could all admire its effect against the cream-coloured blouse her mother wore. "It looks great, Aunty Elsie," Lars told her earnestly. "It's exactly what that blouse needed."

Her father was pleased with his gift too, in spite of all the doubts she had begun to have as to whether he would want to part with his old change purse in favour of a rather shiny new one. To her delight he did so with great enthusiasm, declaring that he'd been wanting to "get rid of that old thing for ages" and at once transferring his coins. For Christina that left one more present to give, and, where that was concerned, it seemed she now had nothing but uncertainty. Why had she been so sure about the blue cravat, for heaven's sake? Deciding in the very first moment she saw it because it happened to be the same colour as his eyes. How silly that had been. She should have looked around for a time as she had done with the other presents. At least considered something else – a belt perhaps. Besides, she was no longer sure that it was the colour of his eyes. There hadn't been much light in the shop, and when she'd looked at it later, it had seemed different, somehow …

"Come Christina," her father urged. "Don't you have another present to give? Pastor Sultmann won't be too pleased if we are late for church on Christmas Day."

"It's for Lars." She picked up the small flat package, telling herself that, since there was nothing she could do now to change what was inside, she may as well get on with the business of giving it to him. She handed it over with a faint smile. "Merry Christmas, Lars."

"Thank you, Christina." With a couple of deft movements he removed the wrapping, holding the cravat up for an admiring inspection before knotting it around his neck. "How about that now?" he enquired, parading back and forth with his head thrown back and his chest pushed out. "Isn't this just the most elegant neckpiece you have even seen?"

"It's very smart," Elsie told him, "and it matches the colour of your eyes perfectly."

Christina darted a quick glance at her mother, but she was watching Lars, an admiring smile on her face. She couldn't have known, she told herself, not when she had never mentioned a word about her reason for choosing the cravat. Or could she? With her mother it was quite possible. She had a way of knowing such things without having to be told. If only he would stand still for a while, then she would be able to see for herself whether it really was the same blue as his eyes.

Almost as though he had read her thoughts, Lars did just that. What was more, he came to stand right in front of her, dropping a soft kiss on her forehead. "Thank you, Christina, such a fine cravat will surely make me one of the gentry."

It wasn't quite the same shade, Christina decided as she glanced up into his face, but it was very nearly so. "I'm happy that it pleases you, Lars, but I think you'll be needing more than that to make you one of the gentry."

Lars looked down at his faded shirt and well-worn trousers with mock dismay. "Isn't this what they are wearing these days?"

"I don't think so, but I wouldn't be worrying about it, you'll be quite in fashion at church."

Lars had presents to give too, but they were not from the small shops in Beenleigh. In the previous week, when Johan Schmidt, with whom he had become very friendly, had taken a wagon load of produce to Brisbane to sell, he'd gone along with him, returning with a bulging sack. Since then it had sat on the floor beside his bed. Now, he dragged it over to the tree, delved in and laughingly began distributing gifts willy-nilly: lengths of voile and gingham, ribbons, stockings, gloves, handkerchiefs, a leather belt, fancy hair clips, a pipe, a lace-trimmed nightcap, a pink parasol, woollen socks, a honey-jar, a set of small china ornaments. When the sack was finally emptied, Christina and her parents stood bemused, each of them with an armful of presents.

"Oh Lars, how extravagant you've been." Elsie protested, her voice catching between laughter and tears. "You should never have bought so much."

"It's not so much, not for a special Christmas and not when you've all been so nice to me. Besides, I've always wondered what it would be like to be old Saint Nicholas."

"It is too much," Simon declared, belatedly agreeing with his wife. "Far too much." Then, stroking his new pipe and grinning, "But I'm not giving this back."

They were still laughing and joking as they set out for church, Christina and her mother in the sulky, her father and Lars on horseback. Elsie carried a small basket containing rosebuds and daisies and, seeing it, the smile on Christina's face wavered and she suppressed a sigh. What an even more wonderful day this would have been had those two little babies lived, and little Anna and Hans also. Such a family they would have been.

Instead, there were just the three of them, and it seemed that was the way it would always be, for hadn't she heard her mother tell her father that she would bury no more babies? Didn't she know only too well what that meant; that she would bury no more babies because she wouldn't be having any more? There was something she didn't know, though, and that was how her mother now felt about God; whether she was still angry at Him or whether she had gone back to thinking that He knew best?

As usual, and in spite of the fact that they didn't go to church all that regularly, the Skov family were warmly welcomed by Pastor Sultmann and the mainly German families who did go to church regularly, a small group of them even taking it upon themselves to join the brief pilgrimage to the two little graves, standing with bowed heads while the flowers were laid against the simple wooden crosses.

The Christmas Day service was always nice, Christina mused, sitting between her father and Lars and smiling to herself as she stretched her neck to see the nativity scene arranged in front of the pulpit. Pastor Sultmann didn't become angry and go on about all the evil and wickedness in the world the way he sometimes did. He didn't go on about the trials and tribulations endured by Martin Luther either. He simply reminded them that the fundamental doctrine of the church, as established by that good man, was that they were justified before God, not through any merits of their own, but through faith in His Son. Then he went on to talk very gently about the birth of Jesus and His love and compassion for all of God's creatures.

It wasn't that she didn't admire Martin Luther, Christina reminded herself as the service progressed with only an occasional mention of his name. She did admire him and, in actual fact, she felt more than a little sorry for him. Not only had he been obliged to resist the dreadful temptations of the devil that came his way, he'd also had to do battle with the Pope and the entire Church of Rome, getting himself ex-communicated along the way. He was a German, of course, and it was a bit strange that he had been the one to give them their religion, but, as her father had said …

Christina's wandering thoughts came to an abrupt halt as they stood for a hymn and she felt someone's eyes on her. Half-turning her head, she glanced cautiously over her shoulder and under the brim of her bonnet. Johann Schmidt! Johann Schmidt had been watching her. Even though he had quickly shifted his gaze, there was no doubt about it, he had been staring at the back of her head. It was just a coincidence that he had been gazing in her direction, she quickly told herself. He had to look somewhere, and it couldn't be at the pulpit the whole time; from where he was sitting that would almost certainly have given him a crick in the neck.

Such assurances weren't enough, however, to keep the warm colour from her cheeks. It's all the fault of Lars Ohlssen, she fumed to herself. If he hadn't said such a ridiculous thing, she would never have given anything Johann Schmidt was doing a second thought. She cast an accusing glance up at the culprit, but he was singing away as though he hadn't a care in the world, paying her no attention whatsoever.

On this day there was none of the usual lingering when the congregation came out of the small church. The men were inclined to stay and talk and the children were immediately involved in a chasing game, but they were rounded up and hurried off by their womenfolk. In every kitchen, Christmas dinners waited half prepared and they were anxious to get back to the tasks still to be carried out. Following one another in quick succession, the sulkies, buggies and carts rolled out on to the road.

Getting away so quickly was something to be thankful for, Christina told herself as her mother urged their horse into a fast trot. If they had stopped to talk, she would almost certainly have come face to face with Johann, and, no matter how hard she tried not to, she would have blushed, so badly, more than likely, everyone would have noticed. What a ridiculous business it was, for heaven's sake. Why, she had known Johann ever since they'd come to the valley; he was a nice friend, that was all. Not someone she'd be wanting to marry, if, that was, she had any intention of getting married. It wasn't because he was a German, she quickly assured herself. After all, Lars was Danish, the best possible thing a prospective husband could be, and she couldn't see herself marrying him either. He was just like one of the family and in a way she loved him, but it wasn't, she was quite sure, in the way you loved someone you wanted to marry. No, that was different. You had to want him to kiss you on the lips and hold you in his arms, even sleep in the same bed with you.

Christina's understanding of the involvements of procreation, still by no means complete, had been acquired in a very spasmodic fashion. As a nine-year-old, she'd taken to kicking the rooster whenever she entered the fowl-run and found him in the process of crushing a hen into the dust, until the day her mother witnessed one such incident and explained that, had the rooster not engaged in such activities, there would be no chickens in the eggs they set for hatching. Christina had found this piece of information almost too incredible to absorb. In fact, had the person telling it to her been anyone other than her mother, she would have felt that a joke was being played on her. Since it was her mother, however, the notion became something to be seriously pondered. Questioning brought no further explanation, her mother simply reiterating that the rooster was doing what nature intended him to do and that she was not to be kicking him.

Although often sorely tempted, Christina did as she was told and took to studying the rooster's behaviour instead. He was conceited, there was no doubt about that, strutting about as though putting chickens into eggs was the most important job in the whole world. Amazingly, the hens seemed to agree with him. Now that she was seeing the fowl-run goings-on in a new light, there seemed little doubt that they didn't mind being crushed under the rooster's heavy body. In fact, quite often when he approached them, they squatted down of their own accord, more or less inviting him on to their backs. When he did that, she noticed that their tails were pushed up, which seemed to indicate that something was being done through a passage beneath to put the chickens into the eggs still inside the hen. But what it was and how it was done remained a mystery.

It was a mystery that didn't confine itself to the fowl-run. Things that had been of little or no account began to be viewed by Christina in an entirely new light: the shimmering dragonflies joined together in flight; the beautiful butterflies alighting on the same leaf, one upon the other; the quarrelsome parrots that had previously seemed to be doing nothing more than claim the same space on a bough; the frogs that slipped, piggy-backed, from the creek bank into the water. The time came when she began to wonder about something else that was taking place, something that seemed, in a way she wasn't quite able to fathom, to be shrouded in similar mystery to all those other things. Every so often, her father drove one or other of their cows over to the Schmidt farm, where they stayed for a day or two before being brought home again. "She's going for a little holiday," he always replied when she asked what was happening. A holiday? At the Schmidt farm? What could be sillier, for heaven's sake? It wouldn't be any different for the cow than staying on their own farm. She would have more cows to keep her company … and the bull! Was that big ferocious creature the reason their cows had to be taken over to the Schmidt's farm? Did they have to be with him before the calves would grow in their bellies?

Even when she was small and lived in Haderslev, Christina had known that babies grew inside their mothers. She had seen her aunts with amazing bulges in front of them and then they'd be gone and there'd be a new baby in their arms. It was the same with her mother when little Anna was born, the swollen belly she'd had for weeks and weeks just disappeared. Everyone accepted that Christina knew, but no explanations were forthcoming and it was left to the little girl to find her own answers to the most puzzling of questions. How did the baby come to be there in the first place? How did it get out when it was time for it to be born? After quite a deal of pondering, she had come to what had, at the time, been quite satisfactory conclusions – God arranged both things. When a woman wanted a baby, all she had to do was tell him, in church more than likely, and he took care of everything.

It was some time before she gave thought to the possibility that the baby's father might also be involved in some way, that it wasn't logical for him to be there simply to provide a home. Once convinced that he was involved, however, she quickly decided that it was enough for him to have slept in the same bed as the mother and put his arms around her. This belief had stayed with her even after she had learned about the task of the rooster. After all, a chicken came out of an egg; it was nothing at all like a baby growing inside of a woman. Then had come the vague understanding of why their cows visited the Schmidt farm and with it a new intriguing thought. The calf didn't come out of an egg; it grew inside the mother cow, probably in the same way that a baby did inside its mother. This notion, in turn, stirred a new and startled wondering; perhaps, after all, the father of a baby did more than just put his arms around the mother …

Thinking about marriage renewed this wondering in Christina's mind, and she sighed quietly beneath her pink parasol. How mysterious it all was. More than a little frightening, too, like that other thing that had happened to her four times now. Not that it was frightening once she understood that it was all part of becoming a woman, just as the swelling of her breasts was. It had been though. When it first happened it had been quite terrifying, all that blood that kept coming no matter how often she sponged it away. Only when Mrs Travis had discovered her frantically and tearfully washing out yet another pair of drawers and explained what it was all about had a fear unlike any she had ever known before released its icy grip on her heart – she wasn't going to die.

Mrs Travis had been very kind, Christina recalled, explaining so carefully what happened in a woman's body when the seed from her husband entered and started a baby. What she hadn't explained though, and seemed to be avoiding, was how the seed got into the woman's body. That was a question that teased her mind and yet, at one and the same time, hardly bore thinking about, so disturbing were the possible answers. It was ever so much nicer, she told herself, to believe that a husband and wife need do no more than sleep with their arms around one another to make a baby. And there was another matter that didn't bear thinking about – the birth of the baby. Ever since she had ridden for Doctor Travis after seeing her mother's blood on the kitchen floor and then returned to find her collapsed on the bed and groaning in agony, she'd known that any arrangements God made in respect of this event left much to be desired; bringing a baby into the world was nothing short of a terrible ordeal.

Simon and Lars, who had ridden on ahead with a couple of other men on horseback, were waiting at the turn-off to the track. "What a beautiful picture the ladies make in their fine sulky," Lars called as they approached.

"You and your flattery." Elsie scolded, but smilingly.

"Ah, but I meant it. Tell them it's true, Uncle Simon. Tell them how pretty they look."

"Well, of course they do," Simon confirmed cheerfully. "But, if we don't get a move on, they are also going to be quite wet, that storm is coming up very quickly."

It was, too, Christina decided, tilting her parasol back so that she could see the sky. It had been only a puffy light-coloured cloud mass when they'd gone into church. Now it was dark and green-tinged, and, instead of hovering idly about the ranges, it was sailing purposefully up into the heavens. Still, they hadn't heard any thunder as yet.

This storm wasn't bothering with the dramatics of distant rumblings. Even as the thought occurred to Christina, a loud clap of thunder burst from the heavens and rolled down the valley. The horse started, throwing up its head and breaking its gait, wanting to gallop off down the track. "Whoa! Whoa there!" Elsie called, expertly tightening the reins to ease the animal back into a trot.

"Flash doesn't like storms, does he?"

"No, he does not, Christina. If I'd thought for one moment there was going to be a storm so early in the day, I'd have asked your father to harness up old Sally. She may not look as smart as this fellow, but she's got a whole lot more sense." Elsie gave a sudden soft chuckle. "Though, if I remember rightly, I didn't credit her with too many brains when we drove her down from Brisbane."

"I remember how she was," Christina smiled. "I was hoping that I was going to be able to ride her and you weren't too sure that was a good idea."

"Well, she learnt quickly enough, dear old Sally."

"And I did get to ride her."

"If that's what you call it. I was always under the impression that when you were on her back she just plodded around making sure you didn't fall off."

Christina laughed softly, her eyes dancing. How she loved to hear her mother talk this way, light-hearted and gently teasing. It didn't happen very often and that made the times when it did doubly enjoyable. "I did fall off once," she recalled, wanting to prolong the precious moments. "Do you remember, Mother?"

"How could I forget, considering what you managed to fall into?"

"I don't think I've ever been so disgusted in my whole life. And there was Father laughing so hard the tears were streaming down his face."

"It was difficult not to laugh, once we knew that the only thing hurt was your dignity, of course. I know I nearly burst my sides trying not to do so when your father brought you back to the pump."

A second loud clap of thunder rang out, clear and sharp, seeming in the bush that crowded in on the track to bounce from tree trunk to tree trunk. Again the horse danced about between the shafts, tossing its head from side to side in anxious frustration. "It's alright," Elsie called soothingly. "A few more minutes and we'll be home."

The first large raindrops splashed to earth in the very moment Simon and Lars, having freed the horses and rolled the sulky into the shed at the back of the house, bounded into the kitchen Right away, hail began to fall, bouncing along the ground, making dull plopping sounds on the roof, slithering across the verandah. Twenty minutes later the storm was gone, disappearing in the direction of the coast, but it left behind a glistening white carpet. In spite of the fact that some damage had been done to crops and vegetable gardens, the hail-stones were gathered up delightedly on farms throughout the valley, dropped into jugs of water, lemonade, orange drink or ginger beer, piled around butter dishes and cream jugs, scattered on to bowls of grapes and around slices of watermelon or simply popped into mouths to be crunched or sucked.

"Oh, what a treat," Christina exclaimed, laughingly scooping up the hail with both hands and dropping it into the basin her mother carried. "Cool drinks in the middle of summer."

"A white Christmas." Lars yelled, flinging a handful of icy fragments into the air. "Just like home."

Just like home … Christina felt her breath catch as she repeated the words to herself. Home … how long since any of them had said that and meant a land across the seas? A long time … well, a long time since they'd done so out loud. She stole a glance at her mother's face. What visions had Lars's words brought to her mind?

Were they of Christmases the like of which she would never again know? Of home as it had been in another time, perhaps still was in her heart? Had the very word, as Lars meant it, brought a crushing ache, a yearning to be back there? Christina saw nothing that resembled answers to her wondering. If her mother's smile had wavered, she hadn't seen it happen, and the shadow she'd thought she'd seen cross her eyes was too quickly gone to be sure that it had ever been.

"Hey, how about this?" Lars was merrily performing an imitation skating act, pushing his booted feet along through the hail, swinging his arms back and forth in an exaggerated fashion. As one, Christina and her parents burst out laughing. But Elsie's laughter soon faded to become a small sigh. "What a child he still is. In spite of all the things he has done, he still seems to regard life as something of a game. I do so wish he'd take things a little more seriously, settle down somewhere or, if he's not going to do that, go back to his parents."

"Perhaps he will settle down before too long," Christina suggested quietly, her own laughter cut short by the concern in her mother's voice. "He might tire of wandering around and get himself some land."

"Do you think he's more likely to do that than go back to Schleswig?"

"Yes, I do, Mother. He really likes Australia."

"He likes the challenge, Christina, the adventure, you might say." She gave another small sigh. "You could be right, I suppose, but I just can't see him wanting to be tied to a piece of ground or to set plans either, for that matter. Just look at how he's going to leave us without the faintest idea where he will go. He hasn't even decided which direction he will take."

Lars left on the first day of the new year, riding off as cheerfully as he had arrived, but leaving on the Skov farm a melancholy void that would take its time about closing.

17

By the time the year 1877 entered its second half, drought once again held the Colony of Queensland in its iron grip. In every direction the land cried out for rain, while those who worked it watched cloudless dawn follow cloudless dawn and wondered whether there would ever be an end to the procession of clear blue skies. On the vast sheep pastures of the western plains, men with sombre expressions hand-fed valuable stud sheep and tried not to see the misery of thousands of others pushing their noses into the parched earth in the hope of finding a fragment of forage, or the stinking, fly-blown bundles that dotted their properties. On the huge, sprawling cattle stations further north, conditions were no better. Most paddocks were completely bare; in others and on the big, unfenced runs only isolated patches of rank, dried-up grass remained. Edible scrub trees were being felled to provide a precarious existence for the stronger beasts. For the weak, it wasn't enough; they went down and stayed down, and, as with the sheep, the stench from their rotting carcases polluted the air for miles around.

In the coastal regions, where more regular rainfalls could normally be expected, the drought was making no exceptions. On the cane plantations and on the dairy and mixed farms, conditions were the worst yet experienced by Queensland's settlers. And, for the sugar industry in particular, the long dry spell couldn't have come at a worse time. Henry Schneider wrote to Christina ...

We need rain desperately. If it doesn't come soon, all our work in replanting with new varieties will have been to no avail. Every farm in the district is in the same position as ours, not that knowing this does anything to ease the concern we are feeling. Father is still optimistic, however. He says that we probably had too much good fortune to begin with and that a setback or two will serve to strengthen our resolve. I don't know about that, but it has certainly served to strengthen our backs, so much work has there been to do.

We still don't have any Coolies on our place, by the way. We would have had, though, if things had gone well last year. Father has become quite keen on the notion, as those farmers who do have them are well enough pleased with their investments in that respect.

Christina looked up, smiling, as three-year-old William Travis pressed his small body against her knee. "Go meet Robert and Lizbeth now?"

"Not yet, love. It's too early. Robert and Elizabeth will still be in school."

"Let Christina read her letter, darling," his mother, also reading a letter from the just-collected mail, told him. "Run along and play with Chippy for a while. We'll tell you when it's time to go."

Christina gave the little boy a quick hug and was rewarded with an angelic smile before he trotted off to rouse his dozing puppy. Not until he had disappeared though did her eyes return to Henry's letter ...

I fear that your farm must also be suffering from the drought, since it appears to be all over Queensland. I hope that, in your case, it is not too bad and that your parents are managing to hold on. That's what Father is always saying we must do ... hold on.

Now for some more cheerful news – Rolf has a sweetheart.

She's a very nice girl, the daughter of a storekeeper in the town and she has managed to bring about some quite remarkable changes in my brother.

Don't laugh, but I think that even you, Christina, would agree that he has become quite likeable.

Christina did laugh, chuckling softly, and Mrs Travis looked up, her eyes questioning over the top of her reading glasses. "Something amusing, Christina? Is it for sharing?"

"Henry writes that Rolf has a sweetheart and that she's brought about such changes in him even I would now consider him likeable."

After almost four years of having Christina live in her home, there was little about the people and events of her childhood that Helen Travis didn't know, and she was well informed as to the different natures of the two Schneider brothers. "Well, it's amazing what love can do," she said smilingly. "It's been said, you know, that it can make mice out of even the strongest men."

"I wouldn't like to think that."

Mrs Travis gave a soft, delighted chuckle. "So you'd like your man to remain a man, Christina? And quite right you are. I can't imagine anything worse than being married to a mouse."

They both laughed, enjoying the small joke, before returning their attention to their respective letters ...

I suppose that, with Christmas drawing near, you are hoping that your friend Lars will turn up again. I hope, for your sake, that he does, since you had such a wonderful time last year. I wish someone from back home would just appear on our doorstep. Well, who knows?

Perhaps one day they might. I have no other news worth the telling, Christina, so once again I send you my best regards and I hope that you and your parents have a very happy Christmas, in spite of the wretched drought. Your friend, Henry."

P.S. People up this way are talking about getting some of the friendly blacks to perform a rain dance to break the drought. They are supposed to be able to do that, you know? Father doesn't approve of the idea, though. He says that, since the blacks are not Christians, they would be appealing to some pagan god or spirit. My own view is that it might at least remind our God that He is supposed to be doing something about sending the rain. Is that blasphemy, do you think?"

Was it? Christina wondered as she refolded the letter and slipped it back into its envelope. It didn't seem so, though perhaps even considering that God needed reminding about the rain might be irreverent. A rain dance would probably be in a corroboree, but what special things would the Aborigines do in order to get the rain to fall? And what a wonderful thing that would be, if they really could.

"Dear … oh, dear," Helen Travis murmured as she came to the end of the letter she'd been reading. "The drought is really severe in New South Wales also. My friend at Forbes writes that they are having a most disastrous time of it."

"They are the people with all the sheep?"

"They did have an awful lot of sheep, but it seems not now. The poor creatures have apparently been dying in their hundreds. What a tragedy it all is."

Christina nodded. "The Schneiders have their problems too. Henry writes that if they don't soon get rain all their replanting work will have been wasted. He says that people up that way are talking about asking some of the friendly blacks to do a rain dance for them."

"Goodness, that would be something, wouldn't it? Especially if it worked."

"Do you think it would be wrong to ask them to do that? Apparently Mr Schneider does."

"Why?"

"Because they aren't Christians and they'd be dancing for some pagan god."

Mrs Travis gave her slim shoulders a faint shrug. "It's hard to see anything that might bring rain to this thirsty land as being wrong, but I suppose he could have a point."

"But, if it worked, surely God wouldn't mind?"

"You wouldn't think so. He can't be taking any pleasure out of gazing down on this land the way it is at present." She sighed heavily as she gathered up her mail. "But, when all is said and done, how can we possibly expect an Aboriginal dance to be more effective than all the prayers being uttered in our churches?"

Perhaps because this has been the Aborigines' country for a long, long time, Christina mused; they might understand the climate better than we do. There was only one true God, of course, everyone knew that. Everyone, except the Aborigines, that was, but, in time, if Pastor Sultmann was right, they, too, would know it. Hadn't that been the aim of the dedicated Lutheran missionaries who had been coming to the

Colony for some forty years now, ever since the time when it was nothing more than a convict settlement ... to tell the people about God and all the other things in the Bible? Christina frowned, her eyes thoughtful. After all that time there must be some of them who knew. There could, in fact, be quite a number who knew about God and the Bible, so perhaps it wouldn't be a pagan god they were dancing for ...

"I wonder what they do in a rain dance," Mrs Travis mused, interrupting Christina's wondering.

"I thought it might be some sort of corroboree, though just what that is I have only the vaguest notion."

"I don't suppose we'll ever get the chance to see one ... " Her voice trailed away as the excited yells of her youngest child shattered the sleepy quiet of the early afternoon. "Smoke, Mama! It's coming! It's coming!"

Christina and Mrs Travis both sprang to their feet and rushed out into the back yard. "It's not from the cane." Christina cried, her voice sharp with sudden anxiety. "It's coming from the hills, the wind must have changed."

"Yes, I believe it has." Helen Travis, too, was gazing worriedly off to the ranges, where, for several days now, wispy columns of smoke had been rising lazily into the air. But no longer ... much thicker and darker, the smoke was now blowing towards the town.

"Father said the only reason the fires were staying in the ranges was that there was very little wind and it was blowing from the coast. He said that, if it changed direction, the fires could come down, perhaps even on to our land."

"That may not happen, Christina. There's certainly more smoke and it is blowing this way, but it still seems to be coming from well back in the hills. Besides, even if the fire did come down, it wouldn't go on to the cleared land, so your home would be quite safe, it's well clear of any bush."

"I suppose so. Father has always made sure that there was no rubbish lying around our house."

"There you are then. There's no call to be worrying about your farm."

"Is it a big fire, Mama?" William wanted to know, his small face reflecting some of his mother's concern.

"We hope not, darling. In any case, it's a long way off, right back in the hills."

The little boy was at once tearful. "Will Christina's house get all burned up?"

"No, of course it won't. The fires are much further back than Christina's house."

But Christina wasn't so sure that the fire wouldn't reach their farm, perhaps even their house. Bush fires could move so quickly, and with the breeze growing stronger all the while and the bush so tinder dry … "If it does reach the farm, Mother and Father might need me to help them. Do you think Doctor Travis would lend me one of his horses?"

"Christina, of course he would. But that's the last thing your parents would want for you to be riding through the bush at a time like this. It would be far too dangerous, and they would never forgive us if we let you do something like that."

They both turned as Doctor Travis joined them, his gaze on the billowing smoke. "Those fires have certainly got a go on. I've just been at the school and Mr Nussey is sending all the children from out that way home."

"I could perhaps go with them?" Christina ventured.

"Christina is worried about her parents," his wife told him as the doctor tuned to her enquiringly.

"Of course." Then to Christina, "You live further out than any of the children, dear, and your parents wouldn't want you to be riding home at a time like this. It would only take a single spark to set all that bush along the track to your farm alight. Besides, there's really no call for you to be worried about them. Even if the fire does come down out of the hills, it will stop when it reaches the cleared land."

"How long do you think it will be before I can go home?"

"That's hard to say, what with bush fires being so unpredictable, but, hopefully, a couple of days should see that blaze burn itself out."

But it was Saturday, four days later, before the fires, deserted by the gusty breezes, finally came to a halt and gradually subsided, and Sunday before Christina went home. Her father came for her, riding his own horse and leading the bay mare they'd acquired earlier in the year. "There's too much rubbish on the track for the sulky or cart," he explained. "Enough on the road, too, for that matter."

Christina gave him a faint smile and found even that difficult. The weariness in his voice and the sight of his drawn face and bloodshot eyes brought such an ache to her heart it was all she could do to keep from weeping. "It's alright, Father," she told him huskily. "I'd much rather ride."

"Helga's a little skittish after the fires and she's not too keen on the smell of smoke in her nostrils, so keep a firm rein on her."

Some distance before they reached the track, the road led them into an alien world; where blue-grey smoke, heavy with the aroma of eucalyptus, wafted about after curling upwards from isolated pockets that continued to smoulder, and where it seemed that a monstrous demon had played a monstrous game, taking eccentric and kangaroo-like leaps to make of the bush a grotesque patchwork. In some places all was desolation: the earth ash-covered, all the undergrowth gone, the young trees destroyed, many of their elders destined to join them when the fires eating slowly but steadily upwards through their great hearts completed their horrific tasks. Elsewhere, nothing had been touched: green leaves rustled unconcernedly in the gentle south-east breeze, even the drought-dulled bracken having survived. And in still other places, there were trees that lived while those all around had died, and those that were velvety-black on the one side, ivory-white on the other, the fierce flames that had licked at them being in too much of a rush to do their job properly.

"Oh Father, how terrible it all is." Christina groaned, easing her mount back to a walk as her father was doing with his. "Will it ever come back the way it was?"

"I would say so, given time. This wouldn't be the first time a bushfire has gone through here. And this one probably hasn't been the worst, either."

"But who would have believed there could be such destruction?"

"I know, it all looks dreadful. But George Hunter was out yesterday afternoon to see if everything was all right with us, and he wasn't too dismayed. He said that for a lot of the trees it's only a temporary death."

Simon nodded at a towering black column, crowned by scorched clusters of leaves. "That one, for instance … see, there's no fire burning inside, so there will very likely still be life there and in time it will send out new buds."

"What about all the smaller trees?"

"Where the flames were fiercest, they are well and truly dead, but others will grow in their place, and they'll get off to a better start with the earth cleared of all the dead leaves and rubbish. It's actually not a bad thing for a fire to go through the bush every few years."

They turned off on to the track and Simon warned, "We have to go carefully along here."

"It's like a fearsome black tunnel," Christina groaned. "Is it like this all the way along?"

"Most of the track is pretty bad."

"It must have been terrible for you and Mother being out here with the fires so close."

"It wasn't pleasant," Simon told her with a brief humourless smile. "But it was only on Thursday that we had cause to feel any alarm where our lives were concerned. That was when the first flames crossed the creek. They came exploding through the tree tops and I was expecting sparks to be carried to the house or shed, but, thank God, that didn't happen."

Christina felt a shiver run down her spine. "Did the flames come very close to the house?"

"Closer than I had expected. The corn stalks I hadn't had time to plough under caught alight and blazed furiously for a time and so did a few tufts of dried grass in the paddocks. And, of course, the fire went through the cane fields."

"On no!" It was a cry of anguish. One field had been ready for cutting and crushing; all they had been waiting for had been advice from the mill as to when it would be required.

Simon shrugged his shoulders, looking away from the dismayed face of his daughter. "It was to be expected. There wasn't anything I could do to protect those fields, running back into the bush the way they do."

"Weren't you able to save any of the cane, after it had been burnt?"

"Not a stalk. As you know, if the cane is to be of any use for crushing, it has to be cut right after a burning. Even if I'd been able to do that, there was no way I could have got it to the mill." Again he shrugged. "It was in poor condition, in any case."

Christina felt her heart lurch, then grow heavy and afraid. There was something about her father's attitude, what was it? Not just the despondency that would have been understandable. No, something more. Hopelessness … ? Oh no, surely not. But why, if it wasn't, was he acting in such a casual, almost uncaring manner? Why wasn't he showing some dismay about losing the cane? It was true that it hadn't been flourishing but it would have yielded some sugar, given him some return for his work. Why wasn't he talking about what he was going to do … replanting, cutting back, or something? Why wasn't he angry about what had happened?

"We have to be thankful that no harm has befallen any of us," he said quietly. "Fortunately, that's the way it is on all the farms out this way, so George Hunter tells me. Nearly everyone has suffered some loss, in some cases, outbuildings and so forth, but no one has died or been seriously injured and that's the important thing."

"Of course it is, Father," Christina assured him gently. "Farms can always be mended."

"I suppose so … "

I suppose so, Christina repeated miserably to herself. Nothing of assurance or confidence, just empty words with no commitment in them whatsoever. Sudden tears stung her eyes. It was defeat that her father was feeling. It was in the way he spoke, in the way his shoulders slumped, and it was written all over his face.

They rode for a time in silence, reining their horses to a halt when, not far from the track, a tall gum tree crashed to earth with a trail of vividly glowing embers spewing from its heart. Christina shuddered, feeling the ache within her grow. It was by no means the first great tree she had seen fall. There had been many on the land her father had cleared and only a handful had been left standing. The others had either been chopped down or ring-barked and left to die, the latter a cruel business she had long ago decided, for the tree not only took a long time to fall, it was stripped of all its wonderful dignity before it finally did so. With the removal of the strip of bark from near its base cutting off the supply of sap the leaves withered and died soon enough, but the stark white trunk and branches remained for a long time, like some tortured naked form praying for deliverance; then the branches fell off, but still the trunk stood erect in its terrible deprived state, sometimes for years and years. But this tree crashing down with its heart on fire at this particular time was, to Christina's mind, worse than that, because, in a way, it seemed to represent the crashing of her father's dreams, something fine and inspiring turned to ashes.

Near the end of the track they reined up again, a strangled cry of dismay falling from Christina's lips. In front of them a badly burned kangaroo tried valiantly to rise while her terrified young joey struggled to get back into her pouch. "What can we do for her, Father?"

"We can put the poor creature out of her misery." Simon was already freeing his knife from the sheath attached to his belt.

"Oh no! Not that!" Christina begged.

"I haven't got a gun with me, Christina, so I don't really have much choice. We can't just leave her in that state and the knife will be quicker and cleaner than hitting her over the head with a lump of wood."

"There might be something else we can do, if we just think for a while."

"What, for heaven's sake? Just look at her. Look at her feet. They've been burned completely away. She's going to die, but it may not be for days. Do you want to leave her in that sort of agony?"

"No, we can't do that."

"You ride on ahead. It will take but a minute."

"What about the little joey?"

"I'll have to kill it, too, of course," Simon told her as he slid from his horse, knife in h and. "It will only starve to death if I don't."

"Can't we take it home with us? It doesn't appear to have been hurt."

"What would we do with it? How would we feed it?"

"We could try at least give it some sort of a chance. It would probably drink cow's milk."

Simon looked from the pleading blue eyes of his daughter to the pleading brown eyes of the kangaroo. Both pleading for the joey, he thought, a wry smile briefly touching his lips: the poor maimed creature who must know that her own life is about to end and the young girl refusing to see that she will very likely be doing the joey a disservice by trying to prolong its now fragile hold on life.

"She wants us to save her baby, I know she does." Christina cried urgently. "That's probably what she was trying to do when she got so badly burnt. She must have come through the fire to bring it here."

"Well, we can try, I suppose." Simon loosened his belt and pulled off his shirt. "We will need to wrap him in something, make him feel that he's in a pouch, otherwise he's likely to die of terror. We don't want to prolong the mother's agitation either, so I'll bring the little one to you quickly and I want you to be ready to ride on for a short distance."

Christina nodded. "Yes, Father, I understand."

She heeled her horse forward the minute the joey, all thrusting legs inside her father's shirt, was handed up to her. "There, little one, it's going to be alright," she crooned softly. "We are going to take very good care of you." She was rewarded with a sharp kick in the ribs and almost lost her grip on the struggling bundle. "My, you are a strong little fellow, aren't you? But you are being quite silly, you know? No one is going to hurt you."

"Well, how are you managing?" her father asked as he rejoined her.

"He's very lively. He almost got away from me, and I've had so many kicks I'm sure my ribs are going to be quite bruised."

Simon reached over to her. "Here, give him to me."

"I think that might be a good idea."

"While I'm cuddling this ungrateful creature, you can be thinking up ways of convincing your mother that we haven't gone out of our minds, that one more animal to feed and care for won't add to our problems."

"I'll make sure he's no problem, Father. If Mother doesn't want him, I'll ask Doctor Travis if I can take him into their place, the children would love him."

"Yes, I'm sure they would, but, before you can think about doing that, we'll have to work out a way to feed him … "

Christina was no longer listening to her father. They had come to the gate and she was staring through horrified, disbelieving eyes, while her heart began a wild thumping in her chest. This was their farm? Oh no, it couldn't be. This scorched brown land almost surrounded by a black, black sea their pride and joy of just a year ago? Dear God, don't let it be, she prayed, closing her eyes, let me having a nightmare from which I might wake.

"Not a very pretty sight, is it?"

Opening her eyes, Christina shook her head, not trusting herself to speak. It wasn't a nightmare. It was all horribly, horribly real … the blackened earth where the corn had been, the acres of useless spindly cane stalks, the long black fingers stretching across the cattle paddocks. Oh, no wonder defeat wrapped itself around her father's shoulders like a cloak too heavy to shake off.

"Will you be able to open the gate, Christina? This little fellow's a bit of a handful."

"Of course, Father." Both posts and the gate's bottom rail were badly charred, but the structure was still reasonably sound and, quickly dismounting, Christina swung it open with little difficulty. She watched her father ride through, his face strangely expressionless. Then, in her mind's eye, saw him as he had been on the day they'd first come to this land, saw him kick away the faded surface soil and scoop up a handful of dark earth from beneath, letting it run through his fingers; saw the excitement on his face and the briskness of his step as he strode about, laughingly making plans. What splendid visions had been his on that now far-off day, she thought with an inwards groan. What fine hopes to be dashed into the dust.

Christina pulled the gate shut and remounted, brushing angrily at the two large tears that had rolled on to her cheeks. Crying would do nothing to help, she told herself sternly, and seeing her do so would only add to her father's misery. What she had to do was try with all her might to revive his dreams. Somehow, she had to make him see that all wasn't lost; that, in spite of the present desolation of their farm, he had, in these long arduous years, achieved something worthwhile. They had a pleasant, snug house and the shed he had built with his own timber. There had certainly been lean times, but they had never gone hungry. They still had their land, with more acres cleared now than when they had arrived. Most important of all though, her father had to be made to understand that no one considered him a failure. Why should they, when all was said and done? What had happened wasn't his fault, it was the fault of the drought and now of the bushfire, enemies that no man could have conquered. But the fire was over and done with, and the drought, too, must soon end. He had to be encouraged to think about that, about how different everything would be when the rains came.

But it was January before the first drought-breaking rains fell, and, by then, Simon was determined to leave the Logan valley. Escape was the only solution, he told himself. He must escape with his wife and daughter from this land which, far from bringing him the sort of life he'd dreamed about, was all set to crucify him. Hadn't it already cost him all his capital and countless hours of back-breaking work? Hadn't it taunted him in a devilish fashion, letting him make a little progress from time to time, and then, in the space of a season, taking back all he had gained? And, hardest of all to bear, hadn't it claimed six precious years out of his life? Six years in which almost everything he had done had been dictated by immediate needs, leaving him no opportunity to lay the foundations of a future prosperity. Six years that had, in effect, been wasted, since all he had really managed to do was survive.

George Hunter tried to reason with him, pointing out that every farm in the valley, in the whole of Queensland for that matter, had suffered from the long months of drought; telling him that good seasons were expected and that the banks were prepared to lend money to tide those on the land over these difficult times; assuring him that the Government could help by deferring rent payments and improvement requirements. Simon wasn't prepared to listen. He had been wrong in choosing the Logan valley, he insisted. With all the best land along the river already taken up when he arrived, he should have kept going, considered the valleys further south. Well, perhaps even now it wasn't too late. On a number of occasions he had heard very favourable reports of the Mudgeeraba district, of its green valleys and the many streams that literally tumbled out of the hills.

"It's certainly a very attractive region," the Lands Officer agreed, "but it's not a completely new area, you know? A few people have been farming there for these past seven years or more, and, prior to that, the big runs of the squatters took in the whole district."

"I know there are a few farms there, George, but, from what I hear, it's nowhere near as settled as the Logan was when we came."

"I grant you that. In fact, there's no township whatsoever, no store, no post office, no school. The nearest centre is Nerang, some eight or nine miles away."

"Those are minor problems. The town will come as soon as there are enough people living in the area. It's the major problem I want to talk about, how do I get rid of my farm here? Can I sell it?"

"Not as things stand at present. You don't have a Deed of Ownership."

"But can I get one? I've paid seven lots of rent. That leaves three still owing, a total of thirty-seven pounds ten shillings. If I could manage to pay out that money, could I get the Deed?"

"It could be possible. The Government is never happy about having land forfeited, since it does nothing to help the development of the Colony. Do you know of anyone who might be interested in buying the farm?"

"I have been led to believe that, if I were free to sell, I wouldn't have too much trouble doing so. Now that the drought has broken a number of cane farmers are apparently anxious to acquire more land."

"Well, having a ready buyer would certainly help your case. The main concern of the Government is that the development of the land should continue, and, if you come up with a buyer, that will obviously happen. There would be the question of the improvements, of course, but I can't see that you would have any concerns in that respect. After all, you've got a sturdy home, a shed and bails, all in good condition, plus improved fencing and the additional acres cleared." George Hunter paused, groaning softly. "Hell, man, you really have accomplished a good deal.

How can you be saying that you've made no progress?"

"I haven't made the sort of progress that will guarantee us a decent future, and look at the situation I'm in now."

"It's no worse than that of many others."

"That may be so, but the fact remains that I'm not prepared to try again on that land. I see it as utter foolishness to go on struggling as we have been doing, hoping that a little lasting good fortune might come our way."

"There's no guarantee that things will be all that different at Mudgeeraba and you'll be starting from scratch again with the land you take up. Clearing will need to be done and a house built. How will Mrs Skov and Christina feel about going back to life in a tent?"

Simon drummed his fingers along the edge of George Hunter's desk, a faint smile curling the corners of his lips. "They may not be required to do that."

"Oh … ?"

"I'm hoping to be able to buy an established place, a small dairy farm. Dairying's the go-ahead industry in those parts, it seems."

The Lands Officer nodded, some of the concern leaving his face. "Yes, it is, and the region does seem to be ideally suited to dairy cattle, especially the low, marshy areas. That just might be a good idea, Simon … getting hold of an established place. You can always work at building it up."

"That's what I have in mind. I'll need to be getting things moving right away if I'm to have a chance at this farm, though. The bloke wants to go back to being an overseer for a squatter on the Darling Downs, and he's anxious to get going."

"That's a reversal. Usually, the men working on the big runs can't wait to get their own piece of land."

"Well, it seems that this fellow has discovered that he prefers sheep to cows. His plan is to work for wages for a time and then see if he can acquire a sheep property for himself."

"And you've got an option on his Mudgeeraba farm?"

"More of a gentlemen's agreement. I haven't even seen the place as yet. There was an advertisement in the Courier and I wrote to him. He's agreed to give me a couple of weeks to see what I can arrange."

"We had best get things under way then." George Hunter pulled a pad from under a pile of papers. "And first things first. The rent money, that's not going to be a problem?"

"Naturally, I don't have that kind of money tucked away in an old sock or under the mattress, but I'll be selling a few things, the cows, a couple pieces of furniture." He grinned suddenly. "I will have it by the time you get your paper work done, George, never fear."

"Fair enough, but don't go rushing into selling anything until I've had a chance to consult with my department."

"I won't. I plan on visiting Mudgeeraba right away though. I want to see for myself what the place is really like."

"Yes, of course. You should do that as soon as possible."

They were going to leave the Logan. Although she had known for more than a month now, Christina still found it hard to believe. Just when everything, drenched with inches of rain, was coming back to life, they were going away. It didn't seem possible somehow, not now that this had become their home. There was one good thing about it though, her father was happy again and perhaps even as excited as he'd been when they had first arrived in the valley. He talked with great enthusiasm, endlessly it sometimes seemed, of rich green pastures tucked in against the ranges and of marshy lands stretching away to the coast; about fat, contented cows whose udders were almost bursting so full of milk were they; about bunches of bananas such as they had never imagined and citrus trees loaded with fruit; about creeks with enough water in them to last through any drought; about milking bails that had a proper roof and a cool dairy adjoining; and about a comfortable cottage with a thriving vegetable garden.

It all sounds too good to be true, Christina thought as she sat on the top step watching the vibrant colours of the autumn sunset. Perhaps it was too good to be true, but it was what she had wanted and tried to bring about in her own way: for her father to recapture his dreams of a bright and prosperous future. It was ridiculous then to be feeling uneasy now that he had done that. What did it matter that it involved moving away from their farm? A second chance in a new place, there was nothing wrong with that, nothing whatsoever. She jumped, then laughed softly as a small head with pointed ears pushed under her arm. "Goodness, you gave me quite a start, Joey. Aren't you supposed to be in bed?"

"He's decided he's not yet ready for bed."

Christina swung around to where her mother had just come on to the verandah. "I didn't hear you either."

"You were very deep in thought, or perhaps lost in that sunset."

"It might be nice to be lost in something so beautiful."

"And to float about forever on rose-coloured clouds?"

"That could become a bit tiresome after a time."

"Yes, that's quite possible, even though it does seem such an attractive idea." Elsie settled herself on the rocking chair Simon had made for her last birthday. "That just goes to show what strange creatures we humans really are. One would think that we are doomed never to be content with our lot."

Christina darted a surprised glance at her mother's face, but then, seeing that it was relaxed and smiling, she smiled too. "Not you though, Mother. You are always content with your lot. Even when things aren't the way you would like them to be you never complain, never rage and carry on … " Her voice trailed away and she turned her head, pressing her teeth into her lower lip. How could she have forgotten that one time, a time so long ago now it seemed almost to have been in another lifetime, and that wind-blown figure on the deck of the Friedeburg not her mother but someone else, someone she had imagined.

"Goodness, you make me sound quite dull."

"I didn't mean it like that. I just meant that you didn't go on about things."

Elsie chuckled softly. "I know what you meant, love. In any case, you are quite wrong, you know? I quite often grumble all the way through milking, you can ask any of the cows."

"I just might do that." Christina told her with a quick grin.

"It always seems…" Elsie broke off with a sharp exclamation and bent over to reach under her skirt. "Come on out from under there, you little rascal."

Christina threw back her head on a peal of laughter as the reluctant joey was dragged back into the open. "Oh, how sneaky he is. He was here with me but a minute ago."

"It has become a favourite game of Master Joey's, I'm afraid. He's even tried to hide under my skirt while I'm walking around."

"He probably thinks that you are his mother and that you have a pouch under there."

"Heaven forbid!"

"Well, you really did mother him and, besides, he may even know that you saved his life. He would have died in those first few days if it hadn't been for your patience in getting him to drink, sacrificing your good kid gloves into the bargain."

"That was an act of sheer desperation. We simply had to find a teat of some sort."

"It was a wonderful idea and it certainly worked. Just look at how he has grown, in leaps and bounds, as Father is so fond of saying." The little kangaroo had returned to her side, and she stroked him gently. "I wonder how he's going to like living in Mudgeeraba."

"I don't think it will bother him one iota, so long as he continues to get the attention he seems to think he deserves." They were silent for a few moments, then Elsie asked quietly, "What about you, Christina? How do you feel about leaving the Logan to live at Mudgeeraba?"

Christina felt her heart skip a beat. This was no idle question, for all that it seemed to have been idly enough asked. "I'm just like Joey," she said, forcing herself to speak lightly. "I'll be happy with you and Father, wherever that might be."

She saw rather than heard the faint sigh, saw it in the slight movement of her mother's head and the almost imperceptible slumping of her shoulders. "It won't be easy for you leaving the Travis children."

"No, that won't be easy." What an understatement that was, Christina thought ruefully, when it was going to be one of the hardest things she had ever had to do. Painful enough with the two older children, but with little William, whom Doctor Travis had placed in her arms when he was not yet one hour old, it would come close to being unbearable.

"Mrs Travis has asked if you might be allowed to stay on with them."

Christina jerked her head around to stare open-mouthed at her mother. "What did you tell her?"

"That it would be up to you, of course, your decision entirely."

Her mother was watching her closely; even in the fading light, Christina could see that. And she was sitting so stiffly and so still the chair made no movement at all on its rockers, almost as though she was holding her breath. Yes, that's exactly what she was doing, holding her breath while she waited to see what her answer to Mrs Travis would be. "Mother," she cried, "you must know that I could never stay in Beenleigh and watch you and Father go off somewhere else. My heart would break."

This time Christina heard the sigh, it came with a long soft release of breath. "Well, your father will be so pleased. He has been almost out of his mind since we arrived home and I told him what Mrs Travis proposed." She got to her feet and came to scoop up the now sleepy joey. "I must tuck this young fellow in." She gave a small laugh. "And also put your father out of his misery."

Christina nodded and pushed her lips into a smile. She longed to cry out, "What about you, Mother? Aren't you pleased too? Aren't you pleased for yourself and not just for Father's sake? Surely this is one time when your own feelings must count for something?" Instead, she returned her gaze, now misted with tears, to the sunset and saw that it was fading quickly and that the flying foxes were astir, hundreds of dark forms against the sky.

"Yours wouldn't have been the only heart broken, Christina. Mine would have been also."

Christina swung around, her breath catching, but saw only a fold of her mother's skirt as she disappeared through the door.

18

The farm, nestling at the foot of one of the numerous densely forested spurs running northwards from the McPherson Range and with Mudgeeraba Creek forming part of its eastern boundary, was everything Simon had promised his wife and daughter. After months of uncertainties and delays, they arrived as the sun was about to set on a balmy Sunday in mid-September and were delighted at what they saw, especially the four-roomed, partly-furnished house, with its detached kitchen and iron roof. "It's a real settee." Christina exclaimed after a hurried examination of a velvet-covered piece of furniture. "It's even got legs."

Simon, staggering in through the front door with a heavy chest, chuckled happily. "Real or otherwise, that settee is not going to be sat on just yet, young lady, not if we are to get all of our stuff inside before dark."

"It is nice though, Father, and so are the chairs with their cane backs. We will hardly know ourselves with such an elegant sitting room."

"Well, it's a good thing the Klinsons decided against taking all their furniture with them, otherwise we would have had a very empty sitting room."

True enough, Christina knew, since they'd sold all of their sitting room furniture to help pay for this farm. Not that having to do so was a big sacrifice since her father had found the time to make only a few basic pieces, except for the what-not, of which he'd been so proud. "There's even a what-not, but it's not as nice as the one you made, father."

"It's a deal more elaborate, but you could be right at that, even if I do say so myself."

"They've left a fine solid wardrobe," Elsie called from the front bedroom. "I wonder that they could bear to part with it."

"But what about the farm?" Simon asked with mock reproach. "The furniture's just a bit of a bonus, for which, let us not be forgetting, we have paid. It's not what brought us to Mudgeeraba."

"The farm looks wonderful," Christina assured him with a quick smile. "I can't wait for the morning to see it all properly."

Her father nodded, pleased with her response, but his glance rushed to where his wife had appeared in the bedroom doorway. "And what say you, good wife? Have we taken the right decision?"

"It would seem so. What we have seen thus far is most pleasing. Everything so beautifully green and the cows so healthy-looking So many fruit trees, what a treat that is going to be. And what a special treat to have such a large tank."

Seeing the smiles on the faces of both her parents, Christina felt her heart come free of the last lingering shreds of doubt. This time everything was going to go really well for them. In such a green, fertile place, how could it be otherwise? They would be very busy though, with only three of them to milk over twenty cows twice daily. And it didn't end there: the milk had to be set out in shallow pans so that the cream could form and be skimmed from it, then churned into butter, which would be salted and packed into wooden kegs to be taken over to Nerang, to be freighted by cutter or steamer to Brisbane.

There was, however, something Simon had neglected to tell his wife and daughter when he had explained the working of the dairy farm, simply because at the time of his inspection it hadn't loomed as being important. As early as the 1840s, timber-getters from the south had ventured as far north as the Tweed River, their goal being the rich red cedar, almost as precious as gold with buyers from Sydney to London clamouring for it. By the 1870s cutters had moved into a number of locations in the McPherson Ranges, where they felled the magnificent trees and marked the logs with their brands before bullock-teams dragged them to either the Tweed or the Nerang River, depending on the location in which they'd been felled. Once there, they were floated to rafting grounds where they were lashed into rafts and floated downstream to where they could either be milled or loaded onto steamers for transport to Sydney or Brisbane.

What Simon had been a little remiss in not mentioning was that the rough road running down from the range and passing not more than half-a-dozen yards from their gate was a major bullock-team route from the Numinbah Valley, with close on a dozen teams hauling cedar and other valuable timbers from the hidden reaches of the valley over the hills to Mudgeeraba and then across to Nerang, from where the great logs were floated down the Nerang River to the rafting grounds where Boobegan Creek joined the river. The slow, ponderous bullocks, drawing the heavily-laden wagons, took three days to make the round trip, which meant that each team ran two loads every week. This, the Skov family soon discovered, resulted in an almost continuous procession of teams past their front gate, and, whenever the road dried out, a seemingly endless ribbon of dust, a certain amount of which, particularly when the north-easterlies blew strongly, drifted across their house, at times making dusting a twice-daily chore. It also meant that when they took their kegs of butter over to Nerang for freighting to Brisbane, the journey was invariably slow and, very often, an unpleasant and dusty outing.

From the very outset Christina felt a deep compassion for the bullocks with their wooden yokes and bowed heads, their dark, sombre eyes patiently regarding the dreary, rutted road over which they hauled their great loads. At the same time there came to her an intense dislike of the teamsters with their foul oaths and cracking whips and of the cattle-dogs that joined their masters in tormenting their unfortunate beasts. These emotions, in turn, brought into her life a strange dilemma. Rain was, of course, almost always welcome. Not only did it keep the farm green and thriving, it settled the dusty surface of the road. But rain, she soon came to realise, brought a worsening of the bullocks' plight. The road, where it dropped sharply down from the range, became slippery and eroded, with sections of the edge often breaking away, while the flat stretches became boggy and treacherous as the ruts filled with mud, in places a foot or more deep. It was at such times that the harsh brutality of the teamsters was at its worst. The cruel whips cracked out a thundering volley, the dogs barked and snarled endlessly, and the swearing and cursing became louder than ever, while the bullocks bellowed in terror and strained their hearts to keep the big wheels turning.

"Sometimes, the way the bullocks are treated makes me almost sorry to see the rains come," she admitted to her father one wet afternoon as they watched yet another wagon bog down where it rolled off the slope to the flat ground. "At least when the road is dry things are a little easier for them."

"I know what you mean, Christina. It sickens me too to see those poor creatures treated like that."

"The teamsters are such cruel men, so rough and uncaring."

Simon nodded his head thoughtfully. "They might seem to be, Christina, but we have to remember that they live hard, rugged lives. What appears to us to be cruel and unacceptable might be to them all part and parcel of a day's work."

"If it is, Father, they must have rocks where their hearts should be."

They were chasing up a few cows too intent on their grazing to have joined the main herd already nearing the bails, and Simon smiled with gentle amusement at the sight of his daughter paddling along beside him, her face flushed and angry beneath the dripping brim of the old felt hat she'd jammed on her head. "It could be that they've had to learn to harden their hearts," he suggested. "I have talked to a number of them, as you know, both on the road and in Nerang, and I must say that, apart from their language which is a bit strong to say the least, I haven't found the men themselves the least bit objectionable. In fact, they are usually extremely interesting to talk to, and let us not be forgetting that they are something of a unique breed."

"Just because they drive bullocks instead of horses?"

"That's only part of it, Christina. I was thinking more about the sort of lives they live and how they came to Queensland from down south, driving their teams over the ranges and up the river valleys to wherever there were stands of cedar. In all of these regions the timber-getters have been the first white men to arrive, you know? So, in a way, they have been explorers."

"But none of that excuses the cruelty of some of the men we have seen."

"No, nothing ever excuses deliberate or unnecessary cruelty, but I think we should try to see … " Simon was left with his mouth open and the rest his words unuttered as Christina darted off in pursuit of a straying cow. He had been about to remark on the difficulties confronting the bullockies, to point out that, with some of the teams comprised of twenty or more beasts, there was simply no other way of handling them. By the time she came back within earshot, however, he had decided that a change of subject might be a good idea. "This is the worst thing about a dairy farm," he complained good-naturedly, "having to get out and milk the cows no matter what the weather."

"At least we do the actual milking with a full roof over our heads, thank goodness."

The smile faded from her father's face. "I suppose I should have extended the roof over the bails at the Logan, but with so few cows it never seemed a priority job."

Christina bit her lip. Not for a moment had she intended her words to be taken as criticism. Surely her father knew that she was remarking on a present fortunate circumstance, not complaining about something not so fortunate in the past. Besides, if it had been anyone's right to complain about the bails at the Logan, it would have been her mother's. She was the one who had done most of the milking, the one who had spent the most hours hunched against a cow's side while wind-driven rain soaked through her clothes to her very skin.

"If I could only have got my hands on a piece of tin at a reasonable price, it would have taken no time at all to do the job."

Smothering a small sigh, Christina forced herself to talk brightly. "Well, we don't have to be concerning ourselves with the Logan farm now, not when we have this lovely place."

"No, that's true enough." Simon hesitated, then asked carefully, "You are happy on this farm, aren't you, Christina?"

"Of course I am, Father." Her eyes, suddenly anxious, searched his face. "I hope I haven't given you reason to think that I wasn't?"

"Indeed you haven't, but I know that you were very distressed to be leaving the Logan, what with having to part from Marie Hunter and the Travis children, especially that little fellow."

Christina nodded her head slowly, for the moment not trusting herself to speak. How readily it all came back. How vivid the memory of the soft arms clinging so tightly about her neck, the tear-damp cheeks pressed against her own, the convulsive sobs shaking the small body. How bleak the feeling of loss. Nothing fades, she thought, feeling tears tighten her throat. More than a month gone by and it's still as though it all comes from yesterday.

"You'll be able to visit them," Simon suggested, regretting having mentioned the Travis children. "You can take the coach from Nerang."

"Yes, I have promised to do that."

"And I'm sure Marie would like to come down here for a visit."

Christina nodded. "Yes, she would."

It wasn't until they were nearing the milking yard that Simon broke the silence into which they'd stumbled. He cleared his throat and said quietly and a little huskily, "There's something I've been meaning to talk to you about, Christina."

Christina, beginning a dash out of the rain, halted in her tracks. Surprised at the sudden solemn note in her father's voice, she waited for him to continue.

"It's about your money … "

"Father, you know I'm only too pleased for you to have it."

"No, I insist that it be a loan only."

"I have no need of it."

"Nevertheless, I intend to repay every penny. And I want you to know that your savings have been quite a help to me. There were so many expenses I hadn't counted on, my pockets were well and truly empty." He gave a small rueful laugh. "And I had run out of things to sell."

Don't apologise, Father, Christina pleaded silently. I know how it was, that this farm cost quite a deal more than you got for our Logan place and that you had to get a new loan from the bank. Moving impulsively to her father's side, she caught his arm and squeezed gently. "Empty pockets belong in the past. There aren't going to be such things here, I just know it."

The tension disappeared from Simon's face and he grinned happily. "I know it too, Christina. I think we were destined to come to Mudgeeraba, to this farm."

"But surely we weren't destined to stand out in this pouring rain, not when there is shelter a few yards away."

"We certainly weren't," Simon chuckled, belatedly pushing the gate of the holding yard shut. "Your mother will be thinking that the rain has washed away our common sense." He caught hold of his daughter's hand and they raced together around the outside of the yard with its milling cows and into the dairy. Elsie, setting pans out on a bench, looked up with a quizzical smile. "I was wondering when you two were going to decide to come in out of the rain, but I didn't expect it to be with such a rush. For a moment there I thought the dairy was under attack."

"By the Aborigines?" Christina asked, grinning.

"I didn't get so far as to thinking by whom."

Simon was pulling off his dripping coat. "Well, the sooner we get started, the sooner we'll be finished."

"I'm running a bit late here, I'm afraid.," Elsie told him. "Joey followed me over from the house and I had to take him back. He can spend a couple of hours in the fowl-run."

"He won't like that," Christina grinned. "But at least the hens won't trample him to death."

Simon heaved an exasperated sigh. "When is he going to learn that the milking yard is no place for him to be hopping about?"

"I'm sure I don't know," Elsie told him with a slight shrug of her shoulders. "I'm more concerned with knowing when he's going to realise that his wet body trying to push under my skirt brings me no great pleasure."

Her husband and daughter both laughed, and Elsie's grimace of recalled distaste gave way to a faint grin. "I'm glad to see that others find it amusing."

"We don't mean to laugh, Mother," Christina assured her. "But it really is funny the way Joey still seems to think that you are his mother. I wonder how big he's going to be before he finally comes to his senses?"

"I shudder to think."

A day of deep sorrow but also one of eventual joy; such, for Christina, was the ninth day of November in the year 1878. A letter, redirected by the postmaster at Beenleigh to the post office at Nerang and brought home by her father, informed them that her Grandfather Christiansen had died peacefully in his sleep on the last day of July. And Kathleen O'Rourke came into her life.

"In his sleep," Simon murmured sadly, resting a hand on his wife's shoulder as she sat with the letter still in her hand. "That is a nice gentle way in which to leave this world."

Elsie nodded, her eyes bright with unshed tears. "He was almost eighty years old, that's a long life." She gave a soft sigh. "In a way I've been expecting this news ever since that winter when he first had the chest trouble. It's ironic though. Each year, when summer began here, I thought about it being winter back in Schleswig and wondered how he would fare. Instead, it happened in summer, and so many months back. I've been writing to him all this time, and he wasn't there."

"I know," Simon murmured huskily, recalling other such letters that had come for him, two of them and only weeks apart. For almost three years now, both of his parents had lain in the graveyard not far from their home in Herning. He knew that he would never visit their graves, but in his mind he saw them, saw the stones and the inscriptions. For his wife it would be the same, only in her mind would she see her father's grave.

"I feel so heartsore for my mother. She will be completely lost without Father, and, with such distances between us, I can do nothing to help her."

"Others of your family will be with her, your sisters, certainly."

"I know, but I still feel helpless, as though I should be doing something, but heaven knows what."

"You could write to her without delay. I know it's nothing like being there, but it is a contact and it might help. Besides, your mother will be anxious to hear from you, to know that you are aware of what had happened. But wait … I have a better idea. Why not send her a telegraphed message? It will have to be fairly brief, of course, but it will get to Haderslev in almost no time at all."

"Do you think that would be possible?" Elsie asked hopefully.

"I'm sure it would. Mr Joseph over at the Nerang post office will show you how to do it."

So it was that, on this warm Saturday afternoon, Christina came to be waiting in front of Lenneberg's Store, which also housed the Nerang post office, while her mother discussed with Mr Joseph the intricacies of telegraphing messages to Europe. The girl was standing only a few feet from her, peering intently at a notice tacked to the wall. She wore a faded gingham dress but, as though defying anyone to consider her dowdy, she had tied a bright green sash about her waist; her boots were well-worn and very dusty; her hat an old straw bonnet which she dangled carelessly by its ribbons. Such things, however, Christina barely noticed. It was the girl's hair which caught and held her attention, bringing a sharp prickling of envy. It was a tangle of red-gold curls that cascaded more than halfway to her waist and glowed like fire even in the shade. It was, Christina had no hesitation in deciding, the most beautiful hair she had ever seen ... or ever imagined, for that matter. The owner of all this glory spun around, and Christina, blushing at being caught staring, saw that her eyes were a brilliant green, her lips full and pink, and that, although freckles dotted her small up-turned nose and rosy cheeks, they did nothing to detract from the girl's stunning beauty.

"Do you suppose they'll catch them now?" she asked in a soft lilting voice, her gaze moving speculatively from Christina's carefully braided hair to her neat blouse and crisply starched skirt.

"Who ... ?" Christina mumbled, more than a little flustered.

The girl nodded at the poster she'd been studying. "The Kelly Gang. They've been proclaimed outlaws now. See, it says so here."

Feeling that she had been invited to do so, Christina moved over to where she too could read the words in heavy dark type. It was true, the Kelly Gang, a major topic of discussion during these past months, were now outlaws. The poster said so very clearly ... as of 1 November 1878, Ned and Dan Kelly, along with Steve Hart and Joe Byrne, were outlaws according to the Felons Apprehension Act.

"Well, what do you think?"

"Perhaps they will be caught," Christina murmured uncertainly.

"I think they will be. People won't have any sympathy for them now, not after what they've gone and done. Three policemen shot dead, can you believe that?"

"It was a dreadful thing to do."

"It most certainly was. A real stupid thing into the bargain. They'll finish up getting hanged now ... you wait and see."

"I suppose so."

"They're Irish, you know? Same as us. But Da says we can't be feeling sorry for them, not now that they've taken to killing people."

"They must be very dangerous men. I'm glad they don't live in Queensland."

"Me too. I'm sure I wouldn't want to be meeting up with them, especially that Ned. They reckon he wears a suit of armour made out of old tin and stuff." She grinned suddenly. "Not only are they Irish like us, but they've got the same name as Ma's family. She was Bridget Kelly before she married Da. We all tease her about them, we tell her she's got bushrangers for kin and so on."

Christina's eyebrows lifted. "Doesn't she mind?"

"Ma ... ? No, of course not! If she did, she'd whop us good and proper. She was feeling a bit sorry for them though, when they were just stealing horses and things like that. Reckoned they were just a poor Irish family who hadn't had a chance to make a respectable living in this country. She's changed her mind now though, you can be sure about that. After what that gang did to those policemen, I think she wouldn't mind going after them herself ... you know, in a posse or whatever." She took a few steps backwards, bending sideways to peer in to the post office through the open door. "That's your ma you're waiting for, isn't it?"

Christina nodded. "She's telegraphing a message to my grandmother. My grandfather has died and we've only just learned about it."

"That's too bad. Was it back in your old country?"

"Yes, in Schleswig."

"Schleswig? Everyone around here has been saying that your family is Danish?"

"We are Danish. Schleswig is ... was ... a duchy of Denmark."

"But it's not now?"

"No, it belongs to Prussia now. There was a war and the Prussians and Austrians won."

A hint of familiar resentment had crept into Christina's voice and the other girl was quick to ask, "And you didn't like Prussians owning your country?"

"Of course we didn't. They are very arrogant and they are the worst warmongers of all the Germans."

"Wars are terrible. I know I wouldn't like to be living where there was one going on."

"I was just a baby at the time and it didn't last very long."

"That's something, I suppose. Some of the wars over in Europe seem to go on for ever and ever." She gave Christina a faintly apologetic smile. "I know someone who is a Prussian."

"Oh … ?"

"He's my brother Danny's friend, but we are all taken with him. He's very handsome and always nice and gentlemanly into the bargain, never arrogant like those you knew. In fact, I sometimes wonder how he puts up with Danny. I mean, we have to, being family and all, but Carl doesn't have to."

"What's wrong with your brother?" Christina asked, wide-eyed with interest.

"It's not that there's anything really wrong with him. It's just that he gets cranky about all sorts of things; you know, things that can't be helped or aren't worth getting cranky about. Like the squatters, for instance. The way he goes on about them anyone would think they'd done him a personal injury."

Christina smiled. "I don't think he's the only one going on about the squatters."

"I grant you that, but there aren't too many as obsessed as Danny is. He's forever raving about how the Government should make them give up more of their land and so forth. But there are other things he goes off his head about as well, stupid things, like I said. The trouble is that he's got a chip on his shoulder." The girl shrugged her own slim shoulders.

"Well, that's what Ma says it is, and she reckons it's because Danny didn't get enough praties to eat when he was little. That's potatoes, you know? Ma still calls them praties."

This astonishing piece of information brought a further widening of Christina's eyes. "Does your brother have a great fondness for potatoes?"

"Not now he doesn't, he can take them or leave them, just like the rest of us. But he lived in Ireland until he was five years old and all the kids there like potatoes. They have to, more or less, since it's mainly what they live on, the grown-ups too, for that matter. Anyhow, when Danny was little, the crop in the district where they were living failed two years running, some sort of local blight. Ma says that he was four years old before he had a really decent feed of praties."

"Goodness, that must have been a worrying time for your parents?"

"It was, I suppose, but that trouble was just in certain areas. It wasn't anything like the great famine in the forties when the potato plants all over Ireland rotted and died, leaving the people with practically nothing to eat. Thousands starved to death and others just managed to stay alive by eating ferns and grass and stuff like that."

Christina was horrified. "Didn't they have anything else to eat?"

"At first they did, their pigs and fowls, but they were soon gone. That was the time when people really started to pour out of Ireland, most of them going to America. But Ma and Da were only kids then. It wasn't until the fifties when they had the new trouble in their district that they decided to leave."

"That's when they came to Australia?"

"Yes, in 1859, just before Queensland became a separate colony from New South Wales. They came on the Shackamaxon – Ma and Da, Danny and Joseph, with Patrick being born on the ship. The rest of us were born here in Australia."

"How many children are there in your family?"

"Eight, five boys and three girls. I'm sort of in the middle, the fifth oldest and the fourth youngest."

"Eight? That is a nice big family."

"It's big alright, but I don't know about it being all that nice, what with the house being so crowded and there being no place for even a little privacy." She heaved a sigh before saying just a little enviously. "You're an only child, aren't you?"

Christina nodded, hoping the conversation would steer away from this unhappy subject.

"How old are you?"

"Fifteen, I'll be sixteen in January,"

"I've already turned sixteen, last month." She grinned cheerfully, her envy of a moment before forgotten. "It does feel a whole lot different from being fifteen, as you'll be finding out for yourself when January comes round. It feels grown-up somehow. I suppose, when you think about it, it really is. After all, Ma got married when she was sixteen. Not that I'd be wanting to be married at sixteen, mind. What's more, I can't see why any girl in her right mind would want to do such a thing. Fancy getting tied down with a whole bunch of kids just when life could be really interesting."

The girl's cheerfulness was so infectious it was well-nigh impossible not to respond and Christina laughed softly. "I've still got a couple of months to wait before I'll know what it's like to be sixteen."

"But you must know even now that you wouldn't want to be married at sixteen?"

"No, I wouldn't want that," Christina assured her, wondering idly what the other girl would say were she to know how very different their reasons for not wanting such a thing were.

"I thought you might be around my age, though you're not very tall for nearly sixteen. Still, that's nothing to be concerned about, not when you're so pretty." She swung her bonnet to and fro, a gently teasing smile coming to her lips. "I can see why Mrs Laver told Ma that you were as pretty as a picture."

"Mrs Laver is a very nice lady," Christina murmured, hoping the warm colour she felt in her cheeks wasn't too noticeable. "Both she and her husband have been very kind to us since we arrived in Mudgeeraba."

"Yes, they would be, they are real nice neighbours for your family to be having. They told us that your name is Christina. Mine's Kathleen … Kathleen O'Rourke."

Christina nodded, deciding that it didn't seem appropriate to be saying "pleased to meet you" or "how do you do?" when they'd already been talking together for several minutes. Furthermore, it appeared to be quite unnecessary to inform this new acquaintance of her surname since she no doubt already knew that. "Are you waiting for someone too?" she asked, seeing Kathleen O'Rourke glance, not for the first time, in the direction of the hotel.

"For Danny. He's over behind the pub watching a game of two-up; that is, he had better be only watching. Ma'll belt him one if he's been playing and loses the money she gave him for a bit of rum for the Christmas pudding she's going to be making."

Christina stared at her. "How can he lose his money in a game?"

Kathleen stared back, open-mouthed with astonishment. "Don't tell me you've never heard of two-up?"

"I don't think I have … "

"Swy then … does that ring a bell?"

Christina shook her head. "No, it doesn't."

"Crikey, how long have you been living in Australia?"

"Seven years."

"Seven years, and you haven't heard about two-up?" Kathleen shook her vibrant head from side to side in amazed disbelief. "Just where in the Colony have you been, for the love of Mike?"

"We were living in the Logan valley, a few miles out of Beenleigh."

"Ah … " Comprehension dawned in the beautiful eyes. "Where all the German people live?"

"Yes, they are mainly Germans in the area."

"It's no wonder then. Those Germans are more than likely all Lutherans, and it's not the way of the Lutherans to be gambling. Nor to do much else either, it's said, except work, of course. Da says they are the most sober-sided people he has ever come across."

Christina opened her mouth to tell the other girl that she was also of the Lutheran faith, but quickly closed it again. After all, she told herself, this bright, cheerful girl already knew more than enough about her, especially since all she had known about the O'Rourke family was that they were Irish and lived on a farm not so very far from their own. "How do they play two-up?" she asked, hoping to move the subject away from the Lutherans.

"They throw two pennies in the air and see whether they come up heads or tails."

Now it was Christina's turn to stare incredulously. This was a game for grown men? Oh surely not. Why, it was something children might play at.

Kathleen threw back her head on a rippling peal of laughter. "Don't be looking so astonished, Christina. I know it sounds ridiculous, but, believe me, the men who play take the game very seriously. They often wager quite large sums of money and sometimes they also have quite large brawls."

"Over two pennies?" Christina shook her head slowly from side to side. "It's very hard to believe."

"Well, you'd really have to see a game to understand what goes on, but you'll have little enough trouble getting to do that. Here in Nerang, with the timber-getters coming down all the time, there's nearly always one going on somewhere." She chuckled softly. "There's quite often a game at Mudgeeraba too, and I know where."

"Oh..?"

"You know where the road that comes down from the mountains past your farm joins up with the main road, where the teams often stop for the night, it's there, just around behind that hill. They've even got a piece of ground cleared especially."

"Why would they need to do that just to toss two pennies?"

"Well, they wouldn't if there were only a couple of blokes playing, of course, but there usually gets to be quite a number and what goes on around the ring they form is important also. You see, the men bet with each other ... " Her voice trailed away as Christina's mother appeared in the doorway. Then she said quietly and just a little regretfully, "I suppose you'll be going now?"

"Yes, we have nothing more to do in Nerang." She smiled as Elsie approached. "Mother, this is Kathleen O'Rourke."

"I'm very pleased to meet you, Kathleen. You also live in Mudgeeraba, don't you?"

"Yes, but further down on the flat lands than your place."

"But on a dairy farm?"

"That's right. We have more than a hundred cows, close to ninety of them in milk at the present time. And quite a few heifers and poddies as well."

"Goodness, that is a large number. Milking must occupy almost your entire day."

"I suppose it would if there weren't so many of us and if we didn't have ten bails. But, as it is, we do have time for other things and we all manage to get a break from time to time."

Elsie smiled at her. "Well, there are only three of us, and we had best keep moving, otherwise we'll still be milking or in the dairy when darkness comes."

Christina and her mother were crossing the road to where their horse and sulky waited in the shade of a large Moreton Bay fig tree when Kathleen called after them, "Will it be alright if I visit with Christina some time, Mrs Skov?"

"Of course, Kathleen," Elsie, half turning, called back. "That would be nice for Christina."

"Isn't she beautiful, mother?" Christina exclaimed the minute they moved off.

"Yes, she certainly is, but her hair is so untidy … she would do well to take a good stiff brush to it."

Christina winced involuntarily on the other girl's behalf, knowing all too well that a brush in that mass of curls would be nothing short of torture. "I don't think she'd ever be able to get her hair into braids, it's much too curly."

"You are probably right, but that's not to say she couldn't do something about tidying it up. Still, she seems a very pleasant girl and it will be good for you to have a friend around your own age living in the district."

Oh, yes, Christina thought, smiling to herself, it will be very, very good.

19

The outcome of Christina's meeting with Kathleen O'Rourke was not only that she gained a friend and confidante of her own age, but also that her general education underwent a considerable broadening, and this, begun on that first day, proceeded rapidly.

On the following Saturday, Kathleen rode up to the Skov farm and enquired very politely whether Christina might go riding with her and share the small picnic lunch she had brought. Christina, delighted that this beautiful, vivacious girl should come seeking her company, waited in an agony of suspense while her mother asked what seemed to be a never-ending string of questions and then extracted an equally unending string of promises. No, Kathleen assured her, they wouldn't be riding along the road; they would follow the creek. No, they wouldn't go deep into the bush either; they would go downstream where the banks made for quite pleasant riding. Yes, they would stay well clear of any blacks they might see; yes, she did understand that some of them could be unfriendly. Yes, they would be home by three o'clock at the latest; yes, she did know where the sun would be at that hour.

Finally, the questions had all been asked and the promises made, and the two girls were on their way, their horses cantering easily in and out of the trees along the creek bank. The moment the house disappeared from their view, however, Kathleen wheeled her mount back in the direction of the road. Christina, hesitating, felt the happy smile slide from her face. Surely the promises they had made to her mother weren't going to be broken the very minute they were out of her sight.

"Come on, Christina," Kathleen called over her shoulder. "And don't be looking so worried, for the love of Mike. We're not going to do any of the things your mother warned us about. We are going to watch a two-up game."

Christina gasped, her feeling of unease at once mushrooming. "Are we allowed to do that?"

Kathleen grinned impishly. "Your mother didn't say that we couldn't."

"Only because it would never have occurred to her that you were planning such a thing. But what I meant was, will the men allow us to watch?"

"Heavens no! Though, come to think of it, there's no real reason why we shouldn't, unless they think it's unlucky or something for females to be watching, Or perhaps it's just because they are not keen for us to know how they carry on, yelling and cursing the way they do."

"Cursing … ?" Christina questioned doubtfully as she brought her horse alongside that of the other girl.

Kathleen considered her closely, a small frown puckering her brow. It was quickly gone, however, and she declared blithely, "But we don't need to listen to any of that. We don't have to worry about the men not wanting us to be there either, because they won't see us."

"Are we going to hide in the bush?"

"No, we wouldn't get close enough to see anything if we did that. You know how I told you that they play at the back of that hill?"

Christina nodded.

"Well, you've probably noticed that there's an escarpment on that side and that's where they play, at the bottom of that. All we have to do is go up the hill from this side and we can look down on them without them ever knowing that we are there." She stood up in her stirrup irons to peer through the trees. "We won't be staying on the road, but we do have to go back across it, so we had best take care. There are no teams on the move or we'd hear them, but we don't want to be running into anyone else either. Can you see any movement along the road?"

Christina looked carefully in both directions, also standing up in her irons. "No, there doesn't seem to be anyone about."

"Good, now here's what we do: once we get out of these trees, we lose no time in crossing the road. Then we go just into the edge of the bush on the other side and stay there until we come to the hill … all right?"

Christina wasn't sure that it was all right, but, before she had a chance to reply, Kathleen had heeled her horse forward, guiding it expertly in and out of the trees, and it seemed there was nothing to do but follow. It wasn't, she told the small protesting voice inside her, that she had any great desire to witness a two-up game. In fact, she couldn't see how it could be anything but boring. It was because she wanted to be with the happy, laughing girl who had planned this adventure so recklessly for her benefit, because, more than anything else, she wanted to be that girl's friend.

Approaching the hill, they caught glimpses of bullocks, still yoked together, nibbling the grass along the side of the road, and of wagons, some still laden with great logs, while others, on their return trip, carried only sacks of provisions. "Three or four teams, I should think," Kathleen reasoned. "But there'll be a few men from the farms playing also, including my da."

"Your father plays?"

"Of course. It's his Saturday treat. Sometimes, Danny does too. And Joseph used to before he got himself a sweetheart."

"What if your father sees you?"

"Then I'll really get what-for and probably need to sit on a cushion for a whole week. But he's not going to see me, no one is. Like I told you, we'll be looking down on the game from the top of the hill." She giggled softly, her eyes dancing. "It will be just like having our own box at the theatre."

Christina giggled too, but more from nervousness than anything else. "I've never been inside a real theatre."

"Neither have I, but I've heard tell how it is." She cocked her head to one side, listening intently. "Can you hear voices?"

"Yes, I can, just faintly."

"That means we have to talk softly from now on. They'd be making more noise than we would, of course, but the breeze is blowing that way and we don't want it carrying our voices around to them. Once we are on the hill, we'll need to be even more careful; we'll whisper or talk very softly all the time."

At the base of the hill, they dismounted and tethered their horses to low-hanging branches. Then, to Christina's astonishment, her companion dropped down on to a log and proceeded to tug off her boots. "It's best we take them off," she explained. "It makes for easier climbing. Besides, when we get to the top, we'll need to crawl over to the edge and I don't want to be going home with the knees out of my stockings." With the boots removed and dumped on the ground, she bundled her skirt and petticoat carelessly into her lap and quickly pulled the oft-darned hose from her long slim legs. "Oh, do come on, Christina," she cried, glancing up suddenly. "Why are you just standing there? No one will see you."

With a faint, none-too-confident smile, Christina sat down next to her and, although her movements were by no means as uninhibited as those she had just witnessed, she, too, was soon barefooted, her smile turning to one of pleasure as she wriggled her toes in the soft, cool grass growing against the log.

The hill was more squat than tall, its southern slope, for the most part, easily climbed. "One thing about them making such a din," Kathleen whispered as they neared the top and a sudden outburst of shouting reached their ears, "they'd be flat out hearing us even if we did make a noise."

"We won't take any chances though," Christina whispered back, feeling a need to have this point reaffirmed.

"No, we won't," Kathleen promised with a quick grin. "We'll be very quiet."

With the crest of the hill gained, they crawled the few feet over to the top of the steep escarpment, and dropped on to their stomachs to peer over the edge. There they were, not more than thirty feet below them: twenty or more men in a ragged, restless circle around a large piece of canvas stretched out on the ground. And the noise, unhindered now as it floated up to the girls, was indeed a din. Well, Christina told herself with more than a little relief, even if they are swearing, there's such a confusion of voices, we won't be able to tell.

"The one on the side of the canvas is Paddy Finnegan; he's acting as the ringkeeper," Kathleen whispered, her head close to Christina's. "He's a bullocky and a good mate of Da's. Many's the time he's had his whole team over at our place."

Christina, having no idea whatsoever what a ringkeeper might be, other than that, in this instance, he was a huge man with a very bald head and a large beard, eyed him curiously and waited to see whether he would perhaps do something that would enlighten her as to how he came to have that particular title.

"He organises what happens, controls the game, you might say. That skinny bloke waiting with the piece of wood in his hand, what they call the kip, is the spinner. He's going to toss the pennies, but watch now and you'll see it all for yourself."

The men had been talking and yelling, calling to one another across the canvas, the deep brogue of Paddy Finnegan sounding out above all the other voices, but now an expectant hush descended upon the group. "All right then?" he called, jamming a battered felt hat back on to his head. "All set? Come in, spinner!"

While Christina gaped, open-mouthed, the long arm of the tall thin man shot out, the fingers expertly flipping the wooden kip. The two pennies flew into the air, gleaming in their brief moment in the sunlight before dropping with a dull plop-plop on to the canvas.

"He's headed them!" Paddy Finnegan cried out, his announcement at once smothered in an uproar: cheers from those already tucking away notes and silver, groans from those watching hard-earned wages disappear into the pockets of others. But the big Irishman was not about to allow time for the celebrating of good luck or the cursing of bad. Right away he called for the centre to be set. "Come on now. He's going for a quid. Anyone want to take tails for a quid?"

A one-pound note was at once flung into the ring, the side bettors losing no time in setting up their own wagers, anything from a shilling to a pound or more.

"Did somebody bet a pound?" Christina whispered, aghast.

"Yes, that was the bet with the spinner, but do you see how the others are betting with each other all around the ring? That big bloke standing just to the right of the ringkeeper is my da, by the way."

"Does he bet a pound?"

"Ma would kill him if he did. No, it's mostly just a couple of bob that he bets."

"Does he win often?"

"Often enough, I suppose, but it's usually just a few bob. Watch now, the spinner's getting ready to toss again. He'll keep doing it until he makes a losing bet, then someone else will have a go."

Again Finnegan's big voice rang out. "Right now? Are you all set on the side?" He picked up the pennies, showing first the heads and then the tails as he placed them on the kip. Then he asked again, "All set on the side? Okay! I'm bringing him in. Come in, spinner!"

"Toss 'em high!" somebody yelled.

And other voices followed …

"Yeah … yeah! Make 'em fly and up with tails!"

"No, stay with heads, you bloody beauty!"

Once more the pennies danced brightly in the air before falling to the canvas. "Heads! He's headed them again!" the ringkeeper called.

Another roar of mingled cheers and groans, another transfer of notes and silver: in some cases, returning; in others, joining that previously handed over. Another call for the centre to be set. "Okay. Who wants to take tails for two quid?" The ringkeeper waited, his eyes darting around the ring of faces. "Any part of it then?"

A note fluttered into the ring, followed quickly by another from the opposite side, and then an enthusiastic renewal of the side betting. "Right? Are you all set on the side?" The ringkeeper paused, his quick eyes noting wagers not yet complete, then he called again, "All set on the side? Okay then. Come in, spinner!"

Again the kip was flipped and the pennies flew into the air.

"Come on tails!" a hoarse voice pleaded.

"No, it'll be bloody heads again! The bugger's on a winning streak!"

"Yeah, heads! Come on … come on!"

Heads it was, bringing gasps, groans and a rising buzz of excitement.

"Is he winning because he's spinning up heads all the time?" Christina asked, still more than a little bewildered by the whole proceedings.

"Yes, but only because that's what he's betting that he will do. He's got to miss soon though. No one can go on spinning up the same thing all the time."

"Will he lose next time, do you think?"

"If he still goes for heads, I reckon there's a pretty good chance of it. I know if I was down there I'd be betting against him, his luck must be due to change."

"Five quid!" Paddy Finnegan yelled dramatically. "Does anyone want to take tails for five quid?"

"He is staying with heads." Kathleen gasped. "Oh, he'll lose this time for sure. He's riding his luck too hard."

Christina's gaze was glued to the notes being flung into the ring. "Goodness, they are betting him five quid."

"Five of them going with a quid each. That's because they think it's time for the spinner's luck to change. Da will be having a couple bob on tails too, bet your life."

Once again the centre was set, the side bets placed, and the ringkeeper called for the spinner to come in.

"It'll be tails this time." someone called, but without conviction.

"Yeah mate. Fair go, eh?"

"I bloody well reckon. You sure you've got tails on them pennies?"

Then a hush, a holding of breaths, as the coins tumbled back to earth. "Heads it is! He's headed them again!"

"Struth, can you believe that?" Kathleeen cried, forgetting to whisper, then clamping a hand over her mouth. Not that anyone could have heard, so great was the uproar around the piece of canvas. In spite of all the shouting and yelling, however, Christina's attention had been caught by another sound – the cracking of a twig, and then the dislodging of a stone. For a moment or two she froze, feeling the chill of alarm run down her spine. Someone or something was on the hill behind them. Slowly, she twisted her body around so that she could look back down the way they had come, her breath at once catching in her throat. He was about a third of the way up, a man who climbed with long purposeful strides and didn't seem to care about the noise he was making. She pushed her arm against Kathleen's, whispering hoarsely, "There's a man coming up the hill."

Kathleen jerked her head around, her eyes wide with a mixture of dismay and incredulity. "Blessed Mother of God, it's Carl! What on earth is he doing here?"

"He's beckoning to us to come down."

Seeing that he had their attention, the young man had stopped climbing and was waving his arm in a beckoning gesture.

"I suppose we'll have to go," Kathleen muttered, wriggling her body back from the edge. "We can't have him coming up here and kicking up a ruckus."

"Will he tell your father that we were here?" Christina was doing her own wriggling and at the same time making a somewhat futile attempt to keep her skirt and petticoat down over her bare legs.

"Oh no, I shouldn't think so. Carl would never be so mean, but, if he's here, Danny could be somewhere around. They went over to Nerang together early this morning."

"Would your brother tell on you?"

Kathleen shrugged her shoulders as she got to her feet. "Probably not, but he'd take it on himself to give me a good dressing-down, and I'd have to be nice to him for days and days just in case he did decide to tell."

Christina was on her feet too, busily brushing grass seeds from her clothes and retying the ribbons of her bonnet. "You could explain that it was really my fault, Kathleen."

"Now why would I be wanting to do that?"

"Because it is my fault, that's why. It's because I didn't know what a two-up game was. If it hadn't been for that, you wouldn't be here."

"Don't be too sure about that. This isn't the first time I've watched the men playing down there, you know? Anyhow, what did you think about it all? Do you still consider it ridiculous?"

Christina stared in bewilderment at the smiling, dimpled face. How could she be so unconcerned when the man named Carl was waiting for them with the deliberate stance of someone taking a very dim view of their presence on the hill; when there was every likelihood that the anger of her father or brother would descend upon her shining head; when, worst of all, there was a distinct possibility that their friendship would be brought to an end almost before it had really begun.

"Well..?" Kathleen prompted, still smiling. "Didn't you find it very entertaining?"

"Yes, I suppose I did. It was certainly quite amazing and at least I now have some idea of what two-up is all about."

Kathleen's smile faded and she sighed in exasperation. "It's just too bad that Carl had to show up before we saw whether that bloke spun up heads again, and before you really got the hang of the game." She linked her arm through Christina's as they started off down the slope. "Never mind, there'll be another time. What we have to do right now is think up some reason for being up here, just in case Carl has decided to be difficult or Danny is lurking around somewhere."

Christina swallowed nervously, sensing that any explanation her new-found friend came up with would need to be viewed with some trepidation. "I really wouldn't mind if you just told him that I wanted to see how the game was played."

"Even if I'd let you do that, it wouldn't work. Carl will know jolly well that the whole idea was mine." She lifted her gaze heavenwards, as though seeking inspiration there. "What a pity it is that we didn't take our picnic with us, then we would have had a ready-made excuse for being up there."

Christina's lips parted in an involuntary smile. "And it would have been just coincidence that where we decided to have our picnic overlooked a group of men playing two-up?"

"Well, why not? Coincidences are funny things, no one can deny that. Handy things too, more often than not." Giggling softly, she glanced back over her shoulder to where they had been. "Who's to say that wouldn't have been an ideal spot for a picnic?"

"Even if we were obliged to lie flat on our stomachs," Christina added, giggling too.

"Yes, even so. But it's too late now to be thinking about that. What the heck? We haven't committed a crime or anything like that, so let's go face the music."

The young man, now waiting in the shade of a tree, had removed his hat, and Christina saw that his hair was thick and curly and of a deep golden colour. She saw, too, that he wasn't quite as tall as she had at first thought, but that his shoulders were broad, straining the fabric of his shirt, and that he was clean-shaven, his chin firm, his skin smooth and tanned. There was no doubt about it, Kathleen had been right when she'd remarked that her brother's friend was handsome. He was, in fact, exceedingly handsome, even though he was, at this particular moment, scowling quite deeply. He was also … familiar? A quick frown creased Christina's brow. Yes, she was sure of it now, the man waiting for them to join him was someone she had seen before, but where? "What's his other name?" she asked out of the corner of her mouth.

"Eichstead … he's Carl Eichstead."

Christina gasped. They were the very same person. This Prussian and the one who had ridden for the doctor on that distant, fear-filled day were one and the same. He was older now, of course, more mature in his appearance, but there was no mistaking him. Besides, there was his name – Carl Eichstead. She could remember hearing her father saying that he spelt Carl with a C instead of a K, and Eichstead with ead instead of aadt.

"So, Kathleen O'Rourke, up to mischief again," he accused in a deep voice as they drew near to where he waited. "I suppose you are getting ready to tell me that you were just taking a stroll up there?"

"We could have been," Kathleen told him, her glance darting about. "Is Danny with you?"

"No, he's gone on home."

"Thank heavens for that!"

The words were uttered with a considerable degree of feeling and Christina saw Carl Eichstead's mouth twitch as he restrained a smile. His voice nevertheless remained stern. "I wouldn't be in such a hurry to be thanking the heavens if I were you, young lady."

"Oh Carl, you're not going to be stuffy like Danny, are you?"

"I believe I owe it to Danny and your parents to say a word or two." His gaze moved to Christina's flushed face. "And to this young lady's parents also, I would think, though I don't imagine for one minute that it was her idea to go spying on a two-up game."

Christina swallowed hastily, his words reminding her that both her mother and father would be most displeased to learn what she had been doing. Nevertheless, she couldn't just stand by and let the blame be heaped on Kathleen's head, she should at least be sharing it. Lifting her chin, she said as firmly as she could manage, "I knew where we were going. It wasn't that ... "

But Kathleen cut her short. "What if we did see a two-up game?" she questioned with a defiant toss of her head. "There's no harm been done and none of the men saw us."

"If any of them had chanced to come around this side of the hill, they could have seen a great deal, believe me. As fine a display of petticoats and bare legs as they might ever hope to glimpse."

Christina gasped, affronted and incredulous. How dare he make such a remark. But her gaze had dropped involuntarily to the bare feet and ankles clearly visible beneath the hem of her skirt and her initial reaction was at once swallowed in an agony of embarrassment. Hot colour rushed to her cheeks and it was a moment or two before she could bring herself to raise her eyes.

"None of them ever comes around here," Kathleen was insisting, her eyes widening in dismay as she realised, somewhat belatedly, just what she had revealed.

A quick grin lifted the corners of Carl Eichstead's mouth and Christina saw that one of his eyebrows had been raised, giving him a quizzical expression. He's enjoying this, she decided with a prickle of irritation; he's actually amused by our discomfort.

"And how would you be knowing that?" he asked, laughter lurking behind his dark eyes. "It wouldn't be that you've done something like this before today, would it?"

"That's none of your business."

"Ah, but I happen to consider that it is. I would be most distressed to see you getting yourself into trouble."

Kathleen heaved a deeply exasperated sigh. "I've already told you, we weren't getting into trouble. We were very careful that no one should see us, and we weren't doing anything wrong, nothing that Christina's mother wanted us not to do."

"You're surely not saying that you actually told her you were going to watch a two-up game?"

"No, of course not. But she … well, she told us a whole lot of things we weren't to do."

"I see, and spying on a two-up game just didn't happen to be one of those things? I wonder why?" But then, as though suddenly overwhelmed by the absurdity of the whole situation, Carl threw back his head on a quick laugh.

Kathleen's scowl changed abruptly to a smile, her beautiful eyes lighting up. "I knew you wouldn't be an old meanie, Carl."

"Not being an old meanie doesn't mean that I approve of what you've been doing, young lady. You'd best see to it that it doesn't happen again, otherwise I might feel obliged to discuss the matter with your parents. You and your friend could be in real danger hanging around in a place like this."

Kathleen's smile disappeared and her chin was thrust out rebelliously. For one dismaying moment Christina was sure there was going to be an angry outburst of defiance, but then she shrugged, saying airily, "Who wants to watch an old two-up game anyway?"

"Good," Carl said easily. "Now that we know where we stand, suppose you show that you do have some manners by introducing me to this young lady?"

"This is Miss Christina Skov." She emphasised the 'Miss', having instantly decided to retaliate by denying him the privilege of informality. Then, nodding in his direction, "And this bossy person is Carl Eichstead, Christina."

Unperturbed, Carl smiled, his fine, strong teeth flashing whitely against his tanned skin. "Miss Christina Skov, I thought perhaps it might be. I'm very pleased to meet you, again. Or have you forgotten that we have met before this day?"

Christina shook her head. "No, I haven't forgotten, Mr Eichstead. How could I, when you may well have saved my mother's life?"

His smile wavered. "That was a sad time for your family and hardly one you'd want to be recalling. I'm sorry I obliged you to do so."

"It's alright, it was a long time ago."

"Yes, some years back now, you were just a child."

Kathleen had been listening, her face all surprise. "I really can't believe this, you two knowing each other."

"It was hardly what you'd call knowing," Carl told her. "Just a very brief encounter." He turned back to Christina. "I have been meaning to renew my acquaintance with your father ever since I heard that you'd moved to this district, but it seems I've been away more often than not these past weeks."

"Father has often mentioned you and I'm sure he would be most pleased to see you again."

"Well, now that the crushing season is just about over, I'll be spending more time in Mudgeeraba and I'll certainly make a point of calling on the Skov family."

"We will look forward to that, Mr Eichstead," Christina told him with what she hoped was polite dignity, then immediately asked herself how any young lady could possibly consider herself dignified when her naked toes were staring up at her.

Almost as though he'd read her thoughts, Carl said, "And now I'm sure you must both be anxious to … ah … replace your shoes and stockings."

"They're at the bottom of the hill," Kathleen informed him before turning quickly and, with skirts and hair flying, racing off down the lower section of the slope.

Christina wished that she could have done likewise, the sooner her feet and legs were once again covered, the better she would feel. What would her mother say, for heaven's sake, were she to see her standing here talking to someone who was almost a stranger without her shoes and stockings? Still, it didn't seem fitting that both she and Kathleen should go rushing off, so she set off more slowly, Carl Eichstead at her side.

"And how are you liking Mudgeeraba, Miss Skov?"

"Very much, it's a very attractive region, but please call me Christina." She gave him a small half-smile. "No one has ever called me Miss Skov before."

Carl returned her smile, his teeth again flashing whitely and Christina felt her heart skip a beat. Prussian he might be, she told herself, but he was still the most handsome man she had ever met.

"Christina it is then, and I shall be expecting you to call me Carl."

Christina nodded. Carl with a C, she thought, for no reason at all.

By the time they'd covered the short distance to the bottom of the hill, Kathleen was already sitting on the log, straightening out her stockings.

"I'll wait for you around on the road," Carl said at once.

"You don't have to do that, Carl," Kathleen assured him. "We'll just go back and ride along the creek for a bit and find a nice spot to have our picnic."

"Well, I'll just see to it that you get to the creek."

Kathleen shrugged, unconcernedly wriggling her toes into the first stocking, "That's not necessary, but suit yourself."

He was waiting on his horse when they made their way back around the hill, and he rode with them until they found what Kathleen considered a suitable place for their picnic. "It's not enough that I have a whole tribe of brothers ordering me around," she complained as they watched him ride off. "I have to put up with Carl as well."

"I thought you liked him?"

"I do. I like him a real lot, but that doesn't mean I have to like having him tell me what I should or shouldn't do." She grinned suddenly. "He'd make a fine beau though, wouldn't he?"

"I suppose so."

"My sister Maureen thinks so, she's real sweet on him."

"Oh … is he sweet on her too?" Only later did Christina wonder why she had found it necessary to hold her breath while she waited for an answer to her question.

"He could be, I suppose. He's certainly always nice to her; you'd never see him trying to boss her around." Kathleeen shrugged as she unwrapped a packet of sandwiches. "But that could be because Maureen's always so nice and sweet about everything. She makes a real business of being ladylike, if you know what I mean?"

Christina wasn't quite sure that she did know, but she nodded, there being other questions that she wanted to ask. "How old is your sister?"

"Maureen? She's eighteen." Kathleen handed over a large cheese sandwich and took an enormous bite out of its companion. After a few moments of vigorous chewing, she mumbled, "It won't do them any good though; even if they are both sweet on each other, they won't ever be able to get married."

Christina quickly swallowed the bread and cheese she'd been munching on, her eyes darting questioningly to the other girl's face. "Why won't they?"

"Because Carl's not a Catholic, that's why. Catholic girls can't marry boys who aren't Catholics any more than Catholic boys can marry girls who aren't Catholics."

"Who said they can't?" Christina asked, wide-eyed with astonishment.

"The Pope, of course."

"Can the Pope do that, stop people from getting married?"

"Sure he can. Hey, what religion are you anyway?"

"Lutheran," Christina told her, the faintest of smiles on her lips.

"Lutheran? Holy cow! And I said all those horrible things. Why didn't you kick me in the shins or something?"

Christina's smile took more definite form. "It didn't matter, and the things you said weren't really so horrible."

"They weren't very complimentary either, if I remember right. Well, you are not stuffy, I can tell you that, Christina."

"Thank you. What about Carl Eichstead, he'd be of the Lutheran faith also, wouldn't he?"

"He just says that he's a Protestant, and I've always supposed he was Church of England. I don't really know why except that he didn't seem to be much like a Lutheran." She grinned apologetically. "There I go again, for heaven's sake."

Unconcerned, Christina grinned back, and for a time they gave their full attention to the disposal of their sandwiches. Then she asked, "Does Carl Eichstead live here in Mudgeeraba?"

"Sort of. When he's not cutting cane down at the Tweed, he stays here and rides over to work on Mr. Muir's plantation on the Nerang River or does fencing or other odd jobs about the place. He's got a tent up in the hills on some land he's hoping to get as a selection."

"Whereabouts in the hills?"

"On Little Nerang Creek." She smiled dreamily. "That's a real pretty creek, Christina, with a waterfall not too far up. We'll ride back that way one day. Would you like some more lemonade?"

"No thanks, I've had plenty. Would we see his land if we rode that way?"

"No, we won't be able to follow the creek that far up. His place is well back in the hills with hardly even a track up to it."

"What will he do right up there, for heaven's sake?"

"For a start, he'll just be clearing the level areas, growing corn and grazing beef cattle. The land's not suitable for dairying and, even if it was, he couldn't go in for it, not when he's away cutting cane half the time."

"No, dairying's a job for every single day."

"You're telling me it is. Sometimes, Christina, I just hate those wretched cows with their great fat udders." She stretched out on the soft grass, and, grinning, Christina did likewise. "So do I."

"Well, we have every right to hate them. Take today, for instance. If it wasn't for the milking, we'd be able to loll about here until sunset and talk about all sorts of things. As it is we have hardly any time at all, just look where the sun is already."

There was, nevertheless, time enough for the asking and answering of a great many questions ... for the reaching out that would begin a special loving friendship.

20

Christina stared aghast at the large mound of mashed potato on her plate. Not even in three meals would she be able to eat so much.

"Better eat it," fourteen-year old Hughie O'Rourke warned, grinning at her from across the table. "If you don't eat your praties, Ma will think you're sickening for something and give you a dose of castor-oil and you know what that will do."

Christina swallowed a quick gasp, the warmth in her cheeks telling her that they were rapidly becoming bright pink. Beside her, Kathleen waved a knife at her brother. "Just you quit talking like that, Hughie O'Rourke. Do you want Christina to be thinking that we have no manners?"

"Well, it's true what I said." He turned in the direction of the short plump woman settling herself at the end of the table nearest the cooking range. "Ain't it, Ma?"

As well as being extremely roly-poly in appearance, Bridget O'Rourke was tousle-haired and generally dishevelled. There were, nevertheless, remnants of an earlier prettiness in the soft rosy cheeks and lips, in the sparkling green eyes and in the glints of auburn in the curls that escaped from the loosely knotted bun at the nape of her neck. She smiled often and, when she laughed, it was in a merry uninhibited fashion. In fact, one thing only prevented her from being almost continually cheerful: her head was full of superstitions, many passed down from Irish ancestors, others of her own inventing, but with the majority designed to bring fear to the human heart. Ireland might be far away, but who was to say that omens, evil spirits and the wee people belonged only to that distant country?

No one, according to Bridget. When the fogs that sometimes shrouded the marshy lands closer to the coast rolled inland and swirled about her house, the smile left her face, for hadn't the Gorta always come in just such a mist – that monstrous creature, seven feet tall, his face a skull, his bones covered by a ragged black cloak, who had walked among the people of Ireland, stealing into their gardens to bring scorch, stench and rot such as those who saw and smelled would never forget?

From time to time, the distant howling of a dingo, familiar after nineteen years of living in Australia, would catch her unawares, causing her to shiver with apprehension, for in just such a way did the banshee wail when someone of importance was about to die. Then there was the strange roaring sound that sometimes came from the swamps behind Burleigh Heads – the old bunyip sounding off again, people joked, but Bridget recalled the many evils which had been abroad in the bogs of Ireland and sighed while others laughed. She sighed even more deeply and reached for her beads when the wind blowing from across the ocean took up a soft singing, for that was surely the mermaids up to their tricks again, trying to entice the sailors from a passing ship into a watery grave.

Now, though, Bridget chuckled and said in a soft, lilting brogue, "Tis the devil of a talker, Hughie be, Christina, comes with him and Mikey being twins and always trying to out-do each other. Don't be paying him no mind whatsoever. Castor-oil for a visitor, indeed. What next will he be saying?"

Christina gave her a small smile. "There's such a lot on my plate, Mrs O'Rourke. I don't think I can possibly eat it all."

"Well, don't be fretting about what you can't eat, love. Just do the best you can."

Returning her attention to her laden plate, Christina's eyes met those of Carl Eichstead, also a Sunday dinner guest, and he gave her a quick, sympathetic smile.

"That's not fair, Ma," Hughie protested. "You always make us eat all our praties."

"Praties are good for growing boys." Bridget was already attacking her own large helping. "Even if they aren't like they were in the old days."

Kathleen gave Christina a small nudge, lowering her head to whisper, "Da will agree with that."

Sure enough, the senior Daniel O'Rourke did. "That's very true," he said, to no one in particular. "You don't get the good old field varieties any more. All the fine old reds, the Devonshires, Perths and Yorkshires, are gone."

"And the Blue Don," his wife added. "That was a mealy pratie if ever there was one. I recall eating them as a small child, and such a fine, rich flavour they had, different altogether from these we are obliged to eat today."

"Were they really all that different, Ma?" Mikey, the twin of Hughie, asked, his merry eyes glinting knowingly. "A spud's a spud, when all's said and done."

"Of course they were different." His mother jabbed a fork with sudden disdain into the creamy pile on her plate. "No thanks would you be giving for these if them Reds and Dons were still with us. A crying shame it is to have lost the likes of those praties."

Hughie grinned and winked at Christina. "Mr Andrews was telling me only the day that there are now more than four hundred varieties of potatoes in the world. There are bound to be some as good, if not better, than those that you and Da talk about."

"No, there aren't. There won't ever again be any as good as them that were lost during the famine." Bridget spoke with unassailable conviction, ignoring the grins on the faces of her younger children. After all, she had asked herself many times, how could they, being Australian born and raised, be expected to appreciate the true worth of a pratie?

It was mid-December and Christina was on her first visit to the O'Rourke home. Her initial impression had been that it was surely about to burst at the seams, not only because of all the people crowded into it, but also because of the noise. It seemed there were no rules in this household about waiting for one's turn to speak. The O'Rourke family, with the exception of Maureen, all spoke whenever they were so inclined, which was often. Even now, although they had set about disposing of their meal in a hearty fashion, talk flowed unceasingly back and forth, jumping, without warning, from one subject to another, and quite often rushing off in a number of different directions at one and the same time.

This, Christina soon found, resulted in a quite bewildering state of affairs. How was she to listen to three or four conversations all going on together, for heaven's sake? Kathleen's father had gotten around to discussing a horse named Midnight with his son Danny and Carl Eichstead; Bridget was relating for her daughters something the priest had told her when he'd come from Southport to say Mass for the family; and the three younger boys were engaged in a lively debate about the latest exploits of Ned Kelly and his gang. The one good thing about it all, Christina told herself, was that no one expected her to make too great a contribution, and this gave her an opportunity to observe the various members of this large and noisy family at close range, without it being too obvious that she was doing so …

Mrs O'Rourke was a nice, kindly lady, who had gone out of her way to make her feel welcome. What did it matter that she hadn't bothered to comb her hair or take off her apron before coming to the table, as her own mother would have done, especially with company present? With so many to cook for, she wouldn't have had the time to spare even a passing thought for such niceties. Her husband was a large man who seemed to be always hitching up his trousers from where they had slipped beneath his roundly protruding stomach. He spoke with a deep brogue and, like his wife, had a hearty laugh. His dark, crinkly hair was peppered with grey, but not so his thick bushy eyebrows. These were black still, and, when he had occasion to scowl, they met above his nose, giving him a quite fearsome expression. He had, according to Kathleen, something of a 'paddy', but, since it was as quick to disappear as it was to flare up, this was of no great concern to his brood, who usually managed to flee before he got his belt off, returning only when they considered he'd had a chance to cool down.

His eldest son, Christina was quite sure, wouldn't be nearly so quick to recover his good humour, if indeed he had any. He scowled often and, being one of the dark-haired members of the family with an olive skin, he seemed to wear an almost continual brooding expression. He looked, in fact, as though he would be every bit as quarrelsome and unpredictable as Kathleeen had warned. He was exceedingly handsome, nevertheless, with the same lean, muscular build as his friend, Carl

Eichstead. Christina brought her gaze back along the table, seeking the next O'Rourke. It would have been Joseph, but he was off visiting Sarah Cassells whom he planned to marry early in the new year. Gentle and kind-hearted, Kathleen had described this brother, her favourite and the complete opposite of Danny.

The other three boys also appeared to be unlike their eldest brother, Christina decided, glancing at each in turn. Patrick looked a little like him, being of the same dark colouring, but there was no brooding expression on his face, it was friendly and smiling. Nor was there any on the faces of the auburn-haired twins, only freckles and cheerfulness showed there.

A smaller version of Kathleen, nine-year-old Eileen, good-natured but with irrepressible mischief shining form her bright eyes, was both the darling and the dismay of her family. Only Eileen, Kathleen had lamented, could put a frog in your bed and then bid you goodnight with an angelic expression on her face. That left Maureen, and Christina had deliberately left this observation until last. Now, as unobtrusively as possible, she studied the girl sitting quietly between Carl and Patrick. She was beautiful, there was no doubt about that, but in a quieter, softer way than Kathleen. For one thing, her hair was so dark it was almost black, and it was tidier, brushed back from the pale heart-shaped face into a cluster of long curls around which she had tied a pink ribbon. Her eyes weren't such a flashing green; they were lovely, nevertheless, the amber-shot grey-green of a mountain stream. She was different from her sister in other ways too. She seemed fragile almost and there was a tenseness to her, especially in the way she was sitting stiffly on the edge of her chair. Was the handsome Prussian sitting beside her the reason for that? Probably, if what Kathleen had said was true. And very probably if the way she appeared to be hanging on his every word was any indication.

Maureen, herself, interrupted Christina's wondering. "You're not going to try to ride that brute again, are you?" she cried suddenly, her eyes wide with alarm.

Carl turned his head to smile at her, a warm smile, Christina saw, affectionate almost. "We have to, Maureen," he told her gently. "We've got less than two weeks in which to get him ready."

"You're still planning to race him on Boxing Day!" Maureen gasped, wide-eyed with dismay.

"It hasn't been looking too promising, that's for sure, but we are hoping to do so."

"We are going to race him on Boxing Day," Danny corrected. "That's the very reason we bought the horse."

His father's laughter boomed along the table. "Plus the fact that you got him for a song on account of no one being able to stay on his back."

"We got a real bargain, he's a fine animal."

"Of course he is. And, I grant you, he's got the makings of a damned good racehorse. But you don't really think old Herb Gilbert would have parted with him if he hadn't come to realise that he was never going to get him to the starting post."

"He gave up too easily."

"I wouldn't be calling getting a broken arm and two cracked ribs giving up easily." He caught the eye of Christina who had been listening with considerable interest. "What do you think of these two, Christina? Crazy, eh? They've got a horse they haven't been able to stay on for more than a few seconds, and they've got him entered for the Boxing Day races on Burleigh Beach."

Christina had begun to understand Maureen's alarm and she shook her head slowly, not sure just how to reply. Hughie saved her the necessity of having to do so. "You're in for a real treat, Christina. Midnight knows at least a half-dozen ways of getting Danny and Carl off his back."

"I'm sure Christina won't want to be watching," Maureen told him. "It's all quite frightening."

Christina was about to agree with her, since she had no desire to see either Danny or Carl being thrown from a horse, but once again she wasn't given a chance to speak for herself. "Of course she will," Kathleen declared firmly. "It will be far and away the best entertainment Mudgeeraba has to offer this Sunday afternoon."

Maureen bit her lower lip and made a half-hearted attempt to finish off the roast beef and vegetables still on her plate. Christina's heart went out to her. The girl was in love with Carl Eichstead and she was terrified that he was going to be injured, anyone could see that. Why, for heaven's sake, did he have to persist in trying to ride the rogue horse? He must know that she didn't want him to do so.

The rogue horse was black and handsome, with bright, intelligent eyes. "He's beautiful," Christina breathed, as she climbed with Kathleen on to the wooden rail of the animal's enclosure.

"He's that all right and he can gallop too. You should see him when he's out in one of the big paddocks, he fairly flies."

"No wonder they are so keen to get him broken and to the races. Who will ride him?"

"Whoever manages to stay on his back. They've got a deal, Danny and Carl, whichever one of them succeeds in getting the better of Midnight will be the one to ride him in his first race."

"Who do you think it will be?"

Kathleen shrugged. "Who knows? One's as good a rider as the other, and they've both broken horses before today." She glanced to where the two young men were struggling to get a saddle on the horse's back, a wide grin coming to her face. "Never a one like Midnight though."

Danny was the first to try. Mounting from the heavy wooden gate, he got a leg over the horse's back and lowered himself gingerly into the saddle. In the next instant, the gleaming black body was a heaving arch and he was flying through the air to land with a thud on the hard, sparsely-grassed earth. Christina gave a horrified gasp, but the O'Rourkes all cheered and yelled encouragement as he regained his feet, a heavy scowl on his face.

"Score one for Midnight!" Kathleen laughed.

"Aren't you worried that they'll get hurt?"

"They could, I suppose, but not seriously. A few bruises perhaps, but after all the tumbles they've already taken their hides must be tough as leather."

"They could still break an arm or leg."

"Like old Herb Gilbert did? No, they are young and strong. He was too old to be trying to ride a horse like this one."

Danny made two further attempts, both of slightly longer duration than the first, but both with the same result. Then it was Carl's turn to be sprawled on the ground. He landed close to the rail from which the two girls watched, and he gave them a good-humoured, but somewhat sheepish, grin as he scrambled to his feet.

"That's four to Midnight," Kathleen reminded him, laughing softly.

Carl's grin widened. "I suppose you're waiting for it to be number five?"

"Not at all. I've decided that it's high time the tables were turned. I'm even going to cross my fingers for you."

"Hmmm, that's bound to help. What about you, Christina, what are you going to do to help?"

Christina looked down into the laughing brown eyes and felt her heart skip a beat; not, by any means, the first time Carl Eichstead's nearness had made it do that. "I'll cross my fingers too," she told him, a little lamely.

"Good." Brushing at the dust on his clothes, he strode over to where Danny had been holding the horse and quickly remounted. This time, the first violent springs didn't dislodge him, and Midnight, surprised at this failure, began to rear and then buck furiously. When this didn't unseat the rider, he threw himself to the ground, trying to roll him off. A sharp kick in the ribs brought the animal to its feet again, and, miraculously, Carl was still in the saddle. The O'Rourkes yelled themselves hoarse, but Christina found that her breath kept catching in her throat and she couldn't make even the smallest sound. She kept her fingers crossed though, ever so tightly.

Again and again the horse arched its back with its head down between its front legs, and sprang off the ground. Again and again it reared high, pawing at the air. Again and again it spun around in a tight circle. Again and again it went into a spasm of wild bucking. But Carl remained in the saddle, clinging grimly with both hands and knees. Finally, the exertions began to tell; head-shaking, snorting and stamping replaced the springing and bucking. Then, abruptly, it all stopped and the horse walked quietly across the enclosure.

"He's done it!" Kathleen was screaming. "He's done it!"

Her father and brothers were also laughing and shouting, their hats following one another into the air. Even Danny, Christina saw, had a wide grin on his face. She watched Carl dismount and gently stroke the horse's sweat-stained neck. It danced away for a few paces, tossing its head nervously, then moved back to him of its own accord. Yes, he has done it, she thought, a soft smile coming to her mouth. It faded as Kathleen, jumping down from the railing, exclaimed, "Oh, for the love of Mike!"

Christina dropped to the ground and spun around, her gaze following that of the other girl. Maureen was racing from the house, her skirts flying behind her slight form, her curls bouncing on her shoulders. Carl saw her coming and climbed out of the yard, waiting with a grin on his face as she rushed up to him. For one breathless moment it seemed to Christina that she was going to fly straight into his arms, but he stopped her headlong flight by grasping her upper-arms and laughingly lifting her off her feet.

Kathleen snorted. "It's disgusting the way she throws herself at Carl."

"She's probably just excited."

"Sure, and aren't we all? Besides, she didn't come over to watch, did she? She's bound to have been peeking out of the back door though, it didn't take her long to get here."

"I think she might be really in love with him."

"Well, that's too bad. If she's silly enough to fall in love with someone she's always known she could never marry, she can't expect to have people feeling sorry for her."

"What if something like that happened to you?"

"It wouldn't, Christina. I'm much too … ah, realistic. Yes, that's the word, realistic." She tucked an arm through Christina's. "Come, let us walk down to the lagoon. The waterlilies are just beautiful right now, and there's something else I want to show you."

"What is it?"

"You'll see in good time."

Normally, Christina would have questioned further, but now there was a subject she was reluctant to leave. "I should think it would be very hard to do that."

"Do what?"

"Be realistic when you are in love, especially if it meant giving up the one you were in love with."

"Probably, but that just goes to show that you should be very careful just whom you fall in love with."

"Well, I think that if I loved someone enough to want to marry him I would do so, no matter what his religion was."

Kathleen tossed her a faintly reproachful glance. "You're only saying that because you don't need to worry about it, you're not in love with a Catholic."

"I'm not in love with anyone, and I don't propose to be either, at least, not for a long, long time. But just suppose that I fell in love with Danny?"

Kathleen threw back her head on a rippling peal of laughter. "Grumpy old Danny? You'd never fall in love with him, Christina."

"Probably not. But what if I did and he fell in love with me and we wanted to get married, what do you think would happen?"

"I know what would happen, nothing."

"Nothing … ?" Wide-eyed, Christina searched the other girl's face, surely she couldn't be serious. "I don't understand what you are saying."

"I'm saying that nothing would happen." Kathleen lifted her shoulders in a faint shrug. "Oh, he could go to bed with you, I suppose, if you'd let him, that is. But that would be all. Even stubborn, contrary Danny knows very well that, if he ever finds a girl willing to marry him, she will have to be a Catholic."

Surprised, Christina stopped walking and stared at her friend. "I think Danny would do whatever he wanted to."

Kathleen shook her head slowly from side to side. "He wouldn't marry a girl who was not a Catholic. How could he? No priest would perform the ceremony."

"He could get married in another church, a Protestant church."

"Then he wouldn't be truly married, not in the eyes of God. He and the girl he was supposed to have married would be living in sin."

"But, if they were married legally, according to the law, they wouldn't be living in sin, they'd be husband and wife."

"No, they wouldn't … oh Christina, what are we doing talking about such things on this lovely afternoon? It's not something you'll ever have to worry about." She ginned impishly. "You're not going to fall in love with Danny or any other Catholic either. You're going to fall in love with Carl."

Christina gasped, the warm colour rushing to her cheeks. "That's a ridiculous thing to say."

"No, it's not. It's not the least bit ridiculous. As a matter of fact, I'd say that you're part-way there already."

"I'm not yet sixteen years old, and, what's more, he's a Prussian. I could never fall in love with a Prussian."

"What's that got to do with it? I thought you said that your parents wanted you to treat Prussians the same as you would everyone else."

"Yes, and that's what I have been doing. That doesn't mean I would ever have to consider one of them as a prospective husband."

"Christina, it was ages ago that they took over your old country; you have to put that out of your mind."

"It wasn't all that long ago; it was 1864 when they came."

"Fourteen years, that's long enough. Besides, like you told me before, you were just a baby when it happened and babies don't hate anyone." She threw out her hands in a faintly impatient gesture. "In any case, it's not something you can hold against Carl, he would have been only a young kid at the time."

"I know, and I haven't been holding it against him, not really. It's just that it's something I've always known, that I could never marry a Prussian." She gave a small, self-conscious laugh. "Actually, I don't think I want to get married, to anyone."

Kathleen's mouth dropped open. "You've got to be joking?"

She flashed the other girl a small teasing grin. "I seem to recall you mentioning that you weren't too keen to get married?"

"Not at sixteen years of age … seventeen or eighteen years, either, for that matter. But I plan on being married before I turn twenty-one. After that age, a girl's on her way to becoming an old maid and who wants that? Not Kathleen O'Rourke, to be sure."

"And who will you marry, Kathleen O'Rourke: tinker, tailor, soldier, sailor?" Christina chanted, anxious to return to light-heartedness. "Rich man, poor man, beggar man, thief?"

"Ah ha! A rich man, of course. Tall, dark and handsome into the bargain. And … " She paused dramatically. "If he owns even one cow I shall insist that he employs a milk-maid."

Laughing, they linked arms once again and continued on their way, heading for the slight rise on which the dairy and bails had been erected and which hid the lagoon from their view. One day, I'll tell her, Christina thought. Then, when she knows about little Anna and those tiny graves, she'll understand. But would she? The doubt came with a rush: how could she understand when, with eight children in her own family, there probably hadn't been even one baby taken from them? How could she be expected to know what it was like to have had four taken?

"You didn't really mean what you said about not wanting to get married, did you, Christina?"

"No, I don't suppose so."

"Of course you didn't. Miss Christina Skov for all the days of your life. You couldn't possibly want that."

Christina felt her breath catch. Someone else had said almost those very same words to her. Lars … ? Yes, it had been Lars. Two years ago and near enough to the very day. Two years in which he was to have made his fortune and returned. Where was he, for heaven's sake? Why didn't he write? One brief note, written in Brisbane shortly after he'd left them, and then nothing more.

"Well, come on. You don't, do you?"

Christina pursed her lips in pretended thoughtfulness. "Miss Christina Skov, it doesn't sound all that bad."

"Oh, you know what I mean." She darted a quick, searching glance at Christina's face. "You're not afraid of being married, are you?"

Afraid … ? Of course she was afraid. Afraid that her babies would die just as those her mother had given birth to had done. Afraid that she would fail her husband who would be looking for sons to help him on his land. Afraid that there would be such anguish in her heart it would simply shrivel away. But Kathleen, she knew, had another aspect of marriage on her mind. "I don't think so," she murmured, somewhat embarrassed and more than a little apprehensive as to where this conversation was leading. Kathleen, she had discovered, had a far more thorough understanding of such matters than she did.

"Some girls are, you know? They're scared half to death about what's going to happen to them when they get married."

Christina swallowed, then smothered a small sigh of relief when Kathleen didn't wait for her to respond.

"But that's quite ridiculous, Ma says, being scared like that." She giggled softly. "And I reckon she ought to know."

Again Christina was spared the need to reply. They had reached the flattened crest of the rise and come around to the back of the dairy, and she caught her breath on a gasp of delight. The lagoon, the largest in a chain of shallow waterholes stretching across the O'Rourke's farm. sprawled before them like a flamboyant carpet: perfect round splashes of pink, mauve and yellow on a glossy green background, over which dozens of long-legged birds strutted. "Oh Kathleen, it's absolutely beautiful!"

"I thought you'd like it. This is the time of day when the flowers are at their best, they begin to close quite early in the afternoon. You can actually see them doing that if you watch closely enough. You can see them opening in the morning too."

"I wish we had the time to stay and watch them close."

"So do I, but we won't have. We do have time to go down there though. It will be a bit squelchy around the edges, but the surprise I have for you is down by the lagoon." She sat down on the soft grass and pulled off her shoes and stockings. "It's best we take them off, we can leave them here."

Christina hesitated and Kathleen, glancing up, gave a quick chuckle. "Do you think Carl is going to come over the hill and catch you barefooted again?"

"He could, or your brothers perhaps."

"No, they won't. They'll all be too busy fussing over Midnight. In any case, what would it matter? My brothers have seen my bare feet often enough, other bare parts of me too, if the truth be known." Her lips twitched and her brilliant eyes danced coaxingly. "The waterlilies are ever so beautiful when you get close to them."

It was enough. A few minutes later they were both at the water's edge, their skirts held up around their thighs, their bare feet sinking into soft mud.. Christina did wonder how they were going to be able to clean their feet well enough to put their stockings back on, but it was only fleetingly, her delight was much too expansive to leave room for the consideration of such a minor problem. "You were right, Kathleen, the closer you get the more lovely the flowers become."

"Don't they, though? And each one you look at seems even more perfect than the last." Her smile faded and she gave a small sigh. "Isn't it a pity the plant is such a pest?"

Christina's eyes, widening in surprise, flew to the other girl's face. "What do you mean?"

Kathleen threw out her free hand. "Well, just look at the way it's choked up this lagoon. It's hardly any time since Da and the boys cleaned it out, and they'll probably have to do it again before Christmas, Da was saying."

"They'll destroy all these lovely blooms?"

"They'll have to. The stuff spreads like wildfire; if it's not checked, it will be in all the other smaller lagoons as well."

Christina looked about her, shaking her head slowly. Something else beautiful that was a pest. The birds with the red beaks were as well; they were the swamp red-bills Carl had told them about when he'd made his promised call at their farm. It seemed there were huge flocks of them in the swamps closer to the coast, especially around Carrara, where they'd quickly taken a liking to the sweet sugarcane sap. A real problem for the owners of the small plantations stretching along the banks of the Nerang River, for the birds came in their hundreds, their strong beaks tearing away at the lower part of the cane stalks, damaging them to such an extent they fell to the ground in the first strong breeze.

"What can be done about them?" her father had asked.

Carl had shrugged his broad shoulders. "The growers have taken to encouraging shooting parties to visit the area. But I can't see that making any great or lasting impression, there are far too many birds for them to be controlled in such a way. To my way of thinking, a much better solution would be to try to drain the swamps in the area. That would not only bring about a decrease in the bird population, it would also provide more land for farming."

"Yes, that could prove to be a good idea, especially if, as you say, it not only meant fewer birds but more available land. If there were less water lying about, the whole region between the coast and the ranges would more than likely be excellent dairying country."

"There's no doubt about that. It's certainly where I'd eventually like to have a farm."

Christina started as Kathleen's laughing voice cut into her reverie. "For how much longer are you going to stand there daydreaming?"

She had walked some little distance ahead and Christina at once hurried to rejoin her. "I was just thinking," she explained with a small apologetic smile.

Kathleen grinned. "That was obvious. What about this time?"

"About the beautiful flowers being so unwelcome and those red-bills being such a problem for the sugarcane farmers."

"They're that alright, they make an awful mess of the cane."

They had begun to walk on, side by side, around the edge of the lagoon when Christina asked, "Have you ever wondered what God had in mind when he created Australia? I mean, He put so many beautiful things here, but gave them such destructive ways?"

A frown came quickly to Kathleen's brow. "We should never question God's ways, Christina."

"I know, and I wasn't really doing that. I was just wondering if perhaps His plans for this land hadn't gone astray in some way."

"How do you mean?"

"Well, perhaps He meant for the Aborigines to have it. After all, they've always been able to live quite happily with everything He provided."

Kathleen's frown disappeared and she laughingly gave Christina's arm an affectionate squeeze. "What notions you dream up, Christina. Just because it was that way with the blacks, it doesn't mean that God meant them to have the land for all time. Such a waste that would have been.

No, it's like Da says … Australia was just waiting through all those years when there only black people here."

Christina raised her eyebrows, a faint smile touching her mouth. "Waiting for the white people to come, do you mean?"

"For the white people who wanted a better way of life for themselves than the ones they already had," Kathleen amended firmly. "It was like God had this land in reserve, so to speak. Then, when He saw the troubles of people in other parts of the world, He bid them come."

"Even though He must have known they would be resented by the people who were already here, that many of them would die?"

"Well, God wouldn't have wanted that, of course. But there were things elsewhere that He wouldn't have wanted either … in Ireland, for instance, when the blight came."

When the blight came, Kathleen repeated the words to herself. How many times had she heard them? Thousands, she was quite sure. All her life she'd been listening to her parents tell of how it was when the blight came: how, as children, they'd stood one morning in their fog-filled gardens less than two miles apart, sniffing a stench so vile it turned their stomachs; how the stalks of the pratie plants were green still but the leaves spotted brown; how, in the trenches, tiny blackened praties were uncovered, while others which at first appeared sound rotted to slime within a couple of days. For the people of Ireland, Kathleen had long ago come to understand, a great disaster had struck. The pratie was more than just their staple food, it was a whole way of life. For centuries it had been eaten at every meal in every cottage throughout the land: roasted in the ashes, boiled in the pot, fried in pig grease, or cold in its skin. With the coming of the blight the barrels by the kitchen doors soon became empty; all that remained were the precious seed praties and these must, at all cost, be kept for the next planting.

For a time, Kathleen knew, there had been cabbages and turnips, the pigs and chickens which had been raised to help pay the rent, fish from the streams, the hares and the moorfowl, previously scorned as inedible because of their toughness, but now seen as delicacies. All too soon though, there were no more pigs or chickens, and, as a result, no eggs either, no more cabbages or turnips; the fish had become scant in the streams and the game which had escaped being eaten thus far had fled to the mountains. In the small, damp cottages of Ireland, berries, nuts, ferns, small plants and grasses became everyday fare. Even the nettles which stung the hands so cruelly, were carried triumphantly home; boiled for a long time they became edible and, while they failed to satisfy the hunger gnawing at the insides of those who ate them, they did manage to dull it.

Then, as though it weren't enough for the people to be dying of starvation, the dreaded black fever arrived, spreading like wildfire from village to village, county to county. And still, every six months, the hired agents of the English gentlemen who owned the land, the hated Sassenah, had come for the rents, evicting and destroying when they couldn't be paid; knocking to the ground or burning the meagre shanties that had at least offered shelter, adding all the while to the numbers wandering the roads – the roadlings.

As a small child, Kathleen had often wept when her parents talked about those desperate times, but, as the years passed, she found she could listen almost dispassionately, so many times had she heard the stories and so far away did it all seem. Now, though, spawned by Christina's questioning, a fierce conviction came rushing: the Irish people had every right to try for a new life in a new land, this land. Not America, or some other place, this land. Why, it could even be that they, having suffered so, were the very reason God had kept it waiting. "As sure as the Lord taketh away He giveth back" … that was what her mother often said when she talked about the famine. So, it was very likely that He had kept Australia waiting so that the people fleeing from Ireland could come here. A new and pleasing thought brought a quick smile to her face. Perhaps he had even given the English the task of discovering the place, in the way of retribution, so to speak.

The two girls had been walking slowly, each caught up in her own thoughts. It was Christina who, feeling a sudden need to explain her feelings, broke the silence into which they had drifted. "At the Logan, when our first corn had just begun to ripen, the cockatoos came over the ranges in their hundreds. At first, when I rushed out of our tent I thought it was just about the most beautiful sight I had ever gazed upon, all those lovely white birds against the blue sky and green corn. Then, in the very next instant, I knew that it was also the most terrible sight I had ever gazed upon."

Kathleen groaned softly, "Oh Christina, did they destroy it all?"

"Enough for the whole field to have to be cleared and replanted."

"That must have been a terrible setback for your parents."

"Yes, it was. They had both worked so very hard and they were so proud of that corn. The other horrifying thing about it was that Father had to shoot so many of the birds before the others would leave. For quite a time afterwards, I saw them, broken and bleeding, every night, the very minute I closed my eyes."

"I know. I've seen things like that happen too, especially when we were living out on the Jimbour Downs station. Out there, kangaroos were shot in their hundreds, sometimes more than fifty in a single night, and lots of them with joeys in their pouches. But it just can't be helped, Christina. If people are to take a living from the land such things have to happen."

"I suppose so, but I can't help thinking that there should be another way."

Kathleen stifled a small sigh. She's too gentle, she thought. If she doesn't learn to harden her heart this land will break her before her life has reached anywhere near its allotted span. "There is no other way, Christina," she said crisply. "You have to accept that. If you don't, your life in this country will be one long heartache. But, enough of such gloomy thoughts." She grinned suddenly and tugged on Christina's hand. "It's in that log, the surprise I promised you."

The log, partly concealed by bracken and tall grass was lying a short distance from the edge of the lagoon. Throwing off her hat, Kathleen was quickly on her knees peering into its hollowed centre. "Good, it's still here."

"What is it?"

"Come, see for yourself." She moved so that Christina could take her place at the end of the log and look into the hollow. The minute she did so, she exclaimed delightedly, "Oh, it's just adorable."

"A baby hare, no more than two days old."

"Goodness, is it really so young? It's certainly little but so … well, complete."

"I know what you mean, but hares are quite different from rabbits. They are born with their eyes open and hair and all, perfect little replicas of the adults."

"They are perfect alright. How on earth did you find this one?"

"The dogs chased the mother in here when I was rounding up the cows a couple of days back. I checked to see if she was alright and the baby wasn't born then, but, when I looked again yesterday, there it was."

"Where's the mother now?"

"She won't be too far away, watching us pretty anxiously, more than likely."

"We should leave then," Christina murmured, reluctantly beginning to rise. But Kathleen caught her arm and pulled her down again. "We can watch for a few more moments. She won't mind once she sees we're not out to harm her little one."

"I hope she won't. I would hate for us to be upsetting her." She glanced around her, looking for movement in the tall grass. Then, seeing none, quickly lowered her head, smiling as her eyes again came to rest on the log's tiny inhabitant. "Wouldn't you just love to cuddle it, Kathleen?"

"I surely would, but it's just a shade too far along to reach. Besides, I don't think the mother would approve of that."

"It's probably just as well we can't reach it, we might not be able to resist if it was closer." A disquieting thought wiped the smile from her face. "What about your dogs, can they get into this log?"

"No, they are too big and not nearly fast enough to catch the mother. I'm hoping the little one doesn't venture far from home until it can run as fast as she does."

They lingered for a few moments longer before getting to their feet. "Well, was it a nice surprise?" Kathleen asked, pulling her hat back on to her head.

"Oh yes, it was a lovely, lovely surprise."

"Now, I suppose, we should be getting back to the house. Carl will be wanting to leave, I should think; it's quite a ride up to his place, and, if he's going to see you safely home ... "

"I don't like taking him out of his way."

"It's only a short distance out of his way and he won't mind in the least."

He didn't mind in the least, Carl assured her as they rode away from the O'Rourke farm together. "As a matter of fact," he added with a quick grin, "I'm very happy to have the pleasure of your company, Christina, but, tell me, did you enjoy your first visit to the O'Rourke farm?"

"Yes, I did, very much."

"They are a fine family, the O'Rourkes, a bit overwhelming at times, but real salt of the earth people, just the type of family Queensland needs."

"Kathleen told me that her parents and the first three boys arrived before Queensland was a separate colony even, when it was still part of New South Wales."

"About two weeks before, so it was an eventful time for them to arrive. Did she tell you where they went when they got here?"

"Yes, to Jimbour Downs. That's a very big station, isn't it?"

"It's big all right. When it was first taken up, around 1840, it was something like three hundred thousand acres, but a few years later, the Lands Commissioner ordered a reduction of the area." He grinned with wry amusement. "To a mere two hundred and eleven thousand acres. Can you imagine a property that size, Christina?"

Christina shook her head, giving him a quick smile as she did so. "It would be enormous."

"Well, does twenty-two miles by fifteen miles give you some idea?"

"Is that really the size of the place."

"Yes, that's really the size of the place. It's owned by a Member of Parliament, Sir Joshua Bell. His father bought the property from the original owner who had lasted only three years before getting into financial difficulties."

Christina glanced curiously at the young man riding beside her. "You seem to know an awful lot about the place."

Carl grinned. "Much of what I know has come from Danny, of course, but I have to confess that I am so fascinated by the very magnitude of

Jimbour Downs I ask questions of anyone who knows anything at all about it. I even know how much old Thomas Bell paid for the property. Three thousand and two hundred pounds, and that included the sheep and cattle and all improvements. Of course, there was no great mansion there then, as there is today."

Christina laughed softly. "You're not thinking to have such a place for yourself one day, are you?"

"Some dream that would be." He shook his head slowly, his face becoming serious. "No, I try not to dream dreams that have little hope of being realised. Doing that, in my book, is sheer foolishness. Not only will it get a man nowhere, it will almost certainly lead him away from the path he should have taken."

"But how is he to know just where that path lies?"

"He knows, and, provided he hasn't got his head too far in the clouds, he also knows there won't be anything too easy about it. This is no milk and honey land, Christina, for all that it might be brimful of promise. On the contrary, it's tough and demanding, and that's the way the path to success and prosperity will also be, tough and demanding." The grin returned to his face. "Unless, of course, a man has a pocketful of cash to begin with, then perhaps it won't be quite such tough going."

What were they, those dreams he hoped to realise? Christina wondered as she returned his grin. To begin with, a selection back in the hills, then later, as she'd heard him tell her father, a dairy farm on the flat lands nearer the coast. But what else? A wife and children? Of course. Such a man would be wanting children, sons especially. She started, realising that he had asked a question which was registering somewhat belatedly in her mind. "What about you, Christina? What dreams do you have?"

"I don't know that I have any that are just mine. Ever since we've come to Australia, it seems that I've just shared my father's dreams."

Carl considered her for a long moment before saying gently, "That's certainly understandable, and, besides, you are still very young. You'll have dreams of your own soon enough."

"I'll be sixteen in January," Christina murmured, then immediately wondered why she had found it necessary to make what sounded, even to her own ears, like an objection to his remark about her being very young. Obviously, it had sounded that way to him too, for, although he was quick to suppress a grin, his eyes danced with gentle amusement. "I know, on the twentieth."

Christina flashed him a surprised glance and he laughed softly. "Kathleen told me."

"Oh … "

"Well, don't you want to know when my birthday is?" he questioned teasingly.

Christina had a sudden urge to tell him that whether she knew or not was of no account whatsoever, but she asked, "When is it?"

"On Christmas Day."

"Is it really?" Her eyes, only half-believing rushed to a searching of his face. "You were born on Christmas Day?"

"It's a fact that I was. On Christmas Day in 1853, which means that I am very close to being twenty-five years of age."

Christina laughed, an amused ripple of sound. "What a day to have a birthday, for heaven's sake."

"I was always under the impression that I had chosen very well. After all, I do some very important sharing."

"Yes, you certainly do that." And then a little apologetically, "It's just that I've never known anyone who had a birthday on Christmas Day."

"I should imagine there are any number of us scattered throughout the world."

"I suppose so." After a moment of two, she asked quietly, "In what part of Prussia were you born?"

"In Pomerania, a small town called Barwalde."

Pomerania, Christina repeated to herself, as they allowed their horses to break into an easy canter. Yes, she remembered now, that time at the Logan her father had remarked that Carl Eichstead was from Pomerania. So, there was no doubt about it. He was a true Prussian, born in the country, raised in the country, and, even though he had left it far behind, a corner of his heart could quite easily still be there. Just as a corner of her own was still in Schleswig. Unbidden, a small melancholy regret stole through her; then, recognised, was quickly ousted. Carl Eichstead was a Prussian and that was that. He had been very nice to her, but that was that also. There was simply no reason why she should feel regretful about anything he was, or did.

But then, almost against her will, she found herself asking, "Why did you decide to leave Prussia?"

"To find a better life in this great new land, of course, for the very same reason thousands of others left Europe and Britain, the Skov family included."

"But was there a reason you especially wanted to leave Prussia?"

Carl reined his horse back into a walk and Christina at once did the same with hers. "Did I have something against my homeland, is that what you mean?"

Christina moved a little uneasily in her saddle. It was exactly what she meant, but there was no need for him to have put it quite so bluntly. "Yes," she said, lifting her head just a little defiantly. "It is what I meant."

"Ah, Christina, let me begin by telling you that I understand why you have no respect for my old country."

Christina opened her mouth, but quickly closed it again. There were no words waiting there, none forming in her mind either. What was she supposed to say, for heaven's sake? That it wasn't so? Of course not, when it was something she had lived with all her life. She certainly wasn't going to start denying it now.

Carl was watching her, a quizzical expression on his face. "You're not going to deny that, are you?"

"No."

"Good. Now that we've got that little problem out into the open I can answer your question, but I warn you, it's not going to be a simple yes or no. I should probably begin by assuring you that, in spite of my country's reputation, I have always hated war. I was actually born during a war, the Crimean, and I spent my last year in Europe fighting in one, against the French. I have also always hated aggression and I know that Prussia has a formidable record in that respect. On the other hand, no one can deny the enormous struggles the state had for its very existence, let alone its rise to power. As you know, most European countries can claim a thousand-year history. Not so Prussia ... only in the 18th century did it gain a definite and consolidated form. However, thanks to two outstanding kings, it was, for that time, a quite brilliant form – a modern, efficient and disciplined state." He paused, as though waiting for Christina to say something. When she didn't, he said, "I was expecting you to add that it was also a military state."

"It was, wasn't it?" Christina murmured, a little guiltily since the words had been on the tip of her tongue. Only the quietly matter-of-fact way in which Carl was telling his story and a feeling that he was trying to lead her to a new understanding had kept them there.

"Yes, Prussia was a military state, but so were Sweden, France, Spain, Austria and Russia, so that, in itself, wasn't remarkable. What was remarkable was the size and quality of the Prussian army. It was the state's most important instrument, and everything revolved around it, everything stood or fell by it. It cost the people dearly, of course ... the highest taxes in the whole of Europe and other deprivations on the home-front, but there were very few who believed that there would be a Prussia without it." He tossed Christina a brief smile, holding up a hand in a small gesture of concession. "And so my country was a military state, just as you've always understood."

Again Christina moved uncertainly in the saddle. There was a purpose to what he was telling her, there was no doubt about that. Yet there was nothing of appeal in the way he told it. On the contrary, it was a challenge almost, as though he defied her to insist that his country had been a tyrant. And now he was waiting for her to say something.

"And you are convinced that it was all justified?"

A quick, thoughtful frown creased his brow. "Justified ... ? I would have preferred necessary, but...well yes, I suppose I am. A country which does something to ensure its very being must surely be justified in doing so."

"But what about..."

Carl quickly held up his hand. "I know what you are going to say, Christina. What about the invasion of Schleswig and Holstein? That all comes down to one name, Bismarck."

Christina heaved an expressive sigh. "I certainly know about him."

"I'm sure you do. Still, to give the man his due, the invasion of Schleswig was not something he wanted. It was a demand of German nationalism, and, because Prussia and Austria were rivals for that country, it was a cause neither could ignore."

"Are you saying that gave them the right to march their great armies into Schleswig and Holstein?"

"No, of course not. But that was all tied up with what was happening in Europe at the time. Actually, I don't think things worked out too badly for Schleswig and Holstein. It was a very short war and, afterwards, there were no sweeping changes in the lives of the people living in those duchies."

"My uncle died in that war when he was just eighteen years old," Christina told him flatly.

Dismay washed over Carl's face. "I'm sorry, I had no idea."

"That's what happens in a war, even a short one, people get killed." The words, meant to be angry, emerged a little tearfully and Christina was at once angry with herself. Why had she listened to him so intently, for heaven's sake? Once a Prussian always a Prussian, she should have remembered that.

"I know that, Christina. I've been in a war and seen people die, it's the most horrible thing there is." His voice was gentle and full of remorse and Christina, surprised, stole a quick look at him out of the corner of her eye. He looked contrite, there was no doubt about that. "I can see that what I said was very badly put and I'm truly sorry. What I was thinking was that, eventually, Bismarck was more of a disaster for Prussia than he was for Denmark and her duchies."

Christina tossed him a faintly disbelieving glance. "How can that be? He was Prussia's most famous statesman."

"That's true, but in the 1860s, he made many blunders. As you no doubt know, he was responsible for the foundation of the German Empire, but it didn't take the form he had intended. Instead of Germany being absorbed into Prussia, it was the other way around, Prussia was absorbed into Germany. The great and independent kingdom that was my homeland became just another German state."

"Didn't the Prussian king become the Kaiser? I recall people talking about it not long before we left to come to Australia."

"Yes, he did, old Wilhelm. But he did so very unwillingly. It seems that, unlike Bismarck, he was able to foresee something of what would happen. In fact, on the night before he was crowned emperor, he is reported to have said, "Tomorrow is the unhappiest day of my life. We shall be burying the Prussian kingdom.""

Christina felt her heart stir in reluctant sympathy; there had been such melancholy in the way he'd repeated the old king's words. "So," she said quietly, "that's why you decided to leave Prussia?"

"Yes, when my brother and I came home from the war, the changes had already begun to appear. Changes we didn't like, so we talked it over and decided to emigrate: me to Australia and my brother to America."

They had reached the turn-off that Carl would have taken, and Christina, reining her horse to a halt, told him, "You really don't need to come any further with me. I'll be quite all right from here."

"Do you want Ma O'Rourke to flatten me? She made me promise I'd see you right to your gate."

"I don't know why when Kathleen rides all over the place on her own." She grinned. "Besides, I wouldn't tell."

"She'd find out, never fear. She has ways of doing such things. Sometimes I think she really is acquainted with a whole tribe of the wee people."

Laughing together, they heeled their horses and set them to a smart canter along the rough, dusty road.

At the gate to the Skov farm, Carl dismounted and swung the heavy wooden structure open, leaning against it while Christina rode through. "It looks as though you're just in time for milking," he remarked, waving to Simon who was rounding up the cows. Then, his smile fading, "I hope I didn't bore you, Christina, talking about Prussia the way I did."

"No, I'm glad you told me."

His eyes, dark and thoughtful, searched her face, then, apparently satisfied, he smiled again. "I expect I might see you again before Christmas, but, if I don't, I wish you a very happy festive season."

"Thank you, I'm sure it will be. And I hope you have a very happy Christmas also and a happy birthday." She laughed softly. "And I hope Midnight remembers what you taught him and wins the race on Boxing Day."

"Two races. Since he's shown himself to be so energetic that shouldn't be too much trouble for him. Besides, he owes Danny and me that much, and I don't mean the money we paid for him."

Christina watched him ride off and was halfway to the house when she realised that she was still smiling. How silly, she thought, pressing her lips together. But that seemed even sillier, especially when the smile seemed determined to remain. Laughing softly, she shook the reins and dug in her heels, galloping off in her father's direction, calling to him, "I'll help you round them up and then I'll go and change my clothes."

"That sounds like a good idea, Christina. Did you have a nice day?"

"Yes, I had a lovely day. I had to eat an awful lot of pratie, but I had a lovely day, nevertheless."

"Pratie … ?"

"Potato," Christina told him. "Something the Irish are very fond of, by all accounts."

"Yes … well, I suppose they've more or less had to be." He looked up at her with one eyebrow raised. "You're sounding mighty pleased with yourself, young lady. That good-looking Carl Eichstead wouldn't have been paying you compliments now, would he?"

"Of course not, father. It's just that I've been thinking about what a happy Christmas this is going to be."

"Ah, that it will be, Christina. Our first on this fine new farm and with everything going along so nicely, how could it be otherwise?"

There would, though, be a shadow over Christina's first Christmas at Mudgeeraba. The letter from Mackay arrived in that very week, a letter addressed to her, but in an unfamiliar hand. "Who is it from, do you think?" she asked, strangely reluctant to tear open the envelope.

Her parents were both waiting, their own mail neglected, their faces anxious on her account. Her father cleared his throat. "It could be Mr. Schneider's writing, but perhaps he has only written the address on the envelope. You should open it, Christina."

"I know, but I have the strangest feeling. It's months now since I've had a letter from Henry." With sudden resolution she quickly tore the envelope along its top edge, pulling the single sheet of paper free with trembling fingers. Then, with tears rolling down her cheeks in huge droplets, she read what Mr Schneider had written..

My dear Christina,

It is with a deeply grieving heart that I write to inform you that our beloved son Henry was drowned on 16 March. As you will have read in the newspapers, Mackay had torrential rain at that time and there was much flooding throughout the district.

Our dear, brave boy took a small boat and went to the aid of two of our Kanakas who had taken refuge in a tree when a large creek broke its banks unexpectedly. Tragically, the boat was overturned by the strong current and all three were drowned.

I know that you and Henry were very close to one another and I am very sorry to have to bring you this sad news. I am also sorry not to have written earlier, but I could not bring myself to do so.

With best regards to you and your parents,

Yours sincerely,

Wilfred Schneider.

21

In the 1870s, Southport, originally known as Nerang Creek Heads and the most northerly of the south coast beaches destined to become famous in the mid-twentieth century as Queensland's Gold Coast, was the Colony's only ocean resort. In order to reach the newly surveyed township, it was necessary, however, either to make the entire journey from Brisbane by sea or to take the Cobb & Co. coach to Nerang, and then complete the journey by boat down the Nerang River. The journey by sea was generally considered the more comfortable of the two modes of transport; in spite of the fact that, for the greater part of the decade, the boat services available were based more on the needs of hardy timber-getters than on those of city businessmen and wealthy squatters and their families. Conditions improved somewhat when, in the late 1870s, Jack Tuesley, the first person to operate a regular cargo and passenger service between Brisbane and Southport, replaced his Iris with the more comfortable paddlewheeler, the Maid of Sker.

The alternative means of reaching Southport, however, continued to be something of an endurance test. Not only was the road from Brisbane extremely rough, winding as it did over some very hilly country, but the Cobb & Company drivers were quite unaccustomed to catering to the needs of the more particular, as a lady writing to the Logan Witness in April 1878 pointed out …

"I desire to call the attention of the proprietors to the disgraceful and dirty state of the interiors of these coaches. It is a common practice for the grooms to put under the seats dirty cans of tar and grease and often oil for the use of Cobb & Co., which filthy compound, by the shaking of the coach, gets driven all about, whereby the dresses of ladies travelling are perfectly ruined at a loss to these passengers of four or five pounds.

Another nuisance is that the spaces under the seats are often filled up with old harness, collars, rusty chains, swingle trees and other rubbish which, belonging to Cobb & Co., should be put elsewhere so passengers can travel with a little more comfort than they have ever done on this line … "

Nevertheless, the difficulties and discomforts experienced in getting to Southport were, in the eyes of most, far outweighed by what they found when they arrived: broad stretches of glistening white sand, beautiful river reaches and the island-dotted waters of southern Moreton Bay. Shooting and fishing were available on an almost unequalled scale, and, at Easter in 1879, the resort was to hold the first of its Annual Regattas.

Christina learned about the regatta on her sixteenth birthday. Kathleen rode over to spend a few hours with her, and, running down to the gate to meet her, she saw that she was bubbling over with excitement. She jumped from her horse's back and fairly ran as she led him through the gate. "Happy birthday, dear Christina," she sang, brushing her lips against Christina's cheek and thrusting a small package tied with a red ribbon into her hand. "Happy birthday to you."

"Thank you, Kathleen, but you shouldn't have … "

"Yes, I should so have. I wanted to and, besides, it's only a small gift." She reached out a restraining hand as Christina untied the ribbon. "Don't open it just yet, Christina. I've got something important to tell you before we go up to the house, something that just can't wait."

"I didn't think it was only my birthday that had gotten you so excited."

"No, it wasn't … " She grinned a little apologetically. "Well, of course your birthday is exciting, especially your sixteenth. But this is something quite different."

"Well, I'm waiting," Christina laughed.

Kathleen took a deep breath in order to give her announcement the dramatic effect she was sure it warranted. "There's to be a great regatta at Southport over the Easter weekend and we are to go on the Saturday."

"A regatta, with ships and boats?"

"Yes, a regatta, can you believe that? There'll be hundreds of boats taking part and they expect thousands of people to attend. Da says they'll be coming from all over the place. Oh Christina, it will be so exciting and

I'm to ask your parents if you may come with us."

Christina felt her breath catch. Go to a regatta with the O'Rourkes, how exciting that would be.

"We'll be driving the big wagon as far as Nerang and from there we'll go down the river in the Maid of Sker. Mr Tuesley is going to make it a real gala trip with music, flags and all the rest of it. For the love of Mike, Christina, don't just stand there gawking. Say something!"

Christina laughed. "You haven't given me much of a chance. Besides, I don't quite know what to say … it all seems like a dream you are talking about. Oh, Kathleen, I do so hope I'm allowed to go with you."

"I don't see why not. Your parents should be able to manage the milking for one day."

"We'll be gone for a whole day then?"

"Yes, from quite early in the morning until late in the afternoon, I should think."

"I don't know that I'll be able to … "

"Of course you'll be able to come. You're a big girl now, sixteen years of age. In any case, we won't be doing anything your mother wouldn't approve of." She giggled. "At least I don't think we will. Never having been to a regatta, I don't really know what goes on."

"For goodness sake, don't say that to Mother or I'll never be allowed to go."

"Of course I won't, silly." She sighed dramatically. "How are we ever going to be able to wait for Easter to come round? I'm sure I'll burst with impatience long before then."

Christina gave her a half-smile, doubts stilling her own excitement even as it stirred within her. There were so many things about the proposed outing her mother would want to know; her father too, more than likely. "Who will be going?" she asked. "Not your whole family?"

"No, Ma and Da and the twins and Eileen will stay for the milking and perhaps go to the regatta on the Sunday. Maureen might stay home too. She wants to come but she's afraid of being on the boat. Can you imagine anything more ridiculous? After all, it's not as though we'll be going out on the ocean or anything like that. Anyhow, that leaves Danny, Patrick and me, Joseph and Sarah who'll be married by then. And Patrick is going to ask Sylvia Weaver since he's a bit sweet on her. Then her mother will probably insist that Sylvia's brother Arthur comes to keep an eye on her, she's a bit flighty, you know? Oh yes, and we'll be meeting up with some others in Nerang – Sarah's cousin Jane and her fiancé, and probably his brother. Then there's Carl, of course, and you." She broke off, laughing and breathless.

"It sounds as though it will be a wonderful day," Christina told her. And then, as casually as she could manage, "Is Carl back then?"

"Not yet. He and Danny are still away on that fencing job, but I know they'll both be keen to come to the regatta. After all, there has never been anything like it in the Colony before." They were walking up the track to the house, leading the horse, and she stopped abruptly. "Hey, you haven't opened your present."

"You wouldn't let me, I seem to recall."

"Well, the regatta is much more exciting than a handkerchief … " She broke off on a dismayed gasp. "Damn, now I've gone and told you what it is."

"Don't worry," Christina laughed. "I'll be seeing it in about two seconds in any case." She folded back the soft tissue paper and held up a handkerchief of fine cambric, lace-edged and with an embroidered corner. "It's lovely, Kathleen, thank you ever so much."

Kathleen grinned, still excited. "It will be the very thing for you to drop at the regatta."

"Why ever would I want to do that?"

"So as some handsome young man can pick it up for you, of course."

"You are such a ninny."

"Then you don't think that it's a good idea?"

"To risk losing my lovely handkerchief? I should think not." She caught hold of Kathleen's arm and squeezed gently. "I do so hope I am able to go with you."

She was. To her surprise, her parents readily gave their permission. She worked hard on the farm, they said, and now that she was growing up it was only fitting that she should be able to go on outings with her friends. Even the suggestion that she spend the night at the O'Rourke's was agreed to as being sensible; though, as her mother said after a delighted Kathleen had left, heaven alone knew where they were going to find room to sleep another body.

The Maid of Sker was already at the wharf close by the recently completed bridge when the big wagon rumbled down the last hill and into Nerang, coming to a creaking halt on the river bank. In the crisp, early morning sunshine, the boat appeared spic and span and cheerfully welcoming; her paintwork gleamed and the bunting and streamers with which she had been decorated fluttered colourfully in a gentle breeze. A renewed surge of excitement rushed through the noisy, laughing group in the wagon, and the young men lost no time in jumping to the ground, from where they held up eager arms to lift the girls down.

Patrick was about to reach for Christina when he was laughingly shouldered aside. "It's my turn for the ladies, yours for the hampers."

She saw Patrick raise his eyebrows and begin a good-natured grin, then Carl's big hands were about her waist and she was being swung through the air so widely she caught her breath, quite sure that, if he were to release her, she would fly for several yards before coming to earth. When he did at last set her down she stumbled a little and his arms went quickly around her, holding her steady. "Hmmm," he murmured, grinning, "there's not much of you, is there?"

"There's enough," Christina replied, trying to sound as light-hearted as he did, which wasn't at all easy, what with her cheeks beginning to feel warm and her heart taking up such a rapid beating. It's all from being swung around like that, she told herself, but didn't even begin to believe it.

"For a farmer's wife?" he questioned teasingly as he finally released her.

Christina lowered her lashes, all too aware that the soft pink in her cheeks had deepened. Now what was she supposed to say to that, for heaven's sake? And didn't it just serve her right for having answered him so pertly? Yes, that was more than likely the way the words had come out, pertly, not light-heartedly as she had intended. "I'm a farmer's daughter," she mumbled with a faint flash of defiance.

"Indeed you are, Christina." The teasing note had left his voice and Christina glanced up quickly.. directly into eyes that were gentle and warm and … and …

"Hey Carl, grab one end of this hamper, will you? It's so heavy I think it must have one of Kathleen's chocolate cakes in it."

Christina watched him walk away with a bemused expression on her face, her mind in a whirl. Had he really been reluctant to release her? That's the way it had seemed. Why else would he have let his hands slide down her arms as he did so, then close his fingers over hers? For the briefest moment only, of course, but it had happened, nevertheless. There was something else that had been more than a little confusing. It was the expression she had seen in his eyes, gentle and warm, but what else? What was it that she had seen there? Something unexpected? Yes, certainly that, and, whatever it was, it had made her heart skip a beat, that much she also knew. She gave herself a quick mental shake. Such things to be thinking, for heaven's sake. And to be just standing in the one place why everyone else bustled about. Thank goodness, though, no one seemed to have noticed. Breathing a small sigh of relief she hurried to help Kathleen retrieve the three cushions she had thrown in quick succession at Patrick and which had come perilously close to flying into the river.

The Maid of Sker moved smoothly downstream, her big paddlewheel churning out a frothy white ribbon to mark her wake, music and laughter floating from her deck. "Oh Christina, isn't this just wonderful," Kathleen exclaimed, bouncing about on her seat as she tried to take in everything that was going on. "The very first boat I have ever been on and I love it."

"That's very obvious," Christina told her. "You don't seem to be able to sit still or stop smiling."

"True enough, I can't. I'm sure this is going to be the most exciting day I ever known. I can feel it in my blood, if you know what I mean? It's fairly racing through my veins."

Christina nodded, her eyes involuntarily searching the forward section of the boat where most of the young men had gathered. Her blood might not be racing through her veins, she thought, but something inside her was certainly behaving very strangely. It wasn't simply due to the excitement of the regatta, either. Which was all quite ridiculous. Just because she had grown to like Carl, in spite of his being Prussian, there was no call for her body to be carrying on in such a disturbing fashion. After all, she liked him as a friend, nothing more.

"I can almost feel sorry for Maureen," Kathleen mused, her smile fading, but only briefly.

"It is a shame that she didn't come." Christina bit her lip, and quickly admonished herself. Surely she could have sounded a little more regretful. No, more than that. Surely she could have felt a little more regretful.

"Well, that's a misfortune of her very own making. Everyone tried to tell her that she would enjoy the boat trip, and, when all's said and done, how ridiculous can you get? Most of the people in this country have sailed half way round the world to get here, across the great oceans and all. Like you did when you were just a little girl, Christina. And there's Maureen too scared to go on a boat down the Nerang River."

"She's a very timid person, so it's probably something she can't help."

"She's timid alright, I won't be denying that. But she should make some effort to overcome her fears, most of which are quite unfounded, I might add."

"Perhaps she does."

"Of course she doesn't. Look at how she still won't go to see Midnight race. He has won three times now and been second once, but just because Danny and Carl had so much trouble breaking him she still thinks of him as a rogue horse out to harm them."

A pleasing recollection brought a soft gleam to Christina's eyes. Maureen might not have seen Midnight race, but she had. On Boxing Day she had gone with the O'Rourke family to Burleigh Beach and cheered just as loudly as the others when the horse won both his races. What an enjoyable outing that had been: standing on the glistening sand dunes to watch the horses race along the flat, damp sand at the water's edge; eating a picnic lunch at the base of the great, densely-forested bluff that jutted out into the ocean at the southern end of the beach; watching the great waves shatter into foam and flying spray as they crashed over the tumbled rocks. And, on another occasion since, she'd been at the Nerang race track when he'd won.

"Well, it's too late now. Maureen's at home, and we are on this wonderful boat." Once again, Kathleen's smile flashed brilliantly. "Did you bring the handkerchief I gave you for your birthday?"

"Yes, I did, but, like I've already told you, I am not going to be dropping it, not on purpose, that is."

"Well, I guess you won't really need to, the way Carl keeps looking at you. As a matter of fact, I don't think he would take at all kindly to someone else picking up your handkerchief for you." She leaned her head to one side and considered Christina critically. "And I must say it's not difficult to see why, you look even more beautiful than usual, if that be possible."

"Oh Kathleen, you are a ninny."

"I mean it. Just look at you: hair like spun gold, and it really becomes you put up like that; eyes bluer than the skies; lovely creamy skin without even a single freckle."

"Not true. If you look more closely, you see that I have at least four or five on my nose."

"They must be awfully faint, I've never noticed them." Kathleen giggled. "I suppose that could be because I'm so used to looking at the O'Rourke variety. Anyhow, I think you should always wear blue, it's most definitely your colour."

"And I think you should always wear that shade of green, it suits you perfectly. Since we are passing out compliments, I must add that you look positively ravishing."

They both began to laugh, then glanced quickly and a little self-consciously around them to see if anyone had overheard their conversation. Satisfied that no one had, they broke into an attack of relieved giggles. When these subsided, Kathleen glanced down at the pretty frock she was wearing, smoothing its folds almost reverently. "Oh Christina, it was ever so nice of your mother to make this dress for me.

I've never had anything like it in the whole of my life before."

"Mother likes to sew, especially now that she has a sewing machine."

"Well, she sews beautifully, so she deserves to have that quite marvellous contraption."

"That's pretty much what Father said when he bought it, after Mrs. Laver threatened to throw it out of her house."

Kathleen grinned. "Poor Mrs Laver, she just couldn't get the hang of it."

"And poor Mr Laver, who'd bought it for her as a birthday gift. How deflated he must have been."

"I reckon, but at least it all turned out well for the Skovs. Have you tried it yet, Christina?"

"Only on a piece of cloth. I didn't try to make anything. Once you understand how it works it's not so scary as it at first seems. I think we have good reason to be grateful to Mr Singer, he's the man who invented it."

"Well, let's hope he invents a few more useful machines, something to milk the cows, for instance."

Highly amused at the absurdity of such a notion, they burst out laughing, and were still giggling when, at Carrara, the Maid of Sker eased into a wharf crowded with people in holiday mood waiting to board. Now, around every sheltered bend, water birds rose in thunderous clouds: hundreds of swamp red-bills, but also flocks of ducks, teal, widgeon and other aquatic species, even a number of beautiful swans. Christina, spellbound, left her seat and moved to the rail in order to miss nothing of the breathtaking spectacles unfolding one upon the other.

"Take care you don't tumble overboard."

With the boat so crowded, Christina hadn't realised that Carl had come up behind her, but she gave only a small start before half turning to give him a radiant smile. "Oh, I can hardly believe this. So many birds, and the swans ... it seems incredible that they should be here in such numbers."

"Well, they've not only got the river, there are all the creeks and lagoons as well; this whole region is a water bird heaven. It was actually known as the Great Swamp before the Stephens family took to draining it."

"I heard you telling Father about them. What a job that must be."

"You're telling me. But what foresight they must have had … first the father and then the son. They took up ten thousand acres comprised mainly of peat swamps surrounded by ridges, believing that, with a decent drainage system, it could become good dairy-farming land."

"And they were right?"

"They certainly were. They've already got a couple of dairies established, and others will soon follow."

Christina smiled at him. "And this is where you'd like to have a dairy farm?"

Carl returned her smile. "Right here would be just fine." He gestured at the land they were passing. "This was all a cotton-growing region at one time, and this was Boobegan Price's place. You can see the house he had built through those trees."

"Boobegan Price … " Christina repeated, a smile coming to her lips.

"You've heard about him, then?"

"Not only that, I've seen him."

"Where … when?" Carl had managed to get to the rail at her side and he stared down into her amused face incredulously.

"In Brisbane when we first arrived. We had some of our meals at the hotel where he was staying, and some people told us about him. Actually, they told Mother and Father. I only took in part of what they were saying, but I remember the name and how he got it … from a creek."

"That's right, from Boobegan Creek. That's it you see running into the river over yonder. Old Boobegan bought the land in 1862 – some twelve hundred acres for himself and another similar area for the Manchester Cotton Company, of which he was the head."

"He was quite a character, by all accounts?"

"He was that alright. Everybody in this part of the world hears his story sooner or later. He was what they call a remittance man. Do you know what that is?"

"Sort of. Aren't they men who have been sent to Australia by their families back in Britain?"

"Yes, by the English gentry, for the most part. They are supported by money sent out to them and which, according to some people, they are expected to turn to good account. But general opinion is that their families don't really care what happens to the money so long as the recipients stay away from hallowed family halls, that these fellows are actually the black sheep of the family. Whatever, for the most part, like Boobegan Price, they don't seem to be overly anxious to make a success of what they do here."

"Perhaps they feel they have no need to do so."

"That's quite possible; bad management was certainly part of the reason for the failure of the cotton."

The river had widened considerably, and the boat was now making its way past a number of great logs lying at the water's edge. "The Boobegan rafting grounds," Carl told Christina. "Those logs will be lashed together on a full tide and a cutter will tow them to Brisbane."

"That would be interesting to see."

"Yes, it is. I've seen any number of rafts being towed down this river and also down the Tweed and I still get a kick out of watching them. It would have been a much more exciting business a few years back though, when the timber-getters first worked the Tweed district. In those days the rafts were only given an occasional tow. Getting to Brisbane depended almost entirely on the tides and currents and, of course, on the skill of the raftsmen." He laughed softly, admiringly. "What a job those blokes must have done."

"You don't mean that they went all that way on logs that were just floating along of their own accord?"

"That they did, Christina, and, believe me, it was a whole lot more involved than just going along for the ride. Their first task was to pilot the raft out over the bar at the mouth of the Tweed River. They did this on the ebb tide, of course, but it had to be at a certain stage of the ebb, towards the end. If the raft went over the bar too early, the force of the tide would take it clear out to sea, beyond the north-bound current and into another which ran south."

"Goodness, did that ever happen?"

"I believe so. But crossing the bar into Moreton Bay for the final leg of the trip was apparently even more hazardous. At ebb tide the water rushes out of the bay through a deep, narrow channel between Southport and Stradbroke Island like a huge mill-race and it's powerful enough to carry a raft well out to sea. Then, on the flood tide, when the sea reaches a certain height at the bar, great billows sweep across it and crash on to the inner beach, and at slack water there isn't enough current to carry the raft into the bay. Those that did reach the bar at such times simply went on drifting north. So it was vital that the raftsmen reached the bar just after the tide had begun to come in, only at that time were they able to pilot their long rafts into the bay. Once in there, of course, getting to Brisbane was a comparatively simple matter, they just drifted on the flood tides and tied up on the ebb."

"What would happen to those who weren't able to get into the bay?"

"Some of them apparently entered on the next tide through the passage between Stradbroke and Moreton Islands. Others drifted right up around Cape Moreton, but still others were lost at sea or had their rafts smashed to pieces on the beaches of the islands."

"What brave men they must have been."

"Yes, they were, a very special breed."

Little Tallebudgera Creek joined the river and it became wider still. Then, almost immediately, it swung northwards, following the line of the coast. Here, cane fields lined both banks, brilliant splashes of living green in some places, dark, freshly-planted in others, and, everywhere the dark skins and fuzzy heads of Kanakas.

"That's Johann Meyer's land you are looking at," Carl told Christina. "He's only been here for a couple of years but he's certainly made a lot of progress."

"Are all those Kanakas working for him?"

"Yes, he has about fifty of them."

"Fifty? No wonder he's made good progress."

The faintly sarcastic retort brought a gleam of wry amusement to Carl's eyes. "Hmmm, that remark tells me that Miss Christina Skov doesn't approve of the Kanaka trade."

"No, she does not." Christina darted a glance of enquiry up into his face. "Do you?"

Carl moved his broad shoulders in a casual shrug. "To tell you the truth, Christina, it's not something I've cared to decide one way or the other. I'm well aware that some people have made a deplorable business of the trade, but, on the other hand, I can see how necessary these Islanders have been for Queensland; there simply wouldn't have been a sugar industry without them. In any case, most planters adhere to the rules and treat them quite well."

"That may be so, but it just doesn't seem right somehow. I know it's not really slavery but it must be awfully close to it."

"A number of people appear to think that way, and it's certainly understandable when you hear some of the stories about those people being kidnapped from their island homes and brought here."

Christina eyed him curiously. "Don't you believe that happens?"

"I think it does sometimes happen that way. Like I said, the trade has a nasty side to it, but I just can't see how it can be done away with, not at this stage of the Colony's development, at any rate."

"What can't be done away with?" Kathleen wanted to know, diving into a small space next to Christina and pushing her even closer against Carl.

"That was the end of a particular conversation," he told her. "And we don't propose to go over it for your benefit, young lady."

Kathleen grinned good-naturedly. "Suit yourself. I only asked to be sociable."

Carl threw back his head on a quick laugh, but Kathleen's attention was already elsewhere. "Oh look, Christina, the ferry's getting ready to cross."

The ferry was just leaving Elston (the later Surfers Paradise) with a full load of horse-drawn vehicles, their occupants, judging by their dress and exuberant mood, also heading for the regatta.

"Old Meyer will make himself a pretty penny this weekend," someone nearby laughed, as good-natured banter flew back and forth between the two vessels.

"He makes himself a pretty penny every weekend," another voice cheerfully responded. "If not from the ferry, then from the House of Blazes, that's always busy."

"And how would you know that, Harry?" a feminine voice questioned.

At once a teasing chorus joined in the questioning …

"Yes, Harry, how do you know?"

"Tell... tell. You must tell."

"I've heard it said … " the man called Harry began, but he was quickly shouted down, "You've heard it said? A likely story."

Harry tried again, but his explanation was drowned in laughter and he finally yelled, "Well, if you must know, I've been there."

Laughing along with the others, Christina asked, "What is the House of Blazes, for heaven's sake?"

"It's the place up there on that knoll," Kathleen told her. "It's an inn of sorts."

It looks innocent enough, Christina thought, her gaze on the large, shingle-roofed building with its wide verandah facing the river, hardly the sort of place that might be expected to have such a name. "Why is it called that?"

"Because it has earned the name, I suppose. A couple of timber-getters built the place in the mid-sixties and all of the raftsmen heading back into the bush after delivering their logs made it their last port of call. Apparently, some pretty boisterous and fearsome times have been had there." Kathleen leaned forward to where her eyes could glint impishly up at Carl. "You and Danny have been there, haven't you, Carl? Why don't you tell Christina what it's like?"

Carl grinned. "I was expecting that, Kathleen O'Rourke."

Unperturbed, Kathleen grinned back at him. "Well, go on, tell her."

"It's really just another hotel, Christina. A bit unusual, I suppose, but an hotel nevertheless. It's true enough what our friend here says, that the place had something of a reputation earlier on and I would suppose that it still has its exciting moments. Most of the time, though, it's just another drinking place, very popular with fishermen and holiday-makers. In fact, it seems that no holiday at Southport is complete without a visit to the House of Blazes."

"And Mr. Meyers owns it?"

"He does now. He bought the place from the original owners some two years back, along with a fairly large parcel of land. Then, last year, when the Government established the ferry service, he took over operation of that as well."

"He means to do very well for himself, it seems."

"Well, I, for one, wouldn't be holding that against him. In my book, he's a man to be admired."

Christina nodded. "Yes, I guess he is."

A number of low-lying, mangrove-covered islands divided the river where it flowed into the Broadwater, and, on the largest of these, a group of Aborigines stood watching the Maid of Sker glide past. The children responded to waves and calls from the boat, but the adults stood silent and unmoving. "Well, at least they're not afraid of us," Christina murmured.

Danny, who had joined them at the rail a few moments previously, shrugged his shoulders. "It's impossible to know what's going on in their minds, their faces certainly don't tell anything. Just look at that lot. You'd almost say that you were looking at a huddle of blackened tree stumps."

"That's an awful thing to say," Kathleen protested, but with a small giggle.

Her brother looked piercingly at Christina. "What about you, Christina? Do you think that it was an awful thing to say or do you agree with me?"

Christina moved a little uneasily under his close scrutiny, but managed to say steadily enough, "I don't think it was very nice."

"You've been out-voted, Danny," Carl told him, smilingly easing the slight tension. "I agree with the ladies."

Danny eyed him with mock reproach. "What a friend. Well, then, perhaps I should try to atone for my … ah … whatever it was by enlightening the ladies as to what those blacks are doing on that island."

"It looks to me as though they are doing absolutely nothing." his sister interrupted.

"If you don't want to know, Kathleen, don't listen. I'll tell Christina, I'm sure she'd like to hear." He raised his dark eyebrows enquiringly, and Christina, relieved to see him in such relatively good humour, nodded. "Yes, I would like to know."

"Good. Well, it so happens that they go to the island for the berries off a bush that grows there. They call it gee-gee, and they've given that name to the island as well." He smiled briefly. "Now isn't that an interesting piece of information?"

"Yes, it is. Do you know a lot about the Aborigines, Danny?"

"No, only bits and pieces. I don't believe anyone knows a lot about them, Christina, not yet."

"Do you think they ever will?"

"I would expect so, but it won't be in our lifetime."

In 1879, the sea had not yet broken through Stradbroke Island at Jumpinpin. The waters from the Logan, Albert, Pimpama and Coomera Rivers and the numerous creeks of the region all funnelled down to the narrow end of Moreton Bay and into the Broadwater, where they met the waters of the Nerang River coming from the opposite direction. They then poured out into the Pacific Ocean between Porpoise Point at the southern extremity of Stradbroke Island and Nerang Head, the northernmost tip of the sand dunes that separated the lower reaches of the Nerang from the ocean.

On Easter Saturday in that year, the Broadwater presented a quite breathtaking spectacle. The Colony's finest yachts were there, as was the entire fleet of the Moreton Bay Oyster Company, plus a vast assortment of paddle-wheelers, fishing boats, cutters, and other craft out of every stream between Brisbane and the Tweed. And they were all at their gayest, brightest best: scrubbed until they sparkled, their masts and wheelhouses draped with flags and brightly coloured bunting; their whistles constantly sounding. The water beneath their keels sparkled too, a vibrant, translucent blue, and, above, as though it would never have dared be otherwise, the sky was at its bluest with only an occasional feather-like cloud sailing across its vastness.

As the Maid of Sker nosed her way into the wharf, Christina found herself staring speechlessly. What a sight it was. So many boats, a hundred or more. Yes, there would have to be. Probably closer to two hundred, with more arriving all the time by the look of things. And there were so many people, on the boats, and on the shore as well. They milled around the tents that had been erected between the trees and spilled on to the sandy beach like a colourful tapestry. A very colourful tapestry, for there were gowns, bonnets and parasols of every imaginable shade: brilliant reds and oranges; soft pinks and mauves; purples and sunny yellows; gentle greens and flashing greens; a dozen or more different blues, There were men, too, who added to the colour, with their cream trousers, pastel shirts and straw boaters. Why, it was like … like … Christina giggled to herself. It was like nothing she had ever seen before.

The first tree the O'Rourke party came to with its shade still unoccupied was some little distance back from the water and not very far from the impressive-looking Pacific Hotel, built only in the previous year. It was, however, on a long, low rise and they took possession in gleeful triumph.

"It's a splendid position." Joseph declared, echoing the general opinion. "We'll be able to see everything that's taking place on the water and yet be far enough away from the crowd to be comfortable." He gave his wife of two months an affectionate glance. "What do you think, Sarah?"

Sarah, involved in a discussion with her cousin as to the best place to put the picnic hampers, gave him a quick smile. "I think we have been most fortunate, Joe love. There are people arriving all the time and, with the sun shining so brightly, they'll all be looking for shady spots." She returned her attention a little anxiously to the hampers. "I think there could be a few ants about, Jane."

"Thank goodness we've got Sarah and Jane to worry about such things," Kathleen murmured in an aside to Christina as they spread a rug over the soft grass. "But she's right, you know? We have been lucky to get this spot. Not that you and I are going to be lolling about here all day, mind. Very soon, we are going to be taking ourselves off on a little stroll. I can't wait to be rubbing shoulders, so to speak, with those very elegant ladies down there. Did you ever imagine such gowns? Or such bonnets? They must have cost the very earth."

"I wouldn't be at all surprised." Then, taking a deep breath. "Oh, I do love the smell of the ocean."

"Mmmm, it is nice, sort of tangy," Kathleen agreed as they settled themselves on the rug and removed their bonnets.

"May I join you two young ladies?"

"Of course you may, Arthur." Kathleen gave the tall young man a dazzling smile and patted the rug at her side. "Sit by me, Christina will be wanting … "

Christina, alerted by the mischievous twinkle in her eye, cut her short. "We were just remarking how pleasant it is here, with the breeze blowing in from the ocean."

Arthur Weaver, lowering his long frame a little awkwardly, nodded. "It certainly is that. I enjoy the smell of the ocean."

"So do I," Christina told him, wondering if he ever really smiled. All the way on the wagon he had worn a serious expression, and on the boat as well. Why, only on one or two occasions, had she seen his mouth even so much as twitch. Perhaps it was the responsibility of keeping an eye on his sister that kept him so serious. She stole a sideways glance at the rosy-cheeked, slightly-plump young girl sitting ever so close to Patrick, her hand on his knee as she leaned forward to gaze into his eyes. Ah yes, it could well be that Sylvia Weaver was a little flighty, just as Kathleen had said. But, on the other hand, perhaps she really cared for Patrick …

"Every so often I get a faint whiff of fish," Kathleen declared, wriggling her nose fastidiously. "Can you smell it. Arthur?"

"Very faintly, and it's not really unpleasant." He shrugged. "The Kanakas will get the blame, more than likely."

Both girls looked at him enquiringly. "Why?" Kathleen asked.

"Because they usually catch more fish than they can eat and then leave the remains for the pelicans, which are too well fed to do a thorough clean-up job."

"If that's what they do, they deserve to get the blame," Kathleen told him.

The faintest of wry smiles touched Arthur Weaver's mouth. "The thing is they've been doing it for quite some time and nobody cared. It's only since Southport has become popular as a holiday resort that the whole thing has come to be seen as a problem. It seems that the wealthy businessmen and squatters visiting here don't take too kindly to the smell of rotting fish."

"And who can blame them?"

"Nobody, but sometimes those very people aren't too fussy what they leave lying on the shore either and they should know better."

"Yes, they should," Christina agreed, sensing that this was a sore point with the young man. "Do the Kanakas often fish in these waters?"

"They come every Sunday, dozens of them. Believe me, Christina, it's a sight to behold. They scatter all over the sand flats as the tide comes in, splashing furiously to stop the fish from escaping into deeper water, then they catch them by throwing spears or shooting arrows. Small sharks and rays are the most favoured as a meal, and, as soon as one is caught, it's taken up to the fires they have burning on the beach, where it's cooked and eaten right away."

"Ugh ... I don't think I'd be enjoying that," Kathleen exclaimed, screwing up her face.

"A young shark cooked on an open fire as soon as it's been caught is very tasty."

"Don't tell me you've eaten one, Arthur?"

"Yes, I have, part of one, that is. Another bloke and I joined the Kanakas a couple of months back."

He grinned ruefully. "We didn't catch a thing, but we weren't allowed to go hungry. Like I said, shark meat can be very tasty."

"You were probably starving, and that's why it seemed tasty." Kathleen suggested.

"I was hungry, I seem to recall, but I don't believe I was starving."

"It would be interesting to see the Kanakas fishing like that," Christina told him with an appreciative smile. "I suppose that, coming from the Pacific Islands as they do, they'd be quite used to getting a meal in such a way."

"I would expect so." His eyes rested thoughtfully on her face for a moment or two as though he wondered whether or not she would be interested in what else he had to tell. Then he said quietly and just a little uncertainly, "They perform a ritual you might find interesting also, Christina, or amusing, perhaps?"

"Oh ... what is it?"

"On every second Sunday, before they begin their fishing activities, they wade out along the edge of the main channel until they are up to their necks in water and then they drink several mouthfuls. They believe that the water from the open ocean has medicinal qualities."

"Salt water? That is interesting. But why do they do that only every second Sunday?"

"Because it has to be at flood tide. Every other Sunday when they arrive it's at ebb tide and the water then contains all sorts of impurities from the rivers and creeks. It's hardly of medicinal quality, so to speak."

Christina smiled at him. "The water out there looks very clean and sparkling to me. Is it flood tide now?"

"No, the tide is more than halfway out, as a matter of fact, but I agree, the water does look quite clear. Still, there are any number of streams emptying into the Broadwater and I suppose the Kanakas should know … after all, they are the ones drinking it."

Again Christina smiled at him, then turned her head to watch some boats lining up for the start of a race.

"I think they must have to go around that buoy over there," Kathleen decided excitedly. "Which one are you going to barrack for, Christina?"

"I don't know. I think I might barrack for all of them."

Kathleen tossed her a glance of mock reproach. "That's not fair. You'll be sure to have the winner if you do that."

Surprisingly, Arthur Weaver smiled. "I think it's a good idea. I'm sure they all deserve a cheer."

With the race over and the noise which had accompanied it subsiding, Christina stole a glance around her. Sarah and Jane, apparently having solved the problem of the ants, were relaxed and smiling as they went back to discussing plans for Jane's marriage to George Hart, an event set to take place in June. That somewhat swarthy gentleman was close by, talking earnestly with Joseph. Patrick and Sylvia Weaver had seized upon the opportunity offered by the excitement of the race to move even closer together, his arm behind her now, her head resting on his shoulder. No wonder her brother seemed so serious. Charged with the responsibility of keeping an eye on that young lady, who wouldn't be?

Not that he appeared to be overly anxious at the moment, he was actually chuckling at some remark Kathleen had made. That left Carl, Danny and James Hart, who was every bit as swarthy as his brother but a good six inches taller. The three men were still standing, discussing the various boats, Christina decided, since they were looking out over the water as they talked. Her gaze lingered, even though the suggestion that this was where it had been headed all along was rejected the very minute it came into her mind. If only he wasn't so terribly good-looking, she thought with a faint sigh, or if he was moody and scowling as Danny often was, then perhaps he wouldn't be so constantly on her mind.

Carl turned his head as he laughed at something James Hart had said and Christina quickly tugged her gaze away, letting it settle once again on the boats moving so busily about. But her mind continued its wandering … to other things that had been bothering her, things that had brought her thoughts into very strange conflict. When she was away from him, she couldn't wait to see him again; yet, at one and the same time, she wanted to avoid him, apprehensive of the pleasure that came with being in his company. It sometimes seemed that, against her will, her life was somehow becoming entangled with Carl Eichstead's. Against her will? Of course it was. Even if she had planned on getting married one day, he wasn't the person she would choose, what with him being so much older than she was and a Prussian into the bargain. And that, she thought, smothering a sigh, was something that was really confusing, the swiftness with which the way she felt about Prussians generally seemed to have changed. All the years of hating them melting away in a single afternoon. How strange that had been, almost as though she had wanted something like that to happen … that she had, subconsciously, been looking for an excuse to stop hating them. Why? Because she had met Carl Eichstead? No, it wasn't that …

Kathleen's laughing voice cut off any further denial her mind might have come up with. "What on earth are you shaking your head like that for?"

"I don't know. I mean … I didn't realise I was shaking my head."

"Well, it certainly looked as though you were taking a big decision about something, didn't it, Arthur?"

"We all have a right to our own thoughts," Arthur said quietly, giving Christina a small, but reassuring, smile.

"I suppose you're right, but Christina's such a one for deep thinking. There's many a time I'd just love to know what's going on in that head of hers."

"Not much that you don't know," Christina told her with a quick grin. "You usually manage to get everything out of me one way or the other."

Kathleen grinned too. "Well, I'm pretty clever at doing that, even if I do say so myself. In any case, why shouldn't I know your secrets? I always tell you mine." She got to her feet, pulling on her bonnet. "I think it's time we took that stroll."

"Would you like me to come with you?" Arthur Weaver asked hopefully.

"Not this time, Arthur. Christina and I are going to be talking about all those fabulous gowns the ladies are wearing and you'd be bored to tears."

He opened his mouth to assure them that he wouldn't, but Kathleen quickly whispered close to his ear, "I really think it best that you stay and keep an eye on that brother of mine. I'm sure he's just waiting for a chance to run off somewhere with Sylvia."

"That was cruel," Christina said, half-reproachful, half laughing, as they made their way down the gentle incline.

"Yes, I suppose it was, but we didn't want Arthur tagging along with us. I do feel sorry for him though, the poor fellow's completely under his mother's thumb, you know?"

"Then why doesn't she keep Sylvia under her thumb also?"

"I think she tries to, but Sylvia won't have a bar of it. She doesn't seem to have much success with the three younger boys either. It's only poor Arthur she manages to keep the reins on."

"Well, he seems very kind and I suppose that could be why he lets her do it."

"Mmmm … could be. Anyhow, it was more or less right what I said. He does need to keep an eye on those two. They are going to get themselves into hot water, sure as anything." An amused grin spread across her face. "That would really be something, wouldn't it? A shotgun wedding for our Patrick."

"Oh Kathleen, what a thing to be saying."

"I'm just being realistic, that's all. Besides, even Ma has said that there's a distinct possibility of that happening."

"Well, if it does, I just hope Mrs Weaver doesn't blame poor Arthur." Christina glanced at the other girl with a teasing smile. "He's really keen on you, you know?"

Kathleen's mouth dropped open. "Wherever did you get such a ridiculous notion?"

"From the way he was acting back there."

"That's silly. He was nicer to you than he was to me."

"But he didn't look at me the way he looked at you, especially when he thought no one was watching him."

"You just imagined it." She threw back her head on a sudden peal of laughter. "I can just picture Mrs Weaver's face if she heard you say something like that. You've got no idea how she watches me whenever we go over to their place for Mass … all the time, more or less, and out of the corner of her eye mostly. It's like she thinks I would be poison for her Arthur."

Christina stared at her disbelievingly. "She doesn't really?"

"Yes, she does, really. Sometimes, when she's watching me and pretending not to be, I get this urge to poke out my tongue just to see her reaction."

Christina tried to act horrified, but giggled instead.

"But, with Maureen now, it's a completely different story. The way she gets fussed over in the Weaver house is something sickening."

Maureen and Arthur? They would make a wonderful couple, what with both of them being so gentle and kind. The thought, born of feelings not yet acknowledged, bounded into Christina's mind, and was quickly followed by another … it would be a very good match for Maureen, since the Weavers had a very nice farm and appeared to be quite prosperous.

"Of course, Maureen's exactly the sort of wife she would want for Arthur," Kathleen continued. "She would just do everything the old battle-axe told her to. I bet that, if they did get married, she wouldn't even want to build them a separate house."

"But Arthur might change if he got married, stand up for himself a bit more."

"He might, but I doubt it. I think he'll always be just like his old man and work like the very devil, but let the old lady make all the important decisions."

"Do you suppose that Maureen and Arthur care for one another?"

"They seem to get along together pretty well, But Arthur has probably been thinking what's the use of hoping for anything more. After all, he'd have to be blind not to see how looney Maureen is about Carl."

Christina swallowed against the sinking feeling that claimed her, annoyed that it had done so. For that was another of the strange things that seemed to be happening to her, the unsettling interest she had in the relationship between Carl and Maureen.

"But that's more than enough about Arthur Weaver. He's old enough to solve his own problems and this is supposed to be a pleasant stroll." They had reached the edge of the crowd stretched out along the shore and an excited sparkle flashed into Kathleen's eyes. "Christina, have you ever imagined such wonderful clothes?"

Christina shook her head, every bit as wide-eyed as her companion.

"And see, there are ever so many in that new fashion with the skirt trailing along the ground."

"Yes, I've noticed." Christina's attention had been captured by an elegant pink gown, the very latest style for a stroll along the beach, though she wasn't aware of that. The bodice was long-sleeved, tucked and braid-trimmed, and it was worn with a short velvet bolero in a maroon colour. The skirt was an intricate arrangement of frills and flounces: three deep flounces caught up in an apron effect over many smaller flounces; a huge bow folded into several layers of pink and maroon over a bustle at the back; and, emerging from under the bow, the frilled train that trailed for a foot or more along the ground. She waited until the wearer of this most fashionable creation had moved a short distance away before whispering to Kathleen, "That must be one of the most beautiful gowns ever, but I should think those styles would be every bit as inconvenient as the crinolines used to be. And how dirty they must get, dragging along the ground like that."

"They'd be a nuisance alright." Kathleen giggled, her eyes dancing. "It would be sort of like being a peacock, except that a peacock would be better off, he could at least get his tail up off the ground."

Christina giggled with her, but at the same time lowered her eyes for a new appraisal of her own skirt. It was full and flowing with a single deep frill at the hemline, but nowhere did it touch the ground, and her shoes were clearly visible. Furthermore, it had no horsehair bustle beneath its folds, though her mother had ever so cleverly arranged most of the gathering under a bow at the back, and this did give almost the same effect as a small bustle would have done. "We don't seem to be quite up with the latest fashion," she murmured with a faintly rueful grin.

"Well, who cares when all is said and done? You can bet we are a darn sight more comfortable than those who are. In any case, our dresses are as pretty as any of them. What we have to do is stroll about with our noses in the air."

"Why?"

"So that people will think we are the daughters of rich squatters, of course." Her smile wavered as she raised her eyes to give the brim of her bonnet a disgusted glance. "If only we could have had new bonnets as well as new dresses."

"We did get new ribbons."

"New ribbons on old faded bonnets while all the smart ladies are wearing hats with the brims swept up at the sides and the back." But her cheerfulness was not to be contained and it came rushing back. "Well, I suppose new ribbons are something." She glanced about her, the ladies in their fashionable attire, for the moment at least, losing their claim on her attention. "Christina, do remember to keep your handkerchief at the ready, and, if I give you a pinch, don't ask questions, just drop it."

Laughing softly, Christina shook her head. "You really are quite impossible."

They made their way through the crowd slowly, with Kathleen staring openly and Christina trying, though not very successfully, to keep her interest as unobtrusive as possible. It was like a grand parade, she mused, especially in the places where the gentry congregated, laughing and talking together before strolling about as though they were more interested in displaying their elegance than anything else that was going on. How they stood out from the local people, the farmers, fishermen, timber-getters and their families. It was almost as though clusters of expensive jewels had been washed up on a shore of pebbles. There were two, though, who seemed to be neither expensive jewels nor pebbles, and Christina found her attention returning to them almost involuntarily. They were dressed more flashily than elegantly, and their hair was of a bright unnatural colour ... on one of them orange almost. Their lips were painted and shining and their cheeks heavily rouged. And there was something else about them that at once caught the eye; it was the deliberate and provocative way in which they walked, their heads held high, their hips swaying. Christina saw that many of the more fashionably dressed ladies gave them scornful glances, which didn't, she also saw, appear to bother the two unusual women in the least. "Have you noticed those two?" she murmured, nudging Kathleen.

"Who could help but notice them?" The women were walking towards them and she quickly took hold of Christina's hand and pulled her away from their path. "They're a couple of those I told you about, I should think."

Puzzled, Christina stared at her.

"Oh, you must remember, it was only last week." Kathleen put her lips close to Christina's ear and whispered, "Prostitutes."

Christina's mouth flew open and she quickly turned her head, trying to see the women again, but caught only a glimpse of purple as they disappeared into a refreshment tent. "How do you know that?" she asked, her eyes wide with astonishment.

"From the way they look, of course, all that paint and stuff on their faces and the gaudy clothes they are wearing. In any case, haven't you noticed how the other women have been reacting, trying to pretend they're not there, sort of," she giggled. "Not the men though, they're getting an eyeful whenever they can be sure of doing so without their wives spotting them."

"Well, they seem to be quite nice. One of them smiled at me when you were getting our lemonades."

Kathleen gasped. "You didn't smile back?"

"Of course I did. What else was I supposed to do?"

Kathleen began an exclamation of dismay, but burst into a fit of giggles instead. "Oh Christina, you are priceless."

"I don't see that it was all that amusing." But in spite of her slight chagrin, Christina felt a faint smile tug at her lips. "I suppose you are going to tell me that no squatter's daughter would ever have smiled at a … at a…"

"At a prostitute," Kathleen supplied, dashing a hand over her mouth when the word emerged none too quietly. Dismayed, they both glanced quickly around to see if anyone had overheard. A smartly attired elderly man was looking at them, a rather startled expression on his face, while the young man with him grinned widely. Kathleen gave them a small, rather sheepish smile, before hurrying Christina away. "I think it's time we went back for our lunch."

They were almost at the tree when Kathleen came to a dead halt, whispering hoarsely. "That would have to be the most gorgeous-looking man I have ever seen."

Christina, following her gaze, gasped, staring in disbelief. They were walking in the direction of the hotel, a tall young man with a beautifully dressed lady on his arm, an elderly lady who was so very familiar. Mrs Klaussen? Oh yes, it was! It was!

Eleanor Klaussen saw her coming, a slim girl in a blue dress literally flying up the incline, her bonnet slipping from her pale gold hair. She paused, recognition tugging at her mind, then, in an instant, dawning fully.

With a soft, joyous cry, she held out her arms and Christina raced right into them. "Oh Mrs Klaussen, it is you! It is you!"

"Christina! After all this time. What a wonderful, wonderful surprise."

They were hugging each other, half-laughing and half-crying, words spilling almost incoherently from their lips, while the young man looked on, puzzled amusement on his face. Finally, Eleanor, wiping tears from her cheeks with the tips of her gloved fingers, held Christina from her and turned to him. "David, this is little Christina, of whom you have heard so much. Christina, this is my grandson, David Charlton."

David Charlton smiled, his teeth flashing whitely beneath his dark, neatly-trimmed moustache. "I thought it might be, though she doesn't seem to be so little anymore." He reached for Christina's hand, shaking it formally. "I'm delighted to meet you, Christina. I've been hearing about you for so long, it seems that I already know you." His voice had trailed away, his eyes, suddenly incredulous, leaving Christina's face to settle somewhere beyond her left shoulder. Kathleen had come up on to the rise, slowly and uncertainly.

The time would come when Christina would recall that moment with startling clarity and tell herself that she should have seen what was happening, that any stranger passing by would have done so, so starkly was it etched on both their faces. For now, though, she was much too excited, too overcome with her own emotions to be aware of those of others. She held out a hand, urging Kathleen to join them, happily making the introductions. The moment they were done, Eleanor said, "We must find a place to talk, Christina. I have so many questions to ask you." She looked around her with a quick frown. "If only there was some place to sit … "

Her grandson smiled at her. "Why don't we invite these two young ladies back to the hotel to have lunch with us?"

"Yes, that's a splendid idea, David. Why didn't I think of it?"

"That would be lovely, Mrs – " Kathleen began, but Christina, glancing back to where Sarah and Jane were unpacking the hampers, cut her short. "That's very kind of you, Mrs Klaussen, but we are with Kathleen's brothers and some friends. We've brought a picnic lunch and they'll be expecting us to share it with them."

"Then you must, of course."

"Perhaps they could come over to the hotel after lunch then, Grandmother. You and Christina can sit on the verandah and catch up on each other's news, you'll have a good view of the races from there. While you're doing that, I'll entertain Miss O'Rourke, that's if she'll allow me the pleasure, of course." He was gazing steadily at Kathleen, his eyebrows raised, and she nodded quickly. "I would enjoy that."

Eleanor glanced at her grandson just a little questioningly, but he smiled reassuringly. "We'll probably go down on to the sand to watch or, better still, beg a ride in one of the boats."

Later, she, too, would wonder how she could possibly have been so blind, especially when she knew this beloved grandson so well. "Christina and Kathleen might have other plans for this afternoon."

"No, we haven't," Kathleen told her quickly. "We were just going to sit around watching the races."

"Good, it's settled then," David Charlton declared with one of his breathtaking smiles. "Shall I come and fetch you?"

"That won't be necessary," Christina told him. "It's that hotel over there, isn't it?"

"Yes, the Pacific, we'll be watching out for you."

They were the last of those who had wandered off to return to the tree and Christina, excitement still bubbling within her, felt a prickling of guilt as her eyes took in the food already set out on a checked tablecloth. "Is there something I can do, Sarah?"

"You can put these sandwiches on a plate if you would, Christina, and perhaps you'd like to slice your cake." She glanced up at her sister-in-law who was staring out over the water with a bemused expression on her face. "And you might see to the glasses, Kathleen."

"What...? Oh, the glasses ... ? Yes, of course."

Danny gave a short laugh. "It seems that meeting up with the aristocracy has left our sister more than a little dumbstruck."

Kathleen gave him a sharp glance. "Don't be ridiculous."

Danny laughed again and shifted his gaze to Christina, who was kneeling on a rug as she unwrapped the sandwiches Sarah had passed to her. "You didn't tell us that you had friends among the privileged and wealthy, Christina?"

Startled at the tone of the remark, Christina looked at him searchingly. He was smiling, but not with his eyes, they were sombre, censuring almost. Surely he wasn't objecting to her talking to Mrs Klaussen and her grandson?

"They are squatters, aren't they?"

"I believe so." She spoke clearly and steadily, in spite of the nervous fluttering at the base of her throat. "Mrs Klaussen's daughter and son-in-law owned a station out west at the time she came to Australia. I suppose they still have it."

"Bet your life they do. They look pretty prosperous to me."

Christina bit back the retort that sprang to her lips, telling herself that Danny was Danny and that she knew very well how he carried on about the squatters. "Mrs Klaussen is a very nice lady who was very kind to me coming out on the ship." She smiled directly into his face. "I don't believe I should stop regarding her as a good friend just because her family happen to be squatters."

Carl, lounging against the tree trunk, gave a quick laugh. "Good for you, Christina. A friend's a friend, whatever. Don't let Danny try to tell you otherwise. Besides, even though he's so against the squatters, he'd have been one himself, given half the chance."

"And so would you, mate," Danny retorted.

"But of course. I would never be so foolish as to deny that. If I had come out to Australia a bit earlier and with a few quid in my pocket, I'd have done just as those blokes did, got myself some sheep and lit out for the great interior. And, believe me, if the land was there for the taking, I'd have taken it."

"Come off it, Carl. You know damned well that such golden opportunities were for the gentry, the English for the most part, not for free passage immigrants."

Carl grinned lazily. "Well, even if the vast rolling acres weren't for us, there's no getting away from the fact that the free passage has really been something. It might be on a smaller scale, but we've still been given the opportunity to make good."

"Of course we have," Arthur Weaver's voice came quietly and surprisingly into the discussion. "And you are not altogether right about the squatters, you know, Danny? It might appear that they were fortune's favoured, but they still had plenty of hard work to do and no end of hardships to endure. Don't forget that they quite often went out into areas that hadn't yet been explored, let alone surveyed, into the unknown, so to speak. Furthermore, they didn't all become rich. What with drought and attacks by the blacks, many of them finished up losing their land, and owing a stack of money to the banks into the bargain."

"Which was probably their own fault. They were just too bloody greedy, grabbing up more land than they needed or could manage. And look at the trouble the Government has had getting them to part with some of it; they've thought up at least a dozen ways in which to evade the requirements of the Selection Acts – dummying, peacocking, pre-leasing, taking out mining leases, to name but a few."

A faint smile touched Arthur's mouth. "But things have changed in recent years. You've only got to look at this area to see that. In the fifties and sixties, one man, W.D.White, held all the land from the Logan to the ocean and from Brisbane to the Tweed – your farm, ours, and how many others?"

"Well, doesn't that make you sick to the guts to think that such a thing could have happened in the first place?"

"Not at all," Arthur told him calmly. "It was something that belonged with that period of development. The land was lying there idle, why shouldn't pastoralists move their animals on to it?"

"I think Danny's met his match," Sarah whispered to Christina. "About time too."

Christina, who had been listening in amazement, nodded. What an unusual man Arthur Weaver was, letting his mother boss him around, then standing up to Danny in such a way. Catching his eye across the sandwiches, scones and cakes, she gave him an encouraging smile, but Sarah was not about to let this particular discussion continue. She clapped her hands sharply together. "Come on, everyone. It's time to eat, and, while we are doing so, we will have more placid conversation, if you don't mind."

"That's my girl," Joseph said, giving her a resounding kiss on the cheek. "Not only the best cook in the whole of the Mudgeeraba district, but real smart as well."

Everyone laughed, and Christina was surprised to see that Danny was no exception. Well, for heaven's sake, she mused to herself, perhaps, after all, his bark is worse than his bite.

The Pacific Hotel was a sprawling but impressive building, which offered its guests not only a breathtaking view of the Broadwater and the islands beyond, but comfortable bedrooms, a well-catered dining room, and three fine sitting rooms. All of which, Eleanor remarked as she led Christina through to the verandah, was something of a surprise, considering the newness of the town. "But Southport is really going to grow, Christina; in leaps and bounds, I should think, now that it has been discovered, as it were." She settled herself in a cane armchair, gesturing to Christina to do likewise with the one next to it. "David and I arrived last Sunday on a steamboat called the Arakoon... late, since it had taken us more than nine hours to come from Brisbane. Even so, it all looked quite lovely with the moonlight shimmering on the water. But, when I woke the next morning and looked out of my bedroom window, I thought that I had surely died and gone to heaven."

Christina smiled. "It is a very attractive place, there's no doubt about that."

"The sort of place where one could live forever without ever wearying of it. But tell me, where are you living? Somewhere close by?"

"We have a dairy farm at Mudgeeraba. That's not real close. We had to go over to Nerang and then take a boat down the Nerang River to get here. This is my first visit to Southport, as a matter of fact."

"Is that so? Then I take it that you haven't been living at Mudgeeraba for all of these past eight years?"

"No, only since last September. We were at the Logan before that."

"Ah, so you did go there. I recall your father talking about doing that when we were on the Friedeburg."

Christina nodded. "Father took up a selection right after we arrived."

Eleanor was quick to see the shadow that had come to the eyes of the beautiful young girl sitting beside her. So, she thought, life in Australia hasn't been too easy for my little Christina and her parents. "But things didn't work out?" she prompted gently.

"Not on the farm they didn't. Every time we made a little progress some setback would come along. It was the big drought in 1877 that finally decided Father to move though; that and a large bushfire in the valley."

"It didn't burn your house?" Mrs Klaussen enquired quickly and anxiously.

Christina gave her a small wry smile. "No, but I don't know how it didn't. It came so very close and burnt practically everything else."

"How terrible that must have been. And I certainly know what the drought was like." She shuddered. "Twenty thousand dead sheep, more than a thousand dead cattle."

"I'd almost forgotten that it was everywhere in Queensland."

"It certainly was, and the wonder of it all is that the land has been able to recover after such a disaster." She was looking out over the water and Christina stole a searching glance sideways. Yes, there were lines in the fine skin and shadows beneath the lovely eyes, just as she had thought this morning when the brim of her hat had made it difficult to be sure. "Have you liked living in Queensland?" she asked gently, not at all sure that she should be asking the question.

When there was no replay for a moment or two, she was sure that she had indeed erred, but then Eleanor Klaussen said quietly, "I have liked being with my family, Christina, that has brought me great joy. But I think that I was too old when I came, too old to become a true Australian, that is. I've come to realise that I am never going to get used to the isolation of this country or its vast emptiness." She lifted her thin shoulders in a faint shrug. "I have given it a great deal of thought, mind, and tried very hard not to be defeatist, but I've come to the conclusion that it's all a question of balance, of one's years, as it were. If too many of them have been spent in one lifestyle, it becomes incredibly difficult to spend those that remain in another, especially when those lifestyles are poles apart in every respect."

"I suppose so," Christina murmured, then waited for her companion to continue. After a short pause, she did so. "I think I might have told you about waltzing in Vienna with Strauss conducting his own wonderful music. Well, that was on my sixteenth birthday, a very special treat my parents had arranged. Do you know what I did on my sixtieth birthday, Christina?"

Christina shook her head, smiling gently.

"I danced the waltz in a woolshed while an old station hand played the Blue Danube on an accordion." She chuckled softly, amused recollection bringing a merry twinkle to her eyes. "And there was my granddaughter, just turned seventeen, waltzing … none too smoothly, I'm afraid… with a handsome young shearer, and with such a rapt expression on her face; as though she was doing the most romantic thing in the world in the most romantic setting in the world. It was that, I think, that finally made me see where my problem lay. This country is not for the old and memory-ridden from other lands, Christina, it's for the young and courageous, whether they be from far shores or born here. And I think this might apply especially to big remote stations like Taldoon.

"Is that the name of your station, Taldoon?"

"Taldoon Downs, actually. My son-in-law named it after a family estate in England."

"Is it very large?"

"Oh yes, thousands and thousands of acres, very few of them ever a true green." She laughed softly. "It's no wonder I'm so overwhelmed by all this colour, Christina."

"Kathleen has told me that the station where she was born and lived as a small child was like that, very brown-looking most of the time. It's a wonder the sheep can live in such places."

"They like the drier regions, of course, though I've often wondered myself how they manage to survive when the ground seems bare almost. On what station was you friend born, do you know?"

"Yes, it was at Jimbour Downs."

"Jimbour? For goodness sake! That's in the same general area as Taldoon, but about sixty miles off. I have been there though. It's an amazing property and the new home the Bell family have built is absolutely magnificent. Two stories high and with twenty-four rooms. That doesn't include kitchen or staff facilities which have been retained in the old homestead. It's all unbelievably lavish, of course, especially when you consider that it has been constructed in the Australian outback."

"It must be very beautiful, but I just can't imagine what you would do with twenty-four rooms."

Eleanor smiled at her. "The Bell family live quite grandly, Christina, and they do a good deal of entertaining, often of very important people. On the other hand, a person doesn't have to be important to be received hospitably at Jimbour; they even have special quarters for travellers and swagmen, with free rations readily available."

Christina nodded. "Yes, Kathleen told me. That used to happen even when they were living there."

"How long ago was that?"

"They left in 1872." Another question had found its way to the tip of Christina's tongue, an important question that refused to wait. "Have you been back to Europe, Mrs Klaussen?"

"No, Christina, I haven't. For one thing, I couldn't bring myself to face up to that long sea voyage again. For another, I've always been afraid that, if I did go back for a visit, I would end up staying there, and that would never do, it would cause too much heartache." She smiled as her eyes took in the gentle compassion on Christina's face. "It's not such a tragedy as all that, dear. After all, I am with the people I love most in all the world, what more could an old woman be wanting?"

Christina opened her mouth to reply, but her mind couldn't come up with the right words, and she closed it again.

Eleanor chuckled. "See, you can't think of a single thing. In any case, we've had more than enough about me and too little about you. Just what have you been doing with your life, apart from growing into a charming and very lovely young lady." Her eyes twinkled. "Which I always knew you would, of course."

Though she blushed, a soft smile of pleasure came to Christina's lips. "Nothing very special, I'm afraid."

"Well, here you are speaking perfect English, and that is certainly something I am pleased to see."

"I still don't write it very well, the spelling always gives me trouble."

"Never mind, that's a minor problem. But tell me about this farm of yours at Mudgeeraba."

"It's very nice, a dairy farm with over thirty cows, and tucked right in against the foothills. Of course it's only been a few months since we arrived, and we've had very favourable weather, but Father thinks we will do well there. He's only sorry that we wasted all that time and effort at the Logan."

"I don't suppose anything we do is ever a complete waste, Christina; it's all experience of a sort. Was there a school for you to go to at the Logan?"

"Yes, in Beenleigh. It had opened not long before we arrived. I didn't attend for very long though, just eighteen months."

"Oh ... why not?"

"Mother was having a baby and I was needed at home." Eleanor opened her mouth, but, before she could say anything, Christina went on with a rush, "The baby died. Then, afterwards, things weren't going very well on the farm, and Doctor Travis offered me a position as nursemaid to his children. So, instead of returning to school, I went to live with them." Seeing the concern on the older woman's face deepen into dismay, Christina gave her a quick, reassuring smile. "I didn't really mind leaving school and it was a very nice job. The doctor and his wife were ever so kind to me and I loved the children. Leaving them and my good friend, Marie Hunter, was the hardest thing about leaving the Logan." A wider smile parted her lips and spread to her eyes. "I'm going back to see them all though, next month, and for a whole week."

"You must be looking forward to that?"

"Yes, I am, ever so much."

Conversation between them continued to flow easily as they recalled and reminisced, questioned and replied, each, in its turn, bringing delight, surprise, amusement, laughter, sadness, sudden tears ...

"What happened to that nice Henry Schneider you were so friendly with on the ship? Did you keep in touch with him? I seem to recall that you planned to write to one another."

Christina bit her lip hard, but the stinging tears filled her eyes, regardless. "We did write to one another," she said huskily. "But Henry is dead now, he died in those big floods at Mackay."

"Oh Christina, I am so sorry."

Christina brushed at the tears that had slipped on to her cheeks. "It happened last March while we were still living at the Logan, but I didn't know until just before Christmas. I had been wondering why I hadn't had a letter from Henry in quite a while, especially since I'd written to tell him that we would be moving. Then Mr. Schneider wrote … he said he hadn't been able to bring himself to do so earlier."

"Poor, unhappy man, I don't wonder. He must have been devastated, his wife also. And how distressing for you too, Christina, you and Henry were such good friends."

Christina nodded, recalling the tears that had dampened her pillow, the ache that had come to her heart. "When I saw the strange writing on the envelope, I had such a strange feeling I couldn't bring myself to open it."

"A premonition," Eleanor sighed. "One of the stranger instincts we human beings seem to have."

"Henry was so interested in the sugarcane," Christina mused sadly. "Every time he wrote he had something to say about what was happening on the plantations in the north, and he had taken it on himself to make a study of the different types of cane."

"I can see him doing something like that, he was a very intelligent young lad."

"And very brave. He went in a small boat to try to save the lives of two Kanakas who had been marooned in a tree, but the boat overturned in the current and they all drowned." She sighed heavily. "If Henry could only have known that was going to happen, perhaps he wouldn't have gone to their aid."

"He would still have gone, dear. It wouldn't have been in that boy to just stand by and watch those men die."

"I suppose not. It's just that when I think of him losing his life in such a way I can't helping feeling that it should never have happened."

"I know, I know." It was a gentle murmur and very carefully the conversation was steered in other directions. By the time a waitress wheeled out a tray with afternoon tea, Christina was smiling again as she told Mrs Klaussen about Joey and his affection for her mother.

"He apparently means to spend his life on your farm."

"It seems so. We'd always expected that, when he'd grown up a bit, he would take off into the bush and rejoin his own kind, but it hasn't happened. Father says it still may, if he sees a lady roo that he finds attractive." She chuckled softly. "But Mother says that Joey's too comfortable in his present situation and that he'd more than likely invite any lady friend he acquired to move in with him."

Eleanor laughed too. "That could present a few problems. They seem to have large families, these kangaroos."

The time slipped by, easily, comfortably, until Christina noticed the Maid of Sker making her way back to the wharf. She glanced a little anxiously up and down the still-crowded foreshore but there was no sign of Kathleen. "I think it's time for us to be leaving. I hope Kathleen hasn't forgotten we have a boat to catch."

A small frown came quickly to Eleanor's brow and her eyes too scanned the foreshore. "David is a very reliable person, so I expect they will be back presently. It appears that one of your party has come for you though."

Christina had also seen Carl come up over the incline and she at once got to her feet, moving to the rail to wave to him. Seeing her, he waved back and quickened his footsteps. "We have to leave, Christina," he called as he came closer to the verandah.

"I know, but Kathleen hasn't come back yet."

"She's on one of the yachts and it's coming in now, we'll meet her on the wharf."

"And who might that handsome young man be?" Eleanor Klaussen wanted to know as they made their way back through one of the sitting rooms to the front entrance.

"His name is Carl Eichstead, and he's a good friend of the O'Rourke family."

"And of yours also, I'm thinking." A merry twinkle had come to her eyes. "Is there something important you have neglected to tell me, Christina?"

"I've only known him for a short time."

The evasive reply didn't fool Eleanor, not when she had seen the warm colour rush to Christina's cheeks. "Well, when you've known him for a little longer, you can tell me more about him, in the letters you are going to be writing to me." She gave Christina's fingers a gentle squeeze. "This time, my dear, we are not going to lose one another."

Christina gave her a rueful smile "You won't be very pleased with my spelling."

"You've learnt to speak English very well and that's the important thing. I certainly won't be worrying about how you spell your words." She laughed softly. "And I promise not to include spelling lists when I write to you.".

"She seems a very charming lady," Carl remarked as he and Christina hurried away from the hotel. "I wish I'd had time to say more than just hello and goodbye to her." Christina had introduced them on the front porch and been more than a little surprised at the instant liking she'd sensed between the two of them. "Yes," she said now, "you would have enjoyed talking to her."

"It's nice that you had an opportunity to renew your acquaintance with the lady."

"Oh yes, it was all quite wonderful, and so unexpected. I'm sorry that you were obliged to come and fetch me though."

Carl grinned down at her. "That appears to be a very elegant hotel, Christina, but I don't think your parents would have been too pleased had we gone off and left you there." He reached for her hand. "And if we don't do a little sprint we could both be left behind."

Kathleen was already on board the paddle-wheeler, but David Charlton still lingered on the wharf. He smiled at Christina and shook her hand. "I hope we see you again before too long, Christina."

Although she didn't see how that was going to be possible, Christina returned his smile and said, "I hope so too. I've had such a nice afternoon with your grandmother."

Kathleen had managed to save Christina a seat but Carl was obliged to stand and he went to join the other men of their party. "Oh Christina, I've had the most exciting time I've ever had in my entire life, or ever dreamed of having, for that matter. We've been out on the Broadwater in a most splendid yacht." She grinned happily. "That's what David said it was, a yacht, not a boat. Well, anyhow, it belongs to friends of his and they were all ever so nice to me. Can you believe it? Me, out on a yacht with all those ever-so-rich people?" The words tumbled from her smiling lips, her eyes sparkling like emeralds, and Christina smiled at her excitement. "I'm glad you had such a nice time, Kathleen."

"I had a wonderful, wonderful time, not just a nice time." The boat was slipping away from the pier and she turned to wave to the tall figure almost lost in the crowd gathering to board another boat. "Isn't he just the most handsome man you have ever seen?"

"He is very good-looking."

Kathleen's brilliant eyes danced knowingly. "But you don't think he's the most handsome man in the whole world?" She laughed teasingly. "No, of course you don't. What a silly thing for me to be asking you."

"I did say that he was very good-looking and he seems to be very charming into the bargain."

"He's that alright. In fact, he has such perfect manners I was in quite a tizzy lest I say or do the wrong thing." Her smile faded and she heaved a resigned sigh. "Which I probably did without even knowing it."

"If you did, I'm sure he wouldn't have minded."

They arrived back at the O'Rourke farm as the moon, full and golden, began its climb into the star-studded sky. Again, it was Carl who lifted Christina from the wagon, but this time he set her firmly on her feet and there was no need for him to put his arms protectively around her. Telling herself that she was relieved about that, Christina watched him swing Kathleen to the ground and then take hold of a hamper Patrick handed down to him. He set it on the ground close to where she was standing. "The end of a perfect day, eh Christina?"

Christina nodded. "Yes, it has been a most perfect day."

He was about to move back to the wagon, but a horse whinnied close by and he turned back to her, taking hold of her elbow. "Midnight has waited up for us. Come and say goodnight to him."

"Shouldn't we be helping to unload the wagon?"

"There's little enough to do and so many falling over one another trying to do it we'd be better out of the way." He was already leading her away from the wagon. "In any case we'll only be gone for a few minutes."

The horse whinnied again and pranced about excitedly as they approached. "Hey there, old fellow, settle down now," Carl called softly. "Here's Christina come to bid you goodnight."

Christina held her hand out coaxingly as she moved to the fence. "Here Midnight, here boy." At once the horse trotted over, thrusting his head over the top rail so that she could run her hand along his satiny neck.

"So," Carl mused, laughing softly, "he really is a very smart horse."

"It's hard to believe that he was once so violent."

"Ssssh ... he doesn't like to be reminded of his bad old days."

Christina giggled. "Oh, excuse me." And then, in a whisper, "Is it alright to ask when he's going to have his next race?"

"Yes, perfectly alright. He likes to hear people talking about his races and how fast he is. Don't you, Midnight?"

Christina gasped as the horse moved his head up and down, then burst out laughing. "You made him do that."

"How can you say that when all I did was tickle him?"

"I thought as much, but you still haven't told me, when is he to have his next race?"

"Not until June, we decided to let him have a bit of a break."

"He has certainly earned himself a holiday." She glanced back in the direction of the barn and the house beyond. "We should be going back, Danny's already putting the wagon away."

"Then there's no need to rush. Besides, Midnight will be offended if we don't spend a little more time with him, won't you, boy?"

Again the horse nodded and again Christina laughed, but this time quietly. What would they all be thinking, for heaven's sake? For her and Carl to be out here on their own when everyone else was back at the house? It was something that was bound to bring a raising of eyebrows, at the very least. "The Weavers and Joseph and Sarah will be leaving, and I haven't had a chance to say goodnight to them."

"They'll be having a cup of tea first, but if you really want to go ... "

"It's not that ... it's just that I think we should." She gave the horse's neck a final pat and turned from the rail. Carl at once joined her and they walked slowly back towards the house.

"It's such a beautiful night," Christina murmured, then wondered whether he had heard the tremor in her voice. Why was she being so nervous, for heaven's sake?

"It's that alright, Christina, beautiful and mysterious, romantic too." He laughed softly. "I've always thought of moonlight as being something of a magic wand able to transform almost anything. Just look at that old pigsty now. It looks quite … ah, quite … "

Christina giggled and finished for him, "Quite a deal better than it does in the broad light of day."

"Exactly."

"That wasn't a very good example, but I do know what you mean."

"What would you have chosen as an example, Christina?"

"Let me see now. I can't say the trees or anything like that because they are always beautiful and don't need to be transformed. The windmill? No, it looks nice enough in the daytime." She glanced about her, considering. "I can't say the barn, that wouldn't be any better than your pigsty. What about that field over there?"

"The one they've just ploughed?"

"Yes, the one they've just ploughed." She was chuckling softly, amused at his reaction.

"Perhaps you could enlighten me as to just what transformation I'm supposed to be seeing?"

"A huge striped blanket. See, light on the ridges, shadows in the furrows."

"And that's supposed to be a good example?" Carl laughed.

"It's the best I could find, unless you'd rather have old Clover?"

Carl glanced to where the old Clydesdale was dozing in the middle of a group of cows. "Very well, but I'm afraid you'll have to tell me what he's being transformed into."

"A fine charger, of course. You have to help the moonlight with a bit of imagination."

"Ah yes, I can see it now, a fine charger with a knight in shining armour about to climb on to his back. I wonder where he's off to."

"He's going to rescue a beautiful princess. She's being held in a tower miles and miles away, but the distance won't worry Clover in the least, you can see how strong and virile he is."

As though on cue, the old horse lifted his head, snorting loudly, and they both burst out laughing. As they did, Carl's arm brushed Christina's and she realised with a start that their slow walk had become even slower and that the rectangle of light spilling from the O'Rourke's kitchen door was still some little distance away. At once she quickened her footsteps, asking, "Will you be staying for a cup of tea?"

"I'm staying for the night, but I think I'll give the cup of tea a miss. Ma's probably got sandwiches and scones to go with it, and I've already eaten enough for one day. In fact, I think I'll stay out of that kitchen and go straight to bed."

"Gosh, I've eaten enough too. I do hope she's not too persistent."

"Be thankful for sandwiches, it could have been a pile of praties."

They laughed quietly together, then Christina asked, "Where will you sleep?"

"I've got a bunk of sorts in the barn. I've slept there on more than one occasion."

"I'll say goodnight then. There's really no need for you to walk me right up to the house." She took two or three steps away from his side, but had she taken the next one, she would have walked right into him, for he'd moved quickly around to block her path. "Do you have to be in such a rush to leave me, Christina?"

"I wasn't."

"It certainly seemed that way, you were practically running."

"I was nowhere near running, for heaven's sake."

Carl laughed softly as she stared up at him in helpless exasperation. Then, giving her no time in which to protest, he caught her by the shoulders and kissed her soundly on the lips. "Goodnight, sweet Christina." In the next instant he had released her and was striding off in the direction of the barn, whistling softly.

Wide-eyed and breathless, Christina watched him go. Then she turned and walked, no longer quickly, across the moon-silvered grass, expecting at any moment to have her trembling knees fold beneath her. The night was alive with its own special sounds: the shrill chirping of crickets, the mournful call of a mopoke, the howling of dingoes, the drowsy hoot of an owl, but these she no longer heard … they had been banished by the wild thumping of her heart and the singing in her ears.

22

At the time Carl Eichstead's application for a selection on Little Nerang Creek was formally approved in July 1879, Queensland was in its twentieth year as a separate colony. Its population had increased to two hundred thousand, its sheep numbers to seven million and its cattle numbers to three million. In spite of the widespread drought two years previously, a period of overall progress and prosperity was being enjoyed.

Brisbane, after disastrous fires which had wiped out much of Queen Street in 1863 and 1864 and a period of financial doldrums between 1866 and 1870, was now a fast-developing city able to supply most of the needs of an expansionist frontier. Throughout the 1870s, stimulated by the entry of new capital and a growing workforce, new industries had been established, and those already set up expanded. And the general economic growth of the capital had been accompanied by the growth of cultural amenities, recreation facilities and important community services such as the press.

Away from the city and its environs, settlement was being consolidated and extended in every direction. On a broad front, sheep-men were thrusting forward into new and drier regions of the interior, while those already established on vast, sprawling acres increased the size of their flocks at every opportunity and built substantial homes to replace the huts or log cabins they had begun with. Hard times they had certainly endured. Floods and bushfires had punctuated the seasons and long dry spells had been all too frequent. They had, furthermore, found it difficult to achieve a happy balance with the natural environment. They had succeeded in driving the Aborigines from their stations and controlling the dingoes, only to find that, in doing so, they had left themselves open to a new challenge – with their natural predators gone, the kangaroos flourished, over-running their properties in plague proportions. Anxious to extend their grazing lands, they had cleared away bush and scrub in a ruthless fashion, then watched in despair as the swirling winds of the dry seasons lifted the surface of their chosen acres and whipped it into dust storms that blotted out the sun. In many cases, such recurring difficulties had resulted in failure and the forfeiture of the land so eagerly claimed. But where the squatter had managed to hold on, determined and enduring, the rewards had come. Ever since the mid-1860s Britain's textile mills had been winning wider markets and the demand for Australian and New Zealand wool had been surging upwards.

Capable and fortunate sheep-men had, as a result, amassed considerable wealth, and their grip on both the land and the Colony's economic and political affairs had grown steadily. As the seventies drew to a close, the squatters on the cattle lands were also enjoying more prosperous times. Although the central and northern regions of the Colony had been thrown open for settlement at a time when there was still a bias in favour of sheep, many pastoralists, finding the conditions unsuitable for the production of wool, had switched to cattle. Others had stocked with cattle from the very outset Setbacks there had certainly been, but there were now a number of men in Queensland who could quite rightly be called cattle kings.

Along the coastal strip, plantation-type agriculture had become firmly established, with sugarcane and banana-growing areas being extended rapidly; still, however, resembling the plantations of other tropical lands with their white overseers and massed native labour. In 1874, the Government, following the lead of plantation owners who had brought in a trial shipment of Indian Coolies, had attempted to obtain indentured Chinese Coolies, but, for various reasons, neither scheme had been as successful as had been hoped, the result being that, in spite of widespread disapproval, the Kanaka trade still flourished.

For the selector on his small farm, however, progress and prosperity at the end of the seventies were still, for the most part, little more than a dream. If he was managing to eke out a living for himself and his family he had cause to be thankful, since this was something many of his kind had failed to do.

Carl Eichstead knew all about such dreams, he had some of his own. But, unlike many of the early selectors, he had very few illusions. His selection, since he had little capital and no chance of borrowing any, was second-class pastoral land: not a selected block reclaimed from a big sheep run which might have allowed him to become a successful wheat farmer; not a rich cattle-grazing area from the Beau Desert, Mundoolin or Nindooinbah stations which would have brought such joy to his heart,; not even a piece of the marshy flatlands termed first-class pastoral, where he could have begun a fine dairy farm. His selection was one hundred and ninety-five acres tucked away between mountain folds, beautiful, with the deep, swiftly-flowing Little Nerang Creek winding its way along part of its eastern and its entire northern boundary, its fern-filled gullies, and tree-framed glimpses of the ocean from its highest ridges. But a hard master with its dense forests where ironbark trees predominated, with its steep embankments and its patches of level or gently sloping land scattered and of no great size. It wasn't, Carl well knew, going to make him rich; for a time, it wasn't even going to provide him with a living. But it was a beginning, a place to get a foothold.

He said as much to Simon Skov when he called to tell the family that his application had been approved, laughing at his choice of words. "Get a foothold? Believe me, that's pretty much what I've had to do, especially when I was clearing a section of the creek bank so that I could bring up water. I was expecting any minute to go tumbling in."

"It's that steep then?" Simon queried, his eyebrows raised.

"Yes, the bank is steep alright, but I suppose it's just as well if flood waters come down the creek the way I've been told they do."

"You'd still need to build well away from the bank?"

"Yes, I've picked out a spot which should be ideal … on a rise, and, fortunately, in an area of fairly open forest, which means I should be able to get started without first having to do a lot of clearing."

"What sort of a house did you have in mind?"

"I don't want to be spending a whole lot of time on it, there's too much else needing to be done. But I still think it would be folly just to throw something up, so to speak. A solid structure will be a double bonus; it won't be needing continual repairs, and it will help with the improvement requirements I have to meet. I've been thinking about something around twenty-four feet by twelve feet with two rooms."

"You'd go with iron-bark for the walls?"

"I'm thinking about slabs of the yellow stringy-bark. I've seen that done in a couple of places and it not only looks quite good, it's apparently very effective. The roof will be bark from the good old box tree."

Simon grinned. "That's quite a job, getting the bark off the tree in decent-sized pieces?"

Carl returned his grin. "Fortunately, I've had a bit of experience at that. My main concern is with the timber for the framework of the house and the pine boards for the floor. It will all have to be pit-sawn on the place since there's no way I can get milled timber up there."

Carl had arrived just as the Skovs were about to begin the afternoon milking. Taking up a bucket, he had insisted on taking Elsie's place, leaving her to see to other chores. Now, with everything done almost an hour earlier than was normally the case, they were gathered in the dairy, out of the bitterly cold westerly whistling through the bails, and with Christina miserably conscious of her muddied boots, faded woollen skirt and well-worm cardigan. Why did he have to turn up just out of the blue like that, she moaned to herself, especially when she'd seen him only twice since the regatta? Twice, in all that time, and neither occasion had been the least bit satisfactory. The first had been over at Nerang when she'd been with her mother and he with Danny; the second at the O'Rourke's, when they'd been literally surrounded the whole time and he had ridden off early, heading for Johann Meyer's plantation where he'd been promised two weeks' work splitting fence posts. Why, it was almost as though she had dreamed what had happened after the regatta.

"Isn't that so, Christina?"

Christina started, her eyes, at once dismayed, flying to her father's face. "I'm sorry, Father, I wasn't paying attention."

Simon chuckled. "Not paying attention to our discussion on house-building after all the assistance you gave me with the doors and windows on the house at the Logan?"

"I was thinking about something else."

"Well, I was telling Carl about Mr Hunter taking you out to see our old place when you had your little holiday in Beenleigh and how a detached kitchen has been added to our house."

Christina nodded, her cheeks becoming warm as she met Carl's gently amused eyes. "Yes, the new people have done that."

There had been other changes too, Christina recalled, even though less than a year had gone by; many more acres cleared and young cane thriving in field after field. "Good seasons," Mr Hunter had said, seeing her amazement, "and the man has three grown sons to help him."

You'll be wanting sons too, Carl Eichstead, to help on that selection of yours and carry on with what you begin ... the thought came unbidden and Christina pushed it quickly from her mind. It wasn't, after all, any concern of hers. With a small inwards sigh of relief, she saw that he had returned his attention to her father. She didn't want him looking at her the way he sometimes did, as though any notions she might be having were being reflected all too clearly on her face.

"Of course, I wish now that I'd done more clearing than I have done," he was telling Simon, "but, as you know, my original application had to be amended and that was something of a blow. I haven't been eager to do a great deal when there was a chance the whole thing might fall through."

"I don't blame you. In the same situation I don't think I would have been doing anything at all to improve the place. What about the road? Have you had any advice about that?"

"Only that a road has been surveyed, nothing about when it will be built."

"So you still don't know when you'll be able to get a cart or wagon up there?"

"No, I'll have to go on relying on Samson's back to get me and my provisions ... and hopefully produce ... up and down those hills. It's just as well that I have only myself to consider ... "

It was near to midnight, Christina was quite sure, and still sleep eluded her. With a small, exasperated sigh, she snuggled deeper into her warm bed, yawning widely and squeezing her eyes tightly shut. But her mind was not about to be fooled by such actions, it went right on imprinting pictures on the backs of her eyelids and obliging her to listen to what it had to say ...

It was clear enough then, it told her, having once again reviewed pieces of conversation from the afternoon – the fact that Carl had kissed her didn't mean a thing. It hadn't, in fact, been anything more than a friendly goodnight kiss. Hadn't he made it clear that there was no place for a woman in his plans, not for years and years, at any rate. Before finally riding off, he'd talked about clearing and fencing, the timber he should be able to sell, the corn and potatoes he would plant, the acres he would only partially clear and leave for the grazing of beef cattle, the time he would still need to spend away cutting cane or doing other jobs, the adjoining land he hoped one day to acquire under the Homestead Act; even about how, in time, he would sell it all and buy a place down on the flatlands. But never a single word about having someone to share it all with.

Didn't he realise that a woman who truly loved him wouldn't care about her home being pretty much in the wilderness, or that there was no real road up to his selection. She'd be able to ride, wouldn't she? As for feeling lonely when he was away ... well, of course she would miss him, but there would be so much to do the time until he was home again would fly by. They would be able to have at least a couple of milking cows, fowls, a vegetable garden, perhaps even a small flower garden. Sighing, Christina opened her eyes again and stared into the darkness. It really was quite amazing that a man who could plan as Carl Eichstead did couldn't see such things. Besides, there was the question of children, of his sons. He'd be wanting those and how was he to come by them without a wife? Giving her pillow a vicious thump, she turned it for the fourth time. It was simply none of her business whether he wanted to be married or not and for it to be keeping her awake was simply too ridiculous. Besides, wasn't it a fact that marriage didn't come into her plans either? Of course it was ...

Christina lowered her gaze from her mother's disapproving frown to the letter in her hand, a letter addressed to her in a bold, sloping handwriting that was no longer unfamiliar. She knew very well what she would find when she opened the elegant-looking envelope – another envelope addressed in the same handwriting, but not to her. Her mother knew too, since this was the fifth such letter they had collected from the post office at Nerang.

"It's deceit she's practising, Christina, and no good will come of it. As I've told you before, it displeases me to see you involved."

"I know, Mother, but what can I do?"

"You could tell Kathleen that you do not wish to be receiving these letters."

"She's my very dear friend, and it seems little enough to be doing."

"It might very well seem little enough, but there's something unpleasant about such secrecy. He should he writing to her at her own home, that's what any gentleman with honourable intentions would be doing."

"He would do that, but Kathleen won't let him. She says there would be a terrible to-do and that her mother might even tell the priest."

"How ridiculous! They are only writing to each other, after all. Surely there is no sin in that?"

"That's what I said, but Kathleen said her parents would think there was something more to it. It seems they really are determined that all of their children will marry Catholics."

Elsie gave her shoulders a small shrug. "Well, that's their business, I suppose, but I cannot, for the life of me, see anything wrong with Christian marrying Christian." She eyed Christina shrewdly. "Is there something more to this than just friendship?"

"How could there be? They've only ever spent a couple of hours together." Christina shifted her weight uneasily from one foot to the other, knowing only too well how evasive her words had sounded.

"And what, half a dozen letters since?"

"This is the fifth."

"Five then, since Easter. That does seem a lot for just a casual friendship. Has Kathleen ever offered to let you read any of these letters?"

"Heavens, I wouldn't want to do that."

Elsie raised her eyebrows. "If they are just friendly letters and considering you know his grandmother, that wouldn't be so unseemly, and he probably has things to say that would be of interest to you."

"Kathleen has told me any number of things that David has written." She gave her mother a small smile, "In any case, as you know, I've had two letters from Mrs Klaussen, and I think they've told me everything that is happening on their property."

"But never a word about her grandson writing to Kathleen. Don't you think that strange?"

"It's alright, Mother, truly it is. No harm can come from letters, and, if it's going to upset Mr and Mrs O'Rourke to know that their daughter is corresponding with a Protestant, then surely it's better for them not to know. After all, with David living miles and miles away, he and Kathleen may never see each other again."

"Love has been known to laugh at distances, Christina, but I suppose you could be right, it would serve no purpose to cause Kathleen's parents needless concern." She smiled wryly. "Let us just hope that it would be needless."

Christina nodded, swallowing against a surge of guilt. Needless? Her mother would never believe that were she to see Kathleen's face when she handed over David's letters. Or if she'd seen the way they had looked at each other that day at the regatta, in the very instant of meeting, no less. How strange it was that that had come back to her, almost as though her mind had taken a picture and stored it away for future reference; then brought it out three weeks later when the first letter arrived, so clearly it had made her breath catch in her throat.

"You don't seem too sure."

The words were more statement than question and Elsie's eyes were watchful on her daughter's face. Again Christina moved uneasily, her mind groping for words of reassurance that wouldn't really be a lie. "I know they shouldn't be worrying, not about the letters, and Kathleen has never said anything about when she might see David again. I'm sure she's well aware just how impossible, how difficult that would be."

Elsie sighed quietly as she returned her attention to her own mail. "Well, you just make sure that you don't get yourself involved in anything more serious than letters. Kathleen is a very nice girl, but she is much too impulsive."

Another wonderful, wonderful spring, Christina mused, her whole face smiling. And, just as other Australian springs she had known had done, it had arrived with no great flourish: no trumpets or sudden bursting forth to proclaim its presence boastfully to the world; just the balmy late-winter days sliding gently into balmy early-spring days and all the countryside quietly changing. New green grass pushing up through that left yellowed by the heavy frosts of July and early August, wild flowers scattered through it; the tree ferns and bracken unfolding new fronds ever so gracefully; the new leaves of the young gum trees pink and fragile, and on those grown tall clusters of red, yellow, or creamy blossoms, their high presence made known by the gum nuts which had covered the buds and now lay discarded on the ground. On the breeze blowing gently from the south-east the salty breath of the ocean mingled with the strong scent of the bush, the rich fragrance of the wattles gone now, having given way to the elusive merging of eucalyptus, new vegetation and honey. And the busy humming of insects and a chorus of bird songs filled the air. Christina held her breath and listened intently. There it was again. Yes, bell birds! Oh, how could such a tiny sound be so entrancing?

Kathleen had heard them too. She was a little ahead of Christina as they guided their horses in and out of the trees along the creek bank, and she glanced back over her shoulder. "Can you hear the bellbirds, Christina?"

"Yes, I can."

"I told you that you'd hear them along Little Nerang Creek." She eased her horse to a halt, glancing about her. "I think this might be a good place to leave the horses. We'll leave our picnic too, and come back to eat it after we've walked for a way along the creek bank."

Christina, too, looked about her, but a little anxiously. "We've come a fair way. Do you think it's all right to go still further?"

"Yes, of course it is. You haven't seen the loveliest part of the creek yet, where the waterfall is. Besides, it's not all that far." She swung from the horse's back, her feet hitting the ground with a small thud.

Christina dismounted too and led her horse closer to the other girl's. "Carl told Father that there are still quite a number of Aborigines in these areas."

"There are blacks everywhere in Mudgeeraba, you know that. But they're not the least bit hostile, not now."

"But what about those who stay in the bush and keep well away from white settlements?"

Kathleen shrugged as she secured her horse on a loose rein. "If there are any hereabouts, they'll disappear into the thicker bush the minute they set eyes on us." She grinned. "And we won't even know they've seen us."

"I suppose that's true enough, but only if they don't want us to see them."

"I'll bet you a half-penny that, right now, there's not a single black within miles of this part of the creek."

In spite of her uncertainty, Christina laughed softly. "You and your half-penny wagers. One of these days you're going to find that you've got quite a reckoning to make."

"Well, I do have a few saved, just for that very purpose."

Side by side, they made their way along the creek bank, setting to flight a flock of parrots which had been feasting on the gum blossoms high above their heads, ducking as the rushing, screeching cloud of brilliant colour swooped low, laughing self-consciously as they watched it rise in a swinging arc to the branches of another tree where it shattered into vibrant fragments as the birds squabbled over positions. "Those parrots are just plain crazy," Kathleen muttered. "One of these days they are going to take someone's head off for sure."

"Well, it's not going to be mine," Christina told her. "I always duck quickly when I see them coming, not that I always mean to, it just seems to happen."

"I know. I do that too, and, sometimes, after they've passed, I take a quick look around to make sure no one's seen how ridiculous I was." Kathleen heaved an exasperated, but smiling, sigh. "Why, for the love of Mike, do they have to make such a racket? Just listen to them now, screeching and bickering away, it's a wonder they ever get round to doing any actual eating."

"They certainly make a noise and, unfortunately, there's nothing musical about it. I remember that was something Mother and I talked about when we first arrived, how the parrots were all so colourful, yet made such awful, raucous sounds, while the plainer birds like the butcher bird and the magpie had such heavenly calls."

"What about the bellbirds?"

"Well, that's such a small sound, and yet it's so poignantly lovely it almost makes me want to weep." She stole a quick glance at Kathleen's face out of the corner of her eye, but there was no bright amusement there. Instead, she looked thoughtful and nodded her head slowly. "I think I know what you mean." Then, smiling again, "You'd be in your element at Carl's place, that's getting into the heart of bellbird country."

"Yes, he told me. He said he'd take me up there one day to hear for myself."

"Ah ha?"

Christina met her shrewd gaze levelly. "There's no call for you to be looking so smug. It was just … well, sort of a friendly invitation. Not even that really, he just said 'one day'."

"Well, he will take up there, I just know it. And I'll bet … " She broke off, grinning. "How many half-pennies do I owe you?"

"I've lost count."

"Well, double or nothing that he asks you up to his place before … ah, before Christmas."

"What does that mean, double or nothing?"

Kathleen considered her with amused exasperation. "You really don't have much of a gambling instinct, do you, Christina?"

Christina grinned. "I know how two-up is played, and I know how they bet on the horses when they race."

"Hmmm, that's something, I suppose. But to get back to this wager I'm proposing. It means that if I win, instead of owing you whatever it is, I owe you nothing. If you win, instead of the amount I now owe, I will owe you double."

"You wouldn't really try to pay me?"

Kathleen laughed. "Pay you what? Come Christmas, I'll owe you nothing, you'll see."

"Even if he does ask me, I may not go."

"Why ever not?"

"Oh, I don't know. I suppose because I wonder whether perhaps – "

Kathleen didn't let her finish. "You wouldn't come to any harm with Carl, you know? He's too much of a gentleman to try to seduce young ladies with respectable reputations." She grinned again, teasingly. "Even if he did kiss you without being given even the slightest bit of encouragement."

Christina sighed. "I should never have told you about that."

"You didn't, actually. I had to extract it from you, remember?"

"Well, I shouldn't have let you do that."

"I would have known in any case. It was written all over your face when you walked into the kitchen. The others would have seen it too, if they hadn't been so busy feeding themselves. In fact, I wouldn't be a bit surprised if Arthur Weaver noticed."

"Oh, for heaven's sake!"

"For heaven's sake nothing. Talking about Arthur reminds me, I've got something really interesting to tell you. He has started calling on Maureen."

Christina's eyes widened in surprise. "Since when?"

"Since about three weeks back after Ma had a word with Father Donavan and Father Donavan had a little talk with Maureen."

"What would they have talked about?"

"What do you think? About Maureen being so stuck on Carl, of course, when there was a fine young Catholic boy available on the very next farm."

"Your mother wouldn't really have told the priest about that?"

"Oh yes, she would ... and yes, she did."

"What about Arthur? Would the priest have talked to him too?"

"I suppose so."

Christina's mind was in a whirl. So perhaps Kathleen was telling the truth when she said that her mother would tell the priest if she knew she was writing to David. She smothered a quick sigh. What was she to do, in that case, about her resolve to try to talk Kathleen into taking her mother into her confidence? This outing would have been a fine opportunity, especially since she now had his latest letter, which had arrived only yesterday, tucked inside her blouse.

"There's no need to be looking so glum about it. Maureen and Arthur are becoming quite attached to one another. And, if you're fretting that you might be getting Carl on the rebound, so to speak, let me assure you that isn't so. He wouldn't have married Maureen even if he had been an eligible Catholic."

"How can you know that?" Christina regretted the question the minute it left her lips, it was such a clear indication of interest.

"Because I know that he's never been in love with her. He likes her well enough, but then everybody likes Maureen, she's that kind of person. But love, that's something quite different."

My opportunity, Christina thought, hardly believing that it had come in such a way. "You know all about love, of course?" She asked the question smilingly but her gaze was glued to the other girl's face.

Just for a moment it seemed that Kathleen had been caught unawares. The grin on her face turned into a soft secretive smile and a dreamy expression came to her eyes. Then she shook her head slowly from side to side, laughing softly, "You are trying to trick me, Christina."

There it was, Christina thought, the thing that bothered her. Kathleen, who was always so open about everything and eager to confide, was quite the opposite when it came to David Charlton. She seemed, in fact, not to want to talk about him. Why? Because she was afraid she would betray feelings her church would frown on? Because she didn't want to admit them, even to herself? "Did you always know that David was a Protestant, Kathleen?" she asked carefully.

"Of course I did. Hey, what is this, an inquisition?"

"I was just wondering why you started writing to him if you knew."

"He asked me to write to him. Besides, we don't have to be concerned about what religion our friends are, you know that. And that's all David is, a very nice friend. We like each other and we like to exchange letters, it's as simple as that."

"Then why don't you tell your mother that?"

"Because she wouldn't understand, that's why. She'd be seeing omens and all sorts of things like that. Then, to ease her mind, she'd have to tell Father Donovan about it, just like she did about Maureen and Carl. I don't want him reminding me about things I haven't forgotten in any case."

"But if you explained to your mother that you and David were just good friends … after all, she would know that you had only seen each other the one time and then only for a couple of hours."

"She still wouldn't understand." Kathleen had looked away, staring off into the distance, but now she brought her gaze back to Christina's face. "Is your mother being difficult about David's letters coming to your place?"

"No, not difficult, but she is a little concerned, on your account mainly." Christina smiled wryly. "I assured her that it was all quite harmless and that, if your parents were going to be worrying needlessly, it was better that they didn't know."

"Exactly. That's just what I think. What did she say to that?"

"She agreed, but – "

Kathleen didn't let her finish. "Well, thank heavens for that," she muttered fervently.

"So long as there really was no need for them to be worrying, of course." Christina went on pointedly.

"Well, how could there be, with me here at Mudgeeraba and David hundreds of miles away?"

Again Christina smiled wryly. "Do you want to know what Mother said when I said that?"

"I'm not sure I do, but tell me anyway."

"She said that love has been known to laugh at distances."

Kathleen laughed softly, her eyes dancing. "Now isn't that a comforting notion?"

Before Christina could reply, she had darted to the very edge of the embankment, exclaiming delightedly, "Look, we could quite easily go down here and walk in the water. As a matter of fact, so long as we're prepared to clamber over a few boulders, I think we might be able to go right along to the falls at the water's edge."

Sighing quietly, Christina joined her. The matter was closed, it seemed, and she had accomplished nothing. "The water does look nice and cool."

"It most certainly does and it's quite shallow near the bank." She sat down on the ground and began pulling off her shoes and stockings. "Instead of carrying them all the way, we'll leave them here and pick them up on the way back."

"Will they be all right, do you think?"

"Of course they will! We can push them into the end of that hollow log if you like." She laughed teasingly. "Just in case a couple of lady roos come along and decide they'd fancy themselves in shoes and stockings."

Christina sat down beside her. "How is it that you seem to be always talking me into removing my shoes and stockings?"

"How is it that you are always so reluctant to do so?"

"Not always, only when I think my bare feet might be sighted by someone."

"Well, there's no one around now, so hurry up, eh?"

Christina did and they were soon scrambling down the bank, giggling happily. "Oooh, it's cold," Christina cried, holding her skirt and petticoat bundled above her knees and dipping her toes into the crystal-clear water.

"That's just because we're so warm. Once we've gotten over the first shock it won't seem cold at all."

They made their way slowly, splashing happily along. Every so often clusters of boulders turned the creek into a series of tumbling cascades and, closer to the bank, loomed out of the water to block their way, making it necessary for them to climb over them. "Phew, that was hot work," Kathleen exclaimed as they jumped down on to a small arc of sand after one such exercise. "I just wish we could … " She spun around to Christina, a wide smile coming to her face. "We could do it, Christina. We could go for a bathe."

Christina stared at her. "You've got to be joking?"

"No, I'm not. Look, the water's not deep just here. The sand has built up against the rocks and you see the bottom for almost a third of the way across. It's like a small pool and it would be perfectly safe."

It would be, Christina thought, even though they couldn't swim, and it would be ever so nice. But she quickly shook her head. "How can we take a bathe when we have nothing to wear?"

"Then that's just what we will wear, nothing."

Her mouth dropping open, Christina stared at the other girl incredulously. What was she suggesting, for heaven's sake? That they should take a bathe in the creek with nothing to cover their nudity? Oh, what a thing to be considering even. It was shameful to display one's naked body. But there was no shame in the way Kathleen was pulling off her clothes. She was doing so with delighted abandon, giggling as she dropped first her skirt and then her blouse on to a large flat boulder close against the bank, taking the time to tuck her still unread letter carefully in between before adding petticoats to the small pile.

"What if someone should happen along?" Christina asked, glancing nervously about her.

"No one will happen along, Christina. Only the birds will see us and perhaps a platypus … oh, and maybe those elegant lady roos who will now be wearing our shoes and stockings." She laughed out loud, but Christina's smile in response was still tentative. "Perhaps we should leave our underclothes on?"

"And how will we get them dry afterwards, for the love of Mike?" Kathleen was already down to her camisole and draws and these she quickly discarded, flinging them carelessly on top of her other clothes. "We'd have to wait around for hours more than likely."

Christina had averted her eyes, embarrassed by her friend's nakedness, but now she couldn't help but see the pale, nymph-like figure dashing into the water, and hot colour rushed to her cheeks.

"It's heavenly, just heavenly." Kathleen was standing waist-deep in water, dashing handfuls over her shoulders and breasts. "A bit cold, but once I'm wet all over, it won't be. Oh, it's so … so invigorating."

Still slowly undoing the buttons on her blouse, Christina took yet another apprehensive look about her.

"Oh, do hurry. You've been ages undoing those buttons."

Christina slipped the blouse off her shoulders, then stepped out of her skirt. The water did look inviting and, if she was to enjoy it as Kathleen was so obviously doing, there was nothing for it but to remove her clothes, and perhaps, if she did so as quickly as possible and then made a quick dash, it wouldn't be too embarrassing. With all of her clothes finally on a boulder, she plunged in, setting up a great splashing with arms and legs.

"You are right, Kathleen, it is heavenly. As a matter of fact, it's quite … quite delicious." They both burst out laughing at her choice of word. "Delicious, delicious, delicious," Kathleen chanted, only her head now above water, her beautiful hair floating in a deep-red semi-circle. "Yes, that's exactly what it is."

The water was shadowed in places, a soft deep green, and gold-splashed in others, a pattern that changed in tune with the gently swaying branches overhead and gave to the bodies of the two girls such an ethereal quality, had they not been indulging in so much laughter and splashing about, they could quite easily have been part of a very tranquil scene.

"Someone is watching us, you know?"

Christina had been about to jerk head around, but she stopped herself, laughing softly. "A kangaroo, I suppose?"

"No, a cheeky little willie wagtail. See him up there peering down at us."

"Where? Oh yes, I can see him now, but I think it might be a her, there's a nest further along the branch. Poor thing, she probably thinks she has built her home in a lunatic asylum."

"Well, she's a bit crazy herself. Fancy building a nest out over the water like that; the young birds could quite easily fall in and drown."

"Somehow all baby birds seem to know not to fall out of their nests, instinct, I suppose." Christina's eyes searched the tree's other branches.

"We might see a pee-wee's nest too … they often build close to the willie wagtail. I'm sure I don't know why though. You'd think they'd be embarrassed at having their raggedy home so close to something as neat as that."

"Well, I guess beauty is in the eye of the beholder, as Ma so often says. But I can't see a pee-wee's nest in this tree."

"I can't either."

For over an hour the happy chatter, laughter and splashing about of the two girls mingled with the bird calls and the melodic sounds made by the creek as it tumbled over the rocks. Then they left the water and stood for a while on the strip of sand, letting the glistening droplets run from their bodies. "I wish now that we had brought our lunch with us," Kathleen mumbled as she pulled her camisole back on. "I'm positively starved."

"I am, too."

"One thing's sure, we won't be going as far as the waterfall today. As soon as we've dressed and dried our hair a bit, we'll make our way back." She giggled. "We'll go along the bank so that we can hold up our skirts and petticoats and let the sun get to our draws."

"Mine don't feel the least bit comfortable, they are sticking to me, as a matter of fact."

"Well, without a towel, we didn't really have a chance to get properly dried. We probably should have waited a bit longer before getting dressed."

"I don't know about that. Frolicking about in the water with no clothes on was one thing, standing about on the shore with nothing on was something else again."

Kathleen chuckled as she climbed on to the flat boulder where her clothes had been and began to comb her dripping hair with her fingers. "I hope you don't have bad dreams about this little adventure, Christina."

"I probably shall, but just what are you doing up there?"

"I'm going to sit here in the sunlight and dry my hair, just for ten minutes or so."

"It won't dry in ten minutes, there's too much of it."

"No, but it will get started. Besides, it's so nice here and we had such a good time, it would be a pity to be rushing off, no matter how hungry we are." She bent her head and began shaking the wild tangle of vibrant curls in front of her face. "You should undo your braids, Christina, your hair will dry much more quickly if you do."

"I suppose so."

They were both on the boulder, swinging their long hair to and fro and running their fingers through it when the sound of a horse approaching reached their ears. As one, they scrambled to their feet, glancing questioningly at one another as they did so. Once able to see over the top of the embankment, however, their eyes became riveted on the horse and rider wending their way at a gentle canter through the trees, some little distance from the creek bank, but coming in their direction. "It's Carl," Christina gasped in a horrified whisper. "You don't suppose he saw us bathing or getting dressed, do you?"

"How could he have done that? Didn't we just hear him riding down from further up the creek? But what on earth is he doing here? The track up to his place is a good half mile away."

"Perhaps we should just duck down and not let him see us?"

"No, we can't do that. He'll see our horses and start wondering what has happened to us. In any case, he has more than likely seen us."

"He doesn't look as though he has … " The words trailed away as Carl glanced sideways and abruptly reined up his horse, staring for a moment or two before heeling it towards them. The big chestnut came through the thicker growth of trees along the bank with small mincing steps, its rider bending low in the saddle to dodge the lower branches. It came to a halt, pawing the ground anxiously on the very edge of the embankment, and Carl was able to peer almost directly down at the two girls. "Christina! Kathleen! What on earth are you doing down there?"

Kathleen gave him a quick smile. "We've just been resting for a while. We left our horses back a distance and walked along at the edge of the water."

"You've come a fair way; you're not planning on going any further, are you?"

"No we are actually going to be heading back, very soon now."

Carl grinned suddenly. "It looks very pleasant down there. It would be a nice place for a swim, I would think."

Christina gasped and Kathleen quickly dug an elbow into her ribs before replying, "Yes, it probably would be. The water is certainly very cool and refreshing to drink."

"I know, I've not long drunk from the creek myself. As a matter of fact, I had a swim as well, up at the waterfall."

Christina saw the mischievous gleam that came to Kathleen's eyes and at once held her breath. "It's just as well we didn't get that far then."

Unperturbed, Carl grinned back at her. "Yes it is." His gaze shifted to Christina's upturned face. "What do you think of the Little Nerang, Christina?"

"It's very pretty, and we've been hearing bellbirds all morning."

He nodded. "They are usually very active when spring comes round."

"Are you going to our place?" Kathleen asked.

"No, I have to go to Nerang."

"Ma's been complaining that we've hardly seen anything of you these past weeks."

"Well, you give Ma my love and tell her that I've been very busy whenever I've been at home." His lips curled in an amused grin. "How did you come to get your hair so wet?"

"Our ... our hair?" For the briefest moment Kathleen floundered, reaching up almost defensively to finger her damp curls. Then she said airily. "We washed it. The water was so clear and clean-looking we both thought it would be a good idea."

Carl raised his eyebrows questioningly at Christina. She swallowed and nodded quickly, but he continued to look at her and she moved uneasily under his scrutiny. "That's why we've been sitting here in the sun, trying to dry our hair." And that, she thought, with a faint flutter of relief, was certainly no lie.

"It looks very pretty like that."

"It looks very untidy, I should think."

"Very pretty, nevertheless." He smiled at both of them. "I must be on my way, unless you'd like me to accompany you back to your horses?"

"No, we'll be perfectly alright," Kathleen assured him.

"Well, don't be too long about starting back."

"We won't," they promised in unison and Carl threw back his head on a quick laugh. "You sound like a pair of schoolgirls, guilty schoolgirls at that. And I see you are both missing your shoes and stockings again."

The gaze of both girls dropped involuntarily to their bare feet, and, before they had time to recover their composure, he'd tossed them a laughing salute and was urging his horse back through the trees to the clearer ground beyond. Here, it swung at once into a canter, disappearing quickly from their view.

"I think he knows," Christina groaned softly.

"No, he doesn't. Never in a hundred years would he suspect that we would take a bathe in the creek without any clothes on. Why, he wouldn't even think that of me, let alone you." She looked down at her bare feet again and at once burst out laughing. "It really is quite hilarious," she gasped when she was able to regain her breath. "There was Carl so amused because he'd caught us without our shoes and stockings, and if … if he'd only known what he would have seen us without if he'd come by just a little earlier."

"Oh Kathleen, how awful that would have been. I think I would have died." But Christina's horrified exclamation was followed quickly by a giggle, and, a moment later, she was laughing just as merrily as Kathleen. They sat down on the boulder again and let their mirth have its way in such ringing peals even the willie wagtail decided to leave. "Now look what we've done." Christina managed to gasp. "We've frightened the wagtail away from her nest."

"What a shame. Poor Willie, poor Carl."

This also appealed to them both as being highly amusing and they dissolved into a new burst of ringing laughter, which went on until the tears streamed from their eyes and their sides hurt. Then, still giggling, they clambered up the embankment and headed back to where their horses waited.

Kathleen lost her wager. Christmas came and went and still Christina had not been up to Carl's selection.

23

Christina was thinking Carl as she picked up the potatoes her father dug from the earth, filling her bucket before trudging to the end of the row to empty it into the big sack propped up and waiting there. Perhaps, she thought, he'd changed his mind about having her go up there. Whenever he came calling, it didn't seem to be to visit her especially, but rather to talk to her father about the house he was building, and that probably showed clearly enough that he wasn't interested in anything more than a casual friendship. But then, if that were the case, she asked herself, what explanation could there be for the strange intensity she'd surprised in his eyes on more than one occasion? Or for the gentleness towards her that he tried to conceal with good-natured teasing? Then there had been that wonderful night just two weeks back when they had taken the sulky and gone with the O'Rourke's to a dance over at Nerang. What a simply marvellous dancer he had proved to be, so light on his feet and with his arms so strong around her.

"You waltz divinely, Miss Skov, but I'm sure you've been told that many times."

"Only by my father, Mr Eichstead; this is the first real dance I have been to." A pretend formality in response to his and with her lips and eyes smiling as his were, but with her heart beating ever so wildly. Oh, however had she managed to keep her voice steady?

"You must be very young then, Miss Skov?"

"I have only recently turned seventeen, Mr Eichstead."

"Only seventeen? And here you are, the belle of the ball."

"Why, thank you, Mr Eichstead, that's very kind of you." But a quick glance around the school-room, converted for the evening into a dance hall, and at the mere dozen or so couples gliding around the floor had brought the laughter spilling from her lips. And he, laughing too, had drawn her closer, ever so much closer.

"Is there something special about that potato, Christina?"

Christina jumped and hastily dropped the potato into her bucket. "I'm sorry, Father, I was daydreaming."

Her father grinned, amusement crinkling his sunburnt face. "It must have been a nice dream. You looked as though you were dancing with that spud."

Mortified, Christina bent down and began gathering up the potatoes he had just dug up. What a thing to have done, she moaned to herself; to be standing in the middle of a potato field, swaying to and fro with what would surely have been a dreamy expression on her face and a potato in her hand! What next would she be doing, for heaven's sake? Well, she certainly knew what she shouldn't be doing and that was thinking about Carl Eichstead such a …

"Oh God, no!"

Her father's sharp exclamation caused Christina to bounce back up, and she followed his gaze to where two men were carrying a litter down the rough mountain road. Another accident at the timber camps … yes, it must have been. Dread closed around her heart. Please God, don't let whoever it is be badly hurt.

"Run and warn your mother, Christina. They'll be looking to her for help, more than likely. You can give me a call if I am needed also. Go quickly now."

Christina did as he told her, jumping over the rows of potatoes still standing. No need to worry about them, she told herself. By this time tomorrow they'll all be uprooted and withering in the sun. A good crop … yes, a very good crop, by far the best they'd had. No wonder her father was so pleased. Think about that, she told herself, and about how well things had gone for them since they'd come to Mudgeeraba. But her gaze kept darting to the men with the litter and her heart had taken up a wild thumping. Why did they have to bring them to their farm? First the man with the deep gash in his leg, then the one with half his face torn away by a branch flying from a felled tree. And now this one would come, probably with an equally horrible injury. Oh God, don't let it be too terrible, please! And, if I'm needed to help, please don't let me faint or be sick, the way I was last time. Let me be calm and strong like my mother.

Elsie was kneading dough at the kitchen table and she looked up frowning as her daughter dashed up the short flight of steps to the open door. "Is something wrong?"

Christina gulped to recover her breath. "Two men are coming down out of the hills and they are carrying a litter."

Her mother sighed, her frown deepening. "Another accident in one of the timber camps. I do hope it's not too serious." She was already wiping flour from her hands, and, by the time the men reached her gate, she was there waiting for them, fearful and anxious as to what was about to confront her, but with never a thought of shrinking back.

"It's his legs, missus, they're real bad. He slipped when the log we were loading got away from us and it went clean over them."

"It happened so quick," the second man added, "me and Jack didn't get a chance to help him."

Christina, hesitating some little distance from the gate, shivered as the men's gruff voices explained what had happened, their eyes on her mother's face betraying their anxiety to have someone more capable than they were take over the responsibility of caring for their injured mate. It is serious, she thought, her mouth going dry. It is very serious, worse than either of those other two, more than likely. She watched through eyes wide with apprehension as her mother bent over the litter … saw her reach out a hand to lift the blood-stained blanket and then stiffen, all the colour draining from her face. Christina blanched too, moaning softly and pressing her teeth into her lower lip. How terrible the injury must be for her mother to be standing there so stricken and with her free hand pressed over her mouth as though to stop herself from screaming. Perhaps he was already dead, perhaps it might even be better if he was.

But no, he wasn't dead. Her mother had taken her hand away from her face and she was speaking to the men, huskily but firmly, "We must get him to a doctor as soon as possible."

"I could ride for the one over at Nerang, missus, if you'd loan me a horse," the man whose name was Jack offered.

"No, I think it best we take him there, to the doctor's surgery. But, first, we must see what we can do to make him more comfortable. If you could bring him up to the house … "

"Of course, Missus … bless you, Missus."

There was only a dull moaning coming from the litter and, as it came abreast of where she stood, Christina saw why; an almost empty whiskey bottle lay tucked into the crook of the injured man's arm and the smell of the liquor was thick about him. The eyes of the man at the foot of the litter met hers and he smiled briefly, apologetically, "Jack gave it to him for the pain, miss, to knock him out, sort of. It did that alright, what with young Lars being not much of a one for the drink."

Lars…? Christina's eyes flew to the face of the injured man and she stared, eyes wide with disbelief and horror, at the chalk-white face partly hidden by an untidy beard. It was Lars! It was! But in the next instant she was shaking her head wildly from side to side, whispering hoarsely, "No, it's not Lars, not our Lars … it can't be!" It seemed that he heard her whisper; for the space of one heart-stopping moment his eyes, bright with a feverish lustre, opened and he stared up at her, faint recognition beginning to dawn. Then they lost their brilliance and were no longer focused. Christina couldn't move, a numbness that had claimed her entire body held her feet glued to the ground. A bad dream? Yes, it had to be. A terrible, terrible dream.

"Come along, Christina, I will be needing your help." Her mother's voice, but sounding as though it came from miles and miles away. It hadn't though, she was only a few yards up the track, hurrying ahead of the litter. And it was no bad dream. It was all happening. Lars Ohlssen had been up in the timber camps and a log had rolled over his legs, but why hadn't they known that he was there, so close by?

"Christina!"

Her mother … oh yes, her mother would take care of everything. She would know what to do. "What should I do?" she asked, scurrying past the litter to her mother's side.

"You could run on ahead. I'll need lots of hot water, the Condy's crystals, cotton wool and that old sheet for bandages. And get yourself cleaned up."

Christina fled, glad of the excuse to remove herself, even briefly, from the harsh reality of the shattered body being carried up the track. She was filling a second large saucepan from the barrel by the back door when the men carried the litter through the front of the house into the kitchen. "I'll be needing a firm, flat surface," her mother was saying quietly, "so we'll put the litter on the kitchen table." She scooped up rolling pin, floured board and ball of dough and dumped the lot unceremoniously on a bench by the fireplace. "Careful now, put him down gently."

They were careful, lifting the litter and setting it on the table with all the gentleness they could muster, but still the scream came, a terrible sound that echoed about the rafters and seemed to Christina to have no end to it. And, while he screamed, he tried to sit up, his arms flailing about as though he would catch at the very air. Shaking uncontrollably, she saw her mother take hold of his hands, speaking soothingly as she gently but firmly pressed his shoulders down on to the litter. Then, abruptly, the screaming stopped and his head lolled to one side.

"He's passed out again, thanks be to the Almighty," one of the men muttered gruffly.

Elsie, the limp wrist quickly between her thumb and fingers, nodded. "Yes, thanks be." Then, more briskly. "Would one of you look for something suitable for splints? There are packing cases in the shed, break up whatever you think will do."

"Yes missus, leave it to me. I know the sort of thing you be needing."

"She turned to the other man. "Would you be kind enough to fetch my husband? You'll see him digging potatoes in the field over yonder." She swallowed hard, her teeth catching momentarily on her lower lip. "Tell him that it's Lars Ohlssen who has been injured."

The man nodded, his eyes warm with sympathy. "I thought you must have known the lad, missus … back there at the gate."

"I have known him ever since he was a babe in arms," Elsie told him dully.

With the saucepan of water on the range and the fire prodded to greater effort, Christina fled the kitchen, a choking sensation at the back of her throat, the scream still ringing in her ears. Please God, let me find everything. Please let me find it quickly And she had to clean herself. A quick glance at her stained clothes and dirt-streaked arms told her that her mother would expect her to do that first. In her small bedroom she pulled off her boots and stepped quickly out of her skirt before tugging her blouse over her head. She poured water from the big jug into a basin and scrubbed vigorously at her face, hands and arms with a flannel cloth, telling herself over and over that she had to be strong, that she couldn't just leave everything to her mother.

By the time she returned to the kitchen, the blood-stained blanket had been removed and a clean rug covered the upper part of his body. The lower part … his legs? Where were his legs? Not that tangle of flesh and blood, bone and mud. No, that couldn't be Lars's legs … !

"Did you find the sheet?" her mother asked, not taking the time to look up from her terrible task of cutting away what remained of Lars's trousers.

Christina gulped, wanting to be sick, to run from the house and heave her heart out. "Yes … yes, I found it." Her voice came thickly, barely recognisable as her own and she kept her eyes averted.

"Good. Now put some water out of the kettle into … " Elsie glanced up suddenly. "Are you listening, Christina?"

"Yes … you want water out of the kettle.?"

"Put it into the big mixing bowl and make sure it's fairly warm. You know how much Condy's crystals, then I'll need you to hold the bowl for me."

"Yes, Mother … " Why was she saying 'yes' when every fibre of her being was screaming 'no'? She didn't want to hold the bowl; she didn't want to be anywhere near that horrible sight. She was shaking so badly, how was she going to keep from spilling the water? What if she should drop the bowl?

For a brief moment, Elsie's eyes, dark with grief, held her daughter's. "I know that it's no easy thing I ask of you, Christina," she said gently, "but we must do what we can, little enough though it may prove to be. If we can clean away some of the dirt and bind the legs on to splints it will help ease the pain and perhaps lessen the danger of infection. I also want to replace those tourniquets the men applied with clean cloth."

Christina nodded, the violent trembling easing as the warmth of her mother's understanding enfolded her. "I'll get the bowl."

Pulling it from its place in the bottom of the cupboard, she set it on the bench next to the discarded dough. The water from the kettle, tested with her elbow, was too hot. She added some cold, a little more. There, that was better. Now the Condy's … the crystals spilled into the water, spreading their purple stain. Enough … ? Yes, it was right now.

Her father burst into the kitchen, his face strained and anxious, turning grey as he moved to the table. "Jesus! Oh Jesus!"

"You must get the cart ready, Simon. We'll take him over to Doctor Davies."

"To Nerang? How can he travel?"

"He has to," Elsie murmured. "It's the only chance he has."

"Wouldn't it be better if I rode over and brought the doctor back here?"

Elsie shook her head. "He could be tied up and not able to come, then we would have lost all that time. In any case, I think he would prefer to tend Lars in his rooms."

Simon nodded slowly, his eyes searching his wife's face. Christina knew that, although no words were spoken, a question had been asked and an answer given; something horrific had been conveyed to her father for he shuddered and squeezed his eyes tightly shut. In the next instant, she knew, with a terrible, choking certainty, what it was: there was no way Doctor Davies could save legs so terribly crushed; all her mother was hoping was that he could save Lars's life.

Through eyes bleak with misery Christina watched the cart roll down the track and out through the gate. Her mother and father had both gone with Lars and so had the timber-getter named Jack, anxious to be on hand should he be needed along the way. The other man had remained behind, hoping to be able to get back to their unattended camp before nightfall. Now, though, he considered Christina uncertainly, reluctant to leave her alone with her sorrow. "I'm real sorry, miss," he mumbled, his hands pushed deep into his trouser pockets. "It was a terrible thing to happen to someone you know."

Christina nodded and brought her gaze around to his face, a weathered but kind face, twisted with compassion. Vague surprise found its way through the numbing horror in her mind. This man was a timber-getter, perhaps even one of those she had seen ill-treating their bullocks, yet he seemed to have such kindness in him ... why, there were tears in his eyes even. But, then again, perhaps he didn't have any bullocks. Not all of the timber-getters had their own teams; some of them just felled the trees, then hired the teamsters to bring the logs down out of the hills.

Samuel Hansen, one-time inmate of Her Majesty's Prison at Port Macquarie, moved uneasily from one foot to the other before Christina's steady, but distant-seeming, gaze. She's had a terrible shock, he thought, and she's in need of a deal of comforting, quite a deal. But Samuel had spent too many of his sixty-odd years away from the softness of a woman to be the one to offer that comfort; the words were no longer in him, so he cleared his throat and mumbled gruffly, "I should be going, miss."

Frowning, Christina pulled her thoughts together. This man would have been hours coming down from the mountains and, even without the litter, he would be hours getting back to his camp, the least she could do was offer him a cup of tea and a bite to eat. "Will you have time to stay for a cup of tea and a sandwich?"

"That would be right kind of you, miss, but I wouldn't want to be troubling you, not at a time like this."

Christina gave him the ghost of a smile. "It won't be any trouble."

The kitchen was a mess, but, thank heavens, her mother had taken the time to scour the table while the men carried Lars out to the buggy. They wouldn't eat there though. She would make the tea and some sandwiches at the bench, then take them out to the verandah. Samuel Hansen had come back inside with her and he busied himself rolling up the strips of sheeting that hadn't been used, his big, rough hands fumbling with the fabric. Christina wanted to think only about the sandwiches she was making, but there were so many puzzling questions troubling her mind. How had Lars come to be in a timber camp in this very region? When had he come? Where had he been these past three years? She stole a glance at the timber-getter out of the corner of her eye. He would have at least some of the answers. Almost of its own accord, it seemed, the first question was falling from her lips, "How long was he … how long was Lars with you?"

"Eight or nine weeks, no more than that. He joined up with us not long before Christmas, as a matter of fact. Me and Jack had taken the team over to Nerang with a load and he was hanging around there looking for a bit of work. We took quite a liking to the lad; he was that friendly and cheerful, even though he was flat broke. We'd been thinking that an extra bloke in our camp would be a good idea. You see, we'd not long come up from the Richmond ourselves and there was just the two of us, that meant there was no one to leave in camp when we brought the logs down. We, ourselves, hadn't had no trouble with the blacks getting off with things, but, from what we'd heard tell, it's always on the cards, so to speak. Anyhow, the long and short of it is that we asked Lars if he'd like to join up with us and he agreed."

And it turned out to be the most tragic decision he ever made, Christina thought, smothering a sigh. "Where had he come from, do you know?"

"Down south. He'd been in Sydney for a time and other places before that, but he came back up this way meaning to visit some folks he knew up at the Logan." His eyes rested questioningly on Christina's face. "That would be your family, I'm thinking?"

Christina nodded, fresh pain joining that already in her eyes. So close … they had been so close, and he hadn't known. "We moved here from the Logan more than a year ago. Lars wasn't the one to be writing letters so we had no idea where he was, otherwise we would have let him know where we were."

"Well, letter-writing's not something I take kindly to, meself. Not that I've ever had much cause to be doing any. Anyhow, I thought you would be the ones when I saw that your mother recognised Lars. Then there was your name, Christina. He was always talking about you, and your parents too, of course. He said you were the only family he had in Australia."

Christina groaned softly, "I can hardly believe that he has been in the district all these weeks and yet we didn't see him. Did he come past here often?"

"Only the once as far as I recall, the time when he first came back with us. He liked being up in the bush and he was always quite happy to stay in camp when Jack and me brought a load down. Reckoned he had more chance of saving his money if he kept away from the two-up games. Besides, staying up there gave him a chance to get on with his sketching."

About to make the tea, Christina turned her head sharply. "He's been painting again?"

"Not painting exactly, miss. Lars doesn't have no paints. Sketching's what he calls it. He uses charcoal from the fire and any piece of paper or cardboard that he can get his hands on, but it's mighty fine work that he does, nonetheless – trees, flowers, animals, people." A faint smile caught his lips. "He's done some very good likenesses of you, I'm thinking."

"Oh … ? I didn't know that he could draw people. Back in Haderslev, back where we came from, he used to paint pictures of the countryside and things like that."

"Was he good at that too?"

"Yes, he was, very good. We've still got one that he did of our house, you'll see it in the sitting room." Christina turned back to the bench where she made the tea and set out the sandwiches, cups and saucers on a tray. "I thought we might go out on to the verandah … "

Samuel Hansen was at once at her side, taking the tray from her hands. "That's a fine idea. And I must say that looks right tempting, it's quite a time since I've eaten and my stomach is beginning to know it."

Some forty minutes later he was on his way, cutting across the paddocks to where the road began its climb into the hills. A teamster, Christina thought with a small, wry smile as he turned to wave, that gentle, kindly man is a teamster.

Carl rode through the gate as Christina was listlessly rounding up the cows. He jumped from his horse and came quickly to her side. "Are you alright, Christina?"

"Do you know what has happened?"

"Yes, I met up with your mother and father in Nerang. I told them I'd come by and help you with the milking, it could be quite some time before they get back."

"Was Lars still alive?" she asked dully, still walking and staring straight ahead..

"Yes, he was still alive."

"His legs are all smashed to pieces, you know? Both of them, and Doctor Davies isn't going to be able to save them."

"He's a fine doctor, Christina."

"He still won't be able to save Lars's legs. My mother knows that, she's just trying to save his life. But what will he do without his legs?"

Carl reached out and caught her arm, bringing her to a halt and swinging her around to face him. "Have you cried, Christina?"

Christina stared up into his face blankly. What a thing to be asking? Had she cried? Of course she had cried. She was still crying, and she would probably never be able to stop.

Carl shook her gently. "You have to cry, shed tears. You can't just keep it all locked away inside you."

But there were tears, her whole being was awash with them. Just because her eyes were dry, burning like embers in her aching head, it didn't mean …

"Are you listening to me, Christina?"

"I am crying … "

With a soft moan Carl drew her into his arms, holding her tightly. "Oh, my dear, sweet love, my dear sweet love." For long moments he just held her, rocking her gently to and fro, but then he asked quietly, "How long have you known Lars?"

"All my life," Christina murmured against his chest. Oh, but it was nice to be held so. It was like being in a cocoon, with everything frightening and ugly locked outside.

"You must have liked him an awful lot?"

Christina sighed quietly. Why was he asking her questions? Why didn't he just go on holding her?

"Christina … ?"

"Mmmm … ?"

"Did you? Did you like him an awful lot?"

"Of course. Not all the time though … when I was little, that is."

"Oh, why was that?"

"He ... he used to laugh at me when I blushed."

"And you didn't like him doing that?"

"No, of course not." Don't talk ... don't talk ... I'm too tired to be answering questions ... just let me stay here.

But he didn't let her stay there ... he held her at arm's length. "But he did that painting of the house for you when you were little ... you must have liked him then?"

"Yes, I did. He gave it to me when ... when ... " She couldn't finish. Tears choked off her voice and filled her eyes before slipping in great droplets on to her cheeks. At once she was back in his arms, his lips murmuring against her forehead. "I'm sorry ... so sorry, but I had to get you to cry, it's much better than trying to shut it all away."

"Oh Carl, it was just awful," she sobbed, pressing her face into his chest and lifting her arms to cling to him. "I wasn't calm and brave like Mother. I wanted to be, but I wasn't. I was terrified and I hated having to hold the bowl and help with the bandaging. I just wanted to run outside and be sick."

"But you didn't. You stayed and helped your mother, didn't you?'

"Yes ... "

"Well, that's the important thing, what you actually did." He continued to hold her in his arms, talking quietly and soothingly and, finally, her wild sobbing eased and she asked huskily, "Do you think Lars will die?"

"I think he might want to, Christina."

"I think so too, he wouldn't want to live without his legs."

Lars died as he was being lifted on to the operating table. "We had to try to save his life," Elsie murmured bleakly as she and Simon walked away from the doctor's house. "But, had we managed to do so, I don't think he would have thanked us."

Simon nodded, unable to speak. A moment or so later he blew his nose loudly and asked miserably, "How are we ever going to write such news to Peter and Maria?"

"We'll find the words ... we have to."

"Do you suppose they'll hold us responsible?"

"Oh Simon, they would never do that."

"I keep seeing Lars running along the platform when our train was pulling out of Haderslev yelling out that we should watch out for him, and I remember what you said about hoping his parents wouldn't be blaming us if he did decide to come to Australia. Now they have so much more to blame us for."

Elsie reached for his hand and tightened her fingers about his. "Lars had a mind of his own, and sooner or later he would have come here, whether or not we had done so. I'm sure Peter and Maria will have realised that."

"Oh God, I hope so."

"If only he'd come back to us, or let us know where he was, what he was doing … "

"A timber-getter of all things," Simon groaned. "What would he have known of such an occupation?" They were nearing their horse and cart, where the man who had come with them waited, and he blew his nose again before rubbing vigorously at his eyes.

Jack Keach had known from the moment he saw them walk from the doctor's house that it was all over, but he left the hint of a question in his remark, "He didn't make it?"

Elsie shook her head. "He died before Doctor Davies could do anything for him."

"I'm very sorry, he was a real decent young bloke." But, though he spoke sincerely, he was thinking just as bloody well, it's every bit as indecent for a man to be buried without his legs as it is for him to try to go on living without them.

Some four weeks later, a bullock team came to a halt at the gate to the Skov farm and Samuel Hansen made his way up to the house, a sugar-bag over his shoulder, an assortment of cardboard and paper held together with a length of string under one arm. "Lars didn't have a lot of stuff," he explained as he handed the sugar-bag over to Elsie, "but there might be something that you want to keep or send back to his family."

Elsie nodded. "I will have a look. Thank you for bringing his things to us, Mr Hansen."

"It was no trouble, Mrs Skov." They were in the sitting room and he peered through into the kitchen. "The young lady's not here?"

"Christina is still over at the dairy, but she shouldn't be too long now." Elsie eyed the untidy bundle, now in his hands, curiously. "Did you have something for her?"

"It's just some of Lars's sketches that I thought she might like to have."

"Oh … well, would you like a cup of tea while you wait?"

"Thanks all the same, but I don't want to be too long. Jack's got the team down by the gate as you can see. If it's alright with you, I'll go on over to the dairy."

Elsie smiled at him. "Of course it's alright."

Christina, setting out clean pans for the afternoon's milking, looked up with a start when he appeared in the doorway.

"I didn't mean to startle you, miss."

"It's alright. I guess I was just daydreaming a little."

Samuel looked searchingly at the lovely young face smiling gently at him. She's fine, he told himself with a small sigh of relief. She's gotten over that terrible shock she took, bless her. Waiting for a time before bringing her the sketches had been a good idea though … he must remember to tell that to Jack since he was the one who had suggested waiting for a bit.

"I've brought these sketches, miss. I think you'll like them, and I know Lars would want you to have them."

Christina took the bundle from him, her eyes warm with gratitude. "Thank you, Mr Hansen, ever so much."

"I didn't bring those that were only half-finished or the ones that were torn and raggedy, only the ones that Lars himself seemed to value."

Christina had lifted them on to a bench and untied the string. "Oh, you were right," she exclaimed. "This girl does look like me."

"It is you, miss."

"But how? How could he do that, with pieces of charcoal of all things and me not even there?"

"Well, he had a picture in his mind, I suppose. How old were you when he last saw you?"

"Almost fourteen."

"Then you wouldn't have changed all that much, in the way you look, I mean."

"I don't suppose so. But I still don't see how he could have done it, how he could have remembered."

"Our minds are very peculiar things, miss; some things they have awful trouble recalling, but, when it comes to someone we ... ah ... someone important to us, they seem to be able to keep very clear pictures indeed."

Christina was looking at the rest of the sketches. "They are all wonderful." She glanced up suddenly, misty-eyed. "There are some of you and Mr Keach. Wouldn't you like to keep those?"

"They'd only get lost or damaged at the camp with only me and Jack to look after them. No, you keep them, something to remember us by."

Christina smiled at him. "I'd be very happy to do that, but don't forget that we are expecting to see you both from time to time. I know my mother has told you that."

"Yes, she has ... your father also, and it's mighty nice of them. Perhaps me and Jack will drop by for a cuppa one day."

Flicking his long whip over the rumps of his lead bullocks and urging them to get a move on, the timber-getter nodded in response to his own thoughts ... if Lars Ohlssen hadn't been quite in love with Miss Christina Skov when she was not yet fourteen years old, he would certainly have been now, just as any man with two eyes in his head and a heart beating in his chest would be.

24

The Kelly Gang was finished. The news hummed along telegraph lines and claimed headlines in newspapers, large and small, throughout Australia. On Monday, 29 June 1880, an armed battle between police and the bushrangers had taken place at the New South Wales town of Glenrowan. Here, at a small wooden hotel owned by a Mrs Jones, the notorious gang had finally been overcome. Dan Kelly, Joe Byrne and Steve Hart were dead, and Ned Kelly, clad in heavy armour and defiant to the last, had walked into the police barrage and fallen, shot in the legs, he was now in captivity.

"What will they do with him?" Christina asked Carl as they rode, side by side, along the level section of the track leading up to his selection."

"Hang him, I suppose, but there'll have to be some sort of a trial first."

"How awful."

Carl tossed her an amused glance. "You're not going to be feeling sorry for the man, surely? He's an out and out murderer."

"I know. It's just that hanging seems such a terrible way to die."

"It's no worse than some of the cold-bloodied killing he and his gang did."

"I suppose not."

"What do you say we forget about the Kelly Gang, for the time being at least? They've caused enough trouble and had more than enough attention these past years; we don't want them intruding into this day as well."

Christina returned the smile he gave her. "No, we don't. It's much too beautiful a morning." And at long last you are taking me up to see your selection, she added to herself, letting the smile slide from her face but feeling it still inside her. This was, after all, a day of special significance? Didn't what was happening tell her all too clearly that she hadn't imagined that Carl had called her his 'dear love' when he'd taken her into his arms on that terrible day when Lars had died. Didn't it confirm that all the time he had spent with her in the weeks that followed hadn't been solely to help her recover from her grief?

They had reached the foothills and Carl heeled his horse forward. "As you can see, it's no longer possible for us to ride side by side. I'll go first, then I can tell you what to watch out for, but it's a very rugged track for the rest of the way, so you'll need to keep your wits about you."

"I have complete faith in Samson. Didn't you tell me that he could find his way home blind-folded?" Christina was riding the big chestnut at Carl's insistence, while he was mounted on one of her father's horses, a sturdy brown gelding, recently acquired.

"You take care, nevertheless."

The track, extremely narrow, twisted and turned as it climbed, at times hugging the very edge of steep declivities, while, on either side the forest deepened into dense, serried ranks of giant gum trees that rose to heights of three or four hundred feet and from the gullies to five hundred feet or more, dwarfing all except the magnificent bunya-bunya pines which, here and there, dared to challenge their supremacy. Occasionally, though, the two riders came out of the shadows into splashes of sunlight and caught glimpses of the lowlands stretching off to the coast and in the distance of the ocean itself. And, from time to time, the track meandered in a downwards direction where one line of hills merged into another or where a gully had been forged by rushing water. At one of these, they dismounted and wandered into a fern-engulfed wonderland, where daylight had become lost and only a green twilight filtered through the interlaced fronds overhead and where a small waterfall spilled into a rocky pool.

"Carl, it's just beautiful," Christina whispered.

"Yes, it is," Carl whispered back before laughing softly, "But I don't think we need to whisper."

"Yes, we do. It's just like being in a church, a wonderful church, a cathedral perhaps." She lifted her gaze to his gently smiling face. "Have you ever been in a cathedral, Carl?"

"No, I haven't."

"I haven't either. I'm sure being inside one would feel just like this though, calm and mysterious, very close to God."

Carl was watching her, an unfathomable expression in his eyes, and she gave a small self-ridiculing laugh. "Close to God … ? In a hollow in the mountains with not even a glimpse of the sky? How silly I am being." She would have turned from him but her hand brushed his and at once his fingers closed over hers. "I know what you mean, Christina. Well I think I do." He hesitated for a moment or two and Christina thought that he was going to let the matter rest there, but then he said, "I believe that God is always close to us, in our hearts, as it were, but that there are times when we feel His presence more strongly than others."

"It doesn't have to be in a church?"

"No, or on a mountain top either."

Christina nodded, a faint smile touching her lips. "In Haderslev we used to go to church every Sunday, but, since we've been in Australia, it seems we've hardly gone at all. I used to worry about that, thinking I would lose God if I didn't go to church regularly."

"But you don't think that now?"

"No, I came to see that it's just like you said. In any case, God would certainly understand how well-nigh impossible it is for people like us to get to a church every Sunday."

"It's that alright." Carl drew her closer to the pool. "Would you like a drink?"

"Yes, I would."

They bent down together, scooping up handfuls of the cool, crystal-clear water and dashing it to their mouths. "Oh, it's freezing," Christina laughed, shaking the droplets from her hands.

"It's always like that, even in summer."

"Do you come here often?"

"No, only occasionally."

"I think I'd be coming often if I lived hereabouts, it's such a special place."

"There's nothing to stop us coming back some other time, but right now I think we should be leaving, we still have a way to go."

They were on what seemed to Christina to be a flattened ridge, with valleys dropping away to both east and west, when Carl eased his horse back beside her with a wide grin on his face. "Well, Christina, this is it. You are now on Carl Eichstead's selection."

Drawing a quick, involuntary breath, Christina looked around her. But there was nothing to see, .they were still surrounded by dense bushland.

Carl laughed at the puzzled expression on her face. "I haven't got round to this part yet, and, since it's where the road will eventually go through, I probably won't be doing too much about it. The best land is a bit further on."

"When do you think the road will be built?"

"I have no idea. But there's more chance of it happening now that the Government has handed over responsibility for roadworks to Divisional Boards. For one thing, there'll be local people on the Boards and they'll have a better understanding of what's required." He grinned cheerfully. "I take it you haven't been too impressed with the track?"

"It's not all bad, and there are some quite lovely views from parts of it."

"This is impressive-looking country, there's no doubt about that." He heeled his mount forward, and, a short distance further on, they rode off the crest of the ridge and came to a halt at a rough wooden gate. Christina joined him as he dismounted to open it, smiling down at him. "I can see your house through the trees and you've even got yourself a driveway."

Carl laughed. "If you can call chopping down a few trees so that I can get from my front gate to my house a driveway."

"Well, at least we are able to ride the rest of the way side by side."

A short distance further on, they came out of the thickly forested area and Christina found herself gazing wide-eyed at the nearly completed house, the stretches of cleared land running off to the creek bank, the sturdy fences, the corn, strong and healthy-looking, the half-dozen cattle grazing contentedly, and the vegetable plots close to the house. But she saw, too, the gigantic semi-circle of huge trees standing up from the bright green sward where the cattle were, the dense scrub into which the cornfield merged, the stumps of felled and fired trees and the great logs not yet turned to ashes. And she knew, with a lurching of her heart, the herculean toil that would have been required to wrest this small oasis from the wilderness.

In front of the house, Carl reached up to lift her from the horse. "Remember, I did warn you… it's not yet complete."

"It looks fine, and it's complete enough for you to be living in it," Christina told him as he set her on her feet.

"Well, it's much better than the tent, that's for sure." With the horses unsaddled, he tethered them in the shade on a loose rein. "Samson will be thinking he's home for the day and go wandering off if I don't restrain him." Returning to Christina's side, he caught hold of her hand. "I don't need to open the door for you, there isn't one."

Christina laughed. "I had noticed. Aren't you concerned about prowling animals?"

"I got used to them when I was living in the tent. It didn't take long to realise that anything remotely edible had to be shut away."

Christina nodded. "I remember how it was when we were living in a tent at the Logan." They had come into the house, and she smilingly looked around her: at the solid looking walls, the two windows, and, most impressive of all, the large stone fireplace. "Carl, this is really very nice."

"Well, this is the kitchen and dining area and it's more or less complete. The bedroom still needs a floor. As you can see here, I've been using pine boards for that, and they have to be pit-sawn. And, of course, pit-sawing requires two men. So, what with Danny doing some work at Yaun's sawmill over in Numinbah valley, I've had to put the bedroom on hold." He grinned suddenly. "Only good thing about it is that he tells me he's getting valuable experience."

"He's been a big help to you?"

"Heavens yes. I'd never be able to pay him for the work he's done, but we have a deal: when he builds a house, he will expect the same from me." He pulled a chair out from the table and took Christina's bonnet from her nervously fluttering hands. "Have a seat for a while. I want to get this fire stirred up and our dinner reheating."

"You should have let me bring some sandwiches."

Carl glanced at her with mock reproach. "When I've made this fine duck stew especially?"

"Well, there must be something I can do to help?"

"No, I have everything under control. I thought it would be a good idea to eat as soon as the stew is hot, then we can spend some time out of doors. There are some really nice areas along the creek."

"I'd like that." She tapped the rough pine table. "Did you make this as well?"

"Yes, and the two chairs." He chuckled softly. "But don't be worrying, they won't collapse on you."

"I had no such thoughts," Christina assured him. "I think you've done very well with everything."

"Well, I'm really only what they call a bush carpenter, not a fair dinkum one. And, of course, it's all had to be built from timber available here. The Yaun's have got that sawmill over in Numinbah valley, but getting milled stuff down from there and then up here would have been well-nigh impossible. In any case, it would have been out of character to have used milled timber. Pretty much all of the cottages throughout these ranges have been built by the settlers themselves with their own timber."

Christina sighed quietly. "It was what Father planned to do at the Logan … "

"Yes, he told me. With him being a true carpenter, he could have come up with something a deal better than a simple cottage. It's just a pity he didn't have the time to do that. He's been so interested in what I've been doing I'm sure he would have enjoyed it."

"He was certainly happy with the things he was able to do – windows, doors and stuff like that." Fond memories of helping with such jobs struggled with a faint regret that that was all her father was able to do on his house, and she quickly changed the subject, "That stew smells delicious."

"It's going to be at the table in around five minutes, so prepare yourself'"

It was delicious, and Christina told him so, as she pushed her chair away from the table. "Since you cooked it and also gathered those yummy wild berries, it's up to me to do the washing-up." She reached for Carl's plate, but he caught hold of her hand, restraining her. "We are not going to waste precious time washing up. I'll do that tonight."

"It wouldn't take long … "

"No, the dishes can wait. We are going to linger on the creek bank and talk." Getting to his feet, he hurriedly gathered up plates, cups and cutlery and stacked them untidily on the bench by the fireplace.

The creek bank was high and so steep Carl had been obliged to cut steps and build a section of rough railing to a narrow strip of lower bank, from which he was able to draw buckets of water, which were then carried first to the top of the bank and then up the rise to the big barrel at his back door. "The worst thing about it," he told Christina, "is the time it takes."

"I can imagine, but there's just no other way of getting it up, is there?"

"Not unless it was possible to set up a pulley of some sort." He grinned wryly. "Even if that could be done, it would be a waste of time and effort; the first flood to come down would wash it all away."

"It's a very fast-flowing stream even without a flood. Is it always in such a hurry?"

"Up here in the hills, it is, because of the steep drop it takes down from its source to the lowlands. It's a bonus in a way as, even in the driest weather, the water is incredibly fresh and clean."

Nearby, a sun-splashed grassy ledge a foot or so from the top of the bank caught Christina's eye. "It's just like a big armchair."

"So it is," Carl agreed. "Designed especially for the whiling away of a pleasant hour or so." He caught her hand, leading her to where she was able to lower herself on to the soft grass.

Spreading the folds of her skirt and tucking her slim legs under her, Christina laughed softly. " I should think it's like being in the balcony at a theatre."

Carl sat down beside her. "Did you go to the theatre when you were a little girl back in Hadersleben … ah … Haderslev?

Christina raised her eyebrows at the slip … the German pronunciation instead of the Danish one, but there was a smile on her lips, and Carl grinned. "Sorry."

"You don't look too sorry, but you're forgiven. No, I didn't go to a theatre back in HadersLEV! Well, not a real one. There was a hall next to the school, where they had concerts and things like that, and I remember going there a couple of times. Have you been to the theatre?"

"Yes, I have, as a matter of fact, in Berlin."

"Goodness, that must have been exciting."

"Well, I don't recall that it was particularly exciting. We saw some sort of opera and it was kind of slow and boring. I was with my brother, and I remember that he kept wanting to leave."

Christina grinned. "And you were a good boy and wouldn't let him?"

"It wasn't quite like that," Carl told her, returning her grin. "We were holidaying with an uncle in Berlin, and, hoping to improve our appreciation of the arts, he had bought the tickets for us. Imagine how he would have reacted if we'd walked out."

"I should think he would have been very disappointed, and perhaps just a little annoyed that he had wasted his money."

"More than a little, believe me."

They both laughed, then Christina asked, "Has there ever been a flood while you've been here?"

"Not a really big one. The water didn't come up over the bank, and I've been told that's only a minor flood, that with a really big one it would be a different story."

"Surely it wouldn't reach right up here?"

"That's what I thought too, but it has, and on more than one occasion apparently, which is why I've built the house well away from the creek and on that bit of a rise."

A pair of ducks glided into view, moving swiftly with the flow of the water and bobbing up and down over the ripples. "Ah!" Christina grinned. "Now I know where our dinner came from."

"It didn't, actually. Danny and I shot a dozen or more over in the swamps, three for me and the rest for the O'Rourke family."

"I know the size of the pot of stew Mrs. O'Rourke makes."

"Actually, I wasn't going to make a stew today. I had planned on giving you a special treat by cooking the ducks the way the blacks sometimes do."

"Why didn't you?"

"Well, even though I was pretty sure you'd be interested, I got to wondering whether perhaps the process mightn't turn you off eating the finished product."

"What do they do, for heaven's sake?"

"They roll the duck in a ball of mud, feathers and all, and put the whole thing in hot ashes. When it's cooked and they remove the mud, the feathers come away with it and all the innards come out as cleanly as you like."

"And it still tastes alright?"

"It tastes great, really tender. I've cooked duck that way on a number of occasions, it's a great time-saver."

"I should think it would be. Plucking a duck, wild or otherwise, is one of the most tedious chores I know."

"Which just goes to show, there are things we can learn from the blacks. The trouble is that many of their ways are beyond us, we just don't seem to be agile enough. Do you know how they catch the ducks?"

"I suppose they hit them with their boomerangs."

"They might do that occasionally, but normally they use their boomerangs to frighten the birds. They string nets across one end of a large lagoon and then hide themselves. When the ducks arrive they throw their boomerangs among them, the ducks think they are hawks and dive down into the nets."

Christina nodded. "I recall Mr Hunter, my friend Marie's father, telling us that they so something like that to catch the parrots."

"That's right, they string the nets from tree to tree."

"They really do have some amazing ways of doing things."

"Including another method of catching the ducks, something Danny and I have tried."

Christina returned the somewhat sheepish grin he gave her. "I can't wait to hear."

"Well, in the summer time, they go into the large waterholes and stand there with the water up to their necks, holding a small bush in front of them to hide their heads. The ducks, being not too smart, think this is just another bush and swim closer and closer as they feed, then, all of a sudden, they're grabbed by the legs and pulled under."

Christina was staring at him, laughter and amazement on her face. "And you and Danny tried that?"

"On two occasions, as a matter of fact."

"And how many ducks did you catch?"

"Not a single one. Those not-so-smart ducks were too quick for us."

When their laughter had died away, Christina asked, "Do you see any Aborigines around here?"

"I've seen a few on the other side of the creek from time to time. They set up their camps further back, because I'm here, I suppose, but they come to those bunya-bunya pines you can see over yonder. They consider the seeds from the cones a great delicacy, apparently."

"So I have heard. Are there any Bora rings in this area?"

"Not just here, as far as I know, but there do seem to be quite a few scattered about in other places. There are several down at the Tweed and some very important ones on the upper Albert River, not far from Tambourine Village."

"Where they held that big corroboree last year?"

"Yes, that's right." He seemed surprised and glanced a little suspiciously at the faint smile curling her lips. "That was to celebrate the death of Wongawallan, the black outlaw."

"I know." Christina's smile widened and her eyes danced mischievously. "I also know that you saw it, you and Danny."

Carl was incredulous. "Danny told Kathleen? I don't believe it!"

Christina laughed softly at his amazement. "No, he didn't. He told Joseph, and Kathleen overheard."

"That eavesdropping little minx."

Even though he was far from being genuinely annoyed, Christina felt obliged to come to her friend's defence. "She wasn't really eavesdropping. She just happened to be passing by the barn and she heard Danny tell Joseph that he'd seen the most exciting thing ever, or something like that."

"And she just had to stop to find out what it was?"

"Well, she didn't see why it had to be such a secret, and I don't either, as a matter of fact."

"It wasn't meant to be, not really. It was just that we were quite impressed with what we saw, and we came away feeling that we had been intruders. So we decided that we wouldn't say too much about having been there and then we wouldn't be required to answer questions about what took place."

The amused smile had left Christina's face and she said quietly, "I understand, and I'm sorry I teased you about it."

Carl took up her hand from where it rested on the grass between them, entwining his fingers in hers. "It's alright, Christina, you have no call to be sorry. I'd like to tell you about it."

"Oh no, you don't have to. I mean there's no need for you to feel that you should do so."

"I don't feel that I should do so, it's just something I'd like to do. It was an incredible experience and I would very much like to share it with you, that's if you'd like to hear about it, of course?"

"Yes, I would, very much."

He began slowly and quietly, "It was in March last year and Danny and I were over at Cedar Creek on a fencing job. You may remember, it wasn't that long before Easter?"

Christina nodded. She did remember and with good reason; she'd been more than a little concerned that they weren't going to be back in time to go to the regatta.

"Well, when all these blacks began to arrive in the area, heading for the Bora rings, we figured something big was on, especially since they'd come from as far away as the Richmond and Brisbane and Ipswich. By the time they were all assembled, there were hundreds of them."

"How did you know when the corroboree was going to take place?"

"We didn't. We went up there on four consecutive nights and saw nothing but groups of blacks squatting around the campfires. Then, on the fifth night, there was a different atmosphere, a sort of subdued excitement which conveyed itself even to where we were."

"Where were you?" Christina asked, wide-eyed with interest.

"In a tree. And none too comfortable, I might add. As a matter of fact, they took so long to get things moving we had begun to think that we had been wrong in thinking that this was to be the night. Then, just as we were about to leave our precarious perches, this peculiar humming noise started. It seemed to be just a couple of men's voices to begin with, but it was soon taken up by others. It's hard to describe what it sounded like. The nearest thing I can think of is a huge swarm of bees and yet it wasn't quite like that, it had a strange throbbing sound." He shrugged his shoulders and gave Christina an apologetic smile. "Best description I can manage, I'm afraid."

Christina smiled back at him. "It's a very good description, I'm sure."

"Well, this humming went on for a time, then a chant of some sort started and about a hundred blacks gathered around a tree trunk which had been cut off about forty feet above the ground, and some thirty of them climbed it, one of them to the very top. They just kept on pushing up the trunk until it couldn't possibly have held another body. They were all wearing these peculiar headdresses: a sort of bow arched from the back of the head to the forehead and which had cockatoo crests stuck in sticks standing erect all along it, making the whole thing look like a giant crest. The next thing that happened was that those on the ground, the women included, began to sing, and, as they did so, the men on the tree all swung halfway around at arm's length, bowing their heads, feathers and all, and then back again. Do you understand what I mean, Christina?"

"Yes, I think I can picture it. It must have looked quite startling."

"It certainly had the most amazing effect. In the light from the campfires what they were doing gave the impression that the tree trunk was being worked around in a groove."

"What did it signify?" Christina asked, suppressing a faint shiver.

"I really don't know. It was all to do with the death of Wongawallan, of course, but just what it meant I have no idea. Danny and I went back to look at the tree trunk a few days later, and it had all these deep notches cut into it for footholds." He gave a short laugh. "It was a strange feeling though; if it hadn't been for those notches, I think I might well have believed that the whole thing had been an illusion of some sort."

"I've always thought I'd like to see a corroboree, but I'm not so sure now. Just hearing about that one made me go all shivery inside."

"Some of them could be quite amusing, the goanna corroboree, for one."

Goanna … barra. It was an involuntary connection and Christina caught her breath, surprised that the word had still been there, tucked away in her mind. Surprised, too, that it should cause a vision to come rushing up through the years – an ugly-looking creature impaled and thrashing about while a young Aborigine danced delightedly around it, crying, "Barra.! Barra!" A strange sensation touched her heart, the ache of not knowing something that mattered. What had become of him? Did he still roam the bush, unclothed, living the old tribal way of life and taking part in ceremonials such as the one she had just heard described? Or had he been caught up in the white man's way of life?

"Hey, why so sombre?" Carl put his fingers under her chin and turned her head so that his eyes could search her face. "Hearing about the corroboree wasn't that depressing, surely?"

Christina shook her head and brought a smile to her lips. "No, it wasn't that. I was just wondering what had happened to the young Aborigine boy who took me home that time I was lost in the bush. You remember, I told you about it?"

"Yes, I do remember. As for what has become of him, I suppose that's something you'll just have to go on wondering about. He may well have been with that big group we saw at the corroboree. On the other hand, he could be miles and miles away by now." Carl still held her hand, and he lay back against the grassy curve of the embankment, drawing her into a reclining position beside him. "You know, I see this little green nest every time I go down to the creek to bring up water, and I've always promised myself that one day I would come and sit here."

Nervously trying to ensure that she wasn't lying too close to him and that the hem of her dress hadn't crept up when she'd unfolded her legs, Christina turned her head in surprise. "And this is the first time you've done it?"

"That's right. Because I always thought that I couldn't spare the time, I suppose."

"And now I've caused you to lose a whole day."

"I've earned myself a day off, and I can't think of a nicer way to spend it. I'm not only sitting in this place. I've got you with me."

Feeling her heart begin to race, Christina shifted her gaze to a cluster of feathery clouds sailing across the sky. "How long are you back for this time?"

"Just this week. The crushing's on in earnest down at the Tweed and all of the growers are looking for cane cutters."

"I thought that you would have been back on Saturday, for Maureen's wedding?"

"I was back on Saturday, but not in time for the wedding. A pity as I was looking forward to seeing Arthur and Maureen become man and wife. The problem was that I had a bit of trouble getting back from the Tweed. You know how I've told you that Samson can find his way home?"

"Blindfolded?"

Carl laughed. "I don't really know about that part of it, but it's certainly true that he can get himself back here with no trouble whatsoever. Well, when I went to saddle him up at crack of dawn last Saturday, he wasn't there. He'd got out of the paddock I keep him in and set out on his own."

"You mean that he came back here, all the way from the Tweed?"

"That's exactly what he did, the ungrateful creature."

"You couldn't get another horse?"

"No, there wasn't one to be had anywhere."

"Goodness, what did you do?"

"Walked, caught the coach for part of the way, then walked again. You see, I had this foolish notion that my trusty mount would have had the decency to wait for me somewhere along the way. But no. Not until I finally got to the gate did I catch up with him. There he was, as innocent as you like, waiting for me to open it and let him in."

Christina pressed a hand over her mouth, but it was no use. A rippling peal of laughter burst from her lips and was quickly followed by another, and another.

Amused, Carl waited for her laughter to subside before remarking with mock seriousness, "So you think that's funny, do you?"

"Oh yes, It's the funniest thing I've heard in a long time. I'm sorry that you had to walk, of course … and that you missed the wedding."

"You don't look very sorry?"

"But I am. It's just that it was such a funny thing to have happened … Samson coming home on his own like that, then waiting to be let in."

"Hmmm … Samson has some amusing ways alright. Saturday wasn't the first time he took it into his head to take off on his own."

Christina considered him questioningly, her lips parted in a smile, her eyes misty with the remnants of her laughter. "Where else did he leave you?"

"Are you sure you want to know?"

"Of course. Why would I not want to know? And I promise not to laugh."

"Well, if you're sure … ?"

"I am … very sure."

"It happened one day last spring. I was on my way over to Nerang and I decided to stop off for a swim in the pool at the bottom of the waterfall. It was very pleasant and I probably stayed in the water a bit long … " He was speaking slowly and deliberately, his amused eyes on Christina's face. As his smile widened, hers faded. "When did you say that was?"

"Last spring, a Saturday, I seem to recall. Anyhow, my trusty steed decided not to hang around waiting for me and took off. It was a funny thing though … instead of going back home or even over to the track, he followed the creek downstream. It was just good luck that he stopped to graze on the bank, otherwise it would probably have taken me ages to catch up with him."

"Oh no!" Christina cried, springing back into an upright position and dashing her hands up to cover her ears. "Don't tell me anymore! Please don't tell me anymore!" She wanted to cover her face too, for she was sure it was the very brightest pink. Oh, when had he been there? Before they had seen him riding through the trees, that much was certain. He must have led Samson back from the bank and then made a pretence of having just come along. But just when had he been there the first time? When they were splashing about in the water? Or when they were dressing? Or, worst of all, when they were just standing there waiting for the water to run from their bodies? A sudden vivid mental picture of each scene as it would have appeared to someone up on the bank flashed through her mind and was instantly followed by a desire to tumble off the ledge and disappear from his sight. "Oh, I am so mortified. I will never be able to look you in the face again."

Carl was laughing, a deep chuckle that sounded very close behind her right ear. Then his hands were on her shoulders and he was turning her towards him. "Close your eyes, then."

She hadn't though, Christina recalled, plumping up her pillow and pressing her cheek into its softness, not right away. Had she done so, she wouldn't have seen the tenderness that merged with the amusement in his eyes. But, when he'd drawn her into his arms and his mouth had claimed hers, and for such a long time … ?

Yes, she must have closed them then, otherwise she would surely have swooned right away, such a whirling had there been in her head, such a fire racing through her body. When the kiss, so unlike anything she had ever known or imagined, had come to an end, he had held her from him. Not something he had wanted to do … one confused, enquiring glance up into his face had told her that, but something he felt he should do. And, in a way, she had understood. Such kisses kindled fires that were apt to rage out of control. It hadn't been easy though, lying back with her head on Carl's shoulder while he told her ever so carefully of his plans. In fact, such an ache of yearning had there been within her, it had taken all the will power she could muster to keep from turning and pressing her body against his …

"By the time two years have passed, Christina, I hope to be in a much more satisfactory situation. I will be applying for a Homestead block as soon as I think I have a chance of getting it. Then, with it and the Selection I'll have almost twice the workable area I have with this place, and I should be able to grow enough produce and raise enough beef cattle to allow me to spend most of my time at home, instead of having to go off looking for outside work. Of course, I don't intend to stay up here in the mountains. Once I'm in a position to buy land outright, instead of acquiring it by paying rent to the Government, I'll move down on to the flat lands, go in for dairying."

"You're a dreamer, Carl, just like my father."

"Naturally. I wouldn't have come to this country had I not been. It's the way it is with free-passage immigrants. Some, though, are impatient dreamers, they want it all pretty much right away. Three or four years they allow themselves, perhaps a little more. Not enough, my love, not nearly enough in a country such as this."

"You're not one of those impatient dreamers?"

"No, I know only too well that's it's going to take time. I may not even live long enough to see all of my dreams come to reality."

"You don't mean that? You can't."

"Ah, Christina, it's not something to be looking so dismayed about. I'll reap rewards, you may be sure of that. In fact, in a way, I've been doing that ever since I set foot on these shores: freedom to do as I please; a good, fulfilling life on the land; opportunities just waiting to be grasped; confidence in the future. But the ultimate rewards we all have our sights on are success and prosperity and it could well be that they will only be for our children."

"How many children do you want to have?"

"A whole batch. At least three sons and a couple of daughters as beautiful as their mother."

Why had she asked? Christina groaned into her pillow. Why was she thinking about that now when she had resolved to think only about how wonderful it was to love and be loved in return. But the little graves pushed past the barrier she had, weeks back, erected so painstakingly in her mind, so stark and clear they might have come from yesterday, and, drifting with them as though it knew only that it had to follow, came the small canvas-wrapped bundle. Dear God in heaven, what had she been thinking of, reaching out with open arms for something that could never be, something that would be so unfair she would never forgive herself for letting it happen. It wasn't enough that she loved Carl with all her heart. Or that she didn't really mind what sort of a house they lived in. Or that she was prepared to work beside him as he cleared, ploughed and planted. Or that she would never complain about the loneliness of that farm so far back in the hills. Why, it wasn't even enough that she would be willing to die for him. No, only if there were children would it be enough, without them all else would be to no avail.

But, even as the tears of hopelessness began to gather in Christina's eyes, the thought stirred … she had two years. He wasn't planning on being married for at least two years, therefore, she didn't have to decide anything now. After all, Carl hadn't actually proposed to her, not in so many words, so it wouldn't be that she was cheating or anything like that. When all was said and done, she couldn't very well go up to a man who hadn't really asked her to marry him and say, "I'm sorry but I don't think I would make you a very good wife." No, of course she couldn't.

25

Unlike the previous year, winter took its final fling in a burst of shocking weather that spilled over into the first days of September. But then, almost overnight it seemed, it was spring – a brilliant spring, awash with colour and gentle warmth. The thought occurred to Christina that this was one of the only two such seasons there would be in two years, but she quickly pushed it from her mind. She was happy, blissfully happy; her skin glowed with an inner radiance, a smile hovered almost constantly about her lips and her heart sang. Carl took her to dances over at Nerang in their sulky, and to the races on Burleigh Beach, where he twice rode Midnight to victory in the main race of the day. He called at their farm far more often than he had been wont to do. And he kissed her, of course, sometimes lightly with smiling affection, but, occasionally, deeply and lingeringly.

From time to time, though, doubts pierced her happiness like sharp arrows, refusing to be ignored. She wasn't being fair to Carl. She shouldn't be holding him with unspoken promises, with smiles and willing lips. She should be sending him on his way so that he could set about looking for a more suitable wife, and there were her parents who seemed to have come to the conclusion that she and Carl had a definite understanding … wasn't she deceiving them as well? Such doubts always succeeded in bringing a sharp ache to her heart, but she would quickly remind herself that no mention of marriage had as yet been made, that, in any case, she hadn't actually resolved to say no. Why, she told herself, it just might be that she and Carl would be married in two years' time. Wasn't it possible that, in the intervening period, something would happen to convince her that all her fears were groundless? She didn't go so far as to think what this something might be; it was enough that her mind had seen fit to accept that there just might be such a possibility.

Kathleen, however, wasn't prepared to accept Christina's assurances that Carl hadn't asked her to marry him. "He has, hasn't he? I can tell just by looking at you. These past weeks you've been positively glowing with happiness."

"I've already told you, he hasn't."

"Well, if he hasn't actually proposed, he must have said something?"

"Such as what?"

"Such as … oh, I don't know." Kathleen threw up her hands in exasperation. "You'll have to tell me."

"There's nothing to tell."

"But you're in love with Carl, you're not going to deny that?"

"No, I'm not going to deny that."

"And he loves you. That's no secret, he's done so for ages. So … " She grinned widely. "Of course you're going to get married. There's just no reason why you shouldn't. You're perfect for one another."

Christina felt the smile stiffen on her lips. No reason … if only that were so. If only it wasn't so important about the children. If only she could bring herself to talk about it with someone, respond to the crying out of her heart for its burden to be shared. She eyed the cheerful girl helping her hang out the washing with a sudden longing. Could she tell her? Would she understand?

"Ah ha! You were about to tell me something. It was on the tip of your tongue. What was it?"

Smothering a sigh, Christina grinned and said teasingly, "It was that I don't know why I chose such an inquisitive person for a best friend, especially when she confides almost nothing about her own romance."

"It wasn't that at all," Kathleen accused. "It was something important, I could tell from the serious look on your face." Her eyes widened disbelievingly. "It's not that silly business about Carl being a Prussian, is it?"

Christina felt a small start of surprise. Just when had that ceased to be a problem, for heaven's sake? And how? Had it simply faded in importance until it was no longer a matter for concern? Or had it just happened abruptly, as it were? She didn't know. And how strange that was. There had been the time when Carl had talked to her at some length about Prussia and the things that had happened there, of course. But, even though she had understood something of his feelings, what he'd said hadn't really changed anything; he was still a Prussian and the Prussians had invaded her homeland.

Kathleen was waiting, concern beginning to cloud her eyes. "It is that."

"No, it's been ages since I concerned myself with the Prussian thing."

"Thank goodness for that. What was it then, what you were about to tell me?"

"What if I told you that Carl is not ready to take a wife yet, that he feels he won't be in a position to do so for two years?"

Kathleen heaved an exaggerated sigh. "And isn't that just like a man, expecting a girl to wait all that time!"

"He hasn't asked me to wait, not in so many words. He just remarked that in two years' time he expects to be in a better situation than he is at present."

"And, somehow, he managed to convey to you that when that happened he would be asking you to marry him?"

"It seemed that way, but it may have been only my imagination, so I wouldn't like you to be saying anything to anybody."

"Of course I wouldn't, silly. It wouldn't have been, though … just your imagination, I mean. I suppose, when you think about it, Carl was only being fair. After all, if you married him now, you'd be up there in the hills on your own half the time, which would be absolutely terrifying."

Christina nodded. "It would be very lonely, his place is ever so isolated."

"So I understand, but how can you bear to wait two years?"

Because those two years might be all I have … the words darted, unbidden, into Christina's mind, so vividly she gave a small gasp, for a moment fearing that she had spoken them out loud. "The time will pass quickly enough," she murmured.

"It won't, you know. It'll drag like anything."

"But I'll be seeing Carl frequently. It's not as if … " Her voice trailed away and her eyes darted to the other girl's face.

The smile came, faintly and ruefully, as Kathleen finished for her, "It's not as if he's off somewhere out of reach, and it's not as though there's nothing to look forward to."

"Kathleen, I'm sorry, I wasn't thinking."

"It's alright, Christina." She grinned impishly. "Haven't I been telling you all these past months that David Charlton is just a good friend?"

"Which you know very well I didn't believe."

"Well, I was trying to make myself believe that, too, you know? In the beginning, at any rate. After all, he was a complete stranger, someone I'd only been with for a couple of hours, and he certainly wasn't our kind of people." The grin came again, but wryly. "Can you imagine that, telling myself that he was just a good friend when I went to sleep every single night with his image on the back of my eyelids and his letters tucked under my pillow."

Christina nodded, compassion touching her heart, but words eluding her.

"I was even stupid enough to believe that after a time I mightn't feel so strongly about him, what with not being able to see or talk to him. When all's said and done, a letter resting against your heart is mighty poor substitution for the warmth of flesh and blood."

"Perhaps if you hadn't been writing to him you might have been able to put him out of your mind," Christina suggested quietly.

Kathleen gave her shoulders a faint shrug. "Do you think I haven't considered that? At one time, I actually did decide not to reply to David's letters, but I just couldn't do it."

"Oh, why haven't you told your parents, Kathleen?" Christina groaned. "I'm sure they'd understand."

"No, they wouldn't." She gave a short, mirthless laugh. "They'd be even less likely to approve now that Maureen and Arthur seem to have settled down to married life quite happily."

"I don't see what you mean?"

"Well, didn't Maureen think herself in love with Carl, with a non-Catholic? Now here she is, after just a little persuasion, mooning over Arthur as though he'd always been the only man in her life. That would be the example I'd have thrown at me. Ma and Da would never believe that what happened for Maureen wouldn't also happen for me, that all I required was for a nice Catholic boy to come calling. Sweet Mother of God, how little they know. Why, I would become a nun before I'd marry someone else."

"Oh no, you couldn't!"

Kathleen laughed softly at the dismay on Christina's face. "No, I don't suppose I could. I'd probably never make the grade, for one thing," A faint smile remained on her face, but her eyes became suddenly watchful. "I could run away from home though."

She's joking, Christina told herself, her dismay threatening to sharpen into alarm, she would never do such a thing. "You know you would never do anything so silly."

"I might." Then, with the bright green eyes even more watchful, "Would you help me, Christina, if I did decide to run away?"

Christina stared at her, no longer so sure that she was joking. "You're not serious, you can't be."

"Running away to David might be the only chance at real happiness I get."

"He's asked you to do that?" Christina gasped incredulously.

Kathleen shook her head. "No, it would be up to me to suggest such a thing. David's much too honourable; he can't think beyond coming to see Da and asking formally for my hand."

"Why don't you let him do that?"

"Don't be a ninny, Christina! You know Da's paddy, he'd go clean off his rocker. He might even take his gun or a whip and chase David off the farm."

"Of course he wouldn't. He'd probably start off being angry, but you know that he usually calms down before too long."

"He wouldn't this time though. In any case, just supposing he did calm down later on, David might be already maimed or even dead."

"That's silly, your father would never do anything to cause real harm to anyone."

"Well, I'm not going to be risking it, Christina, I can tell you that. Even if he didn't go so far as to get his gun, he'd carry on in such a way poor

David would probably take fright and flee for his very life."

A small frown puckered Christina's brow. "How is it that your father didn't take exception to Carl?"

Kathleen waved her hands airily before delving them once again into the basket of wet clothing, "He knew Carl was no threat, that he wouldn't be wanting to marry Maureen."

"How could he have been so sure about that?"

"Well, he's not blind, you know? And I suppose Ma would have been telling him there wasn't any need for them to be concerned." She straightened from the basket, her eyes again searching Christina's face. "You still haven't answered my question?"

"What question?"

"Would you help me if I decided to run away?"

"What could I do, for heaven's sake?" Christina asked with a small, flustered laugh.

"I don't know yet. I'll let you know when I work out a few … goodness, your parents are back from Nerang already."

Christina turned her gaze sharply to where the horse and sulky were moving at a steady clip along the road towards the gate. "I do so hope they've got a letter from the Ohlssens. Father is ever so anxious to hear from them."

"He probably should have telegraphed them," Kathleen declared matter-of-factly.

"He did consider doing that, but then he thought that a letter would be a kinder way of letting them know about Lars."

"I suppose it would be, but it seems awful that they should be all that time not knowing that their son was dead."

"Well, they'll know by now," Christina sighed. "There just might be a letter back from them. Father read in the paper that a German ship arrived in Brisbane a couple of days back."

"It's really taking him a long time to get over Lars's death, isn't it? Seven months, and he's still brooding. Like Ma says, you should really just grieve for a time and then let the dead rest in peace. They wouldn't want you to be going on about them dying."

"It's not so much Lars dying that Father's distressed about. He seems to think that Aunty Maria and Uncle Peter will be holding him responsible in some way."

"That's ridiculous. He wasn't anywhere near Lars when he had his accident."

Christina shook her head. "I don't mean for the accident itself. I mean for him being in Australia. You see, when Father decided that we would come here, Lars got it into his head that he wanted to come too, and he did, a bit later on."

"Well, he was old enough to make up his own mind, and he probably would have come in any case."

"That's what Carl says."

"He should know. After all, he was only eighteen when he came to Australia." The horse and sulky had turned in at the gate and Kathleen gave it a hurried glance before saying, "You won't forget that you promised to help me run away, will you, Christina?"

Eyes widening, Christina stared at her, not knowing whether to be amused or alarmed. "Kathleen, I didn't … "

Kathleen grinned. "Well, you asked what could you do, and I said I'd let you know."

"Oh, for heaven's sake!" Christina chose to be amused and she returned the other girl's grin. "I know you're only joking."

Simon brought the horse and sulky to a halt not far from where the two girls were standing and called to them as he jumped to the ground, "Still not done with the washing, eh? It seems to me there's been quite a deal of chit-chat taking place."

"We've just a few more things to peg out," Christina told him, her gaze flying to the letters in her mother's hand.

There were three from her grandmother, and four from her aunts. All from Haderslev, Christina thought with a small groan, and still nothing from the Ohlssens. Oh, why didn't they write?

"There's a letter from Marie," Elsie said, handing it over. "She's probably got some new plans for your visit."

"That's great, I've been expecting to hear from her." Tucking the letter inside her blouse and quickly picking up one of the few garments still to be pegged out, Christina failed to see the small, thoughtful frown that came to Kathleen's face. "You're going to Beenleigh soon, aren't you?"

"Not until next month. I'm sure I've told you about the visit."

"Yes, you have. I don't recall that you told me the exact date though."

"Oh … well, perhaps I didn't mention it. It's the eleventh, a Wednesday. Now, do let's hurry with these last things so we can go inside and hear all the news."

"I have to be getting home, Christina, it must be close to midday."

"I thought you were going to stay and eat with us?"

"I had thought to, but I've just remembered something I have to do, and, if I leave now, I should be able to get it done before milking time comes round." She smiled. "Besides, I don't want to be intruding into your letter-reading."

"You know you wouldn't be doing that, and Marie's probably got a message for you; she usually includes something to be passed on."

"I'll be seeing you at the dance on Saturday night, you can tell me then what it is."

Christina shut the gate and watched her ride off, a small puzzled frown coming to her brow. What was it that she had to do and had only just remembered? Something that she didn't want to tell her, that was obvious. Well, she told herself as she turned and made her way up to the house, it was none of her business when all was said and done. Christina had, of course, no way of knowing that it was very much her business, that the something Kathleen had to do so urgently was the writing of a letter that would spin the first threads of an involvement into which she had no wish to enter.

They were at their favourite picnic spot on the creek bank when, for the very first time Kathleen opened a letter from David Charlton in Christina's presence. The envelope was torn open and the two pages it contained tugged free with such feverish haste any pleased surprise this might have caused was swamped by swift alarm, and Christina stared incredulously as Kathleen, her breath held in what seemed to be an agony of suspense, sent her eyes racing over the bold handwriting. "Is something wrong?"

"No." The word came on a long expulsion of breath that was part laugh and part relieved sigh. "Nothing's wrong. Everything is wonderful, in fact. Just wonderful." She read on for a moment or two, then lifted her head, tossing the tumbled hair back over her shoulders, and Christina saw that her face was flushed and her eyes ablaze with excitement. "I'm going to do it, Christina! I'm going to run away from home!"

Christina gasped, her disbelief so great she was sure that she must be hearing incorrectly. "What did you say?"

Kathleen laughed, her eyes dancing beneath their long fringe of curling lashes. "Ah Christina, you know very well what I said. I'm going to run away … elope, if you like." She held up the letter in a hand that trembled. "David agrees that it's the only way, the only thing we can do."

"It isn't. It can't be. Please say that you would never do such a foolish thing."

"But I would, and I'm going to." She spun herself around, arms outflung and face uplifted to the sky. "I'm so deliriously happy I'm sure that I have only to flap my arms and I will fly away." Still spinning, she sent forth a rippling peal of laughter. "What a shock that would be for the birds. What a shock for David to have me drifting down out of the sky and into his arms."

Christina stared at her, dismayed, her mind in turmoil. Dear God, there must be something she should say to bring Kathleen to her senses, to make her see the folly in what she was planning. "Kathleen, stop carrying on like that," she said sternly. "You have to think."

"But I have, Christina. I've thunk about everything." She laughed delightedly. "Thunk … that's a good word, isn't it?"

"I think you've gone clear out of your mind." But a faint smile had come to Christina's lips and Kathleen saw it. She stopped her spinning and came to stand in front of her, taking hold of her hands. "That's better. Don't you know that you have to be happy for me? After all, you are my best and dearest friend and you know what it's like to be in love."

"I am happy that you are in love, I think that's wonderful. But I'm not happy about what you are planning to do. I can see it bringing a lot of distress and heartache. Besides, there'll be no end of difficulties. For one thing, what are you going to do about your parents' consent? You'll need that before you can be married."

Kathleen's smile faltered, but only momentarily. "Once they see that I intend to be with David, no matter what, they'll have to give it."

Christina groaned softly. "Ask them first, Kathleen, please."

"And then what? Run away after they've said no, when they'll more than likely have sent for the priest and be watching me all the while?"

"You don't know for sure that they will say no."

"Yes, I do. I've told you that ever so many times."

"I know, but if there's even the slightest chance … "

"There isn't. I just wish you'd understand that."

She turned away, gazing off into the distance, and it seemed to Christina that the slim shoulders had slumped. "I'm sorry," she murmured, tears of remorse tightening her throat. "I didn't mean to spoil your happiness. I just want you to be sure that what you are planning isn't something you'll come to regret later on."

Kathleen spun back again, her eyes fiercely alight. "I'll never do that, Christina … never … never! Even if I had only the briefest time with David, it would be something to cherish, not regret."

"Well, I suppose if you're sure it's the only way … "

"It is, believe me." She hesitated, chewing on her lower lip, then said quickly, "I can't do it without your help, Christina."

Christina started, apprehension rushing through her. "What do you mean?"

"Just what I said, I'll need your help." A small, pleading smile curled her lips. "Please don't let me down."

"I don't know how I could possibly help."

"But I know, I've got it all worked out."

"You've got all what worked out?"

"How we can do it. You're still going to Beenleigh to visit the Hunters, aren't you?"

Christina nodded. "Next Wednesday."

"Well, I could come with you, pretend that I'm visiting the Hunters too. It wouldn't be an unusual thing to be doing. After all, I have become friendly with Marie during her visits to your farm and she has said on more than one occasion that she hoped I'd be able to visit with you one day."

"I know she has, and that would have been really nice … "

But Kathleen, again bubbling over with excitement, was anxious to get on with explaining her plans. "I won't actually be going there, of course, not to the Hunters. We'll take the coach from Nerang together, but, when you leave it at Beenleigh, I'll continue on … "

"To where?"

"Brisbane, of course. David will meet me there."

"You've already arranged all that?" Christina gasped, her eyes wide with disbelief.

Kathleen lowered her lashes, momentarily contrite. "I had to do it this way, Christina. There just wouldn't have been any sense in arranging things with you, only to find that David didn't approve of what I was planning." She thrust out her hand with the letter still in it. "I've only just learned that he does approve."

"But you went so far as to tell him when to meet you?"

"I had to, there wouldn't have been time to get another letter back to him."

Trying hard not to be angry, Christina asked, "Just what did you tell him?"

"That I was going to leave home and take the coach to Brisbane if he was in agreement. If he wrote to say that he wasn't, then I wouldn't go, of course."

Exasperation mingled with Christina's dismay. "What if I'm not prepared to go along with your plan? David will have travelled all the way to Brisbane for nothing. Have you thought about that?"

Kathleen's eyes widened and fixed themselves on Christina's face with an expression that was part fearful, part pleading. "You don't mean that you won't help me?"

Christina hardened her heart against the pleading. "I could very well mean just that," she said shortly. "The whole idea is so preposterous it hardly bears thinking about."

"But it's not, Christina. It's really very simple. When all's said and done, I'm not really asking you to do such a lot."

"Only lie … to my parents, your parents, the Hunters."

"No, not the Hunters … we don't have to tell them I'm coming. Then, after the coach leaves Beenleigh, you can tell them the truth if you want to. You wouldn't be lying to my parents either … I'll be the one to tell them."

"Tell them what?"

"Well, they know that you are going over to Beenleigh for a week, so, as soon as I get home, I'll mention that you've asked me to go with you. I'm overdue for a break from the farm so they can't very well refuse."

"What happens when I come home without you? I'll be the one who has to break the news to them, I suppose?"

"No, of course not. Oh Christina, I would never put you in that situation. I'm going to have a letter already written to Ma and Da and I'll post it in Brisbane. It will have arrived by the time you get back, so they'll know everything."

Christina gave a short mirthless laugh. "And, of course, they'll continue to be friendly towards me?"

"Why shouldn't they? After all, they'll know that it was all my doing." She smiled ruefully. "Please don't be angry with me, Christina; my heart will break if you are not my friend anymore."

Christina ignored this plea, there was still too much of importance to be settled. "I'd have to tell my parents that you were running away," she declared flatly.

Kathleen was aghast. "Oh no! You can't!"

"Well, I'm certainly not going to tell them that you are coming to the Hunters with me."

"It wouldn't be such a monstrous lie, Christina, not when I will be going as far as Beenleigh with you."

Christina was adamant. "Either I tell them the truth or you look for a new plan."

Kathleen stared at her, the colour draining from her face, leaving the freckles to stand out like golden pinheads. "You don't mean that, Christina. Please say you don't."

Christina moved uneasily before the stark dismay on the other girl's face. "I could never lie to them like that. Even if I tried to do so, it would never be successful, they would know right away that I wasn't telling the truth."

"Your father would go straight to Da," Kathleen wailed, wringing her hands together.

"Perhaps, if I explained the situation, he wouldn't do that … "

"Do you think he would understand?" Faint hope struggled with disbelief in the eyes that searched Christina's.

"I don't know." But she did know. There was no way either of her parents would understand. They would both think it outrageous for a young girl to be running off to a man she hardly knew without her parents' consent to marry. Besides, why should they take it upon themselves to incur the wrath of the O'Rourkes by remaining silent?

Kathleen was watching her, the faint hope fading. "You wouldn't be able to convince your parents, would you?" The words, dully uttered, were more statement than question, but Christina shook her head. "I don't think so. Father would consider it his responsibility to go to your parents."

"Then you can't tell him, Christina. Surely you can see that. Da would kill me."

He wouldn't go that far, Christina told herself, but there would certainly be a terrible uproar. What was truly amazing though was that Kathleen's correspondence with David Charlton had remained a secret in that noisy, overflowing household, that she could be on the point of running off to him and still none of the family had become the least suspicious. "I don't understand how your parents haven't realised that something has been going on," she said quietly.

"There hasn't been anything except letters, you know that. I make sure that no one gets to see those."

"You've just been fortunate, you should have been burning them."

"Never. Haven't they been all I've had these past eighteen months or more?" Quickly bringing her emotions under control, she heaved a long deep sigh. "We don't have to be worrying about such things now,

Christina. It's your parents we have to be thinking about. You do see that we can't tell them that I'm running away, don't you?"

Christina moved her head in a reluctant nod.

"What can we do then?"

"I don't know." And then, with faint accusation, "You've thought about how to handle everything else."

"I've thought about your parents too, but I haven't been able to come up with anything that would work, except to tell them that I'm going with you to the Hunter's. Just think about how it would be. Your mother or father will be taking you over to Nerang, that much is certain. As for me, I either go to your place and go with you or one of our mob drives me. Whichever way it happens, your parents will have to believe that I am going to the Hunter's with you, unless ... " She was frowning deeply, thoughtfully. "Unless they were of the opinion that I just happened to be taking the same coach ... to Brisbane."

"I don't see what you are getting at?"

"What if I come over to your place sometime over the weekend and announce that I'm going to Brisbane for a couple of days and that I'll be taking the same coach as you are?"

"What happens when Mother or Father talks to one of your family?"

"Well, they don't really see each other all that often and I'd be hoping that by the time they did meet up Ma and Da would have had my letter. When you think about it, what I tell your parents will be true enough, I will be going to Brisbane, and, in all likelihood, I will be there for a couple of days."

Christina struggled to sort order from the confusion in her mind, to see things clearly instead of through a veil of compassion. Every reasoning instinct dictated that she should flatly refuse to have anything to do with her friend's scheming. But her heart strayed in other directions, reminding her of the warmth and joy Kathleen's friendship had brought into her life, foretelling the anguish her refusal to help would bring, recalling the ecstasy that came with being in the arms of the man one loved.

"Of course, I would have to impose upon your parents to transport me over to Nerang. Otherwise whoever takes you would get to talking to whoever takes me, and that would be the end of everything before we even got started. They wouldn't mind if I came with you, would they, Christina?"

"They certainly wouldn't mind driving you over to Nerang, but I think we are probably rushing things. I mean, it's such a new notion, and we haven't really thought it through."

"It will work, I know it will. I don't know why we didn't think of it before."

"How do you propose to get to our place?" Christina asked, her eyes on the other girl's face quietly challenging.

"Oh, I ... I ... "

"You see, there are other things to be taken into account."

Kathleen nodded, thoughtful but not unduly concerned. "I'll have to get someone to deliver me, I suppose."

"Then whoever it is would still be talking to my parents."

"Not if I get them to drop me off at the gate. It would be all right to do that on the day before, wouldn't it?"

"You know very well that you are always welcome to sleep over."

"Thank you, Christina!" She gripped Christina's hand and swung her around in a gleeful dance. "You are the best friend anyone could possibly have and I love you ever so much."

In the days that followed, Christina's nervousness conjured up a dozen or more potential obstacles, and she told herself over and over that it was a ridiculous plan with no hope of succeeding. Who was to say that her parents wouldn't meet up with one of the O'Rourkes before Wednesday even, let alone before Kathleen's letter reached them? How was she to act when Kathleen arrived and announced that she was going to Brisbane? Wouldn't letting her parents believe that be the same as lying to them? She should, she berated herself, have refused point-blank to be involved from the very outset. It could even be that, in the long run, that would prove to be the very best thing she could have done for Kathleen. Being unhappy for a time now could hardly compare with the heartbreak of being estranged from her family for the rest of her life – a distinct possibility, all things considered. But the days passed and none of the obstacles feared by Christina eventuated. It seemed, in fact, that the luck of the Irish was well and truly with Kathleen and her unwilling accomplice.

Carl called at the Skov farm on Saturday, but, in response to Christina's discreet enquiry as to whether he planned on visiting the O'Rourke's, he firmly shook his head. "Not this weekend, I don't have the time." Smiling, he ran a gentle finger over her cheek. "I wouldn't have come down at all, had you not been going away. I wanted to wish you a happy holiday."

Then, on Sunday afternoon she stood, trying to feign surprise, but speechless with trepidation, while Kathleen excitedly told her mother about her visit to Brisbane. "I'm so looking forward to it, Mrs, Skov. I haven't been to the city in such a long time."

"You're not going on your own, surely?"

"That's why I've chosen to go on Wednesday. I'll have Christina's company as far as Beenleigh."

"That will be nice for Christina too, but what about when you get to Brisbane? Do you have someone to stay with?"

"Oh yes, a good friend, someone I know from out west but haven't seen in such a long time."

"What a pleasant reunion you have to look forward to then."

Christina was hardly able to believe what she was hearing. How had she been able to do it, get it all said without really having to tell a lie? But surely her mother, who knew all about the letters from David Charlton, must suspect who that friend from out west was. But no, it seemed not, for she calmly resumed her darning, saying with a smile. "I'm really quite envious, Kathleen. It will be such a treat being able to visit the big stores."

"Yes, I'm looking forward to that. I have a little money saved so I'll be able to do some Christmas shopping."

"A good idea. Christmas is not all that far off. It will be such an advantage having a friend on hand who is familiar with the city. She'll be able to help you choose wisely."

"I didn't tell a single lie," Kathleen mused with some satisfaction as she prepared to climb on to her horse.

"But misleading someone, that's the same thing really."

"It might be, but it was really your mother who misled herself." She caught hold of Christina's hand, squeezing it impulsively. "Can't you see that it's the best thing that could have happened? I didn't have to make up a whole lot of stuff and she's not going to be worrying about what I might be doing."

"I still can't believe she didn't think about David, especially when she knows he's been writing to you."

"I can't either. As a matter of fact, I nearly died when I said 'from out west'. I was actually trying to infer from Jimbour Downs, but the minute the words were out I realised that had been a mistake."

"A very big mistake ... "

"Oh, I know, I know." She laughed suddenly, happily. "What are we doing standing here holding post-mortems when we should be giving thanks that we are safely over another hurdle?"

"I think we've just been extremely lucky so far."

"So do I. But, just think, Christina, two more days to get through and we'll be on our way."

The obstacle Christina had earmarked for Kathleen's arrival at their farm on Tuesday didn't eventuate. The only members of the O'Rourke family the Skovs saw, apart from Kathleen herself, were Joseph and Sarah, who deposited her, suitcase, basket and all, at their gate.

"Goodness!" Elsie exclaimed, frowningly watching them drive off. "You'd think they'd have at least brought her up to the house."

Christina, already at the bottom of the steps, called back over her shoulder. "They seem to be in a hurry, and Kathleen has probably told them to leave her there."

So it was done. On Wednesday morning, just twenty minutes late, the coach rolled away from Nerang with the two girls sitting primly side by side, Kathleen unable to wipe the smile from her face, Christina breathing easily for the first time in days.

Not until they reached Beenleigh, however, was she able to convince herself that Kathleen had indeed been successful in running away from home. Marie Hunter, all smiles, was waiting to greet her and they hugged each other delightedly before Marie exclaimed, "And you've brought Kathleen with you. How wonderful."

Since there was a fifteen-minute stop at Beenleigh, Kathleen had left the carriage with Christina. "I'm not staying, Marie. I'm going on to Brisbane."

"What a pity. We could have had such a good time, the three of us. But how lucky you are to be going to Brisbane, it's becoming such an exciting city. How long are you there for?"

"Just four days, but, yes, it will be exciting. Right now, though, I think I should be getting back to my seat. I don't want to lose it." She turned and held out her arms and Christina stepped into them, a wave of impending loss washing over her. Kathleen would get back on the coach and go on to Brisbane where the man she loved would be waiting for her and then spend the rest of her days far, far away. It was something she had known all along, of course, that Kathleen would be going out of her life, but there had been too many other things to worry about. It was at the very forefront now, though, causing her heart to feel like a stone in her chest.

"Don't you dare cry, Christina," Kathleen whispered close to her ear, "or you'll have me bawling too, and think what a to-do that would be."

Marie had been watching them, a small puzzled frown coming to her brow … four days? She would only be gone for four days, then why did Christina seem so distressed? Why was Kathleen so tense?. What was there about her trip to Brisbane that seemed suddenly a bit mysterious? "You stay until the coach leaves, Christina … I'll take your things and wait for you in Father's office."

They both watched the tall slim figure walk away, involuntarily delaying the moment when there would be a need to say something.

"I do appreciate your help, you know that, don't you Christina?" Kathleen finally murmured.

"I hope that you are going to be very happy, you and David."

Kathleen smiled wryly. "But you still think that I shouldn't be here?"

"Oh Kathleen, all I'm able to think right now is how much I am going to miss you."

"I'll miss you too, Christina, something awful!"

"We'll be writing to one another, won't we?"

"Of course, we'll write often." There was a sudden catch in her voice and Christina saw that a single bright tear glistened on her left cheek, realising with a start that she had never seen Kathleen cry. Her own eyes filled and overflowed, and Kathleen looked away quickly, making a pretence of watching some children playing. But, after a few moments, with the silence heavy between them, she said quietly, "I wonder if they've done it yet?"

"Done what?" Christina asked huskily.

"Hanged Ned Kelly … it's supposed to happen today."

Christina gasped, her mind flying back to snatch up a vision … a girl with the most beautiful hair she had ever seen intent on reading a notice. Oh God, she prayed, please don't let it be an omen. Just because our friendship began with Ned Kelly, don't let it end with him.

Danny O'Rourke appeared on the Hunters' doorstep on the fifth day of Christina's visit, and it took all of her will power not to cringe before the dark anger on his face. "Where is she, Christina?" he demanded.

"Kathleen's not here."

"No, and she never was, I know that. What I asked was where she is."

Christina's mind whirled. The letter Kathleen had written, had it reached the O'Rourke's so soon? Yes, it must have done, that's why Danny was here. But perhaps not, he might have found out some other way. In that case, he might not know all of it, only that Kathleen had run away from home. "I don't know," she murmured guardedly.

"Come off it." He caught her wrist roughly, holding it in a tight grasp. "I don't have time to be playing games. I want to know where my sister is, and I want to know now."

Christina had the feeling that he was about to shake her and she trembled inside. "She has gone to Brisbane," she said as steadily as she could manage, "but I don't know where she is staying. She posted a letter to your parents and that should tell you all you want to know." Then, glancing down at her imprisoned wrist, "You are hurting me."

Marie had been hovering in the hallway behind her and she asked anxiously, "Shall I fetch Father, Christina?"

For a moment Christina was tempted to let her do so, but Danny had dropped her wrist, leaving red splotches where his fingers had gripped, and he seemed to be making an effort to bring his anger under control. "No, it's alright, Marie."

"Do you know what that letter says, Christina?" he demanded furiously.

"No, I don't, except that it was to tell your family what she was doing."

"What she was doing? Leaving home to be with the man she loved and couldn't live without. That's what it said, nothing more. Nothing about who he was or where she was going. But you know who this man is and where she will be, don't you?"

He had come close to yelling at her, and Christina swallowed before finding her voice, "I've told you … I don't know where she is staying."

"You're lying, Christina."

Christina's lips tightened at the cold harshness of the words, and she muttered, "How dare you say that?"

A faint, sardonic smile flitted over the dark, handsome face. "I do dare, and, what's more, I'll say it again … you're lying. You and Kathleen planned this whole thing, so you have to know."

Christina jerked her chin up, her eyes flashing angrily. "Even if I did know, I wouldn't tell you, Danny O'Rourke." She spun around, intending to slam the door in his face, but he was too quick for her. He reached out and again took hold of her arm, swinging her back to face him. "She's run off to meet one of our fine-feathered friends, hasn't she?"

"She has run off to be with the man she loves," Christina cried, suddenly defiant. "I'm sure that in her letter she also asks her parents to forgive her and give their consent to her marriage."

Danny was staring at her, incredulously. "For the love of God, what sort of a man has she taken up with that he couldn't come to Da and ask for her hand?"

"He didn't do that because Kathleen wouldn't let him; he's not a Catholic."

"How the hell does she expect to marry him then?"

"I suppose she is hoping that your parents will come to see that the love she and David have for each other is more important than the difference in their religions."

"More important?" he exploded. "You don't know what you are talking about, miss."

Christina flinched before his renewed outburst but managed to tug her arm free. "I think you should leave."

"No, not yet." Again he moved quickly, taking a step forward so that his boot would be ready to keep the door from closing. "David, you said. what's the rest of his name?"

"You must know that I won't tell you that, Danny. In any case, you won't be finding them; they'll be quite a distance out of Brisbane by now."

Comprehension dawned and his dark, heavy-lidded eyes widened. "Those squatters, the ones you met at the regatta?"

He was so aghast and for what seemed to be such a stupid reason, Christina had a ridiculous desire to laugh. A wealthy pastoralist wished to marry his sister and here he was looking so horrified one would think she had run off to marry an Aborigine. A smile must have touched her lips, for he almost snarled, "It's nice that you can be amused."

"I was thinking of Kathleen's good fortune, if you must know. She will be living a very comfortable lifestyle."

He gave a short laugh, harsh and ridiculing. "So you think she can be comfortable, living in sin?"

Suddenly dismayed, Christina stared at him. "You wouldn't make her do that," she pleaded. "You couldn't."

"If you'd taken the time to think about it, the pair of you, you would have seen that it's the only way they can live together."

"But, once your parents give their consent … ?"

"They're not like to be doing that, believe me. Just supposing they did, where would they find a priest willing to perform the marriage?"

"A Protestant minister would marry them," Christina told him, trying to speak with conviction, but failing. How well she remembered what Kathleen, herself had said about such a marriage. It wasn't true, of course, but it was what people of the Catholic faith believed …

Danny was watching her, almost pityingly, as though, Christina thought, he thinks I'm too stupid to understand. With her anger rushing back, she accused hotly, "If you, yourself, were in love with a Protestant, it would be quite a different matter, wouldn't it?"

Suddenly white about the mouth, Danny grabbed her shoulders, shaking her and demanding harshly, "Do you really believe that, Christina? Do you? Do you?"

Realising that she had made him very angry indeed, Christina gulped before crying passionately, "Yes, I do. I do think that. You wouldn't let religion stand in your way if you loved someone."

His dark eyes bored into hers and his lips curled cynically. "Well then, answer me this … why do you suppose I've stood aside and let Carl make all the running with you?"

Christina gaped at him, incredulous, speechless. What was he saying? The words were ringing in her ears, but surely they didn't mean … No, that was just her imagination, a trick her mind was playing on her.

As abruptly as he had taken hold of her, Danny released her, almost flinging her from him in his haste to be down the steps and striding off to the gate. Slumped against the door jamb, her entire body trembling and her legs threatening to give way beneath her, Christina watched him swing on to his horse and dig in his heels, then he was gone from her sight.

"What a horrible man," Marie exclaimed, coming to stand at Christina's side. "I'm sure that if Father had been home he would have thrown him off the premises."

"He has always been moody," Christina murmured, trying to still her trembling. "And I suppose he has every right to be angry."

"He doesn't have any right to be angry with you. It's Kathleen who has run away."

"But he knows that I helped her."

"Well, like you said, what else could you do? She's your dear friend and she needed your help."

"Would you have helped her, Marie, if you had been in my place?"

A thoughtful frown creased the smooth young brow, but then she nodded her head slowly. "Yes, I think I would have done just what you did, try to talk her out of it and, when that failed, help her." She sighed. "It's all so ridiculous, you'd think Kathleen's parents would be delighted to have her make such a fine match."

A wry smile touched Christina's mouth. "That's what I keep thinking, but it seems that, for the O'Rourkes, a fine lifestyle is not nearly as important as the right religion."

"What did Danny O'Rourke say to you just before he left? It seemed to give you quite a shock."

"It wasn't anything really. I just misunderstood what he said." She forced a smile to her lips. "Shouldn't we be leaving? Your mother will be wondering where on earth we are."

"Heavens yes. She was to have finished visiting old Mrs O'Halloran at eleven o'clock and it must be past that now. She'll be thinking we've changed our minds about meeting her, and I do so want to steer her in the direction of those heavenly shoes we saw." She turned and sped along the hall. "Let's get our bonnets ... quickly, Christina."

It was true, Christina told herself as she hurriedly tied the ribbons of her bonnet under her chin, she had misunderstood. Why, it was unthinkable that Danny O'Rourke would have come courting her had she been a Catholic, completely and utterly unthinkable.

26

Anxiety, held at bay during Christina's stay at Beenleigh, travelled with her over the miles of her homewards journey, easing a little when her father greeted her cheerfully as she alighted from the coach at Nerang, but growing again when they set off in the sulky and it became clear that he was going to leave whatever recriminations there were to be to her mother.

"Your mother will be speaking to you about it, Christina," he said in response to her half-hearted attempt to bring up the subject of Kathleen's running away. "It's not something I wish to become involved with." He smiled. "Besides, I'm sure you and I have many more pleasant things to talk about. How were the Travis children? Did they still know you?"

"Yes, they did. I spent quite a bit of time with them, which was wonderful."

"And their parents?"

"They're fine. Mrs Travis arranged a musical evening to coincide with my visit. It was ever so delightful, especially since so many people I knew were there." She grinned. "And no babies chose that night to be born, so Doctor Travis was able to stay the whole time."

"It seems you have had a nice time. What about our old farm, did you get out there?"

"No, I didn't, there was so much to do, the time just disappeared. I saw Johann Schmidt though, and he said the farm is doing very well."

"Well, I suppose it would be, what with the excellent seasons we've had these past couple of years. How was Johann, is he married yet?"

"No, but he soon will be, to the daughter of the people who bought our farm."

"Good luck to him. He's a decent fellow, Johann, someone I always liked, which is more than I can say for his old man."

Christina glanced at him in surprise. "I didn't know that you disliked Mr Schmidt?"

Simon shrugged. "I don't suppose that I actually disliked him. He was a helpful neighbour and he's certainly a good, honest man. It's just that I always found him somewhat overpowering." He gave a sudden chuckle. "He called me a blasted fool when I decided to leave the Logan, did you know that?"

"To your face?" Christina gasped.

"Of course. Anything that fellow has to say about you will always be to your face, never behind your back."

"I still think it's dreadful that he should have said that."

Simon chuckled again. "Well, he probably thought anyone who left the Logan was a fool."

"Then I just wish he could see what we have now, that would teach him."

"Ah yes, we have a nice farm, to be sure. But let us not be forgetting that those good seasons haven't only visited the Logan; the weather has been extremely kind to us since we came to Mudgeeraba."

Christina nodded, but absently, and she cast a searching, sideways glance at her father's face. He seems happier than he's been in months, she thought, light-hearted almost. It wasn't just to do with her homecoming; after all, she'd only been gone for a week. No, it was something more than that. "Has everything gone well on the farm while I've been away?" she asked carefully.

"Yes, very well. Young Herbie Martin has been helping with the milking, and I've finally got around to acquiring some pigs."

"Truly … ?"

"A boar and four sows, enough to begin with, I would think."

But it's not the pigs, Christina decided, smiling inwardly at the notion that she was discarding them as the reason for her father's cheerfulness in much the same way as she had done with herself. Something else then. Dare she ask? Dare she take the chance that it was what her mind was suggesting?

She didn't need to. Simon answered the questions without its having been asked. "We've had a letter from Aunty Maria and Uncle Peter."

Christina caught her breath on a rush of thankfulness. "That's nice." Oh yes, it had to be. If it weren't, her father wouldn't be looking so content.

"It seems they have accepted the news of Lars's death very well. They're deeply grieved, of course, but they wrote that it has been a comfort to know that he died in our arms, so to speak, and not off somewhere in the midst of strangers. They are also thankful that he has been properly buried and that we are able to visit his grave regularly."

"It's wonderful that they have written like that."

Simon nodded. "Their letter has taken a load off my mind, Christina, off my heart as well. I called in at the cemetery this morning, and, for the very first time, I was able to stand at Lars's grave and feel at peace."

Christina put her hand through his arm, squeezing gently. "I'm ever so glad, and I'm sure Lars would be also."

The moment Christina had been dreading had arrived. Her father had left the house as soon as they had eaten, leaving her to sit on at the still uncleared table with her heart sinking before the sad accusation in her mother's eyes.

"I had thought never to see the day when you would act so foolishly, Christina."

"I'm sorry if I caused you distress, Mother, I didn't mean to."

Elsie raised her eyebrows. "You set out to deceive me, yet you didn't mean to cause me distress?"

"It wasn't like that," Christina protested, her eyes filling with tears. "I didn't set out to deceive you."

"Christina, you and Kathleen had me believe that she was simply going to Brisbane for a few days to visit an old friend, whereas the truth of the matter was that she was running away from home. If that's not setting out to be deceitful, then I don't know what is." She spread her hands in an impatient gesture. "I'm well aware that no lies, as such, were told, and I suppose it might be said that I allowed myself to be deceived, that I should have been more alert, less gullible. My answer to that is this … it simply never occurred to me that I need be suspicious of something my daughter and her friend, a welcome visitor in our home, were telling me."

Christina longed to cry out that she had done none of the actual telling, but, with the protest quivering on her lips, she gave a small inwards groan and bit it back. She couldn't go asking for all the blame to be heaped on Kathleen. In any case, her mother no doubt knew very well exactly what had happened. It would be the fact that she had been there, clearly approving since she had made no interjection, that made her, in her mother's eyes, every bit as guilty as Kathleen "There wasn't anything else we could do," she said miserably. "If we'd told you the truth, it would have put you in an awkward situation, and Father would probably have gone to the O'Rourke's … "

. "He most definitely would have gone to the O'Rourke's. A girl barely eighteen years of age running off to a man she hardly knows. Any responsible person aware of such a thing wouldn't hesitate to warn her parents."

"But it was all the fault of Kathleen's parents in the first place If she'd been able to talk to them, get them to understand, she wouldn't have had to run away."

This wail of protest brought Christina a sharp glance from her mother. "Get them to understand what?" she asked sternly.

"How very much in love Kathleen is."

"In love? With a man she has been with for … what? A couple of hours at the most?"

"It's true though, she is in love with David Charlton, and he's in love with her. I know that they have only been together for a couple of hours, but I think they fell in love in the very moment they first set eyes on one another. When I look back, I can picture them, just standing there staring at one another, as though they were the only two people in the whole world. Even though they've had to make do with only letters since that day, I don't think anything has changed, for either of them."

Elsie heaved a deep, regretful sigh. "Those wretched letters. I should have insisted that you were not to have them addressed to you. I think I knew in my heart that no good would come of it."

"I somehow don't think it would have made any difference to the way things have turned out. It might even be that Kathleen would have run away before this."

This time Elsie's sigh was heavy with exasperation. "Oh, that foolish, impulsive girl. Why didn't she speak to her parents?"

"She was afraid to, that's why, and she was also afraid to let David do so. She knew that telling them that she wanted to marry a non-Catholic would send her father into one of his rages. In fact, she was terrified that, if David came to ask for her hand as he wanted to do, Mr O'Rourke would use his gun or whip to drive him off the place."

Elsie's eyes had widened incredulously. "You don't believe he would have done that, surely?"

"I don't think he would have harmed him, but I think he might have threatened him."

"Mr O'Rourke wasn't raging when he came here. He was certainly very angry, but he wasn't ranting and raving, so to speak."

Christina tossed her mother a startled glance. "Mr O'Rourke came here?"

"Yes, he came to find out what was going on. Why shouldn't he, when all's said and done? There they were believing that Kathleen was with you at the Hunter's when this letter arrives … "

"He wasn't blaming you and Father, was he?"

"No, he was well aware that we had been misled just as they had been. As a matter of fact, before he left, he apologised."

"He apologised? Christina gasped, "What for?"

"His daughter involving us in her escapade. What he said was perfectly true, Kathleen had no right to involve us, or you either, Christina."

"She needed someone to help her, and I'm her friend."

"Friends are not for using in such a way."

"She was desperate, and she did try to arrange everything so that I wouldn't be held to blame."

"She might well have tried to do that, but, if she'd given the matter any real thought, she would have seen that at least some of the blame would fall on you. After all, it was your support that made the whole thing possible."

"That's what the O'Rourkes think?"

"What else can they think?"

"Well, what did they expect me to do?" Christina cried, her voice both tearful and bitter. "Just turn my back and leave Kathleen with her chance at happiness turned to ashes."

Elsie sighed, her eyes softening. "I appreciate the situation you have been in, Christina, and perhaps, given a little time, Kathleen's family will come to do so as well, but the fact remains that you have allowed yourself to become involved in something that has caused a great deal of distress and is likely to cause even more."

"How do you mean, even more?"

"Well, what's to become of Kathleen? You've both been thinking that she's running away to happiness, and that's all there is to it. But what happiness will there be for her if she can't marry David, if her parents won't give their consent?"

"But they have to. Kathleen is counting on them doing so."

Elsie shook her head in disbelief. "After running away from home, she's counting on them to give their consent to her marriage?"

Christina tried to explain, but it was something she hadn't quite understood herself. "She thought they might relent once they saw that nothing was going to keep her from being with David." Her voice trailed away and she stared unhappily at her mother. "You don't think they will give their consent?"

"I'm sorry, but I'm afraid I don't, and there's something else, what about David Charlton's family? How are they going to react?"

"They would never object to having Kathleen in the family."

"She'll hardly be in the family if she isn't able to marry David, but, that aside, they may very well object. Some Protestant families are no more anxious to take Catholics into their fold than Catholic families are to take Protestants into theirs."

Something tugged at Christina's mind, and not for the first time. Previously, though, it had seemed of little significance, hardly worth considering. Not this time ... this time it brought with it a strange uneasiness and she wondered how she could ever have dismissed it so lightly. Four letters from Mrs Klaussen since the regatta and in not a single one had there been mention of Kathleen. And this despite the fact that she was often mentioned in her own letters. Did that mean that Mrs Klaussen knew that her grandson was in love with her and disapproved, perhaps for the very reason her mother had just mentioned?. Swallowing against the sudden tightening of her throat, she cried, "If it was like that, it would be wrong, not something God would be wanting."

"No, I don't believe He would," Elsie agreed gently. "But it's something we human beings brought on ourselves when we elected to let the importance of being a Christian become overshadowed by the supposed importance of being a particular religion and now, I'm afraid, we simply have to live with the consequences."

"Oh, how silly it all is, and how sad. People who are in love should be able to marry no matter what religion they are, and with the blessing of their families."

Elsie smiled faintly. "It could well be that Kathleen and David will have the blessing of his family. I only mentioned the possibility that they might object to show you that Kathleen may be confronted with difficulties she hasn't bargained on."

Christina groaned softly. "I do so hope they accept her. I think it would break her heart if they didn't."

Elsie rose from her chair with a resigned shrug of her shoulders. "All you can do now, Christina, is pray for her happiness."

"Yes, I will." Misty-eyed, she looked up at her mother. "And I'll pray that you might forgive me for deceiving you."

For a moment or two Elsie remained intent on gathering up the cutlery. Then she said quietly, a little huskily, "There's no call for you to be doing that, Christina."

It seemed to Christina that Saturday took an age to come round and that, when it finally did arrive, its hours had been weighted down with anchors, so slowly did they pass. But, at long last, with the shadows grown to their full length and the sun about to slip behind the ranges, the horse and rider appeared on the road and she was running, her skirt flying about her ankles, down to the gate. She almost fell into Carl's arms, crying tearfully, "I didn't want her to go, not like that."

He held her from him, his eyes tenderly teasing. "Hey, what's all this? Tears when I haven't seen you in two long weeks."

Christina's eyes flew upwards, searching his face. Didn't he know, for heaven's sake? Was she herself going to have to be the one to tell him? It certainly seemed so, for such unconcern could only mean that he was quite unaware that Kathleen had run away. "Don't you know what has happened?" she asked in a small, husky whisper.

"Don't I know that Kathleen has run off to that dashing young squatter she met at the regatta, is that what you mean?"

He was grinning and Christina couldn't believe it. More than a little exasperated, she tried to pull herself free of his arms, and when he wrapped them more tightly around her, beat her fists against his chest, wailing, "It's not something to be laughing about. It's been horrible, just horrible. There's so much to worry about I don't think I'll ever … "

She didn't finish what she'd been about to say. Carl's mouth had claimed hers, shutting off the words, and, when the long deep kiss came to an end, there was no way she could have said, as she had been going to, that she didn't think she would ever be happy again. They had to talk about Kathleen running away from home though, and it had to be now, before they went up to the house. Once there, it would be a couple of hours before she again had Carl to herself. He had taken hold of her hand and already begun to walk up the track, leading Samson. "Now tell me, how was your holiday with Marie?"

"It was very nice, I had a lovely time." Then quickly, lest he ask a whole sting of questions that could wait, "Do you think I'm to blame for Kathleen running away?"

Carl's fingers squeezed hers. "Now why on earth would I think that? It wasn't your idea, was it?"

"No, of course not."

"Well then … ?"

"The O'Rourke's think it's my fault as much as Kathleen's."

Carl shrugged. "I'm sure they're not all blaming you. In any case, you have to remember that they are, for the most part, a somewhat hot-headed bunch. Give them time to cool down a bit and you'll find that they come round to seeing things in their proper light."

"If only Mr and Mrs O'Rourke would see that it was really their own fault that Kathleen ran away. Why, she couldn't even talk to them about David."

"Well, the O'Rourke's are devout Roman Catholics, Christina, and I'm sure Kathleen has always known just what that meant when it came to choosing a husband."

"But she didn't set out to choose a husband. She fell in love."

"I know … I know. But the fact remains that she could have had no illusions whatsoever as to what the attitude of her parents would be. She must have known that their consent to her marriage to a non-Catholic wouldn't be forthcoming."

Christina glanced up at him with renewed despair. "Then you don't think they'll give their consent?"

"No, I don't."

"Even though they must now realise that Kathleen intends to be with David, no matter what?"

"I'm afraid that Kathleen will have to wait until she comes of age to marry her David."

"But that won't be for years. Whatever will she do in the meantime?"

"That's something Kathleen will have to work out for herself, Christina." He lifted her hand, brushing his lips lightly over her curled fingers. "And, since there's nothing we can do to help her, I think you should stop worrying about it."

Christina groaned softly. "I wish I could, but how can I? It's not only that my dear friend is in this unhappy situation … it's that, in a way, I am responsible."

"That's rubbish," Carl told her sternly. "You helped make it possible for Kathleen to run away, that's true enough, I suppose. But you didn't suggest that she do so and I take it you didn't encourage her in any way. You were, in fact, simply responding to a plea for help from a very close friend. Besides, had you not helped her, she would still have gone, the very minute she thought up some other scheme. You must know

Kathleen well enough to know that?"

"I suppose she would have found some way."

Carl grinned. "Of course she would have, nothing would have stopped that young lady once she'd taken it into her head to run off. Now, let me see a smile on that beautiful face of yours. How am I going to enjoy myself at the dance if you insist on looking so glum?"

Christina's head jerked up. "There's a dance, tonight?"

"I thought you would have known, it's four weeks since the last one."

"Four weeks?" Christina repeated vaguely, her mind at once full of dismaying visions. "Yes, I suppose it is, I just hadn't realised. I don't think I want to go dancing tonight, Carl."

"It's just what you need, sweetheart, something to cheer you up."

Christina waved to her parents with a smile on her face, but it was gone the minute the sulky rolled off down the track. It was a beautiful summer evening, warm, but with a gentle breeze drifting across from the ocean, the sky star-studded, a near-full moon just beginning its climb into the sky, but Christina's mind was too full of anxious thoughts for her to be able to appreciate such things. There would almost certainly be some of the O'Rourkes at the dance; what would they do when they saw her? Simply ignore her? Or come right out and accuse her in front of everybody? Whatever they did, it would be terrible and she would be sure to burst into tears, and, if Danny happened to be there ... Christina's heart lurched at the very thought, and she squeezed her eyes shut to try to shut the image of his dark, furious face from her mind.

"Hmmm, that is a grim face," Carl said, laughing softly. "Dare I ask what thoughts lie behind it?"

For a moment or two Christina didn't answer, then she murmured unhappily. "I don't really want to go to the dance."

The smile left Carl's face. "It's going to be alright, love, I promise you."

"Will Danny be there?"

"He said he might be."

"He came to see me at Beenleigh, you know?"

Carl nodded. "Yes, he told me that he went to ask if you knew where Kathleen was staying in Brisbane."

"But I didn't know."

"So he said."

I suppose he just happened to forget to tell you how angry he was, or how rude, Christina thought with a sudden flash of resentment. And he certainly wouldn't have told you what else he said, those strange furious words that had been so unbelievable. She smothered a small sigh. She wouldn't be wanting Carl to know that, in any case, or how Danny had behaved; the two of them were such good friends, she would never forgive herself if she was the cause of a rift between them.

"You've no call to be worrying about Danny, Christina. He rants and carries on from time to time, but, underneath, he's not nearly as hard as people are inclined to think."

"That may be so," Christina murmured doubtfully, "but I still don't have any wish to be meeting up with him, not just yet. I know that it sounds cowardly of me but you said yourself that they needed time to cool down."

Carl looked down into her troubled eyes, his own grown thoughtful. "I'm sure the O'Rourkes at the dance would be decent to you, Christina, but, if it's going to be stressful for you, perhaps … "

Christina gave him a small, wistful smile. "I'd really rather not go."

"Well, if you feel so strongly about it … " He slowed the horse to a walk. "What would you like to do then? Go back home?"

"No, not yet." She looked about her, no longer oblivious to the moonlight spilling over the land, the stars scattered like diamonds across the dark velvet of the sky. "It's such a beautiful night. Couldn't we just go for a drive somewhere?"

"Of course, that's a fine idea. Where do you suggest?"

"We've just passed the turn-off to your place, could we go along that road?"

"It will be okay for the sulky for a short distance so why not? The bellbirds will all be sleeping, but you can sing to me."

"I don't have to, do I?"

"No, but I'd like you to."

"After a while then, when we get to where the bellbirds would be."

They drove along the bumpy road for a mile or so, then bounced off into a section of open forest, where thick summer grasses made for slightly more comfortable progress. The trees, though, made for more intricate progress and they were obliged to weave in and out, in moonlight one minute, in shadow the next, at almost every turn disturbing one or more of the local inhabitants. A startled owl staggered so clumsily from a branch a few feet above their heads it seemed that it was about to tumble into the sulky with them. A koala, about to move from one tree to another, abruptly changed its mind and hurriedly climbed back up the tree it had just climbed down. A family of grazing wallabies looked up in surprise before scattering in all directions, but a large kangaroo wasn't in such a hurry to be off; he waited until they were almost upon him before hopping lazily out of their path.

"He thought he had the right of way." Carl laughed.

"It could be just that he didn't quite believe his eyes. After all, there wouldn't be too many sulkies come through here."

"No, there would not." Carl brought the horse to a halt. "And I think this is as far as this one goes.""

They were in a small glade, around which the trees had closed ranks, the only way out being the way they had come in. "It's very nice here," Christina mused, looking around her. "No wonder the big roo was reluctant to leave."

Carl jumped to the ground and held up his arms to lift her down. "It must be just about time for the first dance. May I have the pleasure, Miss Skov?"

"Why, of course, Mr Eichstead."

"I'm afraid, dear lady, that you will have to help with the music."

"Naturally ... "

They danced a waltz, in a fashion that certainly wouldn't have pleased Mr Strauss any more than would their la-la-la-ing of his Blue Danube; because the grass allowed for no sliding of their shoes, their only alternative was to adopt long, hopping steps. Still, round and round they went, laughing, humming, becoming breathless, until, finally, Carl staggered back against a tree trunk, pulling Christina with him. "If you don't mind, Miss Skov, I think perhaps we should rest for a while."

"I quite agree, Mr Eichstead. That was the most exhausting waltz I have ever danced." Laughing softly, Christina twisted around in his arms so that she could lean back against him, her head resting in the curve of his shoulder. Gradually, she regained her breath, then promptly lost it again when she glanced up sideways and saw how young and handsome he looked, with his fair hair tousled about and his lips parted in a wide smile. A mingling of tenderness and gentle yearning touched her heart and, unable to help herself, she reached back over her shoulder to touch his face with her fingertips, letting them trace, ever so lightly, the outline of his mouth, feeling the smile disappear, hearing, in the next instant, the quick intake of breath. Then his hands were on her shoulders and he was turning her around to face him. "I think we should leave, Christina."

But Christina, with only a vague understanding of the agonised struggle taking place within him, quickly shook her head. "On no. Not just yet. We've hardly been here any time at all." Feeling that precious moments were slipping through her fingers, she swayed towards him, but Carl's hands dropped quickly from her shoulders to her waist, holding her in such a way her body barely touched his. "It's best that we go," he said quietly.

Disappointed, Christina nodded. "Of course, if that's what you want."

"What I want? Oh my God, Christina!" He choked over the words, losing them in a soft groan as he crushed her slight form against his lean hardness. With his mouth claiming hers in a way different from any other time, Christina's eyes flew open and a faint anxiety trembled through her; for the space of a heartbeat only, then it was smothered in an urgent seeking, lost in an equally urgent responding.

Was it really only soft grass beneath her body? No, it was a cloud, a wondrous rose-coloured cloud that lifted her up out of the glade to where it seemed she could touch the stars. For one bewildered moment, when work-roughened hands first touched those most private parts of her person, she was afraid to let the cloud enfold her, but her trembling body was not about to be denied. It paid no heed whatsoever to the warning that buzzed faintly in her head and it quickly overlooked the sharp pain that brought a soft gasp to her lips. Of its own accord, it reached out, responding, clinging, revelling, rejoicing, until the cloud soared so high her whole being exploded in wave after wave of ecstasy.

Afterwards, with the embarrassment of replacing certain articles of her clothing over and done with, Christina stood quietly within Carl's arms, while he pressed his lips to her forehead. "I love you, Christina. I love you with all my heart and I would be very pleased if you would marry me."

Christina stiffened, her heart skipping a beat. Marry him? But he didn't mean right away, surely? Oh no, he couldn't mean that. He'd said two years, in two years' time. Forcing her lips into a smile, she looked up into his face. "You don't mean right away?"

A small, rueful smile touched Carl's mouth. "I don't mean this exact moment, but just as soon as things can be arranged."

"But you're not ready to take a wife yet, you've said so on more than one occasion?"

"I know. I had planned on getting myself into a better situation first, more land, the house completed."

"Well, there's no need for you to change your plans just because … "

"Yes, there is. I didn't intend things to happen as they did, but now that they have … well, I don't think we should wait."

"But we must wait. You've planned everything ever so wisely and I'm not going to be the one to spoil that. It could even be that I would be stopping you from realising your dreams, and, if that happened, I would never be able to forgive myself." She spoke quickly, nervously, and, within her, a small voice cried, Don't let him insist. Please don't let him insist … I was to have had two years.

Carl had taken hold of her upper arms and he was shaking her gently. "Don't you see? You could have a baby, Christina."

"No! Oh no!"

At once he gathered her back into his arms, rocking her soothingly to and fro, his lips against her hair. "It's alright, darling, it's alright. It may not happen, and, if we are married, it won't matter in the least if it does."

Christina buried her face against his chest, her mind racing. May not happen … may not … may not? Oh, it couldn't. Not from just this one time, it wouldn't be fair. Only sometimes, Kathleen had said, only sometimes did a baby begin when a man and woman did such things. But which times were they? How was she to know? Why hadn't she listened more carefully when Kathleen had tried to explain? Paid attention instead of becoming flustered and deliberately changing the subject? Why, it could even be that this had been one of those special times, that the seed which would begin a baby was already nestling inside her?

"Are you listening to me, Christina?"

Christina nodded, her mind striving to recall what it was he had been saying. Something about speaking to her father right away, about there being no point in waiting until she knew. She caught her breath in a small gasp. That was it, she would know. Of course she would, and she wouldn't have to wait all that long either, just until it was that time of the month again. "We could at least wait until I know," she said quickly. "When you come to think of it, that would be the sensible thing to do."

Carl held her from him, her eyes searching her face, a deep furrow between his brows. "Don't you want to marry me, Christina?"

Christina's heart lurched and dismay washed through her. Dear God in heaven, that was the last thing she wanted him to be thinking. Even if it happened that it was never to be, she wouldn't want him thinking that she didn't love him enough to marry him. Smiling gently, she slipped her arms around him. "Of course I want to marry you. I just think it would be better to wait as you've always planned."

"It wouldn't take much to finish the house, perhaps even add a verandah … "

"The house is fine. So long as you were living in it with me, I'd be perfectly happy … " Her voice trailed away as a thought leapt to the forefront of her mind; the excuse she needed was right there, begging to be used. "I would mind about you being away, though."

Carl heaved a deep sigh. "I would have to be away, Christina. As things are at present, I couldn't support myself, let alone a wife as well, if I didn't do outside work."

"I know, it's just that I'd be terrified up there in the mountains on my own."

"I can understand that, the isolation takes some getting used to, even for a man." He frowned suddenly, thoughtfully. "What if we were to get married and you stayed on with your parents for a time? I'm sure they'd appreciate still having your help on the farm."

"But that wouldn't really be like being married, and, in a way, it could spoil things, having such a start. I think it would be much better if we waited until we can begin married life in our own home."

"Of course it would, but we may not be able to wait that long."

Christina nodded her head slowly. "If we can't, then we'll just have to work something out, but I don't think we have to be making decisions right now; we could well be rushing for no reason at all."

"Well," Carl agreed, more than a little reluctantly, "I don't suppose a couple of weeks is going to make all that much difference."

Because her emotions were in conflict, Christina's mind was also in a continuous state of confusion. Guilt had found a niche and lodged itself securely, a two-fold guilt. The first part, sprung from her response to Carl's proposal, had come with her out of the glade and was, in a way, the hardest to bear; sometimes, it seemed that it actually lashed her with accusation, causing hot, bitter tears to fill her eyes. If only he hadn't asked her to marry him. If only he had waited and let her have those two years. It wouldn't have been that she was actually taking anything from him and surely she had a right to borrow two years of happiness. Now, though, everything had changed. He was under the impression that, sooner or later, she would become his wife, and why wouldn't he be, when she had as good as told him so?

The second part of Christina's guilt had to do with what they had done and it had been slightly more tardy in arriving. Not until she removed her clothes to prepare for bed had it caught up with her, nevertheless doing so with drama enough: the sight of blood on her draws and petticoat bringing a horrified gasp to her lips and setting her whole body shaking. What they'd done was wrong, something that should never have happened. Probably wouldn't have either, she accused herself, if she hadn't protested when Carl had wanted to leave the glade. They would have come home and he would have kissed her goodnight, perhaps in a thorough fashion, but then he would have held her from him. In spite of her distress, the ghost of a wry smile came to Christina's lips. At least she didn't have to wonder any more why he always did that.

Regret, however, had no firm hold on her feelings. Sometimes, encouraged by her guilt, it settled for a time, but, for the most part, it was kept hovering by memories of such joy and rapture as she had never believed possible. They lulled her to sleep at night; they greeted her in her first moments of waking, causing her to squirm luxuriously in her bed; and, more often than not, they caused her body to ache with such yearning, it seemed she couldn't wait for what had happened to be repeated. Such an admission, of course, always brought a quick self-reprimand; it wasn't to happen again, they wouldn't let it.

Worry came and went, with Christina refusing to allow it a permanent foothold. In her bedroom, she would undress where she could see her body from the neck down in the mirror hanging on the wall and run her hands over her smooth, flat belly, wondering whether there should be something to tell her what was happening inside, any signs that she should be looking for. There was certainly nothing that she could see, her body seemed to be exactly as it had been before. Surely, she reasoned with herself, there would be some change if there was a baby growing inside her, if not in the way she looked, then certainly in the way she felt. Yes, of course she would know, one way or the other, it was quite unthinkable that she wouldn't. So it was that worry was allowed only brief intrusions and the monstrous fear lurking only a breath away deliberately ignored.

Worry had, in any case, been groundless, as Christina discovered at the end of the first week in December.

But other feelings, other emotions, were not about to release their hold on the course of her life so easily. They continued to confuse and to be in conflict and, worst of all, they betrayed. The guilt chose to sleep when it should have been widely awake. The rapture had taken to recalling itself and did so constantly; the yearning in her body flared into fierce desire, laughing at her attempts to convince herself that she would be content just to be held. Resolve crumbled ...

With the crushing season at the Tweed over, Carl was home, working tirelessly on his own place. Finishing off the house, Christina suspected, pushing aside any guilt she might have felt by telling herself that it would be nice for him to have a completed house to live in. In any case, it seemed that he now understood how she felt about marrying him at this time. He had asked her again, of course, twice. But that, she told herself, was probably just because he felt obliged to do so. It certainly wouldn't have been because he was anxious to rush into marriage ... no, he needed those two years every bit as much as she did.

But the euphoria into which Christina had allowed herself to drift was to be short-lived. The time for evasions and excuses came to an end on New Year's Day; the day of resolutions, she would later recall with more than a little bitterness. She met Carl at the gate and would have run into his arms, but he took hold of her shoulders, his face grim, and said very sternly, "I have something to say to you, Christina, and I will be obliged if you will pay attention."

The smile died on Christina's face and, within her chest, her heart took up a slow thumping, the beat that belongs with apprehension. She felt a sudden urge to tug herself free, to run away so that she wouldn't have to listen to what he was so clearly anxious to have said. Not that she didn't already know what it would be: after last night, it was inevitable that he would want to talk of marriage again. But this time it was going to be different from those other times, she knew that with a sickening certainty. Why else would his face he so set and determined? Why else was he making sure that she didn't snuggle into his arms?

"We must get married." The words came bluntly, and he went on quickly, giving her no opportunity to interrupt. "We can't wait, Christina, surely you can see that. In spite of all the resolutions I make, it seems I have no willpower where you are concerned. I love you so much, the minute I take you in my arms, I am lost."

Feeling her mouth go dry, Christina ran the tip of her tongue over her lips. Oh, what was she to say to him … ?

Carl gave her no chance to say anything. "And you … " he said with a strange intensity, "you want me to make love to you, I know you do." His hands had slipped down her arms and, when Christina would have spun away from him, they gripped her wrists. "It's no use, Christina, you can't hide something like that, your need is as great as mine."

Hot colour had rushed to Christina's face and she quickly lowered her lashes, mumbling, "That's an ungentlemanly thing to say."

Carl gave a short, mirthless laugh. "It may well be, but it's the truth, nonetheless, and you know it. Don't get me wrong, I'm not objecting. Far from it. I think it's wonderful that we should … well, both feel the same way. What I can't understand is why, when such is the case, you don't want to marry me."

"You know that isn't so."

"No, I don't know that isn't so. Not anymore. In fact, it seems to me that you are very happy to be finding excuses." There was bewildered anger in his eyes and his fingers tightened about Christina's wrists. "Tell me, do you love me?"

Christina gasped, staring up at him in disbelief. How could he possibly ask such a question after all that had happened between them? What sort of a girl did he think she was, for heaven's sake? One of those … those … Resentful tears burned the backs of her eyes. Oh, how dare he?

"Do you, Christina. do you?" he demanded, his eyes, dark and piercing, boring into hers.

"You shouldn't need to ask me that." Christina cried bitterly.

Carl groaned and, just for a moment, it seemed that he was about to release her wrists and take her into his arms. Instead, he said bleakly, "You are quite right, I shouldn't."

"It was an insult."

"Oh Christina, don't be silly. You know very well I was only trying to get you to confirm what I know in my heart."

Christina's eyes softened and she said quietly, "I do love you, Carl, I love you with all of my heart."

A faint smile came to Carl's eyes and to his mouth, but still he didn't draw her close. "All right then, we get married."

"Not just yet. You must have a chance to make something of your place just as you've always wanted to do, without the hindrance of a wife."

"I don't believe that I have ever said that a wife would be a hindrance," he said flatly, the smile gone. "My reasons for wanting to put off getting married have been that I felt I didn't have sufficient to offer a wife, that it would be asking too much to expect a woman to live up on my farm with things the way they were."

"A wife would be a hindrance nevertheless. You'd have to change your plans and then it would take ever so much longer for you to realise your dreams."

Abruptly, he released her wrists and, half-turning, gazed back at the mountains. "It may not. I have been thinking about that, about what I could do. It's still going to be a year or so before I can apply for the homestead land, but there's nothing to stop me from doing a bit of clearing and running some cattle there." He pushed his lips into a small wry smile. "Be a kind of squatter until such time as the land becomes mine officially."

Christina swallowed, feeling that walls were closing in around her. No, she begged silently, don't make me decide now. Let me have those two years to think about what I must do. "But you'd still have to be away for a lot of the time."

"Not quite so much, I've been thinking. The cane cutting brings good money and I'd still want to be doing some of that. But there are other jobs closer to home … "

"No, not yet!" Christina cried, dismayed that her chief excuse was on the point of disappearing. "I don't want to get married just yet!"

Carl stared at her. "Why? Why don't you?"

"I don't think I'm ready for marriage."

"What do you mean, you're not ready for marriage?"

"I'm still not eighteen years old."

"Christina," Carl said very quietly and very evenly, "if you are ready to make love, you are ready for marriage, it's as simple as that."

"I think I should be the one to decide whether or not I am ready."

"That's what you believe, that you are not ready?"

Christina wilted before his incredulous gaze, but managed to say, "That's what I feel."

Carl considered her for what seemed a long time before saying resignedly, "Well, Christina, it grieves me to have to say this, but if we are not to be married, we have to stop seeing each other, alone, that is."

"No ... no ... " Though the words were screaming in her head, they emerged as just a whisper.

"It's the only way. What we have been doing is wrong, and, sooner or later, we are going to find ourselves in an unhappy situation, one way or the other."

Christina swallowed the lump in her throat. "We won't do it anymore."

Carl gave a short, harsh laugh. "I've been telling myself that ever since that first time."

"But, if we both ... ?"

"It won't work, Christina."

Christina's heart sank. Dear God, what was she to do? If she let him go, what was left for her? Heartbreak and a sense of loss that would almost certainly stay with her for the rest of her life. If she agreed to marry him, she would at least have happiness for a time and surely no one would begrudge her that. Or would they? If there were no children, wasn't it possible that Carl would begin to feel that she had cheated him? Perhaps even come to hate her for having done so? So, what would she have? At most, a couple of years of love and happiness, to be paid for by how many of resentment and despair? And what of herself? She didn't have her mother's courage, she would die if she had to bury one baby after another.

"Won't I see you at all?" she asked bleakly, lowering her eyes so that she wouldn't see the angry misery in his.

"We live in the same general district, Christina, so we'll certainly be seeing each other occasionally. We just won't be spending time alone together." He was watching her intently, a puzzled frown on his forehead, as though he was trying to read what was going on in her mind. Then he burst out, "Oh, for God's sake, Christina, think what you are doing!"

"I think that what I am doing is best for both of us. It's too soon for us to be married."

Carl groaned and threw up his hands in an exasperated gesture before exploding angrily, "I'm damned if I can understand you, but, if that's the way you want it..."

He wheeled on his heel but at once stopped and stood still ... within reach of her hand were she to hold it out. But Christina stood still too, her hands clenched so tightly into fists the nails bit into her palms. Let him go, she told herself. Let him have the two years to build for his dream. Let him use them also to look for a wife who will know that she can give him strong healthy children. Only when he had swung on to his horse and ridden off did the tears slip in great droplets on to her cheeks.

27

Christina ticked off the dates she had written on a scrap of paper, for the third time. There was no mistake, five weeks had gone by since her last period, not just four as she had been hoping. Five full weeks. But hadn't she been late before? Of course she had. She was almost always a couple of days over and there had been at least two other occasions when she had gone a full week past her time. Christina could find little consolation in such assurances. Other times there might have been, but they had been before she'd known the boundless pleasure of lying in Carl's arms. The five weeks quickly became six, and then seven. Every morning she considered her naked body in the mirror. Flat … flat … yes, her stomach was flat still. But, when she moved closer to the mirror, she saw fear in the pale face staring back at her. Her body might look the same, but it didn't feel the same. There was a strange tingling in her breasts, a soreness when she pressed with her fingertips, and there had now been three mornings when a feeling of nausea had sent her scurrying outside, sure that she was about to vomit.

On one of those mornings her mother had looked at her searchingly as she toyed with her breakfast. "Are you not feeling well, Christina?"

"Yes, I'm quite well, Mother. It's just this heat making me feel a little listless. I don't think it has ever been quite as bad as this."

"You could be right, but then I say something like that every summer. There's no need for you to come to Nerang with me if you don't feel up to it."

"But I want to go with you, and I'm quite all right really."

"Well, it's up to you, of course." She smiled. "I must say that I'm glad you are no longer trying to avoid the O'Rourke family."

Christina returned the smile, but wryly. Avoid the O'Rourke's? How could she have gone on trying to do that, when it seemed that her only chance of seeing Carl was out on the road or over at Nerang. What she hoped to gain by seeing him she had no clear idea. She knew only that there was a great emptiness in her life and that she ached to see him, even if it was only to say hello. She hadn't seen him though, not even once since New Year's Day. She had, however, seen at least some of the O'Rourke's: Patrick and Joseph who had both greeted her cheerfully enough when she'd run into them outside Lenneberg's Store, and Danny who, one day, had overtaken their sulky on the road and bid her a curt goodmorning before exchanging a few words about the weather with her father.

For a time a faint hope stayed with Christina, perhaps it was just that she was going to miss out on a period. It was something that Kathleen had once told her, that, if you were sick or under a lot of stress, something like that could happen. But it gradually faded until she was forced to accept that at some time, probably towards the end of winter, she would give birth to a baby. With that acceptance a great lassitude had taken hold of her. She told herself that she should think about what she was to do, that she should tell her mother for one thing. But she didn't seem to be able to think with any clarity, and she couldn't bring herself to tell her mother, not yet. So she simply drifted along, doing her chores, talking, smiling, occasionally laughing.

Her mother and father saw the shadow in her eyes and heard the brittle ring to her laughter, but they put it down to the fact that she'd had a misunderstanding with Carl, probably a lovers' tiff that would soon resolve itself. Christina, having been obliged to explain Carl's abrupt departure on New Year's Day, had told them that they had decided not to see so much of each other for a time, since Carl wanted to improve his farm before thinking about marriage and she wanted to wait until she was a little older. There was more to it than that, Elsie and Simon told themselves and each other, but it was best not to interfere.

Towards the end of March, Christina received a second letter from Kathleen. The first, written in Brisbane, had been little more than a scribbled note saying that she'd arrived there safely, that David had been waiting for her and that they were both deliriously happy at finally being together again. This letter was much longer …

My dearest Christina,

I am really sorry to have taken so long to write this letter, but I kept hoping that I would have good news for you. No such luck. Ma and Da refuse even to answer my letters. I don't suppose they even read them. Oh Christina, I have become so unhappy I sometimes cry all night. I know David loves me every bit as much as I love him, but here we are, with me sleeping in one bedroom and him in another, and that's the way it's going to be until I come of age if Ma and Da go on refusing to give their consent for me to marry. More than two years – it doesn't bear thinking about.

It's not my idea to be sleeping apart, I can tell you that. In fact, I've even gone so far as to hint to David that he should come to my room after everyone is asleep. But he won't do that. He's just like his parents and grandmother – very proper about everything.

His family are very nice to me, by the way, even though they didn't seem too pleased when David brought me here. For one thing, I don't think they liked the idea of me being a Catholic. What a laugh that is, don't you think? Anyhow, they seem to have become used to the idea that David is determined to marry me and they seem anxious to get the wedding over and done with. I suppose they think it's a bit of a scandal for me to be living here, even if I don't sleep with David.

'Taldoon' is a very fine property. The main house is massive and very elegant, with beautiful carpets and furniture. They also have crystal and silver like you'd never believe, and they really do use it even though they are way out here, miles from anywhere. There are servants, of course, and, do you know, dinner is not the meal you have in the middle of the day – it's the one you have in the evening. I think it's going to take me forever to get used to that. One thing I'm really pleased about, though, is that David insisted on buying me some nice clothes when we were in Brisbane.

There's a dear little church right here on the station and that's where David and I will be married, if he doesn't get tired of waiting for me and find someone else. Oh Christina, however could you and Carl wait for two years when there's really no need for you to do so? Mrs Klaussen talks about you a lot, and she has asked about Carl too. It seems that she took an instant *liking to him, but then who doesn't? Actually, I think she would have been delighted had it been you that David fell in love with. How terrible that would have been for my dear, sweet lamb with you already head-over-heels in love with Carl. Now, don't go trying to deny it – you were, even then.*

I think a lot about what you did for me, dear Christina, and I've come to realise just what sort of a situation I've put you in. I do so hope my family haven't taken it out on you. In my letters I have begged them not to be holding you to blame in any way whatsoever, but, if they haven't been reading them, a fat lot of use that would have been

I miss you something awful. Sometimes, when David is miles away chasing up sheep or inspecting fences, I pass the hours just thinking about the wonderful times we had together. I still burst out laughing whenever I think about Carl seeing us that time we went swimming in our birthday suits. Do you still blush when you think about it? Just kidding.

Please write soon, and I will write straight back, I promise.

Love you.

Your friend forever, Kathleen.

The fragile shell in which Christina had enclosed her heart shattered and, dropping the letter on to the table, she put her hands over her face and wept. At once, her mother's arm was about her shoulders. "Oh, my dear, what is it? What has happened?"

Shaking her head, unable to speak, Christina handed over the letter. Her whole being, it seemed, was awash with sorrow: for Kathleen, for herself, for what they had lost. We had so much joy, she cried silently, so much love in our hearts, so much laughter on our lips.

Now there was such unhappiness, such shadows on their lives, it seemed those days were in another age, not just a few short months ago. There was no going back though, for either of them. No way to undo what they had done. Kathleen would have to go on enduring the dilemma she was in: the uncertainty and the estrangement from her family, the fear that she might lose the man she loved. Just as she herself would have to go on enduring heartbreak and despair: the man she loved already lost; the shame that would come when her condition became obvious and there was no wedding ring on her finger. Somehow, Christina mused bleakly, there was a thread of irony running through the tangle of their unhappiness ... Kathleen despairing at the thought of waiting for two years, whereas that was just what she herself had wanted to do.

"It's not something to be so distressed about, Christina," Elsie murmured as she finished reading. "Obviously, Kathleen's not very happy at the moment, but David's family seem to have accepted her, and that's something. When you come to think of it, she must have known all along that her parents would react just as they have done. She and David are going to have to wait to be married, but that's not such a disaster. They are both young, and, if they truly love one another, they should be quite prepared to do that." She rested a gentle hand on Christina's bowed head. "Love is very rarely a simple, straightforward matter, Christina, you should remember that. In fact, it quite often brings as much pain as it does joy." She hesitated, then went on carefully, "I hope that you and Carl haven't quarrelled because he wants to wait two years before being married?"

Christina had choked off her sobs. She'd had to, her mother was saying something that made her want to laugh. "What did you say?"

"I said that I hoped you and Carl hadn't quarrelled just because he wanted to delay marriage for a couple of years. He's a very sensible young man, you must know that. Anything he does will be with your welfare in mind. Besides, two years is not so very long."

For the first time in her life, Christina found herself overcome with hysterical laughter, and it went on and on, echoing in her ears, setting her head to spinning, hurting her throat. Oh, but it was funny, what her mother had said ... terribly, terribly funny.

"Christina, stop that! Stop it this instant!"

But it took a long while to stop, even with her mother shaking her so hard her teeth rattled. It wasn't that she didn't want to stop. It was just that the laughter seemed to have a mind of its own and it kept welling up from inside her. Finally, though, everything was very quiet, even her sobbing no more than a small, muffled sound coming from deep down in her chest. "I'm sorry, Mother."

"You don't have to be sorry, love. You've been under a lot of stress in recent months, what with Kathleen running away from home, then whatever it was that happened between you and Carl. It's not at all surprising that you've become so tense."

Now, Christina thought, I should tell her now. She felt a strange, indefinable sense of relief; her mother would know what to do and then some of the load would be lifted from her shoulders. But her mother had left the kitchen to go to her bedroom and when she came back she had a damp cloth in her hand and the semblance of a smile on her lips. "Wash your face, it will make you feel better. Then perhaps you'd like to tell me how it was that Carl saw you and Kathleen swimming in your birthday suits?"

Christina gasped and was glad to be able to hide her face in the cloth. It was in Kathleen's letter, and she had handed the letter over to her mother without giving it a single thought. And that wasn't the only thing Kathleen had intended only for her eyes. Oh, what had she been thinking of, for heaven's sake?

"You're not going to stay behind that face-cloth for the rest of the day, I hope?"

There was gentle teasing in her mother's voice and Christina lowered her hands. "I am so embarrassed about what happened, and, if I tell you, I think you will be most displeased with me."

"It can't be as bad as all that, surely, but, if you prefer not to tell me … "

"No, I mean it's not that I don't want to." She gave her mother a small, rueful smile. "It was the spring before last … you might remember since it was the very first time Kathleen and I rode over to Little Nerang Creek."

Elsie nodded. "I do recall when that was. I remember being a little concerned that you were going so far."

"Well, we left our horses and we were going to walk as far as the waterfall, but we came to a place where the creek had a nice sandy bottom and wasn't at all deep … "

"And you decided to take a bathe?"

"Yes, the day was quite warm and the water looked so inviting, but we couldn't very well go in with our clothes on."

"Of course not."

Christina tossed her mother a sharp glance and was surprised to see the corners of her lips twitch. Oh, surely she wasn't amused. "You don't think it was terrible what we did?"

"It's not something I'd like to think you were going to make a practice of, but I'm sure you had a most pleasant bathe. What I am waiting to hear, however, is how Carl came to be there ... quite by accident, I take it?"

"We had no idea he was anywhere near that part of the creek, and, of course, he didn't know we were going to be there either. He was on his way over to Nerang when he stopped for a swim up by the falls, then his horse wandered off and he came down along the creek bank looking for him."

"Goodness! Still, I'm sure Carl would have done the gentlemanly thing and hurried away."

"Yes, he did, we didn't even see him. He came back later, when we were dressed, and spoke to us."

"It should be a lesson to you, nevertheless. It could have been anyone happening along there, and it may not have ... "

Christina's eyes had filled with fresh tears and she turned her head away, but not before her mother had seen them. "It's not something to be getting yourself distressed about."

"It's not that, Mother. It's just that talking about that day has made me recall how happy Kathleen and I were, and I know we won't ever again have times like that."

"Not quite like that, perhaps," Elsie said gently. "But there will be many other happy times for both you and Kathleen. And who knows? It could well be that some of them will be shared, that you won't always be so far apart. Why, you've hardly begun your lives."

Christina smothered a deep sigh. Hardly begun, was that really the way it was? With so much already belonging in the past? What of the empty years still to come – the empty years, empty days and empty hours? They weren't likely to be slipping away as quickly as those that had been joy-filled had done. Not worth the clinging to, they would take their time about passing. "I remember when we were coming out on the ship," she mused tearfully, "Mrs Klaussen said that there were moments in our lives that we want to hold on to, but that they are the ones that go by most quickly of all. I think there's something else as well … sometimes we just don't realise how lucky we are to have those special moments, not when they are actually happening, that is."

"That is no doubt true, Christina, and I suppose it's especially true when we are young. But, when all's said and done, I don't know that we should be wanting to hold back time; well, certainly not just to cling to happy moments. Why, the happiness we know on one day might very well be surpassed on the next."

Christina nodded, but very slowly. "I suppose so."

For a few moments, Elsie's eyes, shadowed with concern, studied her daughter's pale face, then she said quietly, "I want you to promise me something, Christina. It's that you won't be worrying yourself sick about Kathleen. There's nothing you can do to help her in her present predicament, so just be thankful that at least she's with the man she loves and that his family have accepted her."

Tell her now, the small voice inside Christina whispered, tell her … tell her. "Mother … " But the words wouldn't come, they stuck in her throat. It was all too hard to explain, especially her reason for not marrying Carl. How could she possibly tell her mother that she was afraid she wouldn't be able to give him the sons he needed? Wouldn't that be much the same as accusing her of having failed her husband?

Elsie waited a moment or two, then smiled, "If you're concerned about something else in Kathleen's letter she wouldn't have wanted me to read, there's no need to be."

So the days slipped by with no sharing of Christina's frightening secret. Following the outburst of tears and hysterical laughter some of her lassitude had slipped away, and she was surprised to find that, in spite of her worry and heartache, she was feeling quite well. There were no further bouts of nausea, the dark circles disappeared from beneath her eyes and her face was no longer pale and drawn. Only occasionally now, did she study her naked body in her bedroom mirror. The changes were there, and she knew them all too well: her breasts were fuller, with the nipples more pronounced and darker in colour; her waist had thickened, obliging her to shift the buttons on the waistbands of her skirts a full two inches. Inside of her body, too, things were happening; sometimes, when she lay very still, she could feel the faintest movement. Little more than the flutter of a butterfly's wings, but she knew what it was … the baby had begun to make its presence felt.

Christina wasn't sure just when the notion that she should go to see Mrs O'Rourke occurred to her. It seemed that it had been there, niggling away at her mind, for some time before she allowed herself to pay it any attention. She did this the evening she sat down to write to Kathleen and, even though her heart beat faster at the mere prospect, she came quickly to the conclusion that it was something she had to do. "I thought I might go to see Mrs O'Rourke," she said quietly and more than a little nervously.

"There's no call for you to be doing that, Christina," her mother told her.

"I thought if I just talked to her … "

"It will do no good, you must know that. Hasn't Kathleen brought you enough trouble already, without involving you further?"

"She wouldn't be involving me, Mother. I'm sure it has never ever occurred to her that I should go. It's just something I feel that I should do."

"Well, you have no need to feel that way. It's for Kathleen and her parents to solve their problems."

"It's not that I think I can solve their problems. I'm just hoping that I can start Mrs O'Rourke into thinking differently."

At the end of the table, with the Courier spread before him, Simon coughed to clear his throat. "Just how would you be hoping to accomplish that, Christina?"

"I don't know, Father. I will just have to wait and see. Even if I can persuade her to write to Kathleen it will be something."

"It won't, if she's not prepared to give her consent and simply writes reprimanding the girl. That, I would expect, would result in an even greater rift."

"But, if she was going to do that, she could have done so already. She hasn't, Kathleen hasn't had a reply to any of her letters. Perhaps she will think about giving her consent."

"For goodness sake, Christina!" With an exasperated sigh, Elsie slowly shook her head, "I thought you had come to accept that the O'Rourke's are not going to give their consent. Why go over there and leave yourself open to their resentment, as it were? You have no idea how Kathleen's mother might react."

Christina bit her lip before saying quietly, "I would still like to go, for my own sake, as well as Kathleen's. Mrs O'Rourke has always been very kind to me."

Again Simon cleared his throat. "Why don't you think about it for a while, love?"

"I have thought about it, Father, and it's something I really think I should do, have a quiet talk with Mrs O'Rourke."

"How do you expect to be able to do that?" Elsie asked, a little impatiently. "How will you know that Kathleen's father won't be there and fly off into one of his rages?"

"He's out of the house most of the time, and I know, for a fact, that he's rarely home on Saturday."

Simon raised his eyebrows. "Where does he go on Saturday?"

"He goes to play two-up with the bullockies."

"Good heavens!" Simon chuckled. "Does he really do that?"

Christina nodded. "Yes, he does."

"What a thing for a man with a family to be doing." Elsie was not about to share her husband's amusement. "I should think he'd have any amount of other things to do on Saturday."

Christina, anxious to have the question of her visit to the O'Rourke's settled, said quietly, "I think he considers it his reward for a week of hard work, and it would be the best day for me to go to their place ... if you and father think it would be all right, that is..."

She saw the frown on her mother's face deepen and, for a moment, was sure that she was going to say that it most definitely wasn't all right. But she said, "Well, I can't say that I approve and I certainly can't see that you will be able to accomplish anything, but, if you've set your heart on going, then I suppose the sooner it's done the better."

Christina rode nervously up to the O'Rourke home. Her mouth felt dry, her palms damp, and her heart was simply racing. Nevertheless, she kept her back straight and her chin up, telling herself that it was important to at least look a little confident. She kept her eyes fixed straight ahead, even when she saw first Mickey and then Hughie come out of the barn and stand staring at her. A flicker of wry amusement crossed her face. A few months back they wouldn't have been standing there gaping like that, they would have been waving their arms above their heads and yelling to attract her attention. Responding to a sudden tug of devilment, she turned her head and waved to them. They both waved back, then dropped their arms and looked at one another, as though not sure that they should have done so or how it had come about they had. The hint of a smile caught the corners of Christina's mouth. Poor boys, they were probably flabbergasted enough to see her come riding up without having her wave to them as though it was the most natural thing in the world to be doing.

She glanced at the small house the O'Rourke's had built for Joseph and Sarah, and saw Sarah standing in the doorway, her little girl at her knees, her swollen body telling all too clearly that there would soon be another baby. She waved the minute she saw Christina look in her direction, and Christina waved back, the warmth of affection softening her eyes. There would be no resentment in Sarah, she was much too kind and gentle. On a sudden impulse, she turned her horse and headed for the little house. She came to a halt at the fence enclosing a tiny flower garden, but didn't dismount. "Hello, Sarah, it's nice to see you again."

The smile on the other girl's face was warm and genuine. "It's nice to see you too, Christina." She took the little girl by the hand and came over to the fence.

"Goodness, hasn't little Mary grown?"

"She's sixteen months old now," Sarah patted her protruding belly. "In a few weeks, there'll be another one, as you can see."

Christina nodded. ""That's nice for you and Joseph."

"Yes, we are both pleased about it. Will you come in for a cup of tea, Christina?"

"I would like to, Sarah, but I'm on my way to see Mrs O'Rourke." She smiled briefly, "Mrs O'Rourke senior, that is."

"I'm glad you've decided to come and see her."

"You don't think that she'll be annoyed?"

"No, I'm sure she won't. Ma has ways been very fond of you, Christina."

"Is she on her own?"

Sarah nodded. "She should be. I know Da's not there, he rode off right after milking. Joseph and Patrick have taken a load of potatoes over to Nerang, and Eileen has gone to spend the day with Maureen. Maureen is going to have a baby too, did you know?"

"No, I didn't know."

"In August, and it will be … " She broke off, a concerned frown coming to her brow. "Are you feeling alright, Christina?"

"Yes … yes, of course." Christina pushed her lips into a smile. "I should think Arthur will be very pleased about that."

"Oh, he is, you'd think he was the first man ever to father a child." The frown was still there and her eyes searched Christina's face anxiously. "You have become quite pale. Are you sure you won't come in for a while?"

The smile felt stiff but Christina was able to keep it on her lips. "I'm perfectly all right, Sarah. And I'll come and have a cup of tea with you another time."

"You just be sure you do that. Now, where were we? Which of our tribe have I not yet accounted for?"

"I know that the twins are in the barn."

"Good, that's where they are supposed to be. So, that just leaves Danny, and he hasn't been home at all these past three weeks. He's got some work over Tambourine way." She gave a small laugh. "But of course you know that, since Carl is with him."

Christina swallowed, her mind toying with the idea that it would be simpler to let Sarah go on thinking that she did know, but then she said quietly, "No, I didn't know, I haven't seen Carl in quite some time."

"Oh Christina, I am sorry, I had no idea." She sighed heavily. "I hope it hasn't been all this business with Kathleen that has come between you two."

"No, that has nothing to do with it." She glanced across at the main house. "I had best go on over."

Sarah nodded. "Ma has probably seen you here, and she'll be wondering what's going on."

"That's what I was thinking. I wouldn't want her to be getting the idea that I'm here at your invitation or anything like that, for your sake, I mean."

"That wouldn't bother me in the least. As a matter of fact, I think the whole affair is just too exasperating for words."

Bridget O'Rourke was waiting at the kitchen door, as plump, flushed and dishevelled as ever, but not as jovial, Christina was quick to note, and there was a wariness in her eyes.

"I hope you don't mind that I've come to see you, Mrs O'Rourke."

"Of course I don't mind, Christina. Come on in and we'll have ourselves a cup of tea. I've got some scones just ready to come out of the oven."

"Mmmm, I can smell them, and a cup of tea would be very nice."

For a time, while they ate hot scones, dripping with butter and strawberry jam and drank their tea, conversation moved along easily enough: the weather; the huge bunch of bananas strung up and ripening by the back door; the expected grandchildren; little Mary. But the lull came and Christina moved uneasily on her chair, her mind casting about for a way in which to bring up Kathleen's name. Finally, she decided that there was nothing for it but to get straight to the point. "I miss Kathleen terribly and I thought we might talk about her."

Kathleen's mother heaved a great sigh and gave Christina a look that said all too clearly that she had been expecting her to say just that, that she'd had no illusions whatsoever as to the reason for this visit. "We don't talk about Kathleen in this house," she said flatly.

"But she's your daughter." Christina was aghast and her cry of protest emerged much more sharply than she had intended.

"She was our daughter. Now she has chosen not to be."

"You don't mean that?" Christina pleaded in a voice that was little more than a horrified whisper. "You can't."

"Tis the way it be, Christina, and there be no point at all in going on about it."

The set, unrelenting expression on Bridget O'Rourke's face caused Christina to catch her breath, but she went on doggedly, "Kathleen is very unhappy … "

"And doesn't she deserve to be. Running away from home to live in sin the way she's doing?"

"But she's not living in sin. She and David have separate rooms in the Charlton home and that's the way it's going to stay until they can be properly married."

"How do you know that?"

"Because Kathleen said so, in the letter she wrote me."

"Isn't that something she would be saying?" Bridget sniffed.

"I believe her. I also believe that, like she says, she sometimes cries the night away because of the way things are." Christina kept her eyes on the older woman's face, anxious not to miss even the smallest flicker of understanding or compassion. There was nothing to miss; in fact, it seemed that there wasn't even interest. Dear God in heaven, she groaned inwardly, had she really come here with hope alive within her? Had she really expected that this woman would be overcome with love and pity when she heard how unhappy her daughter was?

"She didn't once talk to Da or me about this man. Why didn't she come and tell us if she thought she was in love with him?"

Christina stared at her with a mixture of pity and anger. Didn't she honestly know why? Of course she did. She couldn't help but know. "She was afraid to talk to you," she said, not bothering to keep the accusation from her voice. "She even stopped David from coming to ask for her hand because she was afraid of what would happen."

Bridget drew a deep breath and a furrow appeared between her brows. Nevertheless, she threw out her hands as though the very idea deserved nothing more than to be flung aside. "What rubbish that be."

"No, it's not rubbish, it's true. Kathleen knew that her father would be very angry that she should dare to want to marry someone who wasn't a Catholic and she was also under the impression that you would have had the priest come to admonish her."

"What would have been wrong with that, might I ask? Kathleen is a wilful, inconsiderate girl, and she deserved a good talking-to."

"It would have served no purpose. Kathleen is very much in love with David and she would never have given him up."

"She hardly knows the man." Bridget waved her hands about in an impatient gesture. "One meeting with him and she thinks she's in love for all the days of her life."

"It sometimes happens like that, Mrs O'Rourke, and I know it did for Kathleen and David. I saw them fall in love in the very moment of first meeting, it happened right before my eyes, it were."

"I don't believe that love happens like that, Christina, not real, lasting love. That needs time to grow. I knew Mr O'Rourke from the time I was a toddler, and, when I did come to understand that I was in love with him, I couldn't, for the life of me, have said when that had actually come about. 'Tis like I said, love just grows between a man and a woman."

Christina gave her a small smile. "You and Mr O'Rourke were very lucky to have had so much time in which to fall in love."

Bridget blinked suspiciously. "I'm not saying that it's necessary to have all that time," she said a little tersely. "What I'm saying is that a couple of hours is not enough, not nearly enough. Oh, I know now that Kathleen had been writing to this David." She eyed Christina shrewdly but quickly held up a hand when she would have spoken. "I'm not about to question you about that, Christina, 'tis enough that you've seen fit to become involved in the other business."

"I'm sorry for my part in any distress you have been caused," Christina murmured, moving uneasily on her chair.

"Being sorry is not going to help matters, but don't be thinking that I don't understand the situation you would have been in, what with the two of you being such close friends. In any case, 'tis quite senseless to be blaming you. Once Kathleen had made up her mind to run off, she would have done so, whether you'd helped her or not." Bridget's eyes searched Christina's face and she pursed her lips thoughtfully. "I'm thinking that you've taken to blaming yourself, feeling responsible for Kathleen's unhappiness, as it were?"

Christina sighed. "It's only natural for me to feel distressed when she's so unhappy."

"Kathleen has only herself to blame for her unhappiness, so you can rest your mind in that regard."

"Mrs O'Rourke, have you read her letters?"

The soft, full lips set in a straight line. "What use would there be in doing that? We read the one she sent just after she left, that's all."

"But don't you want to know what's happening to her, to your daughter?"

"'Tis for our consent to her marriage that she writes, Christina, and you be knowing that very well."

Christina groaned softly. "Can't you give it?"

"Of course we can't!"

"Because the Pope says that she can't marry a Protestant," Christina burst out, startling herself with the sharpness of her words. Then, lest she lose the sudden flash of courage, she went on quickly, "I can't understand why that should be. Why would the Pope want to stop two people in love from being married? What reason could he possibly have? I'm sure it's not something God would have told him to do. He would never be so cruel as to keep two people who wanted to be married apart just because they happened to worship Him in different religions. It wouldn't make the least bit of sense, and the Pope should know that..."

She faltered, suddenly overcome with dismay that she was being too outspoken about something about which she knew very little. What did she know about the Pope and the way he ruled over his church, when all was said and done? For all she knew, he could have a whole book filled with reasons why Catholics couldn't marry Protestants.

Bridget's face had become tight with irritation. "The Pope is never wrong in what he decrees, Christina, you would do well to remember that. 'Tis because the Holy Spirit protects him from making mistakes.

So, if His Holiness says that Catholics are not to marry out of the church, then you may be sure that's what God wants."

"But why? Why would God want that when it can bring about such unhappiness?"

"God doesn't have to give reasons and neither does the Pope, and belonging to the Holy Mother Church means obeying its laws, not questioning them. 'Tis something we Catholics know from the time we are old enough to understand and 'tis certainly something Kathleen has always known."

Christina smothered a deep sigh. What was the use? Kathleen's heart might break, yet her mother would still insist that the laws of the church be obeyed. "Kathleen can marry David when she turns twenty-one," she suggested quietly, knowing full well what the response would be.

"No priest would perform such a marriage."

"A Protestant minister would, and in a church. What's more, it would be perfectly legal in the eyes of the law."

"It still wouldn't be a true marriage in the eyes of God."

"I believe that it would be," Christina said carefully. "If it wouldn't be in the eyes of your church, then it seems to me that Catholics must hold God to be hard and uncaring."

"That's an evil thing to be saying."

Although her heart was beating rapidly, Christina said resolutely, "I'm sorry that you think so, Mrs O'Rourke, but I think you should know this: David Charlton's family were no more pleased that he had chosen a Catholic to fall in love with than you were that Kathleen had chosen a Protestant. Nevertheless, they have accepted that it has happened and that he should be able to marry Kathleen. In fact, they are anxious for him to do so, and, believe me, that family won't be considering that it's not a true marriage in the eyes of God. To them it will be, no matter what church it's performed in, or by whom, priest or minister, and Kathleen will not only become David's wife, she will also become their daughter, someone to love and cherish, which will be your loss." She got to her feet. "I should think that you will want me to leave now."

On Bridget's face startled surprise had merged quickly into confusion and, for a moment or two, she stared at Christina speechlessly. Then she waved a hand at the vacated chair. "No, sit down for a bit."

Christina returned to the chair slowly and uncertainly, feeling sure that any faint hope she may have had of getting the O'Rourke's to consent to their daughter's marriage was now well and truly gone.

"Why would the Charlton family have felt that way? There aren't any such laws in the Protestant church about marriage to Catholics, are there?"

"Not that I know of?"

"Why then?"

Christina shook her head. "I don't understand that any more than I understand the way you feel."

"It's different for us."

"Only because your church has seen fit to make laws on the subject, I would think."

"Ah, Christina, you simply don't understand the way it is."

"Perhaps not, but I never will believe that God would want such divisions between Christian religions that a man belonging to one cannot marry a woman belonging to another in a true church ceremony."

"God wouldn't have wanted division in the first place," Bridget replied flatly and pointedly. Then, giving Christina no chance to respond, she asked abruptly, "Are you with child, Christina?"

Christina felt no surprise. Mrs O'Rourke had been eyeing her speculatively for some moments now … ever since she had stood up, intending to leave. Biting down on her lip, she nodded almost imperceptibly.

Bridget's eyes softened and she said gently, "Well, 'tis a fine thing to be carrying the child of the man you love."

The softly spoken words were the key, they unlocked emotions Christina had kept tightly stored away. Tears welled into her eyes and, as they spilled on to her cheeks, she bent her head and wept disconsolately.

"Now then, 'tis naught to be breaking your heart over, lass, not when your man be wanting to marry you."

Christina shook her head, a sob catching in her throat.

Bridget leaned over and patted her shoulder. "Of course he'll be wanting to marry you. Carl Eichstead loves you, everyone knows that. And you love him, don't you?"

"Yes, of course."

"Then there's naught to be fretting about. That little one you are carrying won't be the first, nor the last, short-term baby to be born hereabouts."

"But I can't marry him."

"Sweet Mother of Jesus, why not?"

Christina had to swallow back her sobs before she could answer. "He'll be wanting children, sons to help him on the farm and to follow on after him."

The alarm left Bridget's face as quickly as it had come and she gave a deep chuckle. "Of course he will! Haven't you gotten yourself off to a grand start?"

But Christina's sobs were again coming so thick and fast she choked over them, unable to speak. Bridget brought her a glass of water, her cheerfulness plunged into sudden anxiety. "What is it, Christina? What on earth are you so distressed about?"

"The baby ... it might die."

The older woman's face was at once stricken. "Don't say such a thing, child," she admonished sternly. "Don't even think it. 'Tis tempting the evil ones you'll be doing."

But Christina had no thought to spare for the evil ones. There were others that crowded her mind and now she needed desperately to give them voice. "My mother's babies died," she cried hoarsely. "Three of them just after they were born and little Anna on the ship when she was only a year old."

Bridget's kindly face crumpled and for a moment or two she was at a loss for words. Then she cleared her throat and murmured incredulously. "Four babies? Your poor mother has lost four babies?"

Christina nodded.

Bridget gave a long deep sigh. "That's very sad, Christina, and 'tis no wonder you be worrying about your own baby, but there be no reason at all why it should be that way for you. Look at me now; eight children I gave birth to and every one of them alive and healthy. Yet my own dear, sainted mother lost five babies at birth or in their first year." Five out of sixteen, Bridget added to herself, which wasn't at all bad for Ireland at the time, but there's no call to be mentioning that. "So you see, just because our mothers lose babies, it doesn't necessarily follow that we will do the same when our turn comes."

"I've tried to tell myself that," Christina managed to tell her between sobs. "But I always see those little graves in my mind … it's as though they come there as a sort of warning."

"No, that wouldn't be so," Bridget protested, resolutely pushing aside her own dread of omens. "'Tis because you think about those graves, they don't just come into your mind of their own accord. That be something that has to stop; thinking about them only upsets you; let them stay in the past where they belong."

Christina wiped her flushed, tear-streaked face with her handkerchief and tried to bring her weeping under control. "I'm so ashamed to be carrying on like this."

"There's naught to be ashamed of. You've had a worrying, unhappy time, and a good cry will do no harm at all." She peered at Christina closely. "Would I be right in supposing that you haven't told anyone about the wee one?"

Christina nodded, blinking to hold back a fresh flood of tears.

"Why is that, might I be asking?"

"I've been wanting to tell my mother, but I couldn't bring myself to do so; she'll be so distressed and disappointed in me. And it was hard to explain why I felt I couldn't marry Carl; it would have been like saying it was her fault because she hadn't been able to give my father the sons he needed."

"Yes, I can understand how difficult that would have been, but surely you could have told Carl?"

"I haven't seen him, not since New Year's Day, and I didn't know about the baby then. He wanted us to be married right away, but I thought we should wait for a time. He'd always said that he needed two years before he would be in a position to take a wife … " Fresh tears slipped on to her cheeks in spite of her efforts to hold them back. "I didn't think that he should change his mind just because … just because … "

"He was right to change his mind, I be thinking."

"But I wanted those two years," Christina cried tearfully. "I needed them."

A puzzled frown creased Bridget's brow. "What do you mean, you needed them? Did you feel that you weren't ready to be living up there in the mountains, with Carl off doing outside work a good deal of the time?"

"No, it wasn't that. I wanted those two years to think about whether I would be doing the right thing by marrying Carl, the right thing for him, I mean. I know it would have been unfair letting him believe that I would be marrying him when I wasn't at all sure that it would be so. But it would have been much more unfair to marry him and then not be able to give him the children he needed."

"Carl Eichstead loves you for yourself, Christina, not for the children you'll be giving him. And you will be, believe me." She patted her ample bosom. "I feel it right here in me heart."

Christina wanted desperately to believe what Kathleen's mother was telling her, to let the faint hope stirring within her have its way, yet she hardly dared do so. Was it just possible that she was right? she wondered. Shouldn't she, when all was said and done, know about such things? After all, she had given birth to eight children and lost not a single one, whereas her own mother had lost five. But the fear that had touched Christina's life for years was not about to be put to flight so easily. Held at bay it might be right now, with Mrs O'Rourke's soft, round face alight with smiling confidence. But for how long? Until she rode out through the gate? Perhaps not even that long. Besides, she was wrong about the little graves. It was of its own accord that the vision came and always so stealthily she was powerless to push it from her mind. In any case, just supposing that somehow the faint hope was allowed to grow, wasn't it too late for her and Carl? He had walked away from her, hurt, angry and bewildered and she had let him go, when all she had needed to do was reach out her hand. All those weeks ago, weeks in which she had seen nothing of him, heard nothing from him. She sighed quietly as Bridget's voice interrupted the unhappy memory …

"New Year's Day! You said you've not seen Carl since New Year's Day?"

Christina nodded.

"Then you are further along than I would have thought. You must tell him as soon as possible, Christina."

"How can I do that?" Christina moaned softly. "He was so angry … "

"He was angry because you wouldn't agree to marry him in spite of what had been happening between you. Now that you'll be ready to become his wife he'll have no reason to be angry. On the contrary, he will be as pleased as Punch."

"You don't think he will have changed his mind about wanting to marry me?"

"Of course he won't have changed his mind. Like I said, he loves you. In any case, you have no choice but to tell him." Her eyes narrowed. "Don't tell me you've been thinking to let the baby be born and you with no ring on your finger?"

"I haven't really let myself think about that," Christina murmured bleakly. That, she thought, was near enough to being the truth. The birth of the baby was something too terrifying to contemplate and, besides, it wasn't going to happen until sometime in August, as far as she'd been able to establish. In the meantime, there had been other things of more immediate concern: how to tell her mother being not the least of them; the unhappiness her condition would bring to both her parents another; the swelling of her body and worry as to how soon everyone would know still another. And, always, there was the ache in her heart and the feeling of desolation that made coherent thought about anything, especially the future, well-nigh impossible.

Bridget had been thinking, not very calmly, about what must be done, frowning deeply and glancing about the big kitchen as though she half-expected to find answers lurking in one of the corners. Now, in a voice that brooked no argument, she said, "Carl must come home right away. I will send one of the boys over to Tambourine to fetch him."

Christina gave a quick gasp of dismay. "Couldn't I wait until he comes home?"

"Indeed you cannot. He and Danny might be back next weekend. On the other hand, they could well decide to stay up there until they finish the job. No, we send for him, that's what we do."

"But … what will whoever you send say to him?"

"That he should come home right away because you need to talk to him urgently."

Groaning inwardly, Christina covered her face with her hands, trying to picture Carl's face as it would be when he received such a message. He would certainly have every right to be annoyed that she expected him to drop everything and come running back to her? Or would he be alarmed that something had happened to her, perhaps even guess what it was?

Bridget was still frowning thoughtfully. "On the other hand, it might be best if you wrote him a letter, explaining everything."

Christina dropped her hands from her face, her startled glance flying to the other woman's face. "Oh no! I can't do that!"

"Of course you can, and you must, love. Besides, won't it be easier putting it all in a letter? Not that I think you've any cause to be worrying one way or the other, mind." Getting to her feet, she began rummaging in a drawer of the tall dresser. "I know I have a pad and envelopes in here somewhere. Ah, here they are." She handed the objects of her search over to Christina, then carelessly thrust back into the drawer the armful of odds and ends she'd been obliged to remove: candles, bits of string, a recipe book, a small hammer, some newspaper cuttings. "Now where did I see that pencil?"

All too soon, it seemed to Christina, the pencil had been located and was in her hand. She drew a deep breath and forced herself to concentrate on what she must write … Dear Carl, please come home, I am going to have a baby. No, that was much too blunt. But then, where was the sense in beating about the bush?

"Tis best that I leave you until you've got it done. I'll just busy myself with a bit of cleaning up."

"I don't know how to tell him."

"As simply as possible, I should think."

"I suppose so."

But a good half-hour had passed and three pages lay crumpled on the table before Christina finally signed her name to what she had written …

Dear Carl,

I am sorry to have to write to you like this, but it seems there is nothing else I can do. I am going to have a baby and I would be very relieved to be able to talk to you about what we should do.

Yours sincerely, Christina.

She looked up as Mrs. O'Rourke rejoined her at the table. "Would you like to hear what I have written?"

"No, lass. That's between yourself and Carl. Just put it in the envelope and write his name on it. I'll get one of the twins on his way as soon as he's had a bite to eat."

Giving her a faint smile, Christina got to her feet. "You have been very kind, and I am most grateful for your help. Now I really must be leaving, I have taken up enough of your time."

"I wasn't all that busy and I've been glad to have you visit."

"I'm glad that I came." Settling her bonnet on her head, Christina stole a searching glance at the other woman's face. It seemed pensive and the wide brow was puckered. Was she thinking about what had brought about the visit? she wondered. After all, it was Kathleen's problem that should be the first concern of her mother, not hers. Recalling the note on which that particular conversation had ended, Christina smothered a sigh. She probably hadn't accomplished anything on Kathleen's behalf, but at least she had done her best.

"This family Kathleen's with, they're squatters, aren't they?"

"They are called that, but they are sheep farmers really."

"A good, honest family?"

"I would certainly think so. I only know the grandmother really, but she's a very fine lady."

"Hmmm, and you think she wouldn't mind having a Catholic, an Irish Catholic at that, in her family?"

"I had a letter from her only recently and she wrote that Kathleen was a beautiful girl and that it was clear to all the family that she and David were very much in love." And that, Christina added to herself, was really something, since it was the very first time Mrs Klaussen had made mention of Kathleen in her letters.

"Would she accept a marriage between Kathleen and David as being a true marriage?"

"Oh yes, I'm sure she would."

Bridget's eyes narrowed. "And what would she think about her grandson changing his religion?"

The faint hope that had caused her breath to catch disappeared, and Christina found herself wondering how she could possibly be expected to answer such a question "I don't know," she said quietly, "But I would think that she wouldn't be too pleased, and I don't suppose his parents would be either."

"No, I don't expect so." She waited while Christina tied the ribbons of her bonnet and stepped out on to the small back porch. "You be sure to tell your mother now, and right away."

"I will."

"I expect to be seeing you again real soon, come to tell me your good news. I'm not promising anything, mind, but I'll talk to Mr O'Rourke about Kathleen."

Christina rode home with her thoughts darting about in an erratic fashion … first in one direction, then in another. And what a confusion of emotions they brought. The faintest whisper of elation that perhaps, after all, her visit had done something to help Kathleen. What Mrs. O'Rourke had said was certainly nothing greatly promising, but it was perhaps a move towards a change of heart. There was relief that at last her secret had been shared and, at one and the same time, regret that someone else should know before her own mother and Carl. When she thought about telling her mother, dread loomed darkly, refusing to be thrust aside and insisting that she see in advance the dismay and profound sadness that would come to her eyes. She was glad that Carl would finally know, though, even though she was more than a little apprehensive as to what his reaction would be. Overriding all else, however, there was a wild, irrational joy, she would see him again. Of that she was quite sure. Angry he might be, but he would come to her, just as soon as he was able to.

Her mother was sitting on the verandah, busily knitting. Christina waved to her as she rode up the track, but felt her mouth go dry. By the time she'd unsaddled and freed the horse, her heart seemed to be thumping against her ribcage.

Elsie smiled as she came on to the verandah. "Well, did your visit accomplish anything worthwhile?"

Christina swallowed, not sure whether to be relieved or otherwise that the words being rehearsed in her mind were being obliged to wait. "Mrs O'Rourke is going to talk to her husband about Kathleen, and I suppose that is something, even though she did say that she wasn't promising anything."

Elsie raised her eyebrows. "I must say that's more than I expected. I thought she would simply refuse to discuss Kathleen."

"She started out that way. She said quite bluntly that they no longer talked about Kathleen in that house, but I think that, in her heart, she really wanted to talk about her, not that she was very sympathetic about the situation Kathleen is in."

"Did she blame you in any way?"

"No, not really. She said that Kathleen would probably have run off whether I'd helped her or not."

"Well, I'm glad she's come to her senses in that respect."

For a few moments Christina let her gaze wander over the green pastures to where a heavily-laden bullock-team was making its slow, ponderous way along the road. Then she turned resolutely back to her mother. "There's something I have to tell you, Mother ... I'm going to have a baby."

"Oh no!" It was a cry of astonished disbelief.

Christina felt a surge of anguish rush to her heart. "I'm ever so sorry," she murmured bleakly, tearfully.

Elsie stared at her, dropping her gaze from her pale face to her waist.

"When?"

"Sometime in August, I think."

"Dear God in heaven! Why have you waited so long to tell me?"

Christina groaned softly, tears blinding her. "I wanted to tell you, but I just couldn't. I knew how distressed you'd be, how disappointed in me."

Elsie threw out her hands in an agitated fashion, sending the ball of wool flying from her lap. "Well, I am disappointed in you, in Carl too. I credited you both with … with having more sense."

More sense … the words, echoing in Christina's mind, had an unreal ring to them, the ring of being out of context, of not belonging. Don't you remember, Mother? she cried silently. Don't you remember how it is to be so deeply in love you listen only to your heart?

"I should have known, I suppose. Instead of being pleased that you were putting on a little more weight, I should have wondered about it. That time when you were looking so peaky, if only I'd taken a good look at you, instead of putting it down to your quarrel with Carl and the business with Kathleen." She broke off, her eyes widening with sudden enquiry. "Does Carl know?"

"I've just written to him."

"What do you mean, you've just written to him? Over at the O'Rourke's?"

Christina nervously cleared her throat. "Carl's working over at Tambourine Mountain with Danny. He might not have planned on coming home for a while, so I had to write. One of the O'Rourke twins will take the letter to him."

Elsie's frown had deepened and she shook her head slowly from side to side. "You told the O'Rourke's before you said anything to me, or to Carl?"

"Only Mrs O'Rourke knows, Mother, and I didn't tell her," Christina protested wearily. "She knew, she could tell by looking at me."

"She's a very observant woman it seems," Elsie said dryly.

"She was very kind to me." Christina regretted the words the instant they left her lips, concerned that they might seem to be inferring that her mother wasn't being kind to her, and she waited with held breath for her response.

Nodding her head slowly, Elsie said quietly, "I'm glad about that … that she was kind to you. But you should have told me long ago, Christina. It must have been a terrible burden for you to carry all on your own."

Unprepared for this softened attitude, Christina felt the tears that had been stinging her eyes slide on to her cheeks, and, with a soft cry, she dropped to her knees and lowered her head on to her mother's lap. At once a gentle hand was stroking her hair, soothing her brow. "It's going to be alright, love, it's going to be alright."

Carl was back from Tambourine early on the following afternoon, his chin golden with a two-day growth of beard, dark shadows of fatigue and concern beneath his eyes. Seeing him at the gate, Christina hurried to meet him, her heart racing, her whole body trembling, a small tentative smile of welcome fixed on her lips, and with her mind in a whirl. He'd come so quickly, giving her scarcely any time to think about what she would say to him, what she would do. Why, she'd expected that it would have been at least a couple of days before he got here.

There was no need for such concerns. Carl jumped from his horse in the very instant he reined it to a halt, enfolding her in his arms and whispering in a voice hoarse with emotion, "You should have sent for me earlier. All this time, worrying on your own, while I had no idea. Darling, I'm so sorry. I'm so sorry."

With her heart soaring free of its misgivings, Christina slipped her arms around him. "You don't have to be sorry. It was my fault. I let you leave me and I made you so angry."

Rocking her to and fro, his lips against her hair, Carl groaned, "I was stupid, just stupid. I should have known there was a reason why you didn't want to be married."

Christina tensed, lifting her face from his chest to look up into his face enquiringly.

"Ma O'Rourke wrote me a letter also. She thought there were some things I should know." He smiled gently, ruefully, "And your letter was somewhat brief."

"She told you why I wouldn't marry you?"

Carl nodded. "She said that you were concerned that you may not be able to give me the children I needed to fulfil my dreams." Again he groaned softly, "Ah, my love, if only you had told me."

"Would you still have asked me to marry you?"

"Of course I would. I love you. I love you with all my heart, more than anyone or anything else in the whole, wide world." He gave her a gentle shake. "You do know that, don't you?"

"Yes."

"Well then, isn't that why a man asks a woman to be his wife, because he loves her in such a way."

Christina and Carl were married in the sitting room of the Skov home on 28 May 1881. The Reverend Joseph Whiting of the Congregational Church at Southport, a minister who regularly visited the Mudgeeraba district, performed the ceremony.

28

The Colony of Queensland had come into the 1880s with European settlement spread in every direction. For the Aborigines, though, the battle was still not over; they continued to wage frontier-type warfare that had moved gradually northwards. In spite of its still largely untamed state, however, Queensland had begun the decade in a flourishing economic climate.

The goldfields were enjoying previously undreamed-of prosperity, due mainly to major structural changes in the organisation and technology of the gold mining industry.

Since the big drought of 1877 the seasons had been kind to the man on the land. In the pastoral industry, there was, furthermore, increased efficiency and improvement, one extremely important move being the introduction of wire fencing. This not only helped protect stock from dingoes and the intrusion of the inferior wild herds known as 'scrubbers', but also did away with the need for large numbers of shepherds and boundary riders on the sprawling sheep and cattle stations, which, in turn, resulted in an easing of the labour shortage throughout the Colony.

The sugar industry, also, was moving into an important new stage with technology and southern capital beginning to reach the plantations which now extended as far north as Cairns and Port Douglas.

Everywhere, the smaller landholders cleared, dug and planted their way into the new decade with renewed confidence. With Queensland's star shining so brightly, surely they, too, would succeed, see their dreams begin to merge into reality.

"It seems that we might have chosen a good time to be married," Carl remarked as he and Christina stood, hand in hand, admiring a brilliant winter sunset. "The Colony's really on its way now, striding out, you might say, instead of just stumbling along."

Christina nodded, smiling wryly and lifting her free hand involuntarily to her rounded belly. Not we, she mused to herself. We didn't choose the time, that was done for us by our baby. Our baby ... how things had changed during these past four weeks. Our baby ... whereas previously it had been something she'd hardly dared think about. The fear that had touched her life for years and in recent times done more than simply touch had not entirely gone, though. She told herself over and over that she was going to have a fine healthy baby, and most of the time she believed that, but memory of the little graves still hovered, threatening to intrude into her contentment.

"Now that Britain seems to have realised that Australia doesn't begin and end with Victoria and New South Wales, there's bound to be more and more money invested here. Exciting times, Christina, that's what we are coming into. It might even be that we will have a road up here in no time at all."

"That would be nice, but Father says that most of the money coming here from England is being invested in the goldfields."

"True enough, I suppose, but the benefits will flow on to other things; help the Government, of course, but also encourage people to tackle new ventures. Look at William Laver and the hotel he's planning for the next year or so."

Christina laughed softly. "Hotel, when Mudgeeraba still doesn't have a store."

"That's the way it goes, I'm afraid. First, the hotel, then perhaps a blacksmith or some other small undertaking, then someone will get round to opening a store."

"Someone smart enough to realise that there are things more necessary than drink."

Releasing her hand, Carl put his arm around her shoulders, drawing her closer to his side. "Never fear, Christina, the store won't be all that far behind the hotel. Before the 'eighties' are even halfway through, we'll have a little township at Mudgeeraba, and we'll not only have a road up here, we could very well have the railway from Brisbane through to Nerang. What a bonus that will be." He dropped a kiss on to the top of her head. "None of which means that we don't have longer than that to go before we can consider ourselves truly successful."

Christina nestled against him contentedly. She understood how he felt, knew his dreams, and hoped with all her heart that things would turn out the way he wanted them to. For his sake. As for her own, she was well satisfied with what she had right now. Married to the man she loved, which was, she was quite sure, the most beautiful thing that could ever happen to a woman; living in the house he had built, going to sleep each night enfolded in his strong and loving arms.

"One day, sweetheart, we'll have a fine farm down on the flat lands, and when that day comes, we'll have a decent house, with at least half a dozen rooms instead of just two."

"I'm quite happy with what we have, Carl. Besides, you've forgotten the verandah. I don't know how you found the time to finish off the bedroom and get this wonderful addition built in time for our wedding."

"It was certainly a rush, but I did have a lot of help from the O'Rourke boys, remember? And your father made our handsome front door.'"

"Everyone has been so kind and helpful."

"Yes, they have." He laughed quietly. "A bit more time and I might have been able to get the O'Rourke gang to help me add a detached kitchen."

"What do we want with a separate kitchen when we have such a fine fireplace?

Carl gave her shoulders a quick squeeze. "Spoken like a true settler's wife, and I'm afraid that little luxury will have to wait. I should think the Bailif will be well satisfied with the house as it is and more interested in how much land I've managed to clear and get under cultivation."

"I've heard Father talk about the Bailif."

"The Crown Lands Bailif, a very important fellow where selectors are concerned. He's the one who decides whether or not the conditions for ownership of the land have been met. When he's convinced that they have been, he puts in a report saying so and the Commissioner issues a Deed of Grant. When that happens for us, we will own these acres."

"That won't be for some time yet?"

"Seven more years. I have to pay rent for ten years all told."

Christina nodded. "Four pounds, seventeen shillings and sixpence at the end of every March, I remember hearing you tell Father."

Carl glanced down at her in amused surprise. "That's exactly right. One hundred and ninety-five acres at sixpence per acre, per annum, and, when the final payment has been made, provided we've improved the place enough to satisfy the Bailif, we will truly be people of property. In 1888, that will be our big year, Christina. In the meantime, though, we can apply for a Homestead once the Bailif sees that we are making progress. I'm hoping that we might be able to do that next year, as a matter of fact."

"That will be further up the creek and it's all such dense scrub."

"Not all of it. The land higher up the range is fairly open forest, great for grazing even as it is. There'll be quite a bit of clearing lower down, of course, but the soil is all rich chocolate so it will be worth the effort."

Christina groaned softly. "Oh Carl, why should you have to work so hard? Just look at what you've done today. You've hardly stopped for a minute."

Carl smiled down into her up-turned face. "I don't recall seeing you stop either."

"Well, I did. I had a little nap this afternoon. In any case, I wasn't digging out tree roots."

"I should hope not. You've got to take care of yourself and the little one." He put a gentle hand on her belly and Christina pressed it down more firmly so that he could feel the baby stirring. "Hmmm, pretty lively this evening."

For a time they stood quietly, watching the flamboyant and ever-changing colours in the western sky. Then Carl said on a small sigh, "There's something I have to talk to you about, sweetheart. You know that it's still necessary for me to do some outside work, don't you?"

Christina felt her breath catch, but she nodded.

"This farm wouldn't be able to support us, not yet. I don't want to be going into debt, borrowing money, running up accounts and such like."

"No, of course not." Christina had heard her father talk about the farmers who resorted to borrowing from money-lenders and the trouble they got into; about the storekeepers who let them run up accounts, sometimes adding interest of twenty percent or more, then claiming all the return when the farmer's produce went to market. A terrible vicious circle, her father had called it, not something any man would want to be getting himself caught up in.

"Unfortunately, there's no work available around Mudgeeraba at the present time, which means that I'll have to go further afield."

"Back to Tambourine Mountain?"

"No, Danny finished off that job, there wasn't much left to do. I'm afraid it's back to the Tweed for work with the cane."

"How long would you stay away?"

"I've been thinking that I'd leave early on the Monday morning and then come back on Friday night. That way you'd have only the four nights on your own each week."

Christina swallowed, her mouth going dry. Four nights, up here in the mountains on her own? Five days as well? She couldn't do it. She just couldn't. She would be terrified the whole time.

Carl looked down into her stricken face unhappily. "It's the last thing I want to do, love, leave you up here on your own. There just doesn't seem to be any other way, unless you'd like to go down and stay with your parents while I'm away?"

Christina saw the regret in his eyes, the love and concern on his face, and resolve was born. She was the wife of a selector, wasn't she? Hadn't she known all along the way it would be, the hardships and sacrifices, the loneliness when he was away, the fears that would stalk the dark nights when she was on her own?

"No," she said firmly, pushing her lips into a smile. "I will be staying right here. Why, there's so much to be done I couldn't possibly leave. In fact, I'll probably be so busy you'll be back for the weekend before I know it."

"You will be busy, Christina," Carl agreed quietly, "but I don't want you to be overdoing things."

"I promise that I won't." She laughed softly. "I couldn't be away from here, in any case, not now that we have the fowls to feed and a cow to milk."

"You'll be lonely, Christina, and I'm sorry about that, but there won't be anything to be afraid of, not really. Bluey is a good watchdog as you know, and I'll show you how to handle the rifle, not that I think you'll be needing to use it."

Christina shivered. "I couldn't ever shoot anything."

"I'm sure you won't need to, but I'll feel better if you know about the gun. The blacks hereabouts are quite harmless and they've never ventured anywhere near the house, but, on the remote chance that they did, you'd only have to wave the rifle at them and they'd be off."

"I don't expect that I'd ever be able to hit anything in any case."

Carl didn't tell her that he intended to make sure that was exactly what she would be able to do. Instead, he said, "You'll have Samson, of course, in case you want to visit your parents."

"Won't you be riding him down to the Tweed?"

"No, I'm trading my half-share in Midnight for another horse."

"Oh Carl, you don't have to do that. There's no need for me to have Samson, I don't expect to be going anywhere."

"Well, he has to be here, just in case."

"But how can you bear to part with Midnight. You love that horse."

"I'll still be seeing him from time to time. Danny's father is taking over my share, so he'll be staying at the O'Rourke's." He grinned suddenly. "Actually, Midnight is getting to be a bit lazy, I don't think he'll win too many more races."

"Does Mr O'Rourke know that?" Christina gasped.

"I don't think so."

"But that's trickery."

Laughing, Carl swung her around in front of him. "Is it now, my darling? Then what about the horse Da is trading me in return? As stubborn as a mule and he's thrown the old bloke on at least half a dozen occasions."

Alarm chased the amusement from Christina's face. "You're not going to ride a horse like that?"

"He's a good strong animal, just what I need. Besides, I've had a little talk with him."

"With the horse?"

Carl looked at her with mock reproach. "Don't tell me you've never talked to your horses?"

Christina laughed softly. "What did you tell him?"

"That I knew a timber-getter who uses good strong horses just like him to drag heavy logs out of the bush and that, if he doesn't behave, he'll be doing just that for the rest of his days.'

"What did he say to that?"

"That he would behave, of course."

When their laughter had faded away, Christina asked, "When will you go?"

"Next Monday, I've been thinking. If I go now I'll have gotten in a few weeks before the baby is due. I certainly won't be leaving you on your own once it gets near to your time."

Christina took a deep breath, trying to still the troubling thoughts that at once began to tug at her mind. When they persisted, she quickly admonished herself. Hadn't Doctor Davies told her that everything was going along very well and that he didn't foresee any problems whatsoever with the baby's birth? Wasn't Carl going to take her down to her mother a full week before the baby was due? Didn't the baby move quite strongly within her, even now, when there were still two months to go? Wasn't that an indication that he was going to be born healthy and live for years and years, not just a few hours, a few days? Of course … of course! Everything was as it should be. Everything was arranged. Nothing would go wrong, not with this baby.

"I will be alright, Carl, you won't need to be worrying about me."

"I will worry, love, that's something I won't be able to help. But I'm very sure that, apart from being lonely, you are going to be just fine. You are beautiful, sweet and gentle, but you've come through some rough patches in your young life, and you're a tough little miss." Sweeping her up into his arms, he laughed softly. "Even though there's not very much of you."

"You said that to me once before."

"I know … on the day I decided that in due time I was going to ask you to marry me."

It was worse than Christina had expected, much worse. Life with Carl away was mere existence, loneliness a constant and almost unbearable heartache. Where his presence had seemed to fill the little house, there was now only emptiness and silence. Where, in her heart, there had been gladness at the mere sight of him striding over his land, there was now a bleak yearning. The chores with which she tried to fill the long hours did little to help, always failing to hurry those hours. Friday evening, it seemed, was going to take forever to come round. From time to time, she would hear from the distance the crash of a felled tree or the sharp crack of a teamster's whip, a sound that brought a strange sense of relief, she wasn't alone in the wilderness.

She was thankful that Samson had been left with her. Two or three times each day the big horse would wander up to the house. Looking for Carl, of course, but she let herself pretend that he was checking on her or seeking her company, and she always took the time to pat his neck and commiserate with him. She was glad of the dog, too, even though she had no real affection for him. A blue-grey cattle dog of the same type as most of the teamsters used, it had been acquired by Carl just a week before their wedding, and it still regarded her suspiciously. That it knew its job, though, she had not the slightest doubt; highly prized for their ability to handle cattle, these dogs were, far and wide, even more highly prized as watchdogs.

Nevertheless, Christina's loneliness was quite often joined by fear. This was especially the case at night when, in contrast to the shadowed stillness inside the house, the world outside seemed alive with sound and movement. Often, in the dark hours, the dog would growl softly, menacingly, or rush off barking sharply. She knew well enough that he was probably just chasing some wild creature that had come too close to the house for his liking, but she would still listen anxiously for his return.

Her gaze wandered often to the gun where it rested by the fireplace, and, even though she didn't think she'd ever be able to bring herself to use it, its presence was somehow reassuring. So much so, in fact, she had even considered having it with her when she worked outside, but when Thursday came round this was still nothing more than a notion .

The dew was still heavy on the grass when she went to feed the fowls – a rooster, eight fully-grown hens and a dozen ten-week-old chickens, all recently acquired. But on this morning only nine chickens joined in the scramble for the scattered corn. Frowning, Christina crossed the netting-enclosed run and peered into the open-fronted fowl-house with its nests at one end and roosting perches at the other, calling softly, "Here, chick, chick, chick … "

Then, with a scream choked off in her throat, she saw it – a huge snake coiled into a compact circle a mere two feet from where she stood. In the same instant, her eyes widening with horror, she saw the three bulges at intervals along the creature's gleaming length. The chickens! The snake had eaten their chickens! Swallowed them whole by the look of things. Her mind racing, Christina backed away from the shed. What was she to do, for heaven's sake? It was a carpet snake and they weren't dangerous, or so everyone seemed to think. But this one had eaten three of their chickens and, as soon as it was hungry again, it would be after the others. Why, it hadn't even bothered to move away to sleep off its feast.

Think, Christina instructed herself as she stood in the midst of the pecking and apparently unconcerned fowls, staring in a dazed fashion back at the shed. What would Carl do if he was here? Yes, that was it. What she had to think about. He'd kill the snake, of course, harmless though it might be. He wouldn't let it hang around gorging itself on their poultry. So that was what she had to do, kill the creature. But how? She had seen any number of snakes killed with a stick, their backs broken, but this one was so large a stick would have to be wielded by a strong man for it to have any effect. She'd probably do better with the axe … or the gun? The decision was taken in a flash, she would use the gun and shoot the thing through the head. That shouldn't be too difficult with it lying there dozing, she would be able to fire at its head from only inches away.

The minute she picked up the gun, her somewhat uneasy confidence fled and she began to shake, so badly she could barely hold the weapon, let alone hold it steady. I am not going to be able to do this, she thought distractedly. I'm going to finish up shooting one of the hens or maybe even myself.

The dog had followed her back to the house, where it bristled and growled, sensing her agitation, but confused as to its cause. Christina looked from its dark troubled eyes to the gun in her hands, then closed her own eyes tightly against the tears that stung them and silently berated herself. Where was that toughness Carl had talked about, the toughness she needed to be the wife of a hard-working selector? Not here now, that much was clear. Not when she couldn't even save his chickens from an old carpet snake. Besides, hadn't he taken the time to show her how to use this gun she held? Hadn't he made her fire it over and over until she could, at least occasionally, hit what she was aiming at? Wouldn't he have done that expecting her to take care not only of herself but of the farm as well? Yes, of course he would.

Resolutely, Christina returned to the fowl-run, gun in hand, and with the dog at her heels. It barked loudly and furiously when she shut the gate behind her to keep it out. Not that this was something she wanted to do. Having the dog with her would have been a comfort, but he would be sure to go for the snake and how could he cope with something that size? It was still there, but, dear God in heaven, it was awake! She saw its beady eyes gleam and. when its black tongue darted out, her heart began a new thumping. Somehow, though, she managed to stand still, holding her breath and waiting. Almost at once the snake settled and seemed to be sleeping again.

Losing no time lest her shaky confidence also be lost, Christina crept closer, took careful aim and fired. With the sound of the shot reverberating in her ears and a gasp of mingled horror and triumph bursting from her lips, she saw that the snake's head and that part of its body on which it had rested now resembled a squashed tomato. She was unprepared, however, for the commotion that followed: the whiplash uncoiling, the wild writhing and thrashing about that threatened to wreck not only the nests but the entire shed.

When she rushed from it, it was into an extension of the commotion. The fowls were all cackling, their feathers fluffed in agitation as they fluttered hither and thither, slamming into the netting and one another in their panic. And the dog had gone berserk, tearing around the outside of the enclosure in a frenzy of frustration, barking furiously the whole time. Shaking uncontrollably now, Christina pressed a hand over her mouth to stop the hysterical laughter that had rushed to her lips from escaping. This isn't happening, she thought wildly, it has to be a crazy dream, but her eyes were open and the din she was hearing was real, very real.

In what seemed to have been much longer than the couple of minutes it actually was, it was all over. No sound whatsoever came from the shed, the fowls had resumed their pecking with only an occasional unsettled clucking, and the dog., though it still ran up and down the netting anxiously, had ceased its barking. "It's alright, Bluey" she called, "It's all over so you can settle down."

The snake was dead. Even though a large part of it was hidden beneath a collapsed nest and scattered straw, its tail had stopped twitching. She would leave it for the time being though, Christina decided, come back later and see what she could do about dragging it out of the fowl-yard. What was to become of it after that would have to wait for Carl to decide when he came home on the morrow. She sighed regretfully. She hated snakes, even those that weren't considered dangerous, but she was nevertheless sorry this creature had to die when its only crime had been the sneaking of an easy meal. Still, that was the way things were. It was what happened when a farm was carved from the wilderness. Survival meant that what destroyed must itself be destroyed, she had learnt that early enough.

Christina was on her way back to the house when the dog left her side and flew off to the gate in a new flurry of growling and barking. At once a radiant smile parted her lips and she gave a gasp of delighted surprise. Her father was at the gate, riding one horse and leading another, heavily laden. Yelling at the dog, she ran to meet him, laughing softly when he jumped from his horse and enveloped her in a crushing bear hug. "Father, I am so glad to see you."

"I'm glad to see you too, love. I've been worrying about you up here on your own; your mother has too."

Lifting her shoulders in a faint shrug, Christina gave him a wry grin. "I never knew it was possible to feel so lonely, but I'm surviving."

"Well, being on your own isn't easy, especially when you're not used to it." Simon glanced somewhat anxiously over her shoulder to where she'd left the rifle leaning against a post when she'd run to meet him. "What were you doing with the gun?"

"Shooting a snake," Christina told him, adding with a small rueful smile, "A poor, sleepy old carpet snake, but I had to do it. It had already eaten three of our chickens and it would have taken the others as soon as it needed another feed."

"Yes, it would have, perhaps even a hen if it was big enough. You did the right thing, Christina. You did manage to kill it, didn't you?"

"Yes, I'm sure it's quite dead. I was so close when I fired I couldn't very well have missed. It's still in the fowl-house so you can see for yourself. I thought I'd drag it out later."

"I'll take care of it."

Christina gave her father's arm a quick, grateful squeeze. "You are very welcome to do that." She glanced at the laden pack-horse. "What on earth have you brought up this time?"

Simon chuckled. "Ah-ha, among other things, something very important."

"You've finished the cradle?"

"Not quite, it still has to be assembled. Or have you forgotten that the only way to get things up here is in pieces?"

They laughed softly together, recalling the problems there'd been in bringing up the few pieces of furniture, in particular a bed, Carl had added to his house in preparation for his marriage.

"I've got some other things as well, odds and ends that you may have use for, including that side-saddle I bought when I thought your mother might learn to ride. Not that I'm suggesting you be riding down needlessly, mind. It's just … well, if you feel you need to come down for some reason." A faint smile touched his mouth. "Your mother said I'm to impress upon you that it's the only way a woman expecting a baby should be riding."

Christina gave him an affectionate grin. "Well, you can tell Mother that, when the time comes for me to ride down, it will definitely be side-saddle."

"She'll be relieved to hear that, I'm sure." A sudden scowl formed a deep furrow between Simon's brows. "When are they going to build a road up here? It's indecent that land be thrown open for selection, then such a long time elapse before proper access is provided."

"The road will come. It's just one of the things we have to be patient about, it seems."

"I suppose so," Simon agreed on a heavy sigh. "It's just that the thought of you being up here in your condition and the only way down being on a horse's back causes me quite a deal of concern."

"Everything will be alright, Father."

"Of course." He shook his head as though to brush aside his worrying thoughts, then said brightly, "I've brought you a couple of surprises – a parcel from Kathleen and another from Mrs Klaussen, wedding presents, I would think."

"Oh, how kind of them. I wonder what they've sent."

"Suppose we go in the house and find out, eh?"

"Yes … oh, of course. What am I thinking of, keeping you standing out here like this?" She took hold of his arm, swinging a little awkwardly along at his side as he led the horses up the angled incline to the broad ridge on which the house nestled.

"Ah!" Simon exclaimed as he stepped through the doorway. "What an amazing thing the touch of a woman's hand can be."

Hurrying to stir the slowly-burning fire to greater activity, Christina smiled proudly. It was still, she knew well enough, a meagre little home, but, instead of the sagging stretcher in the bedroom , there was the double bed with its colourful patchwork quilt, a special wedding gift from her mother; beside the bed a rug covered the rough-hewn floor boards, shelves held their neatly arranged clothes, towels and linen, and there were lace curtains at the windows. In the kitchen, a green baize cloth hid the roughness of the table and there were flat cushions made of bright floral cretonne on each of the four newly-acquired chairs; on the pinewood dresser, also brought up the mountain in sections, the dinner service Carl had bought for her contributed further splashes of colour – brilliant yellow daisies and green leaves on a gleaming white background. And there were other things, her own small treasures – the silver and cut-glass cruet set Mr and Mrs Laver, who had been witnesses at their marriage, had given them, the rose bowl from Marie who had been the only other guest, the beautiful lamp with its painted glass base sent by the O'Rourke family.

"How has the roof been?" Simon wanted to know the minute he'd transferred the various things he'd brought inside from his arms to the table.

Christina settled the kettle on its grill over the flames and turned back to him. "Only one leak in that heavy shower we had the other night. Carl's not going to be able to believe it."

"Where did it get through?"

"I don't know, Father, but I know where it finished up, in the middle of the table." She gave him a quick grin. "Which was a whole lot better than the middle of the bed, wouldn't you say?"

Simon returned her grin. "Most definitely." Throwing back his head, he peered upwards. "It ran down the beam, I suppose. I'll have a look before I leave. Right now, I think I'd best unload that cradle."

"I can't wait to see it. But you must wait while I unwrap these presents." Christina's hands were already busy with string and brown paper. "There's something hard inside this one from Mrs Klaussen. What do you suppose it is?"

"I have no idea," Simon laughed. "Unwrap it, for goodness sake."

Smiling happily, Christina did so, gasping with delight when she opened the maroon leather box and saw the six silver teaspoons and matching sugar shovel nestling in their beds of cream satin. "Oh, they are beautiful and so expensive looking."

"They no doubt were expensive. That's fine quality silver, I'm thinking, very fine quality."

"What a dear, sweet lady she is, but I'm sure I'll never dare to use such elegant spoons."

"Well, they can always be for special occasions."

A small, silver-edged card had been tucked into a corner of the box and it read simply, *Christina and Carl … with my best wishes for your every happiness, Eleanor Klaussen.* But, when Christina picked it up, she saw that there was a further message on the back, *so, it wasn't just an old woman's romantic nonsense – you two were meant for each other. Love, E.K.*

Laughing softly as she handed the card to her father, Christina explained, "She met Carl at the Regatta. It was ever so briefly, but she seemed to take quite a liking to him."

The parcel from Kathleen was much lighter, and when the paper was folded back two round crotcheted doyleys came to light, with a letter tucked in between.

"That's nice," Simon said at once. "She's made something for you with her own hands."

Christina's eyes widened, but then she slowly shook her head. "I shouldn't think so; Kathleen hated doing anything like that."

"Well, you read what she has to say while I go and relieve poor old Horace of his load. By then, that kettle should be boiling."

Christina unfolded the three fully-utilised pages with impatient fingers, anxious to know Kathleen's reaction to her marriage and her own news as well. Surely her mother would have written to her by now …

My dearest Christina,

What wonderful news, and what a surprise. I nearly fell over when I read your letter and discovered that you were a married woman. Not that I didn't expect that you and Carl would marry, mind, just that it was a bit sudden. I think it's just lovely about the baby, even though I can understand what a worrying time you must have had. I wish I could have been there to see you married. Even if you didn't dress up as a bride, I bet you looked absolutely beautiful. I hope you like my gift. You'll probably faint when

I tell you that it's all my own work. David's mother has taught me how to crotchet (among countless other things, I might add). I expect that she thinks it will help pass the time and keep me out of mischief?????

Which brings me to my situation...

What a sweet, darling girl you were to go and see Ma. I have had a letter from her and it was simply heaven to hear all the bits and pieces of family news. I cried like a baby. Can you believe that? Anyhow, what Ma suggested was that I should ask David to become a Catholic. She said that would be a fine, clear-cut solution to our problem. Even though I was bawling away I had a bit of a giggle about that – she made it all sound so simple. I couldn't, of course. Even if I hadn't seen the stricken look on his face when I read him the letter, I wouldn't have been able to do that.

So it seems that I'm still in the same situation as I was before, except that I do feel a little more hopeful. At least Ma is writing to me and I have a feeling that she is relenting a little, and, if she does, I think Da will too. I have written explaining to them that I couldn't ask David to change his religion, not when they have their own little church here on the station and hold a service every Sunday. I made a point of saying that it was a private church and not really like one of the formal Protestant churches.

As you will understand, it seemed best not to mention that I have been attending these services. To begin with, I felt like a fish in the wrong pond, but now I rather enjoy going, and, when you get down to what it's really all about, it's not so very different from the Catholic church.

So you see, dear Christina, I still need you to pray for me and I'll try not to be too jealous of you. (At the moment I'm green all over!)

With loads of love and good wishes,

Your friend always, Kathleen.

Simon came back inside as Christina was refolding the letter and she looked up with a small sigh. "Kathleen has had a letter from her mother. Friendly enough, apparently, but no consent to the marriage, just a suggestion that she should ask David to become a Catholic."

"That doesn't really surprise you, does it?"

"No, I don't suppose so, and I guess it's something that she has at least written. It seems Kathleen was ever so happy to hear from her and she does say that she is feeling more hopeful."

"There you are then. Now that she's in touch with her family, it could well be that the matter will be happily resolved."

"Oh, I do hope so," Christina murmured fervently. Then, with a quick grin, "Kathleen did crotchet those doyleys herself."

"So, what did I tell you?"

"I still find it hard to believe. Kathleen sitting down with a crotchet hook and ball of silk. What have they done to her out there in the west?"

They both laughed, a warm, easy sound that reflected the ease and contentment they felt in each other's company, and which would be heard often in the hours that followed. He's the nicest father anyone could possibly have, Christina mused to herself as she held the finely crafted and polished sides and ends of the cradle while Simon screwed them together and then fitted in the base. Always ready to comfort and cheer her, always reluctant to rebuke her, and never had that been more evident than when he'd learned about the baby. Gentleness and understanding had been in his every word, his every gesture, never a hint of criticism or the slightest indication that he was disappointed in her.

"That's all come together pretty well. Now, if we can turn it upside down, I'll be able to fit the rockers."

"Father, it's absolutely beautiful! The most handsome cradle there ever was, I'm quite sure." Her smile faded a little. "It must have taken up a lot of your time?"

"Early evening hours, that's all, and you may be sure that I enjoyed working on this little piece of furniture."

Christina's smile flickered again in response to his, but the troubling thought that had caused it to fade was still there. "Are you and Mother managing all right without me?"

"Ah, Christina, didn't I tell you that you weren't to be worrying about us. We are doing just fine."

"But with just the two of you for the milking?"

"Well, as you know, the milk yield is down, what with it being winter, so that's not a problem at present. What I've decided to do when spring comes round and the cows carrying calves come back into milk is employ young Davey Freeman. I've already spoken to his father and he's quite agreeable."

"That's a wonderful idea."

"Yes, it should work out quite well. Davey's a fine, well-mannered young fellow. "

Christina nodded, having no trouble in recalling the boy. The third eldest in a family of ten children living on a too-small farm and around fourteen years of age now, he was a tall, gangling youth, with a mop of dark curls, flashing amber eyes and a ready smile. He was also, as her father had remarked, extremely polite.

"He'll still live with his family and ride over each day, but, if it works out, I might think about building a small room for him in a corner of the barn."

"That would be a good idea, and I'm sure Davey would like having some space of his own." But Christina was thinking of something else, of how, when farmers had no sons, hired hands were needed and the dream, confined to a single generation, lost much of its purpose. Her father had returned his attention to the cradle, whistling softly between his teeth, and she considered him thoughtfully. Did he ever think about such things, about who was really going to benefit from all the hard work he put into the farm?

"Do you think you could hold this rocker in place for me, love? I've marked where."

"Of course I can." Christina at once took hold of the curved piece of wood, lining it up with the pencil marks on the base of the cradle.

"I hope I haven't made this too big, you've little enough room as it is. But I figured it would be pointless to make something the baby would outgrow in no time at all."

"It will be perfect, Father, and I know just the spot for it, under the window."

"Yes, it should be fine there."

"I can't wait to get it fitted out with all those lovely things Mother has made."

"She has been busy alright, but really enjoying herself, that's for sure. I think she's almost finished knitting yet another little jacket."

Christina smiled wryly. "Too bad I didn't inherit her love of knitting and crotcheting. Do you remember how much trouble I had with that scarf I made for the sailor on the Friedeburg?"

"Do I ever?" Simon laughed. "That would have been a very short scarf indeed, had your mother not helped you."

"I know that I used to measure it every couple of days, hoping that it had grown more than it had. I wonder if he still has it."

"He could have, I suppose, and the jumper your mother knitted."

"He could be still on the Friedeburg, sailing the great oceans of the world."

"And saving other little girls from being washed overboard..."

All too soon it was time for him to leave. The cradle had been completed and moved inside to its allotted space, the snake had been dragged off into the bush and left on an ant nest, the roof had been inspected and some adjustments made to the overlapping of the bark slabs, and, in the early afternoon, he was on his way. Waving to him, Christina resolutely thrust aside the ache of loneliness that threatened to return. Just one more night on her own, she reminded herself, then one more day.

She began listening for the sound of hoof-beats from the time the setting sun took to painting the valley with purple shadows and splashes of gold. He'll be here before darkness comes, she told herself. He'll leave the Tweed early enough to be sure of that. But winter days in Queensland are short and their dusks fleeting, almost illusionary so abruptly are they swallowed up by the darkness of the night. It was just after half past six when Christina heard what she had been listening for, but it could have been the middle of the night, so deep was the darkness through which she peered, straining her eyes in an excited and impatient searching. Then the whistle came, that special sound he'd told her to listen for. She had forgotten about it! Oh, what would he think of that, for heaven's sake? What would he say if he knew that she'd been standing out here even before she'd heard the whistle, before she knew that the man talking to the excited dog was no unwelcome stranger. Next time she would remember though.

She was in his arms the minute his feet hit the ground, her lips lifted eagerly. When their first long kiss came finally to an end, Carl murmured on a sound that was part laugh and part groan, "Now I know why these past five days have been the longest of my life."

"It was more like five months than five days," Christina told him, undoing the buttons of his coat so that she could snuggle closer to his body."

Carl kissed her again before turning her in the direction of the door. "Inside with you now while I unsaddle Finnegan. It's cold out here and the tips of your ears are like bits of ice. Besides, whatever you've got in there that smells so good probably needs your attention."

"It's all under control, just waiting to be served. So, if you don't mind, I'll stay with you. As a matter of fact, I am not going to let you out of my sight this weekend."

They had eaten and she was clearing the plates from the table when she told him, as casually as she could manage, about killing the snake.

"You killed a snake?" he gasped. "Where? How?"

"In the hen-house … a carpet snake, but it had eaten three of our chickens, so I shot it."

Carl shook his head, an uncertain grin coming to his face. "You actually shot a snake?"

"Well, I had the gun so close to its head, I couldn't really have missed. I was a bit sorry to have to do it, though. It was just a poor old carpet snake, but it had eaten those chickens, and it would probably have eaten the others as well if I'd left it."

"Yes, it certainly would have." He caught her hand and, pushing his chair back from the table, pulled her on to his knee. "You did very well, Christina. When did this happen?"

"Yesterday morning, just before Father came up with the cradle. He got rid of it, on an ant's nest, he said. He also fixed up the hen house where the snake knocked down one of the boxes when it was thrashing around after I shot off its head."

Carl's grin disappeared. "Where were you when all that was going on?"

"Outside. I thought the whole hen-house was going to come down."

"God! When I think what could have happened … "

Christina reached up and patted his cheek. "It didn't. And now that's enough about that old snake. I've got some dishes to wash, and, while you're drying them, you can tell me what jobs you have lined up for the morrow."

The first was the back-breaking task of bringing water up from the creek to refill the big barrel at the back door. Watching Carl climb the steep bank with an overflowing bucket in each hand, Christina sighed. How many times was he going to have to do that? And the job didn't end with getting to the top of the bank; the water had then to be carried up the incline to where the house was situated. Oh, if only they had a roof with gutters and a proper tank, like her parents' farm did. That, she told herself, would be the very first thing she would want in a house, not a lot of rooms or anything too fancy – just a tank.

She had been gazing wistfully at the grassy ledge a short distance from where she stood, and when Carl next reached the top of the bank with his heavy load, she asked, "Do you suppose we could sit over there for a while?"

Carl grinned at her. "Are you wanting to be kissed, Mrs Eichstead?"

"Such a notion, for heaven's sake! When all I wanted was for you to rest for a bit."

"Come to think of it, I could do with a bit of a break. You go on over, and I'll empty these buckets and be right back."

Only when they'd been lying back against the grassy ledge for five minutes or so did the thought occur to Christina. When it did she shifted her head on Carl's shoulder so that she could look up into his face. "Do you know something?"

Carl raised his drooping eyelids, amusement touching the corners of his mouth. "No, I'm afraid you'll have to tell me."

"It must be almost a year to the day since that other time we sat here."

"Well, what do you know? So this is an anniversary, that's why you lured me away from my work?"

Christina gave him a gentle dig in the ribs. "How could that be when it has only just occurred to me? Besides, I didn't lure you away from your work. All I said was – "

Carl didn't let her finish. He pulled her closer to him and kissed her tenderly. "Whatever you said was a great idea. But tell me, what names are we thinking about this week?"

"I thought Alice might be nice for a girl and definitely Charles for a boy."

"And what does he get for a second name, this Charles of ours? Simon… ?"

"No!" The word burst from her lips so sharply Carl stared at her, his smile fading. "But you love your father?"

"Of course I do. It's just that Simon doesn't really go with Charles."

"Charles Simon, it sounds alright to me. What does it matter, in any case? Second names are just there, they are hardly ever used."

On tombstones they are, Christina mused bleakly, and small wooden crosses – Madsen Simon Skov, Hans Simon Skov. "I thought Edward might be alright. Charles Edward Eichstead … how does that sound?"

"It sounds great. And now, young lady, it's time to get back to work." He was quickly on his feet, reaching out a hand to pull Christina to hers. "A couple more trips and we'll have enough water to last for well over a week, so how about you go back to the house and make us a cup of tea."

The day passed all too quickly. Carl had a number of jobs he wanted to get done, but they were all in the area close to the house and, for the most part, Christina was able to do what she'd said she'd do and not let him out of her sight. So, over breakfast in the first pale light of Sunday morning, she asked cheerfully, "Well, what are we going to do this morning?"

"How about some more stitching on those baby clothes you showed me?"

"Would you really like to do that?"

Carl spluttered over the spoonful of porridge he'd just raised to his lips. Then, recovering, remarked with mock severity, "You know very well what I mean, woman!"

"You should have seen your face," Christina told him, her laughter spilling over. "It was so … so dumbfounded."

"Didn't it have every right to be?" He spread his large, work-scarred hands on the table. "Can you imagine these with those little things?"

Her eyes shining with love and the remnants of her amusement, Christina shook her head. "Not really, so I suppose I'll have to excuse you. But I'm not going to be doing any sewing today either, that can wait for through the week."

"You'll stay in the house though?

"What will you be doing?"

"I want to do some more clearing, get some of the undergrowth off that area where I've ring-barked a few of the larger trees."

"But that's right over beyond the cornfield, I won't be able to see you from the house." She reached over and took hold of his hands. "Carl, can't I please come with you? I'll just sit on a log and talk to you, and watch out for snakes and things like that."

"And I suppose when you see a snake you'll be wanting to be the one to blast its head off?"

They both laughed, and as simply as that it was settled. Christina went with him to where the southern edge of his cleared land pressed back raggedly into the bush. She didn't, however, spend very much time just sitting down. The bushes, tall bracken and tangled vines that tumbled before Carl's slashing scythe and the branches and small trees that fell before his swinging axe all needed to be dragged into the open and into a pile for burning. The only way, they both knew well, since to let a fire run through the rubbish where it lay would be courting disaster, asking for a conflagration they would have no hope of controlling.

It was when she dragged a tangle of severed brush away from near the base of a tall tree that Christina came across the bird, a young lorikeet. It tried frantically to rise, but, while one wing fluttered strongly, the other hung limply to the ground. Bending down, Christina extended her hand ever so slowly, but the instant she touched the silky feathers the sharp beak flashed and she had a bleeding finger. "Ouch!" she yelped, springing up again.

"Christina, is something wrong?" Carl called from a short distance away.

"There's a parrot here, it's been hurt."

Carl joined her as she examined her injured finger. "What happened to your hand?"

"It pecked me."

"Don't tell me you tried to pick it up?"

Christina nodded sheepishly. "I thought it was just a baby."

"It's young alright, probably not long out of the nest, but that doesn't mean it hasn't learnt how to use its beak." He reached for her hand and inspected the broken skin on her index finger. "It's not deep. Does it hurt?"

"Just a bit." She glanced down to where the parrot had struggled into a new shelter in a clump of bracken. "What do you suppose has happened to it?"

"Who knows? A hawk may have had it and let it drop, or it could have simply fallen out of its nest." He turned away, intent on returning to his toil. "Wrap your handkerchief around that finger, keep it clean."

"But what are we going to do about the bird? It will die if we just leave it here, of starvation if something doesn't kill it first."

Carl hesitated, shrugging his shoulders. "I suppose the kindest thing we could do is wring its neck here and now."

"No! It's not hurt badly enough for that. It's just the one wing, and in time that will mend, more than likely. Couldn't we take it home with us?"

"Do you like having your fingers nipped?" Carl asked with a wryly amused grin.

"Once it understands that we are not out to hurt it, I'm sure it won't do that."

Retracing the few steps he had taken, Carl pushed the bracken to one side and frowningly considered the injured parrot. "I'm not sure that wing will heal, no matter how much time it's given. We could be stuck with an earth-bound parrot."

"We could at least give it a chance to get better."

Carl's grin widened. "I suppose, if it doesn't recover well enough to fly off, you could always teach it to talk."

"Yes, I could," Christina agreed eagerly. "Some people have done that, haven't they?"

"Yes, when they've got hold of one young enough."

"What would they feed them, do you know?"

"There's a bloke at Tambourine who has one that says quite a few words and he gives it bread soaked in water with a bit of honey added, along with some berries and seeds."

"Feeding it wouldn't be a problem then. And it would be wonderful to be able to teach it to talk. It would be good company for me while you are away."

Carl raised his eyebrows and gave a deep chuckle. "That's blackmail, sweetheart. And you don't get them to talk overnight, you know? It's quite a long process from what I hear."

"I wouldn't mind that."

"Well, I suppose, if you want to give it a go … "

The lorikeet, screeching in indignant protest, went home in Carl's hat. Christina's first week on her own had set the pattern for those that followed. The ache of loneliness didn't ease with familiarity; neither did her fears and uncertainties. No more carpet snakes visited the fowl-yard, but a red-bellied black one took up residence in the wood-heap and for three days defied her efforts to strike it down with an axe. But the dog had also become aware of the creature's presence and, held by an instinctive loathing, spent hours waiting patiently. His reward came; with his teeth sunk deeply only a couple of inches from the deadly fangs, he dragged the snake out on to clear ground and shook the life out of it.

There were other problems and upsets. A wombat paid a nocturnal visit to the vegetable garden which had become her pride and joy and left a trail of destruction where it had burrowed in its search for edible roots. A goanna dug a hole into the hen house and ate several eggs. The cow knocked down a section of the rough fencing around the banana trees and ate a number of the new fronds. Then the dog picked up a scrub tick which had buried itself deep in the soft flesh of his neck before she noticed it; there was nothing for it but to take a sharp-pointed knife and dig the thing out. That she was able to accomplish this with little trouble was due entirely to the fact that Bluey seemed to understand that she was trying to help him and made no protest. Breathing a huge sigh of relief, she patted him, "Good dog, well done!" And felt, for the first time, the stirring of what would become a deep affection.

The parrot, named Harry had, for its own protection, taken up residence in a hastily constructed cage, but, within a week, it was possible to leave the door open so that it could go in and out as it pleased. It soon learnt that it was senseless to be trying to peck the hand that fed it and Christina was able to pick it up and settle it on her shoulder. She arranged a graduated series of perches near the cage and encouraged the bird to climb them, and, when it became clear that the dragging wing was going to be a continuing hindrance, she clipped off the longer feathers. The bird's screeching outrage at this indignity soon gave way to what appeared to be delight in its new-found mobility and it took to climbing the perches with great enthusiasm.

Bluey had chosen to ignore this new addition to the household; unfortunately, though, the parrot was not prepared to ignore the dog and never failed to greet his appearance with loud and prolonged squawking.

"Stop that, for heaven's sake," Christina admonished. "You're supposed to talk, not be screeching like that. Come on now … say 'hello', there's a good bird." All to no avail. Though she pleaded and coaxed, saying 'hello', or 'hello Harry' countless times each day, the parrot did no more than put its head to one side and peer at her.

And the weekends continued to take forever to come round and then to fly by once they did arrive.

29

The first pain came as the creeping greyness of predawn robbed the stars of their brilliance. It was fleeting, gone in an instant, but Christina was at once wide awake, a prickle of apprehension bringing a frown to her forehead. The baby … ? No, of course it wasn't. It couldn't be, not when there were at least three weeks of her time still to go. She lay very still, holding her breath and with her hands pressed against her belly in a searching for reassurance. Not yet, little one, it's not time. The minutes ticked by and she began to breathe more easily. A touch of wind, she told herself, that's all it had been; she'd probably been lying in the one position for too long. With a quiet sigh of relief, she snuggled back under the blankets. Another hour before she had to get up, sixty more minutes of warmth and sleep.

The second pain, a replica of the first but not nearly so fleeting, cut into her dozing and brought a quick gasp to her lips. Oh, it was the baby … it was! She clenched her fists as the spasm had its way, its very unfamiliarity putting to flight any hope she might have clung to. Her eyes grew wide with dread and her heart began a rapid pounding. Her baby was about to be born and she was all on her own. No, she tried to tell herself, it couldn't happen like that, not after all the plans they'd made. Her baby was to be born down at her parents' farm and Doctor Davies was to be there … but not until near the end of August. Why, it was unthinkable that she should be having it now, up here in the mountains and all on her own.

With the pain gone, it was almost as though it had never been. But, now, Christina was overcome by the need to act, to do something, and she clambered as hurriedly as she was able from her bed. Her baby was coming, there was no sense in trying to deny that, not when she knew it with a frightening certainty. The pain might have left her, but other spasms would follow, the intervals between growing shorter and shorter. Shivering, she pushed her arms into the sleeves of her robe, reaching with her bare feet for her slippers. Dear God, what should she do? Think! Think! she upbraided herself. Don't just wander around like a half-wit. Light the fire, a voice from the back of her mind advised. Light the fire? Yes, she should do that. With some warmth in the house, she'd be able to think more clearly.

It took a long time. Her hands were trembling so badly she could barely hold the matches, let alone strike one. When she did manage to do so, the twigs she'd gathered on the previous evening defied the small flame and it spluttered and went out in a faint puff of smoke; as did its successor and three or four others after that. While her hands fumbled, Christina's mind raced. Why was this happening? First babies didn't come early; more often than not they were late … everyone said so, even her mother. Oh Mother, why aren't you here? You are supposed to be with me, you promised. But how could her mother be here? How could she possibly get up the mountain when she couldn't even ride? No, it was the other way around … she was supposed to go to her.

But you could come, Carl. It's your baby too and you should be here. Then, out loud, "Light, fire, damn you!"

As though in response to her outburst, the flame caught, searing the twigs into a small blaze, catching at the splinters on the piece of wood she quickly added. Not too much now, she warned herself, just a couple of small pieces to begin with. Rushing with the fire is not going to do a single thing to help. What was it Carl was always saying? Ah yes, many a promising fire has been snuffed out by impatience. She giggled, a small hysterical sound in the still room. What a ridiculous thing to be recalling, for heaven's sake! Carl, please come home. Don't you know that I need you now, that tomorrow will be too late?

With the fire taking hold, Christina crossed the room and, tugging on the heavy bolt, opened the door, catching her breath as the frosty air stung her flushed face. But she saw, with a faint sense of relief, that a rosy glow had begun to creep into the eastern sky and the greyness that lay upon the land was lightening into a soft pearl colour. It would be daylight soon, she told herself, and things never seemed quite so bad away from the darkness of night. All she had to do was force herself to think clearly, and there would be something she could do. Her gaze darted about. A couple of the young steers were a short distance away, ghostly shapes, with only the faint twitching of their tails to show that they were living creatures. Everywhere else stillness reigned and a strange, hollow silence. Well, what had she been expecting when all was said and done, she demanded of herself. Someone to be standing out here just waiting to help her?

A soft snort came from close by and she turned her head sharply. Samson! He was right here at the side of the house and he could help her! She could ride down to her mother. It wouldn't take her much more than two hours ... well, perhaps three. She would go ever so carefully, use the side-saddle her father had brought. Yes, that was a good idea! She would have been doing that in any case, next week when Carl would have taken her down. She hunched over, clinging to the doorframe with both hands as another pain seared through her, stabbing at her spine. Despair surged back, mushrooming.

She couldn't ride for three hours with the baby already coming. He could be born in that time and out on the empty track he would die. And her baby wasn't going to die! He was going to live! Better to stay in the house then, she told herself, clutching at a calmness that eluded her. At least there she would have a bed to lie upon and it would be warm. But horror, stark and heart-stopping, almost folded her knees beneath her. Have the baby on her own? With not a single soul to help her? No, she couldn't do that! She just couldn't! Why, she might bleed as her mother had done, and, with no one to help her, she would surely die. Then the baby would die too, for, even if it were to be born alive, there'd be no one here to care for it.

A grey cloud of misery enfolded her, tears of helplessness spilling from her eyes. In spite of the cold, she continued to stand in the doorway, staring up at the gate slowly taking form, willing someone to be there. Her father..? How many times had he ridden up these past weeks? Six, seven? Almost always unexpectedly. Then wasn't it possible that he would come again today? Wasn't it also possible that Carl would sense that she was in trouble and come home a day early?

But no one came, and when the next pain, sharp and urgent, gripped her and moisture began to run down the insides of her thighs, she closed the door and returned to the fire. It needed more wood, she told herself, something larger now, something to keep it going for a long time. And there were other things she should be doing, other preparations to be made if she was to have this baby on her own. Hot water? Well, the big kettle was full, but it might be as well to fill the smaller one also, and perhaps a saucepan. With the fire set to her satisfaction and the kettles and saucepan in place over the flames, she stood still, looking at the bed and forcing herself to see the way it would be, to determine what she would need. Towels, scissors, a bowl of some sort, something soft and warm to wrap the baby in, something to lie on to protect the mattress.

By the time the morning hours had dragged by, Christina had sunk into a miasma of pain and weariness, in which reality drifted into dream and dream exploded back into reality. She was riding, riding as hard as she possibly could. She had to. If she didn't fetch the doctor quickly her mother was going to die. All that blood and it was spreading everywhere. She woke with a wild piercing scream, frantically feeling the towel beneath her buttocks as another agonising spasm tore through her. It was damp … was it blood? No! Oh, thank God! Thank God!

It was all over. The baby was in her arms, as sweetly perfect as a baby could be. Why, he was even smiling at her. No, it was little Anna who was smiling at her, and she had wings, wings that carried her out of her arms even though she tried desperately to hold on to her. But was it little Anna up there smiling so sweetly down at her, or was it her baby? Pain shattered the dream as she began to shake her head wildly on the perspiration-drenched pillow, and this time she welcomed it. Her baby was still here, still inside her.

There were brief moments when she was sure that Carl was with her, holding her in his arms, and she actually wept with relief and joy, and time and time again she thought she heard hoof beats. They were in her head, she told herself bleakly when she was lucid enough to do so, the hoof beats were in her head. But there came a time in the early afternoon when they had a more defined ring to them and they seemed to be coming closer instead of being always off in the distance, and she knew that this time they weren't in her head. There was someone riding down from the gate, and the dog was barking! A glad cry sprang to her lips. It was Carl! It had to be! He had come home early!

But it wasn't Carl who pushed open the door and stood there uncertainly, a dark silhouette against the afternoon sunlight: the same height and broad shoulders, the same slim hips, yet the voice calling her name wasn't her husband's. It was Danny O'Rourke's!

Christina felt an agony of disappointment unlike anything she had ever known before and a scream of protest rose in her throat, to be choked off on a harsh sob. Danny O'Rourke! Whom she had hardly seen since that day at Beenleigh; who had made a point of avoiding her, of letting her see that he was her husband's friend, but not hers. Now he was here instead of her husband. It wasn't fair! It wasn't fair!

Danny O'Rourke had heard Christina's sob and he strode quickly inside, sucking in his breath as he came to the end of the bed. "My God, Christina! Is it the baby?"

Christina nodded, groping belatedly for the crumpled bed-clothes and pulling them up to her chin. No sooner had she done so than they were being flung aside again as her body contracted and she groaned and writhed, gasping for air.

In an abrupt burst of movement, Danny rushed to the side of the bed. Once there, however, he stood helplessly, his eyes, dark and horrified, taking in the tortured and distended body and flushed, tear-streaked face. "How long?" he asked urgently, his heart thudding against his ribcage.

It was several moments before Christina could answer him; when she did, her voice was little more than a whisper. "Since early this morning." Then, with a new flood of tears welling in her eyes, "I think there might be something wrong "

"No!" It was too sharp a rejection Danny knew at once, and he quickly brought calmness to his voice, "There doesn't have to be anything wrong, Christina. It takes a long time to have a baby, especially a first one." Too late, he was thinking, too late to get her down the mountain. Too late to go for help. Dear Mother of Jesus, what was he to do?

With the contraction running its course, Christina lay back against the pillows exhausted, her eyes closed, beads of perspiration cooling on her forehead and upper lip. The damp cloth moved gently over her face and she raised a hand, intending to take it, but, with a weary sigh, she let it drop again. It was nice to have someone else sponging her face, comforting. Even if it was Danny O'Rourke? she asked herself wryly, and knew instantly that it didn't matter who it was, not now. Danny wasn't her friend, far from it, but he was here, and he stood between her and an aloneness more terrifying that anything she had ever believed possible.

"Christina … ?"

She raised her eyelids slowly, reluctantly, and looked up into his worried face enquiringly.

"I think we are going to have to manage on our own. I can't be leaving you to ride off for help, not with the baby so far along the way."

Christina snatched at his hand. "No, don't leave me! Please don't leave me!"

"I'm not going to, Christina," he told her gently. "I'll stay here and help you have your baby."

For a long, uncomprehending moment Christina stared at him while her tired mind struggled with the implications of what he was saying. Help her have the baby, what did he mean by that? Not that he meant to help with the actual birth? No, of course not! It was inconceivable that he should do such a thing. All he had to do was be here, give her moral support. He could even go outside, just knowing that he was close by would be enough.

"Someone has to help," he said quietly, almost as though he had read her thoughts. "You can't do it on your own."

"Yes, I can. I just need you to be here. You can wait outside when the time comes."

His anger, born of worry, was instant. "For the love of Christ, girl, don't be so bloody ridiculous! You are having a baby and that's a normal, natural thing, not something to be coy about." He glowered down at her.

"Sure I'm not a doctor, but there's no doctor here, none within miles. I'm all you're got!"

Christina quailed before his anger, but murmured doggedly, "I can manage, I've got everything ready." She nodded at the few things she had assembled on the far side of the bed.

Danny gave them a brief glance before bringing his fierce gaze back to her face. "So, you've got the scissors ready to cut the cord, I can see that. But where's the twine to tie it with? Or hadn't you planned on doing that?"

Twine? Twine? How could she have forgotten that? Groaning inwardly, she closed her eyes against the hot, despairing tears that stung them. Danny was right, she couldn't manage on her own. The tears escaped from under her lashes and slid slowly down her cheeks. "Have you ever delivered a baby, Danny?" she asked huskily.

"No, Christina, I haven't." His anger was gone as quickly as it had come and he sat down on the side of the bed, taking her hand.

Christina opened her eyes and looked up at him through her tears, the barest hint of a rueful smile touching her mouth. "That makes two of us."

Danny gave her an encouraging grin. "I have seen a baby being born though, so I have a fair idea of what must be done." There was, he told himself, absolutely no reason to tell her that he had been nine years old at the time. Nine years old! God, what on earth had possessed him? Climbing up to the window like that, hanging there for dear life while that messy scrap of humanity had been drawn from his mother's body and smacked on its bottom. And what a walloping had landed on his own bottom when his da had dragged him down and put him across his knee.

"What time is it now?" Christina asked.

"Almost two o'clock."

"It's quite a while since I put wood on the fire."

Danny got to his feet. "That's my responsibility now. You just lie there and relax whenever you can." About to move away, he hesitated, chewing on his lower lip. "When you have the next contraction, do you think I should perhaps try to see what is happening."

Hot colour rushed to Christina's face, but, after a futile struggle with her mortification, she nodded.

He examined her a couple of times during the three long hours that followed, his hands gentle, his voice encouraging, soothing, telling her not to be afraid, that she was doing well. And Christina, unaware of the fear that clutched at his heart and turned his skin clammy, took confidence from his presence, his ministrations. Until, finally, as the sun was about to drop behind the ranges, her womb pushed its precious contents out into the world.

"It's a boy!" Danny told her triumphantly as she lay back gasping against the pillows, hardly daring to believe that it was all over. "Is he all right?"

There was the sound of a slap and right away a sharp wail of protest. "He looks fine to me and he's certainly got good lungs. I'll just clean him up a bit, then you can have him."

Christina took the small, towel-wrapped bundle into her arms reverently. It felt, she thought, as though her heart were about to burst, so much joy and thankfulness did it contain. This was her baby, hers and Carl's, and he was just perfect: dear, sweet little face, all soft and rosy; tiny tufts of hair clinging damply to his head; long golden eyelashes. She giggled softly as they fluttered. "He doesn't know whether to go to sleep or have a look at me."

Danny smiled at her. "What are you going to call him?"

"Charles … " She hesitated, her smile wavering. In her mind she saw her father's beloved face, knew the delight that would be his. But there was something else there, tugging at her memory. Five days, little Madsen Simon had lived for five days. "Charles Edward," she said quietly, but firmly. "That's who this little one will be, Charles Edward Eichstead."

"Sounds alright to me, a manly name. Now how about a nice cup of tea as a reward for your efforts? And what about something to eat, you must be hungry?

"That would be wonderful."

Only when she saw him light a lamp, did she wonder what they would do now. It was getting dark and he should be leaving. He wouldn't be able to make it all the way down before the light failed, but he could at least have the worst of the track behind him.

Almost as though his thoughts had followed the same course, the minute Danny came back to the bed with her tea and a large sandwich, he said, "I think the best thing would be for me to stay the night, Christina. I don't want to be leaving you on your own and there'd be no sense to it in any case. I could get to your parents, but neither they nor the midwife would be able to get here before tomorrow."

Settling the baby on the bed before taking the cup from him, Christina nodded. "I would appreciate it if you could stay, Danny, but I hope you won't be too uncomfortable with some pillows and a quilt on the floor; as you can see, we have only the one bed."

"No problem, it certainly won't be the first time I've slept on the floor and usually with much less than a quilt." He grinned suddenly, widely. "Isn't Carl in for a shock? I'd certainly like to see his face when he gets home tomorrow afternoon."

Christina glanced up from the tea she was sipping. "I thought you were working down at the Tweed with him?"

"I have been, but I only did two days this week, there were some jobs Da needed me for at home."

"Luckily for me!" Christina murmured fervently. "But you haven't told me what brought you up here?"

"I came to check on you, Ma's idea. She'd taken to worrying about you up here on your own and she woke up this morning with a feeling that something was wrong." Not quite right, he thought wryly. It had been more a conviction than just a feeling. "One of her omens, I suppose."

"Well, I'll be forever grateful to her, and I certainly don't know how I'm ever going to be able to thank you enough."

"All in a day's work, just call me Doctor O'Rourke."

Christina laughed softly. "Have you really seen a baby being born?"

"Yes … Kathleen."

"Kathleen? But you would have been – "

"Nine years old," Danny finished for her.

"Nine! And you remembered!" Although she still smiled, Christina's vision blurred as, unexpectedly, she experienced a strange feeling of longing; she wanted this usually morose friend of her husband's for her friend as well..

Danny saw the moisture in her eyes and the soft melting of her expression and his breath caught. She was dishevelled: her nightdress crumpled and stained, her beautiful hair a lank tangle, her eyes underscored with dark shadows, but she would never know how achingly lovely he found her. My wife, he thought with a sudden rebellious fierceness. She should have been my wife and this should have been my son. She was watching him closely, the beginning of confusion on her face, and he quickly cleared his throat, giving her a faint smile that was part grimace. "And I might tell you that experience of mine was dearly bought. Da thrashed me so soundly I couldn't sit down for two days."

With the tense, tender moment losing itself in their laughter, Danny said briskly, "You probably want to freshen up. I'll bring you some warm water and, if you tell me where to find them, a clean nightdress and sheets."

"Right now I can't think of a single thing I'd appreciate more."

"Not even the sight of your husband standing in the doorway?" Danny teased.

To Christina's amazement, it wasn't her father who opened the door just before midday, it was her mother. "Mother! I don't believe it!" she cried delightedly. "You actually rode up here?"

Hurrying to the bed, Elsie smiled ruefully. "I don't believe it either! I don't think I actually rode. I just sat on the horse's back while your father led him. But how are you, love? And how is the baby?"

"I feel fine. And so does this little one, isn't he just beautiful?" Christina had been nursing the baby and she freed her breast and turned him so that her mother could see him clearly. "I think he is going to look like Carl, don't you?"

"He's certainly a handsome little boy, and he looks like a full-time baby … perhaps you were wrong with your dates."

"I could have been, I suppose. Either that or he decided he didn't want to wait any longer to make an entrance into the world."

"Well, not to worry. We just have to be thankful that everything has turned out well, and especially thankful that Danny came up to check on you." She closed her eyes on a small groan. "I can't bear to think what might have happened, had he not done so."

"Then we won't think about it," Christina told her, passing the baby into her eager arms. "But I'll never forget how wonderful Danny was. I'm sure he was almost as terrified as I was and it must have been very distasteful for him, but he never once faltered. I should think that he ... "

"Now, where is this grandson who couldn't wait for the proper time to be born?" Simon, having seen to the horses, burst through the door and came quickly to the bed. Pressing his lips to his daughter's forehead, he carefully studied her smiling face. "Well, I must say you are looking very pleased with yourself. How are you feeling?"

"I feel very well, Father."

"Yes, but you must take care, look after yourself, you know?" He turned to Elsie who had moved away from the bed. "He's in good shape, the little one?"

"He's fine." She turned down a corner of the shawl. "See for yourself. "

"Gosh, I'd forgotten how little they are."

"He's not so little for a newborn babe," Elsie told him. "Close enough to eight pounds I would think."

Although needed for the milking back on their farm, they stayed until well into the afternoon, leaving only when Christina insisted they do so. "I will be perfectly alright. Carl will be home within a couple of hours."

"He won't be going back to the Tweed next week?" Elsie asked anxiously..

"No, this was to have been his last week down there in any case."

"Well, if you're sure you can manage ... ?"

"I can manage. And, if you don't leave now, you'll have me worrying that you are going to be up half the night milking!" She smiled teasingly at her mother. "You're not afraid to get back on that horse, are you?"

"It's not so much the getting on that bothers me, it's the staying on."

"Would you be better with the side saddle, it's here, you know?"

"No, I think I'd feel even more insecure with that. At least sitting astride the horse gives me a leg on either side, and, even though I'll probably be a bit sore and sorry tomorrow, I think that's the best way for me."

"You did fine, love," Simon told her. "A bit more practice, and you'll be riding up here whenever you feel like it."

Carl was home shortly after sunset, leaving his horse and hurrying to the door when he saw that Christina wasn't there to greet him. Propped up against pillows in the edge of the circle of light thrown by the lamp she had lit, she smiled as he burst through the door, and he breathed a sigh of relief. "Aren't you feeling well, sweetheart?"

"I feel wonderful."

"That's good, just having an early night, eh?" Half way to the bed he came to an abrupt halt, his mouth dropping open. "You … you've got the baby?"

Christina laughed softly. "Don't just stand there. Come and say hello to your son."

"Son … ? We have a son?" But he didn't move, shock and bewilderment held his feet glued to the floor. "He wasn't due yet."

"He decided to arrive a bit earlier than we expected. Oh, come on, for heaven's sake! He's been waiting for you all day" She patted the side of the bed as he edged slowly forward. "Your son and his mother would like you to sit here."

"Oh Christina!" With a small, anguished cry, he dropped down on to the bed "You had the baby here on your own?"

Christina took hold of his hand, squeezing it gently. "It's alright … I wasn't on my own. I thought I was going to be, but Danny showed up." She smiled happily. "Can you believe that? Danny coming just when I needed him, when he hasn't visited a single time since we've been married?"

Carl shook his head slowly from side to side, horrified still. "Only Danny was here … ?"

"Yes, he came because Ma had a feeling something was wrong, one of her premonitions, more than likely. But, when he got here, it was already afternoon and the baby was on its way, so there was no time for him to ride for help, and, besides, I didn't want him to go off and leave me."

"Heavens no! But when was this?"

"Yesterday … the baby was born late in the afternoon."

"Don't tell me that you've been on your own since then?"

"No, of course I haven't! Danny stayed last night, then left very early this morning to tell Mother and Father. They have both been here today." She laughed softly. "Mother rode up … can you believe that? Well, she says she didn't really ride … she just sat on the horse's back while Father led him."

"They didn't bring the midwife with them?"

"No, it seems she was attending another birth, and I really didn't need her. But she's going to come up some time over the weekend, just to check on me and the baby, and then, I suppose, she'll report back to Doctor Davies." She pushed the shawl away from the baby's face. "Oh Carl, isn't he just beautiful?"

"Is he all right?"

"Yes, he's fine. He's no monster, between seven and eight pounds, Mother thinks. But he's a greedy little fellow so he'll soon be growing. Here, hold him, for heaven's sake!"

Awkwardly, and with a good deal of trepidation, Carl took his son into his arms. "My God, he's little all right."

Christina giggled. "Because he's just a newborn baby, silly."

"He's something though," Carl murmured, a slow smile coming to his lips. "He sure is something."

"Charles Edward Eichstead, our little Australian."

"That's right! A fair dinkum Aussie from the moment he came into the world. How about that, little man?"

"When is the mother of this new little Australian going to get her reward? She hasn't even been kissed yet."

"Sorry, love, I've been kind of bowled over, to put it mildly."

"Mmmm, that was a nice reward," Christina purred when his lips finally left hers. She ran her fingers lightly down his cheek. "I love you, Carl Eichstead, with all my heart."

"I love you too, Christina."

"With … " she prompted.

Carl grinned. "With all my heart, of course."

With just three weeks to go to Christmas, Kathleen came home.

Christina's head was bent over the baby sucking hungrily at her breast, but she looked up as Carl came through the door, a quick smile coming to her lips. "Your son grows greedier every day."

Pulling off his hat, Carl returned her grin. "He's a fine little boy and he's going to grow up to be a fine young man, tall and strong, but smart into the bargain."

"Did you hear that, young Charlie? Now you know what your father expects of you, brains as well as brawn." She lifted the baby on to her shoulder, vigorously patting his back.

"Do you really have to wham the poor little bloke like that?"

"You know I do. He won't break his wind otherwise and then in half an hour he'll be screaming his head off. Come on, little one, a big burp so as you won't be sorry later on." The baby obliged and Christina returned her attention to her husband. "Did you see anyone interesting in Nerang?"

"I saw Hughie O'Rourke and I've got news for you."

"Oh … ?"

"Kathleen's home, and on her own."

Christina's breath caught, her eyes, wide with pending dismay, searching her husband's face. "For a holiday, you mean?"

"For good, Hughie said."

"Oh no! I don't believe it!"

"She's home, Christina, you'll have to believe it."

"But why? What has happened, for heaven's sake?"

"I have no idea. Hughie just said that you might like to know that Kathleen was home. She arrived only yesterday, apparently. But it may not be anything to be upset about, perhaps she simply changed her mind about wanting to marry David."

Christina slowly shook her head. "I don't think she would ever do that, but I suppose you could be right, and there's little sense in worrying when I don't know what it is I am worrying about."

Carl raised his eyebrows at this piece of logic, his mouth twitching at the corners as he suppressed a grin. But Christina was getting to her feet with the sleeping baby in her arms and didn't notice. "If that parrot wakes Charlie today, I swear I'll wring its neck myself."

"Poor Harry," Carl murmured, letting the grin spread across his face. "The only bird ever to have incurred Christina's wrath."

Christina sighed heavily. "If only he wouldn't screech so when Charlie is trying to sleep."

"You were supposed to teach him how to talk, remember?"

"And haven't I tried to do so? I'm sure I've said 'Hello Harry' a million or more times."

"Perhaps he doesn't like his name," Carl suggested, tongue in cheek.

"Well, how could we call him Joey when the kangaroo was called Joey? It would have been just too silly, and Harry seemed as good as any other name."

His eyes glinting with amusement, Carl watched her settle the baby in his cradle, rocking it gently when he gave a small whimper. He waited until she straightened then, knowing full well what her response would be, suggested, "We could always take him back to the bush."

"But he can't fly."

"Well, old Harry might make out alright."

Christina quickly shook her head. "No, he would never be able to, he's not nearly smart enough."

Catching her around the waist, Carl swung her into her arms. "We could always send him off with a packed lunch."

"Oh, you're impossible!" Christina cried, laughing, though she tried not to. "You know very well we are stuck with him. And don't you dare say 'I told you so.'"

It was going to reach ninety degrees again, Christina decided, kneading dough and wiping the perspiration from her brow with her forearm. The house was like an oven already and it was only just after eight o'clock. She glanced at the baby gurgling contentedly on a rug by the back door, a tenderly rueful smile coming to her lips. "More prickly heat in store for you, I'm afraid, Charlie."

At the sound of her voice the baby swivelled around, giving her a wide, toothless smile.

"And it's not something to be grinning about, you should know that by now." On the outer side of the doorway, the dog was lying in the narrow strip of shade thrown by the house, tongue lolling. "You don't think being so hot is anything to be cheerful about, do you Bluey?" At once his ears pricked, but only one eye opened and that only partially. "That's answer enough, I suppose," Christina chuckled, "but you should consider yourself lucky with nothing to do but lie about in the shade."

There were nice things about summer though, she reminded herself, especially those early hours when the heat to come was still only a promise. They sparkled for eye and ear alike, crying out for moments to be stolen for simply standing still, seeing and listening. Which is just what she had done a couple of hours back, when she'd finished milking the cow and feeding the hens? Just stood there, feeling positively dizzy with the beauty of her world and the rich smell of the storm-dampened earth?

"It's what you will always know, little Charlie. It won't ever be strange for you, or different from something else. Take Christmas now. As hot as the very devil it's sure to be, but there won't be any other kind for you to be remembering. Christmas in the middle of summer, that's what you … " Her voice trailed away as the dog bristled and got quickly to its feet, listening intently, before dashing off around the house, a deep growl already emerging from its throat. Someone's coming, Christina told herself, although it would be a moment or two before she herself would hear the sound of the approaching horse. Her heart, however, had lost no time at all in taking up the quickened beat of joyful expectation … Kathleen? Yes, it could be. Hadn't she been home for three full days now? She gave the dough a hurried pat before tumbling it back into the bowl and quickly setting about clearing the table and washing her hands and arms. "A visitor, Charlie," she said as she bent to pick up the baby. "And it just might be someone quite special whom you have yet to meet, and you are wet again, for goodness sake!"

She changed him quickly, but by the time she reached the door the horse and rider, accompanied by the furiously barking Bluey had arrived. "Oh Christina, please rescue me from this vicious creature, he simply refuses to believe that I'm a friend."

Laughing softly and a little huskily due to the tears of emotion that had caught suddenly in her throat, Christina reassured the dog and Kathleen jumped lightly to the ground. "Oh, just look at you! The perfect little mother." She pressed her lips to Christina's cheek and then to the pale gold curls on the baby's head. "He is just gorgeous."

"It's so good to see you again, Kathleen," Christina cried, catching the other girl's arm and squeezing gently.

"It's good to see you too, Christina. I missed you like the very devil, you know? And to think that I wasn't here when all these wonderful things have been happening to you; getting married, having a baby." She held out her arms. "Hand him over, I just can't wait to hold him."

Christina passed the baby into the outstretched arms with a smile on her face, but an ache in her heart as she led the way inside. This was Kathleen, this girl with the too-brittle laugh, the too-deliberate cheerfulness and the shadows beneath her once-brilliant eyes? It didn't seem possible.

"This is nice, Christina, very nice, and very comfortable too, I should think."

"Yes, it is. The only problem we have had with the house is a couple of leaks early on; it seems that quite often happens with bark roofs when they are still in the process of settling down."

"The whole place looks pretty good to me. Has Carl applied for the homestead block yet?

"He's hoping to do so early next year, as soon as we feel we can meet the rental payments on both blocks."

"Well, I'm sure you'll get it when you do apply. The old Bailif can't help but be impressed with the way everything is looking. Where is Carl, by the way?"

"He's working three days a week on the Andrews's place, but he's able to get home every night, thank heavens. I spend enough time having one-sided conversations with Charlie and the various animals."

Kathleen laughed quietly. "I can just see you doing that. But, Christina, what a horrible experience for you, having the baby up here and with Carl not home, and fancy Danny showing up the way he did."

Christina gave her a small rueful smile. "It's not something I'd like to be repeating, I can tell you that! But Danny was a tower of strength. As a matter of fact, from the time he arrived and took charge of things, I began to feel that everything was going to be all right."

"Good for him, then, and it's just wonderful that everything turned out so well." She sat down, settling the baby on her knee. "Now, young Charlie, let me have a good look at you. Hmmm, you are like your father, I would think. You've even missed out on your mother's blue-bell eyes." She glanced up at Christina.

"What do you think, that he's like Carl?"

"Yes, very much. Would you like a cup of tea or a lemon drink?"

"A lemon drink, please, it's too hot for tea."

Is she going to tell me what happened of her own accord, Christina wondered as she poured the drinks. Or is she waiting for me to ask, perhaps relying on me to do so?

"Charlie's a good deal heavier than Maureen's little girl."

"He's almost two weeks older."

"Well, two weeks isn't much." She took the glass Christina handed her. "She's a real cutie though, and, of course, both Maureen and Arthur think she's the most beautiful baby ever to be born."

"That's a parent privilege," Christina told her. "What about Sarah and Joseph's baby, is he all right now?"

"Apparently they had a worrying time with him for a couple of months."

"So I believe. It must have been terrible for them. I've been wanting to call on Sarah."

"Have you been down the mountain with this little fellow?"

"Twice, as a matter of fact, but only to our farm, and from there to Nerang to have Doctor Davies check us both out. That was in the sulky of course, but to get down to the farm, Carl takes Charlie in a basket in front of him, it seems to work quite well." The baby had begun to squirm a little fretfully on Kathleen's knee and Christina reached for him. "It's time he was fed and put down for a nap."

Kathleen glanced about her as Christina settled the baby at her breast. "Is that the lamp the family gave you for a wedding present?"

"Yes, and what a lovely surprise that was. As were the presents from you and Mrs Klaussen, but I told you that when I wrote." She is leaving it to me to ask, Christina thought. Either that or she doesn't want to talk about why she came home.

"They are quite valuable spoons, you know? Mrs Klaussen brought them with her from Germany."

"I knew they were very fine quality." Christina took a deep breath. "Why did you come home, Kathleen?"

"I just decided that I wanted to." She lifted her shoulders in a faint shrug. "After all, it's been more than a year since I left, and I guess I was homesick."

"But David? How could he let you go?"

For just the fraction of a second there was hurt on Kathleen's face. Then the shadow of a smile touched her mouth. "There wasn't anything he could do to stop me, not really."

Christina pressed her lips together, cutting off the flow of questions that had rushed there, but her eyes had widened incredulously. Surely David had begged her to stay. Surely he could have found a way to convince her to do so. "He must have been very distressed to have you leave like that?"

"Of course he was. But where was the sense in me staying on at Taldoon when we couldn't be married? Ma did speak to the priest, you know?"

Christina shook her head. "I didn't know."

"I don't know why, she must have known what he would say." Again she moved her shoulders, this time with a faint sigh. "Anyhow, after that, there was no way she was going to give her consent, not unless David became a Catholic."

"You didn't ever ask him if he would do that?"

"I did, as a matter of fact. I didn't want to, but I had become so depressed, what with everything looking so hopeless, I just blurted it out. He was horrified, so much so you'd have thought I'd asked him to become friends with the devil or something like that."

"Oh no! He wouldn't be thinking anything like that, I'm sure! After all, it's not as though you were asking him to stop being a Christian."

Kathleen gave a short, mirthless laugh. "It was strange though, I could almost understand him feeling the way he did. Do you know why?"

Christina shook her head.

"Because there was a time when I would have felt exactly the same way if someone had asked me to become a Protestant. This will probably shock you, Christina, but, when I was little, I actually believed that only Catholics went to heaven when they died."

Christina was shocked. "Oh Kathleen, how could you have ever thought something like that?"

"I don't know. I don't recall that it was ever told to me, so perhaps it was just one of those odd things you sometimes get into your head when you're a child." She made a soft, self-ridiculing sound that was part laugh and part sigh. "What a stupid thing to have believed."

"Where did you think Protestants went, if they didn't go to heaven, to hell?"

"Nothing quite as horrific as that. I suppose I just thought that they went into some sort of limbo and stayed there for all eternity."

"I'm glad you've changed your mind about that," Christina told her with a quick laugh. "Was that when you decided to come home, when David reacted in such a way?"

"I didn't decide right there and then, if that's what you mean, but it could have been when the idea was born, so to speak. But don't be thinking that it was that alone which sent me high-tailing it away from Taldoon. It wasn't, it was a whole lot of things. I just didn't fit in, Christina. No matter how hard I tried, I felt like a bumpkin in that great big house where everyone had such fancy manners they didn't even have to think about the correct way to behave, it just came naturally to them."

"But they were nice to you, weren't they?"

"Sure they were. Every single one of them was nice to me: David, his parents, his grandmother, his brother and sister, the people who came to visit. Too nice, they were all too nice. Sometimes I would get this terrible urge to yell at one or the other of them just in the hope that they would yell back at me, the way it would have happened at home." She gave a sharp giggle. "I really should have done that, it would have been interesting."

Burping the baby before moving him to her other breast, Christina smiled at her. "It was probably the fact that you weren't able to marry David that made you feel that way, frustrated, sort of."

"Perhaps, but, then again, being married may not have made all that much difference. I might have gone right on feeling like an outsider."

"No, you wouldn't have. It was just that it was such an awkward situation for you to be in."

"It was that alright. Can you imagine what it was like sleeping along the hall from the man you love and have him never come to your door in the dark of the night? In the beginning I used to tell myself that it would be only a matter of time, that all I had to do was be patient. Patient, when I was aching all over with wanting him? What a laugh."

Christina felt her face and neck grow warm, it didn't seem proper somehow to be discussing one's intimate feelings in such a way.

Seeing the soft colour, Kathleen chuckled. "You still blush, Christina, and you a married woman. I can hardly believe it!"

"It seems it's meant to be the bane of my entire life, unfortunately. Being married hasn't made the slightest difference."

"Well, as I've remarked no end of times in the past, you shouldn't worry about it, not when you look so adorable with your cheeks all pink and rosy."

"Then you are still a ninny, I'm afraid."

They both laughed, then Kathleen said wistfully, "We had such wonderful times together, didn't we, Christina?"

"Yes, we did ... wonderful, wonderful times."

"You know how they say that you should never look back and sigh? Well, I've come to the conclusion that it's just not possible to look back without sighing."

"I suppose it is sometimes that way, but even if we do sigh about the passing of special times, we still have our memories and there is much to smile or laugh about in them."

"You are right there, Christina. You and I could probably spend the whole day saying 'Do you remember ... ?' and laughing ourselves silly." She gave a deep, throaty chuckle. "We must do that one day, it would be a lot of fun."

"Yes, it would." Christina got to her feet. "Charlie's asleep so I'll just put him in his cradle."

It took but a couple of minutes for her to settle the baby, but it was long enough for Kathleen's brief spell of light-heartedness to have vanished. "I didn't finish telling you about waiting for David to come to my room," she said as Christina returned to her chair.

Christina wasn't sure that she wanted to hear whatever else there was still to tell, but she said quietly, "No, you didn't."

"Well, he didn't come, of course, not even when I suggested that he do so. And I might tell you that I did that on more than one occasion. So, the time came when desperation got the better of me and I decided that there was nothing for it but for me to go to his room."

Christina tossed her a startled glance. "You didn't?"

Kathleen held up her hand, smiling wryly. "You must let me tell you what happened in my own way. It's an interesting little story, believe me."

Christina nodded, not sure that she could speak in any case, what with her breath being caught in her throat the way it was.

"Well, I had to wait for everyone to go to sleep, of course, so I spent the time preparing myself. Even though I had taken a bath earlier in the day, I sponged myself all over from the basin in my room. Nearly froze to death, I might tell you, since I couldn't very well ask one of the maids for hot water at that time of night. Then I put on this really lovely nightdress David's mother had bought for me when she went to Brisbane to do some shopping, brushed my hair until my poor scalp could take no more, dabbed perfume behind my ears and in other places as well, and finally crept out into the hall … trembling and shivering fit to fall apart, some of it from the cold, but most from nervousness and excitement. Still, I got to David's door without falling over or running into anyone. But do you know what, Christina? The door was locked!"

Christina stared at her. "Whatever for?"

"To keep me out, of course." She gave a small, bitter laugh. "Poor David, he'd locked his bedroom door to make sure I wouldn't be tempting him away from doing the right thing, as he calls it. Not that I felt sorry for him at the time, mind. I was so angry I only just stopped myself from banging on the door and waking up the whole household, and what a fine pickle that would have been."

"What did you do, for heaven's sake?"

"I just tapped softly a couple of times, and, when there was no answer, went back to my own room." She gave another small, mirthless laugh. "So, you see, Christina, I can't take the slightest bit of credit for the fact that I'm still a virgin."

"David would have been worrying that you might have a baby, I suppose. Look what happened to me."

"So, what did happen to you? You married the man you love, had a beautiful baby, and will no doubt be happy for the rest of your life. God, what I wouldn't give to have had that happen to me."

Feeling a new rush of compassion well up within her, Christina smothered a sigh and said gently, "Things will work out for you too, Kathleen, I'm sure they will." A sudden anxious frown creased her brow. "You are going to keep in touch with David, aren't you? I mean, just because you've come home now, it's not the end of everything. It can't be, not when you were so much in love."

"He said he'll come for me on the day I turn twenty-one."

Relief and delight wiped the concern from Christina's face. "That's less than two years now, not so very long at all! That's wonderful, Kathleen, just wonderful."

But Kathleen looked at her strangely, a small whimsical smile on her face. "He won't come, you know?"

Christina's smile froze, leaving her lips parted, and it was a moment or two before she was able to stammer, "But you just said … "

"I know what I said, but it won't happen. As a matter of fact, I probably won't ever see David again."

"How can you say that? If he has said that he will come for you, then he will. Why would he say that if he didn't mean to do so?"

"Because he felt obliged to, that's why. Perhaps he did mean what he said, at the time. But two years? That is a long time, Christina, when you are waiting for something to happen. Besides, there's a girl on another station out there David has known pretty much all his life. He likes her a lot and I know that everyone had expected the two of them to marry."

"But he loves you."

"Yes, I believe that he does." She sighed, a small rueful smile on her lips. "Well, he was mine for a time. Not completely and it was for a short time, especially when you compare it to a lifetime, but it was something special to hold on to, you might say. And I can tell you this ... he will be forever in my heart, my one true love."

"Don't talk like that, Kathleen. David is not going to marry some other girl. He's going to marry you."

"Dear Christina, what a loyal friend you are." She spoke gently, a soft affectionate smile on her mouth, but an impish gleam had danced into her eyes, retrieving some of their old sparkle. "But I'm going to win some money from you. I'll bet you a half-penny David is married to Miss Margaret Sanderson before even one year has passed."

30

The rain began to fall over south-east Queensland just after midday on Saturday, the last day of the year; heavy squalls interspersed with periods of sunshine. Off the northern coast a cyclone had been hovering for more than a week, coming towards the land, then veering away again. Now, though, it was on a steady course southwards, staying out to sea, but more or less following the coastline. By Monday morning, the squalls had been replaced by endless veils of heavy raindrops that were buffeted about by the wind before pelting down upon the earth.

"I don't think I have ever seen such heavy rain," Christina remarked as she joined Carl in the back doorway. "It looks as though it's never going to stop."

Slipping an arm about her shoulders, Carl drew her closer to his side. "I expect it will be with us at least until the cyclone either crosses the coast or moves further out to sea, the latter, I hope."

"Oh, so do I, but, if it does come ashore, it will do so further north, won't it?"

"It should, but no one seems to be sure with cyclones. This one has apparently come further south already than would normally be the case."

"What a dreary old world it has brought with it. Not even a scrap of blue sky to be seen anywhere, no blue mountains or green valleys either, nothing but rain and mud."

"Well, it seems to have eased a little at the moment so it could be a good time to get the milking done and throw a bit of feed to those poor half-drowned hens."

Christina moaned softly. "I wish you didn't need to go out in this awful weather."

"At least it's not cold, and we do have only the one cow. Besides, the sun is trying to break through."

The clouds, moving restlessly, had parted momentarily and a pallid sun looked down, a flat sphere which brought no brightness to the drenched earth, but seemed to float despondently, as though it knew it would soon be swallowed up again. It was. By the time Carl had pulled on his boots and reached for the coat and hat hanging by the door, the dark masses which had taken over the heavens had closed ranks and rain was again pouring down. "Hmmm, it didn't give me much of a chance, did it?"

"Something less than a minute, I should think."

"Well, that just goes to show, we can't afford to waste even the seconds." With a quick grin he stomped out into the driving rain, bending his head and trying to whistle, a dolorous sound that was quickly lost in the howling of the wind and the incessant drumming of water on earth.

Christina turned back inside, smilingly shaking her head. Only her husband, she was quite sure, would walk out into weather like that, trying to whistle. Her smile faded as her glance fell on the squares of flannelette strung out before the fireplace. If only there was some other way of getting them dry. If only, occasionally, Charlie would wake up with a dry nappy. If only they had some dry wood and didn't have the smoke to put up with. If only the cyclone would hurry out to sea. If only … if only… she chanted to herself. Then, with a soft chuckle, "If only I could whistle."

Carl wasn't whistling when he later returned with the milk. Instead, his mouth was set in a grim line. "I'm going to have to move the cattle, Christina, bring them well away from the creek."

Christina tossed him a sharp, worried glance. "Do you think the creek is going to come up over the bank?"

"I hope not, but it's risen quite a deal since this morning, and I don't want to be taking any chances, especially not with beef that's almost ready for the market."

"But the banks are so high."

"Yes, of course they are, and it's most unlikely the water will rise high enough to come over the top. It's just that moving the cattle seems a sensible thing to do." He gave her an encouraging grin. "Now, stop looking so worried. We've really nothing to be overly concerned about."

"Charlie's fast asleep, I could come and help you."

"There's no need for you to do that. Bluey and I will have those beasts up on higher ground in no time at all."

The noise had them scrambling from their bed in the hour before daybreak, a monstrous roaring that at once struck terror to Christina's heart. "What is it?" she cried hoarsely, rushing to join Carl who had flung the door open and was peering out into the teeming rain.

"It's the creek, it's coming down in what seems to be an enormous flood."

"Then it will come up over the bank?"

"It would seem so, if that noise is any indication."

"But it won't reach up here, will it?"

"No, we are much too high." He leaned forward, again peering out into the rain-filled blackness. "I can't see a damned thing."

"It seems to be coming closer," Christina murmured, hugging her arms to keep from shivering. "What a terrifying sound."

The raging, debris-laden wave of flood-water had torn away great pieces of the cliff-like banks further upstream, forcing its tumultuous way through and rushing towards their farm faster than a galloping horse. Here, high though they were, the banks were not high enough. The great roar took on a different sound, much like the expelling of a tortured, shuddering breath, magnified a million times over, and Carl and Christina knew that an ocean of water washed over much of their land. They couldn't see it through the teeming rain, but they could hear it, rushing and swirling, revelling in its release from a confined course, and they sensed the destruction being wrought, their insides churning with the bitter pangs of helplessness. Only with the coming of daylight and an abrupt easing of the rain, however, would they know the true magnitude of the setback this night had brought them.

All that remained of their cornfields were flattened stalks, most of them uprooted and strewn about like handfuls of hay. Where their thriving potatoes had been, streams of mud moved sluggishly to the creek bank where they slid over, taking what little still remained of the plants with them; and, everywhere, in the grazing paddocks and cultivated fields alike, logs, uprooted trees with their leaves still green, and huge piles of lesser debris had been dumped by the rushing water. For the space of moments everything seemed to Christina to be out of focus and she gazed upon the devastation with a curious detachment, as though from a long way off. Then, almost against her will, she was projected into a horrifying awareness, and she saw it all with a stark, compelling clarity. A devilish trade, that's what it is, she thought bleakly, all of this rubbish in return for our crops, our fences, our livelihood.

For several long moments neither of them spoke, then Carl said resignedly, "At least the water disappeared quickly enough."

Moving closer to him, Christina slipped an arm around his waist, hot tears rolling on to her cheeks. Why shouldn't she cry? she asked herself. For all the back-breaking toil that had come to nothing; for the dashed hopes; for the terrible waste; and, most of all, for the despair and heartache that must be her husband's? "It's not fair! It's just not fair!" she cried brokenly. The rain continued to fall, but it was no longer torrential, just a grey, mournful drizzle. And by midday, with the cyclone moving away from the coast, a brilliant sun was beating down upon the drowned earth.

"It won't be stopping us, Christina. We'll go ahead with our application for the homestead block, and, what's more, we'll get it lodged right away."

Even though she had only the lamplight by which to do so, Christina saw the glint of determination in her husband's eyes. Nevertheless, she was unable to overcome her own doubts. "You don't think that it would be better to wait for a while. I don't think the Bailif would be very impressed with what we have right now."

"By the time that worthy gentleman gets around to making his inspection we'll have things cleaned up and new crops planted. When all's said and done, it's not as though we have to be felling and clearing virgin bush; it's just a case of getting rid of the rubbish and repairing the fences."

They were both exhausted, having toiled outside until darkness fell, and the smile Christina gave him was little more than a weary flicker. "That rubbish includes some rather big trees, remember?" Then, with a hint of tears in her voice, "There's one lodged right across our little nest."

Carl gave her a wry smile. "Not a priority job, I'm afraid. In any case, there'll be no time for sitting there, not in these coming weeks. But we'll get rid of it one day; it'll make jolly good firewood when it's had time to dry out."

Carl lodged his Application to Select a Homestead with Land Agent Robert Miller of the District of Beenleigh just over a week later, on the 11th of January 1882. To his surprise, it was accepted on the 8th of February without an inspection of the improvements made to his Selection being carried out. The homestead was described by the Government Surveyor as being one hundred and fifty-one acres (two and a half acres having been allowed for the proposed road) in the Parish of Gilston, County of Ward, Land Agent's District of Beenleigh. The whole of the lower area contained within a pronounced bend of Little Nerang Creek, together with a broad band along the southern boundary, was recorded as being covered with dense scrub and the remaining acres as being thickly forested with gums, with a predominance of ironbarks in the north-west corner.

Well aware of the density of vegetation on much of the newly acquired land, Carl was nevertheless overjoyed to have been granted the homestead block, for he was now in possession of some three hundred and forty-six acres of land. Second-class pastoral it all might be, but it was his, or would be before too many years had gone by. Five years only for the homestead, he mused cheerfully, since the yearly payments were to be six pence per acre for five years, and not ten years as was the case with the selection. "Which means," he informed Christina, "that we will have the Deed to those new acres before we get the one to the selection."

"And the homestead will work out as being less expensive. That sounds a bit strange, doesn't it?"

"I suppose it does, and I can't say that I know what the Government had in mind when it set those two sets of rentals, unless it's that the homestead is a sort of reward for occupation and improvement of a selection. Of course, it can never be very large, the maximum area for a homestead is one hundred and sixty acres."

"Well, whatever the reason, five years instead of ten is certainly something to be thankful for."

"I'll say it is, especially as we'll be getting the two Deeds within a year, as it were: the homestead in 1887 and the selection in 1888. Then, my love, our next goal will be a dairy farm down on the flatlands."

Christina, rejoicing for her husband, was also excited about their new land. Until the day she paid her first visit to it, riding Samson, with the baby balanced on the front of her saddle, and following Carl on Finnegan along an old and barely discernible timber-getters' track that wandered through the mountains in the more or less general direction of the Queensland-New South Wales border. It won't all be like this, she told herself, nodding and glancing about her when Carl called over his shoulder that they were now off the selection and on the homestead . There must be some parts where the bush is not so dense, at least some place where we can begin.

There was, but it was little more than a grove in the midst of scrub and towering trees. "This," Carl told her cheerfully, "is where I'll begin the clearing."

Christina, still on the horse, looked around her, her spirits quailing. A farm from this wilderness? It wasn't possible. Her gaze took in a pile of withering vegetation and, in spite of her dismay, a smile curled her lips. "It looks as though you have already begun?"

Grinning, Carl took the baby from her, then held up his hand to help her dismount. "I got a bit carried away when I was here the other day. I pictured how it is going to be and I just couldn't wait to get started." His smile faded and he sighed quietly. "Time, Christina, that's our worst enemy. Not the bush or the floods or even the droughts. Bad enough they all might be, but it's time that's the worst. We have so much to do and it's never done with rushing away from us."

"Perhaps you won't need to do so much outside work this year?" A forlorn hope, Christina knew, hardly needing her husband's reply to snuff out its fragile existence.

"I'll be needing to do a fair bit, what with two lots of rent to be paid and the cost of the additional cattle we'll be buying to run on this place … on that more open land I've told you about further up the range. But until the crushing season starts, I'm thinking to spend most of my time at home. I want to get at least some of these acres working for us as soon as possible."

Christina glanced up at the tall trees that encircled them. "A lot of these will have to come down, won't they?"

"Yes, quite a few of the bigger ones as well as all the smaller stuff. When Danny comes up at the weekend we'll be tackling them with the cross-cut saw. There are a few trees we'll be leaving alone, though, fine hardwood timber that will be of interest to the timber-getters once the road gets built: blackbutt, messmate, the gums, some ironbark and even occasional cedar." He grinned suddenly. "But did you notice the interesting looking tree you are standing under?"

Christina hadn't and she glanced quickly upwards. "It looks like a palm of some sort … "

"It's the bangalow palm, or the piccabeen . According to an old teamster I met down at the Tweed, it's a favourite with the blacks. They not only use the curved leaf base to collect grubs from rotting tree trunks, but also to make a bowl they call a pikki … " His voice trailed away, Christina was staring at him, wide-eyed, her mouth dropping open. "What … you don't think they could do that?" he asked.

"On the contrary," Christina laughed. "I know they can do it. I've drunk from a pikki."

Carl shook his head, slowly, a bemused smile on his lips. "You've drunk from a pikki?"

"Yes, I have. The Aborigine boy who showed me the way home that time I was lost gave me a drink of water and he told me the bowl it was in was a pikki. I think I must have forgotten that, but hearing the name again brought it all back." She laughed softly. "All those years ago, and it seems it was only yesterday." Her eyes widened, delight washing over her face. "I've remembered something else, the water was sweet because he had done something to it, something he seemed to be quite proud of."

"He would have soaked flowers, probably from one of the banksias in the water over-night."

Christina nodded. "I think that idea might have occurred to me even back then." She glanced around her. "I suppose there are lots of things in the bush that they use, apart from the animals?"

"Indeed there are. The Kombumerris are what we whites would call hunter/gatherers, and they would certainly have long ago discovered that bush tucker in this part of the country means good eating."

"Kombumerris … " Christina mused with a whimsical smile. "Did your teamster friend know how that name came about?"

"No, but he did seem to know that the country belonging to them took in the length of the Nerang River valley and from the Darlington Range in the west to the Coomera River in the north, a large area of land, by anyone's account."

"It didn't extend as far north as the Logan then?"

"Apparently not. It seems your little friend may have belonged to another tribe."

"Yes, it does. Carl, you won't have to cut down this tree, will you?"

"It's not a bad-looking tree, Christina, but I don't know how it would look in the middle of a cornfield or a potato patch, for that matter." He gave a deep chuckle. "It will be interesting to see Danny's response to the idea."

Christina's smile wavered. "I didn't know that he was coming this weekend."

"Sorry, love. I should have remembered to tell you. He will be staying over for the whole weekend."

"Well, I expect we'll be able to see that he doesn't go hungry, but I'm sure I don't know where he's going to sleep?"

"We'll figure out something, Danny's not too fussy about where he sleeps."

"He has certainly shown himself to be a true friend these past weeks, what with all that help he gave us clearing away the flood debris and rebuilding the fences."

Card nodded, a sombre expression coming to his face. "Yes, that was really something, wasn't it? I don't know how we would have managed without him … "

"It would certainly have taken a good deal longer than it did to get things back in order."

"I'll say it would. Here we are with just seven weeks gone by since the creek tried to wash us out of the mountains and already our place is looking like a farm again." He passed the baby into the arms Christina held out for him. "I'll be glad of his help with these trees too, I can tell you. There are more giants among them than I had realised."

Settling herself on a patch of soft grass, with her back against the bole of a tree and the baby at her breast, Christina tried to close her mind against a now familiar uneasiness, but it wasn't to be denied. There was something about Danny O'Rourke that bothered her and there was little sense in trying to tell herself that she was just being fanciful. Not when it was something so persistent and, furthermore, something that prevented her from slipping into an easy friendship with him, as she had been wanting to do ever since the time of Charlie's birth. In fact, such kindness had he shown her then, such understanding and gentleness, it had seemed inevitable that, afterwards, a special kind of friendship would be there between them. Instead, it seemed that all they had was a stiff, uneasy relationship they both had to work at.

Not that he ever did or said anything that she could take exception to. Unless it was the way she sometimes caught him looking at her or Charlie, such a strange staring, with his eyes narrowed and his whole countenance dark as though with anger or pain. The worst thing about having him look at her in such a way was that it caused her to remember what he had said that day at Beenleigh when he'd come looking for Kathleen.

Christina's sigh was so deep the baby's soft lips released their clinging grip on her nipple and he looked up into her face enquiringly. "It's a funny old world we live in, Charlie," she told him with a wry smile. "You'd do well to remember that."

The baby gurgled happily, dribbling milk from the corner of his mouth, and Christina tickled him gently. "So, you think the whole business is a laughing matter, do you? Then tell me this, do you think your father would have a similar opinion?"

Squirming happily on her lap, he gave her a wide grin, then abruptly turned his head and pressed his nose back into the soft flesh of her breast, his lips quickly finding what they sought.

"Shame on you, Charlie," Christina reproved, laughing softly. "You're more interested in being a glutton than you are in your mother's problems." But her laughter was short-lived and it was with a thoughtful expression on her face that her gaze shifted to where Carl was busily marking trees with the axe he had brought with him. What would he do if she were to tell him? she wondered. Say that she was being silly, that Danny often looked strangely morose and brooding? Or would he be concerned, distressed even? She sighed again, but quietly this time, her lower lip caught between her teeth. What was it that she'd be telling him, in any case? That Danny seemed to think that he was in love with her? Dear God in heaven, no! Even to infer such a thing would be too much. Something she would never be able to bring herself to do, so full of conceit would it make her appear, for one thing, and so embarrassing would it be, for another; a married woman with a man who wasn't her husband in love with her? What next, for heaven's sake? Don't think about it then, she told herself sternly. Even if Danny will be here for the whole weekend, don't think about it. When all's said and done, he's only coming to help Carl and, God knows, he can do with all the help he can get. All that wilderness to be cleared from his land, fences to be built, land to be ploughed. Responding to a sudden need to reach out to the man who was her hard-working husband, she called out, "Time for a break. Come and talk to Charlie and me."

Straightening from where he'd been chopping at the exposed roots of a small tree, Carl, grinning, pushed his battered hat to the back of his head, "A break when I've only just started." But he let the axe drop, wiped the perspiration from his brow and came to sit beside her. "We've still a long way to go, Christina, but we'll get there, never fear."

"I know we will," Christina told him softly. How could they not? she asked herself, when a man such as her husband said they would?

The days, never long enough, sped by, as did the weeks and months. But gradually the nucleus of a farm began to emerge from the homestead's primordial wilderness. The small patch cleared of scrub early in the piece grew larger and larger; the earth was turned and planted with corn, potatoes and pumpkins. A stretch of forest on a gentle slope was thinned out to provide a grazing area for six young steers. And a number of trees had been bought, felled and marked by timbermen, convinced that a road to the Tweed would soon be running through these hills and they'd be able to get them out.

Christina was very proud of what they had accomplished, and the only blot on her happiness was that, when the crushing season down at the Tweed was in full swing, Carl was only home at the weekend. The fact that she now had her baby to share her isolation became something of a mixed blessing. She was alone in being responsible for him, for his very life, as it were. What if he were to become sick, or if there should be an accident? Now that he was crawling all over the place and climbing up on things, wasn't that always a possibility? But Charlie, more by good luck than good judgment, managed to avoid any major mishaps, and, apart from a sneeze or two that had his mother holding her breath, never even looked like being sick.

Christina began to relax. She talked to him endlessly, of course, and, to her delight, he began to reply with "Mama … Mama" or "Papa … Papa".

Not to be outdone, the parrot decided that it would also talk. This, however, brought Christina no delight whatsoever. On the contrary, its first coherent attempts had her diving out of the back door to stare at the bird in wide-eyed dismay. It wasn't possible, she tried to tell herself. He had just been screeching. He hadn't really said what she thought she'd heard. But he had. The parrot, running boastfully back and forth along its perch lost no time in telling her so, "Shut up, fevens sake! Shut up, fevens sake!"

"Oh no! No! You are not supposed to say that!" Christina cried distractedly. "You're supposed to say 'Hello Harry.'"

"Shut up, fevens sake! Shut up, fevens sake!"

"Stop it, do you hear? Stop it at once! If you can't say 'Hello Harry', then don't say anything!"

But the parrot was happy with this new sound it was able to produce and had no intention of relinquishing it, not when it gained even the dog's bewildered attention and set to flight those of its relatives who came out of the bush and tried to steal its food.

Christina couldn't wait to tell Carl, and the minute he swung from his horse on Friday night she burst forth with her woeful tale, fairly bristling with indignation, which wasn't helped by his reaction. He threw back his head on a loud guffaw, laughter exploding from him.

Christina stared at him, disbelief causing her eyes to widen and her mouth to drop open. "You can't think it's funny?"

"It's more than just funny, it's downright hilarious."

"It's not. It's not the least bit funny even. For one thing, just think what Mother will say. She has always hated to hear anyone say 'shut-up'. She says it's almost as vulgar as swearing." She wrung her hands together and finished on a wail, "I never used to say it, not until that wretched bird started screeching when Charlie was trying to sleep."

"I know, love." It was a sympathetic murmur, but his shoulders were still shaking with laughter.

"How could it learn words it had no business learning when it's too dumb even to say its own name? And it's not only Mother we have to worry about … what about other people who come to visit?"

"There's not one of the people who visit us who won't be amused."

"What about the Reverend Whiting? He told Mrs. Laver that he hopes to be able to ride up here to see us. What's a minister going to think when a parrot screeches at him to shut up?"

"Well, he might be a little affronted to begin with, I grant you that. But, once he's had a chance to think about things, he'll be wanting to acquire our clever bird for himself. Just think what a godsend he would be when people talked during his services."

Christina sighed. "Don't think I wouldn't be happy to let him have him."

"You wouldn't?" Carl gasped in mock dismay. "The most unusual parrot in the whole of the Colony and you'd part with him just like that?"

"I most certainly would." Then, with the semblance of a smile curling her lips, "Can you picture the good Reverend walking around the countryside with Harry on his shoulder?"

"Not just at the moment, but I'll work on it." Carl pulled the saddle from his horse and dropped it on to the verandah before catching her around the waist, a wide grin on his face. "That may not be such a good idea. After all, he's a man of truth, so what would he say when people far and wide asked him who taught Harry to talk?"

Christina dashed a hand over her mouth, her eyes twin pools of reflected horror, but Carl went on cheerfully, "Of course, if you really would like to get rid of him and the Reverend doesn't want him, I'm sure they'd love a talking parrot over at the Nerang pub, and we could probably convince them that they shouldn't tell where he'd come from." He sighed heavily, but with the grin still on his face. "It would be a pity to do that though. Most people can only teach their birds to say 'hello Joey', 'pretty cocky', or things like that, so you could become quite famous."

The very idea was too much, for both of them, and their laughter echoed free and clear down through the valley.

31

It was Christina's twentieth birthday, and she delightedly held up the pair of open-work stockings that had emerged from the small, ribbon-tied parcel Kathleen had brought her. "They're lovely. Where on earth did you get them?"

"Where do you think?"

"I've never seen anything like this at Lenneberg's."

"They didn't come from Lenneberg's."

"You've been to Southport then?"

"No, I got them from the Afghan hawker, as a matter of fact."

"Oh, he's been again!"

It was a wail of disappointment and Kathleen grinned. "Well, if you will live up here in the mountains with only a bridle track to come and go by, you have to be prepared to miss such rare treats, you know?"

"But I did so enjoy his visits. Was it the same old fellow?"

"Yes, and he still looks a hundred years old, so does his horse. That tarpaulin top he has on his cart still looks as though it's going to topple over, and, of course, according to Da, he still sells nothing but trash."

"So, like everyone else with such an opinion, he bought nothing from the old hawker?"

"If a pen-knife, a new belt and a mouth-organ, of all, things, can be regarded as nothing."

They both laughed and Christina, shaking her head slowly, mused, "It's always such a long time between his visits, I wonder how far he goes."

"Hundreds of miles, I would think." The smile left Kathleen's face and she said quietly, "You almost lost that bet I made with you." The traces of amusement still hovering on Christina's face were gone in an instant. "What do you mean?"

"It didn't take very much more than a year for David to write and tell me that he's going to marry Margaret Sanderson, just one month more, as a matter of fact."

"Oh no! He didn't!"

"Oh yes, he did. I got the letter last week."

"I can't believe it," Christina groaned. "I just can't believe it."

"Well, I didn't really have too much trouble believing it, not when I'd been more or less expecting just such news. It still didn't stop me from kicking up a right royal shindy, though. I bawled and bawled, so loudly the whole of Mudgeeraba could have heard me. In the end I had Ma and Eileen wailing along with me and Da swearing that he would take his gun to the villain." She grinned with wry amusement, her eyebrows raised. "Isn't that like a true Irishman? If David had come to fetch me like he said he would, Da would more than likely have taken his gun to chase him off the place and yet there he was threatening to shoot him because he hadn't come."

"Who would be blaming him, nevertheless?" Christina murmured, her heart aching for her friend but at a loss as to what words to say.

"After the performance his wife and daughters put on, no one, I should think. Poor old Da must have been bewildered clear out of his wits. To make matters worse, we had a visitor at the time."

Christina's mind had been quick to summon up a picture of the scene as it would have been, dismaying enough, but now, with someone from outside the family entering into it, even more so. "Who was it?"

"A timber-getter new to the district. Michael Sheehan is his name and he's only been out from Ireland this past year. Da met him at a two-up game and, when he found out that he hails from County Cork, insisted that he call on us the next time he brought a load down. Poor chap, he must have thought he'd been invited to visit a mad-house."

"He certainly didn't choose a very good time. What did he say, for heaven's sake?"

"For a time I think he was too overcome with amazement to say anything. In any case, he wouldn't have been heard, not unless he'd shouted, that is. But, afterwards, he had plenty to say … to me. When he figured that I'd had enough of a go at letting my feelings be known to all and sundry, he grabbed me by the arm and marched me clear out of the house, leaving the others standing there in the kitchen gaping for all they were worth. Then he gave me this lecture on how I should think about exactly why it was that I was carrying on in such a way, whether my heart really was broken as I'd been declaring over and over, or whether it was just my pride that had taken a beating."

"Goodness, that was a bit arrogant of him, wasn't it?"

Kathleen lifted her shoulders in a faint shrug. "I suppose it was when you think about it, but he certainly brought me to my senses, made me think about things, you might say." Charlie, now a confident toddler, came to lean against her knee, proffering a soggy, half-eaten biscuit. She smiled down at him, her eyes at once gentle. "You eat it, darling. It's not something Aunty Kathleen fancies right now."

Unperturbed, the little boy gave her a flashing smile before making his way to the back door where he leaned forward to peer out.

"There's no use hoping to unload it on Bluey, either," his mother told him. Then, more clearly so that he would understand, "Bluey's not here, Charlie, he's gone with Papa."

"Where is Carl?" Kathleen asked.

"He's gone over to Nerang for the cattle auction. He wants to buy a few more steers for fattening, if he can get them at a reasonable price. He should be home by midafternoon at the latest."

"I might get to see him on the way down, if not here. You've done all right out of your beef cattle, haven't you?"

"We got a good price for those we had here at the time of the flood and the new lot over on the homestead will be ready for market before winter arrives."

"You've got quite a few young beasts here, as well."

"Six of them, but they've quite a way to go before we can sell them. That's why Carl is hoping to acquire a few more, preferably nearer to being fully grown and just needing to be fattened."

"Well, you certainly seem to have enough feed for them. But to get back to Michael Sheehan … like I already said, he obliged me to think about things. Not that I changed my mind about my heart being broken, mind. It was … is, I mean. After all, how could it not be when the man I love with every single bit of it is going to marry someone else? But I did come to the conclusion that wounded pride had something to do with the way I'd been carrying on, and I must admit that I got to feeling a bit ashamed. I even tried to offer an apology of sorts, but Michael said that pride was a good thing to have but a bit of an unholy nuisance at times, so there was no call for me to be doing that, apologising, that is."

Her mouth had curved into a smile that was only faintly rueful and Christina considered her thoughtfully, "How old is this fellow?"

"He told me that his father was sent out here as a convict in 1838 and that he was born three months after he left, so he has to be in his mid-forties. Not that he looks it, mind. He's a strong, striking-looking bloke who could quite easily pass for thirty or thereabouts. He's come out hoping to find his father, as a matter of fact, if he's still alive, of course."

"He doesn't know?"

"No, he's heard nothing from him in years and years, not since he escaped from the prison at Port Macquarie. It seems that he just disappeared into the blue, or, as Michael has been hoping, into a timber-getters' camp somewhere. He has been told that a lot of ex-convicts became timber-getters, including some of those who blew through before they'd finished serving their time."

"Well, I know that Jack Keach and Samuel Hansen are both ex-convicts. They aren't escapees though, at least I don't think they are."

Kathleen frowned. "Who on earth are you talking about?"

"The two timber-getters who brought Lars down from the mountains when he had his accident. They told us they had been convicts one day when they stopped in for a cup of tea. I think they felt obliged to do so. As a matter of fact, I have a feeling they were at Port Macquarie also."

"Then they might have known Mr Sheehan, or perhaps something about him. I wonder if Michael has met up with them yet."

"How long has he been in this area?"

"Only about three weeks, I think. Gosh, I must get Da to tell him to look them up. What are their names again?"

"I suppose they could be around the same age as Mr. Sheehan would be."

"He would be in his mid-sixties now, he was only twenty at the time he was deported."

"Only twenty, how terribly sad, and the wife he left behind expecting his baby would have been very young also, I suppose."

"She was just seventeen. She's dead now, though … these past five years, Michael said. God, Christina, can you imagine waiting all those years for your husband to come home? That's what she did, apparently, just waited and waited, never giving up hope."

"I wonder what kept him from going back after he escaped."

"Michael thinks that he probably thought that he'd be picked up again and hanged for escaping."

"Why was he deported in the first place, do you know?"

"Because he was supposed to have plotted against the English; for high treason, as they call it. Do you know what that high treason was, Christina, what he and five others were really plotting to do?"

Christina shook her head.

"To steal some grain so that the people in their village wouldn't starve. That was all they intended to do, steal some lousy grain! For that, three of them were hanged and the other three sent out here on a convict ship, one of them a sixteen-year-old boy whose older brother was one of those hanged."

"They were terrible times, Kathleen," Christina sighed. "But they are in the past now, thank goodness."

"Are they? I wonder. Oh, I know that Irish men, women and children are no longer deported from their homeland to Australia, but they can still be thrown into prison for almost no reason at all. They have only to be suspected of trying to upset the so-called peace, for instance, and in they go. They don't have to do all that much to get themselves hanged either."

A little uneasily, Christina murmured, "I thought conditions in Ireland had improved during these past years. Haven't new Acts of Parliament been passed to lower rents and help those families who get into arrears?"

"A big deal that is, when Irish farmlands go on being owned by the English gentry." She spoke with a sting of bitterness that Christina found both surprising and disturbing. Never before had Kathleen spoken in such a way. Even when she'd referred to the potato famines in Ireland, she had done so in an off-handed manner as though she saw those times as being over and done with and not worth fretting about. There was nothing off-handed in the way she had spoken just now, though.

"It won't always be that way, Kathleen," she said, feeling somehow compelled to say something reassuring.

"Of course it won't. The Irish people will see to that." This time the words were uttered with a fierce conviction, but, even as Christina caught her breath, Kathleen was laughing softly. "What are we doing discussing such matters? It's your birthday, so let's talk about something cheerful." She arched her eyebrows enquiringly. "The new baby, for instance, is it definite yet?"

Christina nodded, a smile coming to her lips. "It seems to be, another August arrival."

"That's wonderful. I'm ever so pleased for you and Carl." Her grin widened teasingly. "You're not going to do what you did last time and have it up here in the mountains, are you?"

"I certainly hope not."

Kathleen shook her head slowly from side to side. "I never cease to be amazed about that, you know? Our Danny acting as midwife, it really does come close to being unthinkable."

Christina's smile faltered and warm colour rushed to her cheeks, but she said steadily, "I owe Danny a great deal, Kathleen. I could very well have lost Charlie and perhaps my own life as well, had he not been with me."

"Oh, I know, and don't think I'm not thankful that he did show up just when he was needed. It's just that … well, for it to have been Danny, of all people. You must admit that he hardly seems the sort of person capable of proving useful in such a situation."

"Who knows what a person is capable of doing in a particular situation, any person?" Christina got to her feet. "I think it's time we had ourselves a cup of tea and a slice of the birthday cake Mother made for me."

"And I know you've made some of those wonderful ginger biscuits,

I've been smelling them ever since I … " She broke off with a delighted chuckle as the parrot screeched, "Shut up, fevens sake! Shut up, fevens sake!" Then burst out laughing when Charlie hurried to the door and yelled at the offender … what he said sounding very much like what the bird was saying.

Christina, setting out the cups and saucers gave an exasperated groan. "You wonder why I'm not on speaking terms with that wretched bird."

"You've an affection for him, nevertheless. You can't be denying that now, can you?"

"I can't quite bring myself to wring his neck, if that's what you mean."

"You know very well that's not what I mean. You're a bird-lover way out of the ordinary, you always have been. So, how could you not be fond of Harry, the cleverest of them all?"

"So clever he's teaching my son to talk boldly, as you just heard."

"Well, the poor fellow doesn't know that he's talking boldly." Her eyes danced with mischievous laughter. "All he knows is that you taught him how to talk and he wants to reciprocate by teaching Charlie."

Christina grinned in spite of herself. "I suppose I have to be thankful that you didn't say that it was poetic justice or something like that?"

They were sipping their tea when Kathleen remarked, "Danny's going away."

"On a job?"

"Yes, but more or less permanently. He's off to New South Wales to become a shearer."

Relief, unbidden but unmistakable, swept through Christina, but she asked, "New South Wales? Why couldn't he become a shearer in Queensland?"

"He thinks he might be better off down there, to begin with, at any rate."

Christina swallowed against the guilt that arrived rather belatedly to challenge her relief. Was he leaving because of her? No, surely not. "Does he know how to shear?" she asked, a little uneasily.

"He did quite a bit at Jimbour Downs when he was younger, so he shouldn't have too much trouble getting the hang of it again. As a matter of fact, he reckons he can become a ringer before too many weeks have passed." She gave her shoulders a quick shrug. "He probably will, too, him being as determined as he is."

"What does that mean, to be a ringer?"

"A ringer is a champion shearer. He's the one who scores the highest tally of sheep shorn at a particular shed in a given time, usually during a season."

"How many would that have to be?"

"That would depend on how good the opposition was, but it would certainly have to be a good deal more than two hundred a day. Out at Taldoon there was a bloke who put up tallies of two hundred and fifty-four, two hundred and fifty-five, and two hundred and fifty-six on successive days."

"Heavens, that many?"

"Well, it's contract work, so the way to make good money is to go like the very devil. A pound for every hundred sheep, that's what a shearer gets."

"I can see that it could be a quite profitable occupation, though I can't imagine how anyone could shear so many sheep in a single day."

"It's not something I'd like to be trying, I can tell you that. But I think Danny looks on it as being something of a challenge."

"How do your parents feel about him going away?"

"They don't mind. In fact, if the truth be known, they are probably feeling quite relieved. Sooner or later, some of the boys will have to leave the farm. They can't all get married and live there, not unless they want to starve."

"Patrick and Sylvia are still at the Weaver's, aren't they?"

"Yes, and he seems to have stopped threatening to gather up wife and baby and come on home, thank goodness. Because Arthur has seen to it that they now have their own little house, I suppose. But there are still the other four boys at home and it seems only right that Danny should be the one to leave, what with him being the age he is and not married, and, what's more, not looking to be."

This time Christina found herself obliged to swallow very hard before she could speak, not only because of the notion that seized upon this opportunity to resume its pestering, but also because she was being eyed ever so speculatively. "Danny probably enjoys being a bachelor," she remarked as lightly as she could manage.

A small secret smile touched the corners of Kathleen's mouth. "I don't think so, well, not especially, at any rate. No, I think the only reason he isn't planning on getting married is that he can't have the girl he wants."

Christina's heart skipped a beat before beginning an uneasy pounding. What was Kathleen getting at, for heaven's sake? What was she thinking with that look on her face? "I don't know what you mean."

"You are that girl, Christina, the one he wants."

"No! Don't say that!"

The anguished plea had burst from her lips and Kathleen's eyebrows shot up. "You knew?"

"No, I didn't know! I mean … there isn't anything to know! It's ridiculous what you said!"

"It happens to be true, nevertheless. Danny loves you and I have a feeling that he has done so for quite some time."

Christina, biting her lip, set her cup shakily back on its saucer. She wanted to protest further, to insist that it wasn't so, but her mind wasn't about to let her do that, not when it had so many incidents to recall and certainly not with her heart knowing the truth of the matter. She lifted her eyes disconsolately to those of her friend and drew a long sighing breath. "I've tried to tell myself that it wasn't so."

"How long have you known?"

"It's just been a feeling, not something definite, so I don't think I can answer that."

"He's never actually said anything or tried to make a pass at you?

Christina was at once indignant. "Of course he hasn't! Danny is Carl's friend, he would never do anything like that!"

"No, I don't suppose he would," his sister conceded, nodding thoughtfully. "But how did you come to know then? Or get a feeling, as you say? There must have been something?"

Christina moved uneasily on her chair, her eyes unhappy, her face awash with soft colour. "It was the way I've sometimes caught him looking at me, or at Charlie. The first couple of times it happened I was a bit surprised but I didn't pay it too much mind. After all, I wasn't really sure just what it was that I had seen on his face. It was something more than the brooding expression he so often wears, I knew that much, but he turned away so quickly I didn't really catch more than just a glimpse."

"But, since those first times you've felt differently?"

Looking into the gently questioning face, Christina momentarily wondered what she was doing telling Danny's sister such things when she'd been so intent on keeping them locked away; her secret, bewildering and distressing, for sharing with no one. Then, with a small inwards sigh, decided that she wanted to tell her; longed, in fact, to have the uncertainty and niggling guilt brought out into the open.

"Since then," she began slowly, "there have been enough times for me to know that it wasn't just my imagination, as I had been trying to tell myself, and I haven't been able to stop myself from thinking back to that day in Been– " She broke off, her long lashes swooping upwards as she realised that Kathleen's question as to whether Danny had said anything hadn't been quite truthfully answered. "Danny did say something, that day he came to Beenleigh looking for you. Not the sort of thing you would have been meaning, though. In fact, he yelled at me and what he said was so strange I was sure I had misunderstood." She hesitated, pressing her fingertips together in steeple fashion and considering them frowningly. "I'm still not sure exactly what his words were or if he really meant what he seemed to be saying. It's only the fact that he's taken to watching me in such an odd way that I've come to be concerned about them."

Kathleen's curiosity got the better of her. "For the love of Mike, Christina, what did he say?"

"Well, he was going on about how you and David would never be able to marry because he wasn't a Catholic and I retorted that it would have been a different story had he been the one in love with a Protestant. He became so angry he looked as though he was going to explode and that was when he said it, something about why did I think he'd stood aside and let Carl make all the running with me."

"Struth! Fancy Danny coming out with that!"

Christina groaned softly. "I keep wishing I hadn't said what I did. I know that I shouldn't have, not when you'd told me that he would never marry a non-Catholic, but he was being so ... so ... "

"Obnoxious," Kathleen supplied with a wry grin. "I can imagine how he would have been going on, believe me, and, when all's said and done, it was entirely my fault." Her grin spread a little. "Not Danny's falling in love with you though, I wasn't responsible for that."

There was no answering smile on Christina's face. "That was none of my doing either. I've never done anything to encourage Danny to think that I might ... well, care for him in a special way."

"I know that, Christina. What's more, I don't think the fact that he's in love with you is anything for you to be getting so agitated about."

"I don't want him to be unhappy on my account."

"If he is, it's his own doing. Even apart from the religious business, he must have known that he didn't have the ghost of a chance with you. He's not blind, after all, so he couldn't help but see the way it was with you and Carl from the very beginning." She laughed softly, encouragingly. "Why, even when you were protesting that you could never marry a Prussian, your heart didn't believe you, did it?"

Christina managed a faint smile. "It seems that it didn't."

"Just as well too. Look at the happiness the two of you would have missed out on. And no Charlie, what a tragedy that would have been." Her smile wavered and she gave a small sigh. "The trouble with me was that I let my heart have too much of its own way. I didn't give my head a chance to say a single word."

"It's just terrible that things haven't worked out for you and David. I'm so sorry I feel like weeping for you."

With the smile quickly back on her lips, Kathleen threw up her hands in mock horror. "Please don't. If you do, you'll get me going again, and I've told you the kind of performance I can put on."

Responding to this attempt at light-heartedness, Christina brought a smile to her own lips. "I certainly wouldn't want to bear witness to something like that."

"No, you wouldn't, and I'd probably scare Charlie half to death. In any case, there's no call for you to be weeping for me. Even though it hurts like the very devil just to think about it, I have come to the conclusion that it might not be such a terrible thing for David to be marrying someone else, from my point of view as well as his. Like I've said before, I wouldn't have really fitted in that family."

"If you and David had been able to marry, of course you would have fitted in."

Kathleen slowly shook her head. "You know what Mrs Klaussen is like … well, David's mother is every bit as elegant, and the thing is that it all seems to be so easy for her. She's always so calm and collected she seems to run that big house simply by lifting her hand, if you know what I mean. There's never any fuss or bother even when really important people, Members of Parliament and such like, come to stay. It was agony for me just trying to imagine how I would be in her situation, and I would have been one day if I'd married David."

"You would have learnt how to handle it."

"I doubt it. I think you have to be born to that station in life. If you're not, the best you can hope for is to be able to muddle along, and that wouldn't make for very much happiness, I've been thinking. In fact, I didn't realise what a strain I was under the whole time I was out at Taldoon until I got home again. Just being able to say what I thought and act in my own natural way was like being freed of shackles."

"You probably tried too hard to be like David's family."

"Perhaps I did, but I hate to think what would have happened if I had behaved like an O'Rourke."

"That's silly. You have a very nice family, and they don't behave any differently from countless others."

"Well, they behave differently from the Charltons, I can tell you that." She giggled suddenly. "In fact, even after just a year away, life back home was a bit of a shock in more ways than one. It's like Michael says, I suppose; we get into new ways of looking at things without even realising it has happened."

Christina, whose gaze had wandered to her son playing on the small verandah, brought it back questioningly to the other girl's face. "You must have spent quite some time talking with this Michael?"

Kathleen's grin was, surprisingly for her, a little sheepish. "It wasn't only the one time that I saw him. He took me over to the dance at Nerang on Saturday night, to cheer me up, he said."

Christina's eyes widened, her lips pursing over a silent 'oh'.

"There's no call for you to be looking like that, like someone who's just found the answer to a riddle or something. It was just a friendly gesture on Michael's part. After all, he's old enough to be my father almost." Her grin spread, no longer sheepish. "He doesn't dance like my father though, he dances divinely."

"So, you had a nice time at the dance?"

"I most certainly did, a much nicer time than I expected to have."

"Does Michael have a wife somewhere?"

"No, he has never been married."

"Why not?"

"Oh, I don't know, Christina. Perhaps he's never met anyone that he wanted to marry. That can happen, you know? In any case, it's none of my business. He's a friend, that's all."

Smiling, Christina reached over and patted her hand. "Of course he is, and I'm ever so pleased for you." It was true, she told herself, she was pleased that Kathleen had found someone to help her through this unhappy time of her life, and there was no reason whatsoever to be feeling even the slightest bit alarmed.

The months slipped by, merging summer into autumn and autumn into winter. With the new baby growing inside her, Christina's old fear returned, not as forcefully as previously, and she was quick to scold herself. Hadn't she already given birth to one healthy child, and under the most trying of circumstances? Hadn't the doctor again assured her that everything was going along exactly as it should be, that she had no need to be the least bit worried? Yes, yes, yes. Everything was going to be fine. But, ever since the birth of Charlie, not a single day had gone by on which she had failed to give thanks to God, and now this fervent thanksgiving was joined by an equally fervent pleading, "Please God, let me keep this baby too … please… please."

Alice Maria Eichstead was born in her grandparents' bed on the 15th of August 1883, just three days before her brother's second birthday. Doctor Davies was on hand to help her into the world and smack her tiny bottom, an indignity to which she took such exception not even Christina doubted that she had come to stay.

To Christina and Carl the year 1883 had given a second child; to the Colony of Queensland it had given a new goldfield. Back in 1880, a stockman named William Mackinley had discovered gold on a dome-shaped mountain rising twelve hundred feet above sea level, some twenty-five miles from Rockhampton. For some time little was done about the discovery because the deposit differed from that with which most prospectors were traditionally familiar: the gold on the mountain was not mixed with quartz but with ironstone; furthermore, the surface gold was difficult to recognise because, in the first place, it was extremely fine, and, in the second, it was often coated with oxide of iron. In 1882, however, Thomas Morgan, an experienced mining man, and his brother had pegged out some six hundred acres. In early 1883 they brought the mine into production, and during the year enormous quantities of gold were extracted. This would be, it was widely agreed, the greatest goldfield of them all. It wasn't, after all, a creek bed, or an exposed section of an elusive reef, it was a mountain – a mountain that appeared to be, at least in goodly part, made of gold.

On the Colony's political front, changes were pending that would have far-reaching effects. Since 1878 the Conservatives, under Thomas McIlwraith, had been in power, and these had been years of prosperity, especially in the Tropics. However, growing scandal about the way labour was being obtained for the cane fields had gradually weakened McIlwraith's position. At the same time, Samuel Griffith, new leader of the Liberals, had been whipping up support, particularly in Brisbane, by pledging to clean up the 'blackbirding' traffic, and in the general election held towards the end of the year he won handsomely and became Premier.

32

Christina considered the water level in the barrel frowningly. However had she managed to use so much? Here it was only Thursday … Thursday morning at that, with the barrel almost empty. And Carl had seen to it that it was full to the brim before he'd left on Monday morning. Well, there was nothing for it, she would have to fetch up more water from the creek. She glanced to where her son was intently examining a large tomato displaying its first hint of redness, calling absently, "Don't pick it, Charlie, it's not ripe yet." What on earth was she to do with him while she fetched the water? She couldn't leave him in the house with the baby; he'd be bound to try to pick her up or feed her something. The fence around the garden certainly wouldn't keep him in; he'd shown on more than one occasion that he had no trouble whatsoever in clambering over that. He could get out of the house too, for that matter. So, he couldn't be simply left either in the house or in the garden, he would have to be restrained in some way.

When his mother first produced the stocking and tied one end around his leg, Charlie thought it was a game and chuckled delightedly. But his laughter was quickly gone when the other end was tied securely around a table leg. "No, Mama, no tie Charlie up," he pleaded tearfully.

Christina swallowed the lump that came to her throat and hugged him to her. "It's just for a little while, darling. Mama has to fetch some more water from the creek."

"I come too, I come too." He was tugging at the stocking, trying to free himself.

"You can't, Charlie. I can't hold on to you and carry up buckets of water as well. You know how steep the bank is, you could fall in and how terrible that would be."

"No fall in, no fall in. Come too, Mama … come too!"

Biting her lip, Christina resolutely eased the sturdy little boy struggling in her arms down on to the cushion she'd pulled from a chair on to the floor. "I'll tell you what I want you to do to help Mama, darling," she cajoled. "You sit here like a good little boy and talk to baby Alice if she starts to cry, and you can have a little picnic. I've got some biscuits and an orange drink all on a tray. That will be nice, won't it?"

Charlie didn't think so and he wailed miserably, "Go wif you, Mama, I go wif you."

With the tips of her fingers, Christina gently brushed the tears from his cheeks. "Do you know what I'm going to do after I've brought up the water? I'm going to saddle up Teddy so that you can have a ride."

Teddy, a cream and tan Shetland pony, had been Charlie's birthday present and was the source of the greatest joy ever to reach his two-year-old heart. The tears were quickly blinked from his eyes and his quivering lips steadied into a smile. "A long ride?" he questioned eagerly.

"Yes, a real long ride." Christina got to her feet and set the tray down beside him. "You'll see … Mama won't be gone for very long at all."

"Just a little time?"

"Yes, just for a little time."

But there was no way any worthwhile quantity of water could be brought up in just a little time, it was much too difficult a task. The steps Carl had cut into the creek bank and the handrails along the more tortuous sections of the steep path helped in that they lessened the possibility of a tumble into the swiftly-flowing stream, but they didn't do a great deal to ease the arduous task of getting buckets full of water up the bank. Christina had decided that the most she would be able to accomplish would be to half-fill the barrel, but, scrambling up the bank for the third time she had changed this hopeful estimate to one third. One bucket at a time was all she could manage and it was taking too long, much too long.

The splash, accompanied as it was by a child's astonished scream, came as an explosion to her ears, causing her to spring upright, the bucket she'd been on the point of filling slipping from her suddenly nerveless fingers, her heart racing, her eyes darting about in a frantic searching. Seconds later, the current brought the small fair head, flailing arms and ballooning clothes abreast of her. Oh God, it was Charlie! He was in the creek!

Flinging herself into the water, Christina lunged toward the bobbing form, her hands reaching desperately for the dress that was keeping her son afloat. She touched it … lost it … felt it again … grabbed at the wet fabric. She had him! Oh, thank God, she had him! Now, if she could just manage to pull him to her, get her arms around him. But Charlie, gulping water each time he opened his mouth to scream, was too terrified to see anything other than a new threat in the clutching hands that held him against the creek's flow and caused even more water to splash over his face; he thrashed about wildly, fighting to free himself. The current, too, fought Christina, not only for possession of her child, but for her own body as well. Already in water up to her armpits, she struggled doggedly to keep her balance and avoid being swept out of her depth. But the current was a formidable enemy. It washed her skirt heavily about her legs and sucked at her water-filled boots; it eddied powerfully about her tensed upper body and tugged at her straining arms. Finally, threatening to loosen her grip on her son's clothing, it induced her to take another step forward. That single step gave it victory.

Christina had been standing on the very edge of the deep water channel and now she floundered into it, losing her hold on Charlie, swallowing water and with her lungs screaming for air. She lived, it seemed, through an eternity before strong arms closed around her and dragged her to the surface.

She was alive! By some miracle she was alive! But, oh God, where was Charlie? What had happened to him? Even as she took the first painful gulps of air, the screaming rose from her throat, "Charlie! Charlie! Where are you, Charlie?" On and on it went, but no one answered. She was pulled to the shore and lifted bodily on to the narrow, flattened lower bank, but the only sounds reaching her ears were her own piercing screams. She tried to get to her feet, to rush back into the water, but her legs wouldn't support her and she dropped to her knees, shivering violently. Her eyes, aching and wild with anguish, searched the water, but there was no fair head to be seen, no billowing clothes … nothing, nothing! He was gone!

Her little boy was gone! The screams died in her throat and she bent her head, sobbing harshly.

The hand on her shoulder shook her, gently at first, then more persistently. Whose hand was it? she wondered incoherently. She turned her head slightly, still without raising it, and saw the long, bony fingers – black fingers! She lifted her head slowly and the anxious black face bent over her broke at once into a smile. The man who had pulled her from the water? Yes, it must be, since he seemed to be the only one here. She should thank him then, for saving her life. But, dear God in heaven, why hadn't he saved Charlie's instead? Fresh sobs choked her and she again lowered her head, covering her face with her hands. At once the long fingers pressed back into her shoulder, hurting her. What was he doing, for heaven's sake? Pulling at her, trying to push her. Why didn't he just let her be? Now he was saying something as well … talking, talking, expecting her to understand his strange words. Something about them wasn't strange, though, the way he said them! Excitedly! He was talking excitedly!

This time Christina's head was jerked up and, still on her knees, she swung around as she was being urged to do, a glad cry falling from her lips. A black boy, no more than eleven or twelve years old was making his way along the bank with a wide grin on his face and Charlie, pale but very much alive, on his shoulders. Christina struggled to her feet and tried to run, stumbling over her sodden skirt and hindered further by her squelching, water-filled boots. She covered only a couple of yards, but it was enough. Charlie was in her arms, wet, cold and sobbing huskily, but with his chubby arms tight about her neck.

Her rescuer waited a moment or two, then unclasped Charlie's clinging arms and took him from her. He screamed loudly and Christina only just managed to stifle her own wail of protest. She wanted to keep him close to her, to hold and hold and never let him go. But she saw at once what the man had in mind. Charlie's shivering body needed to be warmed and he was seeing to it; the wet clothes were peeled away and his hands moved rapidly but gently, rubbing, rubbing … first the face and chest, then the rest of the small body, even his blue-tinged buttocks. When, finally, he set the little boy back on his feet, the colour had returned to his face and the blood was once again coursing warmly through his veins.

Christina, though, was still shivering, and her rescuer considered her worriedly. Oh no! she thought, just a little hysterically, he can't do that to me! He didn't try to. He swung Charlie on to his shoulders and strode back to where the path began its upwards climb, beckoning to her to follow.

The young boy stayed with her, waiting patiently each time she stumbled or was obliged to stop to regain her breath. At first he didn't touch her, but, when she came to a halt only a short way up the embankment, she felt his hands tentatively touch her backside, then push gently. By the time they reached the top, he was, however, pushing with a good deal more vigour and Christina knew she could never have made it without him.

The man, with Charlie still on his shoulders, was more than halfway to the house, and Christina, her breath ragged but with a new anxiety spurring her on, grabbed a handful of her sagging skirt and set off after him. The baby … ? Oh, how long had it been since she'd walked out of that door? An hour … ? Two … ? She had no idea, but it was certainly too long ago for the poor little mite to be still asleep. She was more than likely crying her poor little heart out, but there were no tears on the baby's rosy cheeks. She was wide awake, but contentedly engaged in a bemused study or her own tiny fingers and she gurgled happily when her mother's face appeared over the cradle.

"What a dear, sweet little girl you are," Christina murmured huskily, "but Mama can't pick you up just now, she's all wet."

Christina had rushed past the Aborigine hesitating by the door and warily eyeing the softly growling Bluey, but now she returned to him, Charlie clinging tenaciously to her skirt, her eyes, warm with gratitude, going at once to his face. "Thank you," she said fervently. "Thank you from the bottom of my heart. I will never forget you, or your son." He nodded, seeming to understand, but within Christina a voice groaned that it was far too little. A few words in exchange for hers and Charlie's lives. What else could she do? Give him something? What? He was welcome to anything she owned. But what was there that would be of benefit to him and not a hindrance to his way of life? Some eggs, bananas, oranges? Perhaps he would be glad of such things and at least it would be a gesture. A gesture, she repeated wryly to herself, a small, small gesture … some eggs and fruit when what he really deserved was the return of this valley to the way it had once been.

The boy had remained on the creek bank, thoughtfully eyeing the horse grazing a short distance away. He wasn't afraid of these animals the white people had brought with them from across the seas; the first of them so long ago now there were none of his people left who could remember when it had been. Even his grandmother, who was very, very old, said that they were already here when she was a little girl. Edging closer to the horse, the boy chuckled quietly, his eyes dancing with amused recollection. The old woman was afraid of them though. Hadn't she, only two moons back, run off into the night, wailing and tearing at her hair, just because one had wandered by her sleeping place … going so far it had taken her all the next morning to make her way back again?

Samson lifted his head and gave a startled snort at the gentle touch on his shoulder. The boy caught his breath but didn't remove his hand and, when the horse resumed its nibbling of the soft green grass, laid the full palm of his other hand on its neck, moving it slowly back and forth while he crooned the name he knew the white man had for the animal, "Horse, horse." One day, he told himself, I will climb up on the back of one such as this and go as fast as the wind. Then everyone will see that I'm not afraid.

The faint smile left his small dark face, a frown taking its place. He had been afraid today though … very afraid. When he'd felt the strength of the water and the weight of white child, his heart had beaten like the wings of a hawk inside his chest. He hadn't let the little one go, though; he'd hung on to him even when his arms felt as though they were being torn from his body. And he had remembered what his father had told him to do when the water became too strong … instead of trying to fight it, to wait until it swirled in close to the shore. His father would be pleased that he had remembered to do that. He'd be pleased that he'd been able to save the white child too, and proud of him. Yes, even though he'd been afraid, his father would be proud of him. He might even tell him so.

Charlie told Carl before Christina had a chance to do so. Giggling and squealing as his father first threw him into the air, then tickled his neck with his newly-grown beard, he regained his breath long enough to yell, "Charlie fell in the creek!"

The laughter was wiped from Carl's face and his eyes, ablaze with urgent enquiry, flew to where Christina patiently awaited her turn to welcome him home. She nodded and he at once lowered Charlie to the ground and came to her. "He said that he fell in the creek?"

Christina bit her lip and nodded again. "It's true, he did fall in the creek."

"For God's sake, how? What was he doing there?"

"I tied him to the table when I went to bring up some water, but he freed himself somehow and he … he…" Her voice trailed away before the look of incredulity on her husband's face.

"Fetch some water? Why? The barrel was full when I left on Monday morning."

"I know, but there's been such a lot of washing to do, what with all the baby's things, and, with the weather so hot and sticky, I've been bathing both her and Charlie every day." She sighed unhappily. "I know I should have been more careful with the water."

Carl caught her by the shoulders and drew her to him, pressing his lips to her forehead. "Tell me what happened," he invited, sudden gentleness driving the urgency from his voice.

To her dismay, Christina found she was unable to do so without becoming tearful. Two days with only the children for company and a long, sleepless night in between had done nothing to erase the horror that was as a living thing in her mind. If anything, it had become even more intensified. Every heart-stopping moment had been relived and relived; every horrific possible outcome envisioned over and over, and now she had to inflict it all on her husband, set his heart to thumping, his face to twisting with grim anguish. If only she didn't have to do that.

If only she could spare him the knowing that he could have come home to find his wife and son drowned in the creek and his baby daughter more than likely lying dead from neglect in her cradle, and if only she could now put it all from her mind, just stay here with his arms holding her close …

But her husband wasn't about to let her do that, he wanted to know it all. "Christina, what happened after Charlie fell in the creek?"

"I went in after him, of course." She heard and felt the sharp intake of breath and went on quickly, "The skirt of his dress was billowing out and it sort of kept him floating."

"You were able to reach him without going into deep water yourself?"

"I wasn't out of my depth when I first caught hold of his clothes, but I couldn't pull him in, the current was too strong and Charlie was struggling so."

"And you got out of your depth?" The words burst from Carl's throat as a harsh groan that begged for denial.

Christina nodded, tears choking her. "I knew I should stay where I was," she murmured, "but the water was pulling Charlie away, I could feel his clothes slipping out of my hands, and the next thing I knew the water was over my head … "

Finally, it was all told and Christina was able to give herself up to soft, unrestrained weeping. For a time Carl let her be, rocking her gently in his arms, saying nothing. These, he knew, were tears that needed to be shed. Were they not, they would be as a wall holding in the tensions brought to his wife by her ordeal, allowing them to grow. When he did at last speak, he did so quietly, lifting a hand to stroke her silken hair. "It was a terrible thing to have happened, Christina, a fearful experience I would have given anything to have spared you. But it's over now and we have to learn from it, then let it find its place in the past. Thanks be to God and the black man and boy, whoever they were, I have you and Charlie here with me still. I want to rejoice about that, not grieve about what might have been." He gave a soft chuckle as Charlie, having had enough of being ignored, squeezed between him and Christina. "And you have to agree that no lasting harm appears to have been done where this young rascal is concerned."

Christina glanced down at the small upturned face pushing its way through the folds of her skirt, blinking back her tears and shaking her head on a wondering sigh. "How can he have forgotten how terrified he was so easily? Look at how he told you. It's almost as though he's proud of the fact that he fell into the creek."

Carl reached down and hauled the small wriggling body up into one arm, retaining his hold on Christina with the other. "You know that you were a very naughty boy to go to the creek, don't you, Charlie?"

"Mama tied Charlie up."

"Yes, and that was so as you wouldn't follow her to the creek and fall in, but you did go to the creek and you did fall in, didn't you?

Charlie nodded, his eyes growing wide and solemn at the stern note in his father's voice.

"You would have drowned, you know? If the black boy hadn't been there to save you, you would have gone under the water and been lost for ever and ever. Then Mama and Papa would have had no little boy."

Christina gave a small moan of protest, but Carl, squeezing her shoulder, said quietly, "He has to understand these things. We have no nursemaid to be following him around and we certainly can't be watching him every single minute ourselves, so he must learn where danger lies."

"But he's still only two years old, little more than a baby."

Carl gave her a wry smile. "Do you think that young black who saved our Charlie's life got to be two years old without being well aware that only with extreme care should he venture on to a steep creek bank?"

For a moment or two Christina didn't reply. In her mind's eye she was seeing another young black boy – one who had known the wild, tangled bush like the back of his hand and may very well have saved her own life. "No," she said finally, "I don't suppose he did."

Later, when the dark of night had claimed all the lower regions of the valley and only the ridges and hilltops still basked in the soft rose-grey still lingering from the day, Christina and Carl sat on their small verandah and spoke again of the young black boy and his father. "About eleven or twelve years old, you said?"

"I think that would have been about his age." Christina sighed softly.

"So very young to be saving someone's life."

"Well, that's another thing about the blacks, they seem to be able to swim from a very early age, and that's something I've been thinking Charlie should learn to do before he's much older, next summer perhaps."

"You wouldn't try to teach him here though?"

"No, it would have to be further downstream." He grinned suddenly. "Perhaps you could suggest a nice safe spot?"

Christina tossed him a glance of mock reproach. "I am not going to reply to that."

"I wonder why," Carl laughed, leaning back in his chair and stretching his legs out in front of him. "I wonder why."

Christina watched him through eyes warm with love. How good it was to have him home, and what joy to think that there were only two weeks to go to Christmas, after which would come the quiet time for the sugar industry, those wonderful months when he wouldn't be riding off to the Tweed every Monday morning, and, apart from other odd jobs, would be here with her all the time.

"They would have come from the far bank, of course."

Christina brought her mind back from its blissful contemplation of a time when loneliness would be ousted from her life. "I suppose so, though I don't really know, they were just there."

"They would have," Carl affirmed, nodding. "I saw a few of them over there only last weekend. They've come for the bunya nuts, more than likely."

"I saw them too."

Carl considered her thoughtfully. "You didn't tell me."

"No, and you didn't tell me."

"I didn't want you to be worrying when I was sure there was no need for you to do so."

Christina's lips curved into a smile. "And I didn't want you to be worrying that I might be worrying."

They both laughed softly and Carl reached for her hand, squeezing it gently. "I'm glad you weren't afraid of them. After all, they are just people trying to get on with a way of life their race has known for centuries and which we have made very difficult for them."

Christina nodded, the laughter fading from her face. "I thought about that when I was trying to think of what I could give the man to express my gratitude to him and the boy?"

"Did you think of anything?" Carl asked, his eyebrows raised.

Christina shook her head. "Not really. I did point to that bunch of bananas, but he just shook his head, smiled and was gone. I almost wished that I had a magic wand so that I could change the valley back to the way it used to be."

"Almost?" Carl queried with a wry smile.. "Almost wished?"

"Well, in my heart I knew that, even if I did have a magic wand, that was something I'd never be able to bring myself to do, not after all the work you've done to bring this farm into being, not when it has become our home."

"It's really only a small area that we have, Christina, when you compare it to all the land still untouched in these parts."

"I know, but there are new settlers coming all the time. You've said yourself that land is being taken up in all the valleys and well up into the ranges."

Carl nodded. "Yes, that's true enough."

"And what about when the roads are finally built?"

"That will certainly open up more and more land for settlement. Talking of which, I've got news for you, they are to begin building the road up here early in the new year."

"Early in the new year?" Christina repeated incredulously.

"Hey, I was expecting you to be overjoyed."

"Oh, I am, believe me. It will be just wonderful, especially now that we have little Alice as well as Charlie. It's just that I can't help thinking that where the blacks are concerned it will prove to be a major intrusion into their way of life."

"The road would have come, Christina, even if we hadn't been here, and it won't be the only one winding its way through the mountains. Roads, bridges, railways … the Colony can't progress without them, and the Government is well aware of that."

"Progress for the white man, but what for the black man?" Christina mused wryly. "What is the word that's the opposite of progress, do you know?"

"Retrogress, I suppose." Carl eyed her frowningly. "I think you're exaggerating, sweetheart. In any case, if you are going to look at it that way, you have to remember that the blacks have had thousands of years in this country and have made no progress whatsoever; they are still one of the most primitive races on earth."

"Perhaps they were content with things just the way they were."

"It's not in the nature of man, whatever the colour of his skin, not to want to better his way of life."

Christina tossed him a surprised glance. "I always thought you had a good deal of respect for the blacks' way of doing things?"

"For their way of doing some things," Carl corrected. "They are superb hunters, no one will be denying that. But, if their ancestors from ten ... perhaps even twenty ... thousand years back were to return, I'll guarantee they'd be able to join in the hunt and know at once what was going on. Because all those years before, they would have hunted in the very same manner with the very same types of weapons."

"Well, if a way of doing something is successful, where is there need to change it? You're surely not suggesting that they should have gotten around to using guns?"

Carl gave a short laugh. "You are being very difficult, my love. All I'm trying to do is point out that the Aborigine hasn't improved his lot even though he's had all the time in the world in which to do so. But, I grant you, that wasn't a very good example. Where the hunt is concerned, his spears and boomerangs have no trouble competing with our guns." He ran a hand over the thickening growth of golden beard on his chin. "I think I might do better to get you to consider their overall situation, especially how, after all this time, they still rely for their living solely on what nature provides of her own accord. Somewhere along the line they must have come to recognise the pitfalls in such complete dependence on something so unreliable, but have they done anything to overcome them? No! No soil has been turned, no seeds planted. What nature hasn't supplied unaided they have simply gone without."

"But wouldn't that have been because they know this land is big enough for them to survive by moving from place to place as it became necessary? I remember you telling me that a large area of land belonged to the Kombumerri people."

"Yes, that's right, but, believe me, to live off nature and make a success of it as the blacks do, a large area of land is essential. Even in a rich and fertile location, the number of individuals who can survive there for any length of time is exceedingly small. The result of such a way of life is, in fact, almost always a sparse population, and you can see that with the blacks. We don't know how many of them there actually are scattered throughout Australia, but there's no getting away from the fact that, when you take into account the thousands of years they've been here, their numbers aren't all that great."

Christina sighed quietly. "What some people have said might be true then, that they were a dying race even before the first white people arrived."

"It could well be, I suppose. On the other hand, it might be that there have never been great numbers of them."

"What do you suppose will eventually happen to them, the ones who are still living their old way of life, I mean? I know what happens to those who have taken to living around the townships, trying to adopt the white man's way of life."

"Yes ... well, there's much about that we can only regret, of course."

"Oh Carl, it's nothing less than tragic. What we see over at Nerang is apparently only a small instance compared with other places. Marie writes that there are dozens of them living in shanties on the outskirts of Beenleigh and more joining them all the time. She says it should never have been allowed to happen."

Carl shrugged his broad shoulders. "It's all very well to be saying that now, Christina, but how was anyone to know that things would turn out the way they have? People saw that there were blacks not only willing to be peaceable but to be friendly as well, so they gave them cast-off clothing to cover their nakedness and introduced them to the white man's way of life. It was a perfectly natural thing to want to do. Who was to know that, whereas the blacks wouldn't be all that keen on the idea of work, there were other things they would take a great liking to, booze being at the top of the list."

"That does seem to be behind most of the problems with them. Marie says that they would sell their ancestors' bones for a bottle of rum."

"She could be right at that, at least where some of them are concerned." The corners of his mouth twitched. "I wonder what you'd do with a bundle of ancient bones if you did happen to acquire them?"

Christina, half exasperated and half amused in spite of herself, shook her head at him. "That's not very funny!"

"I was just wondering."

"You should be wondering about what will happen to those Aborigines who are still trying to live in the old way when all the bush comes crashing down about their ears. That was what I asked you."

"Well, you may be sure that it will be a long, long time before there is a shortage of bush in Australia, or of unoccupied spaces. By then, there will hopefully have been time for some more satisfactory form of relationship with the blacks to have evolved. I'm not about to be trying to predict just what that might be, but you have to remember that this isn't, by any means, the first country in which there has been a situation such as we have; we should be able to learn something from the experience of others."

"It seems we are doing that already, learning from the Americans at any rate. According to Father, there are now quite a lot of people who think that reservations are a good idea."

"That's just talk. I'm sure the authorities will come to see that reservations, even though they might have a point or two in their favour, aren't the answer."

"What point or two?"

"Well, they'd be protected areas and the blacks would be able to continue their way of life without interference from us whites. The trouble is that there are so many different tribes, all with different dialects, and all with attachments to particular regions, it would be necessary to have reservations from one end of the country to the other for them to be a satisfactory solution."

"I would hate to see them confined, even if it did mean they could keep their old ways and customs."

"I'm not even sure that's desirable. I know that all association with us has meant thus far is degradation and a confused helplessness, but surely it can be made to benefit them, to bring about improvements in their standards of living, for instance. Like I said, they've made no progress in thousands of years, but it could be that the time for change has arrived and that it's up to us to help them adjust. After all, there wouldn't be too many places in the world where time has literally stood still as it has here"

"How would we bring about these beneficial changes?" Christina asked with a faint smile.

"I wish I knew. I should think that in the first place we would have to convince them that it's not necessary to do something in a certain way just because it's been done that way down through the ages." He gave a short, soft laugh. "I'll give you an example of what I mean. You know the sort of hut the blacks build with sticks and ti-tree bark? Well, considering they're only ever intended to provide shelter on a temporary basis, they serve the purpose very well. Except for one thing … the placement of the doorway has nothing at all to do with the way the prevailing winds blow, it always faces the direction from which the group has come. Even in winter, when the westerlies are so bitterly cold, if they have come from the west, it's on that side of the hut that they will have their doorway."

"Why on earth would they do that?"

"I doubt whether they'd know why themselves. It's just something they've always done."

"I'm sure there must be a reason."

Carl grinned. "Well, if you ever find out what it is, I'd be much obliged to be enlightened."

"Perhaps that's what we should be doing, trying to find out more about them, about why they do the things they do."

"I suppose if we could manage to do that, it would be something."

"You don't think we would be able to?"

"Not to any worthwhile extent, I'm afraid. The blacks live in a world in which myths and superstitions have become so entangled with reality it would be well-nigh impossible for an outsider to understand their reasoning, just supposing, of course, that they were willing to try to explain."

Christina heaved a long exasperated sigh. "What a dilemma it all is!"

"Things have a way of working out," Carl told her, reaching over to give her a reassuring pat on the knee. "Often, all that's needed is a little time and patience."

"It's almost a hundred years since the first white settlement in Australia. That seems to me to be a great deal of time."

"It is, of course, but not when you consider it from the point of view of the changing ways of human beings. When you do that it's but the blink of an eyelid. Besides, you have to remember that for a goodly part of those years the blacks were the enemies of the white settlers, and still are in some areas. There's another thing ... those who came before us were for a long time fully occupied with ensuring their own survival; they had too much on their plates, what with droughts, failed crops and such like, to be worrying as to what the eventual lot of the country's original inhabitants might be."

Christina nodded slowly, thoughtfully. "I have heard Father say much the same thing."

Carl gave her a tender smile. "I know you feel indebted to the blacks, Christina. I do too, and so we should, there being no doubt that we almost certainly owe them both yours and Charlie's lives, but ... "

"It could be that I owe them my life twice over."

"Yes, it could. A little girl lost in the bush might well have died. Even so, I don't think you should let yourself become depressed about what might become of them. For all we know, that man who pulled you from the creek and his companions could be feeling sorry for us ... toiling from daylight to dark, stuck here in the one place, bundled up in clothes even in this stinking hot weather."

A smile tugged at the corners of Christina's mouth. "The young boy was naked, but the man did wear something, one of those apron-type things made out of skins."

"Hmmm, I'm glad to hear that," Carl told her with a quick grin.

"Not half as glad as I was to see it, after we got back to the house, that is. Before that, I couldn't have told you whether he was wearing anything or not."

For a time they sat on in an easy silence, their hands clasped. Then Carl said quietly, "I had company on the way home from the Tweed."

"Oh, who?"

"Michael Sheehan."

"What was he doing down there?"

"He didn't say, and it was really none of my business so I didn't ask him. He still means to return to Ireland though, he did tell me that much."

"I don't know why he doesn't do so then. It's months now since Jack Keach told him that his father has been dead for years and years. Why is he waiting around when he's so sure that Ireland can't manage without him?"

Carl chuckled. "Ah-ha, my love, your claws are showing."

Christina gave him a small rueful grimace. Not even to herself was she able to deny the dislike she felt for Michael Sheehan, a dislike which had begun the first time Kathleen brought him up to meet them and grown during subsequent meetings. This in spite of the fact that, dismayed by her reaction to someone her friend obviously admired, she'd taken herself to task in no mean manner and made a genuine effort to find something likeable about the man. There was, she had finally concluded, nothing whatsoever. He was a man so choked with bitterness and anger it was as though there was no room left within him for any other emotion. Not once had she heard him really laugh and only very rarely did he smile. On the other hand, his mouth was ever so quick to curl sardonically, so sardonically, in fact, it made similar expressions she'd seen on Danny O'Rourke's face seem almost angelic in comparison. It was that, Christina had decided, that she disliked most about him; that and the piercing scrutiny of his strange yellow-flecked eyes. It's positively indecent, she told herself, for a person's eyes to try to bore into someone else's mind the way his do, as though trying to search out its innermost thoughts.

"Well, are you going to tell me what you are thinking behind that sombre expression, or is it better that I don't know?" Carl teased.

Christina gave her shoulders a faint shrug. "For one thing, I was thinking that he has the eyes of a hypnotist."

"He's not a bloke to be comfortable with, I grant you that, but in a way I feel a bit sorry for him; it must be terrible to have such hatred eating at your innards."

"I've tried feeling sorry for him, and I've never denied that he has reason enough to be resentful of the English." An impish grin touched her mouth. "After all, I know what it's like to have one's country in the hands of foreigners."

"I seem to recall that I had to do quite a deal of talking to get you to understand that those particular foreigners weren't all monsters as you seemed to think."

Christina's grin widened into a smile. "At least you convinced me that one of them wasn't."

"Only one? I thought I'd done a better job than that!"

"Well, perhaps there were a few more. I know you got me thinking that the Kaiser wasn't such a wicked old bloke after all."

They both laughed quietly. Then Christina, a smile still on her lips, mused, "I wonder how Michael Sheehan would react to a lecture from an Englishman?"

Carl tossed her an amused glance. "Lecture eh? Is that what it sounded like?"

"Almost, either that or a history lesson."

"Hmmm, after that, I don't think I'll tell you what Michael Sheehan would do to an Englishman daring to give him a ... ah, a lecture."

"You don't need to," Christina told him, still chuckling. "I know what he'd do. He'd knock the poor fellow's block off before he got to say more than a few words."

"Without too much trouble. He tells me that he's done quite a deal of boxing in his time. That's what happened to his nose, as a matter of fact, it was broken in a fight. Not that it's made all that much difference to his looks. Crooked nose notwithstanding, he's a handsome enough bloke."

"Kathleen seems to find him so. It could even be that she has fallen in love with him."

Carl shrugged. "She's impressed with the fellow, that's clear enough, but I hardly think she'd go falling in love with him, he's old enough to be her father."

"She won't be thinking about things like that if she loves him." Her laughter of a moment before suddenly gone, Christina sighed, "She has changed, you know?" Dramatically, she added to herself as Carl nodded in agreement. This past year she has changed dramatically, into a restless, tormented young woman who seems to have taken into her very soul the misery that was Ireland's; a fiercely determined crusader convinced that she and Michael Sheehan will be the ones to put right the wrongs of centuries. "I have a feeling she means to go back to Ireland with him," she murmured unhappily.

"Michael Sheehan has hinted as much, but suppose we wait and see. Even though she does appear to be taken with the fellow, she must know that she'd be very foolish to give up the life she has here for one in a land awash with tears." Getting to his feet, Carl pulled Christina to hers, slipping an arm about her shoulders and yawning widely. "It's past my bedtime, I'm afraid. It's been a long day, and Kathleen's problems, if such they be, will have to wait."

Rubbing her cheek against the hand resting on her shoulder, Christina sighed quietly, "I think she will leave us."

33

Thinking that Kathleen might go to Ireland with Michael Sheehan was one thing; knowing that she would do so something else again. Christina, resisting an urge to put her hands over her ears so that she wouldn't hear, felt her body almost shudder with the dismay throbbing through it.

"You're supposed to be pleased for me, Christina. I'm not going to be an old maid after all."

"Oh … I am, Kathleen." Belatedly she leaned forward to kiss the other girl's cheek. "I'm very pleased for you and I wish you and Michael every happiness."

Kathleen gave her a quick grin. "But you're not happy that I'm off to Ireland? Well, you're not the only one, you may be sure about that. In fact, it could very well be that the only people truly happy about it are Michael and me."

"I thought perhaps your parents might be?"

"Pleased to have one of their brood returning to the old country, as it were? Well, they are not. They think I'm crazy or something. Ma even came right out and said that the evil ones had stolen my wits."

"Well, when you think about it, you'll be a long, long way from them, and that's not something for them to be happy about."

"No, I don't suppose it is," Kathleen conceded with a sigh. "I just wish they'd see that it was meant to be though; for me to meet Michael and go back to Ireland with him. As a matter of fact, Christina, I think everything that has happened to me has been part of the scheme of things leading up to what I'm about to do now."

"I'm not sure what you mean?"

"That thing with David Charlton, for instance. Looking back, it all seems to have been a silly charade, and it sickens me to think that I could have let myself be belittled in such a manner."

"For heavens' sake, Kathleen, it wasn't like that! You were in love! You weren't belittled!"

"Yes, I was, Christina, and it was exactly like I said, a charade. They had me acting, didn't they? Like some person I wasn't and could never be, just so as I would fit in with their way of things and not be an embarrassment to them. More horrific than all of that even, I was going to marry an Englishman, a Sassenah, without giving a single thought to what his kind have done to the people of Ireland."

Christina stared at her, her eyes wide with disbelief. What was she saying, for heaven's sake? Surely not something that she truly believed? "David Charlton is an Australian, Kathleen, just as you are; he was born in this country, and has lived here all his life."

For just the fraction of a second Kathleen's face reflected confusion, then she said flatly, "He's still English, just like his father, and his mother is more English than German. In fact, except perhaps for Mrs Klaussen, the whole family is as English as can be. I can tell you, it fair makes me weep with shame to think that I was so anxious to become one of them." She shook her head, tossing her vibrant hair about her shoulders, almost as though the recollection was so unbearable she sought to fling it from her mind. Then, abruptly, the scowling expression left her face, replaced by one that was smilingly tranquil. "I'm not to be fretting about it, Michael says, not when it happened at a time when I was still so young."

What does he mean by that? Christina wondered more than a little angrily. That Kathleen did, in fact, have something to be ashamed of? That, had she been older, she would have been required to see herself as something of a traitor? Was there no limit to the arrogance of the man, to the hatred smouldering within him? Or, far worse, was there no limit to his hold over Kathleen? Michael says … Michael says … Michael says. It was almost as though she could no longer think for herself, and there seemed little doubt that she had absorbed not only Michael Sheehan's ideas, but also his turbulent state of mind.

Drawing a deep breath to still the quivering she knew her growing anger would have brought to her voice, Christina said as calmly as she could manage, "It's just ridiculous for you to be thinking, even for a moment, that you have anything to be ashamed of. You fell in love with a very charming, handsome young man, and he with you. Unfortunately, you weren't able to marry him and, because of that, things didn't work out. That's all that happened, you didn't betray anyone or anything."

For a moment or two Kathleen didn't reply, and, dismayed, Christina saw the mist of tears in her beautiful eyes. Then she gave her shoulders a shrug and said with the semblance of a smile, "You're a very dear friend, Christina, but you don't understand why I feel the way I do about that thing with David."

Christina, feeling tears prick the back of her own eyelids, bit her lip. Her heart felt heavy and in her mind there was a confusion of words crying out to be said. Finally, though, the only ones to find their way to her lips were, "With all my heart I wish you didn't feel the way you do."

Again, for just a moment, Kathleen seemed taken aback, a little uncertain. Then she grinned. "Hey, stop sounding so glum. All that is in the past now and I've already told you I'm not going to be fretting about it. Things worked out the way they were meant to and that's what matters, what's really important. It's like Michael says … things like that happen because no man is the master of his own life."

Sensing the futility of arguing further, Christina brought a faint smile to her lips. "I thought you were a woman."

Kathleen grinned. "You know very well what I mean, the same goes for a woman."

For a time they talked of other things, drank tea, and laughed and played with the children. But, as was inevitable, their conversation wound its way back to that which was uppermost in their minds. "When will you be going?"

"In May, early May. We are to be married on the last Saturday in April and sail just a week later."

"But that's only … what? Five … six weeks off?"

"Just under six."

"Why go so soon? Couldn't you and Michael stay on for a time after you're married?"

"Not really. Michael says that what with this being a time of change for

Ireland, there's a great deal to be done. He's very impatient to get back there as a matter of fact."

"He hasn't seemed to be in too much of a hurry?" Unable to help the small jibe, Christina immediately regretted it. "I mean … he has seemed quite content to stay on here."

"He has had things to do here. Since he was coming to Australia to try to find his father, he was asked to see if he could rally support among the Irish families here for the new movement he's involved with. It's called the National League."

"What do you mean by rally support?"

"Well, for one thing, encourage them to donate money like the Irish people in America do, thousands and thousands of dollars they give."

"Was he successful?"

"Not very. Well, not where the money was concerned at any rate. Most Irish families in this country are pretty poor still, and, of course, he hasn't been able to cover all that much territory in the time he's had. Still, Michael feels that he has accomplished something, even if it has only been to remind us all that the fight for independence is still going on in Ireland." She paused, sighing heavily before continuing. "You wouldn't think people would need to be reminded about something like that, would you? At least not those like Ma and Da who grew up back there and saw it all for themselves, the famine and the way the English so-called gentry treated them. But it seems that a lot of them have quite put it out of their minds." Again she sighed heavily, this time with exasperation. "How can they do that when they know that a million people died during the three years of the great famine while a further million went fleeing out of the country? All of it the fault of the Sassenah!"

"The failure of the potato crop wasn't the fault of the English," Christina felt obliged to remind her.

Kathleen stared at her, the beginnings of an impatient frown on her brow. "Well, of course they didn't cause it, but did they do anything about it, anything to stop the famine from becoming the disaster that it was? No, of course they didn't! Michael says that, far from being concerned, they were glad to see it come because it got rid of so many Irish people."

Christina shook her head slowly from side to side, finding it impossible to believe what she'd just been told. It was true enough, she supposed, that a good deal more could have been done to help the Irish people weather the great famine, but to suggest that England would have viewed it as a blessing in disguise was just too much. "Whatever reason would they have had for wanting to be rid of the Irish people?"

"Well, they knew how hostile towards them the Irish people had become and there were getting to be too many of them; growing numbers meant big trouble for the Sassenah and they knew it. In the long run, the famine didn't do them all that much of a good turn though. It might have cut the Irish population quite dramatically, but Michael says that, afterwards, those who remained were tougher and more able to stand up for their rights, especially those who were children during the great famine."

"Like Michael?" Christina queried quietly. "He would have been a child at the time, wouldn't he?"

"Yes, like him." Kathleen's chin lifted with a hint of pride. "He says that he became a rebel when he was just ten years old."

"And he's still one?"

"Of course, but it's different now. They are more organised, with the mass of the Irish people behind them, and supporters in parliament even. There's not the violence that there used to be, which is just as well since Michael has to be careful what he does. He has already spent time in prison and the English aren't likely to be forgetting that."

Christina's eyebrows flew upwards. "He's been in prison?"

"In Mountjoy Prison in Dublin; it was in the 1860s. He was arrested as a conspirator in the Fenian uprisings, but he wasn't in jail for all that long. The uprisings didn't accomplish all that much and the Sassenah, thinking the movement over and done with, soon got round to releasing most of those they'd arrested." She gave a short, mirthless laugh. "What fools they were! If only they had known!"

"If only they had known what?" Christina asked, her breath catching in her throat.

Kathleen considered her pensively. "Perhaps I shouldn't be talking to you like this, Christina, but you are my best friend, and you are certainly not English." She hesitated only a moment before going on, "The truth of the matter is that, whereas the Fenian movement might have been finished under that name, it wasn't by any means over and done with. All of those who had been associated with it were still determined to achieve its objectives, even if they were obliged to change their tactics. In fact, Michael says that I'd never believe the things they've done in the years since, had to do if there was to be any hope of a decent life for the Irish people."

"He didn't tell you what sort of things?"

"No, even though I asked, he didn't tell me. He said that, now that they've begun to see the results of their efforts, it's best to let such things rest in the past and hope that they are never again necessary. That doesn't mean the struggle is over though. Michael says that it's only been in these past three or four years that they've really begun to get somewhere and that it's much too early to be thinking that everything will go well from here on. What has happened has been due, for the most part, to a movement known as the Land League which was founded by a Michael Davitt. It has now become the National League and they've got this Mr. Parnell, who's in parliament and is considered a true leader of the Irish people even if he does happen to be a Protestant. There's something else that's very, very important, like finding a four-leafed shamrock almost ... Mr. Gladstone, the British Prime Minister, is in favour of Home Rule for Ireland."

Christina couldn't believe what she was hearing from Kathleen's lips. She knew so much. How clever her teacher had been, and what an apt pupil he had taught. "So now the whole matter can be left to parliament and there won't be any call for rebellion?"

A small scowl came quickly to the other girl's face. "It would be good if that were the case, of course, but Michael says that, even though big gains have been made, what with the Land Act and such like, it won't do to become complacent. For one thing, they have to work to make sure that Mr. Parnell gets re-elected next year. For another, they have to go on intimidating those landlords who still have bad reputations where their tenants are concerned, and, as hard as it may be to believe, they have to keep at the people too, make sure they don't begin to see the battle as being won just because some control is now being exercised over the rents they have to pay."

"I hope it all works out well, Kathleen. Everyone knows that Ireland has had more than her fair share of troubles through the years."

'It will, Christina. Ireland is well on the way to becoming independent, you may be sure about that. When that happens, the Irish people will finally be able to own their land instead of being obliged to rent it from the Sassenah landlords." She seemed suddenly to be caught up in emotion and her gaze wandered out through the open door in an aimless fashion.

Watching her, Christina tried to ignore the feeling of unease that refused to go away, but without success. It's because I can't think of Michael Sheehan as someone who is right for Kathleen, she told herself unhappily. If I could, it wouldn't seem nearly as bad for her to be going so far away from all those who love her. That was another thing, did Michael Sheehan truly care for her? He desired her, of course, but did he have it in him to love her, or any woman, for that matter? How could one tell with a man like that? A man whose eyes pierced the minds of others and burned with bitterness, but were always wary, revealing nothing of what was going on in his own mind? And Kathleen? Was it love she felt for him? Or was it simply admiration that not only overwhelmed, but misled? Or perhaps something else again … a strange gratitude that he had awoken an awareness within her, given purpose to her life, as it were?

Although she continued to gaze out through the door, Kathleen's voice interrupted Christina's wondering. "You know, Christina, I've sometimes thought that God kept Australia waiting for the Irish people, that all those years when there were only blacks here, He had it in mind that this would be a fine place for all those leaving Ireland's shores. I even went so far as to think that He had set the English the task of discovering the place by way of punishment."

"It could have been so," Christina told her, her voice gently humouring.

"No! I was wrong. It wasn't like that at all."

The denial came so sharply, with Kathleen swinging back to face her so abruptly, Christina started, her eyes widening before puzzlement again narrowed them. "I don't understand."

"God didn't mean them to come here, or to go to America either. He meant for them to stay and fight for their country, not run away from it."

Christina stared at her, at a loss for words.

"It's true," Kathleen went on, nodding solemnly. "They should never have left. Michael says the fact that they did has brought a lasting shame to the Irish race."

"What were they to do then?" Christina gasped incredulously. "Stay there and die?"

"Stay there and resist."

"Oh Kathleen, you don't really mean that, you can't."

"Why can't I? Because my own parents were among those who left?"

Christina spread her hands helplessly. "I wasn't meaning that, but … well, surely you're not ashamed of them?"

"Of course not! They were simply victims of something that was bigger than they were. An exodus born of fear, that's what Michael calls it, and he says it's that failing of Irish courage we have to be ashamed of, not the individual people who packed up and left."

"It could be that they needed even more courage to pack up and leave than they would have to stay there," Christina suggested, just a little tersely. "After all, it was no easy life that awaited them, either here in Australia or in America."

"I know that, and I'm not denying that it would have taken courage to set out for a distant land, but it still doesn't alter the fact that they were running away, forsaking their homeland."

"What about my family then? Do you believe that in leaving Schleswig we were forsaking our homeland?"

"That was different."

"Not really. We weren't starving or being badly treated, but we were under the rule of a foreign power just as Ireland is. Denmark had already fought one hopeless war. What else do you think the Danish people could have done to keep Schleswig out of Prussian hands?"

"I don't know, Christina. It's not the same. Your family left because they wanted what Australia had to offer, not because they felt there was nothing but misery for them back there."

True enough, Christina thought. They had come here because her father wanted to be a farmer on a decent-sized piece of land, not because the Prussians were depriving them in any way. She realised suddenly that she'd been holding something in her mind, a notion that she'd been considering almost subconsciously, but with something akin to alarm. "That's not why you're going, is it?" she asked frowningly. "Because you feel you have to make some sort of retribution?"

"Of course not! What a thing to be saying, for the love of Mike!"

"I just thought that perhaps you might be feeling obligated in some way."

"What about feeling obligated to go where my husband goes? Doesn't that count for anything?"

"Of course it does," Christina murmured, then, with a soft groan, "Oh Kathleen, it's such a long way to be going."

The set expression left Kathleen's face and her lips curved into a rueful smile. "I know and I just can't imagine what I am going to do without you. I'll still be able to write to you though and I'll probably come back for a visit one day."

Probably, Christina repeated to herself. At least Kathleen wasn't making a promise as she herself had done … one day I'll come back. Not probably, but will … will! Well, she'd been only eight years old, after all; a child to whom it hadn't seemed possible to be leaving one's homeland for ever and ever. How could that child have known that, in the strange and distant land to which she was going, new bonds would be woven in such a fashion as to come about almost imperceptibly, at the same time obliging the old ones to tug at the heart with less and less insistence.

"You don't think I will come back, do you?"

Christina lifted her gaze to the other girl's suddenly anxious eyes and summoned a conviction she was far from feeling. "Of course you'll come back. You're a fair dinkum Australian, aren't you? Besides, what has there ever been to stop Kathleen O'Rourke once she set her mind to doing something?"

Kathleen brightened, her lips parting in a quick smile. "And I'll have plenty of time for a number of visits. After all, I'm still only twenty-one years old."

So am I, Christina told herself, so who's to say that there won't come a time when I'll go back to Schleswig, with my husband, of course, and just for a visit.

Since the Catholic church at Nerang was still in the process of being built, Kathleen was obliged to choose between being married at home or travelling to Southport, where a church had been completed two years previously. She chose the latter, even though it meant that not all of her family would be able to attend, explaining that both she and Michael had always wanted a church wedding. Christina wasn't able to be present either and she didn't know whether to feel relieved or regretful. Visiting her parents on the following day, she said as much to her mother.

Elsie, the baby settled contentedly on her lap, gave her shoulders a small shrug. "Then it's probably just as well the decision as to whether you should go or not was made for you. Kathleen wouldn't have expected you to go all that way with two small children."

"No, she understood that it was well-nigh impossible for us to be at the wedding."

"Well then, there's no call for you to be concerning yourself in that respect."

"What about feeling guilty because I'm not sure that I really wanted to be there?" Christina questioned with a small wry smile.

"I don't think you need do that either. We all want those we love to be happy, so it's only natural we should shrink from watching them do something they might come to regret."

"Perhaps I'm looking on a gloomy side that just isn't there. It might be that everything will turn out just fine for Kathleen and that she will be extremely happy. She has certainly been keen enough to marry Michael Sheehan and go off to Ireland with him."

"Yes, she has. She came to say goodbye to us, you know?"

"She told me she was going to. Was Michael with her?"

"No, she came on her own." For a moment or two Elsie gave her full attention to her granddaughter, rocking her on her knees and talking to her gently. Then, so quietly Christina at first thought she was still talking to the baby, she said, "There was something rather disquieting about her behaviour. Your father thought so also. He said that she seemed to be working at being happy. It seemed a strange comment to make, but, when I thought about it, I found myself agreeing with him. That's exactly what Kathleen was doing, working at being happy." She sighed quietly. "I suppose it might be said that there's nothing all that wrong with that, but it shouldn't be necessary, certainly not for someone about to be married, and certainly not for someone like Kathleen who has always been such a spontaneous person. But then, who knows? Perhaps, given time, what she has now will turn into the kind of happiness that springs from the heart."

"I hope so, oh, I do hope so."

Elsie considered her daughter, a faint smile touching her mouth, thankfulness in her heart. What greater content could there be for a mother, she asked herself, than that which came with knowing her daughter had found complete happiness in her marriage? Even the fact that hard work and a home that was just a cottage in a virtual wilderness were of no account, not when it was clear that she was truly loved and returned that love in like measure; not when, apart from her work-roughened hands, she glowed with a new loveliness that told of an inner radiance.

"I just wish Kathleen had decided to come back to Mudgeeraba for these last few days," Christina murmured wistfully. "It would have been nice to have seen her again after the wedding."

"Yes, it would have. But then I suppose it's a good idea to have a couple of days in Brisbane before their ship sails."

"I can't believe that I won't be seeing her again … well, not for years and years, at any rate."

Elsie lifted the drowsy baby to her shoulder, gently patting her back. "Such things happen, love. People have their lives to live and, if it's to be across the oceans from loved ones, there's nothing for it, either for those leaving or those left behind, but to bear with the heartache. In time it will fade."

Christina bit her lip, her eyes searching the lined face pressed to her baby's curly head. Had it been like that for her? Had the heartache only faded as the years passed, never completely leaving? Thirteen years, that's how long it had been since they'd sailed away from all those who loved them. What had her mother been thinking on that distant day while she, herself, had been silently vowing to come back? That there would be no coming back? Or had she also made herself a promise?

"Have you ever thought about going back to Schleswig, Mother?" The words emerged slowly after trembling for a moment or two on her lips.

"I'm sure that everyone who leaves his or her homeland for a new country thinks, at one time or another, about going back, Christina. Very few ever do."

"Because it's so far to go," Christina murmured on a soft sigh.

"That's usually the main reason, certainly for those who've come to Australia. But there are others. I think; for one, it's that, by the time it becomes possible, going back hardly seems worthwhile."

Christina's eyes widened in surprise. "I don't think I know what you mean?"

They were on the verandah and, for a time, Elsie let her gaze wander over the cattle-dotted fields to where river gums and willows marked the course of the creek. "Nostalgia is a very demanding emotion," she said finally. "It sets us to yearning not only for a particular place but for that place as it was in another time … in other words, as we remember it. Which is, of course, out of the question, something that just can't be. Time doesn't stand still back where we've come from any more than it does where we are at present, and, because it doesn't, there as here, even a day brings changes while the years bring many. Most noticeably in the people we've left behind. There are those who die, some of them very dear to us, others whom we recall with affection, still others who were simply there and part of what we remember. Those still living grow older and, more often than not, become different beings from the ones we knew, not only in the way they look, but in the things they do and in their very approach to life. That's something we find difficult to envisage, simply because we haven't been there while these changes have been occurring. We see some of it in the pages of the letters we receive, of course, and we can do our best to send off our own word pictures by recounting small, everyday events as well as the more important things in those we write. But letters are, at best, a small substitute for being together. When they have oceans to cross and take ages to arrive they are a very weak bond, not something that will keep people we haven't seen in years and years from becoming more or less strangers to us. That's what I mean, Christina … going back after a long time would be … well, like going back to visit people we hardly know any more."

Christina nodded slowly, the mist of tears blurring her vision as her mind saw the truth in what her mother had said. People did die … all of her grandparents were gone now, along with her Uncle Mads, one of the cousins she had played with as a child, and the kindly minister who had said goodbye to them with his round pink cheeks damp with tears. There would have been others they hadn't heard about. Which just went to show that what her mother had said about letters was also true; they didn't really do very much to bridge what was an ever-widening gulf. How could it be otherwise when there was so much they didn't say, when, by the time they reached their destination, much of what they did say was either forgotten by the writer or no longer seen to be of any consequence? A bond of sorts, that's all they really were, a ribbon that was becoming more and more fragile as the years passed.

"I'll put little Alice down, she's fast asleep."

"I can do that … " Christina moved to get to her feet, but her mother was already on hers. "No, you stay there. Pour yourself another cup of tea, it should still be hot enough."

"With that cosy, I should think so. Shall I pour another one for you too?"

"Of course. When have I ever knocked back a second cup of tea?"

Smiling, Christina watched her leave the verandah with the baby in her arms, but, the minute she was alone, a thoughtful expression came to her face. There was something else, though, something more than what her mother had talked about. Of course the people left behind and what had become of them was important, just as she had said. But there were other things to draw a person back, like Haderslev itself. Why, a hundred years might pass and it would be hardly changed at all. The cobbled square would still be there, along with the school, the church, perhaps even her grandfather's little shop and their own house …

"She didn't even stir, dear little lamb."

Brought abruptly back to the present, Christina smiled at her. "Our Alice is a sound sleeper, there's no doubt about that."

"You've been lucky in that respect, with both her and Charlie. Is he still happy with his little bed?"

"Oh yes, he loves it. It was such a good idea of Father's to make it for him. A full-sized bed would have taken up too much space, probably in the kitchen, but the little bed fits nicely in the bedroom, along the same wall as the cradle."

Elsie spooned sugar into her tea, stirring it for longer than was necessary. Finally, her eyes clouded, she said quietly, "We had some sad news this week … Peter Ohlssen has died."

"Oh no!"

"It seems that he hadn't enjoyed good health for quite some time. In the end though, it was a major heart attack that took his life."

Sudden understanding had joined the dismay in Christina's eyes. "That's why Father has been so quiet this morning?"

"He's very distressed about it, as I am too, of course. Such a dear friend and such a strong man to be taken when he was not yet sixty years of age."

"Father's not thinking that Uncle Peter's death had anything to do with what happened to Lars, is he?"

Elsie moved her shoulders in a faint shrug. "I don't really know, Christina. He says not, and I keep telling myself that the grief he feels is a natural thing and no different from what I am feeling, but he has become so morose I can't help but wonder."

"I hope he's not going to be the way he was after Lars died," Christina groaned.

"Goodness, so do I. That was a most miserable time for your father. I had begun to think that … " She broke off as Charlie raced through the house on to the verandah, yelling, "Charlie saw the little pigs! Charlie saw the little pigs!"

"How many?" his grandmother asked, drawing him against her knee and smiling down into the excited little face.

"Lots 'n lots! Hundreds!"

"Well, I must admit when they all get to squealing at the same time it sounds like hundreds."

"How many are there really?" Christina asked.

"Twenty-six. One sow has fourteen and the other one twelve."

"Heavens! No wonder Charlie is so impressed."

"Charlie can't find Joey," the little boy interrupted, suddenly doleful. "He's not anywhere."

"I think Joey has gone to live with other kangaroos."

"Where? Where did he go?"

"Off in the bush somewhere, that's where kangaroos like to be."

"Will he get some bread in the bush?"

"No, he'll just eat grass like all the other kangaroos and wallabies do."

"Joey won't like that, Grandma, he likes bread better than grass."

"But he'll be happy being with animals that are like him instead of with cows and horses and dogs?

"And pigs?" Charlie yelped. "I don't think he would like pigs."

Watching him scamper off the verandah, Christina smiled at her mother. "Do you remember when Joey was just a little fellow and always wanted to be hiding under your skirt?"

"I recall that he was still wanting to do that when he was no longer a little fellow. But he finally grew out of it, thank goodness!"

"You don't think he'll come back this time?"

"He has never been gone for so long before, so perhaps he has finally realised that living like a normal kangaroo has a few advantages." Elsie sighed quietly. "On the other hand, he has passed the kangaroo life span of six to eight years … "

Christina nodded, the thought that Joey might well be dead having already occurred to her. "When you think about the start he had, he's done very well."

"Yes, he has … hardly a normal life for a kangaroo, but I think he has been happy enough."

"Why wouldn't he have been when he was spoiled rotten?"

They both laughed. Then Elsie, the smile still on her face, changed the subject, "It's just such a relief to know that you are finally to have a road. You'll be able to visit more often and ever so much more comfortably than you do now."

"It would be more of a relief if it was progressing a bit more quickly. It's four months now since they started working on it and it's still not even halfway up to our place."

"It does seem to be taking a long time, but it's getting there, that's the important thing. And, just think, I'll be able to visit you in the sulky instead of on the back of a horse."

Christina gave her an affectionate smile. "You have been very brave about that, Mother, and you have become a very good rider."

"I wouldn't say that, but at least I'm now able to stay on board with some degree of assurance."

They both turned as Carl and Simon appeared from around the side of the house and Carl asked cheerfully, "Well, have you ladies caught up on all the local gossip yet?"

"We've done our best," Christina told him, returning his grin. "Have you and Father found time to discuss anything other than the pig business?"

"We have indeed! We've been talking about all the building going on over at Nerang. The Methodist church finished and the Catholic one nearly so. That will be three churches for a township the size of Nerang, can you believe that? And apparently another hotel is also on the cards."

"Three churches and three hotels," Elsie mused. "It's almost like a competition, with the churches determined not to be outnumbered by the hotels and vice versa. I wonder where it will all end."

Christina had been studying her father and, catching her eye, he came to sit beside her. "Mother has told you about Uncle Peter?"

"Yes, it's such terribly sad news."

"It was his heart, you know?"

Christina nodded, longing to cry out that a heart attack didn't mean a broken heart, but, instead, saying quietly, "It seems that big men like Uncle Peter are sometimes prone to heart attacks."

"Yes, so Doctor Davies told me. I happened to run into him over at Nerang on Friday. He remembers Lars, of course."

Christina groaned inwardly. So, he had more than likely asked the doctor whether Lars's death could have brought about his father's. "Yes, I suppose he would remember."

Simon shook his head slowly from side to side. "Four years. It doesn't seem that long since that terrible day, does it?"

"No, it doesn't, but it has been four years, Father, and that's quite a long time. Lars wouldn't have wanted us to be still grieving on his account."

"That's true, he wouldn't have."

"Mother didn't say just when Uncle Peter died."

"Mid-January, the fifteenth. It was just as he was about to sit down for supper, it seems." Simon rubbed a hand wearily over his eyes. "What a state of affairs. Here we are, just beginning to grieve for him and he has been four months in his grave."

"It's happened like that with all the grandparents and with Uncle Mads," Christina reminded him gently. "It's just the way things are with so much distance between us and those we left behind, but there is something of relief in not knowing right away. At least, by the time we do, we know that those closest to whoever it was who died have had time to put their sorrow behind them. We feel deeply for them, but we can also feel thankful that, for them, the time of that wrenching first grief is over. It would be like that for Aunty Maria; she would have been stricken at Uncle Peter's death, but I'm sure that she's now getting on with her life."

"She wasn't the one who wrote, it was your aunt."

"Well, that's understandable, but she will write. In fact, she has probably already done so."

Simon groaned. "God, the time it takes for the wretched mail to arrive."

Christina gave him a gentle smile. "It takes ever so much longer when we become impatient to receive it, Father."

Some of the tension left Simon's face and the corners of his mouth twitched. "I told you that."

"Yes, you did, and now I'm telling it to you because it's perfectly true. You told me something else too."

"I'm sure I've told you no end of things through the years."

"Yes, you have, and I remember ever so many of them."

"What was this particular one?"

"It was that we each have a path to follow through life and that only God knows where it will lead or how long it will be because only He has all the maps."

Simon chuckled softly. "When did I tell you that?"

"The night you told me that we were to leave Schleswig and come to Australia. I was crying when you came to say goodnight and I wanted to know why we couldn't come back to Haderslev after we had been to Australia, and you said that no one could really say that we wouldn't because … "

"Only God had all the maps," Simon finished for her.

"It is like that, Father, and Uncle Peter died because he had come to the end of the path he had followed, just as Lars did with the one he had followed."

Simon nodded, but for several moments made no reply. Then, with Christina about to go and help her mother prepare dinner, he said ever so quietly, "Sometimes the paths we are set to follow require a great deal of us, and there is often much that we find hard to accept."

Christina felt her breath catch, but she turned back to him and said gently, "If it was all too straight-forward and easy, Father, where would be the challenge? Then, if there was no challenge, how could we be proud of what we have achieved?"

Simon considered her thoughtfully, a faint smile coming to his lips, "I didn't tell you that."

"No, you didn't, that's something I have told myself."

34

By the end of the year the road had passed through both the selection and homestead blocks held by Carl. By March, tending in a south-easterly direction, it had joined another road which, confronted with the main bulk of the McPherson Range, veered off towards the coast, heading for the twin towns of Coolangatta on the Queensland side of the border and Tweed Heads on the New South Wales side.

Apart from a few cuttings and the low plank bridges built over shallow waterways, the road was little more than a widening of the track. To Christina, however, this was of no account whatsoever; the rough dirt strip winding its way through the ranges was every bit the blessing her mother had said it would be. For one thing, her husband was able to travel to and from the Tweed in a good deal less time than it had taken him previously. For another, they were able to acquire a buggy and it was no longer necessary for them to go everywhere with the children perched on the saddles in front of them. For yet another, people who had found it well-nigh impossible to visit before were now able to do so. Among these were Joseph and Sarah O'Rourke and their two children. Their first visit had been in early January, and since then they'd made Saturday visits on a fairly regular basis. Both Carl and Christina were always pleased to see them drive up, while Charlie was almost overcome with excitement; other children to play with was a rare treat indeed.

On a visit towards the end of May, Sarah asked gently, "Have you heard from Kathleen yet, Christina?"

Christina shook her head unhappily.

"Well, Ma has finally received another letter and she has sent it up for you to read."

"I couldn't do that, Sarah."

"Of course you could." She pulled the letter out of the oversized handbag she always carried. "There's nothing ... well, private in it. Something interesting though, but I'll let you read that for yourself."

Christina took the letter held out to her reluctantly, a soft sigh falling from her lips. "I don't know why Kathleen hasn't written to me, she said she would."

"And she no doubt will. It would seem that she's been so busy traipsing all over the place with Michael, she just hasn't gotten around to doing much letter-writing. This is only the second letter that Ma and Da have had from her and she's been gone a full year now. At least she's not quite as bad as Danny. It's more than two years since he left for New South Wales and he's still only written twice. On both occasions at Christmas, as though it's a chore he feels he must do at that time of year. But do go on, read what Kathleen has to say."

"I don't feel right about reading a letter written to someone else, Sarah, it's sort of like an intrusion."

"That's being silly. Besides, what would Ma say if I took it back and told her you refused to read it?"

Christina gave her a small resigned smile and drew the folded pages out of the envelope. "It was very kind of her to think to send it up for me to read and you must thank her for me."

"I will," Sarah promised, her eyes smilingly watchful. She had to wait only a moment or two before Christina looked up, a delighted smile on her face. "She's going to have a baby!"

"Yes! Isn't it wonderful?"

"But, in mid-June? That's only a couple of weeks off." She gave a soft laugh that was partly sigh. "There she is with the baby almost due and here we are only just hearing about it."

"I know, and, to some extent, that's Kathleen's fault. She could have written to tell us before she was some five months along the way. Still, the fact that we've only just found out makes it all the more exciting. We haven't been obliged to go through all those dreary months of waiting."

"We'll still have to wait though, after the baby is born. It will be weeks and weeks before we know how things have gone for her, or even whether she has had a boy or girl."

"It may not be, Christina. There's a postscript at the end of the letter … it says that Michael is going to see if he can telegraph the news through to us."

"What a good idea!"

"Yes, isn't it? The very minute we hear from him, I'll have someone come up to tell you."

"That would be ever so kind of you, Sarah."

"Not at all. It's only right that you should know as soon as possible, what with you and Kathleen being such close friends."

Christina sighed quietly. "I do miss her terribly. It was bad enough when she was away that other time, but she was still in Queensland then, miles and miles away, but still within reach, so to speak, and able to come home without all that much trouble. Now she's on the other side of the world and there's no way she can come home without a great deal of trouble. It's as though she has gone right out of my life."

Sarah nodded. "I know. I feel that way about her too."

"Do you think she'll ever some back?"

"I don't know, Christina. She seemed confident that she would do so before she left, but I wonder if she truly appreciated how very far away Ireland is. Besides, I don't think it's very likely that Michael will be wanting to come back, not when he's so involved in everything that's happening over there."

"From what Kathleen writes here it appears that she has become very involved also."

"Yes, it's like I was saying, she has been all over the place with Michael. She seems to have been having such an exciting time she may not want to come back." She chuckled softly. "Meeting members of parliament and such like, can you imagine that happening to our Kathleen?"

"No, I can't. But it's good that it has all been so interesting for her; she has probably hardly had the time to be homesick."

"She'll have the time now though. Her traipsing about days will be well and truly behind her, I would think." Sarah got to her feet. "You finish reading the letter. I'll just go and see what the menfolk and children are up to."

Kathleen had filled three pages, telling of places she had visited and the people she had met: the beauty of the Irish countryside; the widespread success of the National League; and the popularity of Mr. Parnell, who was, she wrote, not only a most thorough gentleman but a very likeable person. Left to herself, Christina read slowly, thoughtfully, her mind's eye striving to picture the Kathleen she knew in this new world she had entered. One good thing at least, she told herself, there seemed to be no regrets. On the contrary, Kathleen seemed well satisfied with what she had done, what she was doing. Now there was to be a baby and a new and very special happiness for her.

Sarah reappeared in the doorway, chuckling quietly. "They are all very busy extending the fowl-pen, even little Alice."

"What is she doing, for heaven's sake?"

"Transferring nails from one tin to another, very seriously, I might add."

"With her father's approval, I hope, he has a real thing about his nails."

"Don't all men? I know Joseph does about his. Poor little Sean has practically to beg whenever he takes it into his head that he'd like to do some hammering."

"Sean's looking much stronger, Sarah."

Sarah nodded, the smile on her face gentling. "Yes, he's coming along nicely now, thank God. I don't mind telling you, Christina, there have been times when I was sure we were going to lose him, but he seems to have grown out of those wretched bronchial attacks he was having."

"Apparently, children quite often do that." Not all of them, though, Christina added to herself. But then, perhaps even for little Anna, there would have been a chance had it not been for the choking dust of the Sirocco.

"That's what Doctor Davies has told me, but I think there were times when he was close to despair where Sean was concerned."

"You really have had a time of it, Sarah, and, believe me, my heart has done quite a deal of aching on your account. I know the state I would have been in had it been Charlie or Alice having those turns."

Sarah sighed heavily. "We can only pray that it's all in the past now,

Christina, and I truly believe that it is. Sean has become a different little boy altogether from what he was. He has ever so much more energy now and, in the past six months, he's had only the one quite mild attack."

"I've seen a change in him even in these past few weeks and I'm sure you are right; he's going to be just fine from now on."

"What a blessing that will be, especially as it seems that Sean will be the last child I have. He's four years old now, and, apart from that one time when I had that early miscarriage, I just haven't been able to conceive."

"It might just be that your body needs a little more time," Christina consoled gently, "after all the worry you've had with Sean."

"I suppose it could be something like that, but in my heart I feel that I will only ever have Mary and Sean."

"Well, if it does happen that way, you still have them to be thankful for."

"Oh yes, and I am thankful. After all, it could have happened that I had no children at all." She grinned suddenly. "Joseph says that it might be that the good Lord has decided that it's necessary to put some restrictions on the O'Rourkes, lest their offspring be over-running the place."

"There are certainly getting to be quite a few little ones in the O'Rourke clan, there's no doubt about that."

"They are appearing like mushrooms, as Ma is so fond of saying. Maureen is on the way again, due some time in November. With Therese and the twins, that will be four for her. Perhaps even five, since it's always on the cards that she could have twins again. Then there's Patrick and Sylvia with three already, and now young Hughie is married and about to become a father also. And there's still Mikey and Eileen to marry and begin their families." She laughed softly. "You had better remember never to have a feud with the O'Rourkes, Christina. You'll be well and truly outnumbered!"

"I will remember that, Sarah," Christina told her with a quick smile before holding up Kathleen's letter. "Would it be alright if I took down her address?"

"Of course it would, and what a good idea! You'll be able to write to Kathleen without waiting for a letter from her."

Christina began her letter just half-an-hour after the O'Rourke buggy rumbled through the gate and rolled off down the road. But an hour later, when she put it aside to see to other matters requiring her attention, only a single page had been completed, whereas a good half-dozen, incomplete and crumpled, had been flung into the fireplace. She took up pen and pad again that evening, leaning forward into the arc of lamplight thrown on to the table with a frown of concentration on her brow.

Watching her, Carl asked with tender amusement, "Is writing that letter such an ordeal?"

Christina glanced up, the frown still lingering. "It's not easy thinking of things to write."

"She's been gone more than a year, there must be a hundred and one things to tell her. Why don't you just put down any little piece of news that comes into your head, just as you would tell it to Kathleen if she was sitting there with you?"

"But she's not sitting here with me and it's different with her being so far away. For one thing, I think I should take care not to be writing in a way that might make her feel homesick. For another, she has been living what seems to have been a very exciting life, so she may not be interested in hearing about our small everyday events." She sighed quietly, a small rueful smile touching her lips. "Then there's my spelling. I don't want to be sending off a letter that's full of mistakes."

"For goodness sake, Christina! Kathleen's not going to mind that!"

"I know, but Michael might read the letter?"

"So what?"

"He'd laugh about it, that's what. I just know he would."

Carl gave a deep chuckle, rocking back on his chair. "Then be generous. Include a few outrageous mistakes so that he can have a really good laugh."

Christina tried to glare at him, but, as was usually the case, his sense of humour was much too contagious and she found herself grinning instead. "I'll be doing that without intending to, never fear." Then, considering him thoughtfully, "How is it that you learned to speak English without having trouble spelling the words?"

"I don't have trouble because I don't worry about it, but that's not to say that I don't make mistakes."

"Hmmm … and you don't write too many letters in English, do you?"

"No," Carl told her with cheerful unconcern. "I fill in the forms the Government requires and tell them what I've been up to, and that's about it."

"You don't write too many in German either," Christina scolded gently.

"I write to the family every so often."

"Not often enough, not by a long way."

"Well, they know that I'm alive and in good health, that I have a beautiful Danish wife who has given me two fine children, and that we live on a farm in the mountains. What else would they want to be knowing?"

"I'm sure you'd think of a few things if you put your mind to it. Why don't you write to them now instead of sitting there watching me?"

"How can I? You have our only decent pen." He chuckled quietly. "And, at the rate you are going, you'll be needing all of that pad to finish your letter."

Christina glanced at him reproachfully. "However am I going to concentrate on what I'm writing when you're in such a light-hearted mood?"

"Leave it then. Talk to me instead."

"In a minute. I've just thought of something else to tell her." She scratched away for a few minutes, then looked up with a smile. "It is wonderful that Kathleen is going to have a baby, isn't it?"

"Yes, it certainly is. She deserves that kind of happiness, though I must say that I find it extremely difficult to picture her with a baby."

"Oh, I can do that very easily, a beautiful little girl with hair the same glorious colour as her mother's. I can hardly believe that it will be in just a couple of weeks though."

"So Michael is going to telegraph the news when it happens, eh?"

"What Kathleen actually wrote was that he would try to do that."

"I can't see that he would have any problems, it should be simple enough."

Mid-June came and went, then all the days of the second half of the month, and still no message from Michael Sheehan found its way along the nine thousand miles of submarine cable connecting the rest of the world telegraphically with Australia. The O'Rourke family gave up asking at the Nerang post office for such a message and began the long worrying wait for a letter. When it finally came, it had been written by Kathleen herself, a single page telling briefly that the birth had been difficult and the baby born dead, that she had been quite ill for a couple of weeks but was now well on the way to being fully recovered.

Christina, dry-eyed but with her throat aching with tears, stared disbelievingly at Joseph O'Rourke. "Is that all that she wrote?"

Joseph nodded unhappily. "Apart from a few words telling Ma and Da that they weren't to be worrying about her and that she would write again as soon as she felt stronger." He turned his head, gazing off down the valley, but not before Christina had seen the glint of tears in his gentle eyes. "She didn't even say what the baby was," he murmured brokenly. "Or whether it had been given a name."

Christina gulped as the knot of tears in her throat swelled, choking off her voice.

"Can you imagine that, her not saying whether she'd given birth to a boy or a girl? Sweet Mother of Jesus, what a state our Kathleen must be in!"

"It would be natural for her to be distressed, and if she's not been well since the baby was born … " Christina let her husky voice trail away, not sure what it was that she was trying to say.

Joseph took a crumpled handkerchief from his pocket and blew his nose loudly before turning back to face her. "Da says that we are not to be forgetting that the letter was written in early July, which means that Kathleen has had ample time in which to regain her health." He shook his head slowly. "Ma doesn't believe that she is well, though. You know how she is, Christina, with her premonitions and such like. Well, she seems to have had one where Kathleen is concerned, even though she hasn't actually said so. I know we've always laughed about her superstitions, but it's ever so strange how many times she's had a feeling about something and it's turned out to be right. I just hope to God this isn't one of those times."

Christina felt a cold chill run down her spine and, in spite of the sunshine beating down on her, it was all she could do to stop herself from shivering violently. It was true, what Joseph had said. Didn't she know that for herself? Hadn't it been a feeling of Mrs O'Rourke's that had sent Danny to help her when Charlie was being born? "If only she wasn't so far away," she groaned softly. "If only we could see her ... "

"That's what Sarah and I keep saying to one another ... if only, if only. If only someone had told Michael Sheehan about his father being dead for years and he'd never come to Australia. If only Da had never met him at that two-up game. If only that squatter Kathleen was in love with had chosen some other time to write and tell her that he was going to marry another girl. If only Ma and Da had given permission for Kathleen to marry him, even if it had to be in a Protestant church." Joseph gave a short mirthless laugh before adding on a heavy sigh, "There seem to be a hundred 'if onlys', Christina."

"They are bothersome words in all our lives, Joseph, especially when they apply to events that are over and can't be changed," Christina told him sorrowfully. "They spell regret, you might say, and, whereas it's fitting that there are things we feel that way about, all those 'if onlys' are not something we should be taking upon our shoulders to carry though life. We can't undo what's already done, so there's really no sense at all in torturing ourselves by thinking about how things might have been."

Joseph sighed again, but quietly this time. "You are right, Christina. What's done is done. That's the fact of the matter and there's just no getting away from it."

"No, there isn't, so, instead of dwelling on the past, we have to think about Kathleen's future. We must pray that she has regained her health and also for her happiness."

"She did seem to be happy enough when she first got to Ireland, at least it seemed that way from what she wrote. I must say that I was relieved about that. I'd had this feeling that she'd no sooner get there than she'd be wanting to come home again."

"I don't think she had time to think about coming home; it seems she was here, there and everywhere, having a quite exciting time of it." They were standing mid-way between the house and the gate, Christina having run there when she'd seen Joseph turn in off the road, and she now gave him a small apologetic smile. "Do let's go into the house, Joseph, so that I can make you a cup of tea."

"Thanks all the same, Christina, but I won't stay. I've quite a few things to do over at Nerang, and I'd like to be home in time for milking," He whistled to his horse which was grazing just a short distance away, and it at once pricked up its ears and trotted back to him.

"I would like to visit your mother, Joseph. Do you think it would be alright or should I wait for a while?"

"Ma's always pleased to see you, Christina, and I don't see that there's any reason why you should wait."

He swung himself into the saddle, smiling down at her. "You haven't seen Hughie's baby yet, have you?"

Christina shook her head. "Sarah tells me he's a fine, sturdy little boy."

"The finest that ever was, according to Hughie."

"I'll be looking forward to seeing him, and your mother."

Only when Joseph O'Rourke had ridden off did the tears knotted achingly in Christina's throat burst free and well into her eyes. "Dear God, let her be alright," she prayed huskily. "Please, please let her be well and full of life, the way she has always been. Help her to recover from her sorrow and be happy again." And then, because it suddenly seemed that, in some way, Kathleen's happiness depended upon it, "And please let things go well for the people of Ireland."

Things had gone well for the people of Ireland, but, with the bright star they reached for seemingly within their grasp, it once again slipped away. The National League had proved itself to be a very efficient electoral machine. Charles Stewart Parnell was returned to office, his followers becoming the whole of the Irish representation outside the Protestant north-east and the representation of Trinity College. Parnell, with a following of eighty-five pledge-bound members now held the balance of power in the House of Commons and it had seemed that the time was ripe for Prime Minister Gladstone to introduce a bill granting Home Rule to Ireland. It wasn't. The majority of English electors and even many of Gladstone's followers couldn't bear the thought of such a state of affairs. The Home Rule bill was defeated with a section of the Liberals breaking away to vote with the Tories.

Christina knew nothing of all this, but Kathleen's mother, informed by her husband, knew a little. "They still haven't got Home Rule over there, you know?" she remarked during Christina's visit. "They might have powerful forces in parliament and that Mr. Gladstone on their side but they still haven't got Home Rule and the English people aren't about to let them have it, I be thinking."

"I was hoping that Kathleen and Michael might have had something to rejoice about."

Bridget O'Rourke shrugged her plump shoulders. "Well, I suppose they should at least be feeling some satisfaction, a great deal has been accomplished, it seems." She paused to sip her tea and nibble on a biscuit, a thoughtful frown appearing on her wide brow. "I wonder, though. I think it might be like Mr. O'Rourke says, Michael won't ever be content with anything less than Home Rule."

"He's certainly very dedicated to that cause."

"He's that alright. I can tell you, Christina, there have been times when I've thought there was nought else in the man's head." She flung out a hand, almost upsetting her cup. "Oh, I know that there have to be people like that. There wouldn't ever be a successful cause if there weren't, but I wonder whether they ever know what it is to be truly happy." Again she flung out a hand and again the cup escaped by only the narrowest of margins. "Of course, they'd say that they were happy in what they were doing, and I suppose, in a way, they might be, but, when you think of all the things they keep shut out of their lives or pay little mind to, I have me doubts."

Christina moved uneasily on her chair. What was she saying? Something that wasn't at all like anything she herself had ever said and yet seemed to echo her feelings where Kathleen's husband was concerned. A man with his entire life pledged to a cause, with his mind too full of the one thing for there to be room for anything else, and with his heart unable to remember how to beat with tenderness … that was how she saw Michael Sheehan and now it seemed that Kathleen's mother saw him in much the same way.

"The trouble is, Christina, that it's very difficult for others to be really happy with such people, for any length of time, at any rate."

Christina smothered a small sigh. "But, if they take up the same cause, surely that would help?"

"If they took it up at the same time, I suppose that it might. But, where one has carried a particular banner for thirty or forty years of his life and the other just picks it up, not even sure what it's all about, do you really think they are going to be able to go along side by side, in step as it were?"

"They might be able to." It was a reply ringing with uncertainty, for all that she was remembering how much Kathleen had learned about her husband's cause.

Bridget O'Rourke opened her mouth but immediately closed it again, sighing resignedly. For a long moment she eyed Christina steadily, saying nothing, a strangely wry expression on her face. Then she sighed again and said sorrowfully, "I don't believe that our Kathleen has been happy in Ireland, Christina, and I don't mean just since she lost the baby."

It was Christina's turn to stare and she did so open-mouthed, her breath caught in her throat.

"It surprises you then to hear me say that?"

Christina swallowed, searching for her voice. Surprise her? What Kathleen's mother had just said had done more than that, it had stunned her into speechlessness. In view of what Joseph had said, she had been more or less expecting Mrs. O'Rourke to confide that she was concerned about her daughter's health, but for her to come right out and say that she didn't believe she had been happy? It was … well, bewildering, to say the least. She nodded, clearing her throat as she did so. "Yes, it does surprise me. Kathleen seemed happy when she wrote that letter you sent up for me to read."

"She was happy about having the baby."

"But the rest of it? All that travelling about with Michael, meeting so many interesting people? I'm sure she would have enjoyed that."

"She may well have done so, but it takes more than such things for a person to be truly happy. The Saints preserve us, you must know that!"

"But how can you know that there hasn't been more? What makes you feel as you do?"

"Her letters, Christina, they are what make me feel uneasy like. 'Tis not easy to explain. 'Tis just there between the lines … in what she doesn't write, you might say." She sighed quietly. "I was thinking that, what with you being so close to Kathleen, you might have sensed it also."

Christina shook her head, her eyes unhappy, her teeth pressed into her lower lip. "Perhaps if she had written to me … "

"Perhaps that was the reason she didn't write to you, because she thought you would see beyond what she was writing and realise that she was unhappy. But I tell you this, Christina, Kathleen is going to write to you and, when she does, she's going to pour out her heart, she won't be able to help herself."

"Oh no! I'm sure you're wrong about that."

"I could say that I hope I am, but I'm not going to. If Kathleen is unhappy as I feel she is, I want to know about it. It could be that in time she will write and tell her Da and me all about it, but I don't think so. I think she will write to you, and, when she does, you must tell me. Even if she asks you not to, you must tell me."

"But why? Where would be the sense in telling you something like that when she doesn't want you to know and it would only distress you?"

"We would bring her home, Christina. Already I have put aside some money and Danny has sent some also. I'll have no daughter of mine dying of a broken heart on the other side of the world, in me own homeland though it might be." She was silent for a moment or two, tapping her fingers on the table as her thoughts strayed. Then, with a slight shrug of her shoulders, she gathered them again and went on, "I have even thought of sending the money off right away, but I can't very well just write and say that I'm sending money for her passage home because I feel that she is unhappy over there. Besides, as much as she might want to do so, she may not yet be ready to give up and come home, and then, by the time she does, the money could well be gone. No, I have to wait, Christina, I have to wait."

"But, even if Kathleen has been unhappy, it could very well be the sort of unhappiness she'll get over, homesickness perhaps."

"It's more than that, I'm afraid, and I don't think it's something she'll be getting over, but we shall see." She reached over and enfolded both of Christina's hands in hers. "You must promise though. You must promise that as soon as you get a letter from Kathleen you will come and tell me."

Christina swallowed, hesitating, but Bridget O'Rourke's normally gentle eyes were boring into hers with a commanding intensity and she slowly nodded. "If she writes to me I will bring the letter to you."

So it was that Christina began waiting for a letter she hoped would never come. Over and over again, she told herself that it was only a feeling Kathleen's mother had, that there had been no cry of unhappiness ringing from the letters as she seemed to think. But always the doubt came. Had there been something in the letter she herself had read? Oh, if only she could read it again. Or if her mind would recall the flow of words. Different from that in the letters Kathleen had written her from Taldoon? Yes, of course it had been, but wasn't that only natural? She was writing to her parents, after all. But so very different? Stiff almost? Was there really any need for that? Oh, dear God in heaven, there was something about that letter!

And there was something other than the letter, her own feelings about Kathleen marrying Michael Sheehan. Hadn't she been fretting and worrying that she might not find true happiness with him? Hadn't she even wondered whether there was really love between them?

The year drew to a close as it had begun, in weather that was hot and dry. There had been some good general rain during the intervening months, but in most areas not nearly enough. The sequence of incredibly good seasons had come to an end, there was little enough doubt about that. Heaven forbid, though, that another long drought was about to begin.

35

Henry Simon Eichstead came into the world on 3 April 1886. From the very outset it was clear that he wasn't as robust as his brother and sister, and Christina felt her heart stand still on more than one occasion during the first few days of his life. He was so small, barely six pounds in weight, and he sucked so feebly at her breasts, it was as though he had no strength whatsoever. His cry, too, was thin and weak, more like the mewing of a kitten than the cry of a baby. I should have waited, she told herself tearfully as the old fears returned, there was no need to have decided on a name so early.

Elsie, coming into the bedroom and quick to see the dampness on her daughter's cheeks, said gently, "Fretting won't do you or the baby the least bit of good, Christina."

"I'm so afraid that we are going to lose him."

There was only the barest hesitation before the sternly reassuring words came, "You are not going to lose him and it's just ridiculous for you to be thinking that way. It was a normal birth and you know very well that Doctor Davies can find nothing wrong with the baby."

"But he's so tiny, so fragile."

"Well, he'll grow. Tiny babies often do so very quickly."

Christina brushed at the tears on her cheeks with her fingertips. "Doctor Davies did say that, didn't he? That there was nothing wrong with him?"

"Yes, he did," Elsie told her, busying herself with tidying up the room and trying desperately to choke off the voice within her that cried … That's just what your doctor told you when you held a baby the very image of this one in your arms.

Almost as though she had heard the silent cry, Christina lifted her gaze from her baby's tiny face and considered her mother thoughtfully, a faint frown creasing her brow. Did seeing her with a baby at her breast remind her mother, cause her to see those little graves with pain stirring in her heart? Yes, it must. No matter how many years had passed, the pain would still be there and even her mother wouldn't be able to keep it always locked away. Twenty-five years. Yes, in August, it would be twenty-five years since that first small grave was dug beneath the old oak tree back in Haderslev, and not since she'd been just a small child had she spoken to her mother about that baby's brief life.

She had never really talked to her about the other two lying in small graves back at the Logan either. There had been times when she'd wanted to, especially during the time when it seemed that it would be wrong for her to marry Carl. But she'd been afraid to, afraid to hear the answers to the questions she would ask.

It was the same now. She longed to have her mother tell her that there had been something else about the babies she had lost, that it hadn't just been because they were small and frail, but she couldn't bring herself to ask. That little boy back in Haderslev had been ailing, she hadn't forgotten hearing her mother say that. But what had she meant? Ailing in what way? Biting her lip against a fresh flow of tears, Christina let her eyes rest once again on her baby's face. Such a perfect little face, she thought, her heart melting, so tiny but just so perfect.

"Your father should be back with Charlie and Alice soon."

Christina gave her mother a brief smile. "Those two are not going to be too keen on going home, I'm afraid."

"They certainly enjoy taking the butter over to Nerang."

"They enjoy a few other things about being down here as well, being spoiled, for instance."

Elsie gave a small chuckle. "That's a special privilege grandparents have." Then, her face becoming serious again, "Why don't you stay on for another week? There's really no need for you to be going home on Saturday."

Christina struggled with temptation. Three weeks away from home, one before the baby was born and two since, was more than enough. She wanted to be back there, taking up her chores again so that her husband could get on with his own work. She wanted to be near him on the precious days he was home, to go to sleep at night with his arms holding her. On the other hand, it was such a comfort having her mother help her with the baby and to know that Doctor Davies was not so far away should he be needed. "No, she said quietly, "I have been away long enough. Carl has been able to do only the odd days of outside work and he'll be wanting to get back to the Tweed."

"But he's been able to get some more land cleared and fenced, and I'm sure he would agree that you should stay on for a bit longer. So do think about it."

"I will. He'll be coming down on Saturday in any case, so it won't be a wasted trip if I decide not to go back with him." She gave a sudden small chuckle. "At least this baby won't have to go home on horseback the way little Alice did."

"Oh, don't remind me, please! It almost caused me to have a heart attack!"

As she had known she would even as she agreed to think about it, Christina went home on Saturday, her fears tucked away behind a bright smile. A week passed, then a month, two months, and Henry Simon, though he seemed not to care one way or the other, clung to his frail little life and gradually grew stronger, a soft plumpness coming to his cheeks and stick-like arms and legs. Finally, Christina, her heart soaring, was able to believe what she'd tried to tell herself a hundred times or more ... he was going to live.

The blessings that had come with the building of the road were, Christina had soon come to realise, of the mixed variety. For one thing, the timber-getters came with their bullock-teams, setting clouds of dust spinning out over the valley, while their cracking whips and harsh oaths all too often smothered the calls of the birds and the gentle noises of the bush. During the years since settlement of the river flats and lower slopes of the mountain network stretching northwards from the McPherson Ranges had begun, the deep green valleys and precipitous gorges of

Springbrook had remained aloof and undisturbed. Here, there was a wilderness beyond belief, dense green jungles that were shunned even by the Aborigines, for they shut out the light and sunshine and walled in the 'debil debil'.

The timber-getters had known of the veritable fortune reaching skywards from the jungle floor for years, but had been obliged to turn their backs on it. They might well have been able to fell the giant cedars with their sharp, biting axes and crosscut saws, but to do so would have been a waste, not only of time and effort, but of the valuable timber itself, for there was no way to get the logs out. Now, though, it was a slightly different story. The great majority of the sought-after trees were still in inaccessible pockets deep within the jungle's fortressed walls, but some had come within reach … in places where bullock teams could be brought in and the great logs dragged out to the road.

"I think we just have to be thankful that there are fewer logs heading for the Nerang River than there are going the other way to the Tweed," Carl mused one fine spring morning as he and Christina watched a bullock team trundle past their gate before the dust stirred by the one ahead of it had had a chance to settle.

"That's something, I suppose, but there are still a lot coming this way, and it was all so peaceful before."

"I know, but we always knew the road would come." Slipping an arm around her shoulders, he drew her close to his side. "Let us not be forgetting that some of those logs being hauled away are from our land and what a bonus that is. They plan to take out a large cedar and some of the already felled stuff today, as a matter of fact."

"Will that come this way?"

"No, it's on the homestead block, and the teamsters working that area find the road to the Tweed a better proposition." He gave her a quick hug. "Exciting times, Christina, even if the road does have its downside."

For another thing with the road, there was the matter of visitors, a mixed blessing in itself. It was, of course, just wonderful having people call in from time to time, but Christina, Carl and the children weren't the only ones who thought so. Harry, it soon became clear, took great delight in letting visitors know how clever he was. On more than one occasion, Christina had been so mortified, she'd felt like crawling under the table, but never more so that when the Methodist minister, seeking to enlarge his flock now that he had a fine new church, rode over from Nerang to call on her.

"I could have died," she wailed to Carl, wringing her hands together at the mere recollection of what had happened. "I could have just sat down on the nearest chair and died."

Carl, just home from the Tweed and trying to pull off his boots with the children climbing all over him, grinned up at her. "So the good pastor got a bit of a shock, did he?"

"It's not funny! It's not the least bit funny!"

Carl tried, not very successfully, to wipe the grin from his face. "Well, the Reverend Whiting was a bit startled the first time he met our Harry, but he was soon laughing about him."

"This minister is very different from Reverend Whiting. He's very serious."

"So he didn't laugh. He probably doesn't have a sense of humour, that's all."

"Oh, you don't know what happened! You just don't know!"

"Well, suppose you tell me. All I've heard so far is that this minister called and Harry told him to 'shut up, fevens sake', and that it was all so terrible you could have died." With his boots removed, he straightened and patted his knee. "Come, sit here and tell me all about it."

But Christina had become too agitated to accept her husband's invitation and she paced to and fro as the full story tumbled from her lips. "The first time Harry screeched out … well, what he does, the poor man got such a shock his head jerked around and his glasses fell off his nose and on to the floor. Then, when he was bending down to pick them up, that wretched bird did it again, and he … he stood on them!"

Carl choked, then had a deliberate coughing attack while he struggled to restrain the laughter wanting to burst from him. There was nothing funny about a man standing on his own glasses, he tried to tell himself, but the circumstances and the picture conjured up in his mind by his wife's account of the event made the whole thing nothing less than hilarious and the laughter refused to be denied. It exploded from him in such a loud guffaw, Charlie and Alice both stared at him, their small faces full of enquiry. "Why are you laughing like that, Papa?" Charlie wanted to know.

Christina glared at her husband before heaving her shoulders in an exasperated sigh. "Your papa has a very strange sense of humour, Charlie, that's why."

"What's that?"

"It's … oh, never mind!"

Charlie turned back to his father. "What is it, Papa … what Mama says you have?"

Carl managed to recover some semblance of composure, but chuckles still rumbled from his chest. "A sense of humour is what makes you laugh, Charlie, sometimes when you shouldn't."

"Why shouldn't you?"

"Well, if it's not funny, you wouldn't want to be laughing, would you?"

"I don't suppose so."

Alice had climbed on to her father's lap, touching his face with one small hand to ensure his attention. "I laugh when you tickle me, Papa."

"Like this do you mean?"

Watching her squirm and giggle as she was gently tickled, Christina felt her indignation at her husband's response to her unhappy tale begin to melt. Not sufficiently, however, to keep the smile from her lips when the thought occurred to her that she was going to be able to retaliate. There was something she had to tell him and she had been regretting having to do so. Not now, though. Now, she would tell him with considerable relish. "I think we should tell Papa the surprise we have for him, don't you, Charlie?"

Charlie looked at her blankly.

"You know, about Sunday," Christina prompted.

The little boy's face broke into a smile as he remembered and he grabbed his father's arm excitedly. "We are going to church, Papa!"

Carl's smile froze and his eyes flew from his children to his wife, the enquiry in them giving way to dismay at the expression on her face. "Not this Sunday?" he groaned. Christina nodded, just a little smugly. "Yes, this Sunday."

"But it will take all morning to get over to Nerang, go to church, then come home again, and I was counting on having the whole weekend at home. That rubbish is dry enough for burning and I really do need to get those potatoes planted."

Christina's smile of gentle revenge wavered. It was true, he had been planning on getting a whole lot done this weekend. It disappeared altogether when the twinge of guilt came. They didn't make Sunday visits to her parents very often, but they had done so only last Sunday, because she had been worrying about her father who had strained a muscle in his back. "I couldn't very well refuse his invitation," she murmured, "Not after what happened."

"I don't suppose so. You didn't say that we'd go every Sunday, did you?"

"No, I said this Sunday and then, after that, just when we could spare the time."

"Well, I should think that's fair enough recompense for a pair of glasses." His grin returned. "It might be a short service if he hasn't been able to get a new pair."

Christina tried to give him a reproachful look, but knew from the widening of his grin that she had failed. One day, she promised herself, I will stay angry with him, for more than five minutes.

As was inevitable, the road eventually brought visitors who weren't at all welcome. During the 1880s, with the alluvial gold petering out in most of Queensland's fields, the Chinese seekers, abandoned by their recruiters in Hong Kong, Canton, Macau and elsewhere, had been moving south. Some of them took up market gardening, others sought work on farms or with railway gangs, but a lot simply drifted from settlement to settlement, town to town. The two who found their way on to the road did so on a cold day in August, just four months after the birth of baby Henry. They shuffled along on bare, dirt-ingrained feet, the loose tunics they wore over their trousers stained and filthy, coolie-type straw hats on their heads, and small bundles tied to sticks over their shoulders. It was late afternoon before they reached the gate to Carl's farm and they were through it and on their way to the house before the dog's barking drew Christina to the door and she saw them.

They had come to a halt, huddled together, their eyes fixed fearfully on the circling, growling Bluey. Nevertheless, Christina felt a chill that seemed to creep through her very bones, and her mind began to race. The gun, should she get it? No, not yet …the sight of it might just antagonise them. Best to wait and see if the dog was going to be able to chase them off, or if they would just go when she told them to. Charlie had followed her on to the verandah and she pushed him back inside before stepping over to the edge. "What do you want?" she called out, her voice hoarse with nervousness.

The two men took their eyes off the dog to glance in her direction, then began chattering to each other in an excited fashion, a strange, gibbering sound that was, after a moment or two, directed at her.

"I don't know what you are saying! Go away!"

Christina caught her breath as they responded by inching closer, and then, in the midst of the strange sounds issuing from them, she heard one she recognised – whisky. "No whisky!" she yelled at them, her heart beginning to thump against her ribs. "No whisky here!" And to Charlie, who had crept up behind her, "Go inside, Charlie. Close the back door and pull the bolt across. Then stay inside and make sure you keep Alice there too."

"Who are they, Mama?"

"I don't know, love, but we are going to make them go away. Now, be a good boy and do as Mama told you."

Sensing her anxiety for all that she had spoken calmly enough, Charlie scurried off, and Christina heard the door slam, the bolt slide across. She breathed a faint sigh of relief, but Bluey had become uncertain, barking furiously still, but looking back to the house as he waited to be told what to do, and the two Chinese men, sensing his uncertainty, were able to take several steps forward before he again blocked their way, snarling and growling deep in his throat.

"He'll bite you if you don't go away," Christina called. "I have only to tell him to and he will sink his teeth into your legs."

As before, the men looked questioningly at one another, obviously puzzling over what it was that she had said. Then they again began gibbering away. This time, though, it was another word she knew that reached Christina's ears – money.

"No! No money!"

"Give money, you give money."

Christina gasped at the sharp demand. I have to get the gun, she told herself. They have worked out that the children and I are here on our own, and they are not going to leave. "Hold them, Bluey!" she called sharply to the dog. "Hold them there!"

The dog knew the command. He'd been hearing it all his life, had been bred to hear it. These weren't cattle he was holding, but he knew what he had to do nevertheless. He barked loudly two or three times acknowledging the command, then crouched, growling, his eyes glued to the men.

Christina loaded the gun on the verandah, her actions deliberate in spite of the fact that her fingers were trembling so badly she could barely hold the cartridges. Let them see that I'm serious, she told herself, that it's no empty weapon I'm going to be pointing at them. Back on the verandah's edge, she raised the gun and settled the butt into her shoulder, steadying the barrel as her finger curled over the trigger. At once, the men began waving their arms and calling out in what appeared to be angry protests, but they backed off a few feet. "Keep going!" Christina yelled. "Keep going or I will shoot you both!"

When they didn't move, she lifted the nozzle a fraction and fired over their heads, the sound of the shot bouncing down the valley much as that of a great rock falling into a canyon would do. By the time the echoes died away the two Chinese were bolting for the gate, the dog snapping at their heels.

That night, Christina didn't go to sleep at all. She didn't even try to. She lay on the bed, fully-clothed and wide-eyed, the gun beside her, and, as she hadn't done in a long time, she heard, in the night's thousand voices, things that weren't there. Exhausted, she waited for the first light of day. As soon as it arrived she opened the door to the frosty air, and, with the dog at her side and the gun in her hand, made a careful and thorough search. They were gone … yes, she was sure of it. She bent and patted the dog's head. "You're a good fellow, Bluey, a real good fellow."

The letter from Kathleen arrived just over a year after her mother had made Christina promise to bring it to her, and Carl handed it over to his wife reluctantly. "I almost didn't bring it home. I'm not sure that you should read it."

All the colour had drained from Christina's face and she stared at the envelope in her hands through wide, bleak eyes, but she shook her head slowly. "Kathleen wrote it for me to read and that's what I have to do." She bit her lip, then, with her eyes quietly pleading, murmured, "I would like to do so on my own if you don't mind."

"Of course I don't mind, but are you sure … ?"

"Yes, I am. Please let me read it on my own."

Sighing softly, Carl gently squeezed her shoulder before turning to Charlie and Alice who were busily unpacking the boxes of groceries he'd brought from Nerang. "Leave that for now. It's time we checked whether any chickens have hatched out yet. Today's the day, remember?"

Christina watched them head off for the fowl-run before sitting down at the table and tearing open the envelope with trembling hands …

Dear, sweet Christina,

I have started to write to you a hundred or more times, but always I wept so much I set the ink to running and never got the letter finished.

This time it will be different. For one thing I have no more tears left to shed. For another, I know now that I am dying and I want to say goodbye to you and tell you that I have never stopped loving you dearly.

I had a little baby, Christina. It took two full days for her to come into the world and, when she did, she was dead. Since then I have never been really well. I think it's because something happened inside of me when the baby was being born. Whatever it is, I am now so weak I can hardly stand.

Sometimes I think that, if I could only get up off this bed, I could go home. But I can't do that, so I close my eyes and pretend that I am there, and it almost seems to be true. Instead of being cold through to my very bones I feel the sun warm on my skin and I can even smell the gum trees. I can see you all so clearly it seems that all I have to do to be able to touch you is reach out my hand. But, of course, when I do that, you are never there and I am cold again.

Michael is hardly ever here. He has so much to do and sometimes it takes him away for weeks at a time. He is not at all happy about the way things are going. Everyone seems to think that Mr Gladstone will be defeated in the next election and the Tories returned to office , and that will mean the end of Home Rule for Ireland ... for a long time, at any rate. I don't worry about it anymore. It's too much like chasing something you are never going to catch. Like those tiny fish we used to try to scoop out of the creeks with our hands. Do you remember, Christina?

We would be so sure we had them, but always they would slip through our fingers and be gone.

I received your latest letter only this week. It has been ever so sweet of you to go on writing to me when I haven't replied to any of your letters, but I've already told you why that was. Three children now! How very lucky you are! And a kind and loving husband into the bargain, Prussian though he might be! But then you deserve it all, all the happiness there is.

Goodbye, dear, dear, Christina. Remember me, but don't be grieving for me.

Your loving friend, Kathleen.
P.S. I never did pay you all those half-pennies I owed you.

Christina folded her arms on the table, put her head down on them, and wept bitterly for several minutes. Then she dried her eyes, walked purposefully to the fireplace and dropped the pages, one at a time, on to the slowly burning fire. "Too late, Kathleen," she murmured softly, sadly. "You wrote too late."

The letter Bridget O'Rourke had said would come had arrived two weeks after the telegraphed message informing her that her daughter had died.

36

Troubled years for the Australian wool industry had begun in 1884, and, by 1886, prices had plummeted from twenty pounds to seven pounds a bale. Far and wide, pastoralists, reeling at this new setback in a time of drought, responded by attempting to reduce the contract price for shearing from one pound per hundred sheep to seventeen shillings and sixpence – a reaction that was as a red rag to shearers and other bush workers who had begun to question the extremely hard conditions they had previously accepted as part of the established order of outback life. It was time, they saw now, to extend the familiar and cherished sentiments associated with the concept of mateship to something less casual – to a determined standing together that would ensure they all got a fair deal from those who employed them.

Before the year ended organisations had sprung up spontaneously in three widely-separated bush towns – Ballarat, Wagga Wagga and Bourke. And, before the first month of the new year drew to a close, these three separate groups had merged to form the Amalgamated Shearers' Union. William Guthrie Spence, Chairman of the Ballarat group, became President, and, under his leadership, the union mushroomed, rapidly recruiting thousands of members. Spence would later write: Unionism came to the Australian bushman as a religion. It came bringing salvation from years of tyranny. It had in it that feeling of mateship which he understood already and which always characterised the action of one 'white man' to another.

In his heart, though, he knew that another ingredient had been every bit as important as mateship. It was that of leadership. Always, and at every level, there had to be leaders. And, in this great sprawling country, in every district there had to be leaders. Without them the movement would have failed. All the resolve, all the good intentions would have flared as brightly as the campfires, but only for a time. Then they would have been smothered to ashes by talk that went round and round, never hitting out in any worthwhile direction. William Guthrie Spence would have liked to have been able to say what it was that made a man a leader. But, even though he, himself, was one, he was unable to do so. There had, of course, been times when he'd thought he knew … when it seemed that he saw in a particular man all that was desirable. But then, along would come another … gentle whereas the other had been hard and tough, softly spoken whereas the other had urged and bullied, but respected and trusted by his colleagues in no less degree. And he would be obliged to concede that it was all as much an enigma as ever.

Among the leaders he had met though, there was one he had come to deeply respect – a man dark-eyed and sombre of face, who was possessed of an almost missionary zeal. A ringer known far and wide for his record-breaking tallies in the sheds, respected as a hero and only needing to raise his hand to have men follow him. Intelligent into the bargain and not afraid to speak up or to use his fists if the need arose. Yes, Danny O'Rourke had it in him to be the one who stood out from all the rest … the perfect leader. If only, deep inside, he wasn't more obsessed with harming the lifestyles of the pastoralists than he was with improving the lifestyles of those who worked for them.

"I wonder if Danny has got himself involved in all this union business." Carl was reading a week-old Courier, sharing the circle of lamplight with Christina, who was tackling her darning, her most disliked chore. She snipped off a thread and looked up. "Are they still going on about that?"

"It's important news, Christina. Even though the Amalgamated Shearers' Union is not Australia's first union, it looks as though it's going to be its most powerful."

"And you think Danny might be in it?"

"He'll almost certainly be a member, but I'm wondering whether he's had anything to do with getting the thing going."

"I suppose he could have. If it's something the squatters didn't want, then I'm sure Danny would have been all for it."

Carl chuckled. "You could be right at that."

"Five years? It seems incredible that he could have been away all that time and never once come home." Christina held her breath, an old guilt stirring, as she waited for her husband's reply.

"Danny's hardly the type to be concerning himself with visits home, not when it's such a distance for him to come, at any rate."

"It would be a long way, I suppose." And that, Christina told herself, was the reason Danny hadn't been home, because it was such a long way for him to travel. It had nothing whatsoever to do with her. Even if it was true that he had once believed himself in love with her, that had been ages ago. He'd since had plenty of time in which to realise that it was nothing more than a silly notion on his part.

"I'd like to see him again though," Carl mused. "We used to enjoy each other's company."

"I know. You were very good friends."

"Mates ... we were very good mates."

Christina returned his grin, but regret quickly washed away her attempt at reassurance. And still would be, she thought unhappily, if it hadn't been for me. A silly notion it might well have been, but, even so, it had been enough to make Danny decide to leave Mudgeeraba, there was little doubt about that.

"Well, I'm sure he'll come back one day. It may not be until he's an old man, but he'll come." Carl ran a hand thoughtfully over his thick golden beard. "I wonder if he has grown a beard." Then, grinning again, "And I wonder why he hasn't gotten himself married to a squatter's daughter? He's certainly handsome enough to have swept any number of them off their feet."

"That would be a joke."

"Yes, I suppose it would, but funnier things have happened, and it certainly wouldn't have been the first time a visiting shearer has stayed on as a son-in-law."

"But Danny ... son-in-law to a squatter?"

"It is a bit hard to imagine," Carl laughed. "He would need to have quite a change of heart, that's for sure."

Seeking to change the subject, Christina asked, "Is there anything in the paper about the ship running aground at Southport?"

"It's actually on Porpoise Point and there's quite a bit about it, as a matter of fact. It's a barque called the Scottish Prince, and it seems that, in the middle of the night, she was tacking up the coast under full sail and came too close inshore. She touched bottom and stuck fast."

"And they can't get her off again?"

"They hadn't been able to at the time this paper went to print, but it seems they were waiting for a higher tide to try again."

"Well, I hope they do manage to do that. It would be a shame if this ship finished up like the one on Main Beach."

"The old Salamander, what a phenomenon, she is."

"She's become quite spooky, if you ask me … disappearing under the sand the way she does and then coming out again. Not just the once, but over and over."

Carl laughed softly. "You've been listening to Ma O'Rourke, my love. There's nothing spooky about the Salamander. It's just that the sand builds up and then gets either blown or washed away again. It's all to do with tides and the weather."

"It seems impossible that the sand could build up high enough to cover an entire ship."

"It's hard to believe, but that's exactly what it is doing. There's no way the ship is burrowing itself into the sand, then getting itself out again as some people appear to think."

Christina gave her shoulders a small shrug. "Well, whatever the explanation, it still seems an indecent way for a ship to end its days, like a freak of some sort." She pulled a sock out of her mending basket, considered it thoughtfully, then put it back again.

"What was wrong with that one?" Carl asked with a quick grin.

"It's done for, I'm afraid."

"Why don't you throw it away then?"

"I might have another look at it when I get to the bottom of this lot."

"We are not so poor that we can't throw a sock away, you know?"

"It might be useful for something or other if it turns out that it really can't be mended."

The gently teasing smile on Carl's face became suddenly knowing. "A coat for Harry, for instance?"

Christina's startled glance flew to his face. "How did you know I was thinking that?"

"I just supposed that you might be, that's all."

"Oh Carl, when the cooler weather comes we will have to do something for him. He's got hardly any feathers left and he's not growing any new ones as far as I can see."

"Old Harry is a pathetic sight alright, but I should think that going on for six years is pretty old for a parrot. We might do him a kindness by … "

"No! Not yet! Not while he is still able to talk. It would seem like murder almost."

"Christina, for goodness sake!"

"It would seem that way to me, and I don't want you to do it yet."

"Well, if you're sure? But just because he's become rather decrepit looking, it doesn't mean that he's going to stop talking, mind. Look how he was carrying on while we were having our tea."

"Yes, but it's more of a squeak than a screech now, and he doesn't say 'shut up, fevens sake' nearly as often as he used to. He'll stop talking, you'll see. Then he might even die of his own accord."

Carl raised his eyebrows. "Of his own accord? How does one get to do that?"

"You know very well what I mean, Carl Eichstead."

"Well, he certainly doesn't appear to be too upset about his near-naked state. In fact he's probably realised that he's got it made in this hot weather."

"Which he has. I don't think I've ever felt as hot as I have these past few days and February has hardly begun."

"It's hot alright and humid enough for a storm, but I think we're going to miss out again."

"There might be one later, there's still some lightning about."

"Yes, but it seems to be out at sea now and I don't think we'll get a storm from that direction. It may have given somebody something to cheer about on the way there though." He gave a short laugh. "What a contrast. When we applied for the homestead block, we'd just had a huge flood, and here we are, about to apply for the Deed of Ownership in the middle of a drought."

"Nevertheless, it's a good feeling, isn't it?" Christina questioned, looking up from her darning with a smile.

"It's a good feeling alright. As Da O'Rourke would say, just about the grandest feeling a man could have, owning his own bit of land." Carl leaned back in his chair, flexing his shoulder muscles, revelling in his thoughts. "The homestead this year, Christina, and the selection next year. Then we can decide what we do next."

"I suppose we have done enough improvements to meet both sets of requirements?"

'We will have for the homestead. I've been led to believe that they'll be asking for seventy or eighty pounds worth, and we would have a deal more than that. Thirty acres of scrub felled to begin with, and, even though it's not all cleared, it should be credited at fifty shillings an acre. That gives us seventy-five pounds right off. Then there's the fencing, the cultivation … "

Christina nodded, her smile widening. "So we become true land-owners?"

"That we do, my love."

The Homestead Deed was granted on 14 April, 1887, the formal document being issued six months later, on 19 October.

In the meantime, all efforts to refloat the Scottish Prince had proved unsuccessful, and the people of this south-eastern corner of the Colony forgot, for a short time, the troubles the drought was heaping upon them and followed with more than a little amusement the drama taking place on Porpoise Point. Nine days after the barque had run aground she began to break up in rising seas and disgorge her cargo – a huge quantity of whisky! Case after case and many loose bottles washed ashore and the word spread like wild-fire. From all along the coast boat crews, seeking a share of the bounty, converged on the point. The more impatient snatched up the bottles, knocked the tops off and drank themselves senseless. The more provident, however, carried off cases by the dozen, hiding them along the banks of shady creeks to be drawn on for future imbibing. And the local hotel-keepers obtained supplies that would keep them going for months.

Customs officials were sent down from Brisbane, but, by the time they arrived, the spoil was gone. They searched and searched but found little, and many were the gleeful stories told about how they had been outwitted. "They went through our camp with a fine comb," recalled an old oyster man from Stradbroke Island, "but they found nothing and the silly buggers never gave a thought to looking down our water wells."

Later, though, there would come a story fit, it was generally agreed, to make a grown man cry. One boat party had salvaged a dozen cases of the whisky from under the very noses of the Customs officials. Moving them along the coast, they'd taken bearings as the pirates of old had done and buried them between two prominent sand dunes, intending to return for them when all the fuss had died down. When, several months later, they did so, it was to find that the prevailing south-easterlies had resculpted the dunes and raised a huge ridge comprised of tons and tons of sand over their hoard.

Christina couldn't believe what she was hearing. Her father was saying that he was going to sell the farm and move to Bundaberg. Oh, surely not. Surely her ears were deceiving her.

"Your mother and I are getting on in years, Christina, and the farm has become too much for us."

"But you could share-farm it. You've talked about doing that and it seems such a good idea."

"I know, but the way things are now the farm wouldn't support two families. In any case, I don't think I want to farm any more, not when this drought could get worse and go on and on. What I have in mind is to sell the farm and go into the carpentry business."

"The carpentry business? You wouldn't have to move to Bundaberg to do that."

"I've been talking to a fellow who has spent quite a deal of time there, and he tells me there's no end of work for a carpenter as the district is progressing rapidly. He's going back and he has asked me to go into partnership with him."

"It may not continue to progress rapidly, Father, and it's such a long way off. If you really want to return to carpentry, surely there'd be work enough for you around here?"

"There's not enough of a lasting nature in these parts, especially now when everyone is keeping a cautious eye on their expenditures. I've really looked into it, believe me."

"Brisbane then? That man we met when we first arrived said that he'd always have a job for you."

"That was a long time ago, Christina, sixteen years. And you have to remember that these are difficult times for Queensland. There's certainly any amount of work still needing to be done, but the well has run dry, so to speak … the money's no longer available with which to do it. Why, the Government itself is existing on borrowed funds."

Christina groaned softly. "Why did this terrible drought have to come now, just when things were going along so well?"

Her father gave her a wry smile. "In this country droughts have a habit of doing that, as you must know by now. But I'm afraid we can't be laying all the blame for the Colony's present economic problems on the weather. A lot of it we can, but by no means all of it."

"But they aren't problems that have affected you, are they? You're not in financial trouble or anything like that?"

Simon shook his head. "No. I still owe money to the bank, of course, but I've always been able to meet the repayments on time. It's just that I feel I need to make this move. It's a new dream I have, you might say." He tried to smile but the result was little more than an agitated twitching of his lips, and his fingers, already drumming on the table, took up a more rapid beat.

Christina stared at them, fighting an urge to reach over and still them with her own hands. He has become afraid, she thought, so afraid he's taken to clutching at another man's dreams. "It's such a nice farm, Father," she said gently, her eyes warm with compassion, "and it has been ever so good to you."

"I know it has, Christina, but we can't be forgetting that, until this past year, the weather has for the most part been really kind to us." Simon cleared his throat, his gaze dropping from his daughter's face to his hands. "Since I'll be needing money to begin again in Bundaberg, I have no alternative but to sell the farm. I would like to be able to hand it over to you and Carl, but I … "

"Oh, for heaven's sake, Father! We would never expect you to do anything like that! We wouldn't let you."

Simon gave her a faint smile. "It would have been nice to have been able to do so."

Christina smothered a sigh, wanting to reassure him further, but unable to find the words.

"If you would like to buy the place, you'd have first chance, of course, and I'd set the price as low as I possibly could."

"That would be up to Carl, but I don't see that we would be able to. We won't own the selection until next year, and, while we still have to work that land, it would be pointless trying to sell the homestead. Besides, we'd never get enough money just for the homestead to be able to pay for your farm."

"It might be possible to arrange something. You talk it over with Carl and see what he says."

"Yes, of course. Oh Father, do you really need to go so far away?"

"It's not really all that far, Christina. With the railway line now through to Nerang, we'll be able to go all the way by train, and you'll be able to visit from time to time."

"When do you expect to be leaving?"

"Early in the new year. We thought to have Christmas with you and Carl and the children and leave soon afterwards … that's if we've got the farm sold by then, of course." He stopped tapping the table and ran a hand distractedly through his hair. "You will discuss it with Carl as soon as he gets home, won't you?"

Christina nodded. "He'll probably go down to talk it over with you on Saturday."

"Good … that will be good."

He stayed for only a short time and Christina watched him ride off with her vision blurring and her heart heavy. Whatever was she going to do without them? And what was to become of her father now that he had no dream of his own? He could have been a carpenter in Haderslev, she thought sadly. There had been no need for him to come to the other side of the world to do such work.

Charlie, who had accompanied his grandfather as far as the gate, running along beside his horse, came back and at once asked bluntly, "Why is Grandpa going to sell his farm, Mama?"

"Because he is tired of waiting for the rain to come, Charlie, and he doesn't want to be a farmer anymore."

"Is he going back to Schleswig?"

"No, he and Grandma are going to Bundaberg. That's in Queensland but further up north. Grandpa is going to be a carpenter there."

"Won't he be a farmer ever again?"

Christina smiled down into the upturned face with its brown eyes and bridge of fine freckles across nose and cheeks. "We can't know that, darling. Perhaps one day he will get another farm, but what he's going to do now is be a carpenter."

Little Henry, who'd been sitting on the step with his sister, got up and ran to tug at her skirt and Christina lifted him into her arms, kissing his soft cheek "And what do you think about it all, little one?"

"Henry's too little," Charlie told her with all the superiority of his six years, "He doesn't think anything."

"Of course he does, Charlie. Just because he doesn't talk very much yet, it doesn't mean that he doesn't think. He thinks about lots of things. Isn't that so, Henry?"

The toddler smiled at her and tightened his arms around her neck, and Christina felt the heaviness melt from her heart, a flood of tenderness taking its place. No matter how many children I have, she thought, or how much I love each and every one of them, this one will always be special, able to turn my heart with a single glance from his gently dreaming eyes or the briefest of his angelic smiles.

Alice, deserted by her charge, had been frowning thoughtfully, elbows on knees, chin in hands. Now she asked, "Will Grandpa and Grandma be going on a big ship?"

"No, they won't be going on a ship, love." Christina, with Henry still in her arms, sat down beside her daughter. "They don't have to go across the ocean, so they'll go by train."

"Can we go in a train?"

"One day we will. After Grandma and Grandpa have been at Bundaberg for a time, we might even go up there to visit them. That would be nice, wouldn't it?"

"Yes, that would be real nice."

"Alice would be too scared to go on a train."

Christina gave her first-born a severe glance. "That's silly, Charlie. Now, why would you say something like that?"

"Because it's true. She's a girl and girls are always scared."

His sister bounded to her feet and took a swipe at him, but he ducked neatly, leaving her hand to swish through the air. "Tisn't so! Tisn't so!" she cried hotly. "I'm not scared! I'm not! I'm not!"

"Then why do you scream your head off every time you see a snake?"

"Cos I don't like snakes, that's why."

"Because you're scared, that's why."

"That's enough, Charlie," Christina warned him sternly. "It's right that Alice should call out when she sees a snake."

"She doesn't just call out. She screams and screams."

"Well, that's alright. When I was a little girl, and not as little as Alice either, I used to scream whenever I saw a snake. Once, not long after we came to Australia, a big carpet snake came into our tent and slept on the bottom of my bed, and I screamed for so long, grandma had to put cold water on my face to make me stop."

Charlie stared at her incredulously. "And it was just an old carpet snake?"

"Yes, it was just an old carpet snake." Christina smiled at the look on his face, eyes wide, mouth agape. Then, with her smile widening, "And now I'm going to make you scream. Henry is going down for a nap. Alice is also going to have a little rest, and you and I are going to do some lessons."

"Oh no, Mama! Not this afternoon! We did lessons yesterday!"

"We should do them every day ... well, every week day. If you were able to go to school, that's what would happen."

"But that would be different. I'd have to do them."

Christina's eyebrows lifted. "And you don't think that you have to do them this afternoon?"

Charlie opened his mouth, but a second look at his mother's set face had him changing his mind about what he'd been about to say and he mumbled resignedly, "I suppose I do."

Christina's eyes softened at the sight of his crestfallen face. "You know that you have to learn how to write and read and do sums, Charlie," she reminded him gently. "Even to be a farmer you must be able to do such things."

"That's what Papa said." He grinned suddenly, impishly. "How do you spell mousetrap in just three letters, Mama?"

"In just three letters," Christina repeated, crinkling her brow into a frown. "I'm sure I have no idea."

"C-A-T!" Charlie yelled, bursting into giggles.

"Well, for heaven's sake!"

"Papa told me, it's a joke." His grin faded. "I should have remembered to trick Grandpa."

"I tell you what ... if you do good work this afternoon and tomorrow, you can ride down with Papa when he goes to see Grandpa on Saturday."

"On my own horse?"

"I think Papa will agree to that. You can handle her well enough now, can't you?"

The horse, a small gentle mare, was new and Charlie's very own, having replaced the Shetland pony which had been handed on to his sister. His eyes gleamed. "Yes, I can, Mama. And I will do real good work, you'll see."

And that, Christina told herself, is what you call bribery, but it was with an inwards chuckle and she didn't feel the least bit guilty.

As she had promised her father and to forestall her son who usually managed to be first with any news, Christina told Carl about her parents' plans as soon as he arrived home. Not until later, though, when the children were in bed, did they discuss Simon's suggestion that they might be able to buy his farm.

"It's a very nice farm, Christina, and, had this happened in a year's time, even though I've always had it in mind to be further over towards the coast and with something larger, I would have given serious thought to buying it. But, right now, it would be well-nigh impossible for us to do so."

"I know. I told Father that I thought it would be out of the question at the present time."

"And you're not too disappointed?"

"Of course not. I'm not disappointed at all."

They were on the small verandah and Christina left her chair to walk over to the railing, an addition since the arrival of the children, placing her hands on it and leaning forward to gaze out at the wondrous night. When they had first come outside the stars were already bright in the vast dome of the sky, but the glow from the departing sun had been still lingering pinkly about the western horizon. Now, though, such a short time later, the soft light of the moon was flooding the entire valley, the shadows becoming dark and impenetrable, the taller trees standing out blackly against the sky. It's always changing, she thought, never quite the same from one moment to the next ... with the breeze, with the angle of the sun's rays, with the movement of the shadows cast by passing clouds, or with the climb of the moon into the night sky. She felt Carl come up behind her and she took her hands from the railing to draw his arms around her, leaning back against him with a soft sigh. "I can never quite decide when this valley is at its most beautiful."

"Christina, I know how you must feel about your parents leaving the district," Carl said quietly, his lips against her hair. "My heart aches for you and I wish there was something I could do to help."

"Oh Carl, I'm going to miss them ever so much, but it's not myself I'm worrying about just now. It's Father. He seems so at odds with himself. It's as though he's not sure of anything, even about what he plans to do next, as though he's afraid somehow."

"Afraid of what?"

"Well, the drought, for one thing. He seems to think that it's going to go on and on. But it's not only that. I think he's actually afraid that the Colony isn't going to make it, as it were."

"Good Lord! Did he say that?"

"Not in so many words, but he talked about economic problems and the Government having virtually no money and so forth." She half turned her head so that her eyes could search her husband's face. "Are things really as bad as Father seems to think?"

"The Government has financial problems, there's no doubt about that. For one thing, they borrowed too much for railways, and now they aren't paying their way. And, for another, they've taken to leasing out land instead of selling it, which means that, in the short term, they haven't got the cash coming in as it would otherwise have done."

"What will happen, do you think?"

Carl chuckled softly. "To Queensland? It will grow and prosper in its own good time. You have to remember that it's not yet thirty years old, and what has happened, you might say, is that it tried to run before it could walk. With the result that it has fallen to its knees. Not flat on its face, mind, though there are some who might think so … only to its knees. It's going to get up again, and, when it does, it will be a whole different story, you'll see."

What had actually happened was that, throughout the 1880s, Queensland's economy had grown unevenly, with investment patterns out of balance. Money had literally been poured into the sugar industry which had failed to produce the returns expected, and, for the first half of the decade, there had continued to be highly speculative investment in gold mining. In addition, too much money had been invested in residential and pastoral properties, with the pastoral industry, which had previously led the economic expansion, beginning to falter in 1883. The Government's new land policy, introduced in 1884 and blocking the outright purchase of Government-owned land, had, of course, helped to dampen enthusiasm. At the same time, first floods and then droughts did their part to undermine confidence and add to the uncertainty.

Furthermore, the whole economy had been too narrowly based, with emphasis upon a limited range of exports at a time when world prices were tumbling. And there had been too much confidence in the expansive capacity of that economy, with the Queensland National Bank and other finance bodies failing to exercise sufficient caution in their lending policies. The Government, for its part, had borrowed lavishly for development purposes and then run into difficulties in servicing the debt. Since 1885, when land and railway revenues had fallen, it had been chalking up deficits and living on borrowed money. Its total deficit, when the decade drew to a close, would be more than one and a quarter million pounds.

37

On 26 January 1888, one hundred years since the first white settlement in Australia, a Centennial Exhibition was held in Sydney and various other celebrations elsewhere in New South Wales. In the other colonies, however, little attention was paid to the fact that this was a memorable day. Federation was still a dozen years in the future – nationhood and oneness nothing more than dreams in the minds of a handful of far-seeing men. New South Wales might be one hundred years old on this day, but for Queensland, Victoria. South Australia, Western Australia and Tasmania, owing their own separate allegiance to the Crown of England, such a birthday was still to come.

There was little else to celebrate. In three successive years now, the good soaking rains had failed, and drought was once again doing its destructive best, scorching its way over outback plains and through coastal valleys alike; over the vast grazing spreads, the normally lush sugarcane plantations and the small farms, creating a new and frightening precedent as even the most reliable rivers and creeks dried up. It was 1877 all over again, but worse. And in Queensland the disaster of the drought was aggravated by a new problem – the rabbit had arrived.

In 1859, the year of the Colony's separation from New South Wales, a shipment of rabbits had arrived from England for a landowner in the Geelong district of Victoria. Once liberated, they had multiplied rapidly, spreading quickly across the well-grassed lands of the south, then moving north in hordes, advancing up to seventy miles a year on a broad front and penetrating deeper and deeper into the interior. Everywhere they appeared they caused enormous damage. But this was particularly the case in areas where friable soil was ideal for their burrows and sweet grasses provided ample food. None of the mainland colonies was to be spared. By the mid-1880s the prolific and destructive little foreigner had advanced across the west of New South Wales and into South Australia, and from there into Western Australia, while, in the north, the advance guard had crossed the border into Queensland. Now, just three years later, there were rabbits spread over vast areas of the Colony, robbing sheep and cattle of much needed forages and doing even more serious long-term harm by biting off all the living plants and scratching into the top soil in search of roots.

And an old problem had mushroomed. The earlier good seasons had brought about such an explosion in the kangaroo population they were now present, especially on the western plains, in numbers that had reached plague proportions.

Will it never rain? Christina wondered wearily, pausing to brush beads of perspiration from her brow before plunging her hands once again into the hot soapy water in the washtub. Is the valley to stay brown and dreary-looking instead of being lush and green? In the next moment, she was reprimanding herself. They were better off than many. For one thing, they didn't have the rabbits and huge mobs of kangaroos. For another, thanks to the ranges which had teased occasional low-flying clouds into spilling their moisture, it had taken some time for the full force of the drought's searing breath to reach them. And, most important of all, although it was no longer rushing, the water in the creek was still deep and clear.

So, what if they did now have only half a dozen cattle grazing the sparse grass on their land? They'd received a good price for those they'd been obliged to sell, hadn't they? And just as well, too, since there was no outside work to be had and the final rent on the selection was due to be paid. There had been no return from their maize, though. It had all been a write-off, and, with the earth so dry, there was no sense whatsoever in trying to replant. And what a pity that was … for once it was bringing a decent price. Nothing from their potatoes either, but they had at least been able to fill a few bags for their own use.

Christina winced, dashing a soapy hand to her side as the baby she was carrying kicked out cruelly. Then the shadow of a smile touched her mouth. This was a strong baby within her, there was little doubt about that. And now, thanks to the kindness of Doctor Davies and his wife, there was no longer the worry as to what was to be done when the time for its birth came round. Not that she was any too keen on the idea of moving into the good doctor's home, it seemed such an intrusion. But he was insisting and now that her parents were gone she didn't really have any other choice. Christina sighed softly, her eyes clouding. Almost four weeks now since they'd set out for Bundaberg, but, such a void had their going left, it seemed ever so much longer. I'll get used to it though, she told herself sternly, I'll get used to having them live all those miles away.

Annie Margaret Eichstead made her entry into the world on 12 March, 1888. Almost eight pounds, Doctor Davies guessed as he handed her over to Christina, and perfect in every respect.

On the very last day of autumn, Harry died. In Christina's opinion, because he couldn't face the prospect of another winter huddled in an old sock. And that, as she pointed out to Carl, was dying of his own accord, so to speak.

But when, a couple of weeks later, he tipped another young parrot out of his hat on to the table, she took one look and said flatly, "Take it back."

"Take it back where?"

"Wherever it came from, of course."

"It came from a nest in a very tall tree, it must have fallen out." Amusement danced from his eyes. "You want me to climb up there and put it back?"

"No ... no, of course not. Are there still others in the nest?"

"It would seem so. The mother bird is still busy up there, if that's what you're wondering."

Christina nodded. "I was thinking she might leave the nest and look after it, but if there are ... Don't touch it, Henry. It will peck you." The little boy had climbed on to a chair, holding a small hand out to the bewildered bird. He pulled it back quickly. "It's a pretty bird, Mama."

"Yes, I know, love, but it will still peck you if you touch it, because it's frightened and doesn't know what else to do."

"Will he be able to talk like Harry did?" Charlie wanted to know, the question causing his mother to groan softly and his father to turn his head in order to hide the grin he couldn't keep from his face.

"Harry's in heaven now," Alice, also on a chair, reminded her brother solemnly. "Mama said that, even though he didn't have feathers to fly with, he would still get to heaven."

"I know that, Alice. People don't have feathers and they still go to heaven when they die." He turned back to his mother. "Will he, Mama? Will he be able to talk like Harry did?"

Christina gave her shoulders a helpless shrug. "I don't know, Charlie. I mean … no, he won't be able to talk like Harry did." Then, with her voice regaining its firmness. "He's not going to talk at all. Papa will take him back where he belongs."

"But Papa won't be able to put him back in his nest."

"No, but he can leave him in the bushes where the mother bird can come down and feed him. He might even be able to look after himself since it seems that he's nearly ready to fly."

Charlie frowned. "I don't think the mother bird would do that and he's still too little to look after himself."

"How will his mother find him?" Alice asked, sudden tears shimmering in her eyes. "And, if he's not in the nest, how will he keep warm at night?" The tears spilled over, sliding down her rosy cheeks in great droplets.

"Don't cry, Ally," Henry pleaded, his own eyes swimming.

In sympathy with his beloved sister, Christina knew, rather than with concern for the young parrot. But it didn't matter. The tears were there, so the parrot stayed. And, after a great deal of discussion on the part of the children, was named Wally.

"Hello Wally … hmm, that shouldn't be too difficult for him to say."

"Well, you may be sure that I, for one, will not be trying to teach him to talk," Christina told him. "And I really don't think that any of us should be doing that."

"Why not?"

"Because, as soon as he's able to fly, he'll more than likely take off."

"Not if we clip one of his wings."

"We are not going to do that, Carl. It was different with Harry, he was crippled to begin with."

"The children will be disappointed if he leaves."

Christina sighed softly. "They'll just have to understand that it's not right to be deliberately maiming a bird,"

"Well, if he likes it here and takes a fancy to bread and honey he might hang around in any case."

"If he does so, that's fine, but, if he takes to screeching when the baby is trying to sleep, I promise you I'm going to throw a bucket of water over him."

"Not water," Carl laughingly pleaded. "It's much too scarce."

"A sugar-bag then."

"Poor Wally, someone will have to warn him."

In June the setbacks that had come to Queensland took their political toll. Samuel Griffith's Liberals were defeated and Thomas McIlwraith's Conservatives returned to power.

"It was bound to happen," Carl remarked to Christina when the election results became known. "There's no denying that Sam Griffiths has been unlucky though. He took office in a time of prosperity and pretty much right away, things started to go wrong."

"It seems that, among other things, politicians need to have the weather on their side."

"Well, there's certainly little doubt that the drought has contributed greatly to Griffith's defeat."

"And how terribly unfair that is. When all's said and done, what could the poor fellow have done about it?

"Nothing, of course. It wasn't the only reason, mind, but, had the good seasons continued, he might have had a better chance of getting a favourable reception for his policies."

"Father will be disappointed. He thought Mr.Griffith was a very good Premier, even though his government got itself into financial difficulties."

"Well, it all begun before he took office, and he was more or less committed to continuing the development works that were the main source of the problem. At least he did appear to favour the smaller land-holders."

"And he did try to bring the Kanaka trade to an end." Christina looked up from the small garment she was stitching. "What will happen about that now that he's no longer in office?"

"That Act has been passed so I should think the trade will still have to come to an end. There could well be some changes to what Griffith had in mind though. As a matter of fact, he might have found it necessary to make some changes himself had he stayed in office. It has become clear enough that the sugar industry is not going to be able to survive without the Kanakas, certainly not now that the return is so much lower than it was to begin with. I should think that even those who have been most against the trade would have come to realise that. Then there's the fact that a number of the Islanders simply don't want to return home and would be quite content to stay on here in Queensland."

"If they want to stay, I don't see why they shouldn't be allowed to do so."

"They just might do that … for a time, at any rate. It seems that there's talk of putting back the dates that Griffith set." Carl gave a sudden deep chuckle. "I'm thinking that your father wouldn't want to be saying too much in favour of that worthy gentleman up at Bundaberg. There are some big planters in that region and it seems that they really do hate the man. Both there and further north, whenever they are drinking their rum, they apparently make a special toast to him."

"What's wrong with that?"

"Plenty. They don't say 'For he's a jolly good fellow', or anything like that. They say 'DSG' … Damn Sam Griffith!'"

They were silent for a moment or two, then Christina asked carefully, "Did I hear William say that Father should never have left Mudgeeraba?"

Carl smothered a small sigh of discomfort. William Laver had ridden up to the farm simply, he suspected, to discuss the election results, but somehow he'd got around to the subject of Simon Skov and his move out of the district. "You know how the Lavers are about this district, Christina. William's family have been hereabouts for close on twenty years, and he'd taken up his selection on the Little Nerang before I even applied for mine. And, of course, they've got the hotel, which seems to be going along nicely in spite of the drought."

"I know, and they are all really nice people, but it doesn't give them the right to be criticising Father because he has left the district."

"William wasn't really doing that."

"Well, whatever he was or wasn't doing, I hope you told him that Father is doing quite well as a carpenter in Bundaberg."

"I most certainly did," Carl assured her. "He was pleased to hear that."

"Did he say when we are to get a proper store in Mudgeeraba?"

"No, but a church is about to be built, Presbyterian. And, according to William, it will be used as a school during the week."

"That will be progress, but not much help to us. Charlie is still too young to be riding all that way to school." She sighed and Carl gave her an encouraging smile. "Come now, you know that you've done very well with Charlie."

"But what's going to happen in a year or so if he isn't able to go to a proper school?"

"I think you'd still manage to teach him."

Christina tossed him a wry grin. "When I'd be wasting half of every lesson checking to see whether or not what I was teaching him was correct?"

"Well, by then, it may not be a school in Mudgeeraba that we are looking for, but one further over towards the coast."

Christina's eyes softened, a genuine smile replacing the grin. "It's just wonderful that the Deed to the Selection has been approved."

"It certainly is. I might tell you that I was a bit worried as to whether it would be, what with the place looking so poorly."

"That's because of the drought and the Inspector would have known that."

Carl nodded, then sighed contentedly. "Now we have it, Christina: land that we own, land that we can sell. All we have to do is wait for the rain to begin to fall so that we can smarten this place up and then keep our eyes open for the sort of farm we have dreamed about."

Along the coast the rain began with early summer storms; then, in the first months of the new year, became general, drenching the thirsty earth. In the far north the 'wet' set in with all its old fervour and appeared intent on atoning for its poor showing in the previous three years. Only out in the west did the drought continue, giving to vast areas a new name – 'heartbreak country'.

With the children watching her, round-eyed with curiosity, Christina pulled the old wicker case out from under the bed and took it into the kitchen where she set it down on the table.

"What's in it, Mama?" Charlie asked, eyes wide with interest.

"Some things that I wanted to keep." Christina smiled at her eldest son. "As a matter of fact, Charlie, it's so long since I've opened this case I've almost forgotten just what is in it." There was one thing she hadn't forgotten though and, as she set about untying the cord that held the case together, guilt stung sharply. How long? Eight years, and she hadn't looked at it in all that time. Dear God in heaven, how could that have happened?

At the time of moving from her parents farm to Carl's selection, Christina had been dismayed to discover that the edges of Lars's painting had thickened and begun to split, and, worse, that the painting itself had faded drastically. Stung with remorse that she should have let this happen, she'd wrapped it carefully in a piece of soft cloth and put it into the case, telling herself that she would only take it out from time to time. Never had she intended, though, that the first time would come after eight years. It's not that she had forgotten it, she told herself, her fingers fumbling with the knot. It's just that the time has gone by so quickly. "Oh, what's wrong with this cord, for heaven's sake?"

"You've pulled it into a knot, Mama."

"I can see that, Charlie."

"I can undo it for you."

Christina lifted her eyes from the knot to her son's confident young face, and moved to one side with a small sigh. "Very well. You see if you can."

In a matter of seconds, while his mother watched open-mouthed, he had the knot undone. "Papa says there's no sense in just tugging. You have to look and see just which way the string goes."

"Yes … yes, of course. Thank you, Charlie."

The painting was on the top and had to be removed first, but she put it aside, still wrapped in its piece of cloth.

The little boat had been long since forgotten, but now, as she lifted it out of the case, Christina's eyes became soft with tender memories. Then, seeing the eagerness on the face of her son, she handed it to him, watching while he ran his fingers almost reverently over the smooth wood. "It's very fine work, Mama. Who did it?"

"A young Swedish boy who came to Australia on the same ship as I did. He had brought some pieces of wood on to the ship with him and the ship's carpenter gave him some odds and ends. He was always carving something or other. He made some amazing animals, but I think it was really boats and ships that he most liked doing."

"It would have been good to have something like that to do when he was on the ship for such a long time. Where would he be now?"

"I don't know, Charlie. Still somewhere in Queensland, I would think, but I have no idea just where." And no idea where most of the others from the ship are either, Christina added to herself. The Schneiders were still in Mackay … that much she knew, since her mother had sent her a newspaper cutting about their huge plantation. And the Eisemanns were still at the Logan, her father had kept in touch with them for quite some time and Marie occasionally mentioned them in her letters. After meeting up with her at the Regatta, she had kept in touch with Mrs Klaussen, of course, but she had been dead for almost two years now. They were the only ones … the others had walked off the Friedeburg and out of her life.

"One day I might be able to carve a boat like this."

"I'm sure you will, Charlie. In the meantime would you like to have this one for your very own?"

"Yes … oh yes, please, Mama."

"Very well, it's yours then." She turned back to the case. "And I know there's something in here that Alice would like."

The little girl caught her breath, her sky-blue eyes becoming so wide and bright they seemed to be on the point of popping from her head. "What is it, Mama?"

"Something pretty for a pretty little girl, but I have to find it first." The small box, tucked away in the corner of the case, was quickly located by Christina's searching fingers. "Close your eyes, Alice, and hold out your arm."

Alice was quick to obey, screwing up her whole face to ensure that her eyes were closed tightly enough … letting them fly open again and widen with delight the minute Christina fastened the bangle around her wrist. "Oh Mama, it's just beautiful."

"My grandmother gave it to me when I was a little girl and now I'm giving it to you. You must look after it though."

"Oh, I will … I will. I'll look after it ever so carefully."

Smiling, Christina was about to turn from her excited daughter back to the case when she caught her breath, her heart sinking. Henry's eyes were on her face, full of trust and telling her all too clearly that he was patiently waiting for his turn. Dear God, what did she have that would please this gentle little boy? Nothing probably. Nothing at all. Oh, how stupid she had been, not to have thought of that before she'd given Charlie the boat and Alice the bangle. Right in front of his eyes, no less. And now she had nothing to give him. Her mind raced, trying to recall the various things she'd put away during the years. There had to be something. There just had to be.

There was. It bounced up out of the confusion of things her mind's eye was seeing … so vividly it might have come from yesterday and so unexpectedly it brought a gasp to Christina's lips. Something Henry would love, of course it was. But the very thought of bringing it out, touching it again, brought a coldness to her heart. I can't do it, she thought. Even after all this time, I can't do it. Something else? There must be something else. The eyes fixed on her face were becoming uncertain and disappointment had begun to tug at the soft under lip.

Christina groaned softly, then took a deep breath and forced herself to say brightly, "And I've just remembered something that Henry will like." She began bundling things out of the case, letting them spill on to the table in a haphazard fashion. Hurry. Now that she had decided, she had to hurry. If she didn't, the fragile courage she had summoned would desert her. "It's down near the bottom, I think."

There was no mistaking the strangely coloured packet and, at the very sight of it, Christina's mind went spinning back over the years ... seeing the young girl racing along the deck of the Friedeburg with it in her hands ... seeing her again at the door to a familiar cabin, wide-eyed with terror and disbelief ... and then again, the packet still in her hands, but with tears blinding her as she stared at a desert sunset and pleaded with God, "Please, please don't let her die. Please don't take this baby from us."

"Have you found it yet, Mama?"

Christina started, for a moment staring almost unseeingly at the anxious little face. Then she swallowed the lump in her throat and murmured huskily. "Yes, I've found it, darling." Resolutely she lifted the packet out of the case and, after only a moment's hesitation, drew the soft fur donkey out into the light of day for the first time in eighteen years. Tears caught in her throat and stung her eyes, but her son held out his hands with such a look on his face, a swift surge of thankfulness swept through her, bringing a smile to her lips. This could be the reason, she thought, the reason she had kept it all this time.

"Mama, it's a little horse."

"No, it's a little donkey, love. See, it has long ears."

"Yes, I see." He hugged the soft toy to his chest, chuckling delightedly. "A little donkey. It's a little donkey. Is he mine to keep?"

"Of course he is."

The smile he gave her melted the last particles of ice from Christina's heart. It was right that he should have the donkey, she told herself, that it should finally be brought out from hiding. But had she really kept it for him, as it had seemed a few moments back? Had some instinct told her that the day would come when it would bring joy to the heart of another child dear to her? Slowly Christina shook her head, a small wry smile coming to her lips. It would be nice to think that it had been that way, but it hadn't, not really. The truth of the matter was that she had kept the donkey because she'd never known what to do with it. At first she'd thought that she should give it to her father and let him decide, but something told her that to do so would only add to his grief. Then she'd considered throwing it into the ocean and had almost done so, but a strange and frightening rebuke that seemed to come from nowhere had stayed her hand in the very moment it moved to release its grip on the packet. Was she thinking that she was throwing the donkey to little Anna? a stern voice had seemed to be asking. Oh, for shame, for shame! When she wasn't in the deep, dark water at all, but up in heaven with God.

And so the little donkey, still in its packet, had gone to Mrs Klaussen's cabin and stayed there until they reached Brisbane. It had come ashore pushed into the basket she was carrying, and, in the years since, had been moved from one hiding place to another. For quite a time she had continued to think about what she should do with it, but all the ideas that came to her were rejected for one reason or another, until finally she no longer thought about getting rid of it. Her mother had known that she had the donkey, of course. It had been inevitable that she would come across it, but just when she had done so for the first time, Christina had no idea. She had always left it wherever it happened to be, saying nothing.

"What are these, Mama?"

"They are sketches, Charlie, done with pieces of charcoal."

He was going through the small bundle, looking at each sketch in turn, but with no particular interest, when, suddenly, his head jerked up and he frowningly considered his mother's face before again dropping his eyes to the sketch in his hand. "This one looks a bit like you."

Christina smiled at him. "It is me ... when I was younger, of course."

"How old were you?"

How old? Christina repeated the question to herself as her mind began recalling. Sixteen? No ... seventeen. It would have been around the time of her seventeenth birthday that Lars had done the sketch. But he had never seen her at that age! So it was really of her as she'd been just before she turned fourteen ... as he had remembered her from the last time he'd seen her. "I think it's of me when I was around fourteen."

"It doesn't look like someone who is only fourteen."

Christina reached out a hand and took the sketch from him, appraising it critically. Charlie was right. It didn't look like someone who was only fourteen. It wasn't really the likeness of a child at all … it was that of a young woman. A faint frown creased her brow and she picked up the sketches her son hadn't yet looked at. "I just want to see the others he did of me."

She flipped through the untidy pile quickly: trees, birds, bullock teams, Jack Keach and Samuel Hansen, more birds … Ah, here they were, four of them. The frown on her forehead deepened. Four sketches and four different expressions, but not one of them such as a young girl not yet turned fourteen would wear. "You wouldn't have changed all that much … in the way you look, that is," the timber-getter had remarked at the time he'd given her the sketches, and that had seemed to explain why they looked so much like her as she was then. But in those previous three years she would have changed, she could see that now. Perhaps not so much in her features as such, but in the way she used them. And that change was right there … on the charcoal faces spread on the table before her. To begin with, the eyes weren't the bright, innocent eyes of a fourteen-year-old. They were warm and melting, seeming to smile with a secret knowing.

Christina smothered a quick gasp. They were the eyes of a woman in love. Lars had given her the eyes of a woman in love. It was the same with her mouth, for heaven's sake. Her gaze darted from sketch to sketch and back again, seeing the soft, pleased smile on one, the lips parted invitingly on another. And her hair tumbled in curls about her shoulders when it should have been in braids. Why had he drawn her that way? And how … how had he done it, when he would never have seen such expressions on her face or her hair unruly like that?

Unless he had somehow seen her during the time he was at the timber-camp? No, that wouldn't have been possible. Not only had Samuel Hansen told her that Lars had spent all his free time at the camp, there was also the fact that, had he ever been close enough to their farm to have seen her, she would surely also have seen him. What then? How had he done these sketches that were unmistakenly of her and yet were not really of her as he had known her? Simply by chance? Yes, it had to be.

It was the only possible explanation … he'd done them simply by letting his imagination run free.

"I think there's something written on the back of that one," Charlie told her, nodding at the sketch she had picked up and was holding in her hand.

Christina whipped it around. The writing was in pencil and so faint she had to hold it to the light to read the words – *Seventeen today. Happy Birthday, Christina.*

"What does it say, Mama?"

Feeling tears prick at her throat, Christina bit her lip, and it was a moment or two before she could read the words out loud, explaining huskily, "Lars must have done this sketch on my seventeenth birthday."

Charlie stared at her, his small brow wrinkled in confusion. "But you said you were fourteen?"

"Well … yes, I know. But I haven't looked at these sketches in years and years, and I must have forgotten how old I was. If it says here that I was seventeen, then I suppose I was … when this one was done, at any rate."

"Was the Lars who did these sketches that same Lars who is in the cemetery over at Nerang?"

Christina tossed her eldest son a sharp glance. "I didn't know you had been to the cemetery?"

"I went one time with Grandpa, just me and him."

"When was that?"

"One day when we took the butter over to Nerang, but I don't remember exactly when."

"You never said a word about going to the cemetery?"

Charlie wriggled uneasily on his chair. "I … I didn't think to."

"Did Grandpa ask you not to say anything?" Christina hated the question, but couldn't keep it from her lips.

"No, but he cried while we were there and I didn't think he'd want me to tell you that. I didn't think he'd want me to tell anyone."

Christina gave him a gentle, reassuring smile. "No, I don't suppose he would have, but we have all cried for Lars, you know? He was very dear to us."

Charlie nodded soberly. "I know, Grandpa told me." He waited a moment or two, then asked again, "Was he the same one who did the sketches?"

"Yes, Lars Ohlsen. He was very clever at things like that." Christina reached for the painting. "He gave me this painting when we were leaving Haderslev to come to Australia. It's of our house." She removed the cloth covering carefully, mindful of the fraying edges of the cardboard, groaning softly when the painting came to light. "It's quite faded now, Charlie. It seems that water colours don't last forever, not when they are on cardboard, at any rate. But you can still see what our house looked like."

"Yes, I can, but I wish it was still nice and bright. Do you still remember what it was like, living in Haderslev?"

"Yes, but not as clearly as I would like to do." And never a whole picture, she added to herself with a faint sigh, just bits and pieces, as though all she had left of Haderslev and Schleswig were just fragments of memory.

A screeching racket began in the trees outside the back door and Alice and Henry, who'd been sitting on the floor playing with the donkey, scrambled to their feet and rushed to the door, crying excitedly, "Wally's here! Wally's here!"

Smilingly getting to her feet, Christina gave her eldest child a quick hug. "We'd best go and say hello to him, Charlie."

"I reckon or we'll be in real trouble," Charlie told her with a wide smile. There would, he knew, be a hundred or more parrots out in those trees, come in the hope that his mother would have some bread soaked in honey and water for them. One of them just might be Wally who had flown off after staying only two weeks, but that was something nobody knew for sure. Alice and Henry, though, always said they recognised him, and that was why he and his mother played this little game, pretending that they did too. It was real nice, he thought, to be sharing this pretence with his mother; it meant that he wasn't just a little kid anymore.

38

The new decade brought troubled times for the Colony of Queensland. During the investment boom of the first half of the 1880s, foreign funds had become more and more available – an influx of capital that led to Australians experiencing the highest per capita incomes in the world. By the end of the decade, however, overseas investors had become concerned at the difference between expected and actual returns on their investments and were withdrawing further funding. The boom times were soon giving way to the beginnings of depression.

Rising unemployment and failing businesses became the order of the day, and in Queensland, there was another matter also causing concern. As the wool industry grew, so did the number of shearers disgruntled with poor working conditions. By 1890 tens of thousands had joined the Australian Shearers Union and thousands of shearing sheds had been unionised. Discord began when the union laid down a new rule prohibiting members from working alongside non-union members. Shearers at Jondaryn station on the Darling Downs stopped work over this issue, and on 5 January 1891 a strike was declared.

In response, local graziers, hard hit by the long drought and falling wool prices, met in Barcaldine and formed the Pastoral Employers Association. Claiming 'Freedom of Contract', they announced severe wage reductions and refused to negotiate, thus ignoring unions and effectively challenging their right to exist. The unions responded by setting up headquarters in a huge camp at Barcaldine with strike camps also at Clermont and Hughenden.

In 1890, Samuel Griffith, whose government had lost the elections two years previously, had again become Premier at the head of an unlikely alliance with Thomas McIlwraith in a conservative colonial government which fully supported the pastoralists. No time was lost in sending more than a thousand armed soldiers and special constables to Central Queensland. By mid-March 1891, these, along with unionists and strike-breaking labour pouring into Barcaldine had raised the population of less than a thousand to well over five thousand, causing all manner of problems.

Christina was finding it hard to believe what Carl, the Courier spread on the table before him, was telling her. "Soldiers? Why on earth would they be needed?"

"They are supposed to provide military escorts for those non-union men who want to work in the sheds – the 'scabs' or 'blacklegs' as they are called. It seems the Government is concerned that confrontations between them and the union blokes could end in a bloodbath."

"Oh, surely not! They would never be so stupid!"

"You wouldn't think so, but things are really tense out there apparently, and now that the Shearers Union has the support of not only the Workers' Union but also the Maritime Union, it would only take a couple of hot-heads to start something really nasty. In the meantime, how about we leave the unionists and the non-unionists to sort out their problems and use this child-free couple of hours to talk about something more cheerful?"

Christina glanced at the improvised beds in which Alice and Henry were sleeping, and then into the bedroom, where Charlie had his small bed and little Annie still slept in the cot. A tender smile came to her lips. As much as she loved them, it was nice to have this time just with her husband. Bringing her gaze back to him, she asked smilingly, "Does the paper have any cheerful news to report?"

"Not really. It's pretty much all doom and gloom about the depression. No one seems to be hopeful that it will be soon over, which is a blow when we are ready to sell the farm." Carl grinned wryly. "It will be a bit of a bonus when we come to buy a place, though … it seems there are quite a few properties with owners anxious to sell and they'll know not to expect top prices."

"Which means that we won't be getting a top price either?"

"That's right, but we don't have to rush, and, if we are able to buy at a good price, we'll be able to accept a bit less than we are hoping for here. We'll wait a while and see how things work out." He grinned suddenly.

"There is a bit of what we might call cheerful news in the paper."

"Well, are you going to tell me what it is?"

"Some very clever Swedish fellow has invented a cream separator."

Christina stared at him, a small, disbelieving smile on her lips. "You don't mean something that will get the cream out of the milk without having to set it out in pans."

"That's what it says. You pour the milk into a big bowl at the top of the device, turn the handle so that some part of it spins around, then the cream comes out of one spout and the separated milk out of another."

"Just like that?"

"Yes, just like that. Think what a bonus it will for us on our dairy farm."

Christina shook her head. "I'm afraid I'll have to see it before I believe … and see it working, no less. It just sounds too good to be true."

At Barcaldine there were minor instances of sabotage and violence on both sides, but no bloodbath. The strike began to lose momentum in March when thirteen strike leaders were arrested, charged with sedition and conspiracy, and sentenced to three years hard labour on St Helena Island in Moreton Bay. In April, three hundred and seventy-seven 'scabs' from New South Wales and Victoria arrived on two trains, heavily escorted by military personnel. With shearing now under way using non-union labour and the strike leaders removed from town, the morale of the unionists took a deep plunge. On 20 June 1891, its resources exhausted, the union declared the strike at an end.

On the last day of June, Danny O'Rourke rode up to the Eichstead farm. From her front doorway Christina watched as he leapt from his horse and grabbed her husband in a bear hug. She heard their laughter and knew this was a reunion dear to both of them. I am happy for them, she told herself, really happy.

"Who is it, Mama?" Charlie wanted to know.

"That's Danny O'Rourke, you've heard Papa speak about him."

"Yes, I have … he helped build this house and clean up the farm after the big flood, didn't he?"

And he helped bring you into the world, Christina added to herself. "That's right. He has been a very good friend to both your father and me."

It was easier than Christina had expected. Danny gave her a quick hug, kissed her on both cheeks, then smilingly glanced down at the children clustered around her, "Well done, Christina. I'm glad to see that the first effort didn't put you off having a family. But how do you all fit into this little house?"

Christina returned his smile, his cheerfulness causing her slight uneasiness to disappear. "It is something of a crush, especially with a bed in the kitchen, but we manage. Come on in and you'll see for yourself."

For a time they talked about the farm, the drought and the depression. When the conversation did get around to the strike, Christina was surprised to see that Danny didn't seem bitter about the outcome.

"It was too poorly timed to have any worthwhile effect on the shearing season," he told them, "but it was a significant event nevertheless. That march on the 1st of May, for instance. Over thirteen hundred men took part, and it's one of the first such marches to take place anywhere in the world … can you believe that?"

"But what did it really accomplish?" Carl asked. "Pastoralists are continuing to cut wages and employ non-union labour and if unionists want to work, they have no choice but to work beside them."

"That's the way it is now, but it won't be for long. The strike may have failed in accomplishing its goals, but it has already marked the beginning of renewed efforts to pursue the union's cause … not necessarily with another strike but through the ballot box. That's what we need, representation in parliament, and, mark my word, before too long, we'll have it."

"Do you intend to stay up here?" Carl asked.

"Not this time. There are still things I have to do down south, but I'll be back before too long. It's going to be in Queensland that exciting changes take place and I want to be part of that."

Danny was right. A by-election in 1892 in the seat of Barcoo provided the unions with their first seat in parliament. The death of local member, Francis Murphy, a staunch supporter of the squatters' cause, saw shearer Tommy Ryan, who had been arrested but acquitted, win the seat of Barcoo and become the first Labor parliamentary representative in Queensland.

39

It was spring again, the spring of 1892. And in the south-eastern region of Queensland, the season had arrived with a confidence that had been sadly lacking in recent years. It's just the way spring should be, Christina decided as she stole a moment on its fifth morning just to stand and gaze about her. And what a beautiful day this particular one was going to be; all soft breezes, blue skies and brilliant sunshine. The smile on her lips widened and she murmured, "Just the most perfect day for a surprise."

A small hand slipped into hers and she glanced down, her smile gentling. "So you are ready, Alice?"

"Yes, I am, Mama. Do I look pretty?"

"You look just beautiful, darling."

"Is little Annie going to wear her best dress too?"

"Yes, of course. Papa says we must all look our best because this is a very special day."

"Why is it a special day?"

"Because he has a surprise for us ... a wonderful surprise, it seems."

"Is it a present?"

Once, Christina recalled, smiling a little wryly to herself, she had questioned her mother in just such a way, and the surprise her father had had for her was that they were leaving their home to go to the other side of the world. What a heart-stopping surprise that had been.

"Is it, Mama? Is it a present?"

"I don't know what it is, Alice. We just have to wait and see. I do know that we are all going off in the buggy though and taking a picnic with us. That will be fun, won't it?"

The little girl's eyes became large and round with excitement. "We might be going to play on the sand, like we did that other time ... the sand where all those big waves are."

"How about we just wait and see what the surprise is? I think I had better get a move on though, don't you? Papa might go without me if I'm not ready."

"Yes, he might."

Christina raised her eyebrows, amusement tugging at the corners of her mouth. "So you think he would do that, do you?"

"If you're not dressed, he might." She giggled suddenly. "Henry looks funny in trousers."

"Oh, he doesn't, Alice. He looks a real little man."

Alice was unconvinced and she screwed up her face thoughtfully. "Why does he have to wear them?"

"Because he's too big now to be still wearing dresses."

"Well, I'm glad I'm not a boy." She swished her skirt to and fro, then held up her arm. "My bangle looks nice, doesn't it?"

"Mmm, it certainly does. But don't be forgetting your bonnet. You don't want any more freckles, do you?"

"No, I don't. Charlie says I have two new ones on my nose."

Christina bent down to peer into her daughter's face. "Let me see. Ah, just as I thought, Charlie was teasing you. There's not even one new freckle on your cute little nose."

"Will the fairies really come and take them all away one day?"

"Of course they will. They took the ones I had when I was a little girl, didn't they?"

Alice nodded. "What did they do with them?"

Just for a moment Christina was back in Eleanor Klaussen's cabin on the Friedeburg and she smiled at the memory. "Perhaps they sprinkled them on the faces of other little girls. Why, it might even be that you have some of mine on your face."

Giggling, Alice sped away, calling out "I'm going to tell Charlie that."

They came down from the mountains in the midmorning. Excitement travelled with them, and the jolts and bumps that had the buggy bouncing them about brought only laughter. Once out of the foothills Carl set the horse to a smart trot and they rolled merrily along the narrow dirt road that crossed the marshy flat lands in the direction of the coast.

"We are going to the sand," Alice exclaimed delightedly. "I remember that it's this way and I can smell the sea."

"Not this time, Alice," her father told her.

The little girl was silent for a few moments, but not yet defeated. After a whispered, mainly one-sided conversation with her little sister, she announced, "Annie said that she would like to see the sand."

Laughing softly, Christina glanced over her shoulder to where the children were sitting on cushions on the buggy floor. Goodness, how they were all growing. Charlie eleven years old now, and even little Annie had turned four. And how beautiful they all were.

"You look like the cat that got all the cream," Carl mused, his brows raised questioningly, "Perhaps you'd care to tell me what it is that suddenly brought that ever-so-satisfied look to your face?"

"I was just thinking what beautiful children we have."

Behind them, Charlie groaned, and his father laughed. "I was just about to say that you'd better not let number one son hear you say that."

"Sorry, Charlie. What about beautiful daughters and handsome sons?"

"That's better," Carl told her, before adding softly, "I don't think their mother knows just how beautiful she is herself though, or that, right now, she looks no more than sixteen or seventeen years old."

Christina flushed with pleasure, but responded playfully, "You are ever so kind, Mr. Eichstead sir, but you do exaggerate, you know?"

"Not at all. You look much too young to be the mother of four children."

"Well, I must confess that this morning I do feel young. It's such a beautiful day and here we are with nothing to do but enjoy ourselves."

They had been travelling in a mainly north-easterly direction, the land on both sides of the road, low-lying and lagoon-dotted, a meandering line of trees up ahead marking the course of a creek. Here and there, fat cattle grazed the green marsh grasses, and they passed three farm houses set on slight rises well back from the road. Presently, the creek, taking a sharp turn northwards, appeared only a dozen or so yards from the road, obliging it to swing to the north also.

"Boobegan Creek," Christina mused. "What a pleasant-looking waterway it is." And then, glancing about her, "Wasn't there cane all through here?"

"There was, but not anymore. Once the price of sugar dropped the way it did, most of the small growers around here gave the cane away. Even Johann Meyer is no longer growing cane on his land along the Nerang. He's selling it off as allotments, as a matter of fact."

"First cotton, then sugarcane. What will it be next?"

"Something much more permanent," Carl told her, unable to keep the grin from spreading across his face. "Next it will be dairy farms."

Christina stared at him, eyes wide, mouth dropping open. "I know," she gasped. "I know what the surprise is."

Carl gave a deep chuckle. "I couldn't have kept it from you much longer, in any case. Not when it's on the other side of this gate we're coming to."

The property was at the junction of Boobegan Creek and the Nerang River, in an area known as Carrara. In places untidy clumps of long-neglected cane slumped drunkenly. In others, grass, interspersed with weeds, had spread luxuriantly. In still others, the scrub had again taken hold and was reclaiming with a vengeance. The house, at the end of an overgrown track and facing the river, was more than twenty-five years old, and had received little attention during that time, but, constructed of fine hardwood timbers, it was still as solid as the day it had been built.

"I can't believe this," Christina cried, breathless with astonishment as Carl swung her down from the buggy and set her on her feet. "It's Boobegan Price's place."

"It was at one time and others have owned it since, but now it's ours."

"Since when? And how?"

Chuckling, Carl helped the children from the buggy and tried to answer a few of their hundred and one questions before turning back to his wife. "Since just this last week. How? Because we have bought the place, that's how, with a bit of help from the bank, of course."

"It's definite?"

"Yes, I've already signed on the dotted line … several dotted lines, in fact, since I had to sell our place first."

"You've done that, sold the selection?"

"Along with the homestead." His grin widened. "To a bloke who was so intrigued at seeing a bangalow palm growing in the middle of a cornfield he couldn't resist."

Laughing, Christina spun around, arms outflung, her bonnet slipping from her head to dangle by its ribbons. "This place is ours? Oh, it's not possible. It's just not possible."

Carl caught her hand, drawing her towards the house in the wake of their scampering children. "It hasn't received much attention in recent years," he told her, "and there are a few repairs we'll need to be making, but it's a fine solid structure."

"And it's so large, and up off the ground with verandahs on three sides." Christina came to a sudden halt, her breath catching as delight washed over her. "And it has a tank. Oh Carl, it has a tank."

"Two tanks! And why not when it has an iron roof with guttering all around?"

"I must be dreaming. I must be. Water out of a tap and no more beds in the kitchen."

Carl laughed. "The house will be great, Christina, and so will the land. It's only a relatively small part of the area Price originally owned, but it will be a good size for the sort of dairy farm we'll be able to manage."

Charlie came running back to them. "There's a jetty, Papa, just over there where the river is."

"I know, Charlie. The Maid of Sker and other boats stop here if there's anyone to be let off or picked up."

"The Maid of Sker stops here?" Charlie gasped, his eyes wide with incredulity. "Right next to our place. Will we be able to go on it?"

"Of course. We might even go to the next regatta at Southport."

"That will be so exciting, Papa."

"Yes, it will be." Carl slipped an arm around Christina's shoulders, drawing her close to his side. "Your mother and I went to the very first Southport regatta."

"Was that a long time ago?"

Carl's eyes searched his wife's face, teasing her into remembering something about that day that had nothing to do with boats. "What do you think? Was it a long time ago?"

"Right now it seems that it was only yesterday," Christina told him with a soft laugh. Then, seeing the puzzled expression on her son's face, she added quickly, "It was before you were born, Charlie."

With the inspection of the house completed, they had their picnic in the shade of a tree not far from the water's edge, Christina and Carl lingering, the children rushing, impatient to be on their feet and off again.

"It's ever so pleasant here with the river flowing past," Christina remarked dreamily. "Not as spectacular as up in the mountains, but it will be very nice living here."

Carl looked about him, pleased, proud of what he had accomplished. "This place is going to make a fine dairy farm, Christina. It's only eighty acres, but all the land is usable, pretty much every square foot of it."

"There's a fair bit of clearing to be done though."

"Yes, but it's only small stuff, nothing like the jungle that had to be cleared from the selection and homestead."

Christina nodded, but a small doubt had begun to nibble at the edges of her contentment and her eyes became thoughtful. "You're not concerned that we might be making this move at the wrong time. I mean ... isn't everyone saying that the economic problems of the Colony are going to get worse with an even bigger slump just around the corner?"

"I've thought about all that, Christina, believe me. But I'm going on for thirty-six years old and I simply can't afford to be waiting around for what may be termed a better time. Besides, sometimes a man can be too careful." A sudden smile drove the seriousness from his face and, leaning to one side, he nipped a dandelion flower from its stem. "Here, let me show you something. Hold out your hand."

Christina did so and he placed the dandelion on her palm.

"What am I supposed to do with this?"

"That's your dream you're holding."

"It doesn't look like ... oh, why did you do that?"

Carl had given her hand a tap from underneath and the flower had bounced up and fallen to the ground. "Because I wanted to show you what happens to dreams when you don't hold on to them," he told her. "Would you like to try again?"

"Yes, I would."

This time, the minute the dandelion was on her palm, Christina closed her fingers tightly around it. "I won't lose it this time."

"No, you won't. I can see that, so I'm not going to try to make you do so." He reached for her hand and gently uncurled her fingers. "But look at what you've done. You've crushed the very life out of your dream."

Christina lifted her gaze from the crumpled petals to his face. "I don't understand … "

Removing the dandelion, Carl raised her hand to his lips and pressed a light kiss on the spot where it had been. "When you have a dream, my love, you have to hold on to it in such a way as to make sure it doesn't get away from you, but you must also give it a chance to breathe, to take nourishment, you might say."

Christina shook her head slowly, wonderingly, pride and love shining from her eyes. "You, my husband, are the sort of dreamer the Colony needs, especially now, and I am ever so proud of you."

For a time, while the sun moved into the western sky, they sat on under the tree, keeping an eye on the children and quietly making plans: for the more urgent repairs to the house and fences, the clearing, the construction of bails and dairy, and the move down from the mountains which would take place at the end of the month. Then they gathered up the remnants of their picnic and, while Carl went to replace them in the buggy, Christina wandered over to where Alice was playing with the two younger children, the three of them romping about gleefully on a stretch of thick green grass. She scrambled to her feet as her mother approached, pleading, "Play 'Ring o'roses' with us, Mama. The grass is ever so nice and soft to fall on."

Smiling contentedly, Christina took hold of the small outstretched hand, then reached down to pull little Annie to her feet. Henry positioned himself between his sisters, catching their hands, and round and round they went, singing, "Ring a ring o'roses! A pocket full of posies! Tisha! Tisha! We all fall down!"

Charlie, who had been throwing pebbles into the river, came to watch them, standing to one side with a half-smile on his face, uncertain as to whether the enjoyment to be had from the babyish game was worth the sacrifice of his eleven-year-old dignity. But, when his father arrived and joined in, he lost no time in doing likewise.

"Ring a ring o'roses! A pocket full of posies … " On and on it went, with the children falling down and rolling about in fits of laughter, their parents laughing with them but falling only to their knees. Then up again, hands reclasping, and round and round once more. "Ring a ring o'roses … "

Across the circle Christina's eyes laughed into her husband's. "Next year we'll have an even larger ring. Tisha! Tisha! We all fall down!"

On his knees and with his eyebrows raised quizzically, Carl let his gaze drop from her flushed, laughing face to her waist. "Another one?"

Christina had time only to nod before getting back to her feet. "Ring a ring o'roses … " Then, chuckling softly at the expression on her husband's face, she mouthed, "In autumn again, early March, I should think."

Grinning back at her, Carl leaned into the ring so that she might hear him over the noise the children were making. "Just how many children are we going to have?"

"Tisha! Tisha! We all fall down!" Once again the ring collapsed, but this time it was only the children who went down. Taking care not to stand on any small body parts, Christina took the few steps needed to slip her arms up around her husband's neck and have his arms close around her. "We will just have to wait and see, but I should think that six will be a nice family."

The End

Afterword

The real Christina and Carl Eichstead had ten children. Henry, the third eldest, was never as robust as his brothers and sisters; he didn't marry and died in his early thirties. The others all married, presented Carl and Christina with a total of thirty-two grandchildren, and lived long, industrious lives.

Christina died on the 7th of January 1941, having survived her beloved Prussian by eight years. They lie, side by side, in the old Southport cemetery.

The economic slump that had been threatening at the time Christina and Carl began their first farm on the flat lands did eventuate, and would prove to be one of the worst in Australia's history. Between 1891 and 1895 banks crashed and production fell by thirty percent, with employment and incomes dropping drastically as a result. The Eichstead family certainly endured their share of hard times, but, unlike many of the large plantations and pastoral properties which had become heavily mortgaged, their Carrara farm was relatively unencumbered, and they were able to hold on and, through the years, extract a comfortable living from it, as they did also from a second dairy farm they later acquired at Merrimac.

Christina never did go back to Schleswig to reclaim the corner of her heart that she had left there. There was really no need to do so … it had rejoined her of its own accord.

As for what happened to the impoverished Colony? Let the great State of Queensland speak for itself!